Advance praise for *Livin*

"Beautifully illustrated, relatable, and genuine.

–Molly Brooks, creator of *Sanity & Tallulah*

"Heartfelt and fun, *Living With Viola* is
going to mean a lot to an awful lot of kids."

–Eleanor Davis, creator of *Stinky* and *You & a Bike & a Road*

"*Living With Viola* is told with both compassion and humor.
Livy is a character with whom many readers will identify, and
even more will empathize, as they accompany her on her
journey through school, friendship, and family. Delightful."

–Lisa Brown, creator of *The Phantom Twin*

"How does one exist when everything appears to be against
us, especially ourselves? Through this beautifully drawn,
and at turns funny and heart-wrenching story, Livy finds her
way. Rosena Fung's deeply moving and empowering book
is sure to enter the kids' Graphic Medicine canon."

–Fiona Smyth, creator of *Sex Is A Funny Word*
(with Cory Silverberg) and *Somnambulance*

"*Living With Viola* is an explosion of colors and emotions
Rosena Fung has artfully woven into a heartbreakingly
familiar tale many of her readers will feel in their bones. I'll
be tucking this important read onto my bookshelf to share
with my own child so she can see how words can wound,
even, maybe especially, when you turn them on yourself."

–Britt Wilson, author of *Ghost Queen*
and *Cat Dad, King of the Goblins*

"*Living With Viola* . . . fearlessly takes young readers
into the darkness of Livy's panic, anxiety, fear, and sense
of being alone but, like the allies that Livy will find, is also
there to guide them back into the light. One of the best
debuts I have ever seen."

–Jeffrey Canton, children's book
columnist for *The Globe and Mail*

To Mark, for your love,
and Mom and Dad, for your sacrifice.
—R.F.

Cover art by Rosena Fung, designed by Rosena Fung and Paul Covello
Interior designed by Rosena Fung and Paul Covello
Edited by Serah-Marie McMahon
Copyedited by Mary Ann Blair
Proofread by Doeun Rivendell
Expert read/Cantonese language review by Ambrose Li

If you or someone you know is dealing with anxiety, panic, or any other mental health issues, know that you are not alone. In addition to confiding in a trusted adult, you can find support in Canada through Kids Help Phone at kidshelpphone.ca or by calling 1-800-668-6868. For Canada and the US, you can find support through the Crisis Text Line at crisistextline.org or by texting 741741. Both resources will connect you to trained counselors.

Annick Press Ltd.

We acknowledge the support of the Canada Council for the Arts and the Ontario Arts Council, and the participation of the Government of Canada/la participation du gouvernement du Canada for our publishing activities.

Canada

ONTARIO ARTS COUNCIL
CONSEIL DES ARTS DE L'ONTARIO
an Ontario government agency
un organisme du gouvernement de l'Ontario

Library and Archives Canada Cataloguing in Publication

Title: Living with Viola / Rosena Fung.
Names: Fung, Rosena, author.
Identifiers: Canadiana (print) 20210188596 | Canadiana (ebook) 20210188618 | ISBN 9781773215488 (hardcover) | ISBN 9781773215495 (softcover) | ISBN 9781773215518 (PDF) | ISBN 9781773215501 (HTML)
Subjects: LCGFT: Graphic novels.
Classification: LCC PN6733.F86 L58 2021 | DDC j741.5/971—dc23

Published in the U.S.A. by Annick Press (U.S.) Ltd.
Distributed in Canada by University of Toronto Press.
Distributed in the U.S.A. by Publishers Group West.

Printed in China

annickpress.com
rosenafung.com

Also available as an e-book. Please visit annickpress.com/ebooks for more details.

LIVING
WITH
VIOLA

ROSENA FUNG

annick
press
toronto · berkeley

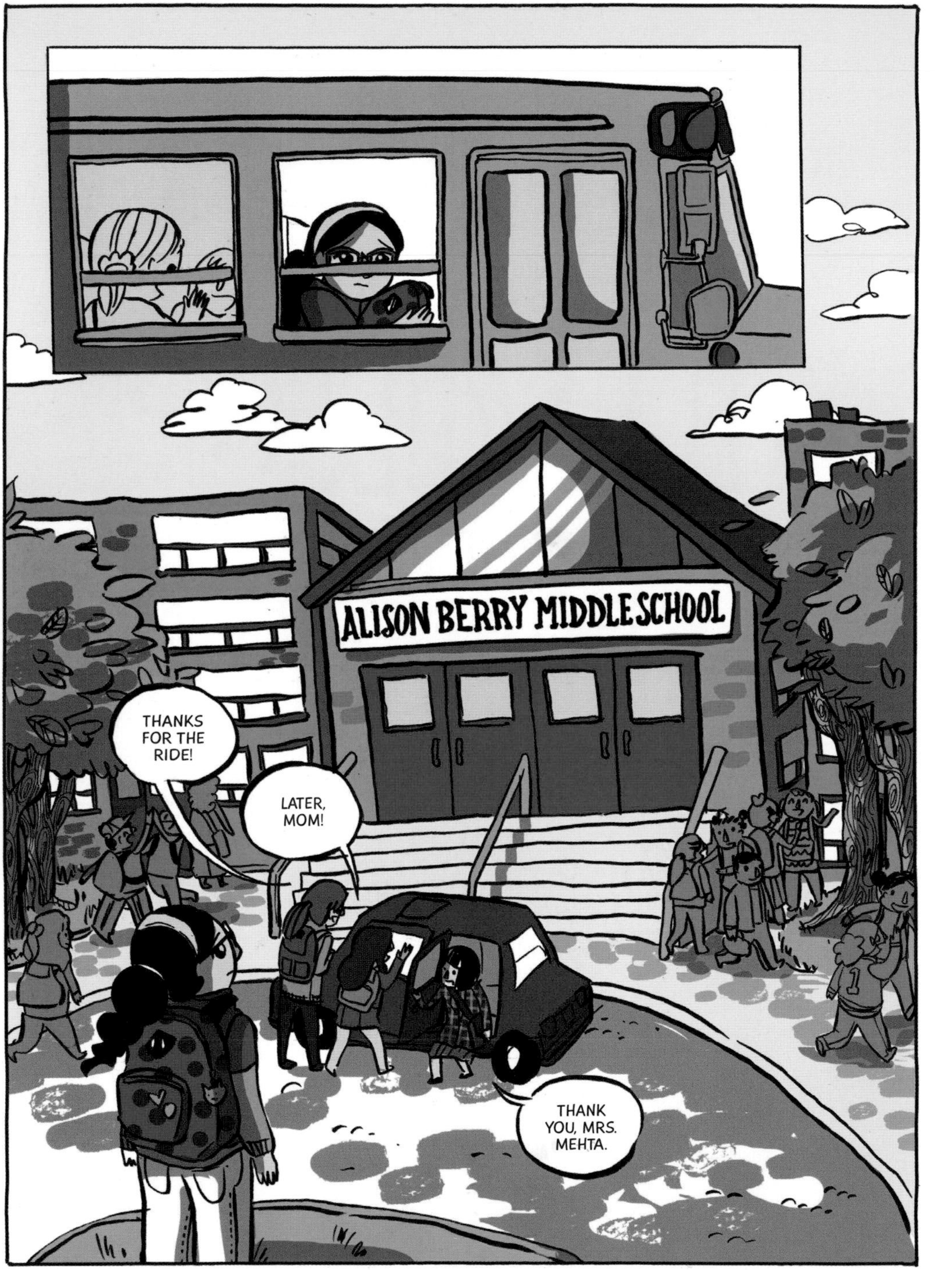
ALISON BERRY MIDDLE SCHOOL
THANKS FOR THE RIDE!
LATER, MOM!
THANK YOU, MRS. MEHTA.

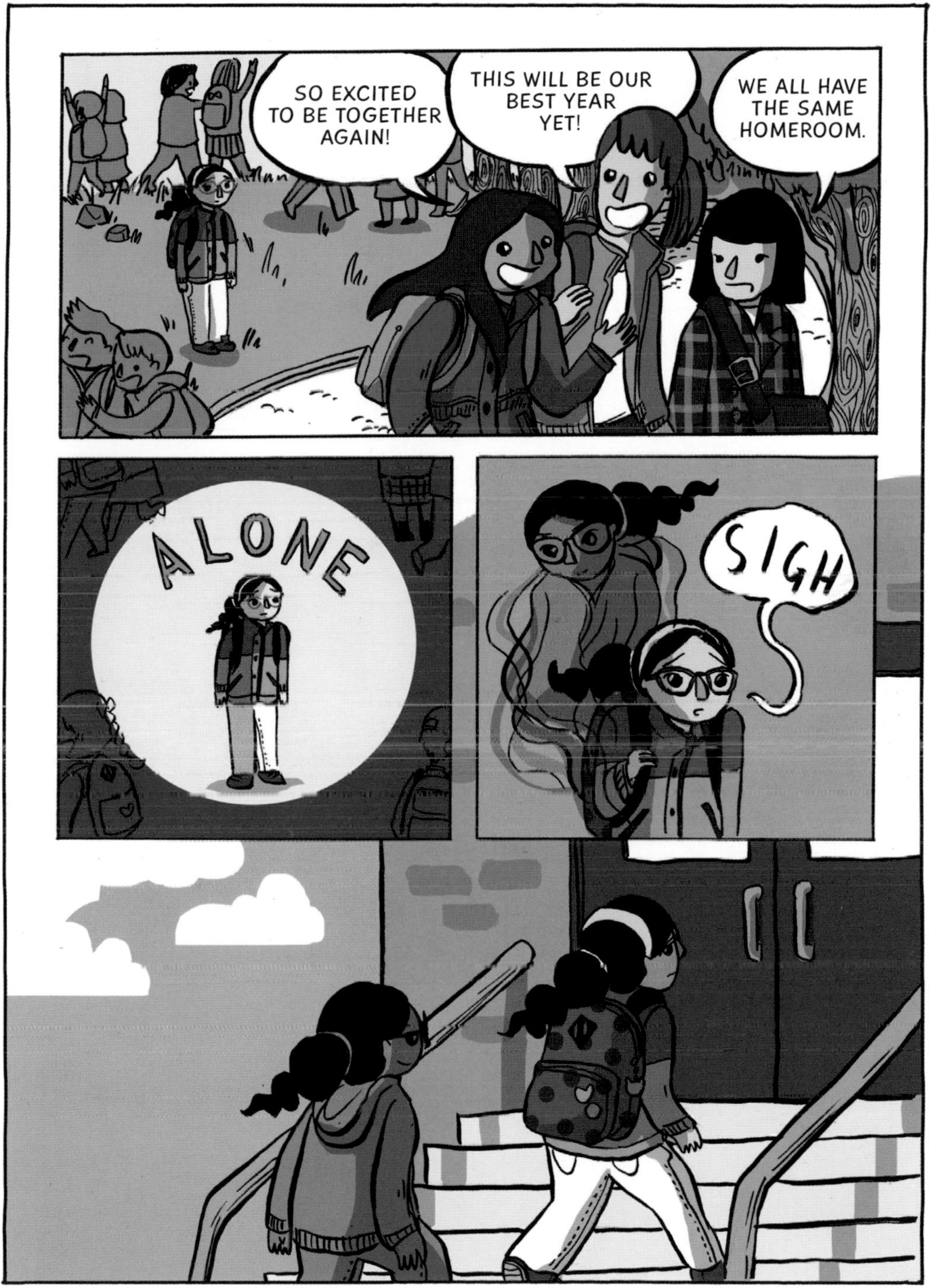
SO EXCITED TO BE TOGETHER AGAIN!
THIS WILL BE OUR BEST YEAR YET!
WE ALL HAVE THE SAME HOMEROOM.
ALONE
SIGH

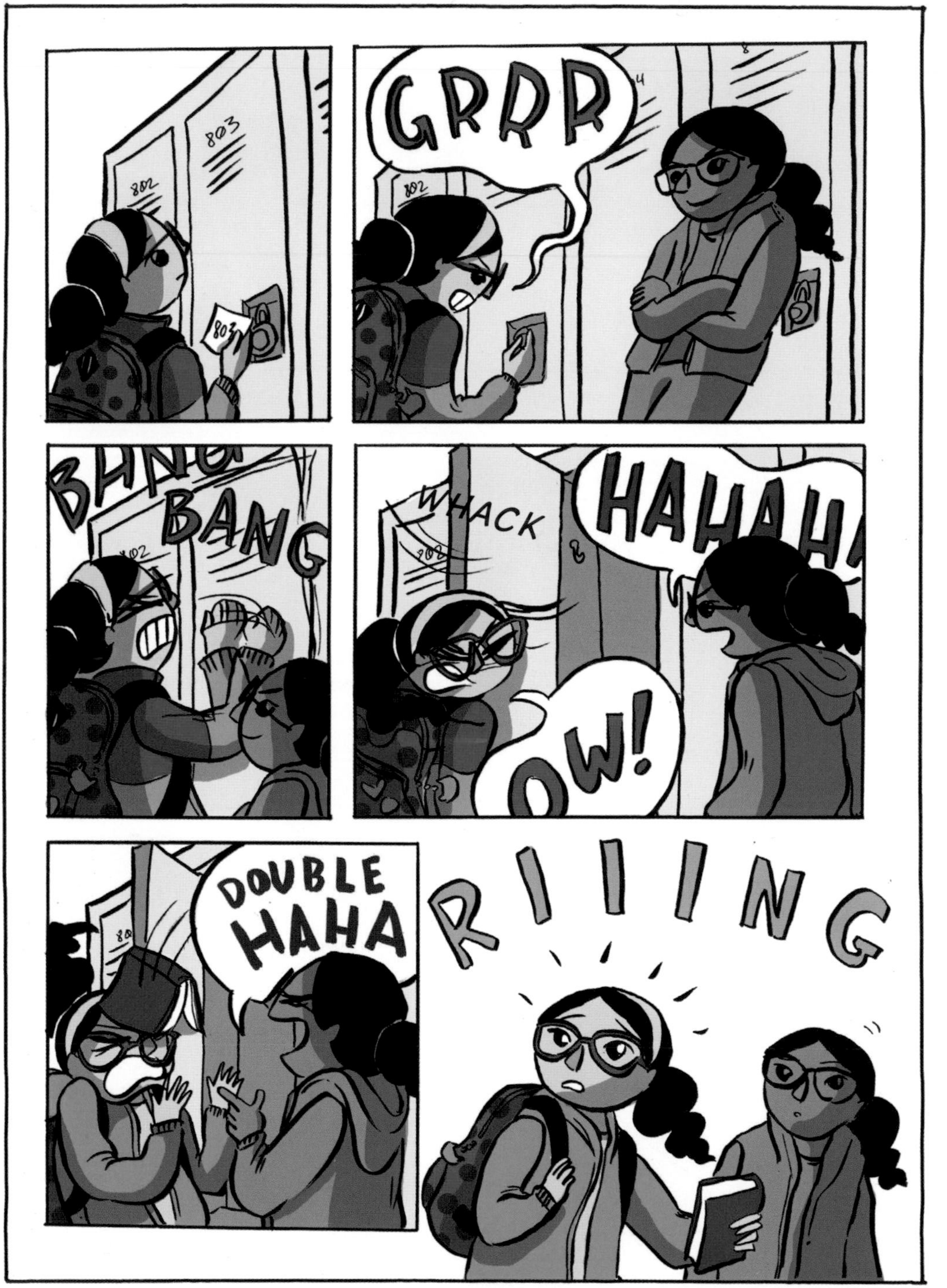
GRRR
BANG
BANG
WHACK
HAHAHA
OW!
DOUBLE HAHA
RIIING

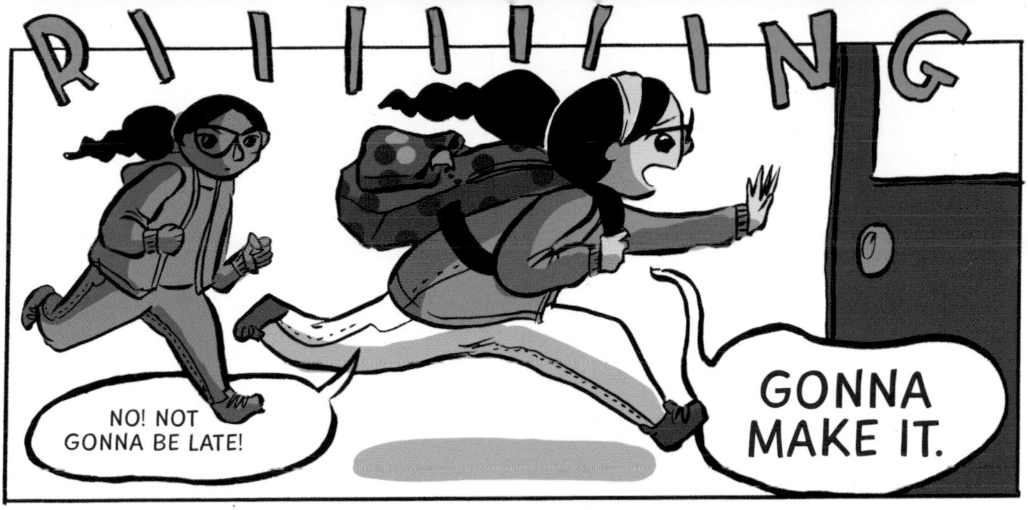
RIIIIIIING
NO! NOT GONNA BE LATE!
GONNA MAKE IT.

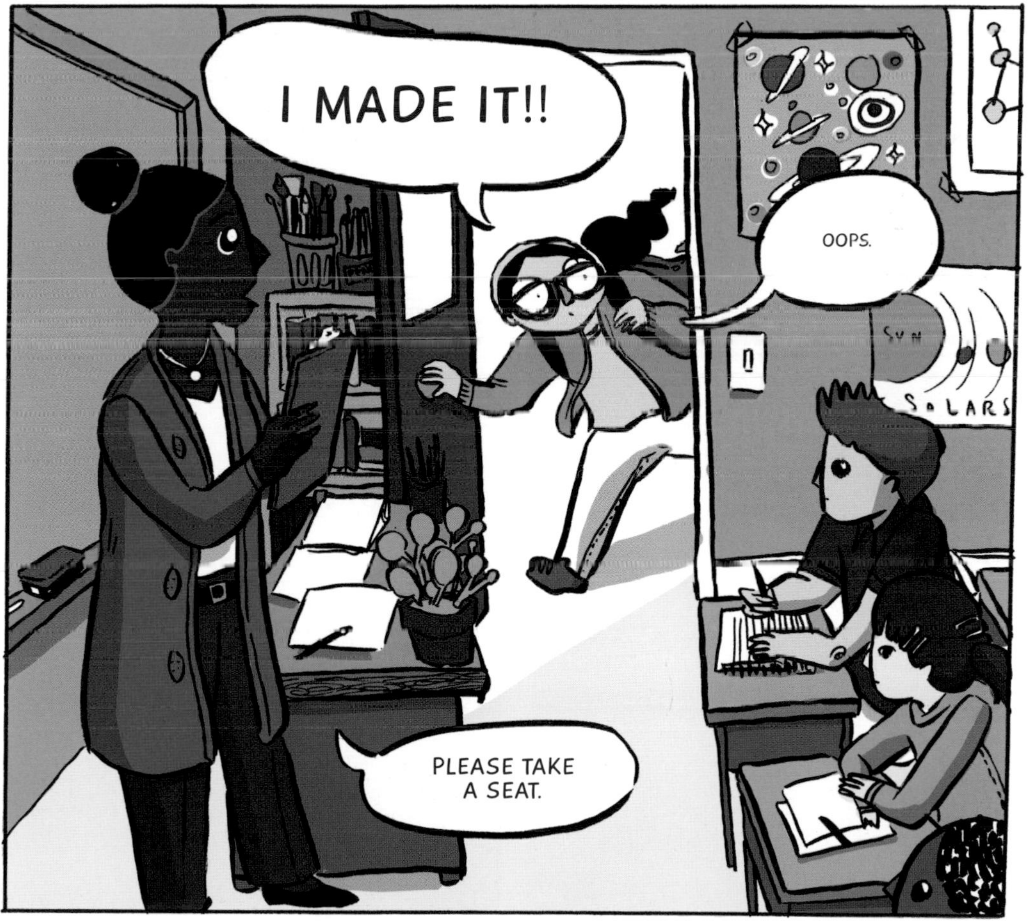
I MADE IT!!
OOPS.
PLEASE TAKE A SEAT.
SUN
SOLARS

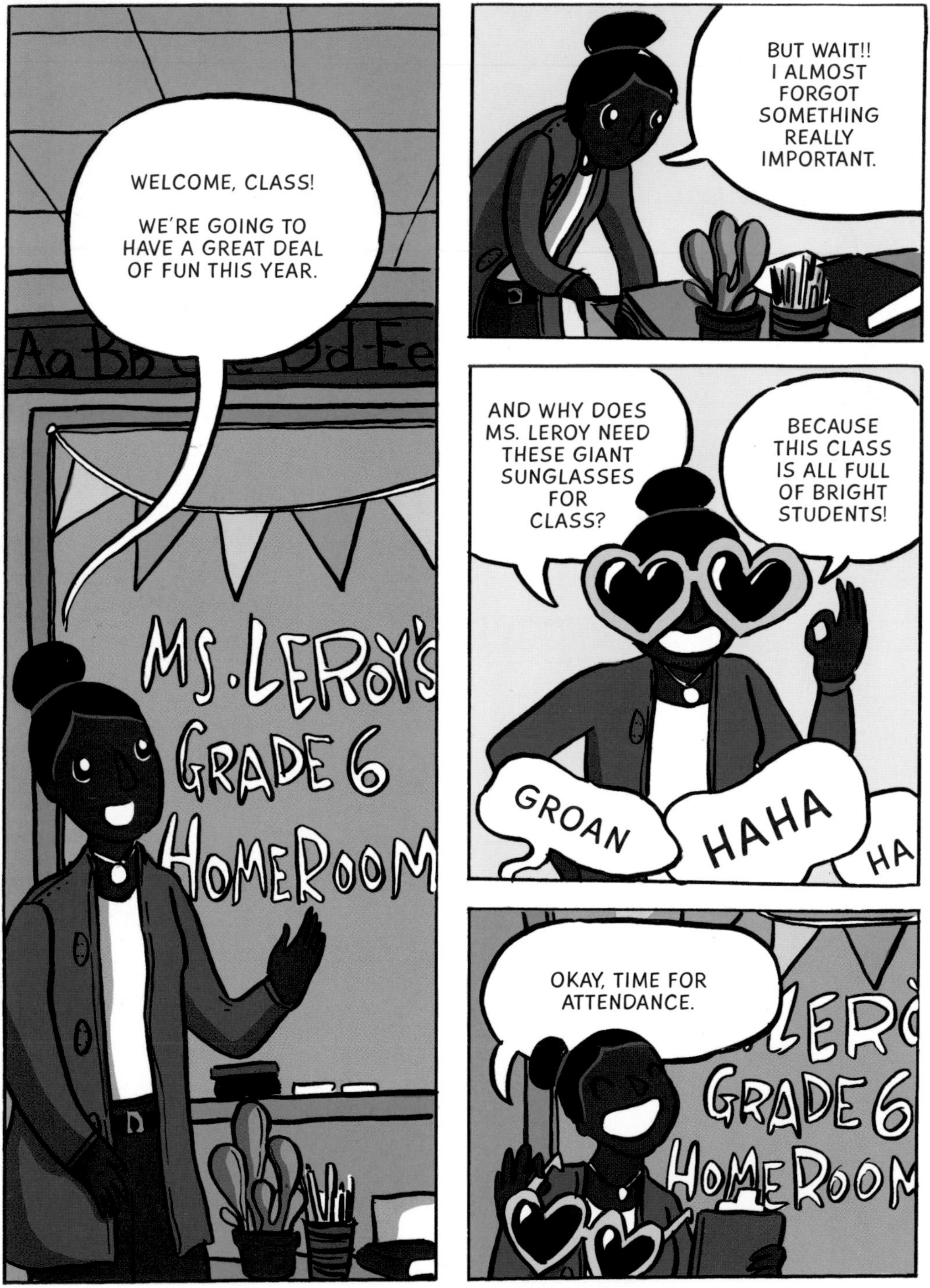
WELCOME, CLASS! WE'RE GOING TO HAVE A GREAT DEAL OF FUN THIS YEAR.
Aa Bb Cc Dd Ee
MS. LEROY'S GRADE 6 HOMEROOM
BUT WAIT!! I ALMOST FORGOT SOMETHING REALLY IMPORTANT.
AND WHY DOES MS. LEROY NEED THESE GIANT SUNGLASSES FOR CLASS?
BECAUSE THIS CLASS IS ALL FULL OF BRIGHT STUDENTS!
GROAN
HAHA
HA
OKAY, TIME FOR ATTENDANCE.
GRADE 6 HOMEROOM

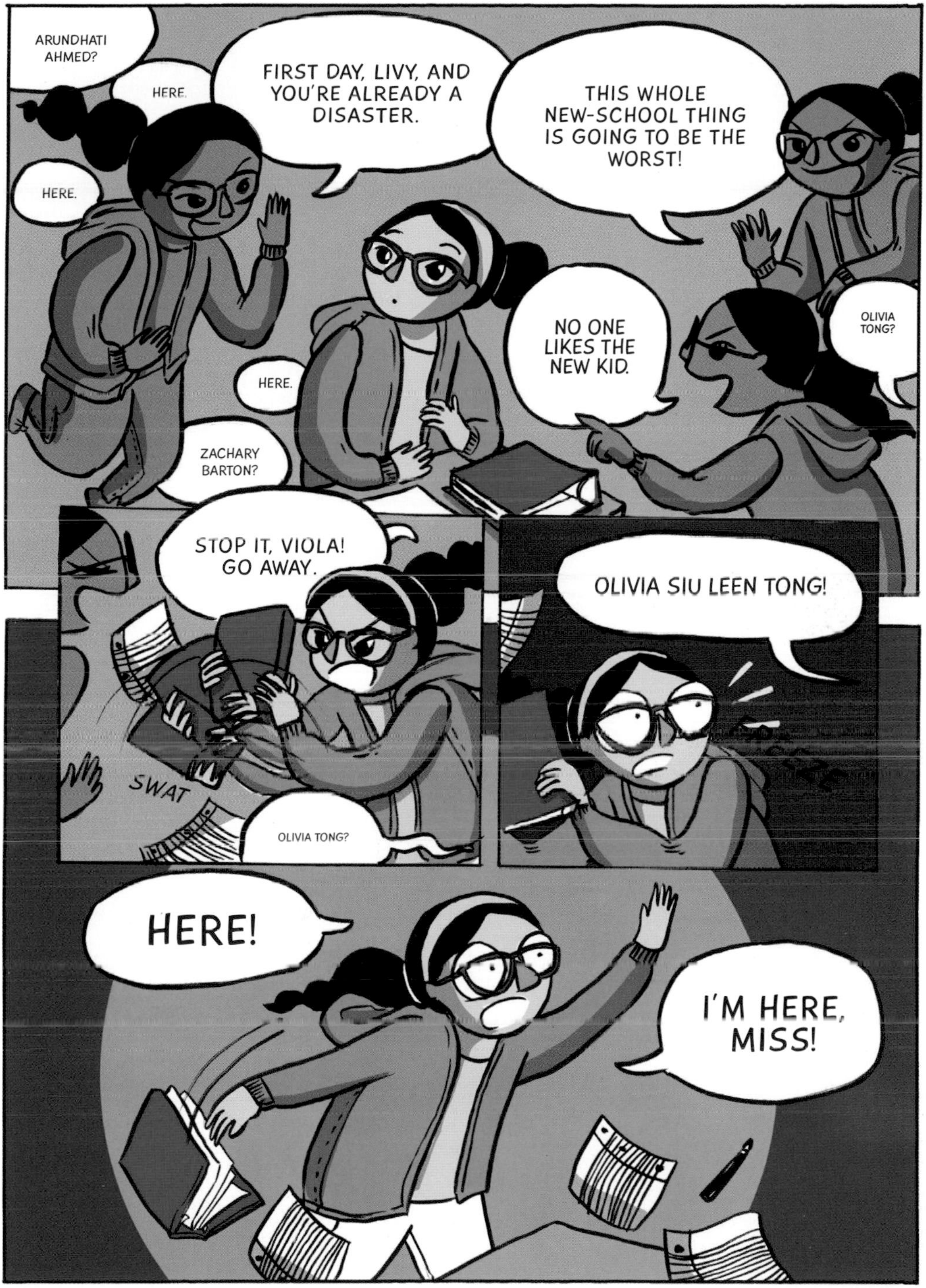
ARUNDHATI AHMED?
HERE.
FIRST DAY, LIVY, AND YOU'RE ALREADY A DISASTER.
THIS WHOLE NEW-SCHOOL THING IS GOING TO BE THE WORST!
HERE.
HERE.
ZACHARY BARTON?
NO ONE LIKES THE NEW KID.
OLIVIA TONG?
STOP IT, VIOLA! GO AWAY.
SWAT
OLIVIA TONG?
OLIVIA SIU LEEN TONG!
HERE!
I'M HERE, MISS!

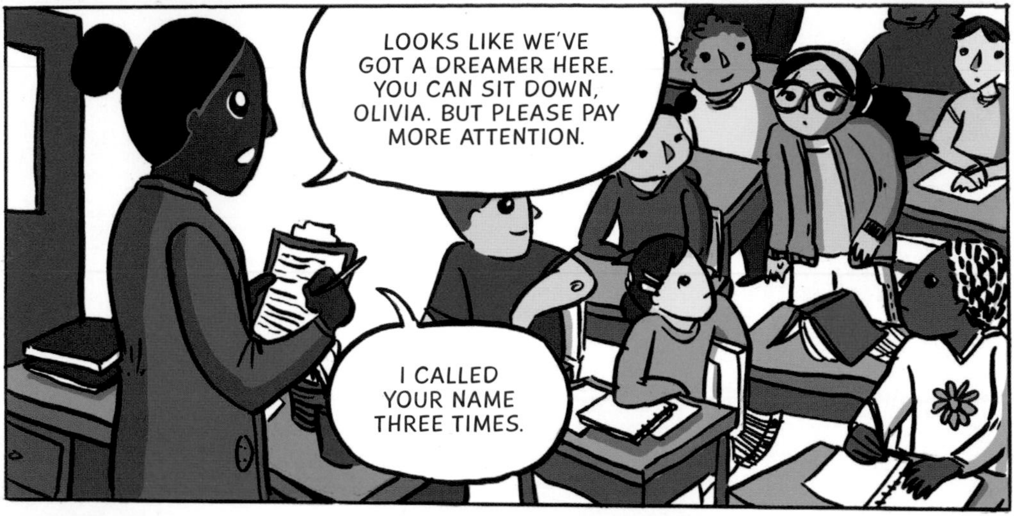
LOOKS LIKE WE'VE GOT A DREAMER HERE. YOU CAN SIT DOWN, OLIVIA. BUT PLEASE PAY MORE ATTENTION.
I CALLED YOUR NAME THREE TIMES.

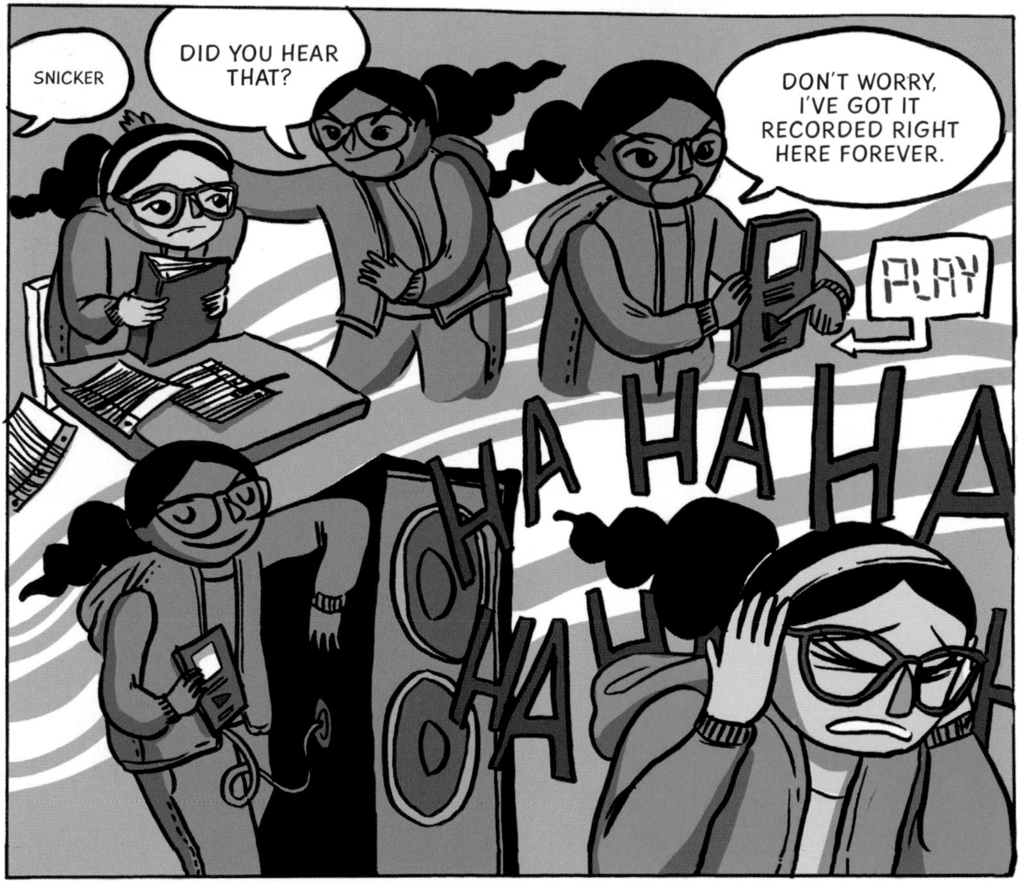
SNICKER
DID YOU HEAR THAT?
DON'T WORRY, I'VE GOT IT RECORDED RIGHT HERE FOREVER.
PLAY
HA HA HA HA
HA HA HA

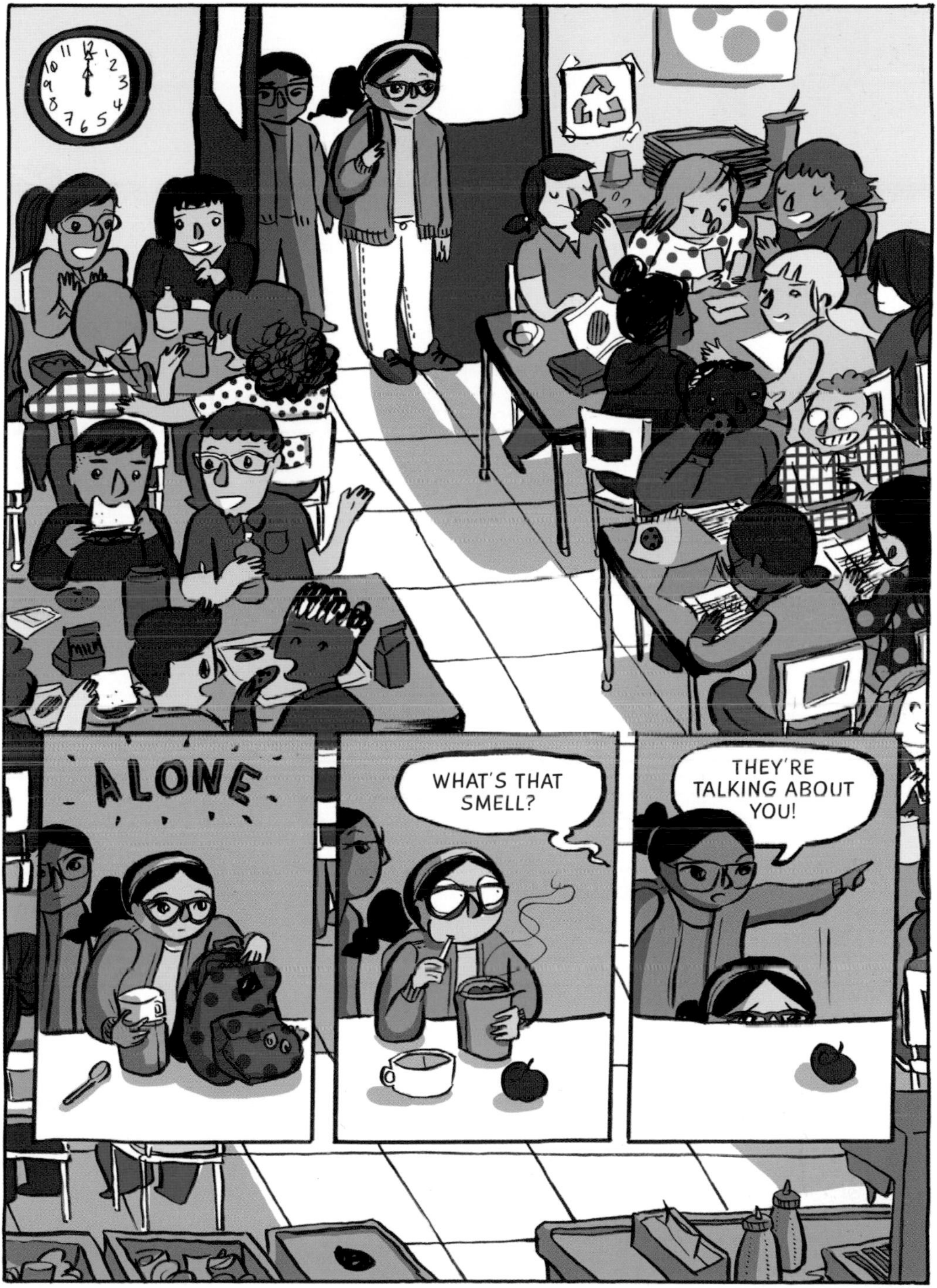
ALONE
WHAT'S THAT SMELL?
THEY'RE TALKING ABOUT YOU!

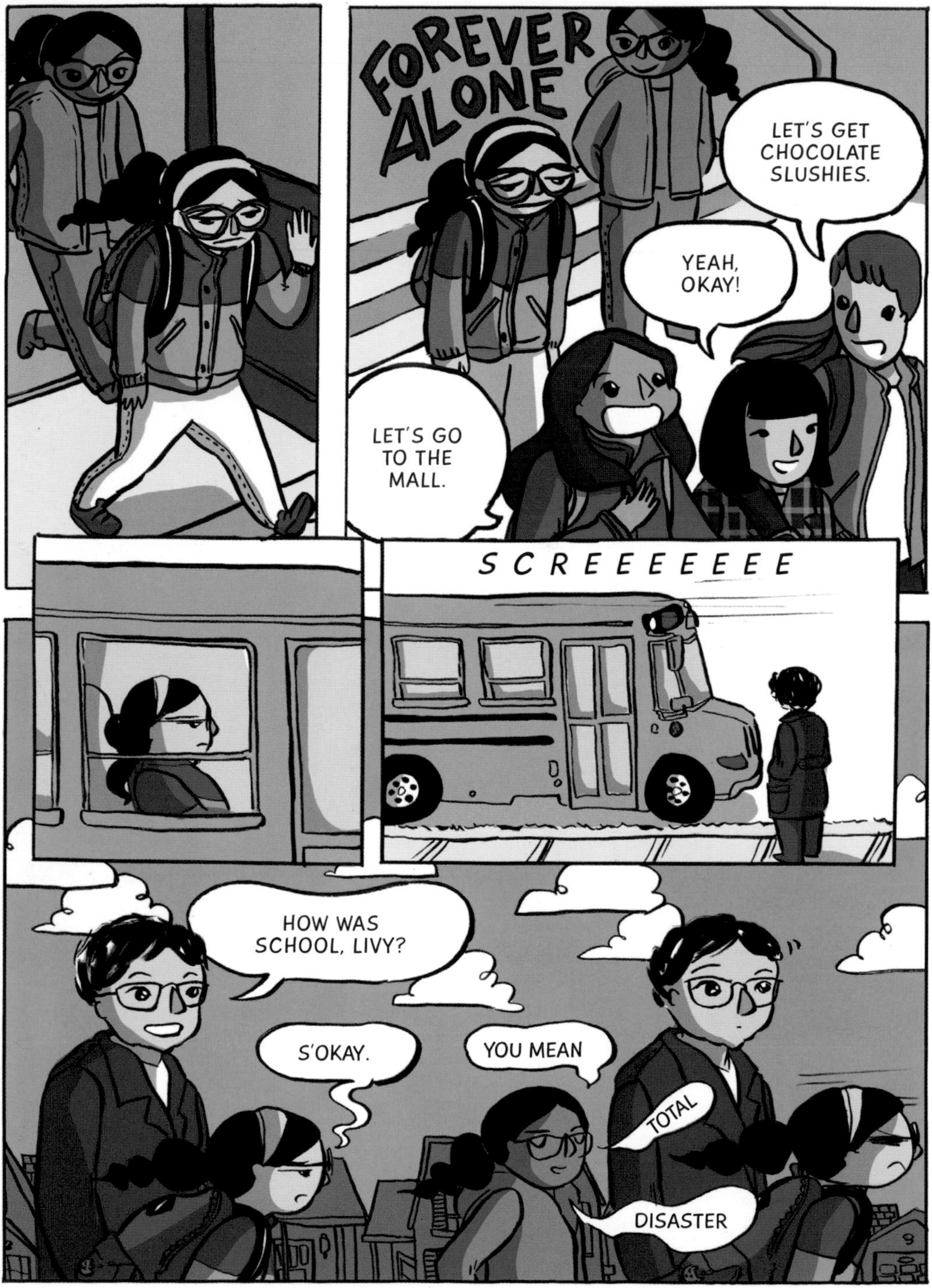
FOREVER ALONE
LET'S GET CHOCOLATE SLUSHIES.
YEAH, OKAY!
LET'S GO TO THE MALL.
S C R E E E E E E E E
HOW WAS SCHOOL, LIVY?
S'OKAY.
YOU MEAN
TOTAL
DISASTER

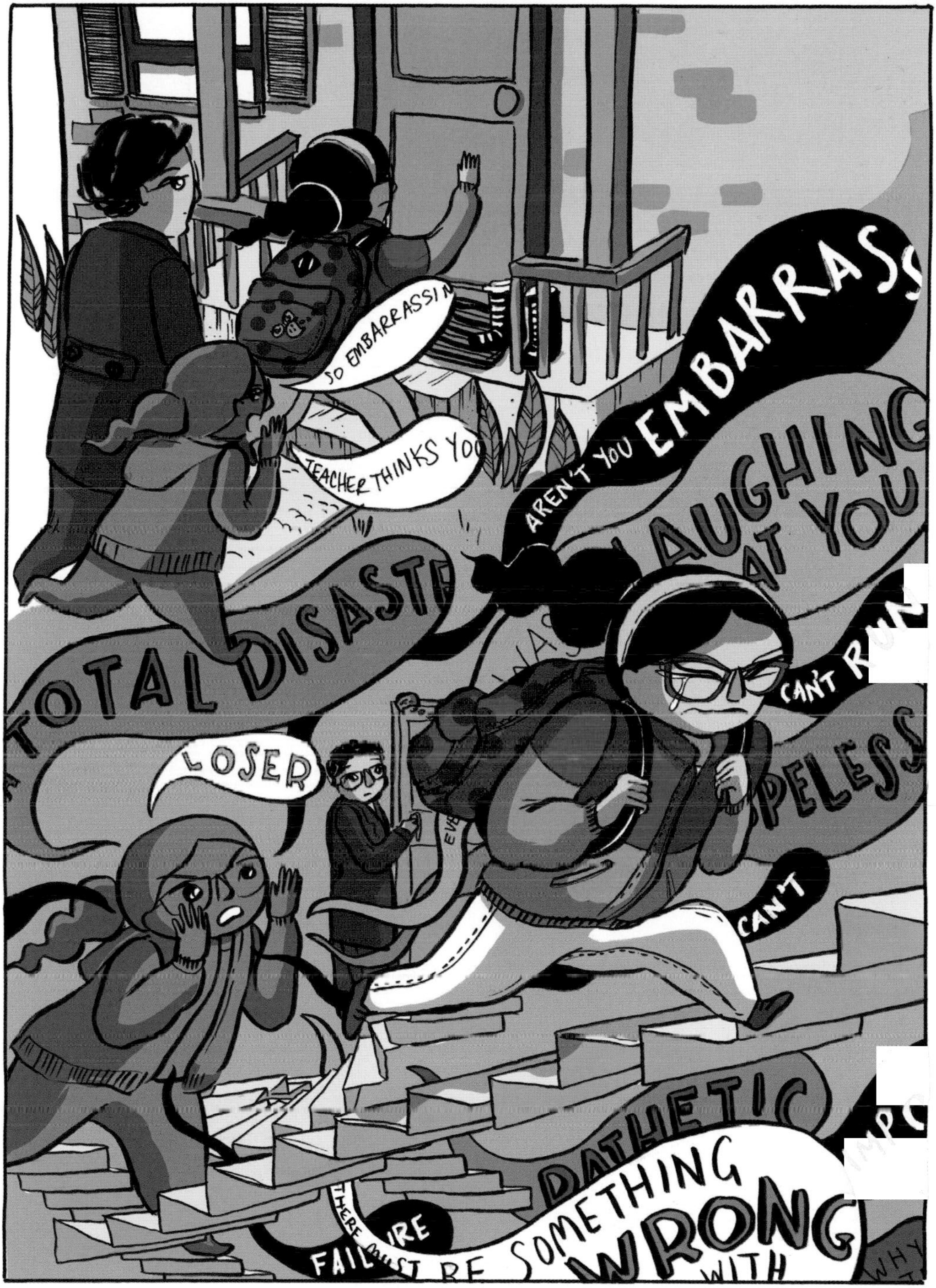
SO EMBARRASSIN
TEACHER THINKS YOU
AREN'T YOU EMBARRASS
AUGHING
AT YOU
TOTAL DISASTE
CAN'T RU
PELESS
LOSER
CAN'T
PATHETIC
SOMETHING
WRONG
WITH

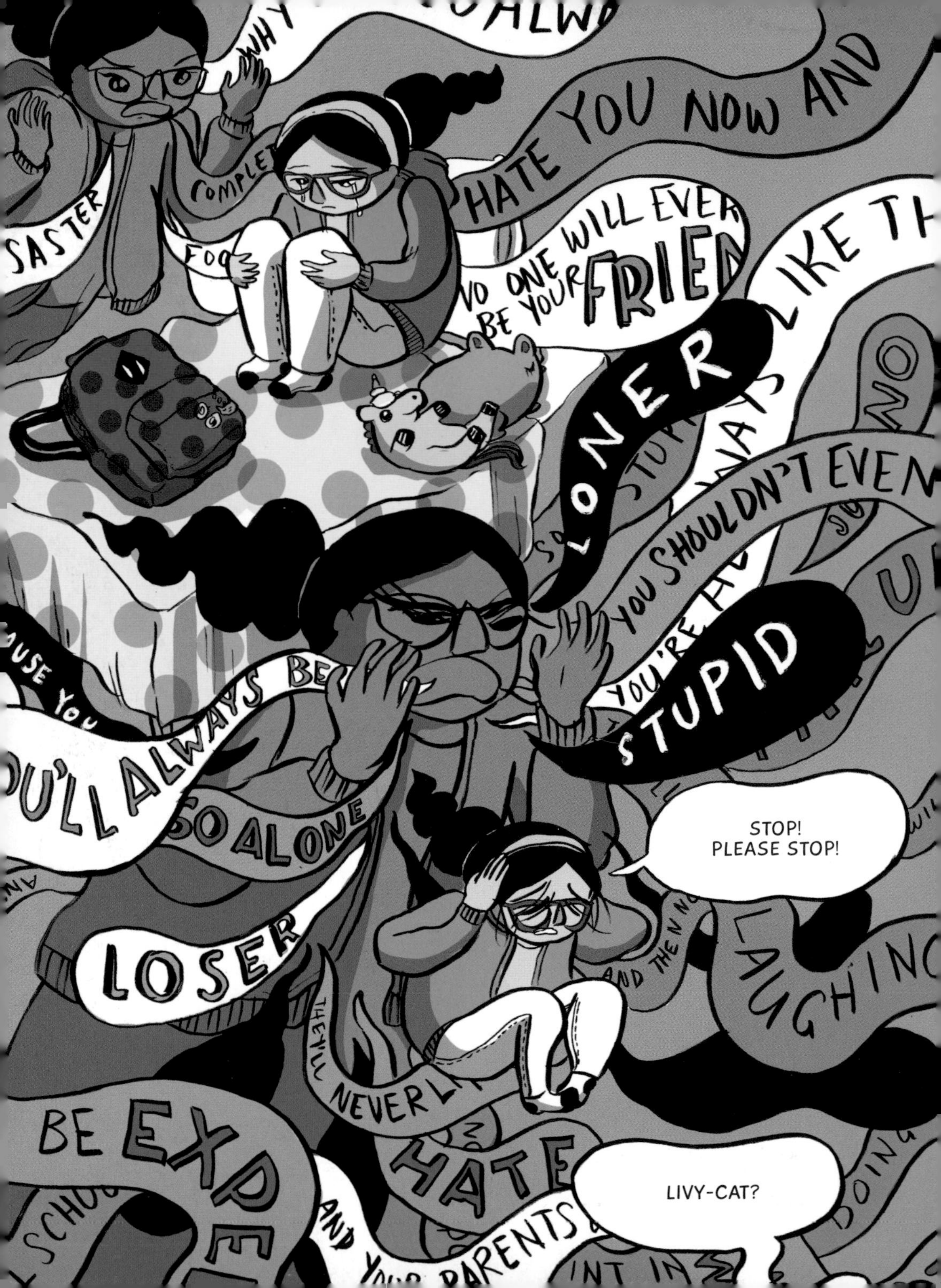
WHY
HATE YOU NOW AND
BE YOUR
LONER
YOU SHOULDN'T EVEN
STUPID
SO ALONE
LOSER
AND THEN
LAUGHING
NEVER
HATE
AND YOUR PARENTS
STOP!
PLEASE STOP!
LIVY-CAT?

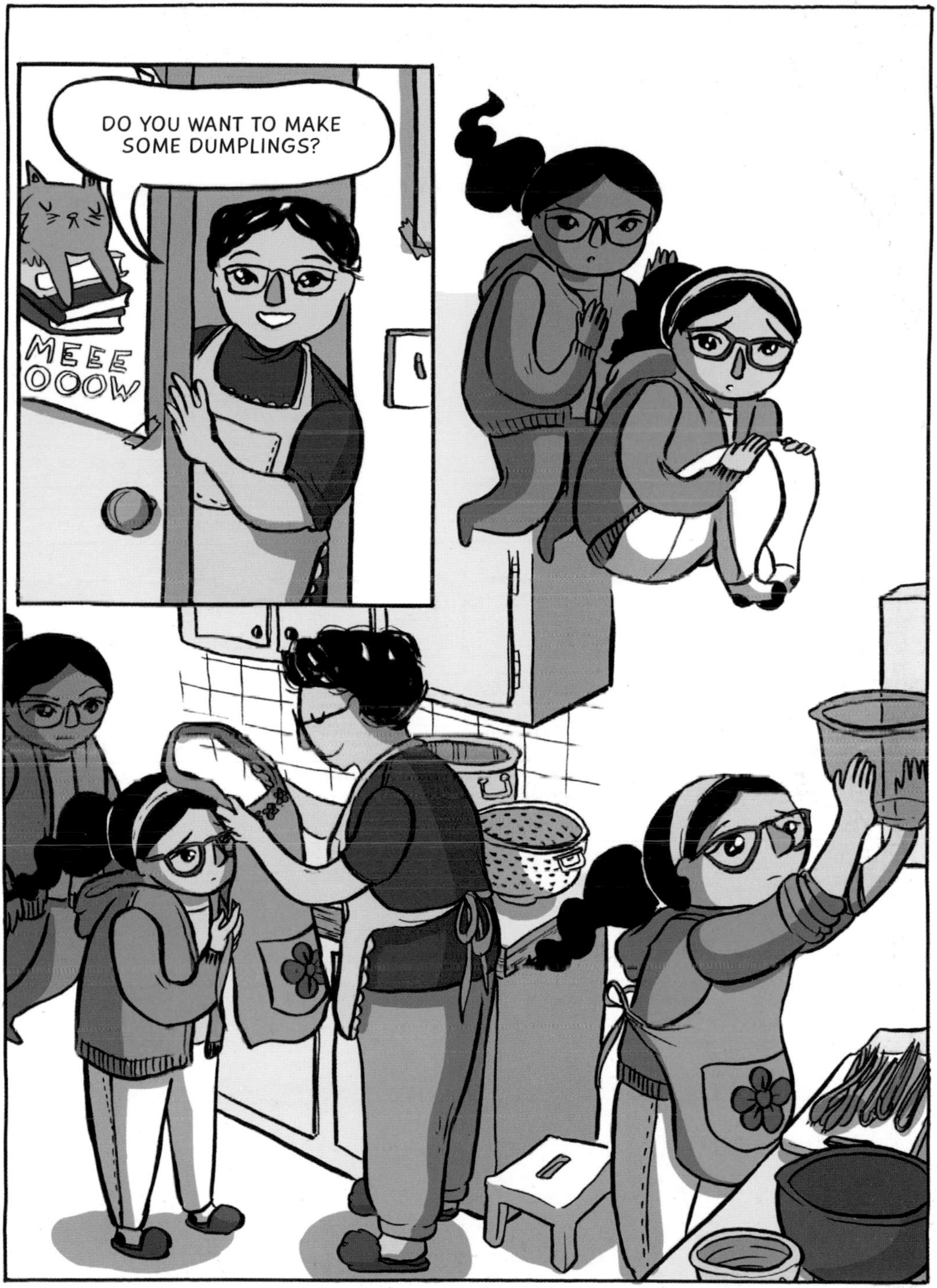
DO YOU WANT TO MAKE SOME DUMPLINGS?
MEEE OOOW

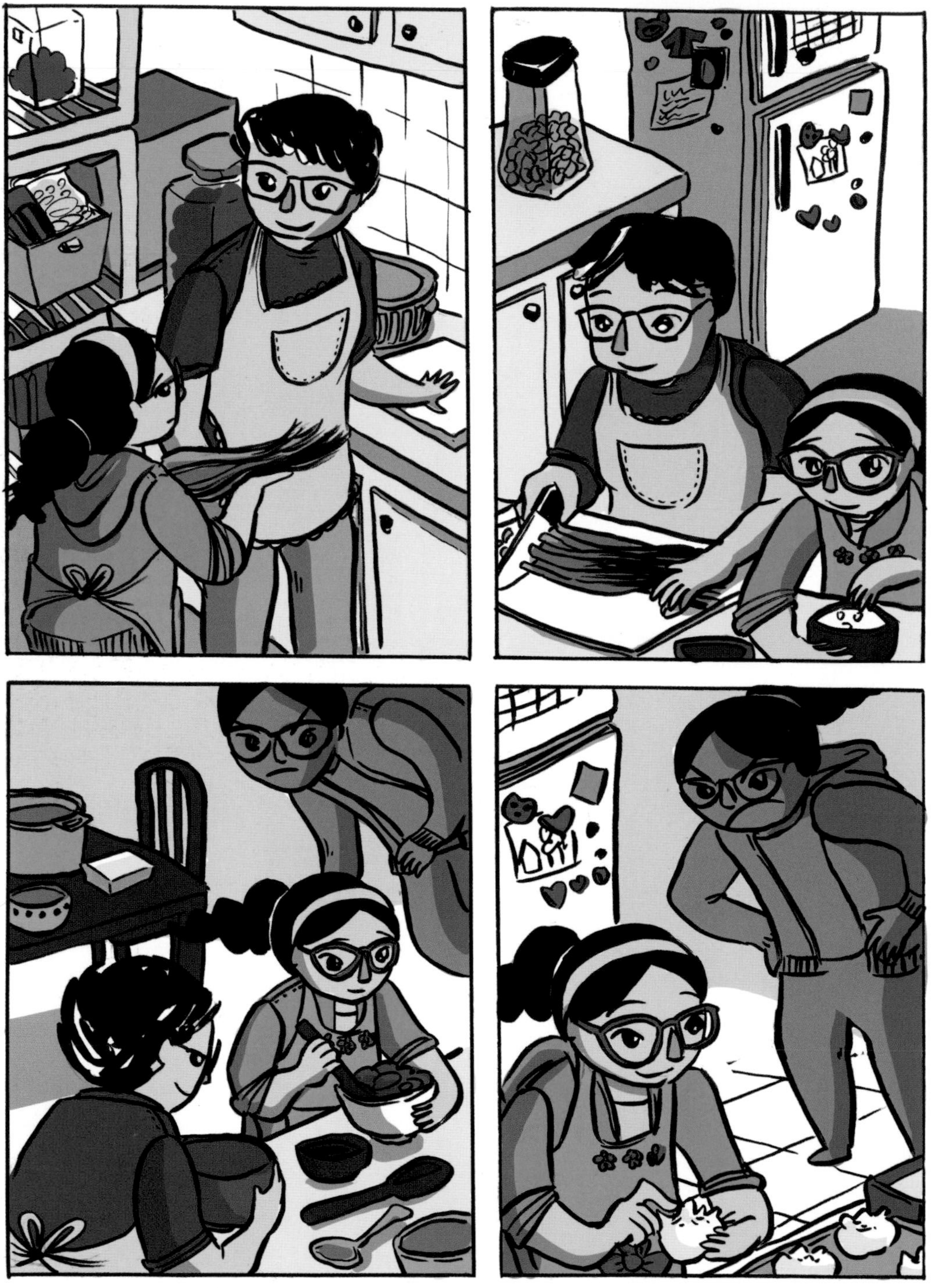

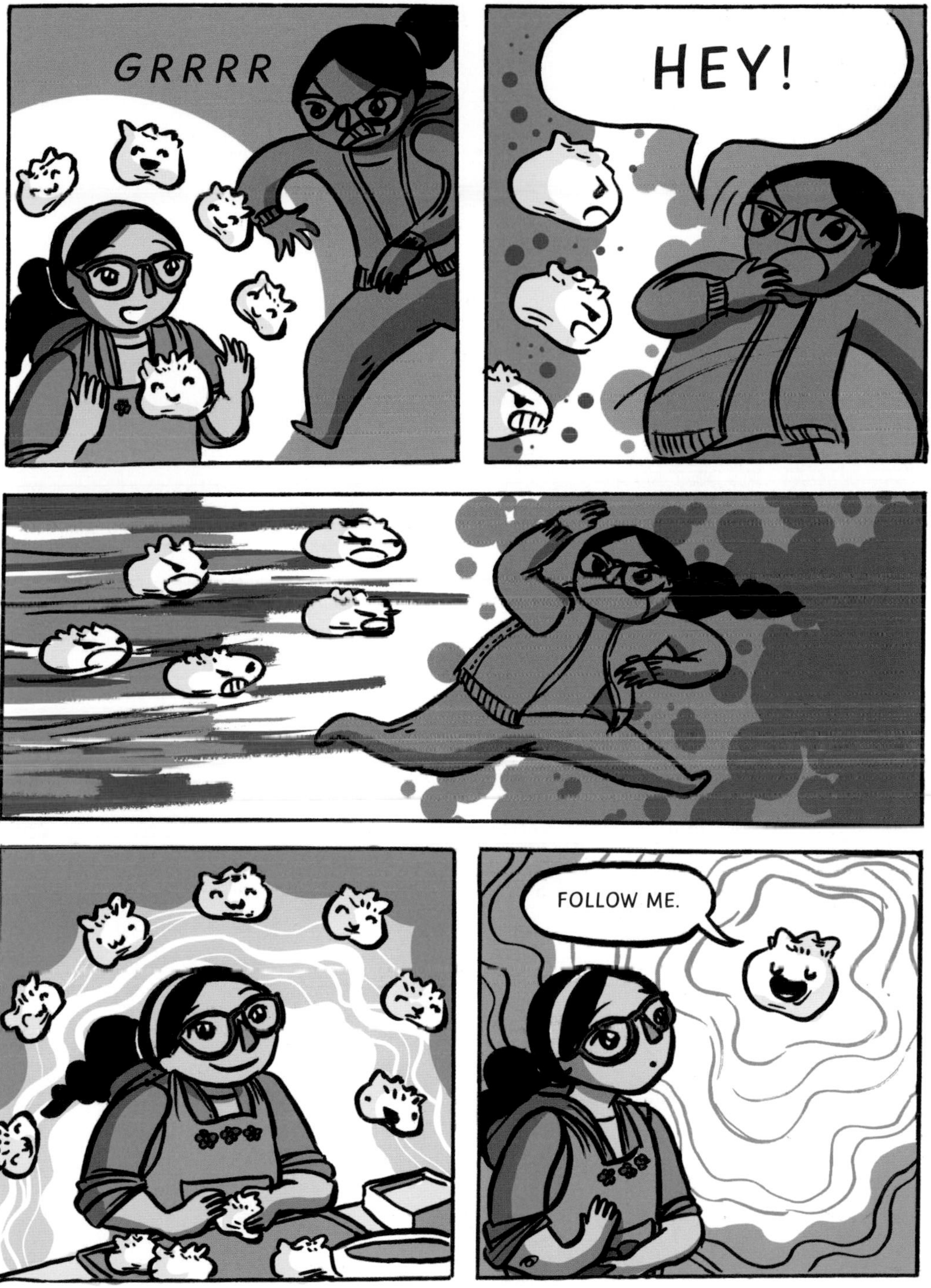
GRRRR
HEY!
FOLLOW ME.

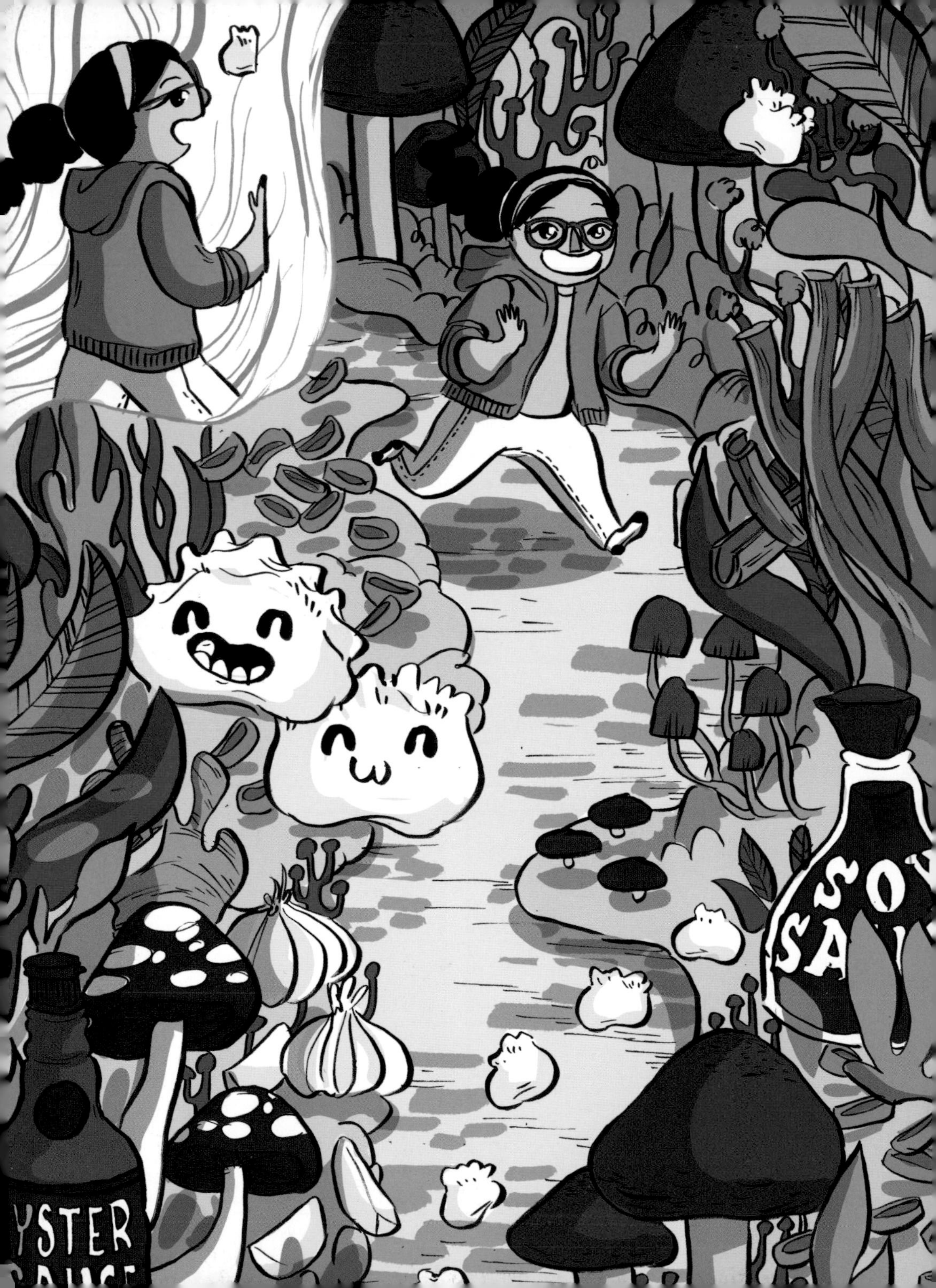
SO
SA
YSTER

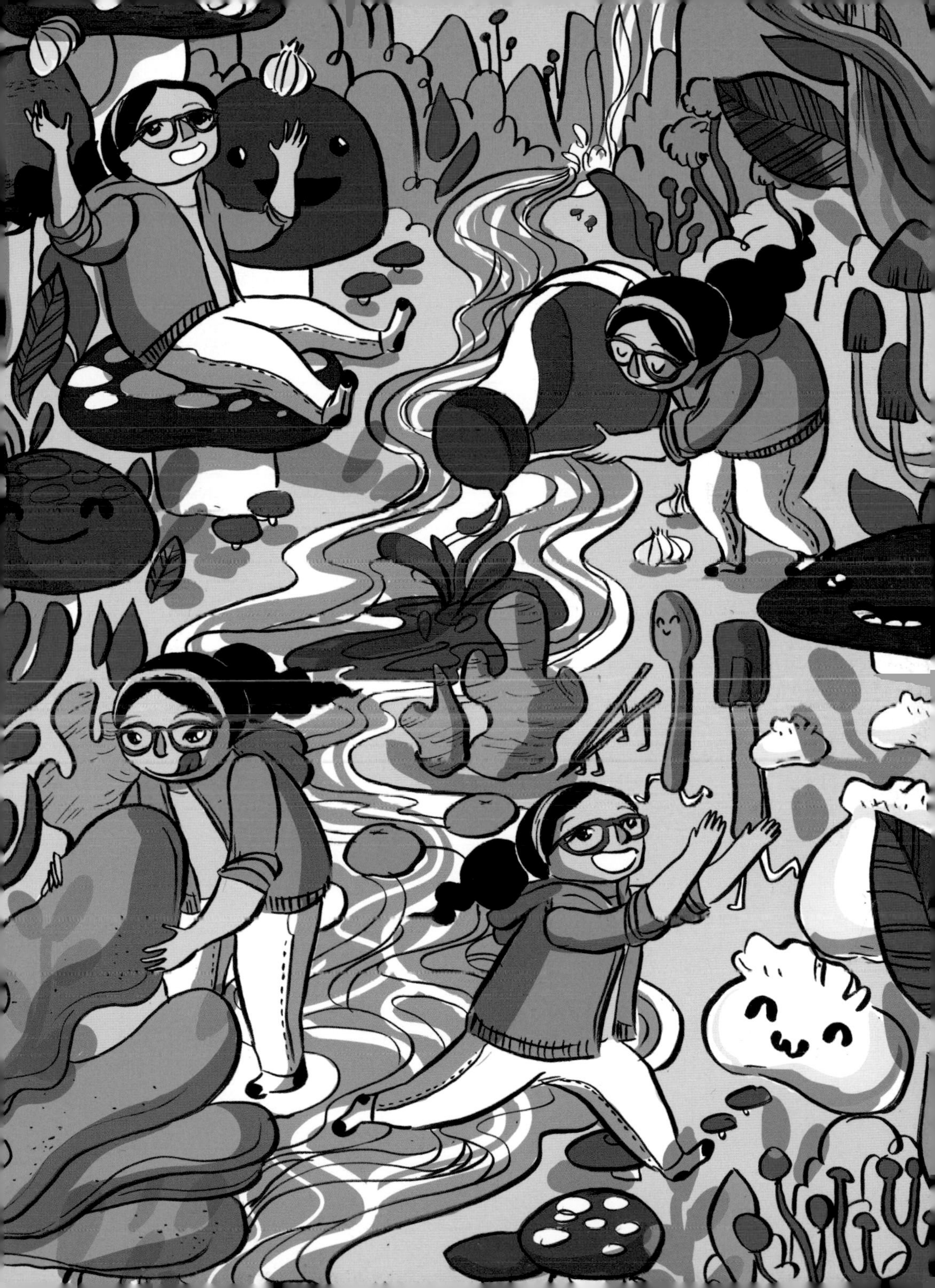

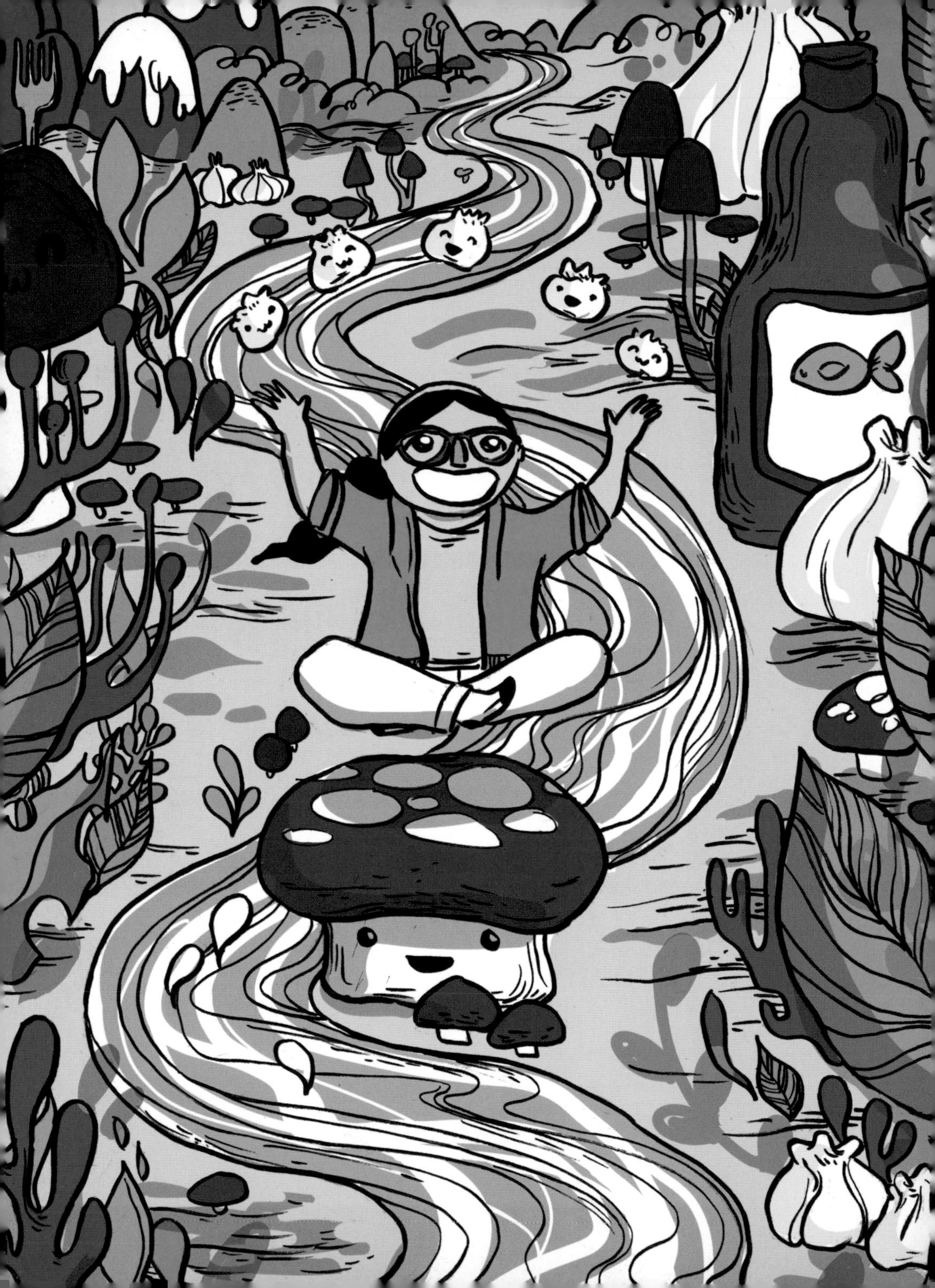

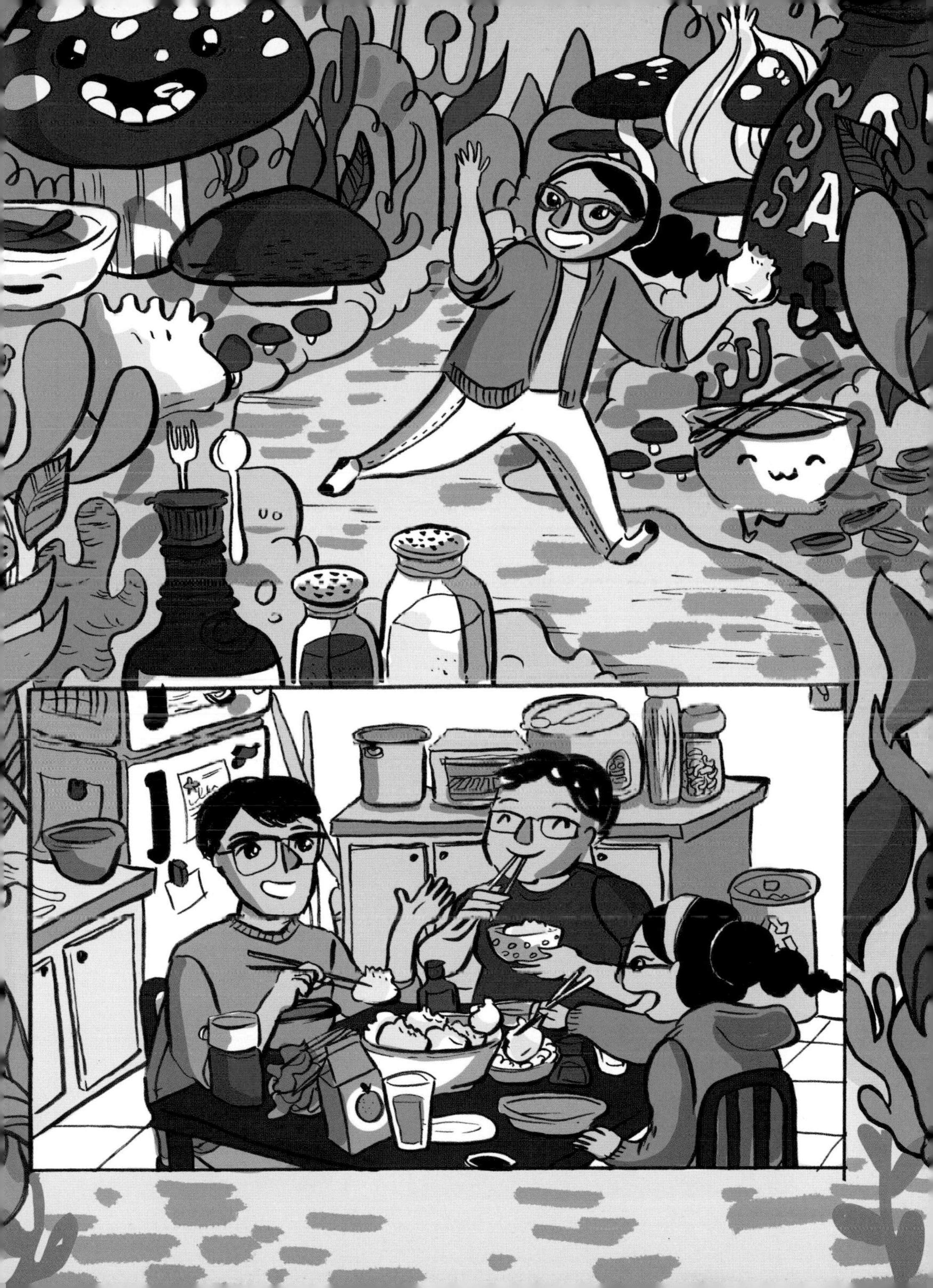

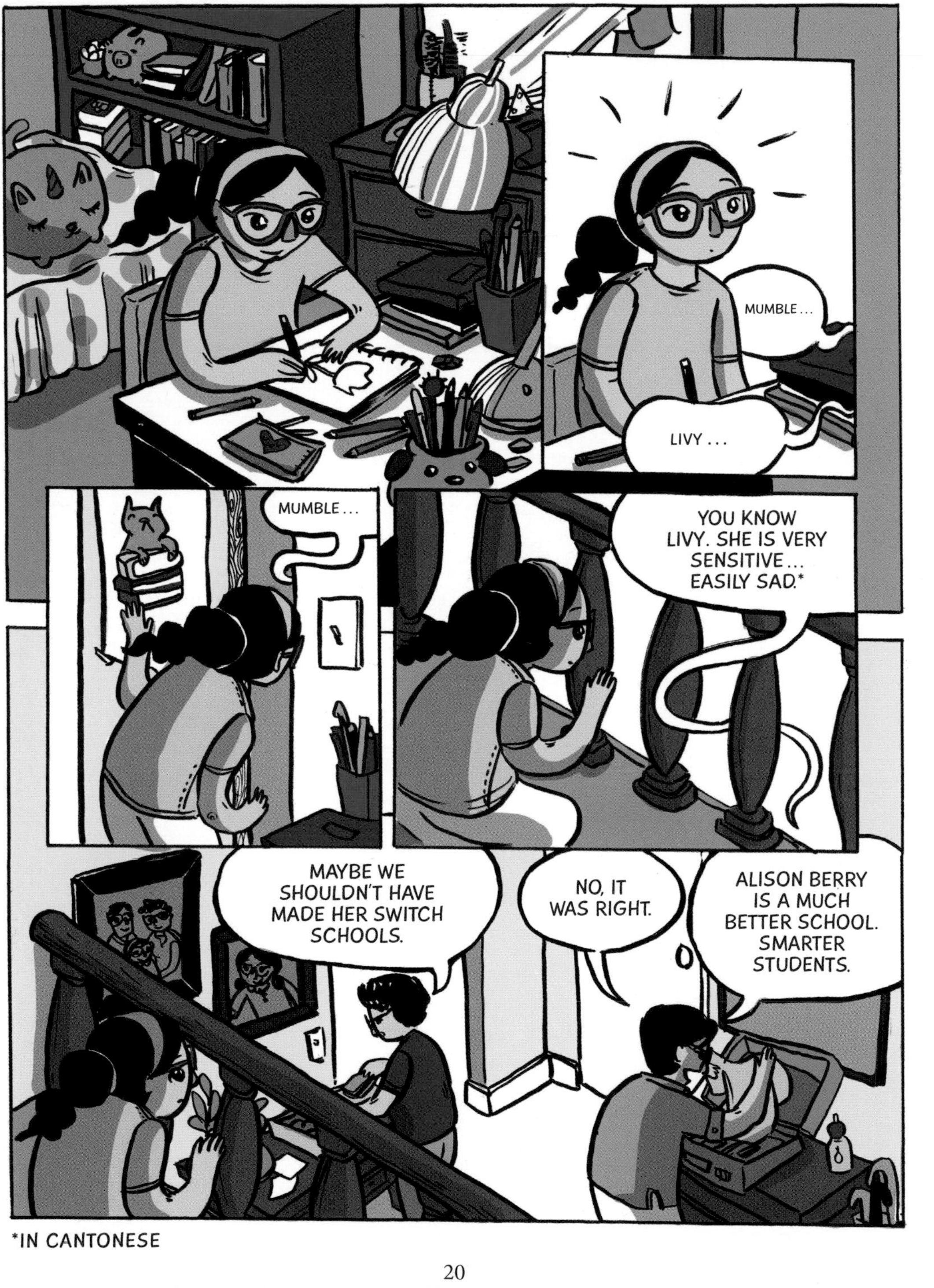
MUMBLE . . .
LIVY . . .
MUMBLE . . .
YOU KNOW LIVY. SHE IS VERY SENSITIVE . . . EASILY SAD.*
MAYBE WE SHOULDN'T HAVE MADE HER SWITCH SCHOOLS.
NO, IT WAS RIGHT.
ALISON BERRY IS A MUCH BETTER SCHOOL. SMARTER STUDENTS.

*IN CANTONESE

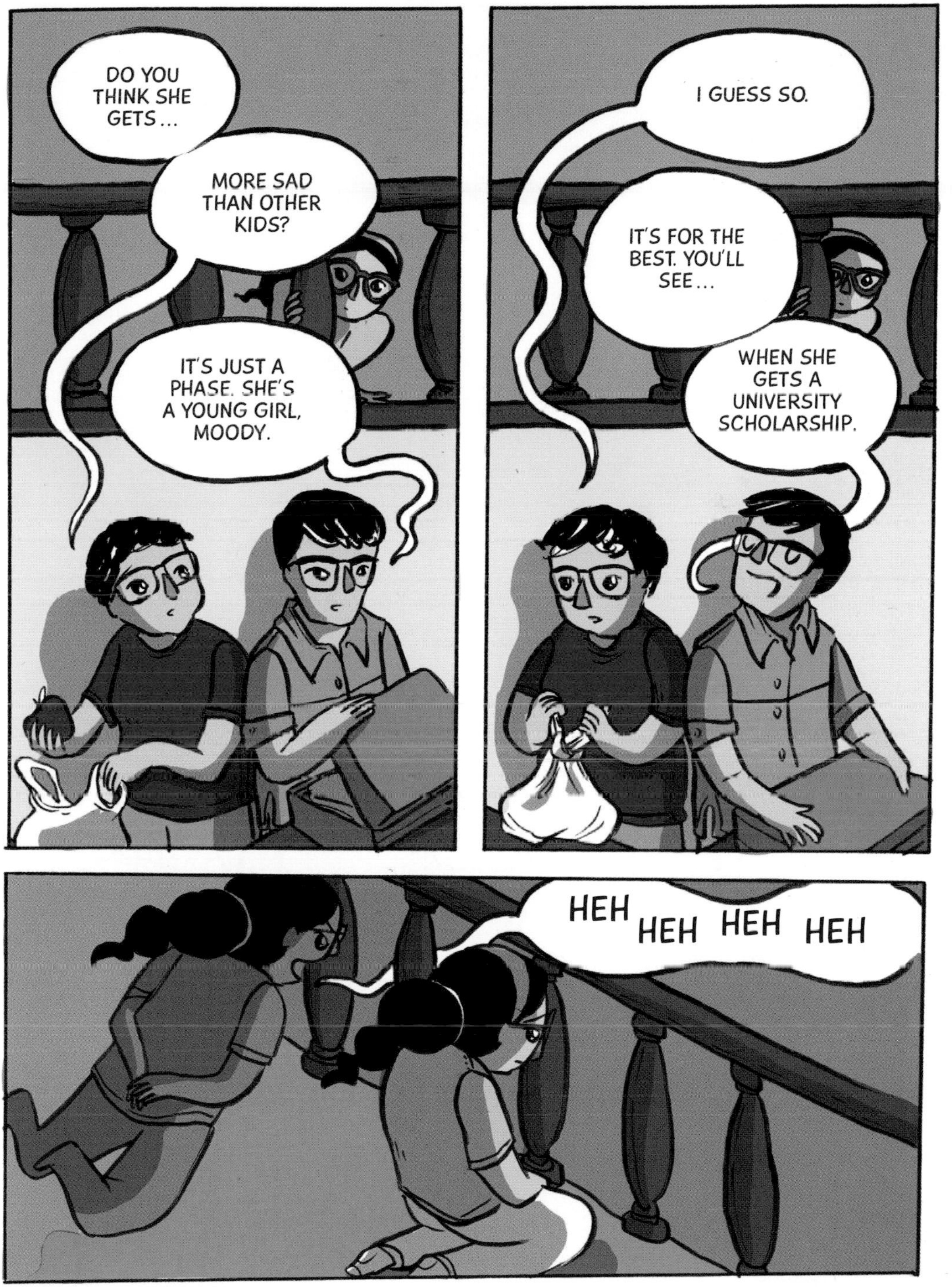
DO YOU THINK SHE GETS...
MORE SAD THAN OTHER KIDS?
IT'S JUST A PHASE. SHE'S A YOUNG GIRL, MOODY.
I GUESS SO.
IT'S FOR THE BEST. YOU'LL SEE...
WHEN SHE GETS A UNIVERSITY SCHOLARSHIP.
HEH HEH HEH HEH

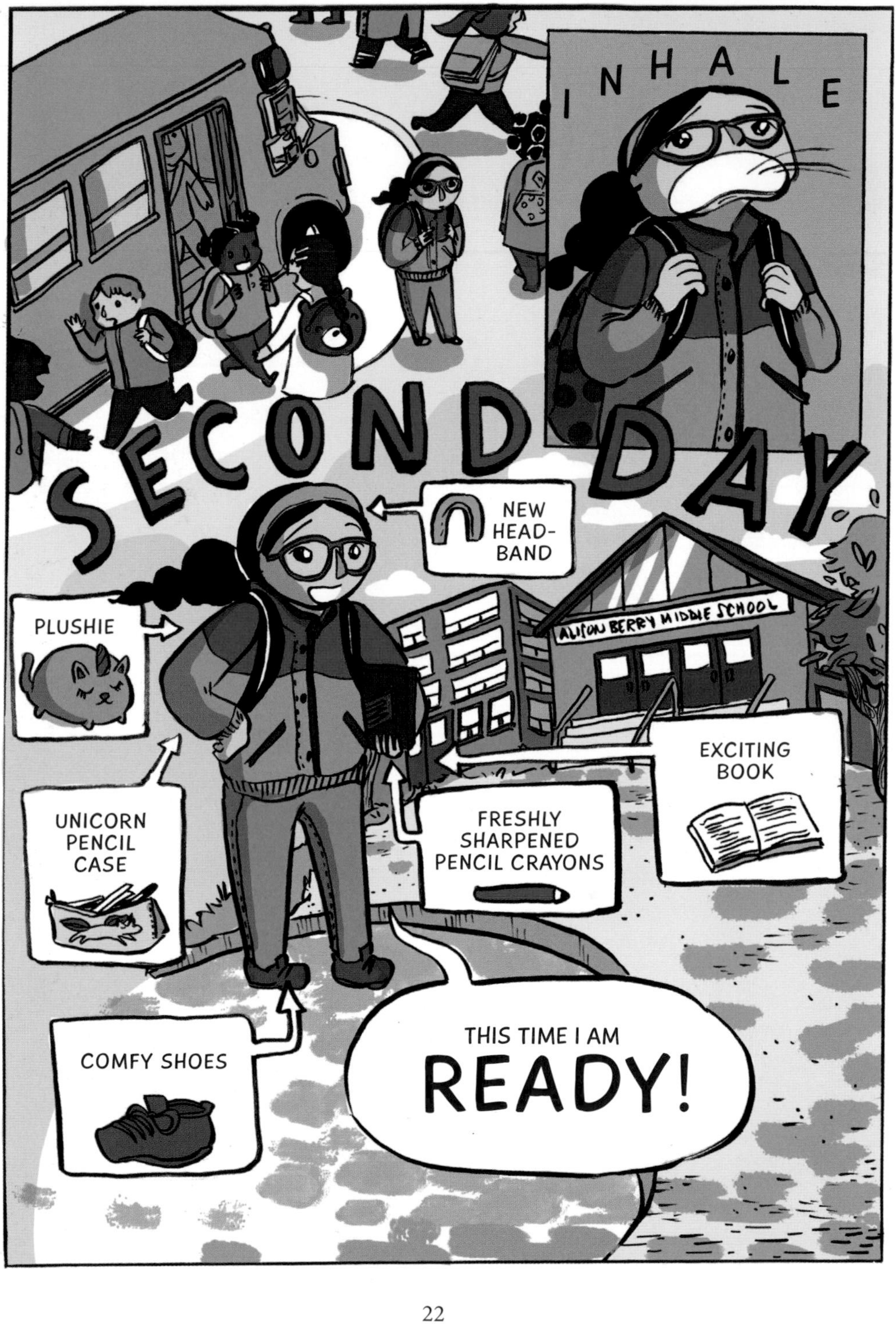
INHALE
SECOND DAY
NEW HEAD-BAND
PLUSHIE
ALISON BERRY MIDDLE SCHOOL
UNICORN PENCIL CASE
FRESHLY SHARPENED PENCIL CRAYONS
EXCITING BOOK
COMFY SHOES
THIS TIME I AM READY!

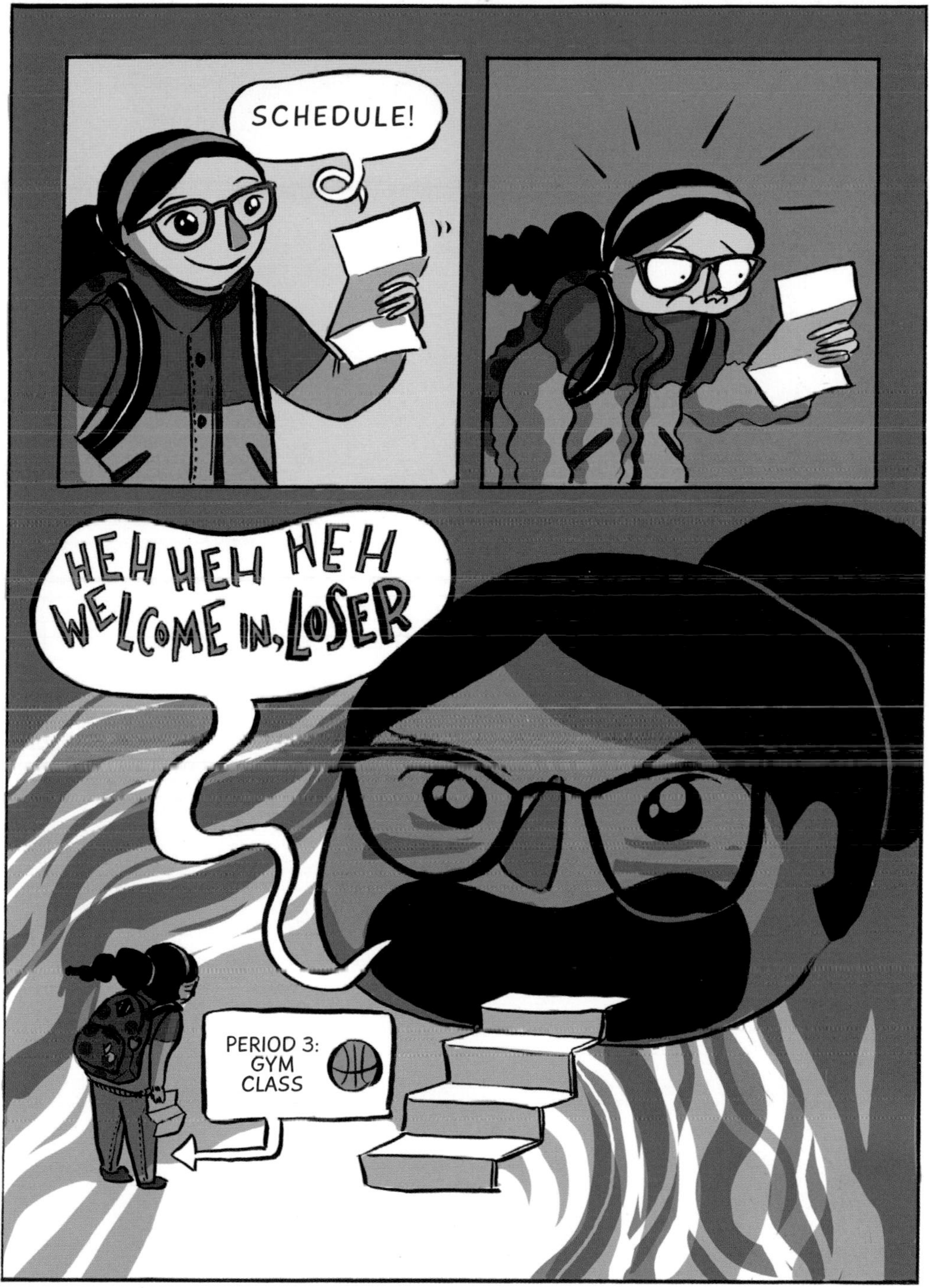
SCHEDULE!
HEH HEH HEH
WELCOME IN, LOSER
PERIOD 3:
GYM
CLASS

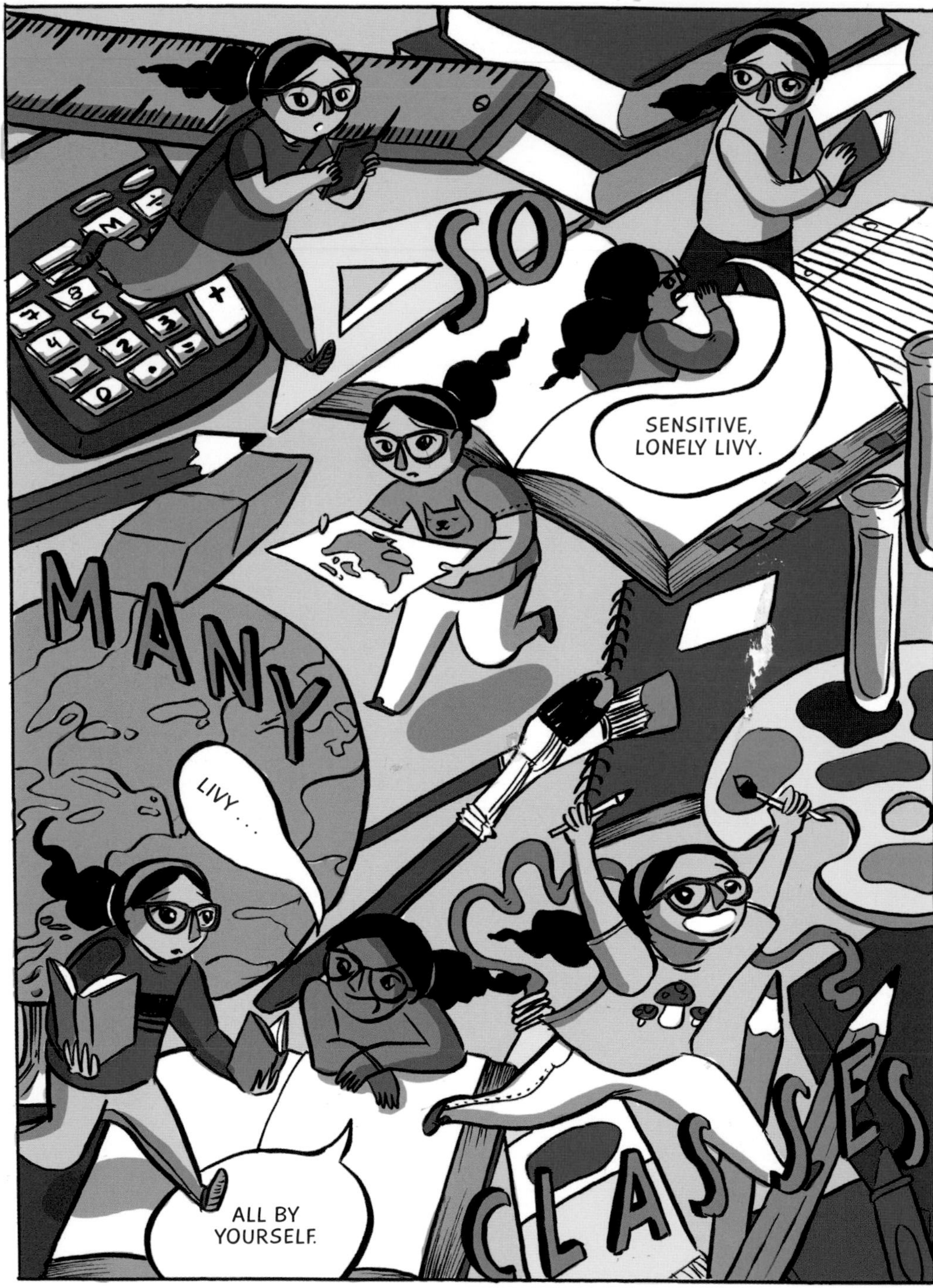
SO
SENSITIVE,
LONELY LIVY.
MANY
LIVY . . .
ALL BY
YOURSELF.
CLASSES

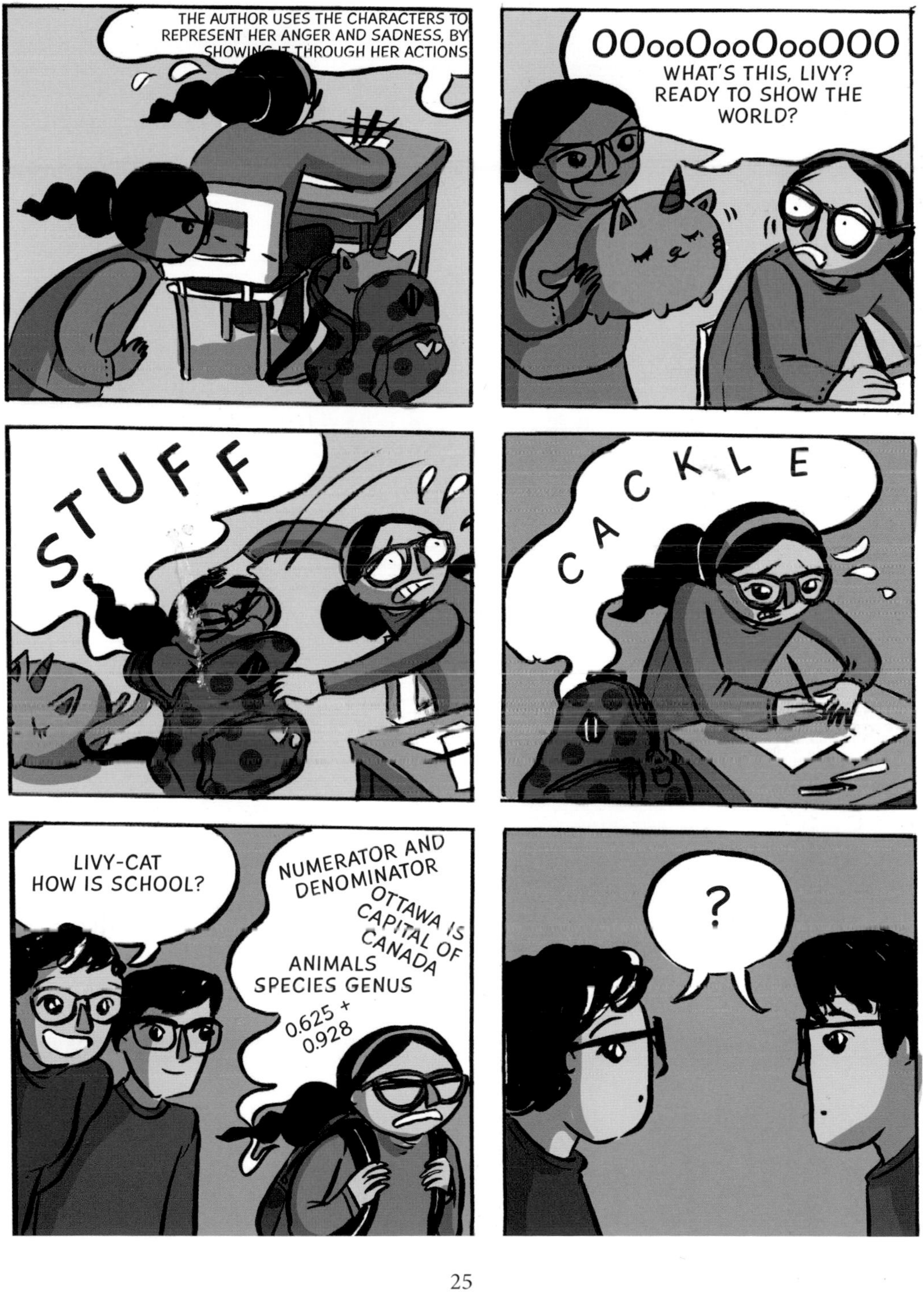
THE AUTHOR USES THE CHARACTERS TO REPRESENT HER ANGER AND SADNESS, BY SHOWING IT THROUGH HER ACTIONS
OOooOooOooOOO
WHAT'S THIS, LIVY? READY TO SHOW THE WORLD?
STUFF
CACKLE
LIVY-CAT HOW IS SCHOOL?
NUMERATOR AND DENOMINATOR
OTTAWA IS CAPITAL OF CANADA
ANIMALS SPECIES GENUS
0.625 + 0.928
?

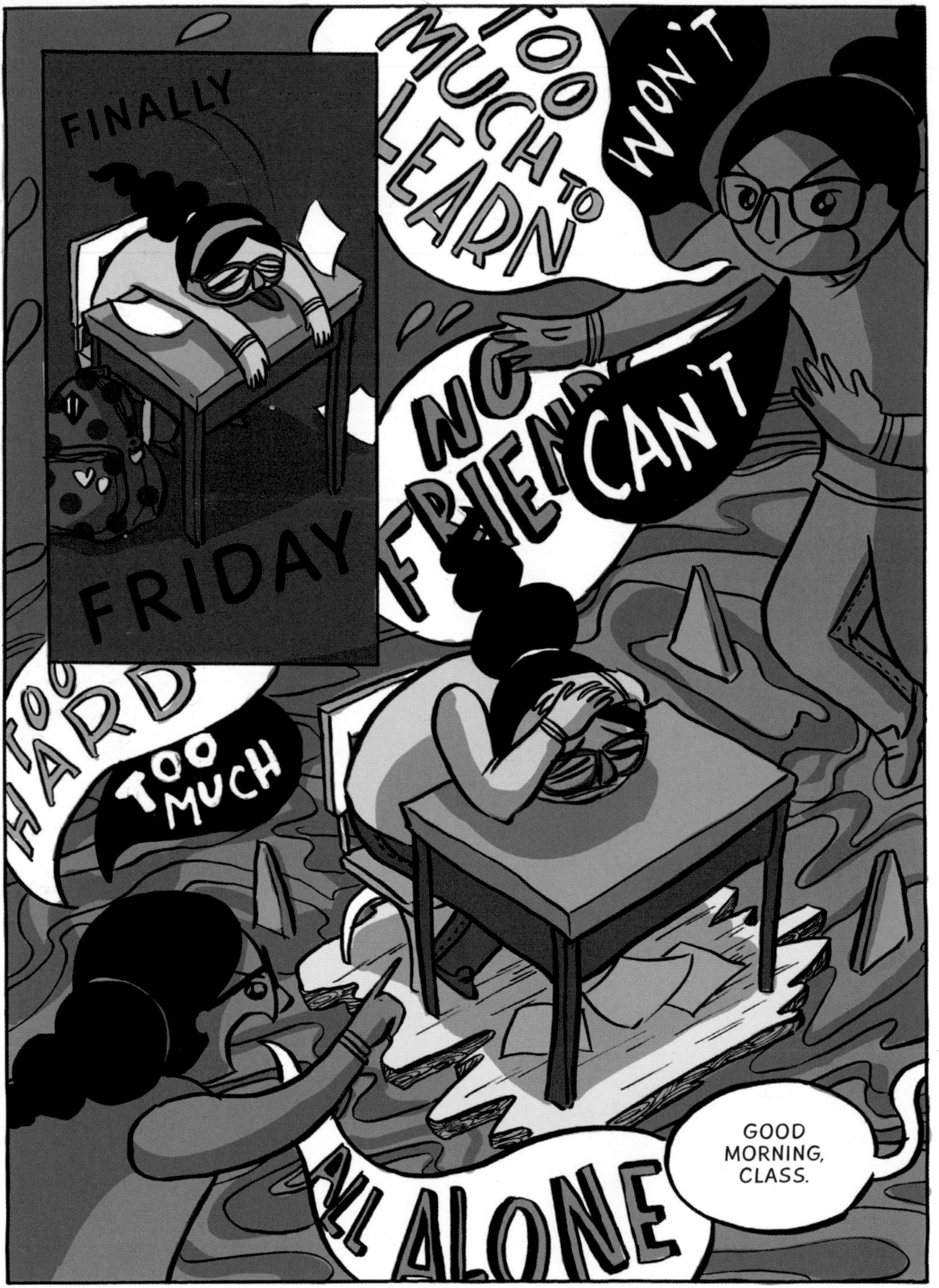
FINALLY
FRIDAY
TOO MUCH TO LEARN
WON'T
NO FRIEN
CAN'T
TOO HARD
TOO MUCH
ALL ALONE
GOOD MORNING, CLASS.

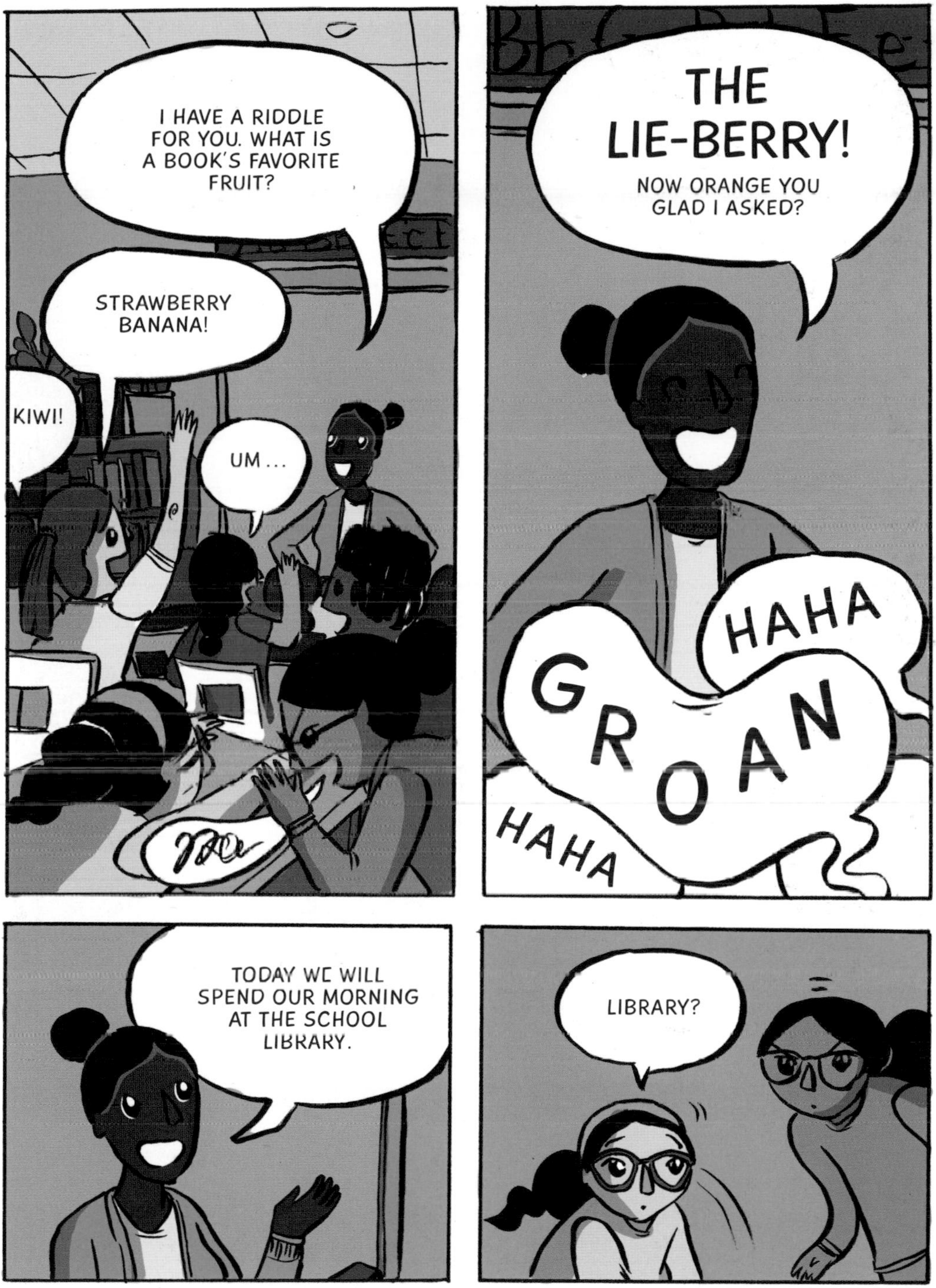
I HAVE A RIDDLE FOR YOU. WHAT IS A BOOK'S FAVORITE FRUIT?
STRAWBERRY BANANA!
KIWI!
UM . . .
THE LIE-BERRY!
NOW ORANGE YOU GLAD I ASKED?
HAHA
GROAN
HAHA
TODAY WE WILL SPEND OUR MORNING AT THE SCHOOL LIBRARY.
LIBRARY?

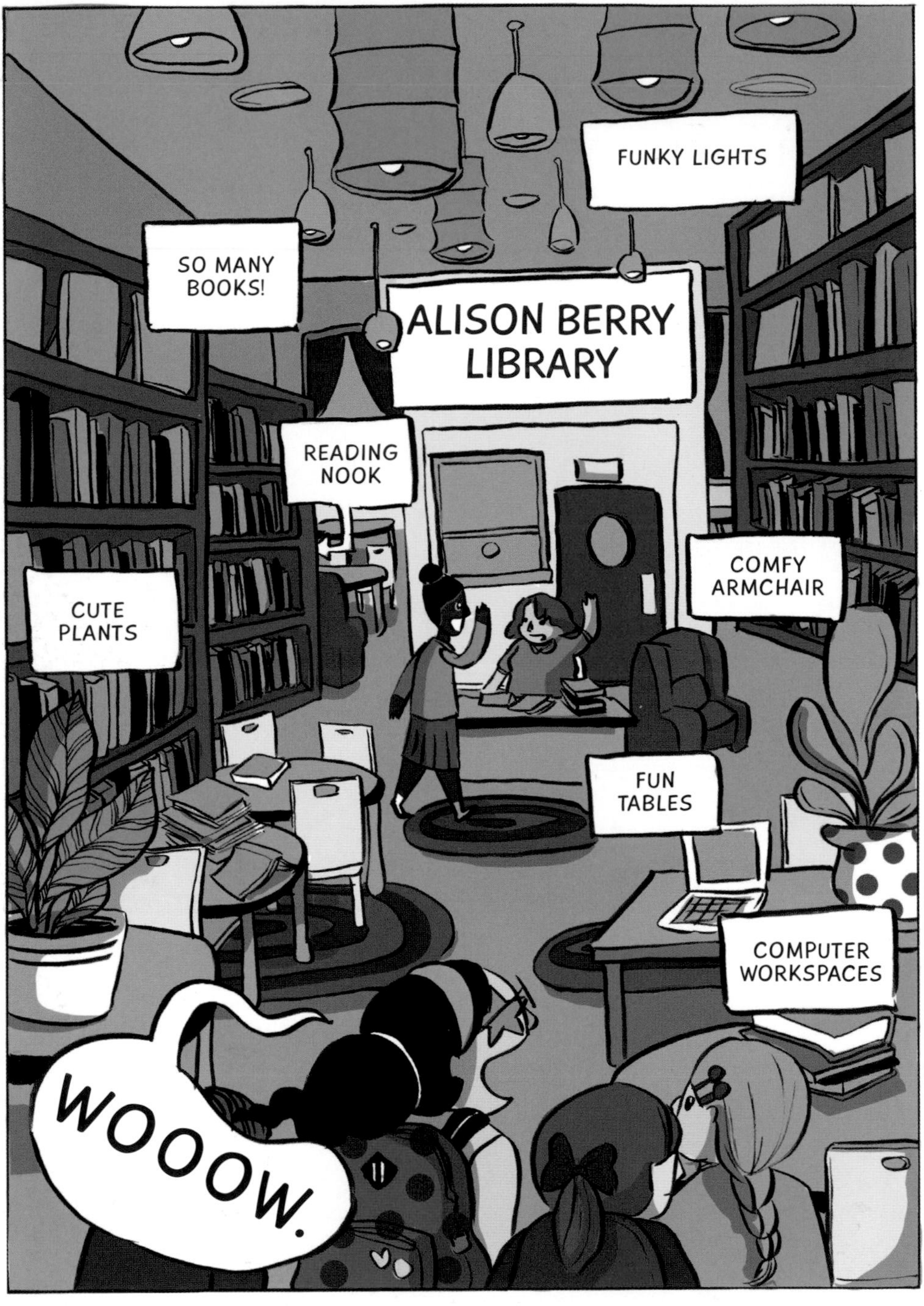
FUNKY LIGHTS
SO MANY BOOKS!
ALISON BERRY LIBRARY
READING NOOK
COMFY ARMCHAIR
CUTE PLANTS
FUN TABLES
COMPUTER WORKSPACES
WOOOW.

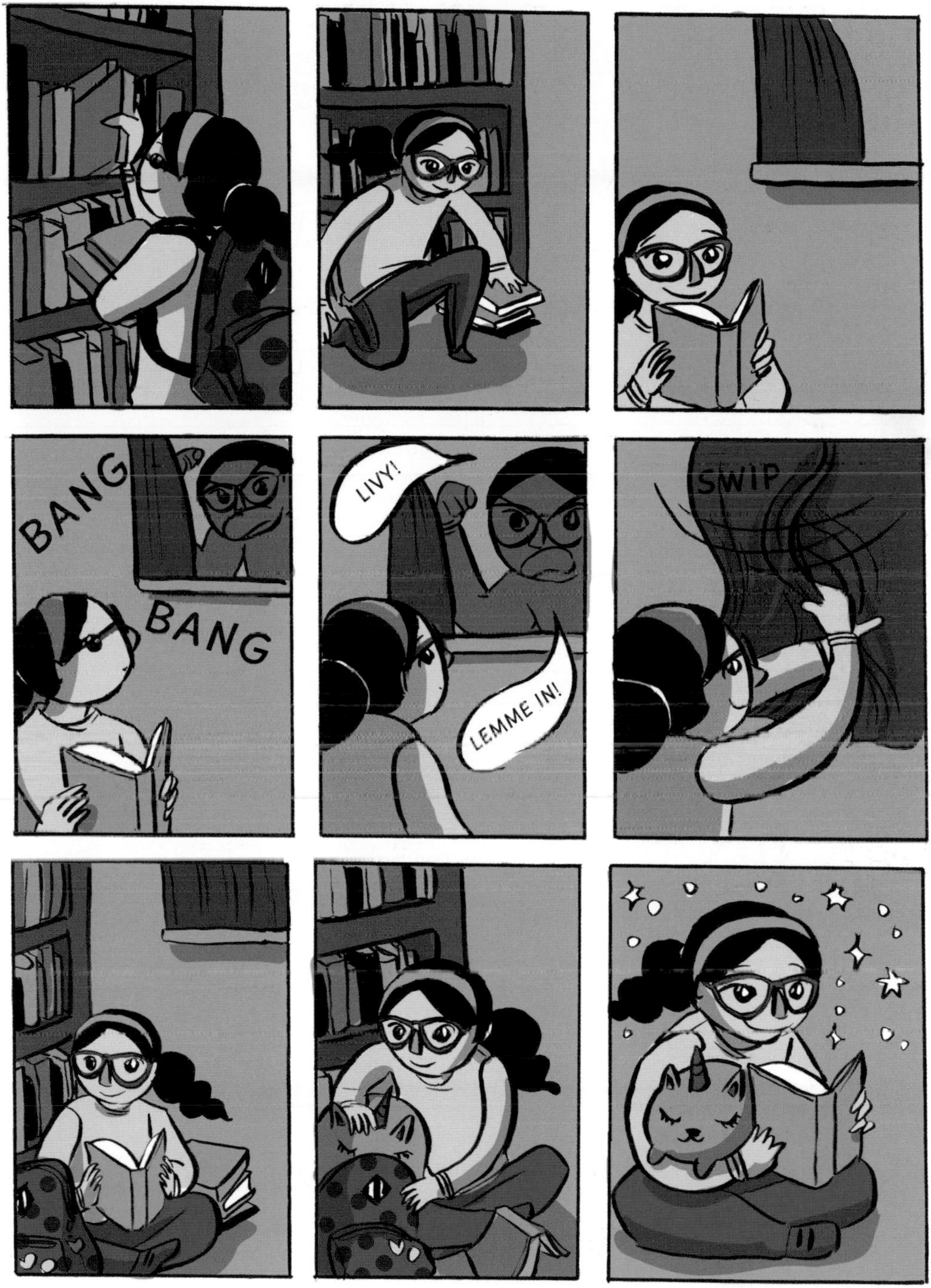
BANG
BANG
LIVY!
LEMME IN!
SWIP

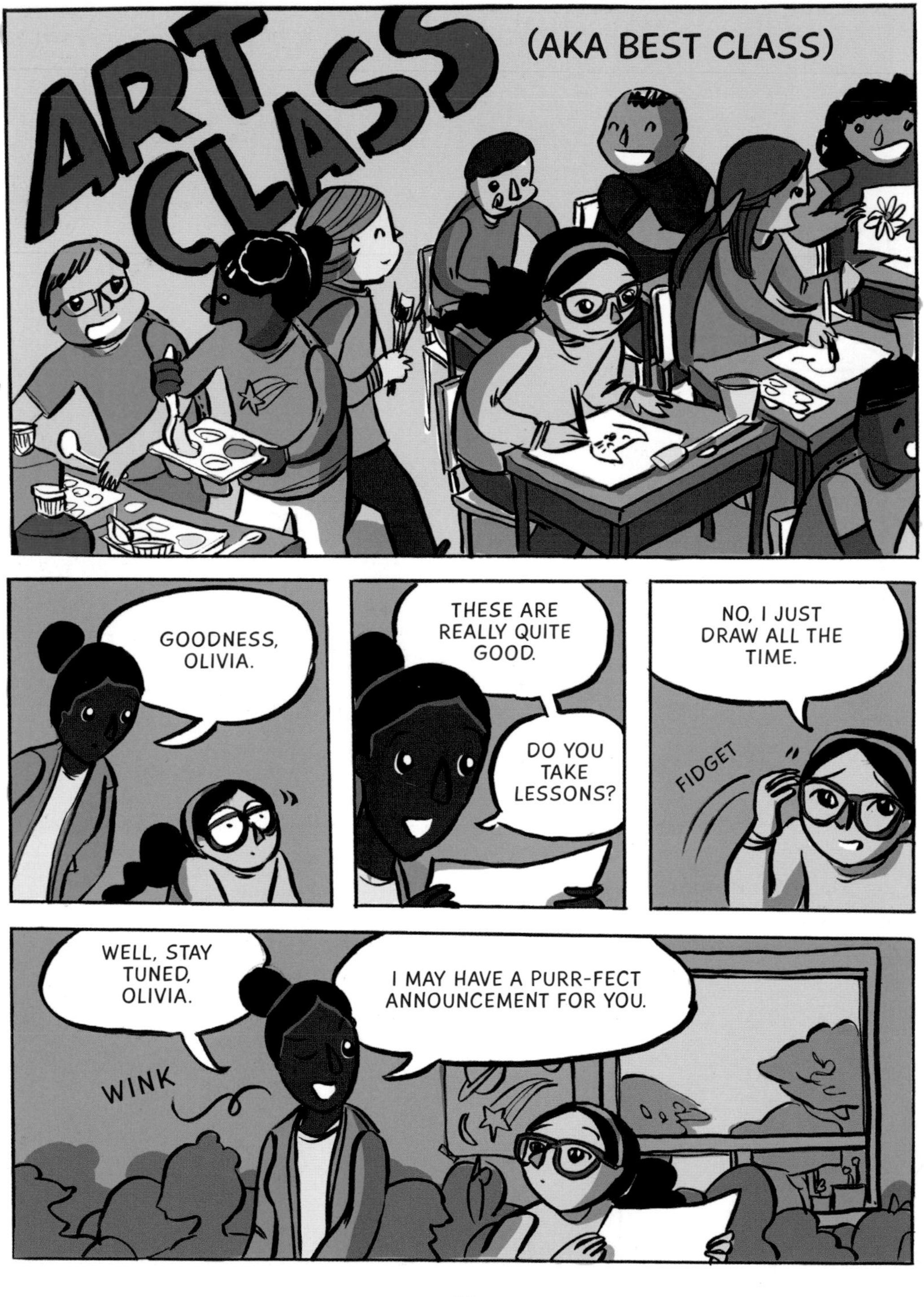
ART CLASS
(AKA BEST CLASS)
GOODNESS, OLIVIA.
THESE ARE REALLY QUITE GOOD.
DO YOU TAKE LESSONS?
NO, I JUST DRAW ALL THE TIME.
FIDGET
WELL, STAY TUNED, OLIVIA.
I MAY HAVE A PURR-FECT ANNOUNCEMENT FOR YOU.
WINK

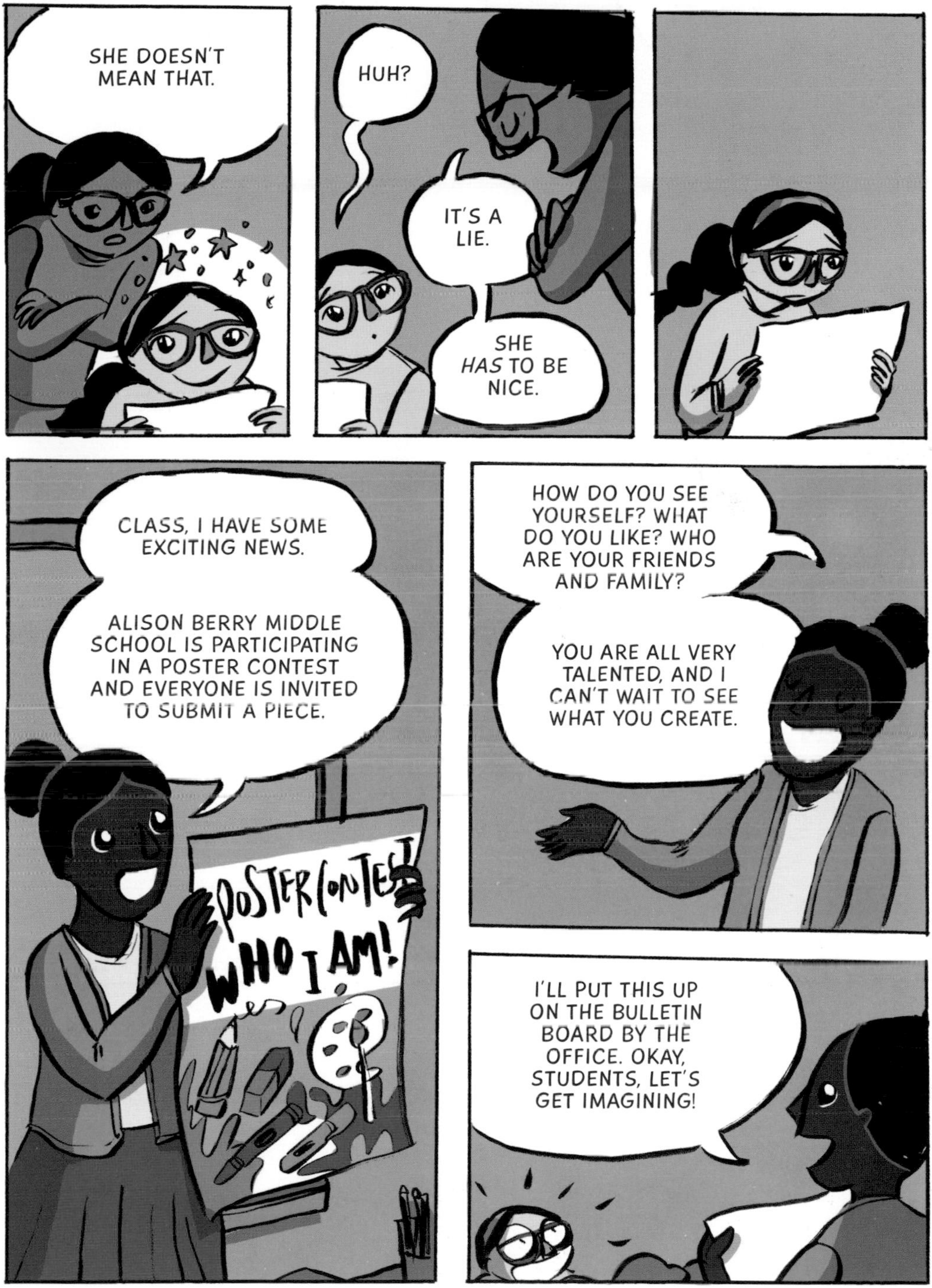
SHE DOESN'T MEAN THAT.
HUH?
IT'S A LIE.
SHE *HAS* TO BE NICE.
CLASS, I HAVE SOME EXCITING NEWS.
ALISON BERRY MIDDLE SCHOOL IS PARTICIPATING IN A POSTER CONTEST AND EVERYONE IS INVITED TO SUBMIT A PIECE.
POSTER CONTEST
WHO I AM!
HOW DO YOU SEE YOURSELF? WHAT DO YOU LIKE? WHO ARE YOUR FRIENDS AND FAMILY?
YOU ARE ALL VERY TALENTED, AND I CAN'T WAIT TO SEE WHAT YOU CREATE.
I'LL PUT THIS UP ON THE BULLETIN BOARD BY THE OFFICE. OKAY, STUDENTS, LET'S GET IMAGINING!

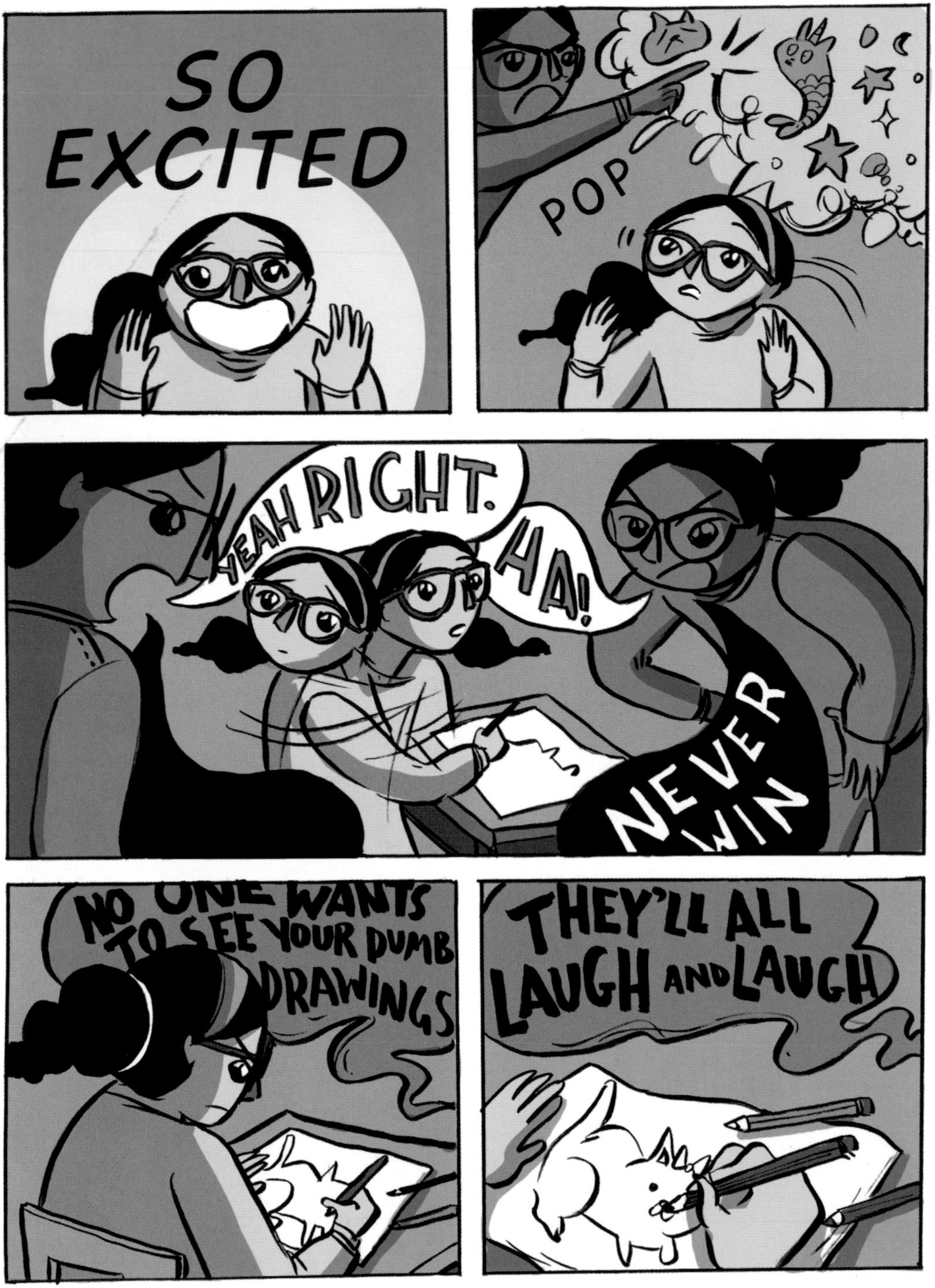
SO EXCITED
POP
YEAH RIGHT.
HA!
NEVER WIN
NO ONE WANTS TO SEE YOUR DUMB DRAWINGS
THEY'LL ALL LAUGH AND LAUGH

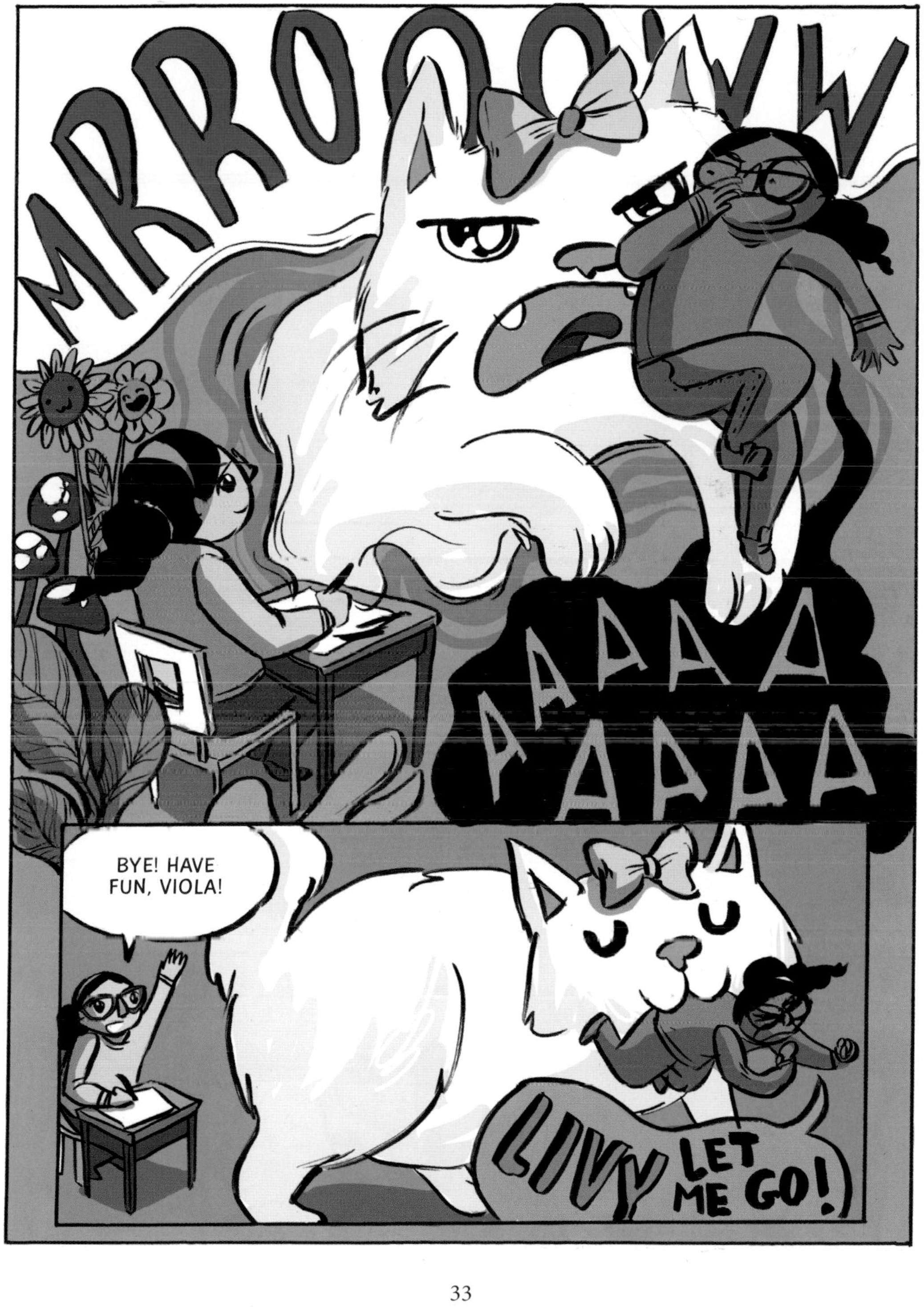
MRROOOWW
AAAA AAAAA
BYE! HAVE FUN, VIOLA!
LIVY LET ME GO!

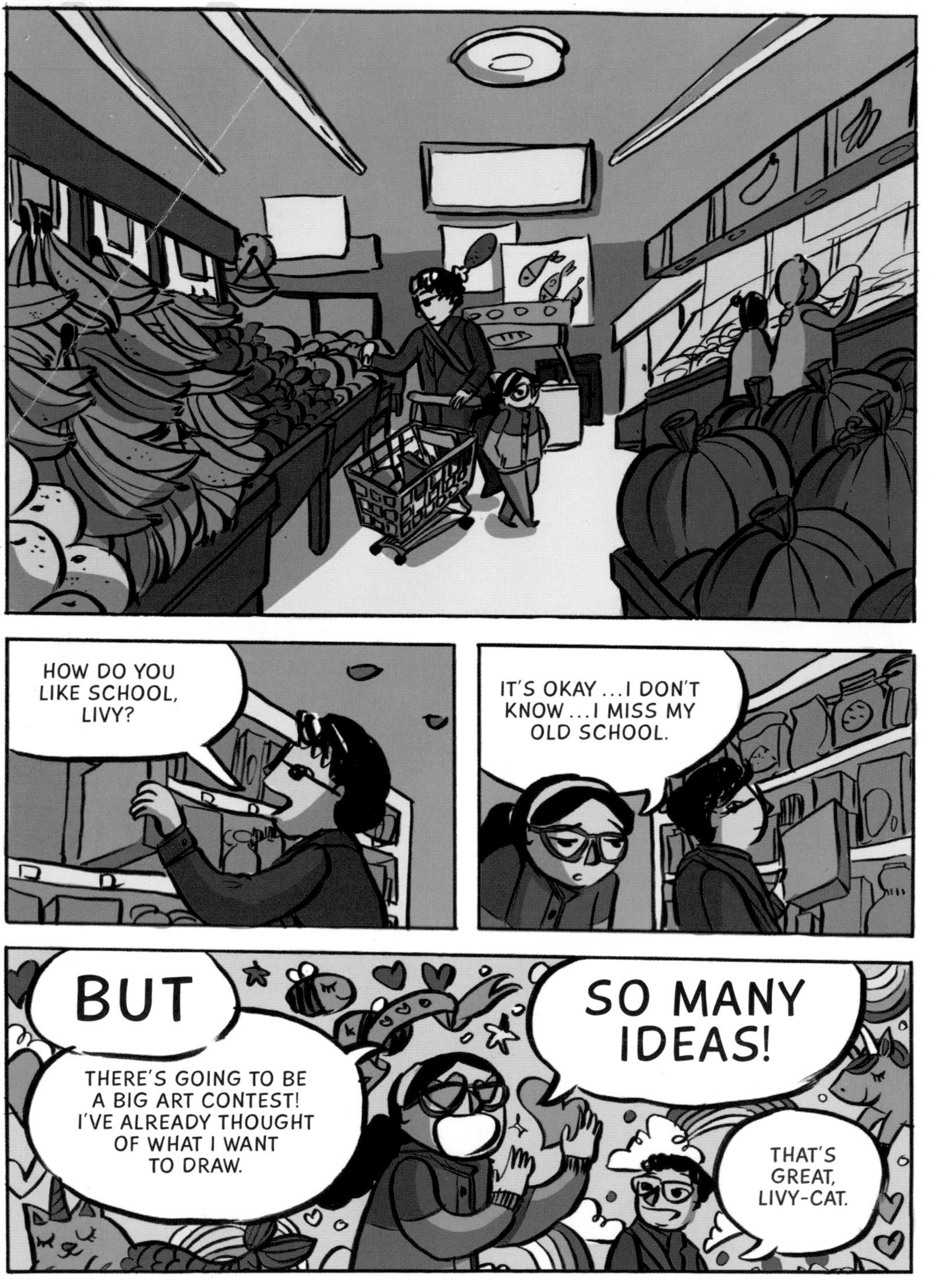
HOW DO YOU LIKE SCHOOL, LIVY?
IT'S OKAY ...I DON'T KNOW ...I MISS MY OLD SCHOOL.
BUT
THERE'S GOING TO BE A BIG ART CONTEST! I'VE ALREADY THOUGHT OF WHAT I WANT TO DRAW.
SO MANY IDEAS!
THAT'S GREAT, LIVY-CAT.

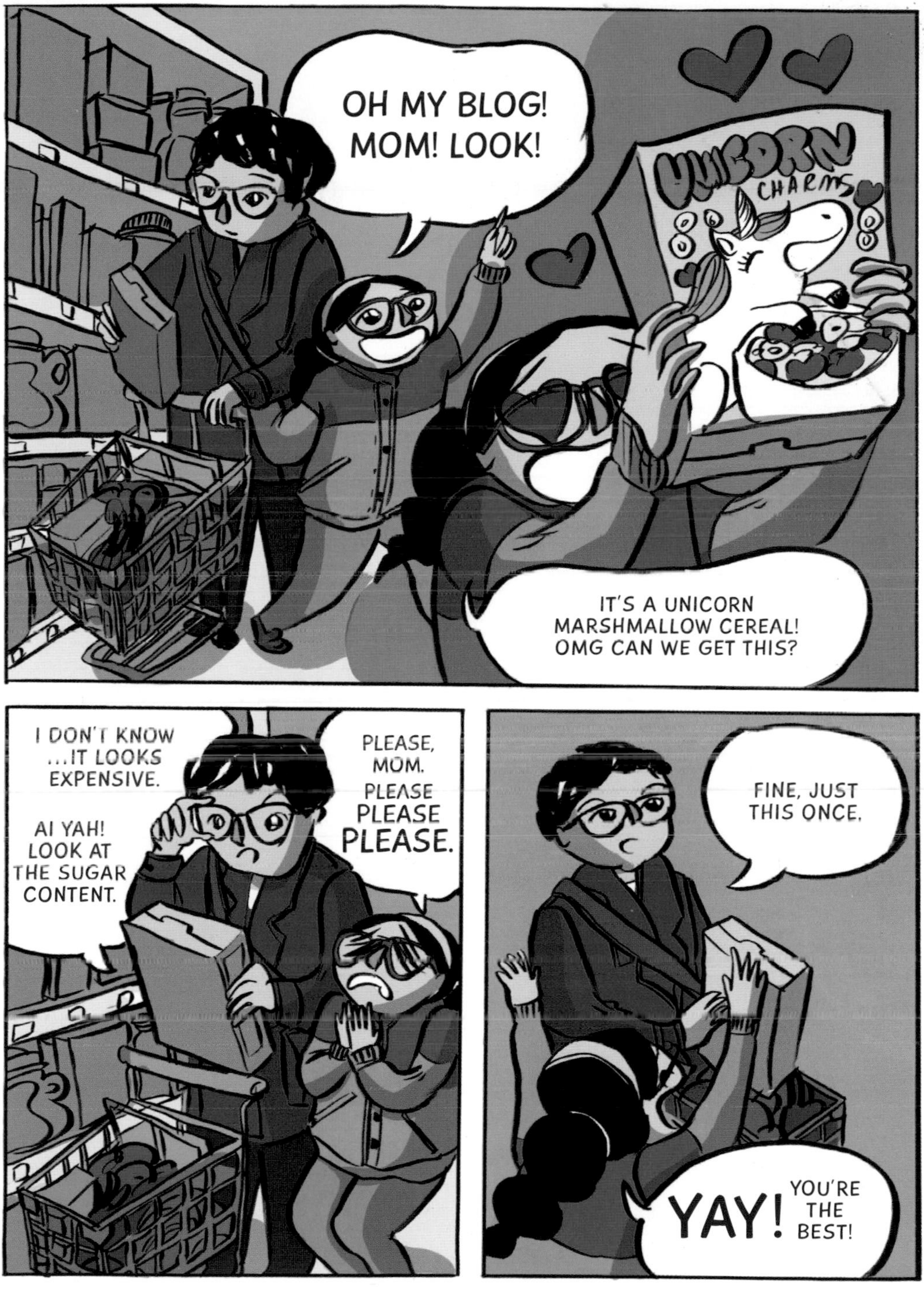
OH MY BLOG! MOM! LOOK!
UNICORN CHARMS
IT'S A UNICORN MARSHMALLOW CEREAL! OMG CAN WE GET THIS?
I DON'T KNOW ...IT LOOKS EXPENSIVE.
AI YAH! LOOK AT THE SUGAR CONTENT.
PLEASE, MOM. PLEASE PLEASE PLEASE.
FINE, JUST THIS ONCE.
YAY! YOU'RE THE BEST!

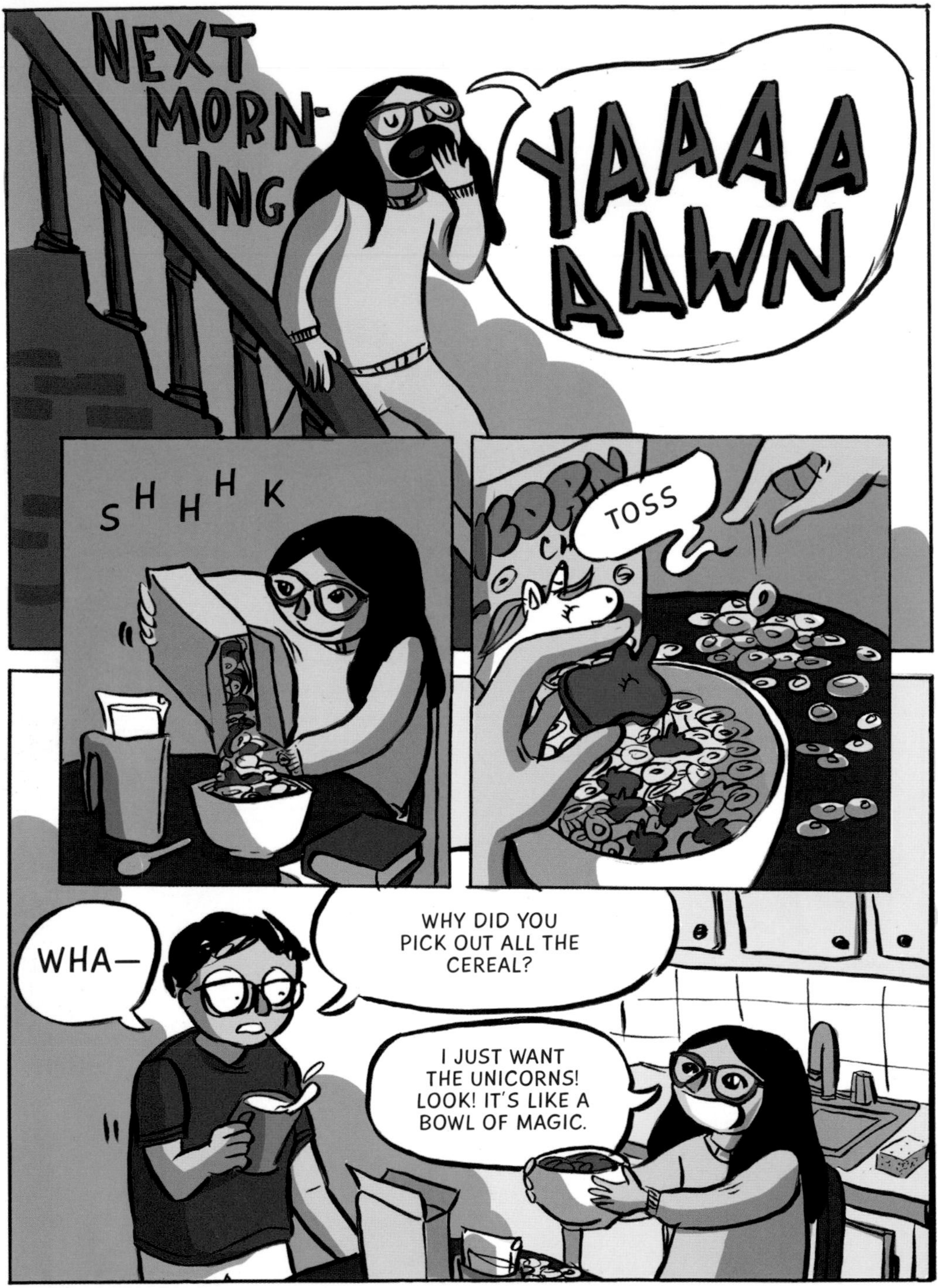
NEXT MORN-ING
YAAAA AAWN
SHHHK
TOSS
WHA—
WHY DID YOU PICK OUT ALL THE CEREAL?
I JUST WANT THE UNICORNS! LOOK! IT'S LIKE A BOWL OF MAGIC.

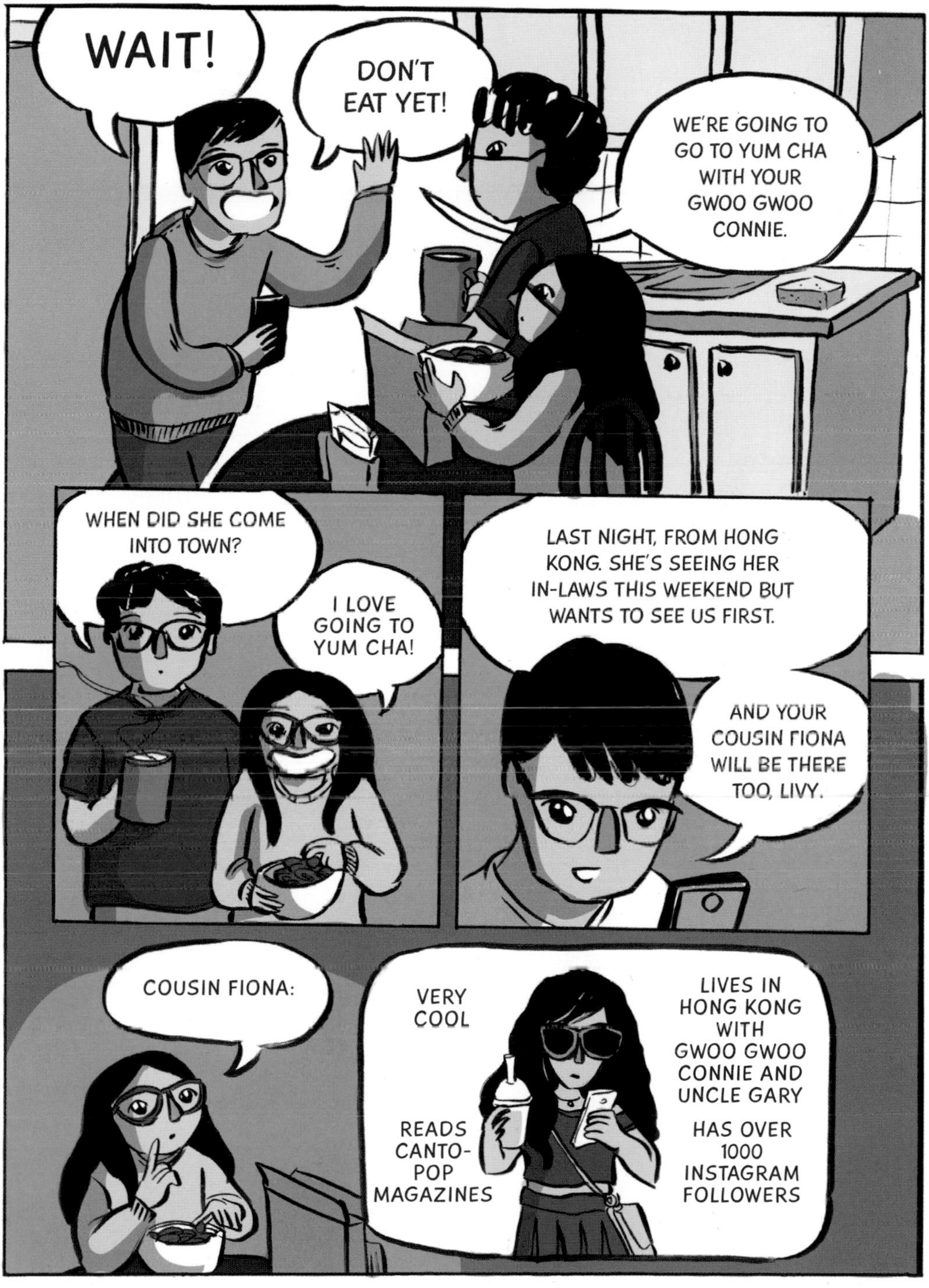
WAIT!
DON'T EAT YET!
WE'RE GOING TO GO TO YUM CHA WITH YOUR GWOO GWOO CONNIE.
WHEN DID SHE COME INTO TOWN?
I LOVE GOING TO YUM CHA!
LAST NIGHT, FROM HONG KONG. SHE'S SEEING HER IN-LAWS THIS WEEKEND BUT WANTS TO SEE US FIRST.
AND YOUR COUSIN FIONA WILL BE THERE TOO, LIVY.
COUSIN FIONA:
VERY COOL
LIVES IN HONG KONG WITH GWOO GWOO CONNIE AND UNCLE GARY
READS CANTO-POP MAGAZINES
HAS OVER 1000 INSTAGRAM FOLLOWERS

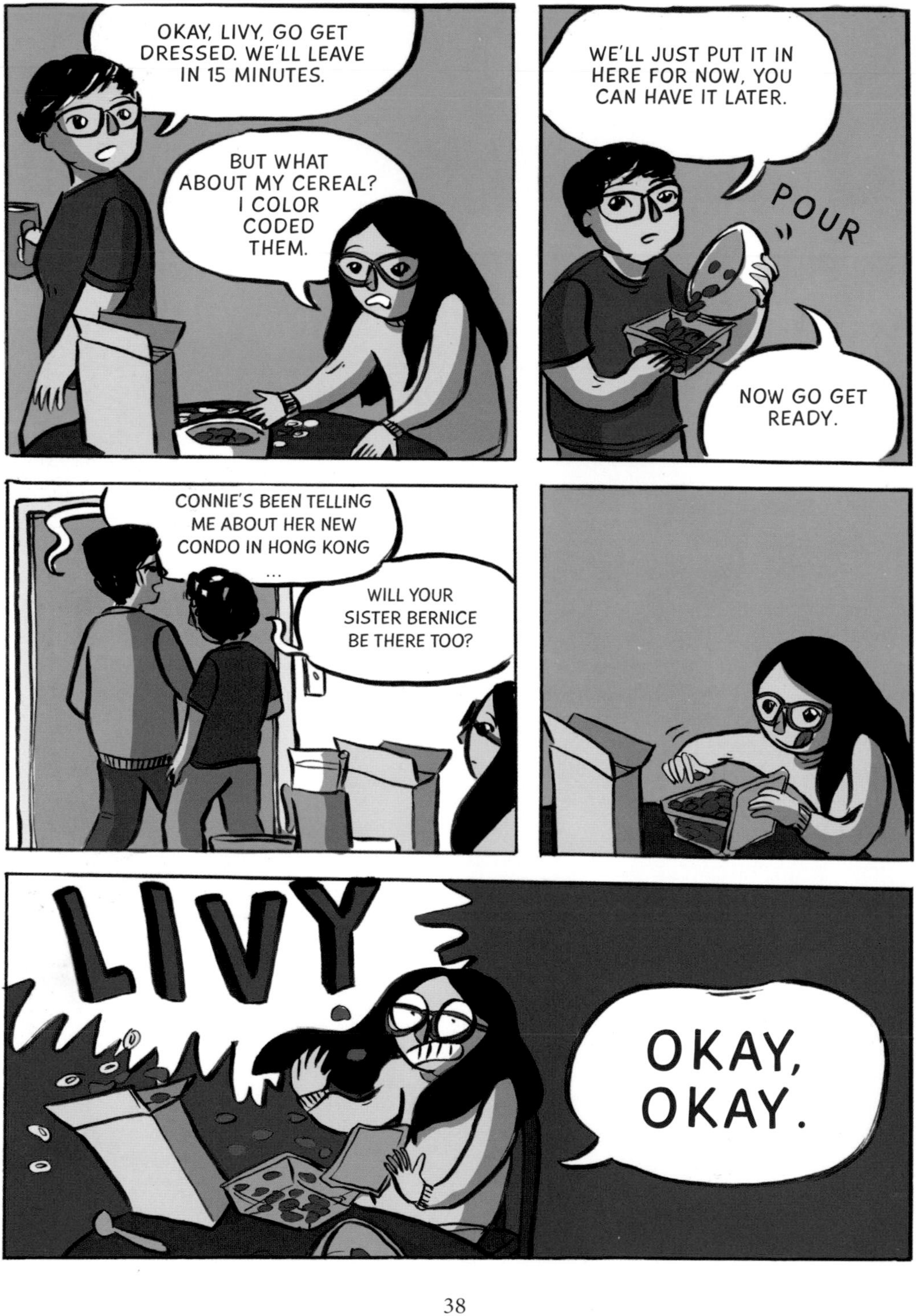
OKAY, LIVY, GO GET DRESSED. WE'LL LEAVE IN 15 MINUTES.
BUT WHAT ABOUT MY CEREAL? I COLOR CODED THEM.
WE'LL JUST PUT IT IN HERE FOR NOW, YOU CAN HAVE IT LATER.
POUR
NOW GO GET READY.
CONNIE'S BEEN TELLING ME ABOUT HER NEW CONDO IN HONG KONG ...
WILL YOUR SISTER BERNICE BE THERE TOO?
LIVY
OKAY, OKAY.

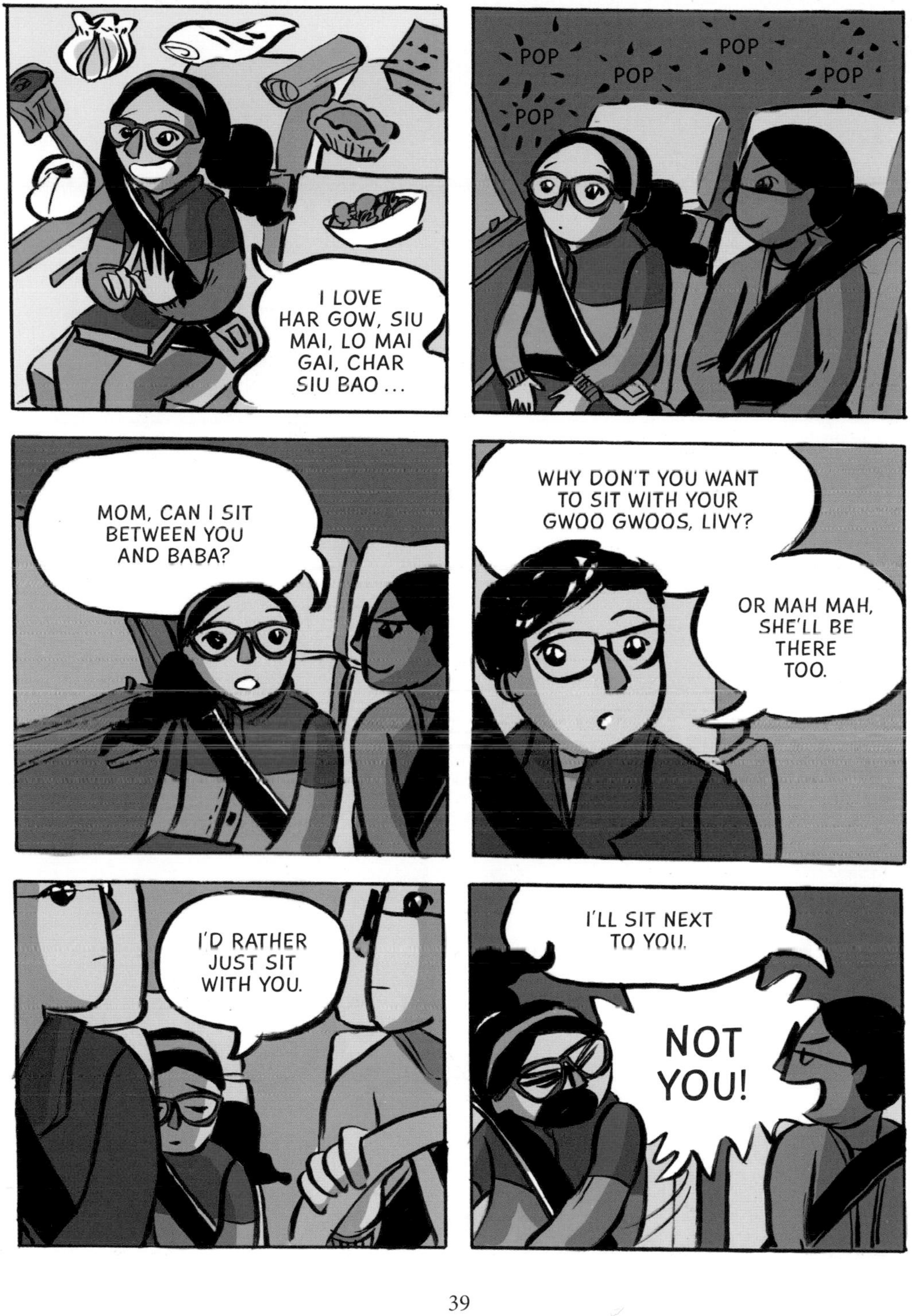
I LOVE HAR GOW, SIU MAI, LO MAI GAI, CHAR SIU BAO ...
POP
POP
POP
POP
POP
MOM, CAN I SIT BETWEEN YOU AND BABA?
WHY DON'T YOU WANT TO SIT WITH YOUR GWOO GWOOS, LIVY?
OR MAH MAH, SHE'LL BE THERE TOO.
I'D RATHER JUST SIT WITH YOU.
I'LL SIT NEXT TO YOU.
NOT YOU!

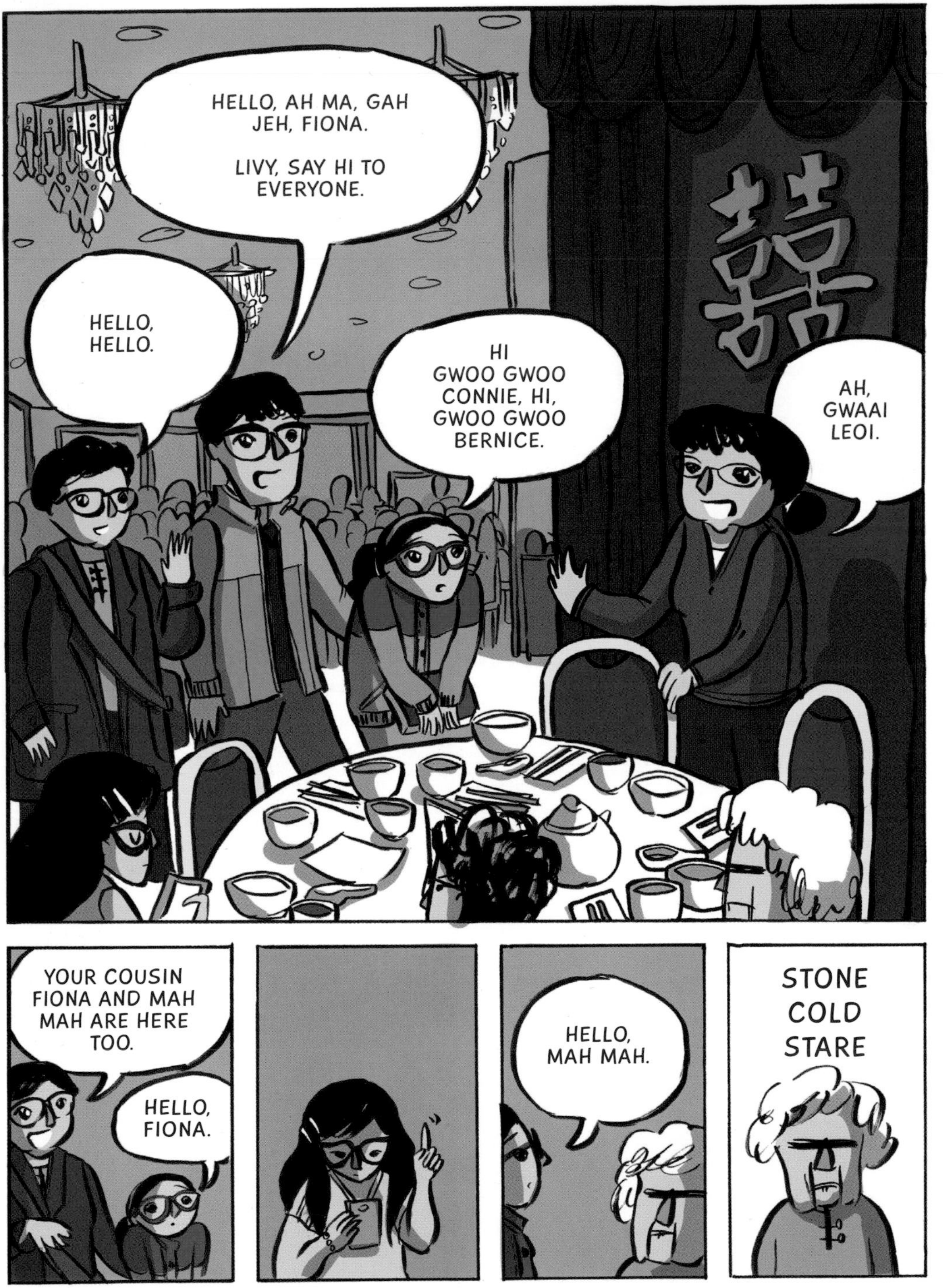
HELLO, AH MA, GAH JEH, FIONA.
LIVY, SAY HI TO EVERYONE.
HELLO, HELLO.
HI GWOO GWOO CONNIE, HI, GWOO GWOO BERNICE.
AH, GWAAI LEOI.
YOUR COUSIN FIONA AND MAH MAH ARE HERE TOO.
HELLO, FIONA.
HELLO, MAH MAH.
STONE COLD STARE

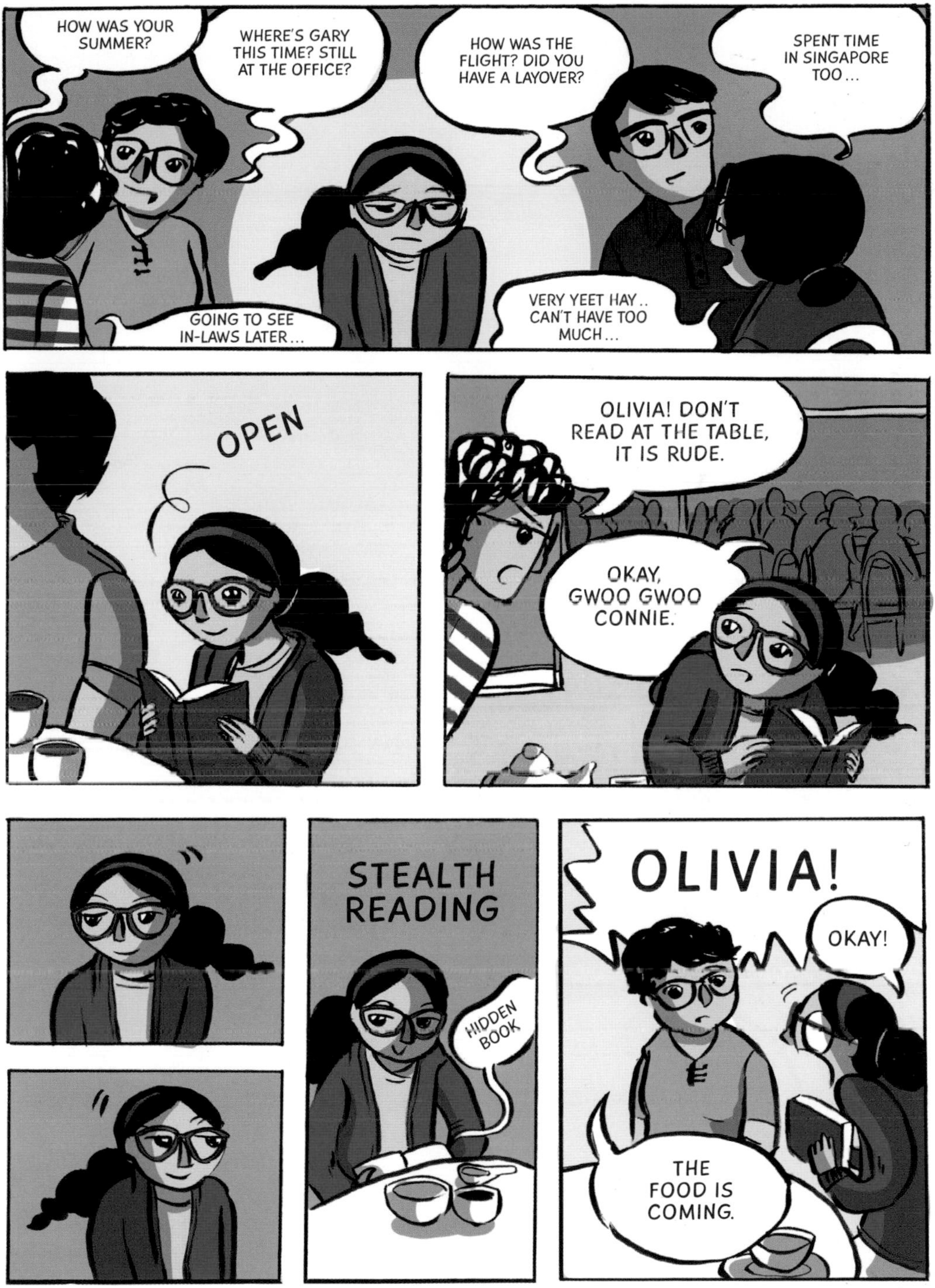
HOW WAS YOUR SUMMER?
WHERE'S GARY THIS TIME? STILL AT THE OFFICE?
HOW WAS THE FLIGHT? DID YOU HAVE A LAYOVER?
SPENT TIME IN SINGAPORE TOO...
GOING TO SEE IN-LAWS LATER...
VERY YEET HAY.. CAN'T HAVE TOO MUCH...
OPEN
OLIVIA! DON'T READ AT THE TABLE, IT IS RUDE.
OKAY, GWOO GWOO CONNIE.
STEALTH READING
HIDDEN BOOK
OLIVIA!
OKAY!
THE FOOD IS COMING.

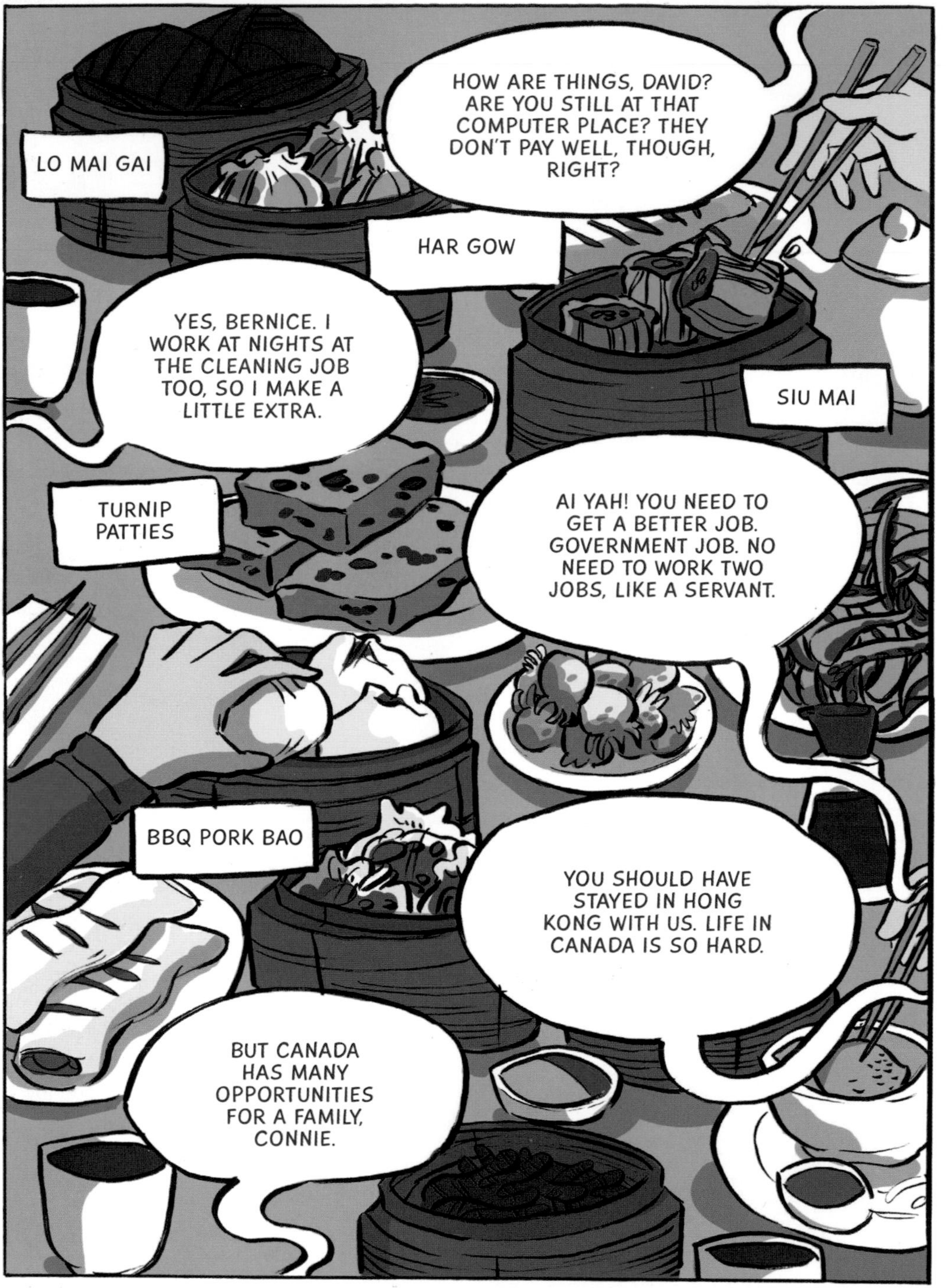
LO MAI GAI
HOW ARE THINGS, DAVID? ARE YOU STILL AT THAT COMPUTER PLACE? THEY DON'T PAY WELL, THOUGH, RIGHT?
HAR GOW
YES, BERNICE. I WORK AT NIGHTS AT THE CLEANING JOB TOO, SO I MAKE A LITTLE EXTRA.
SIU MAI
TURNIP PATTIES
AI YAH! YOU NEED TO GET A BETTER JOB. GOVERNMENT JOB. NO NEED TO WORK TWO JOBS, LIKE A SERVANT.
BBQ PORK BAO
YOU SHOULD HAVE STAYED IN HONG KONG WITH US. LIFE IN CANADA IS SO HARD.
BUT CANADA HAS MANY OPPORTUNITIES FOR A FAMILY, CONNIE.

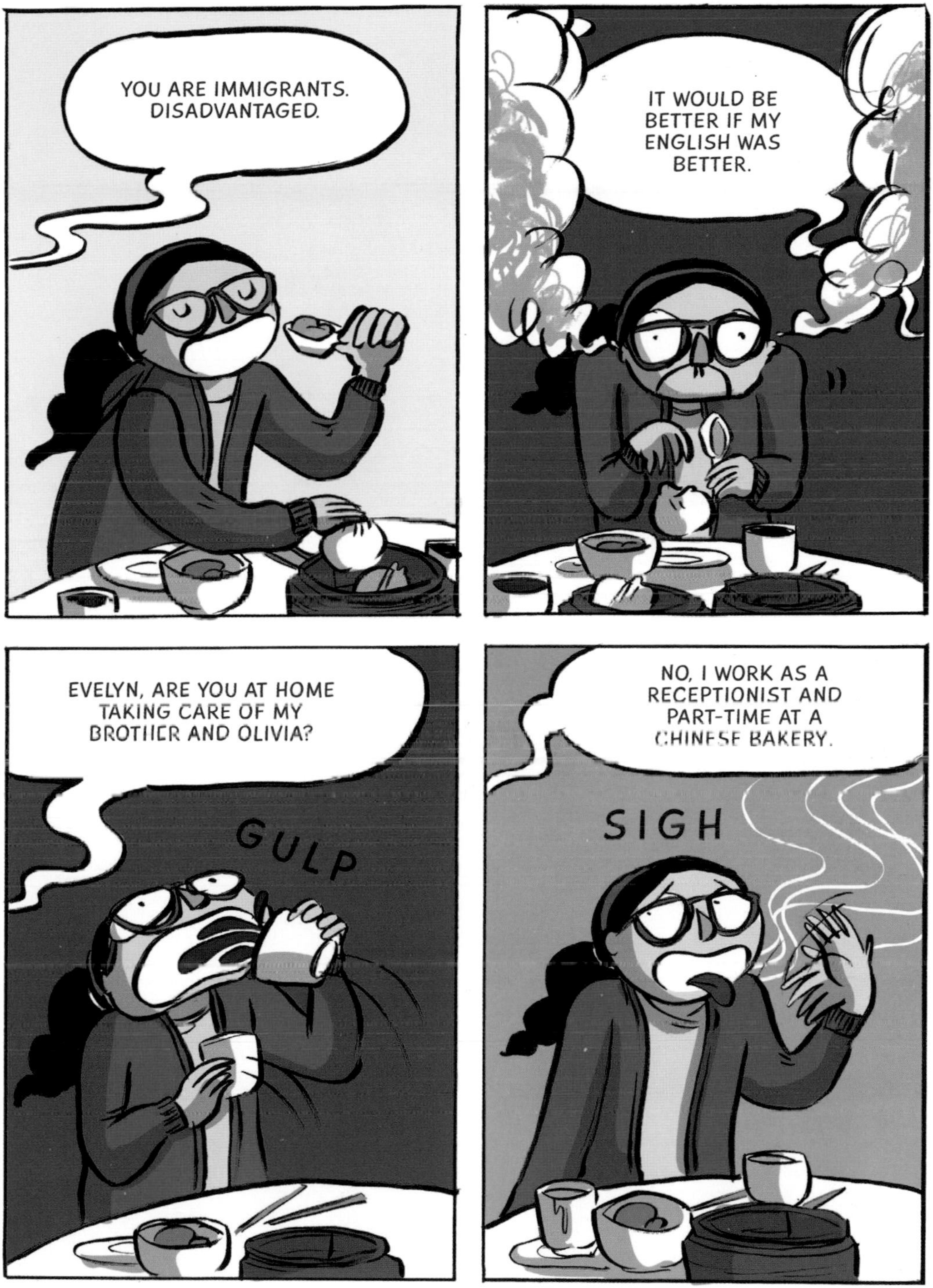
YOU ARE IMMIGRANTS. DISADVANTAGED.
IT WOULD BE BETTER IF MY ENGLISH WAS BETTER.
EVELYN, ARE YOU AT HOME TAKING CARE OF MY BROTHER AND OLIVIA?
GULP
NO, I WORK AS A RECEPTIONIST AND PART-TIME AT A CHINESE BAKERY.
SIGH

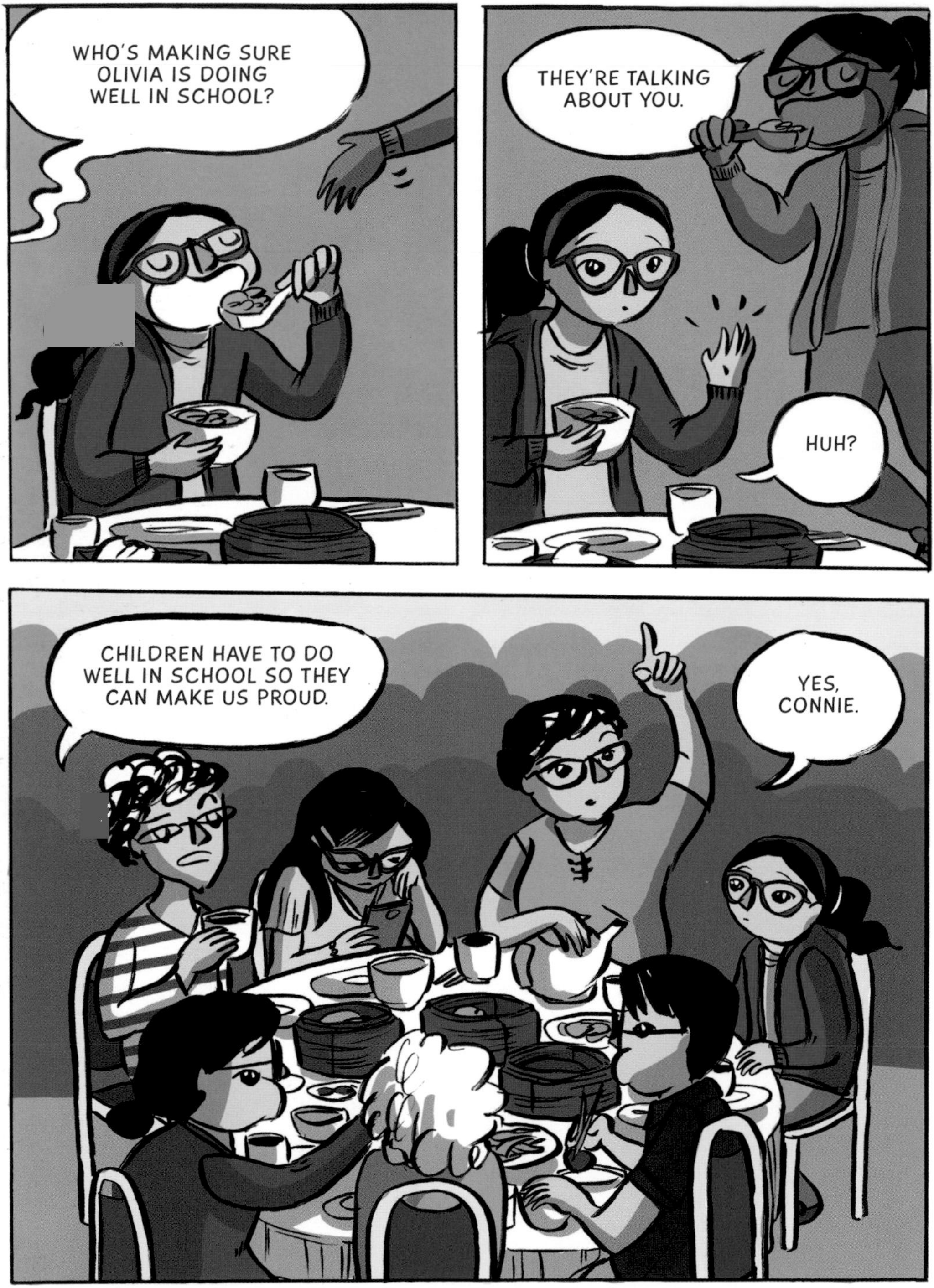
WHO'S MAKING SURE OLIVIA IS DOING WELL IN SCHOOL?
THEY'RE TALKING ABOUT YOU.
HUH?
CHILDREN HAVE TO DO WELL IN SCHOOL SO THEY CAN MAKE US PROUD.
YES, CONNIE.

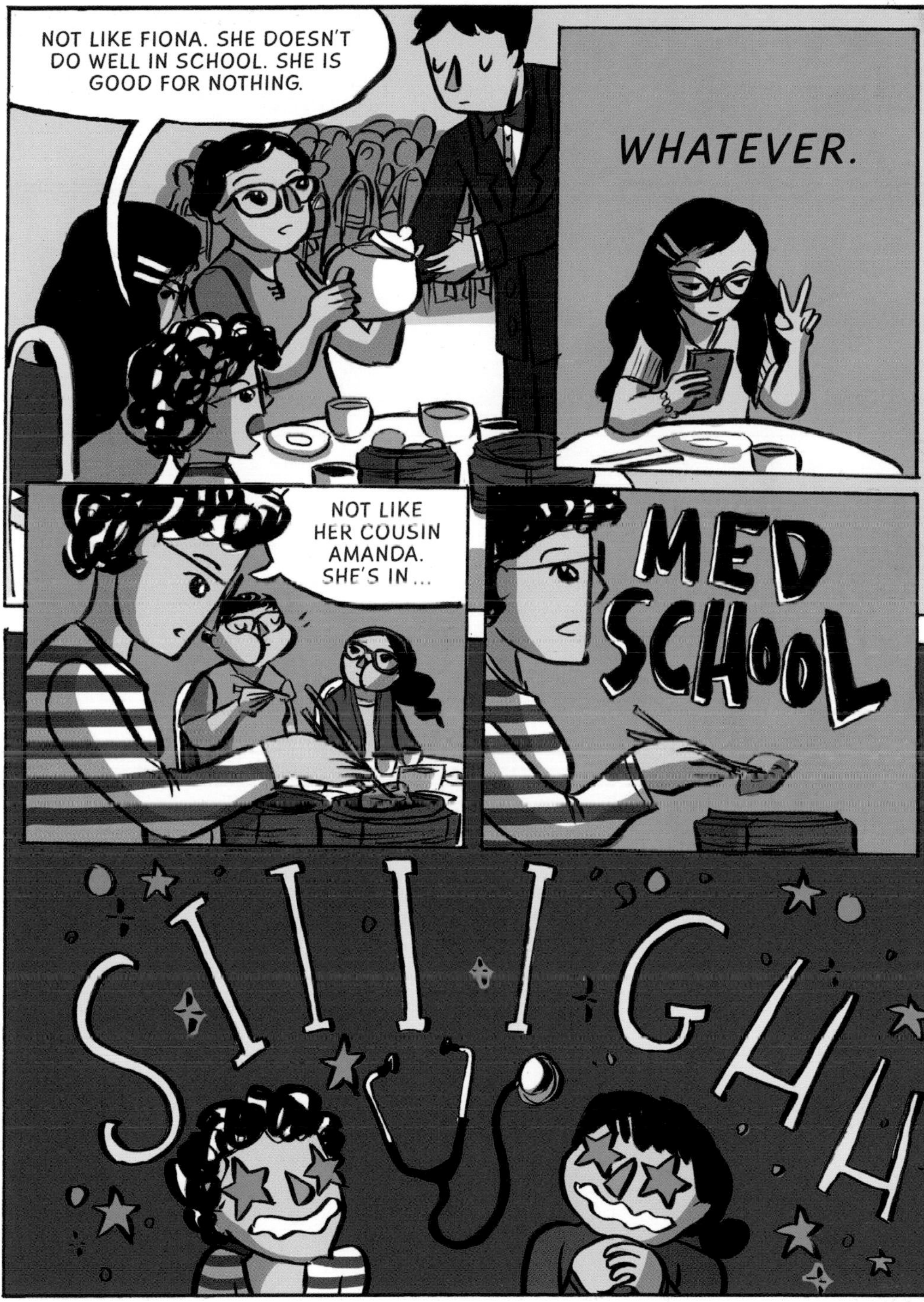
NOT LIKE FIONA. SHE DOESN'T DO WELL IN SCHOOL. SHE IS GOOD FOR NOTHING.
WHATEVER.
NOT LIKE HER COUSIN AMANDA. SHE'S IN...
MED SCHOOL
SIIIGHH

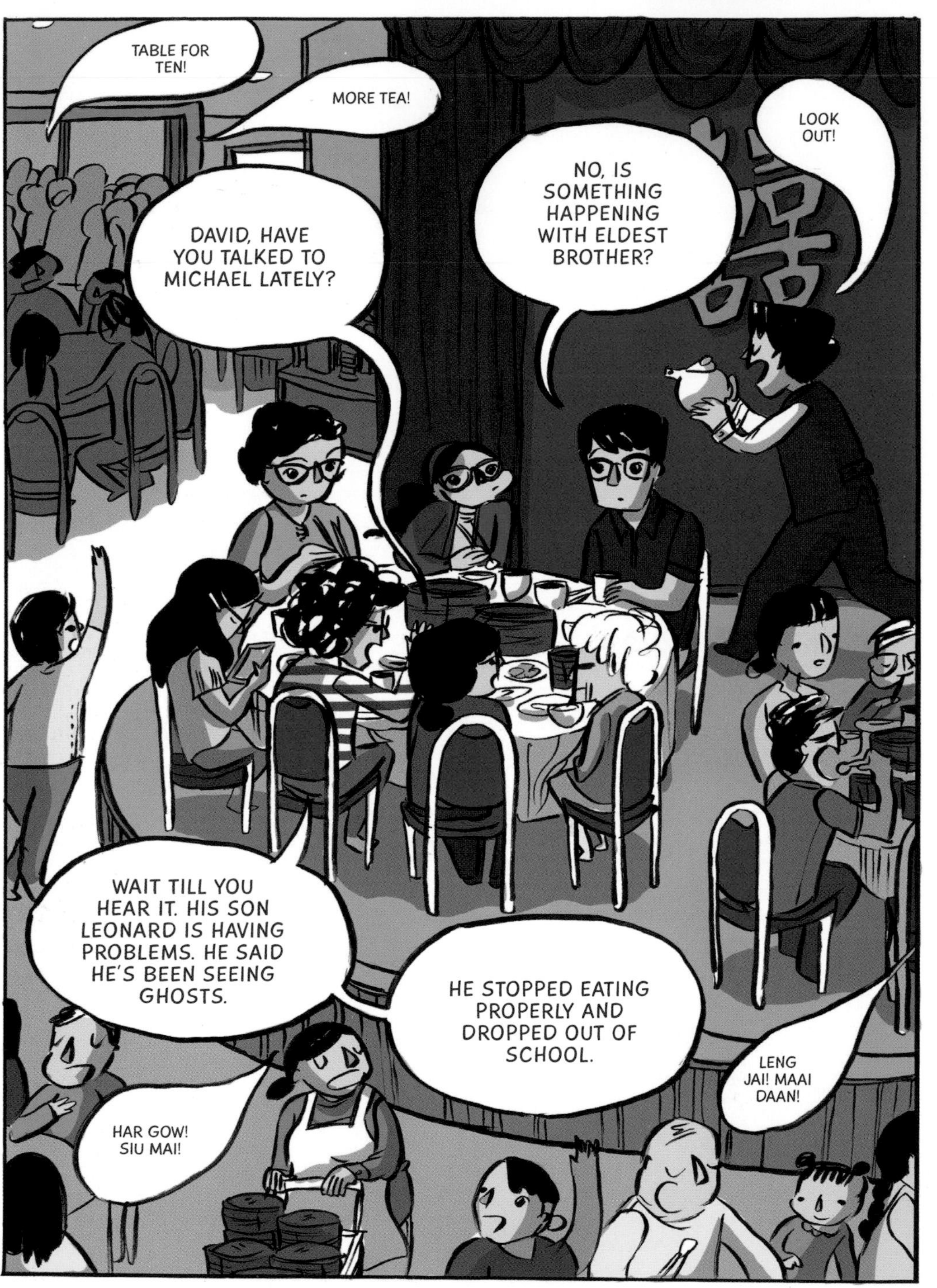
TABLE FOR TEN!
MORE TEA!
LOOK OUT!
DAVID, HAVE YOU TALKED TO MICHAEL LATELY?
NO, IS SOMETHING HAPPENING WITH ELDEST BROTHER?
WAIT TILL YOU HEAR IT. HIS SON LEONARD IS HAVING PROBLEMS. HE SAID HE'S BEEN SEEING GHOSTS.
HE STOPPED EATING PROPERLY AND DROPPED OUT OF SCHOOL.
HAR GOW! SIU MAI!
LENG JAI! MAAI DAAN!

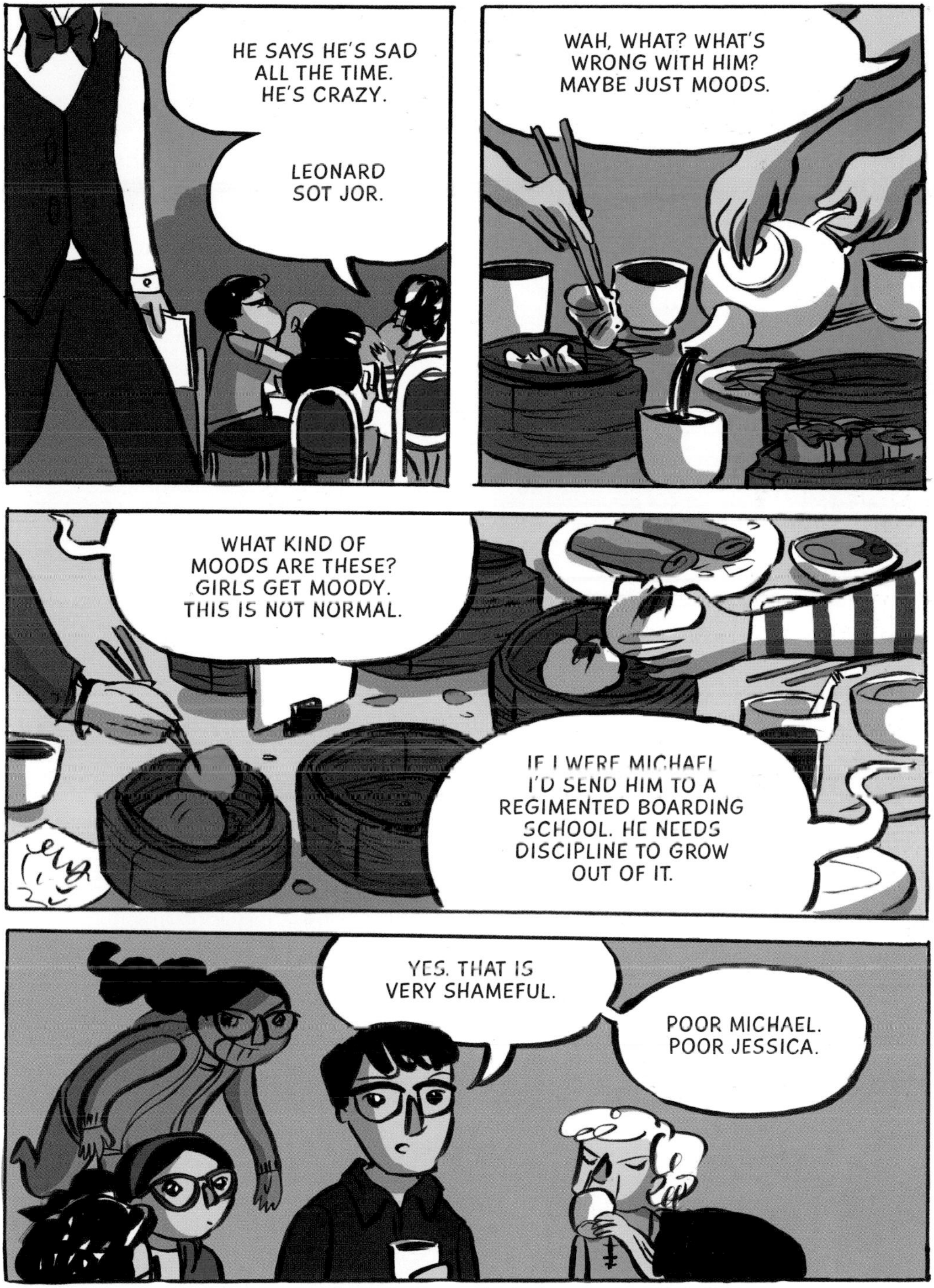
HE SAYS HE'S SAD ALL THE TIME. HE'S CRAZY.
LEONARD SOT JOR.
WAH, WHAT? WHAT'S WRONG WITH HIM? MAYBE JUST MOODS.
WHAT KIND OF MOODS ARE THESE? GIRLS GET MOODY. THIS IS NOT NORMAL.
IF I WERE MICHAEL I'D SEND HIM TO A REGIMENTED BOARDING SCHOOL. HE NEEDS DISCIPLINE TO GROW OUT OF IT.
YES. THAT IS VERY SHAMEFUL.
POOR MICHAEL. POOR JESSICA.

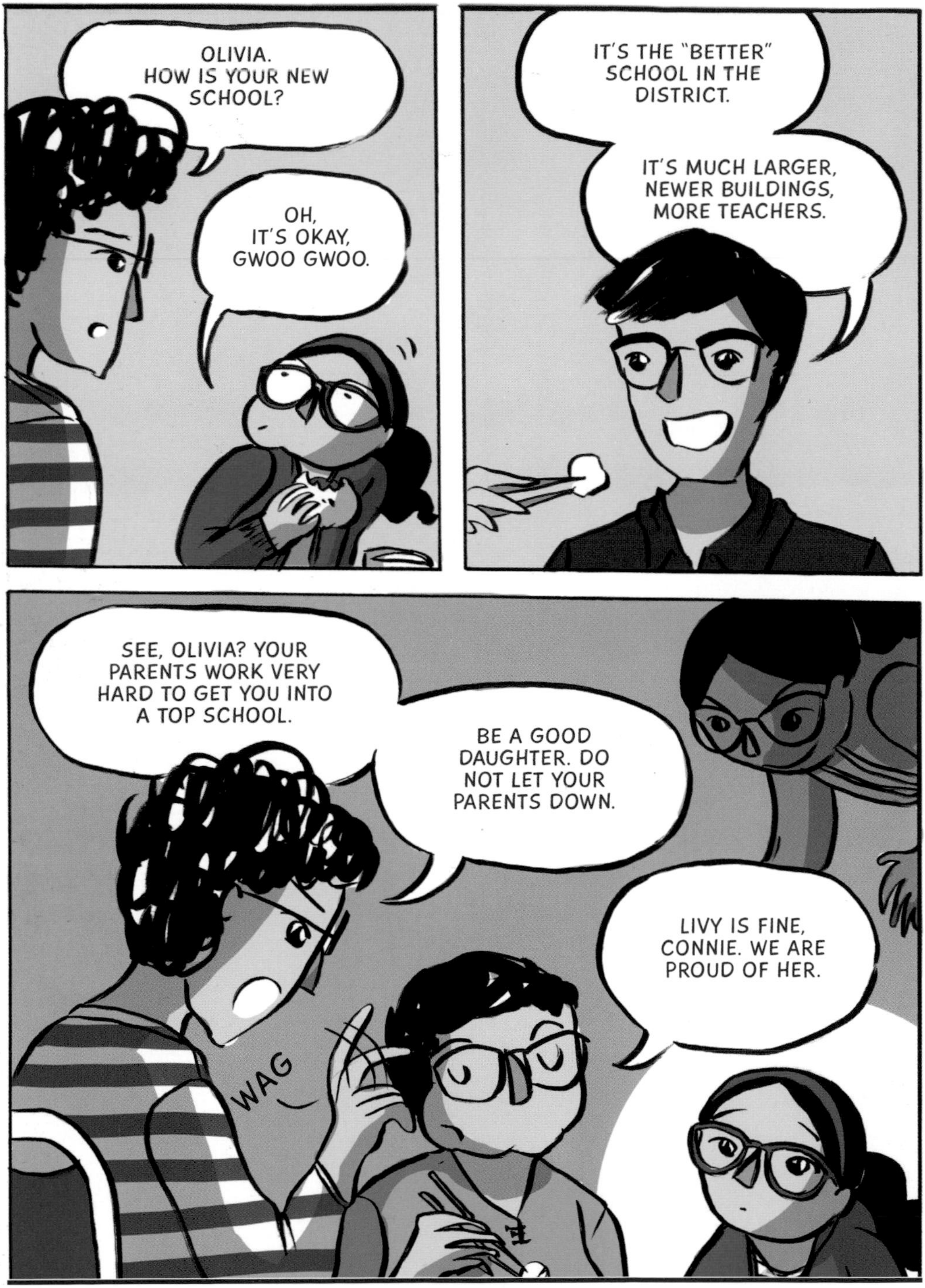
OLIVIA. HOW IS YOUR NEW SCHOOL?
OH, IT'S OKAY, GWOO GWOO.
IT'S THE "BETTER" SCHOOL IN THE DISTRICT.
IT'S MUCH LARGER, NEWER BUILDINGS, MORE TEACHERS.
SEE, OLIVIA? YOUR PARENTS WORK VERY HARD TO GET YOU INTO A TOP SCHOOL.
BE A GOOD DAUGHTER. DO NOT LET YOUR PARENTS DOWN.
WAG
LIVY IS FINE, CONNIE. WE ARE PROUD OF HER.

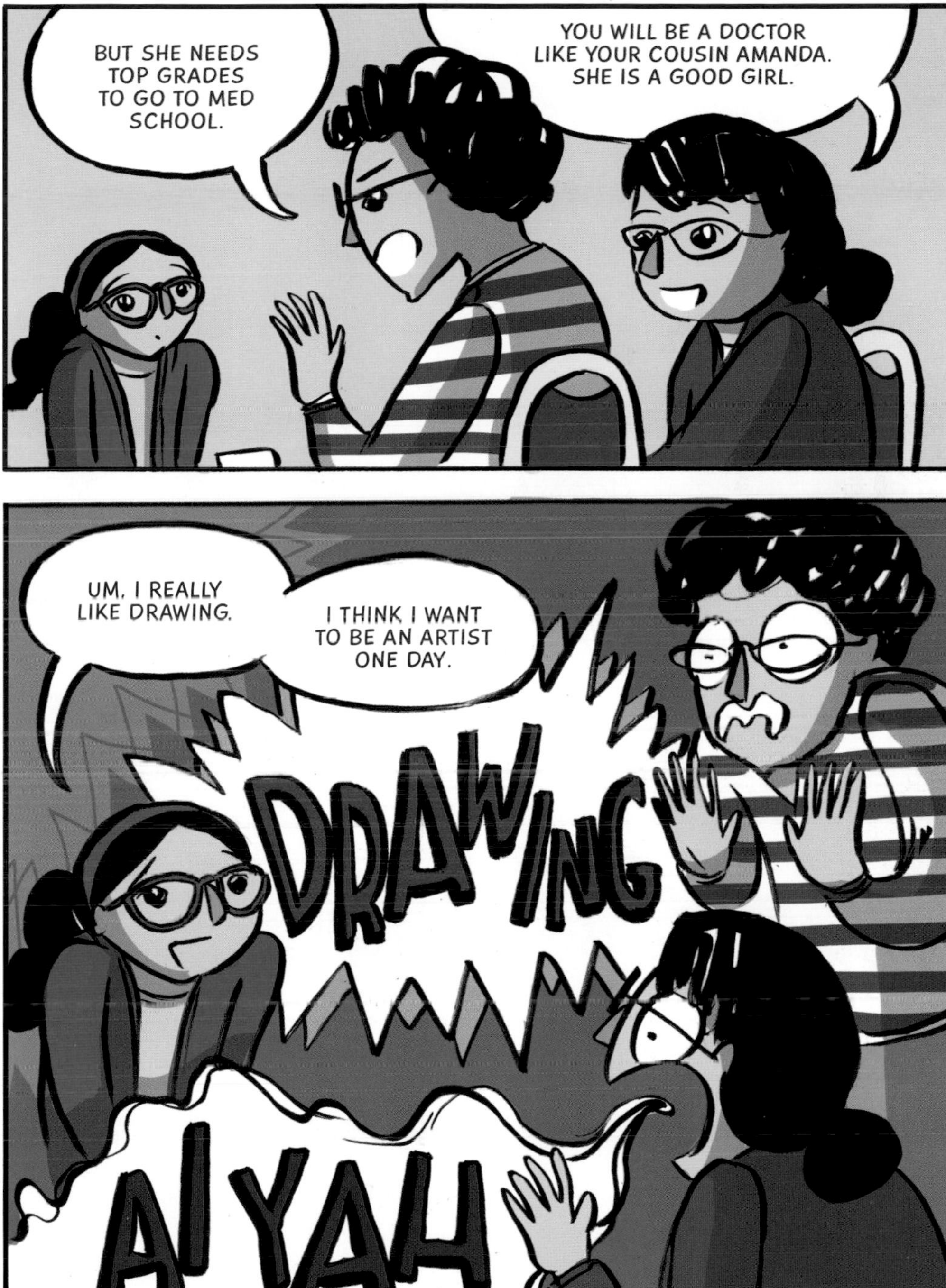
BUT SHE NEEDS TOP GRADES TO GO TO MED SCHOOL.
YOU WILL BE A DOCTOR LIKE YOUR COUSIN AMANDA. SHE IS A GOOD GIRL.
UM, I REALLY LIKE DRAWING.
I THINK I WANT TO BE AN ARTIST ONE DAY.
DRAWING
AIYAH

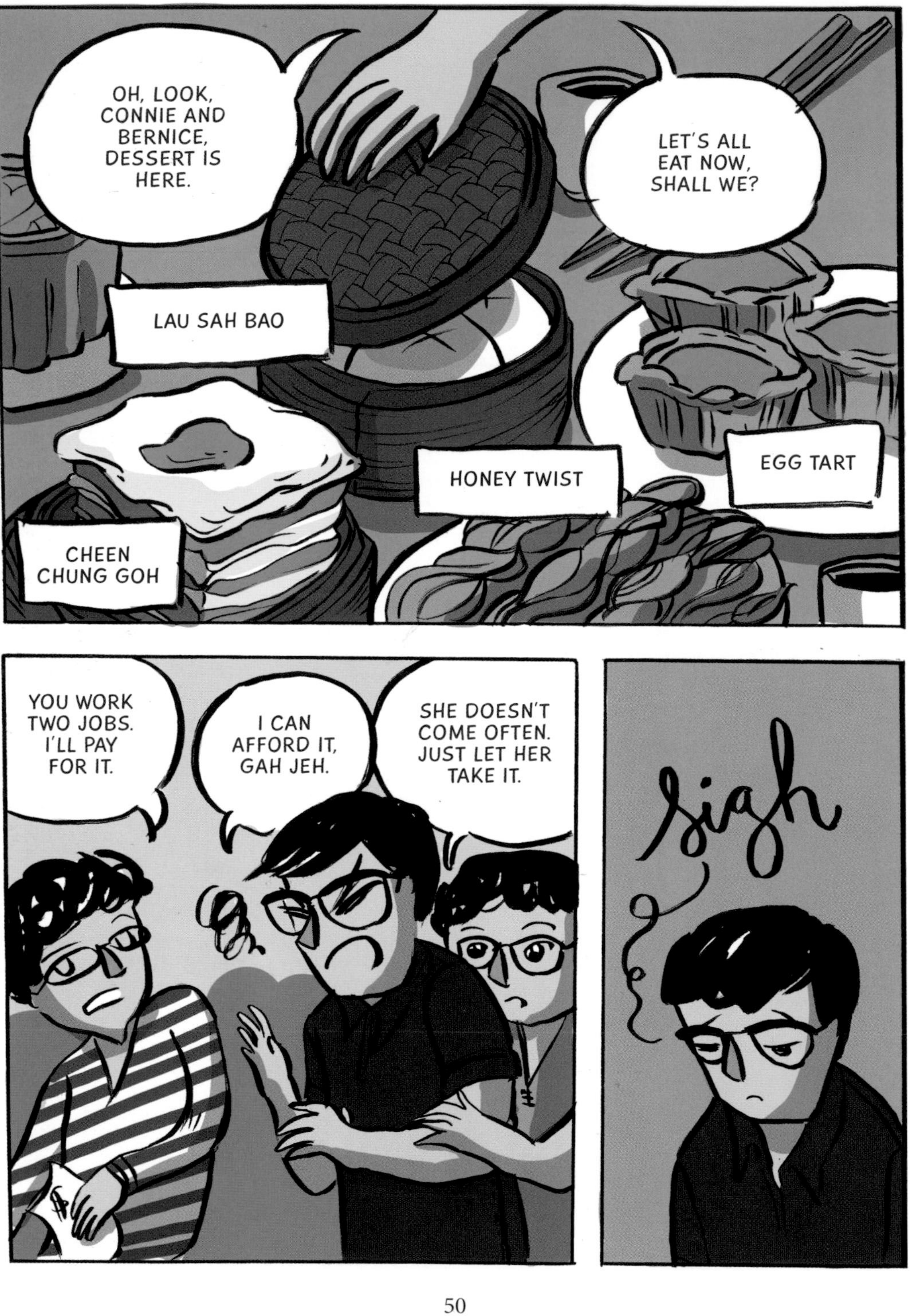
OH, LOOK, CONNIE AND BERNICE, DESSERT IS HERE.
LET'S ALL EAT NOW, SHALL WE?
LAU SAH BAO
HONEY TWIST
EGG TART
CHEEN CHUNG GOH
YOU WORK TWO JOBS. I'LL PAY FOR IT.
I CAN AFFORD IT, GAH JEH.
SHE DOESN'T COME OFTEN. JUST LET HER TAKE IT.
sigh

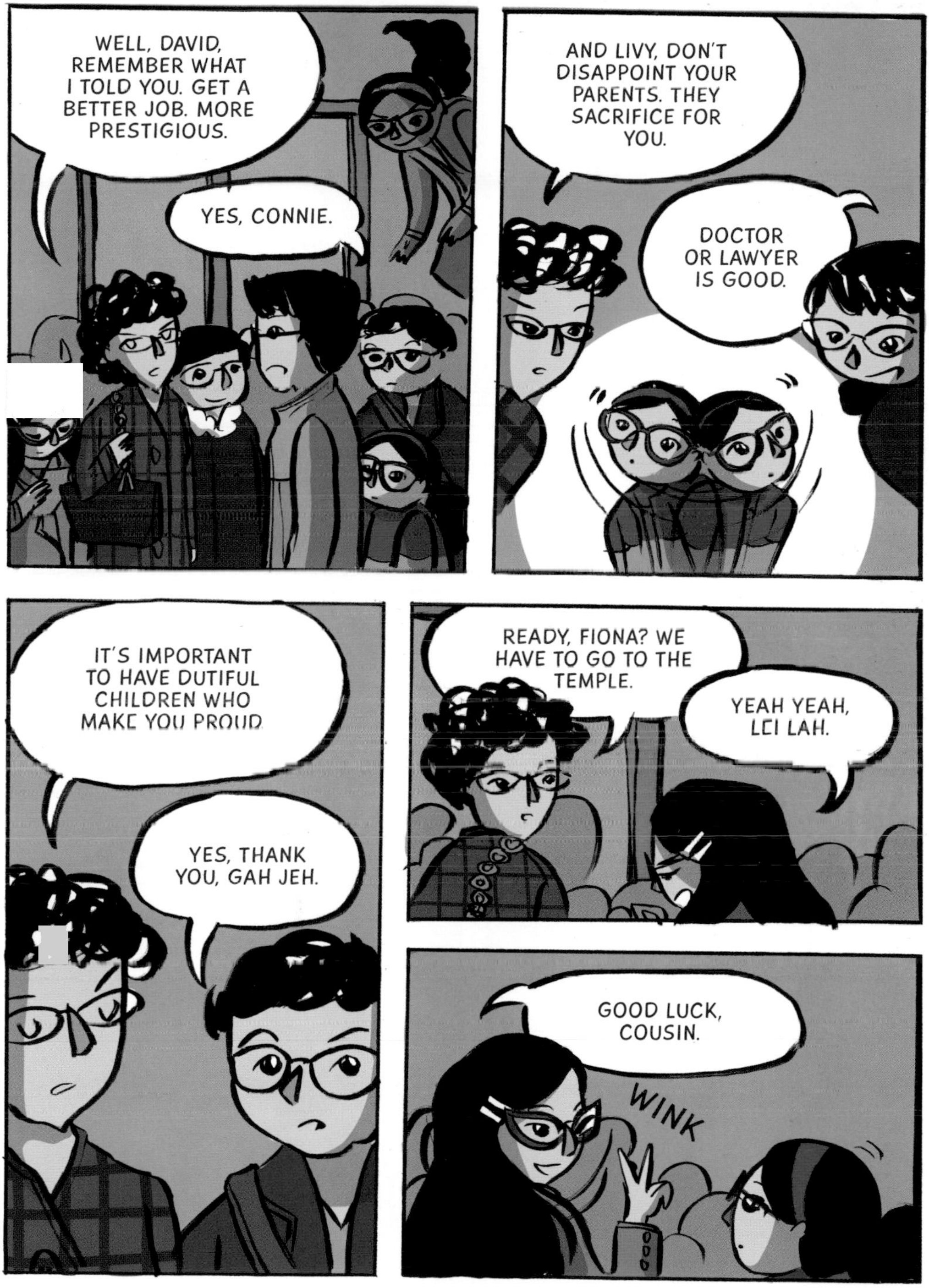
WELL, DAVID, REMEMBER WHAT I TOLD YOU. GET A BETTER JOB. MORE PRESTIGIOUS.
YES, CONNIE.
AND LIVY, DON'T DISAPPOINT YOUR PARENTS. THEY SACRIFICE FOR YOU.
DOCTOR OR LAWYER IS GOOD.
IT'S IMPORTANT TO HAVE DUTIFUL CHILDREN WHO MAKE YOU PROUD.
YES, THANK YOU, GAH JEH.
READY, FIONA? WE HAVE TO GO TO THE TEMPLE.
YEAH YEAH, LEI LAH.
GOOD LUCK, COUSIN.
WINK

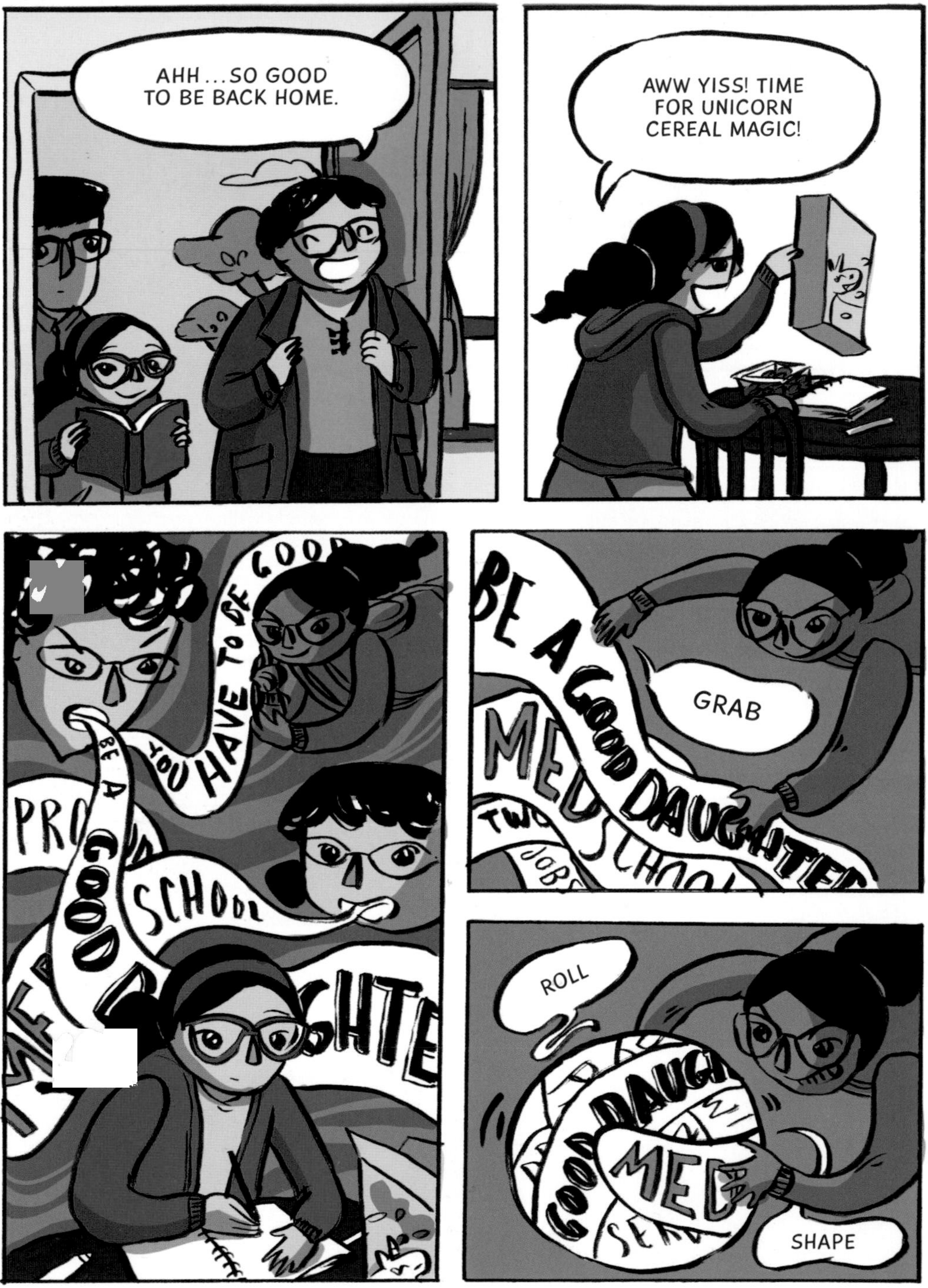
AHH . . . SO GOOD TO BE BACK HOME.
AWW YISS! TIME FOR UNICORN CEREAL MAGIC!
YOU HAVE TO BE GOO
BE A GOOD
PRO
SCHOOL
GHTE
BE A GOOD DAUGHTE
MED
SCHOOL
TWO
JOBS
GRAB
ROLL
DAUGH
GOOD
MED
SHAPE

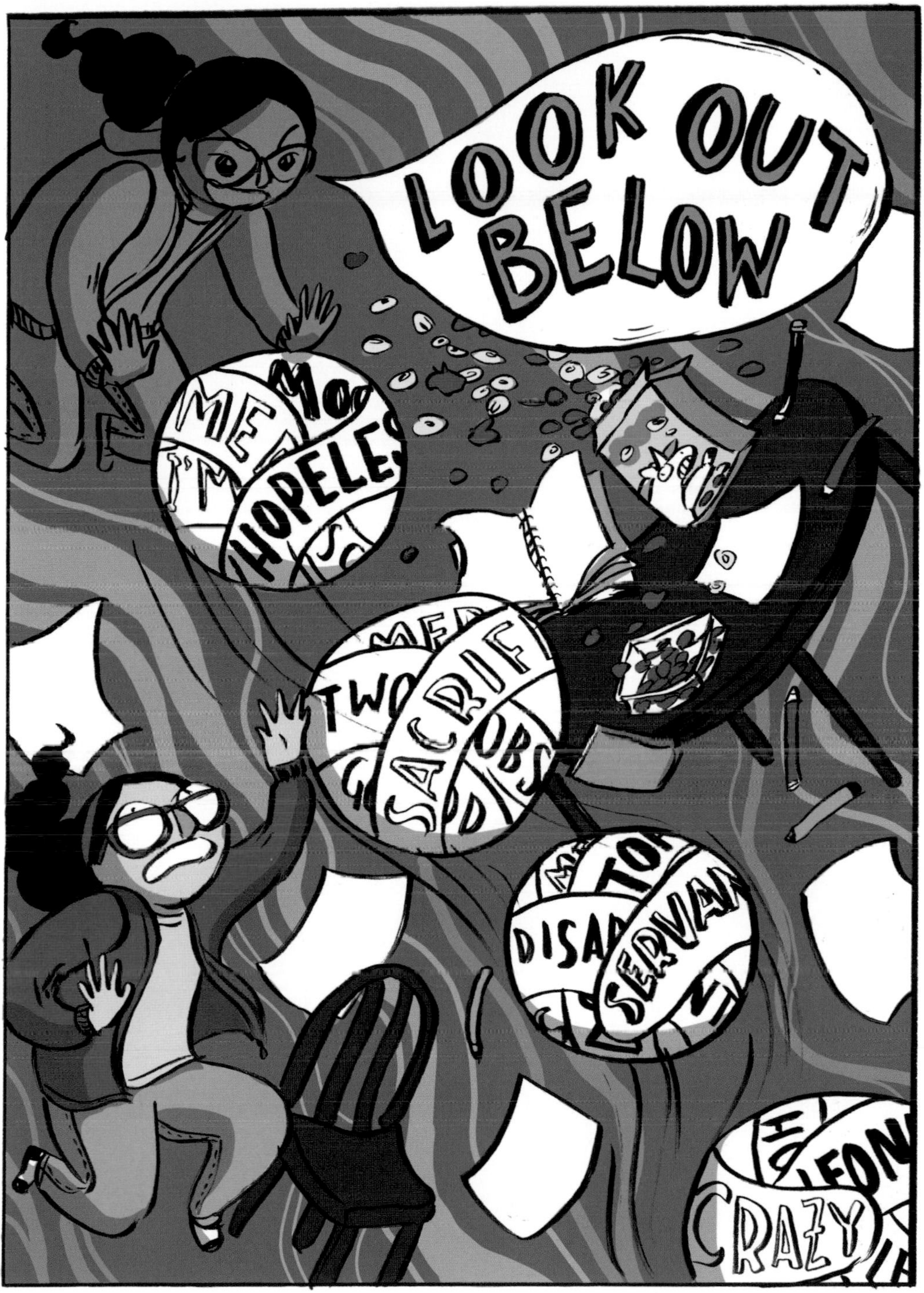
LOOK OUT BELOW
CRAZY

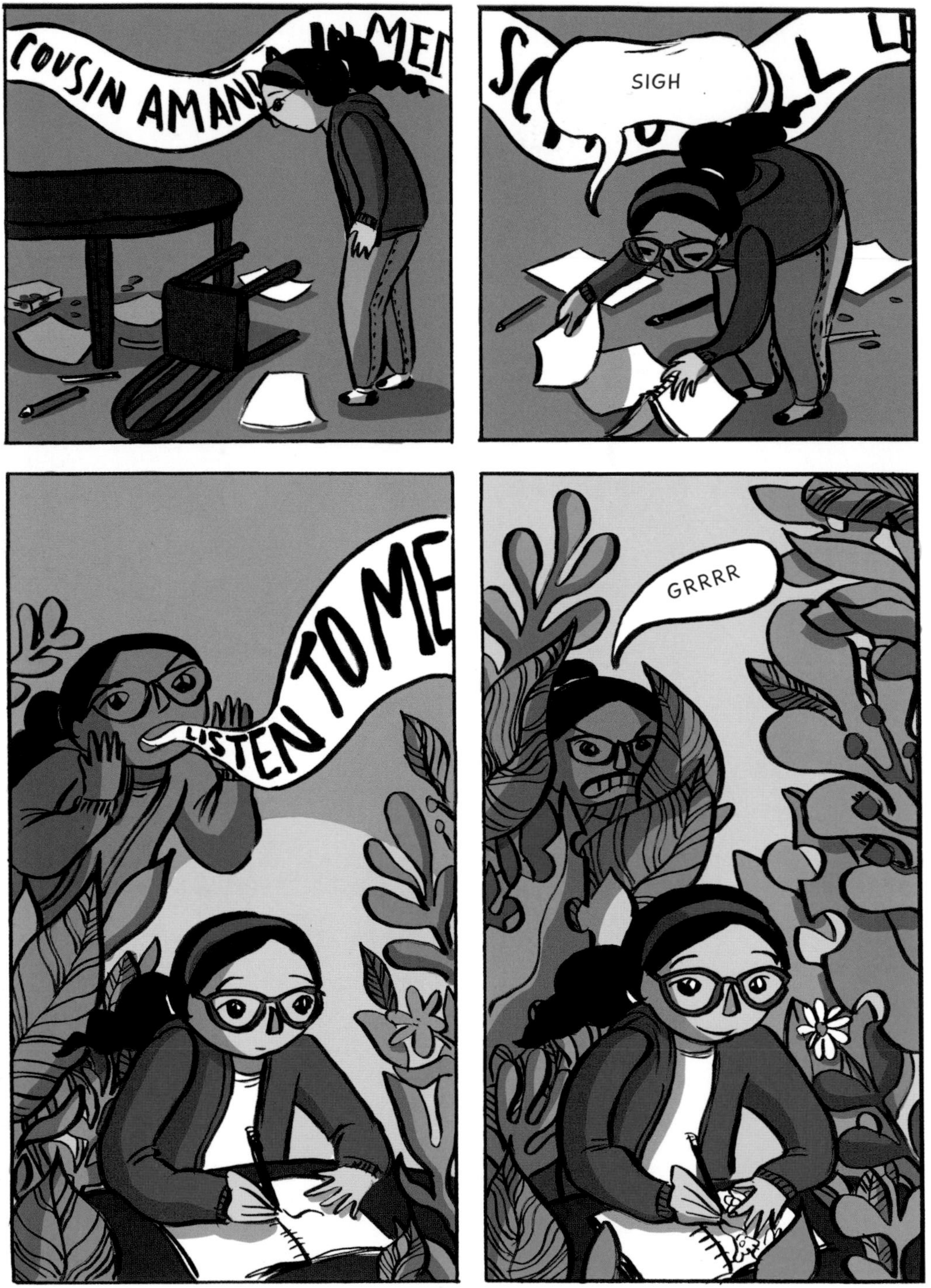
COUSIN AMAN
SIGH
LISTEN TO ME
GRRRR

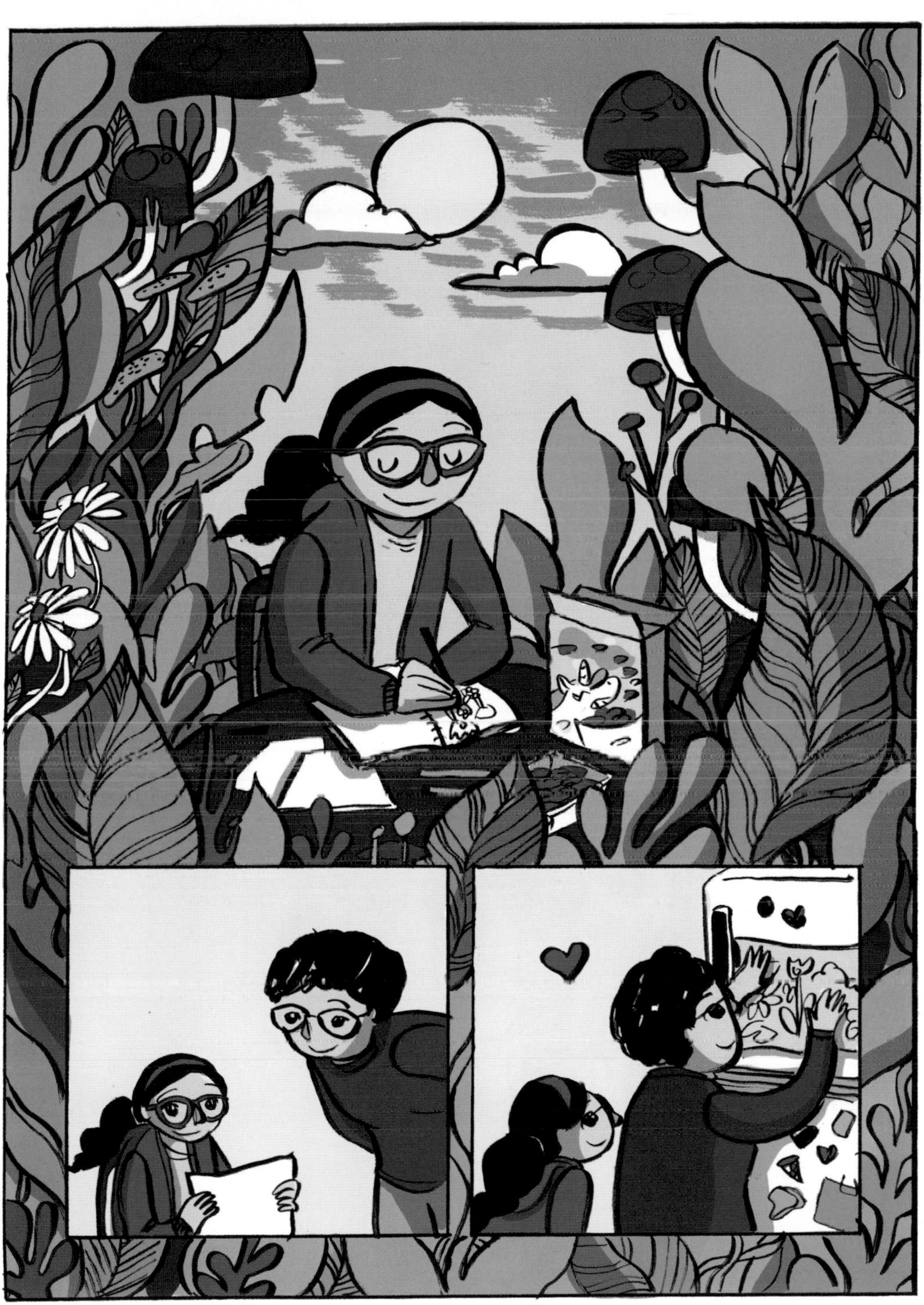

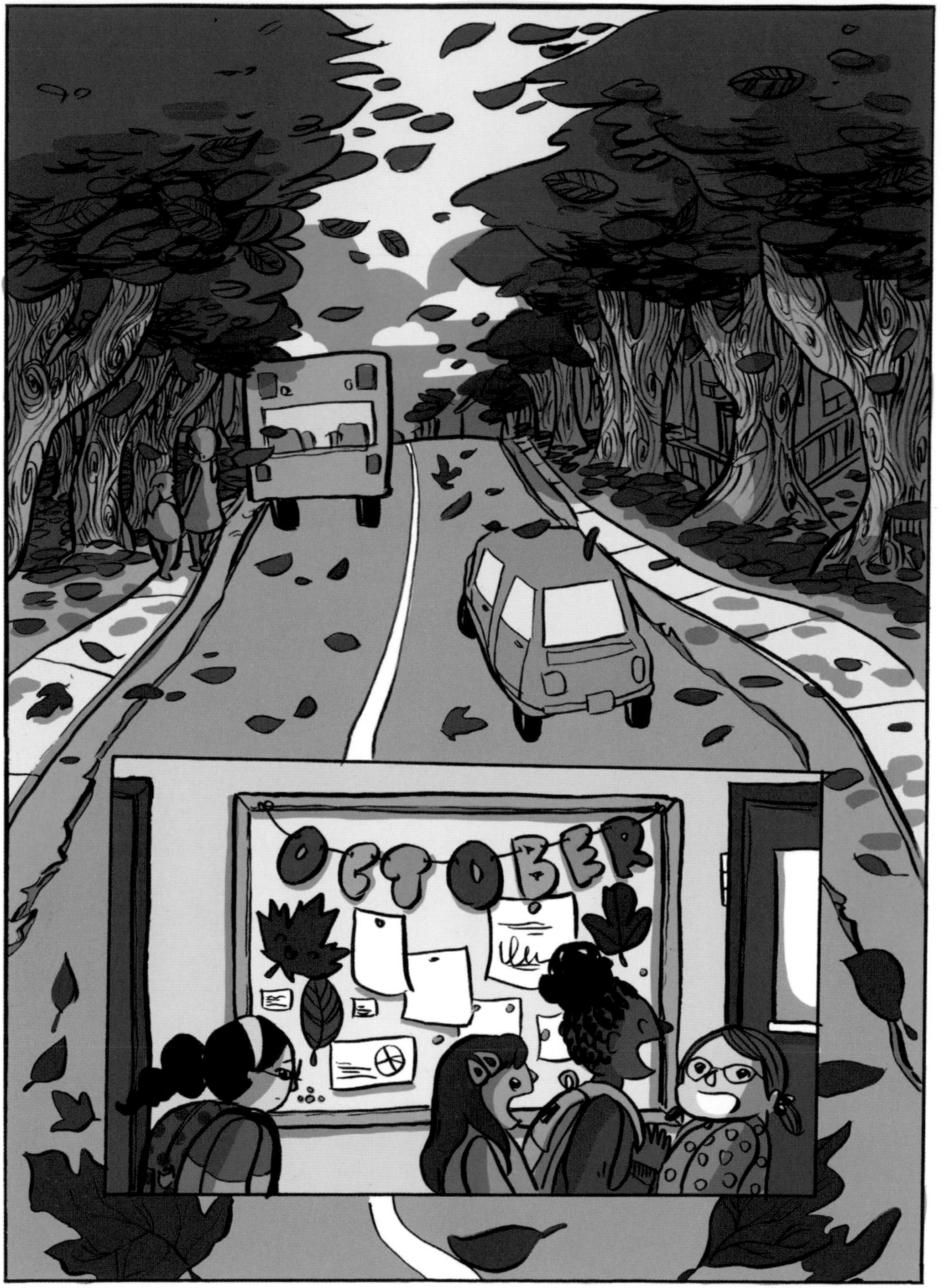
OCTOBER

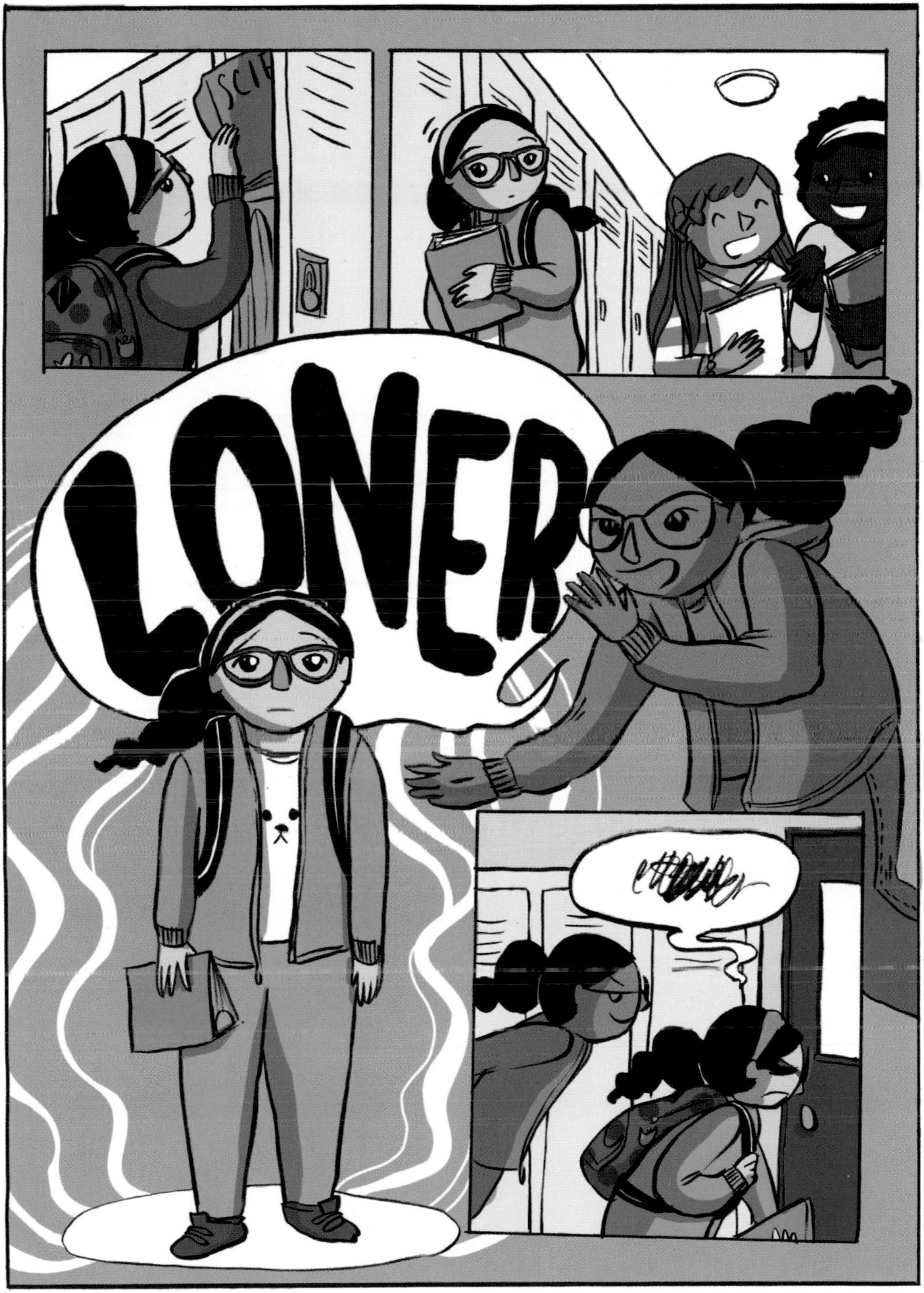
LONER

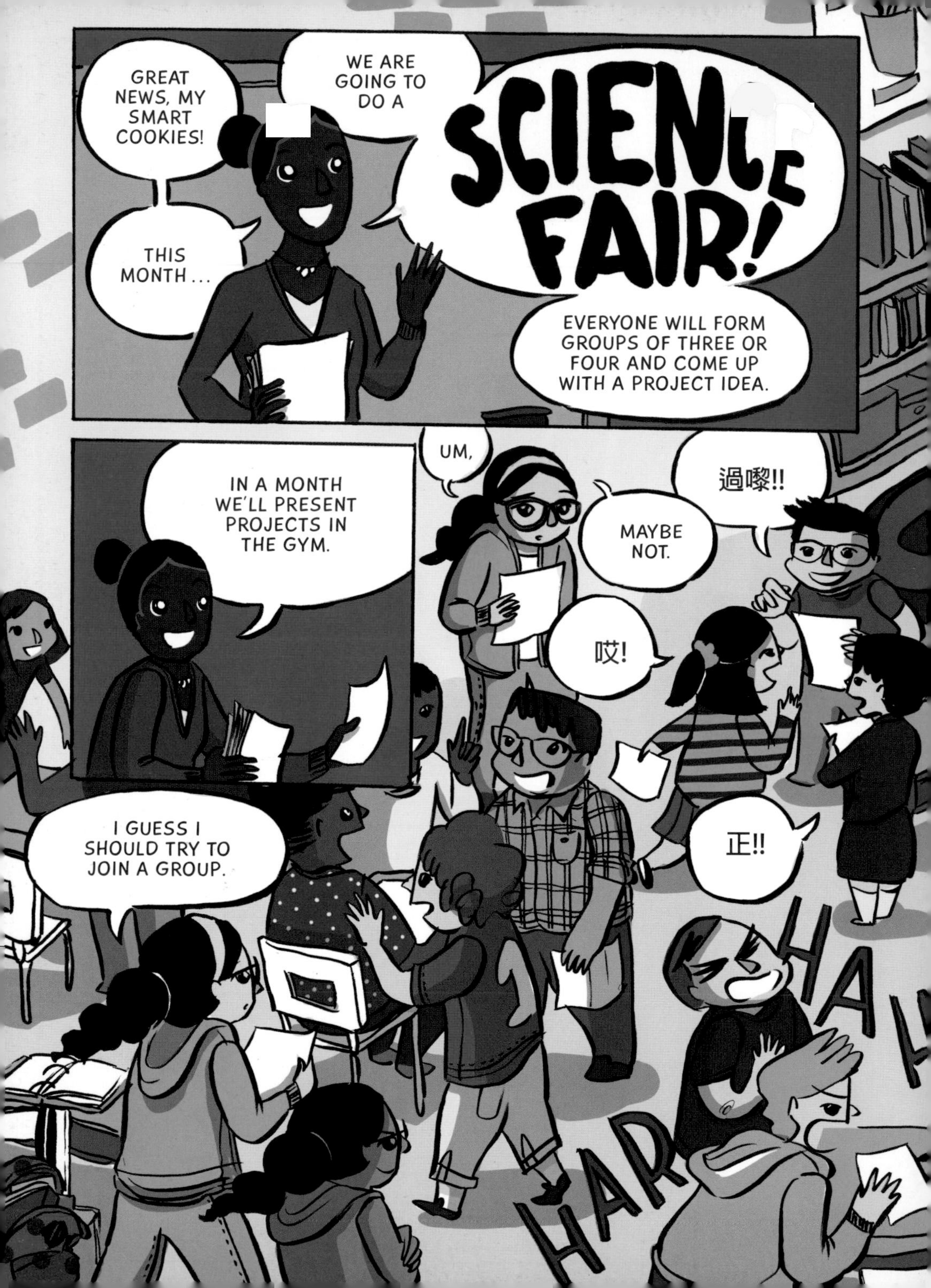
GREAT NEWS, MY SMART COOKIES!
THIS MONTH . . .
WE ARE GOING TO DO A
SCIENCE FAIR!
EVERYONE WILL FORM GROUPS OF THREE OR FOUR AND COME UP WITH A PROJECT IDEA.
IN A MONTH WE'LL PRESENT PROJECTS IN THE GYM.
UM,
MAYBE NOT.
過嚟!!
哎!
正!!
I GUESS I SHOULD TRY TO JOIN A GROUP.
HA HA HA
HAR HAR

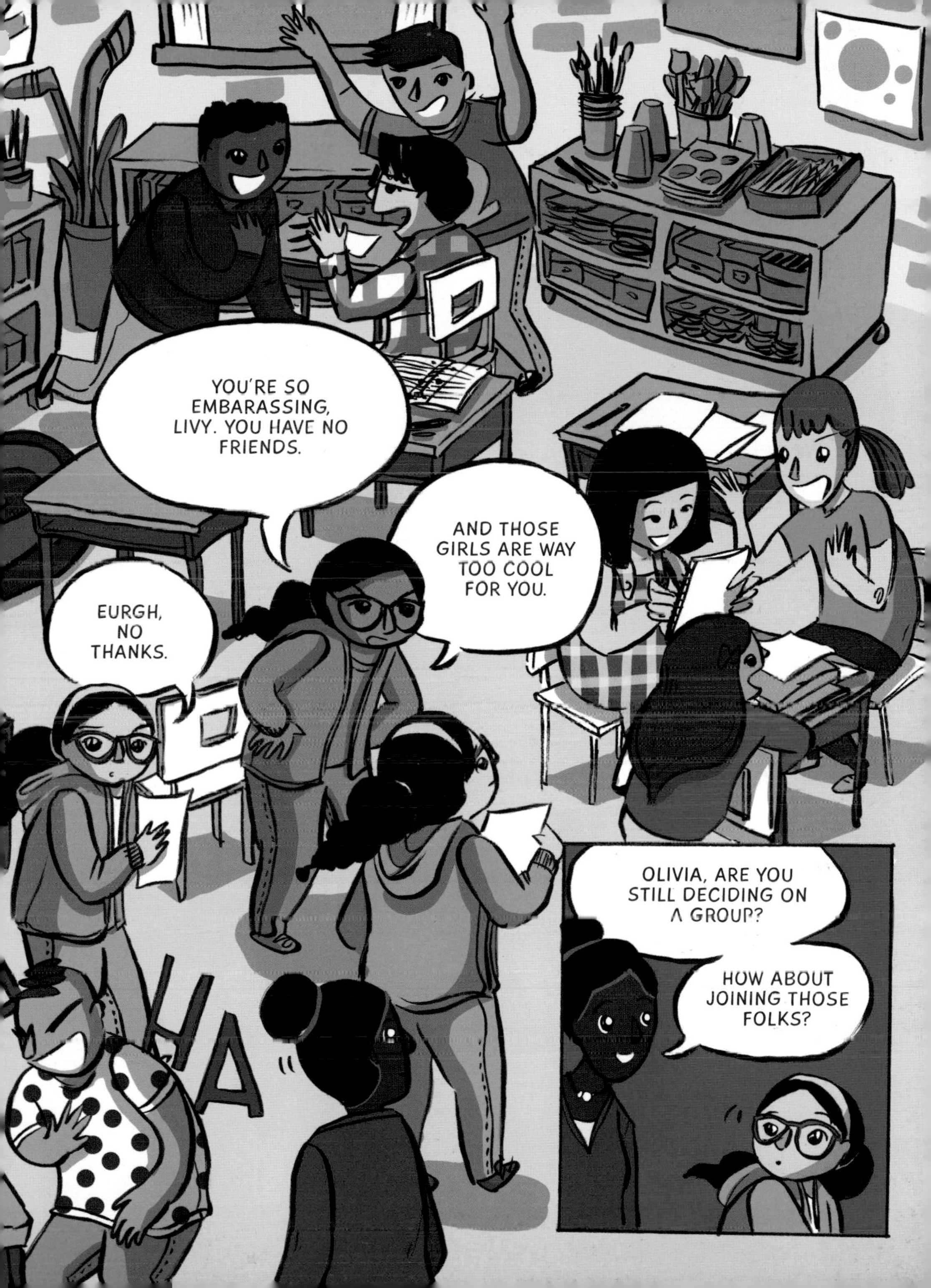
YOU'RE SO EMBARASSING, LIVY. YOU HAVE NO FRIENDS.
AND THOSE GIRLS ARE WAY TOO COOL FOR YOU.
EURGH, NO THANKS.
HA HA
OLIVIA, ARE YOU STILL DECIDING ON A GROUP?
HOW ABOUT JOINING THOSE FOLKS?

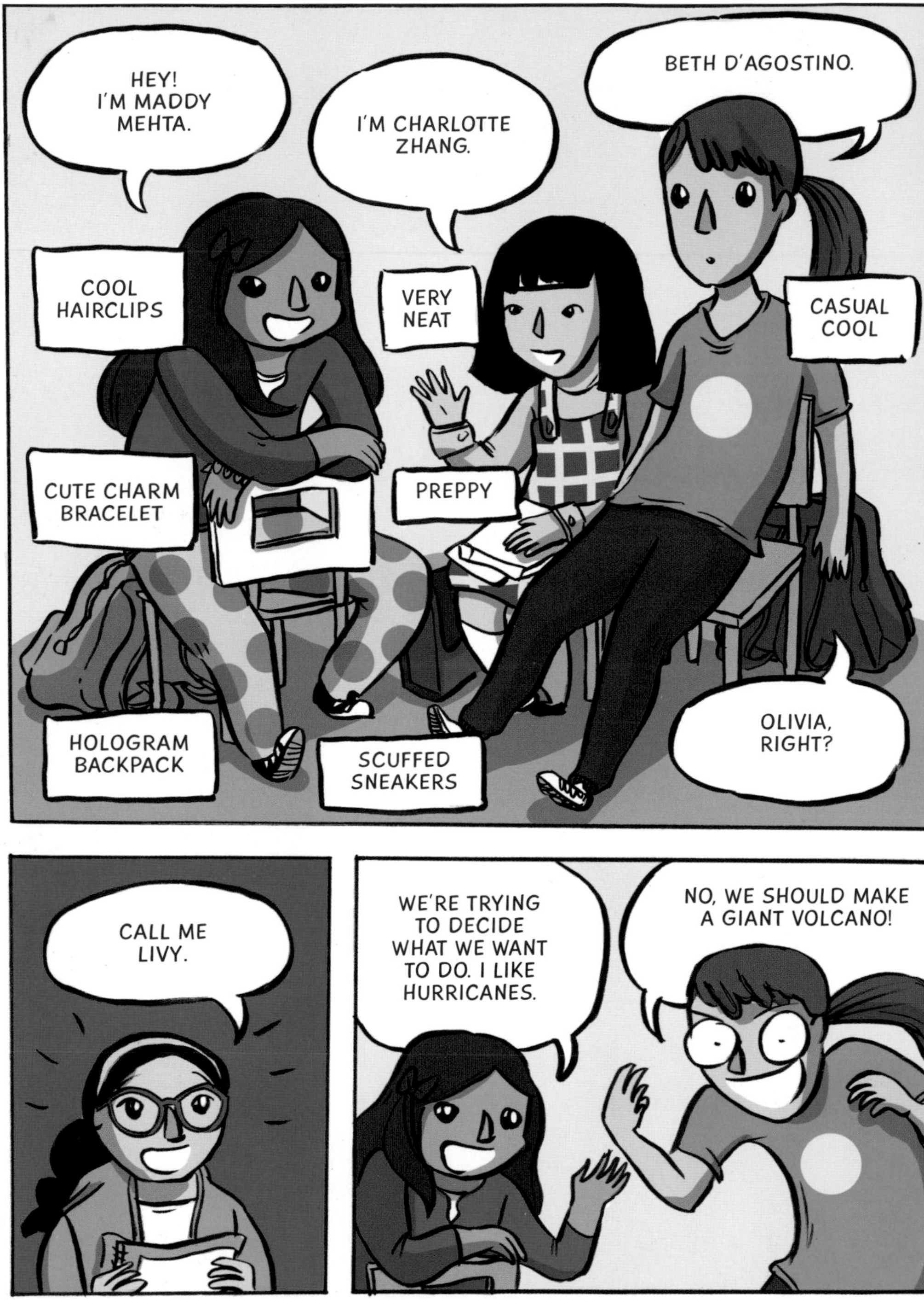
HEY! I'M MADDY MEHTA.
I'M CHARLOTTE ZHANG.
BETH D'AGOSTINO.
COOL HAIRCLIPS
VERY NEAT
CASUAL COOL
CUTE CHARM BRACELET
PREPPY
HOLOGRAM BACKPACK
SCUFFED SNEAKERS
OLIVIA, RIGHT?
CALL ME LIVY.
WE'RE TRYING TO DECIDE WHAT WE WANT TO DO. I LIKE HURRICANES.
NO, WE SHOULD MAKE A GIANT VOLCANO!

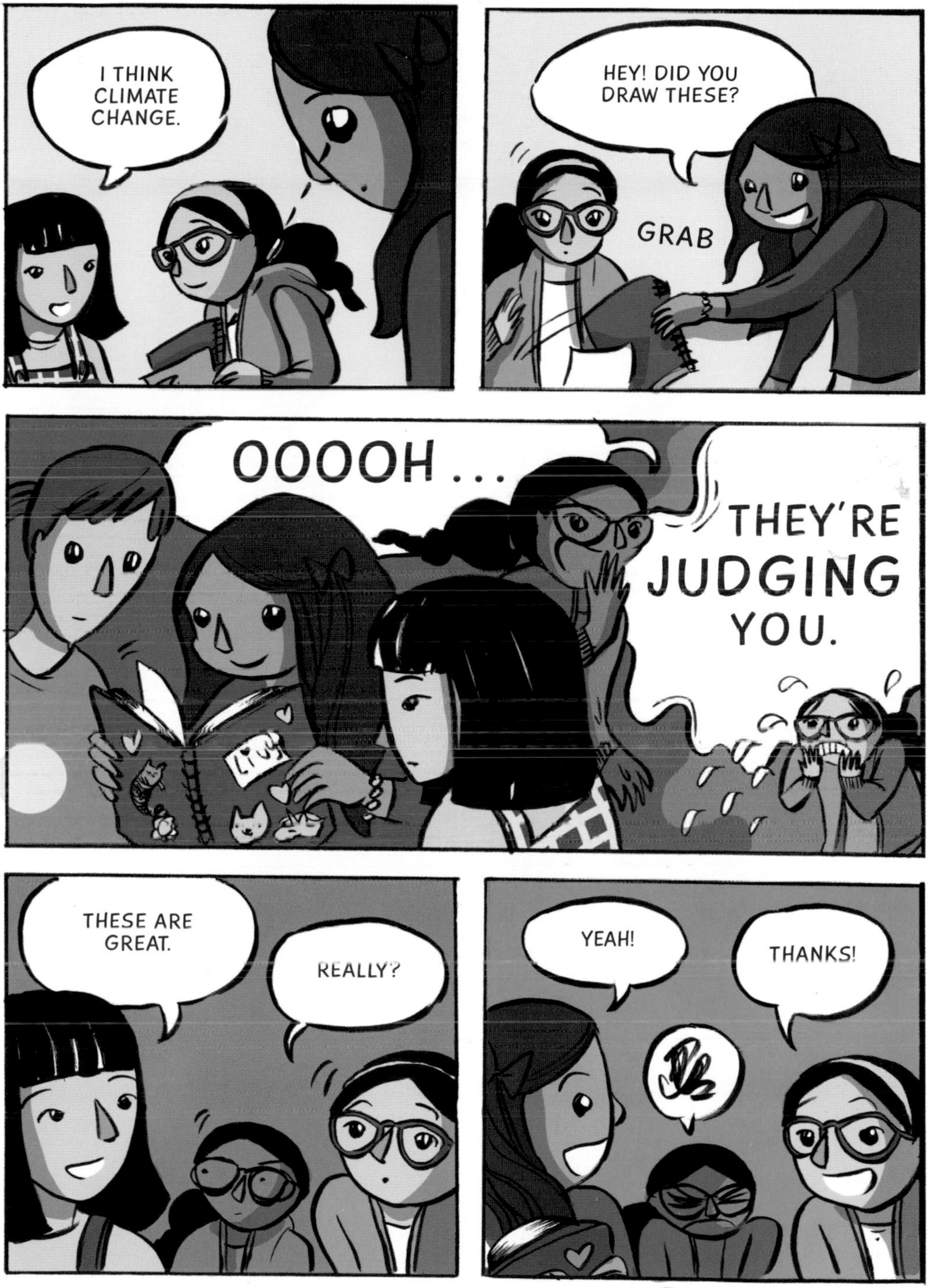
I THINK CLIMATE CHANGE.
HEY! DID YOU DRAW THESE?
GRAB
OOOOH . . .
THEY'RE JUDGING YOU.
THESE ARE GREAT.
REALLY?
YEAH!
THANKS!

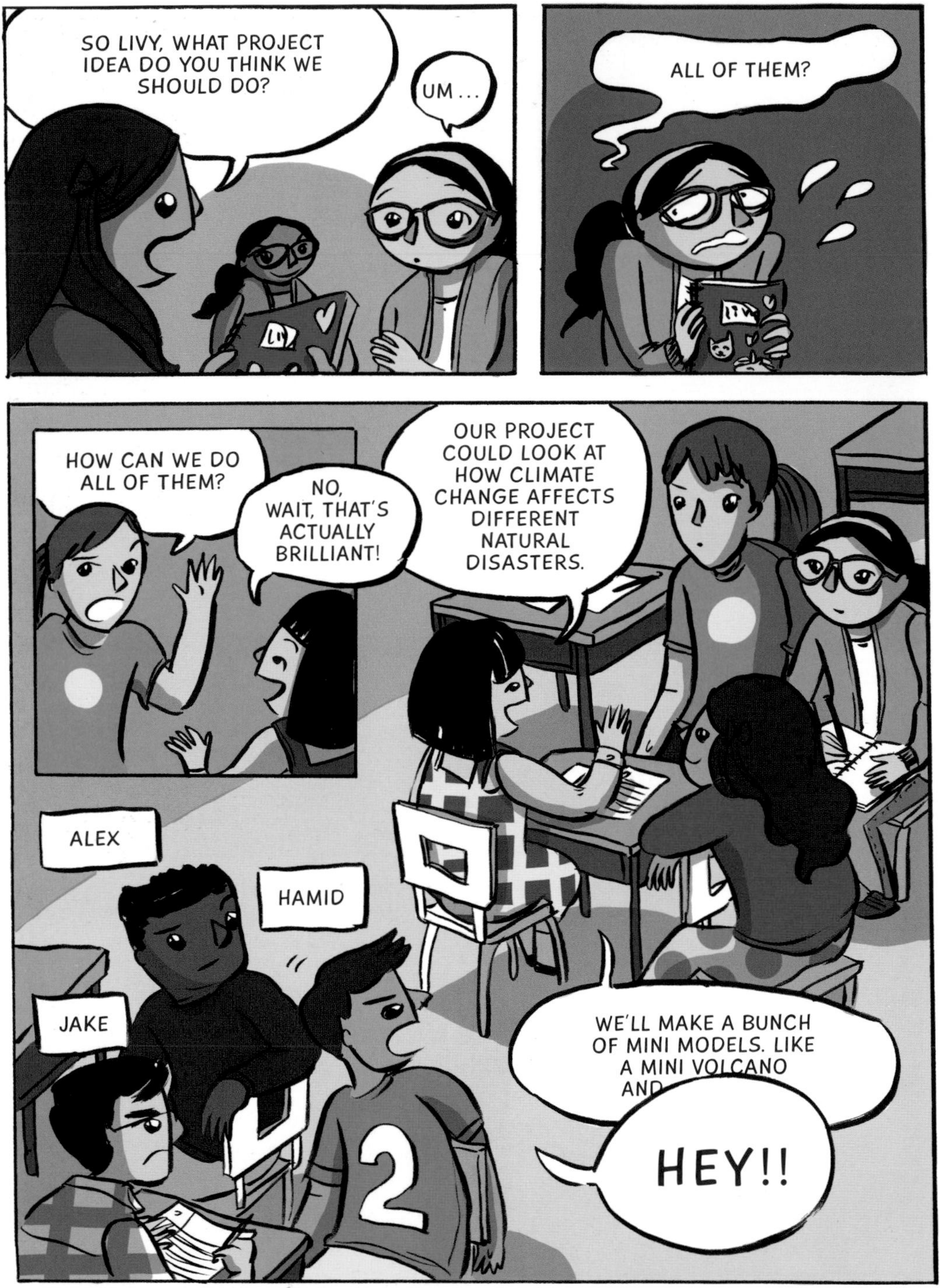
SO LIVY, WHAT PROJECT IDEA DO YOU THINK WE SHOULD DO?
UM...
ALL OF THEM?
HOW CAN WE DO ALL OF THEM?
NO, WAIT, THAT'S ACTUALLY BRILLIANT!
OUR PROJECT COULD LOOK AT HOW CLIMATE CHANGE AFFECTS DIFFERENT NATURAL DISASTERS.
ALEX
HAMID
JAKE
WE'LL MAKE A BUNCH OF MINI MODELS. LIKE A MINI VOLCANO AND
HEY!!

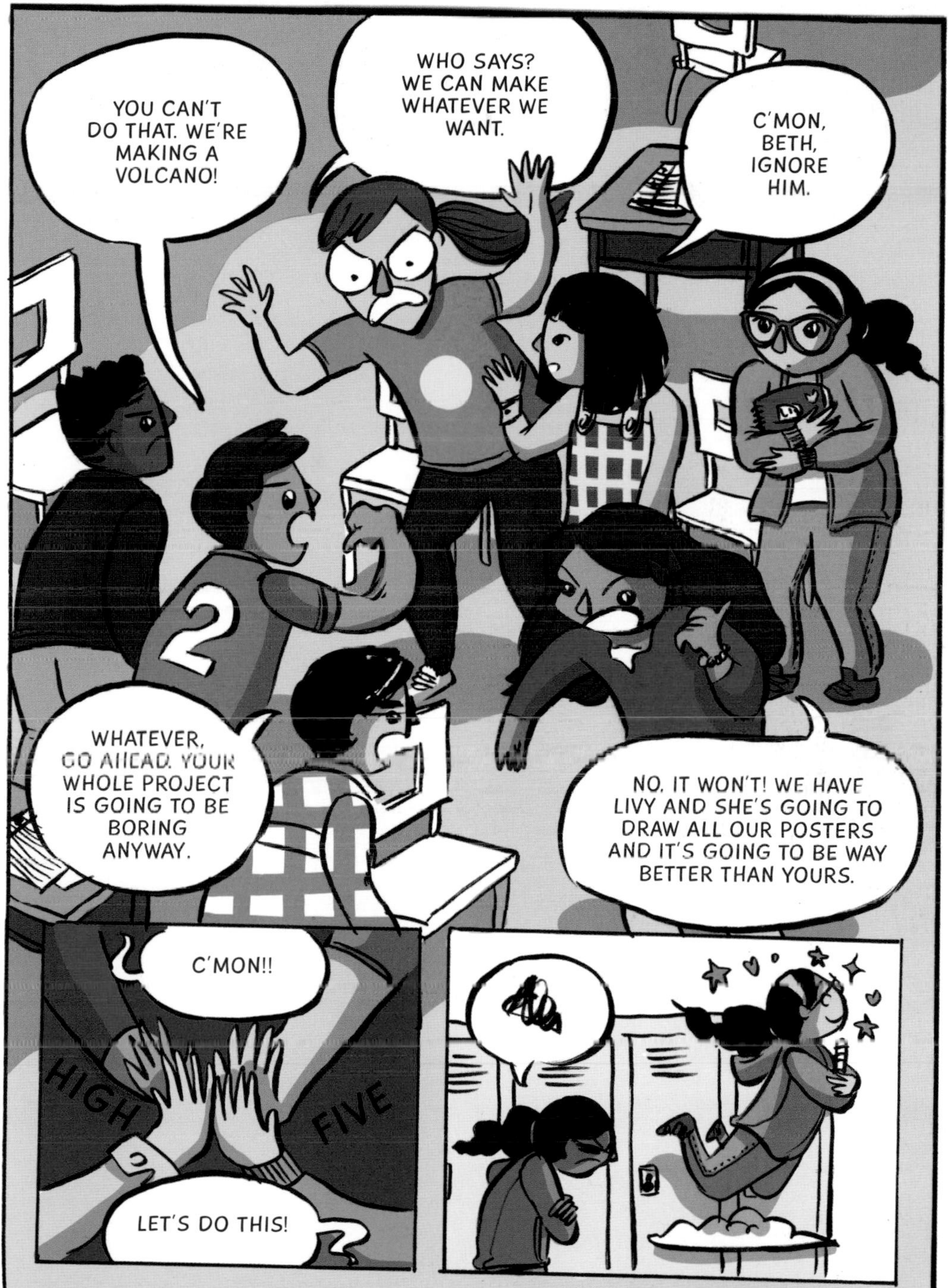
YOU CAN'T DO THAT. WE'RE MAKING A VOLCANO!
WHO SAYS? WE CAN MAKE WHATEVER WE WANT.
C'MON, BETH, IGNORE HIM.
WHATEVER, GO AHEAD. YOUR WHOLE PROJECT IS GOING TO BE BORING ANYWAY.
NO, IT WON'T! WE HAVE LIVY AND SHE'S GOING TO DRAW ALL OUR POSTERS AND IT'S GOING TO BE WAY BETTER THAN YOURS.
C'MON!!
HIGH
FIVE
LET'S DO THIS!

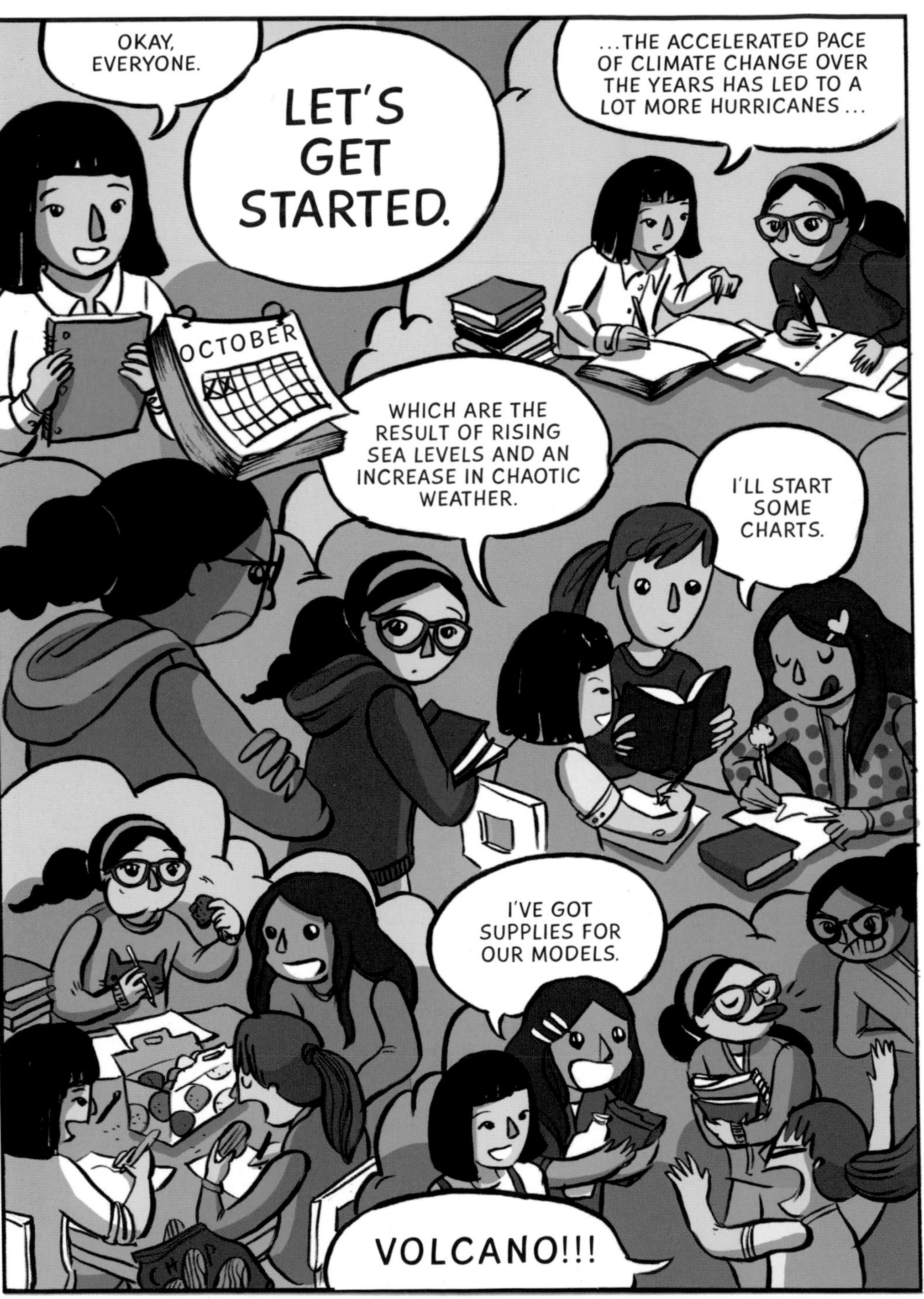
OKAY, EVERYONE.
LET'S GET STARTED.
...THE ACCELERATED PACE OF CLIMATE CHANGE OVER THE YEARS HAS LED TO A LOT MORE HURRICANES...
OCTOBER
WHICH ARE THE RESULT OF RISING SEA LEVELS AND AN INCREASE IN CHAOTIC WEATHER.
I'LL START SOME CHARTS.
I'VE GOT SUPPLIES FOR OUR MODELS.
VOLCANO!!!

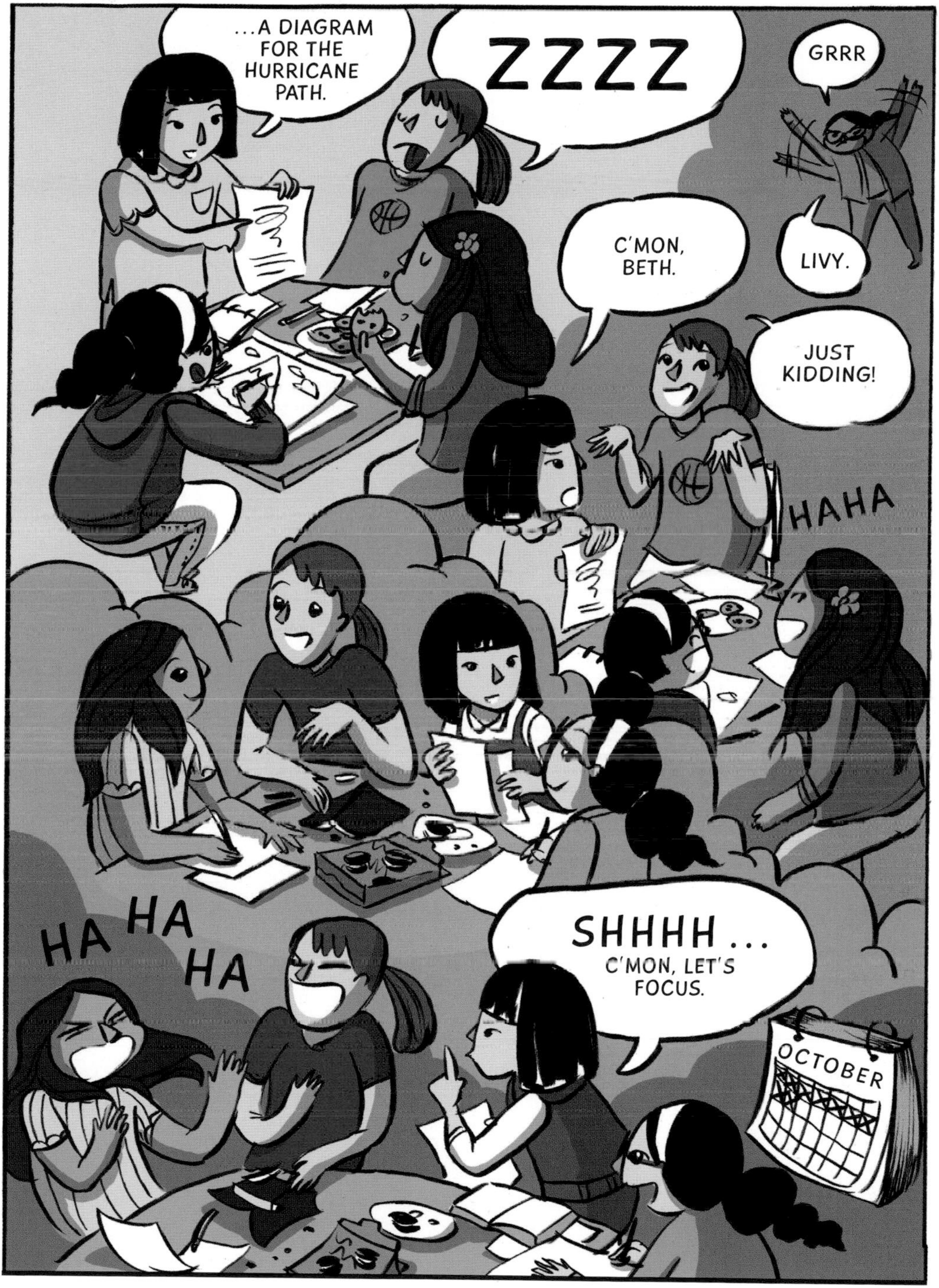
...A DIAGRAM FOR THE HURRICANE PATH.
ZZZZ
GRRR
C'MON, BETH.
LIVY.
JUST KIDDING!
HAHA
HA HA HA
SHHHH ... C'MON, LET'S FOCUS.
OCTOBER

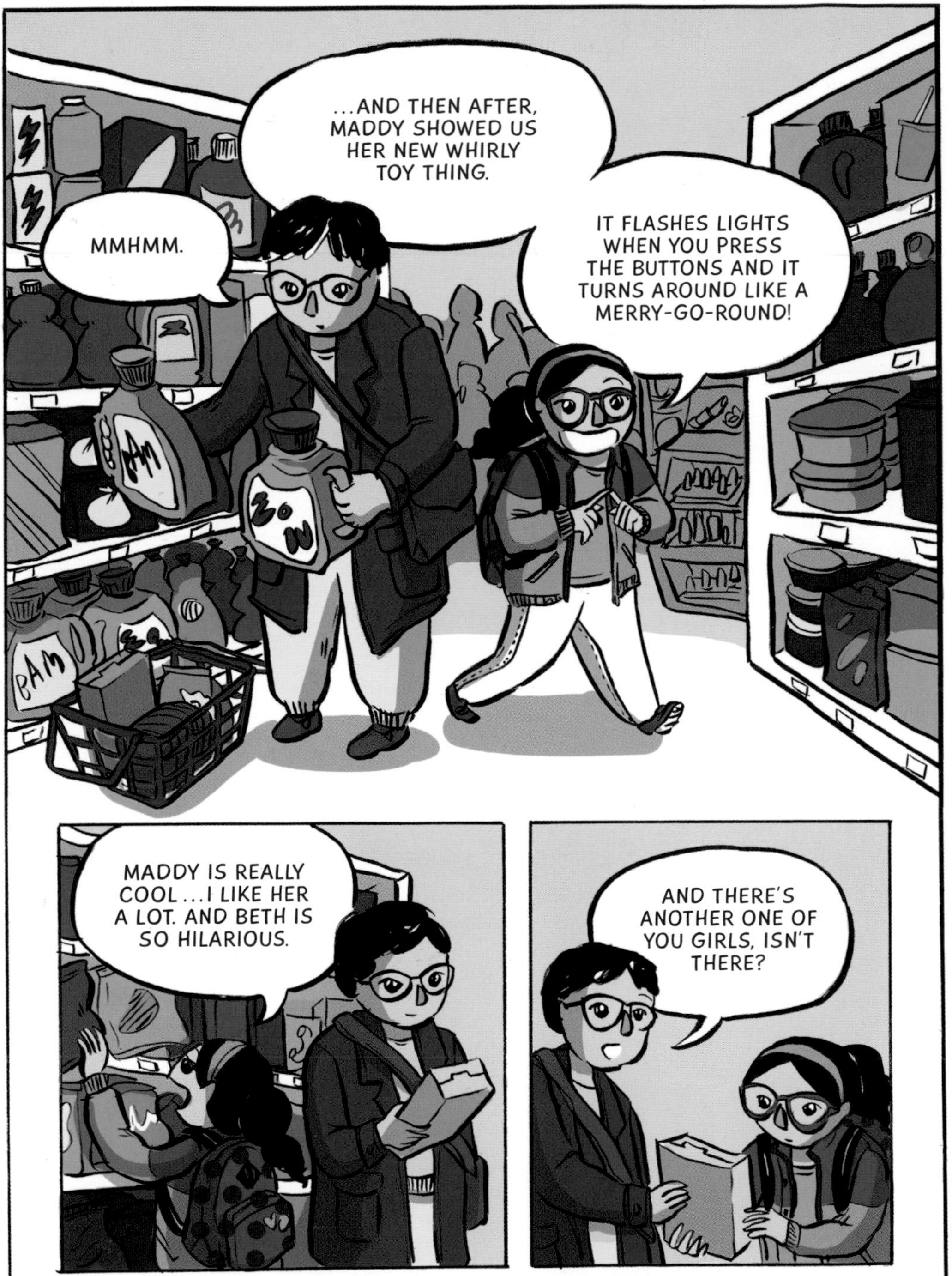
...AND THEN AFTER, MADDY SHOWED US HER NEW WHIRLY TOY THING.
MMHMM.
IT FLASHES LIGHTS WHEN YOU PRESS THE BUTTONS AND IT TURNS AROUND LIKE A MERRY-GO-ROUND!
MADDY IS REALLY COOL...I LIKE HER A LOT. AND BETH IS SO HILARIOUS.
AND THERE'S ANOTHER ONE OF YOU GIRLS, ISN'T THERE?

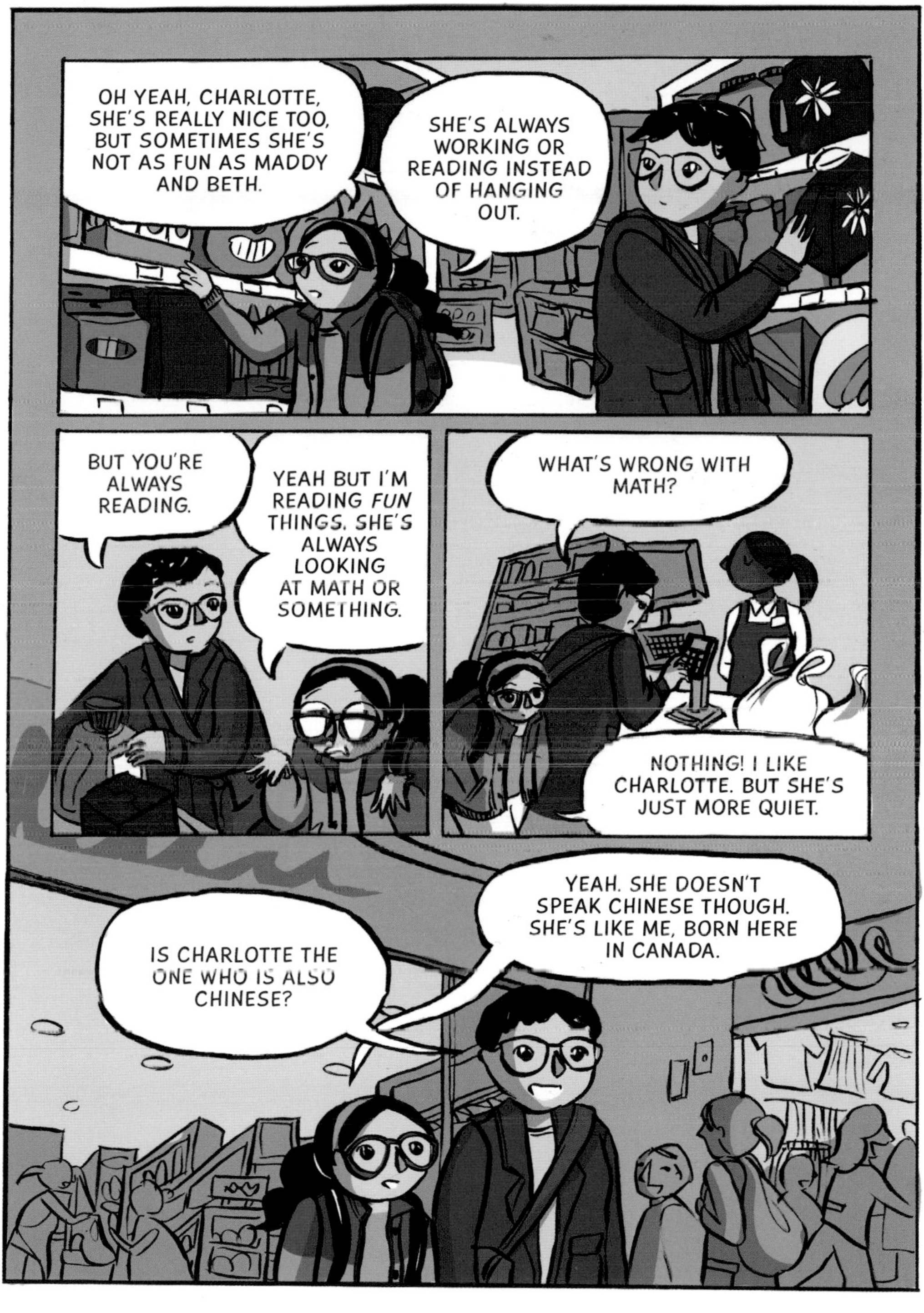
OH YEAH, CHARLOTTE, SHE'S REALLY NICE TOO, BUT SOMETIMES SHE'S NOT AS FUN AS MADDY AND BETH.
SHE'S ALWAYS WORKING OR READING INSTEAD OF HANGING OUT.
BUT YOU'RE ALWAYS READING.
YEAH BUT I'M READING *FUN* THINGS. SHE'S ALWAYS LOOKING AT MATH OR SOMETHING.
WHAT'S WRONG WITH MATH?
NOTHING! I LIKE CHARLOTTE. BUT SHE'S JUST MORE QUIET.
IS CHARLOTTE THE ONE WHO IS ALSO CHINESE?
YEAH. SHE DOESN'T SPEAK CHINESE THOUGH. SHE'S LIKE ME, BORN HERE IN CANADA.

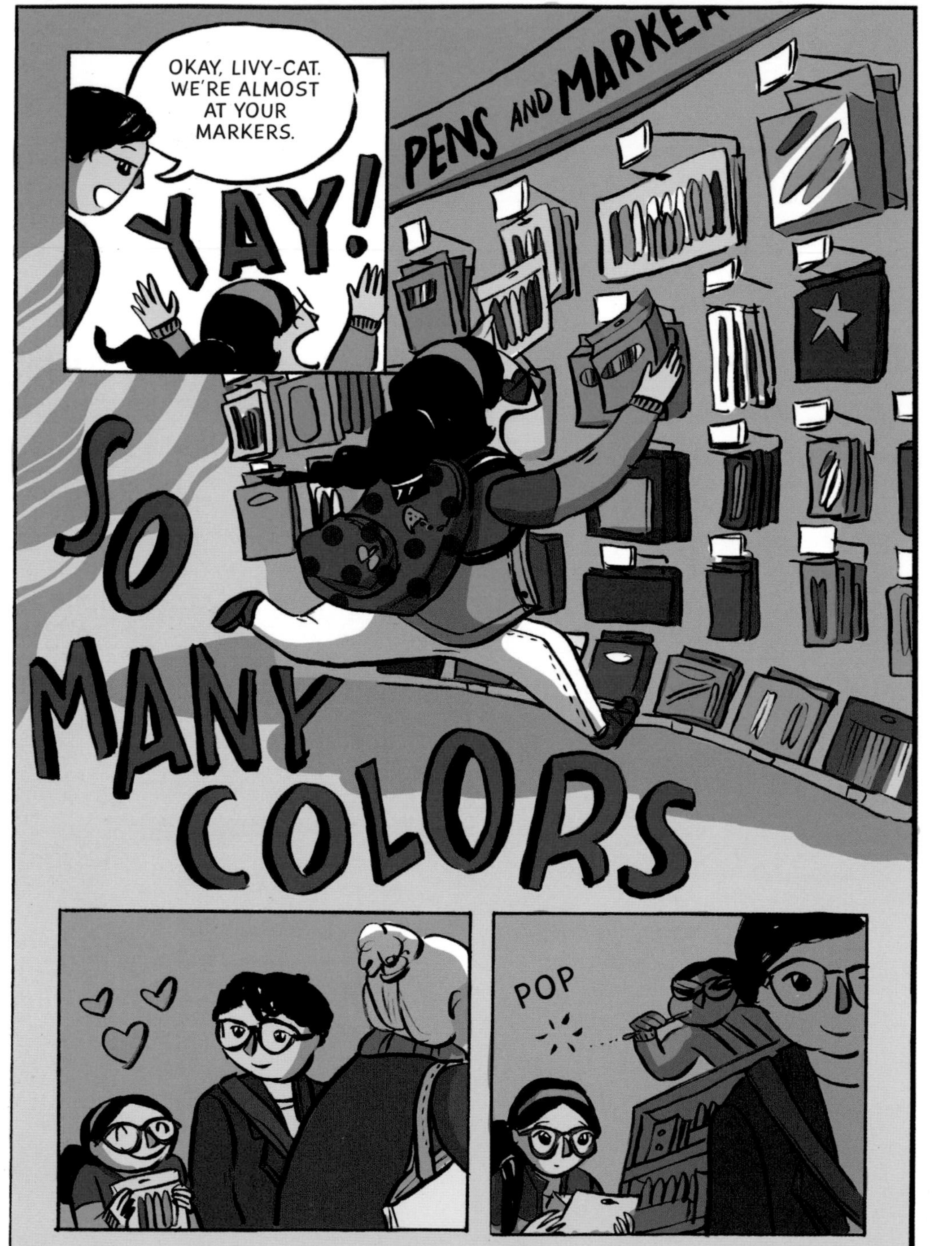
OKAY, LIVY-CAT. WE'RE ALMOST AT YOUR MARKERS.
YAY!
PENS AND MARKE
SO MANY COLORS
POP

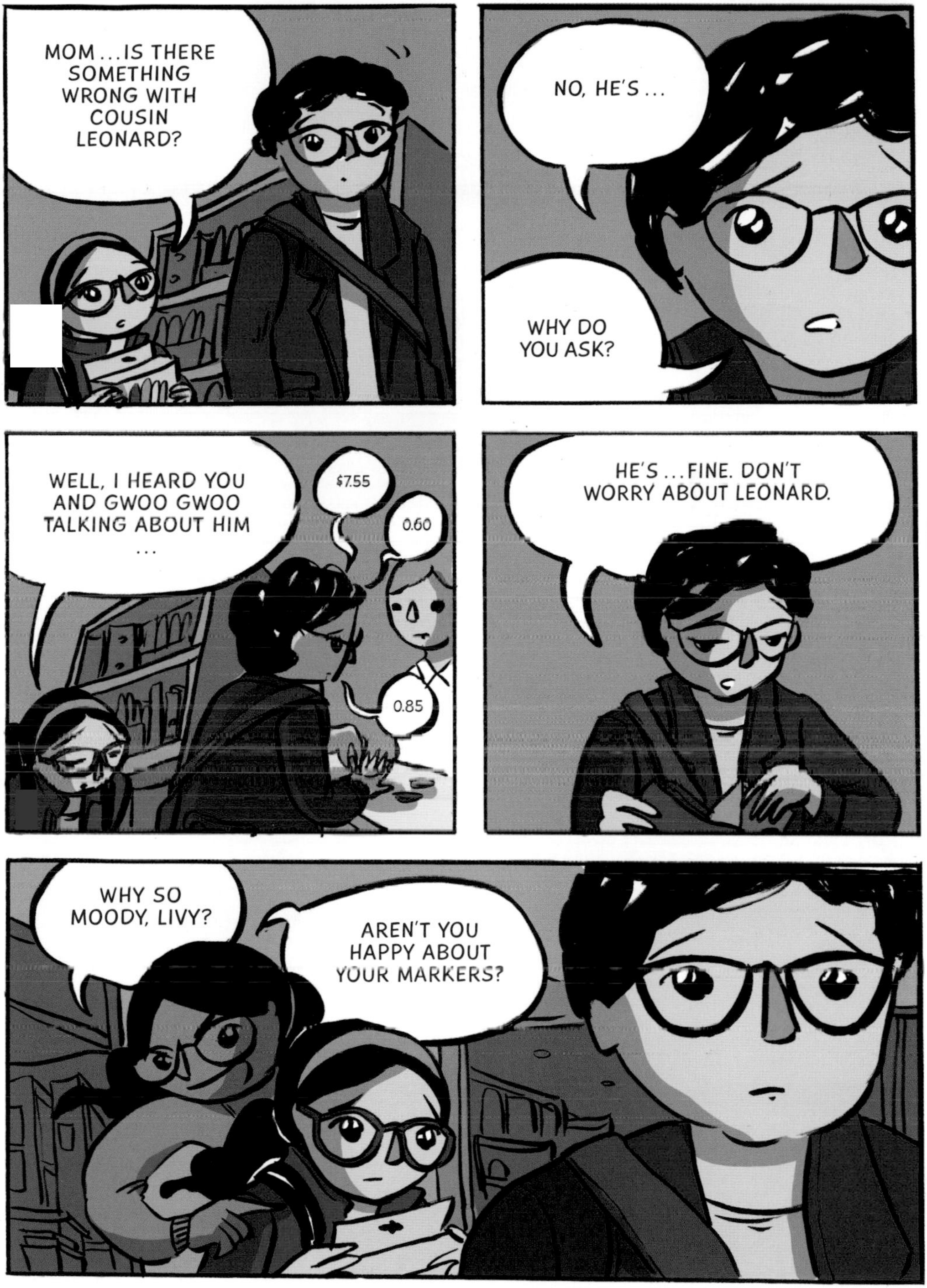
MOM ... IS THERE SOMETHING WRONG WITH COUSIN LEONARD?
NO, HE'S ...
WHY DO YOU ASK?
WELL, I HEARD YOU AND GWOO GWOO TALKING ABOUT HIM ...
$7.55
0.60
0.85
HE'S ... FINE. DON'T WORRY ABOUT LEONARD.
WHY SO MOODY, LIVY?
AREN'T YOU HAPPY ABOUT YOUR MARKERS?

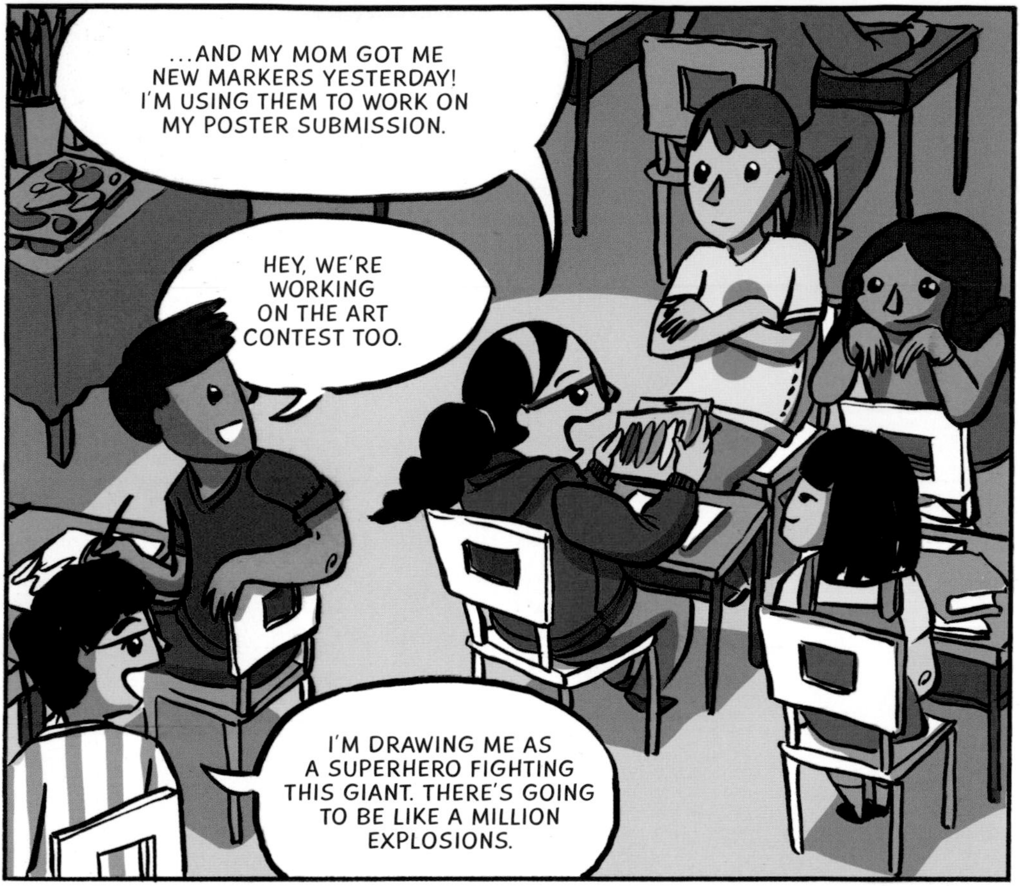
...AND MY MOM GOT ME NEW MARKERS YESTERDAY! I'M USING THEM TO WORK ON MY POSTER SUBMISSION.
HEY, WE'RE WORKING ON THE ART CONTEST TOO.
I'M DRAWING ME AS A SUPERHERO FIGHTING THIS GIANT. THERE'S GOING TO BE LIKE A MILLION EXPLOSIONS.

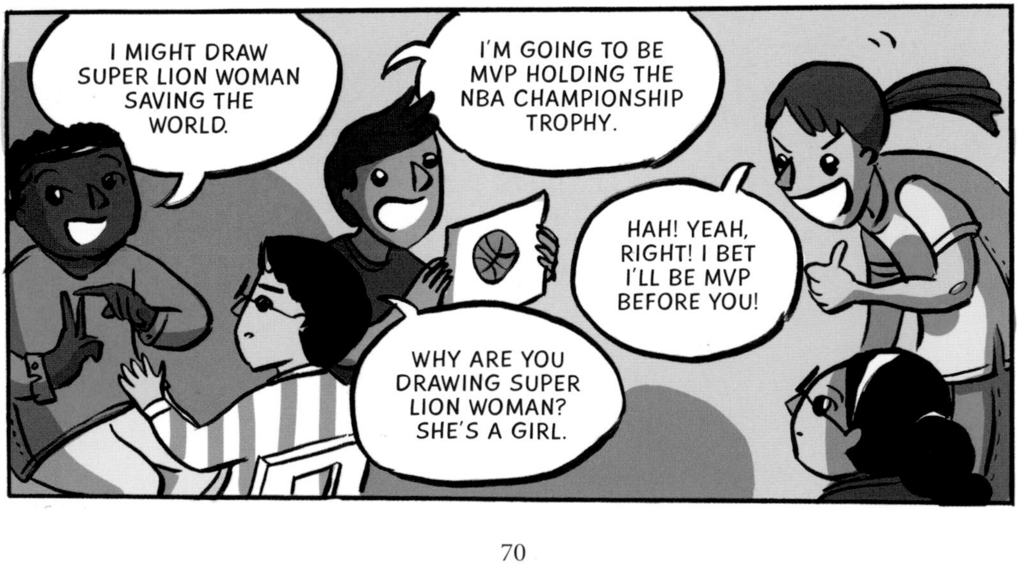
I MIGHT DRAW SUPER LION WOMAN SAVING THE WORLD.
I'M GOING TO BE MVP HOLDING THE NBA CHAMPIONSHIP TROPHY.
HAH! YEAH, RIGHT! I BET I'LL BE MVP BEFORE YOU!
WHY ARE YOU DRAWING SUPER LION WOMAN? SHE'S A GIRL.

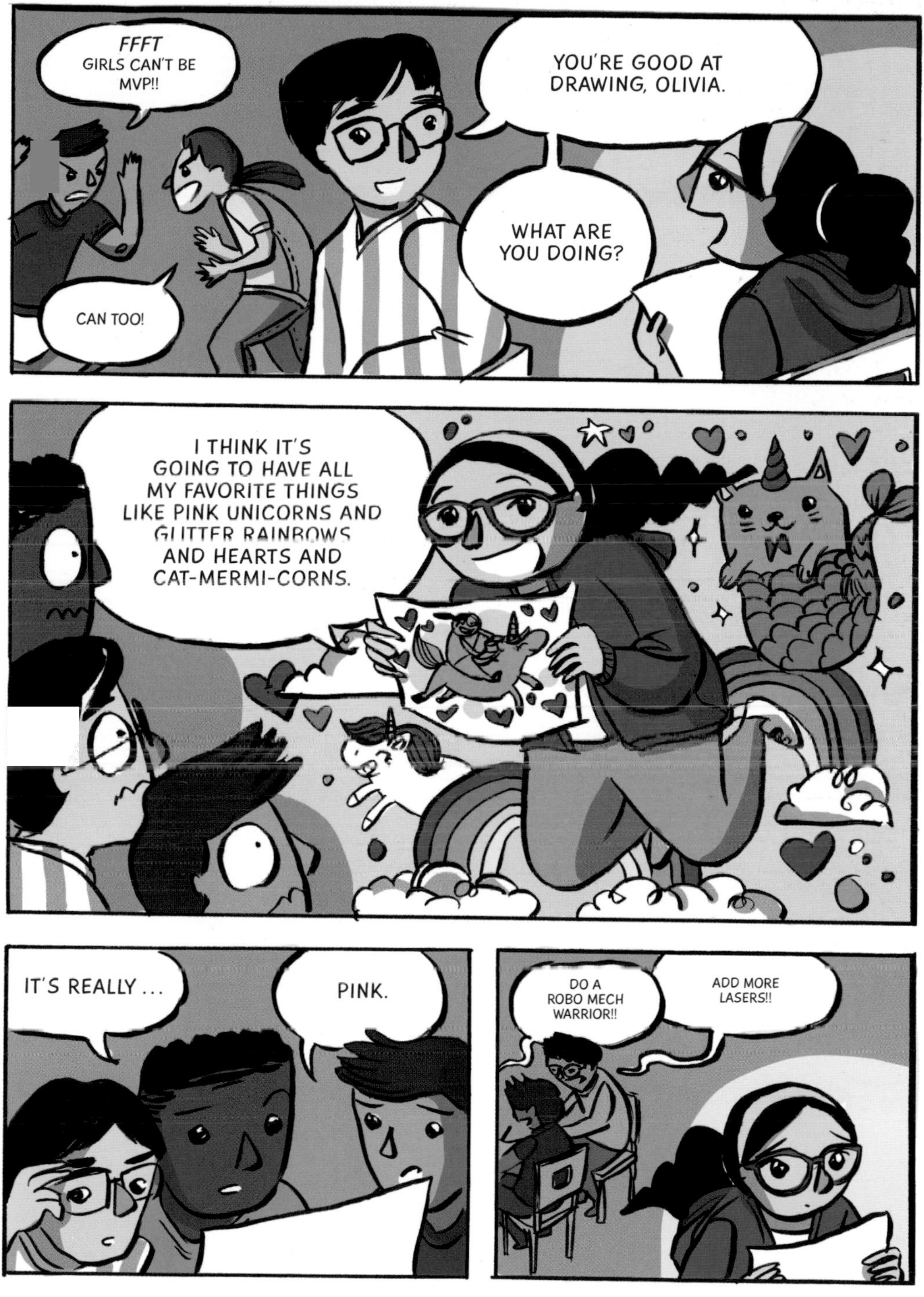
FFFT
GIRLS CAN'T BE MVP!!
CAN TOO!
YOU'RE GOOD AT DRAWING, OLIVIA.
WHAT ARE YOU DOING?
I THINK IT'S GOING TO HAVE ALL MY FAVORITE THINGS LIKE PINK UNICORNS AND GLITTER RAINBOWS AND HEARTS AND CAT-MERMI-CORNS.
IT'S REALLY ...
PINK.
DO A ROBO MECH WARRIOR!!
ADD MORE LASERS!!

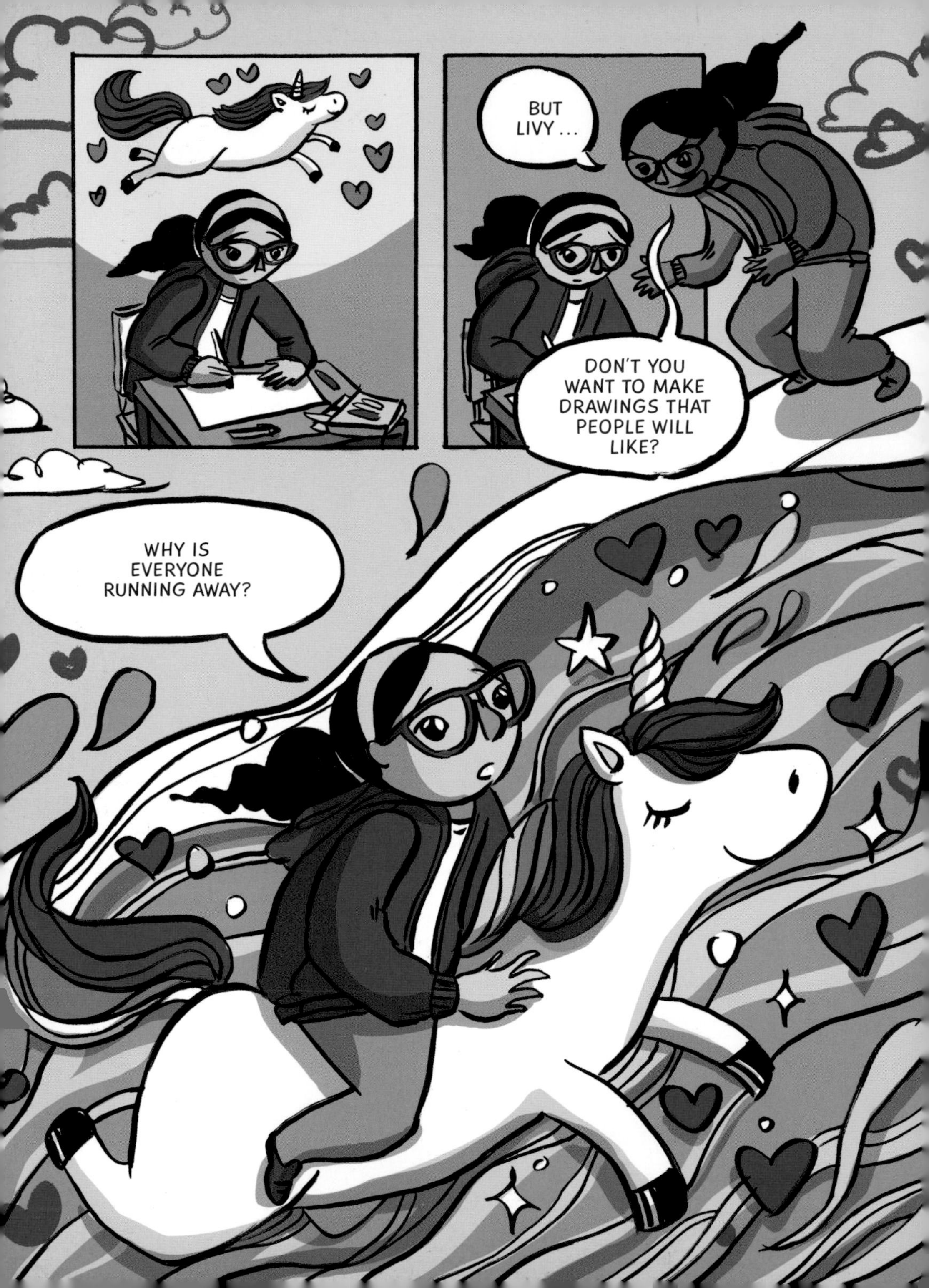
BUT LIVY . . .
DON'T YOU WANT TO MAKE DRAWINGS THAT PEOPLE WILL LIKE?
WHY IS EVERYONE RUNNING AWAY?

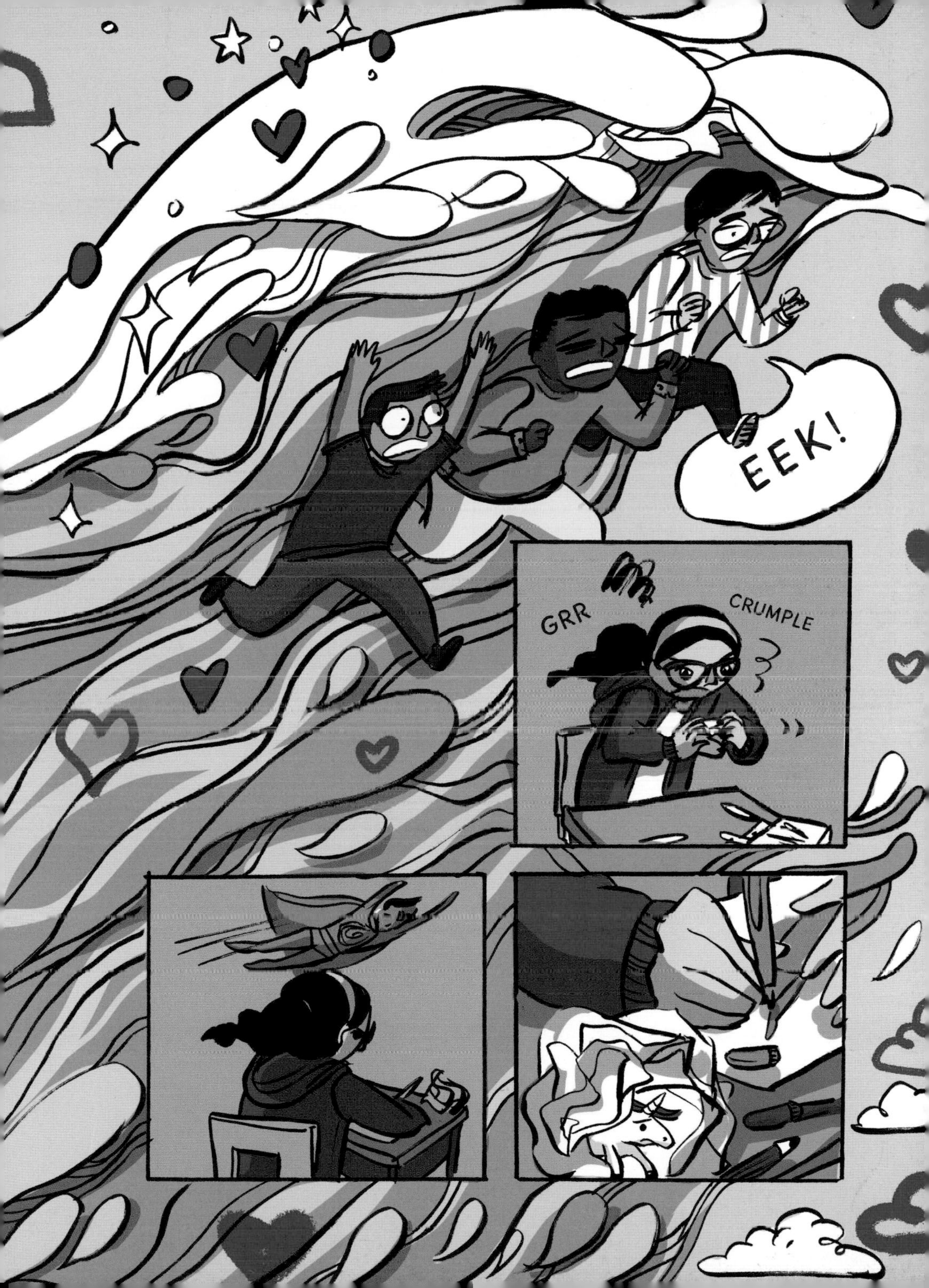
EEK!
GRR
CRUMPLE

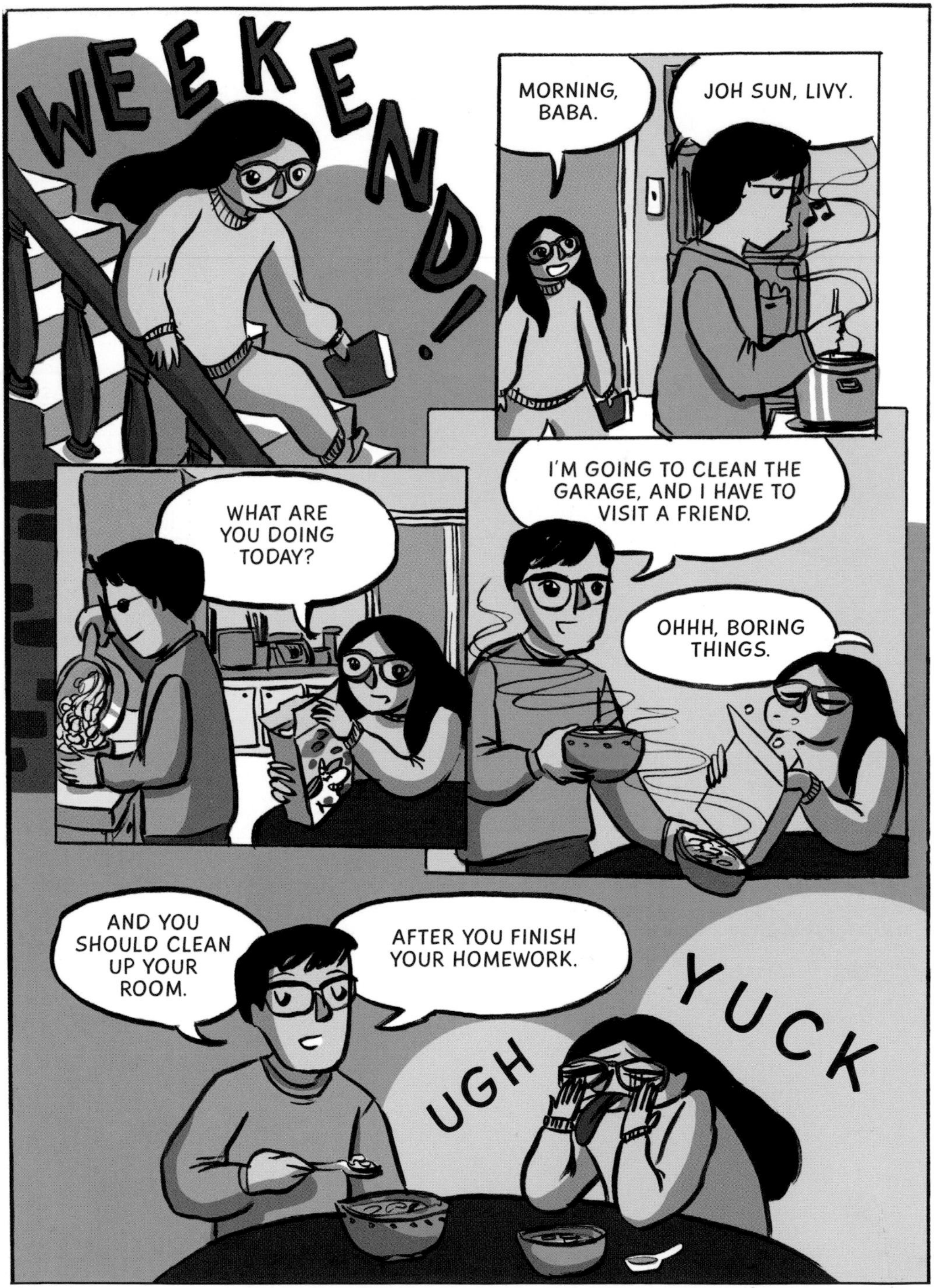
WEEKEND!
MORNING, BABA.
JOH SUN, LIVY.
WHAT ARE YOU DOING TODAY?
I'M GOING TO CLEAN THE GARAGE, AND I HAVE TO VISIT A FRIEND.
OHHH, BORING THINGS.
AND YOU SHOULD CLEAN UP YOUR ROOM.
AFTER YOU FINISH YOUR HOMEWORK.
UGH
YUCK

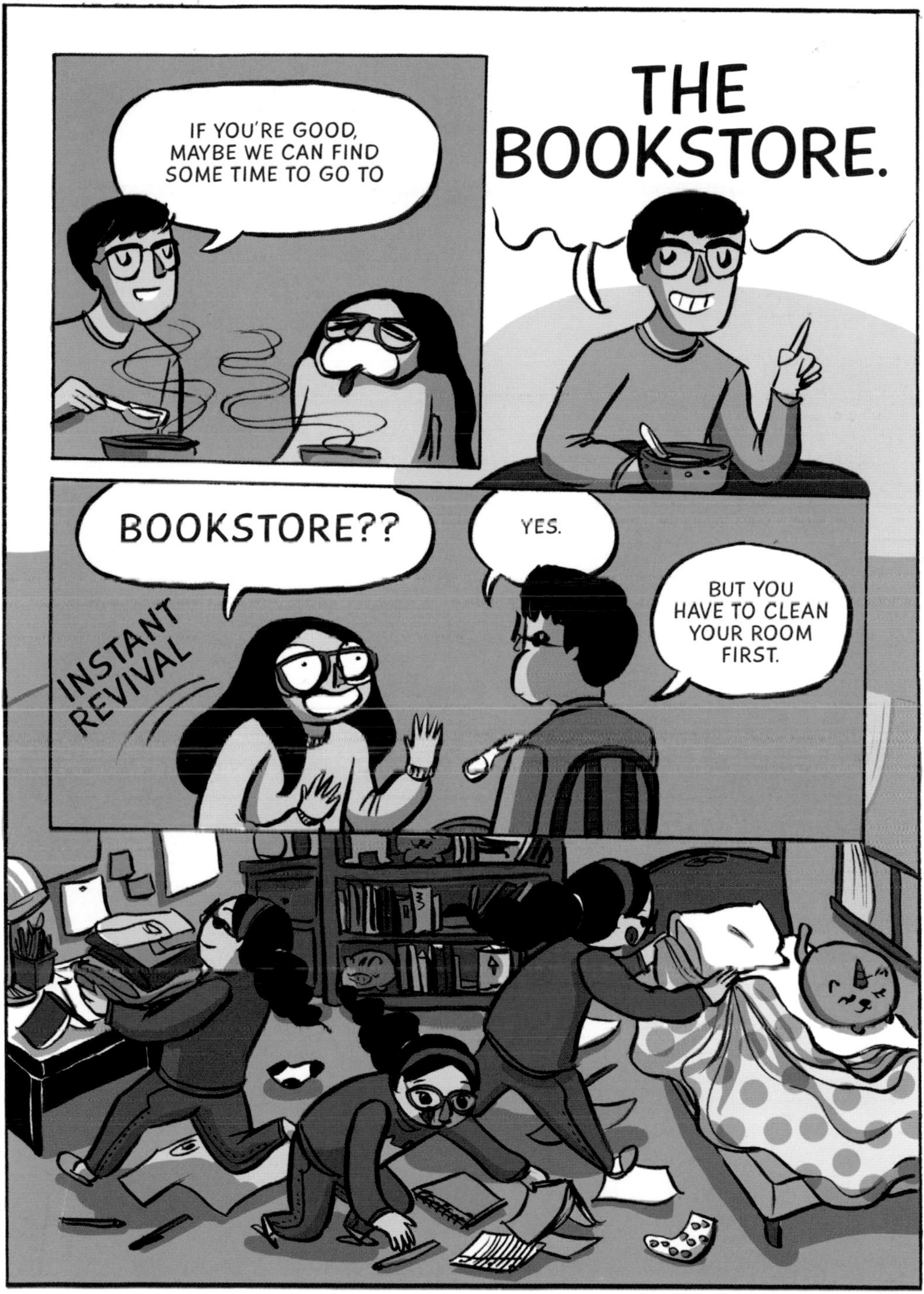
IF YOU'RE GOOD, MAYBE WE CAN FIND SOME TIME TO GO TO
THE BOOKSTORE.
BOOKSTORE??
YES.
INSTANT REVIVAL
BUT YOU HAVE TO CLEAN YOUR ROOM FIRST.

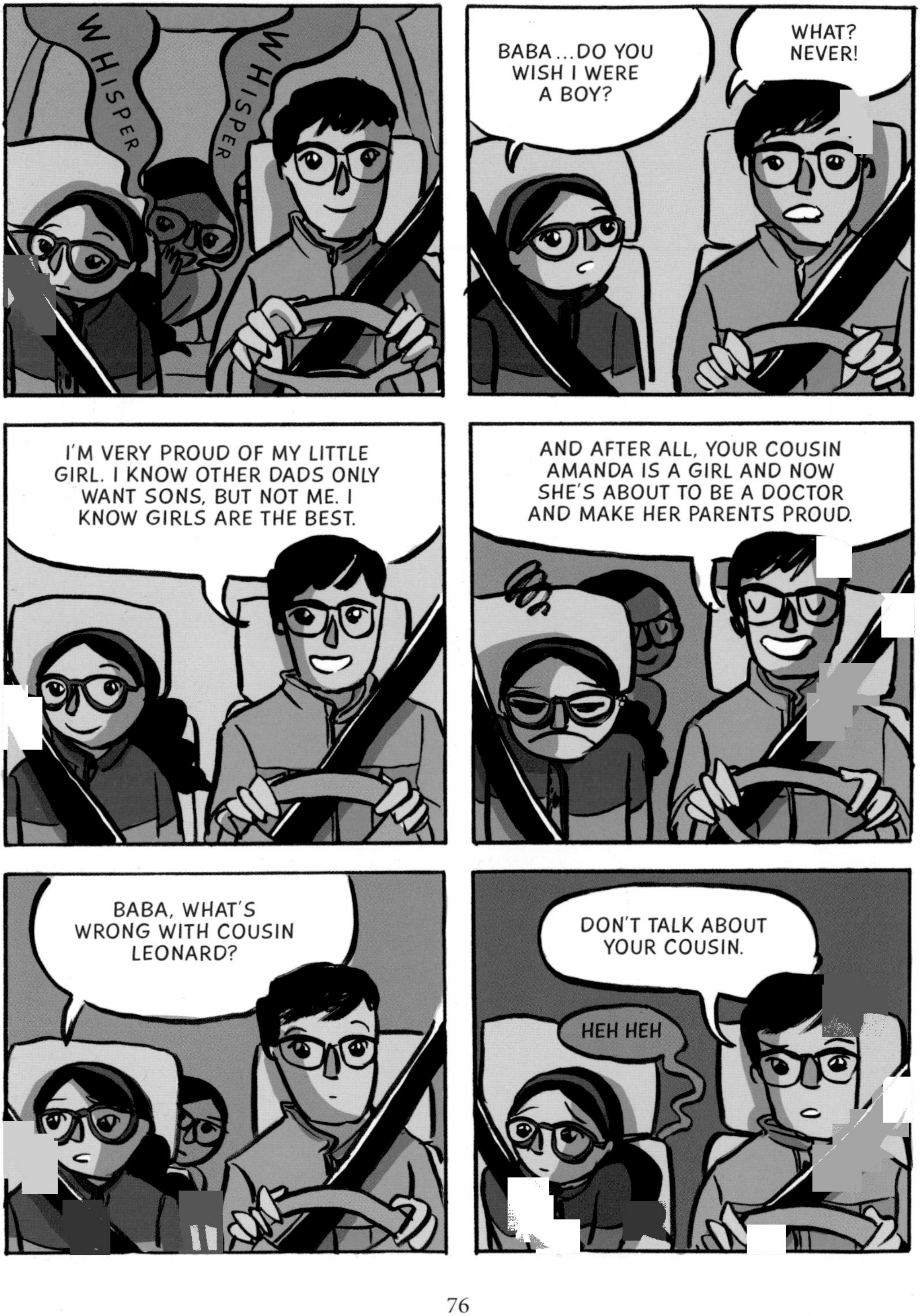
WHISPER
WHISPER
BABA...DO YOU WISH I WERE A BOY?
WHAT? NEVER!
I'M VERY PROUD OF MY LITTLE GIRL. I KNOW OTHER DADS ONLY WANT SONS, BUT NOT ME. I KNOW GIRLS ARE THE BEST.
AND AFTER ALL, YOUR COUSIN AMANDA IS A GIRL AND NOW SHE'S ABOUT TO BE A DOCTOR AND MAKE HER PARENTS PROUD.
BABA, WHAT'S WRONG WITH COUSIN LEONARD?
DON'T TALK ABOUT YOUR COUSIN.
HEH HEH

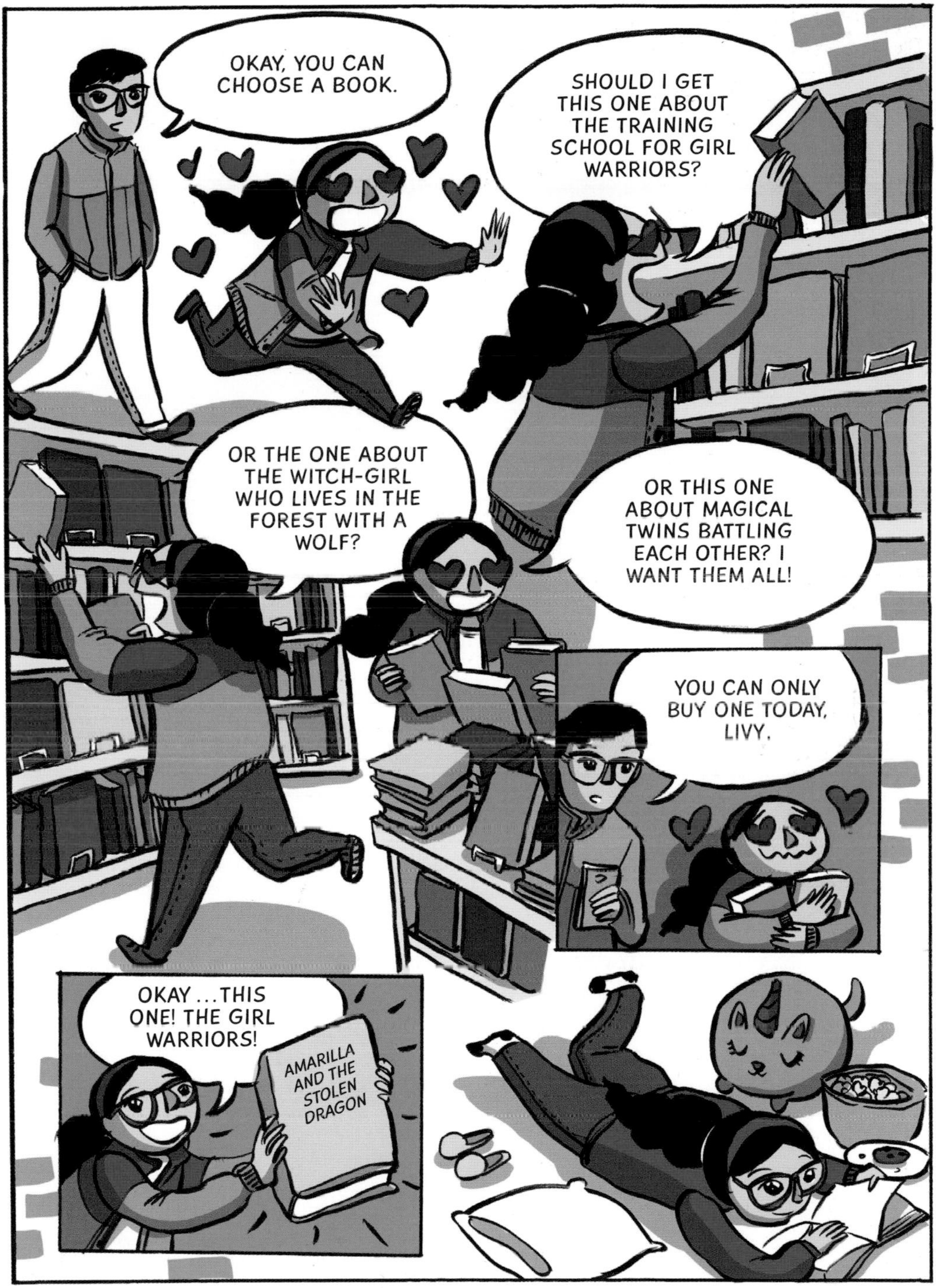
OKAY, YOU CAN CHOOSE A BOOK.
SHOULD I GET THIS ONE ABOUT THE TRAINING SCHOOL FOR GIRL WARRIORS?
OR THE ONE ABOUT THE WITCH-GIRL WHO LIVES IN THE FOREST WITH A WOLF?
OR THIS ONE ABOUT MAGICAL TWINS BATTLING EACH OTHER? I WANT THEM ALL!
YOU CAN ONLY BUY ONE TODAY, LIVY.
OKAY ... THIS ONE! THE GIRL WARRIORS!
AMARILLA AND THE STOLEN DRAGON

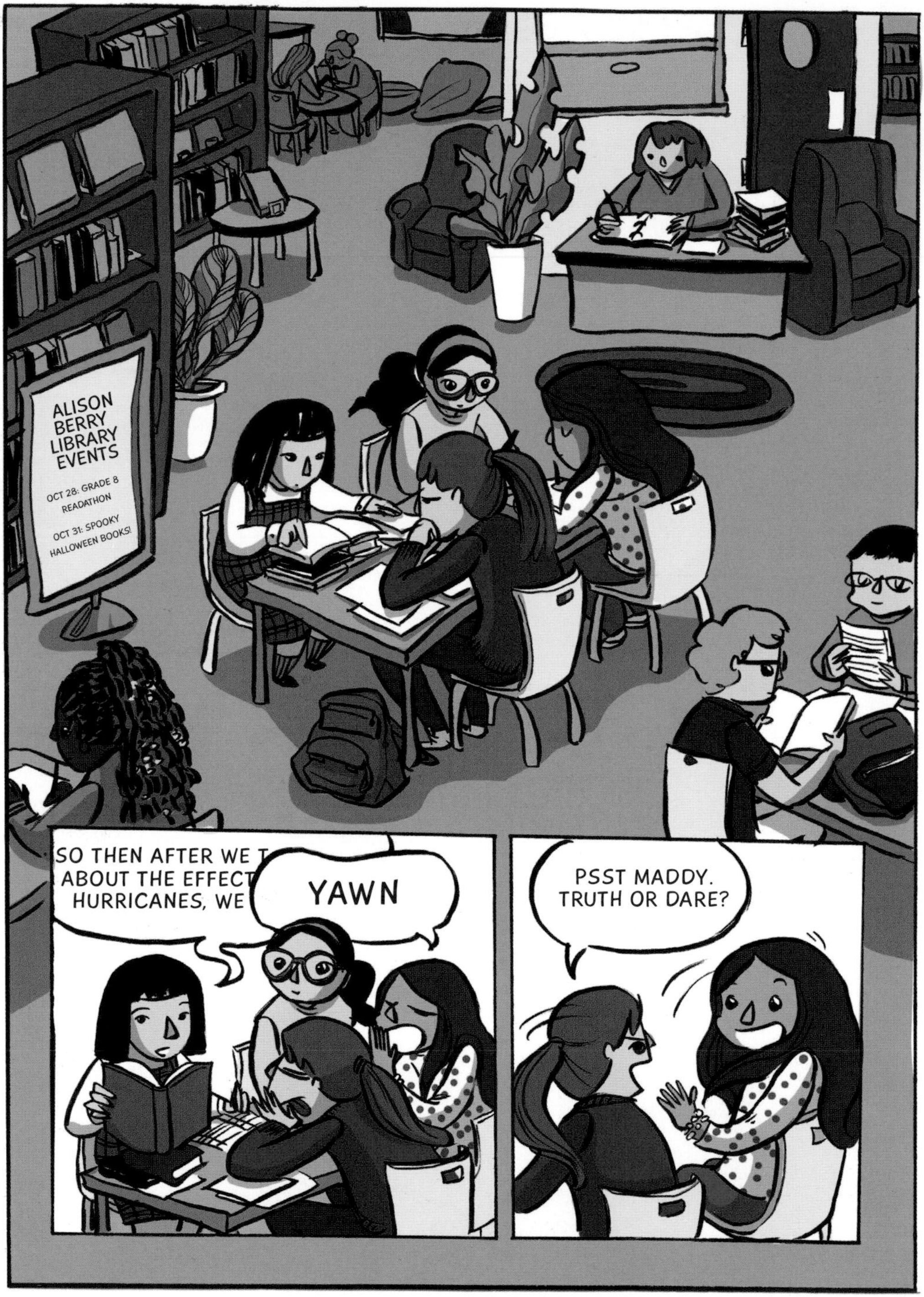
ALISON BERRY LIBRARY EVENTS
OCT 28: GRADE 8 READATHON
OCT 31: SPOOKY HALLOWEEN BOOKS!
SO THEN AFTER WE T
ABOUT THE EFFECT
HURRICANES, WE
YAWN
PSST MADDY. TRUTH OR DARE?

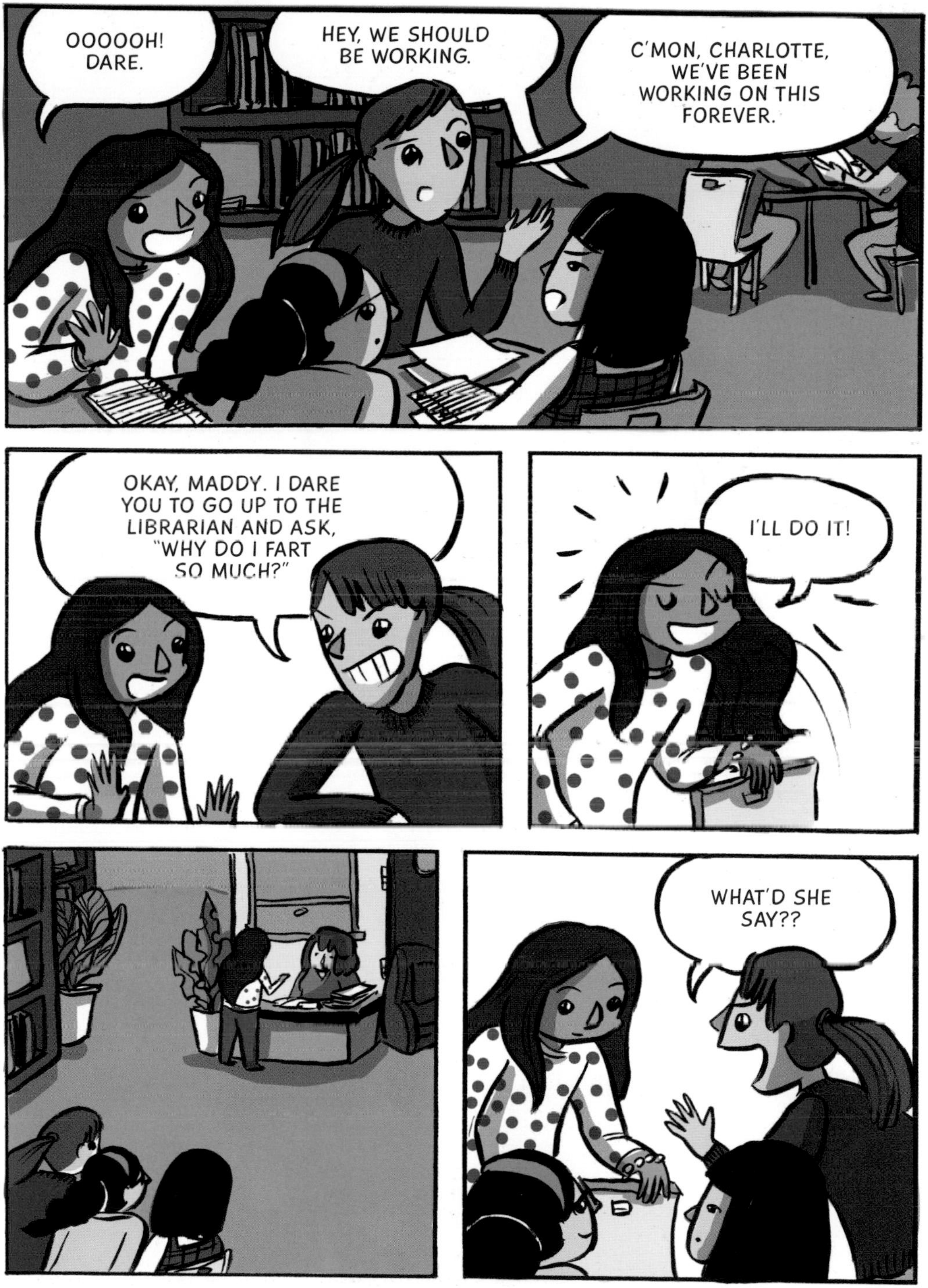

OOOOOH! DARE.
HEY, WE SHOULD BE WORKING.
C'MON, CHARLOTTE, WE'VE BEEN WORKING ON THIS FOREVER.
OKAY, MADDY. I DARE YOU TO GO UP TO THE LIBRARIAN AND ASK, "WHY DO I FART SO MUCH?"
I'LL DO IT!
WHAT'D SHE SAY??

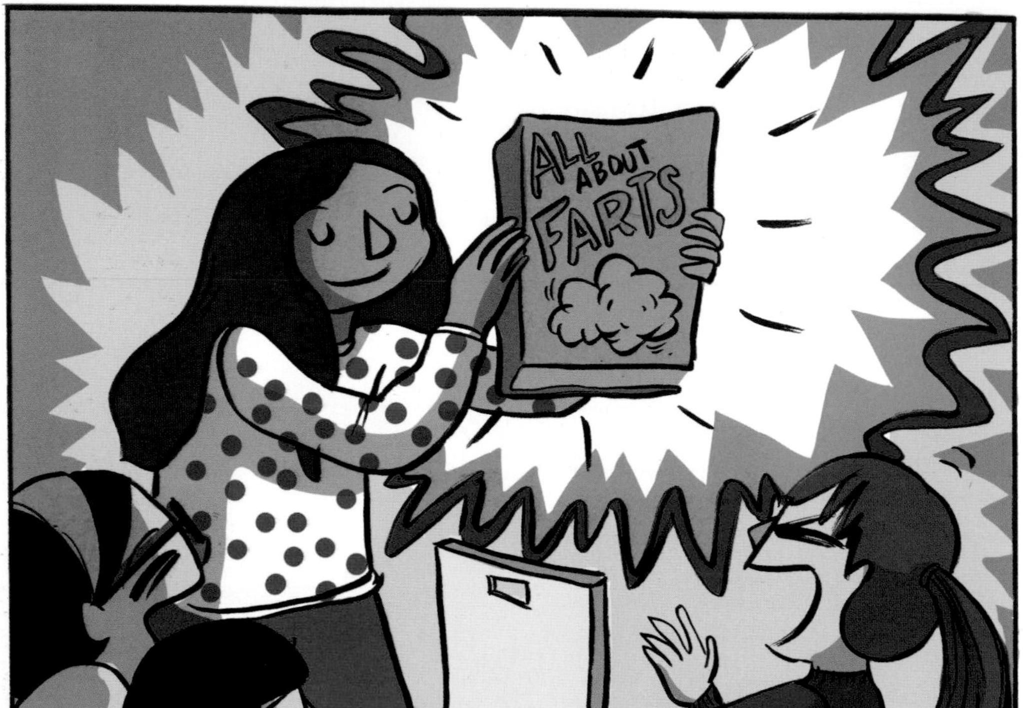
ALL ABOUT FARTS

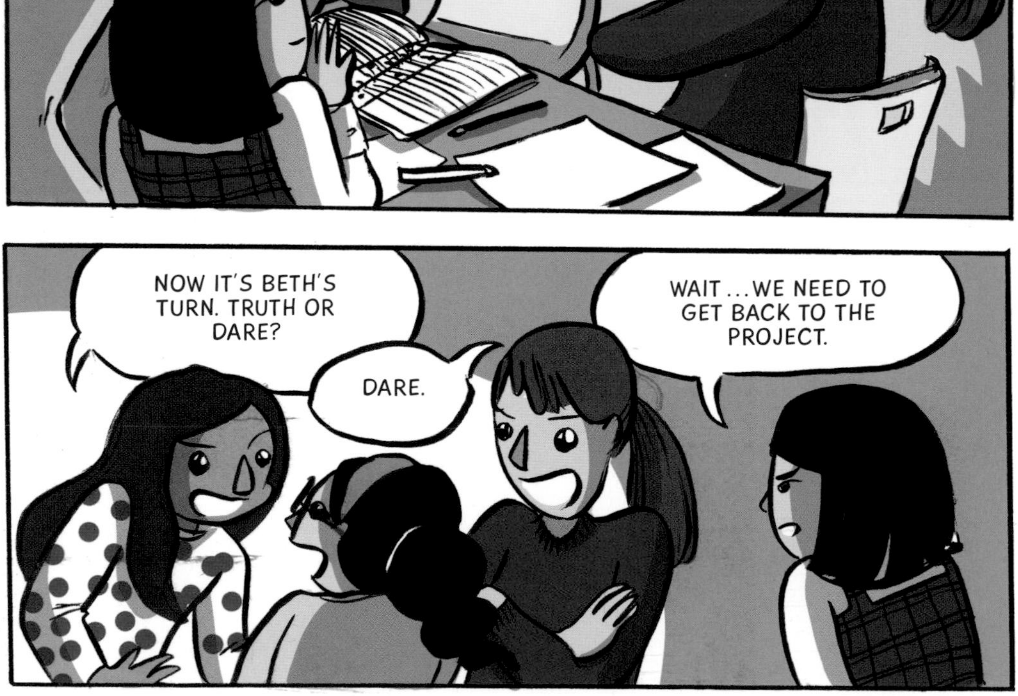
NOW IT'S BETH'S TURN. TRUTH OR DARE?
DARE.
WAIT . . . WE NEED TO GET BACK TO THE PROJECT.

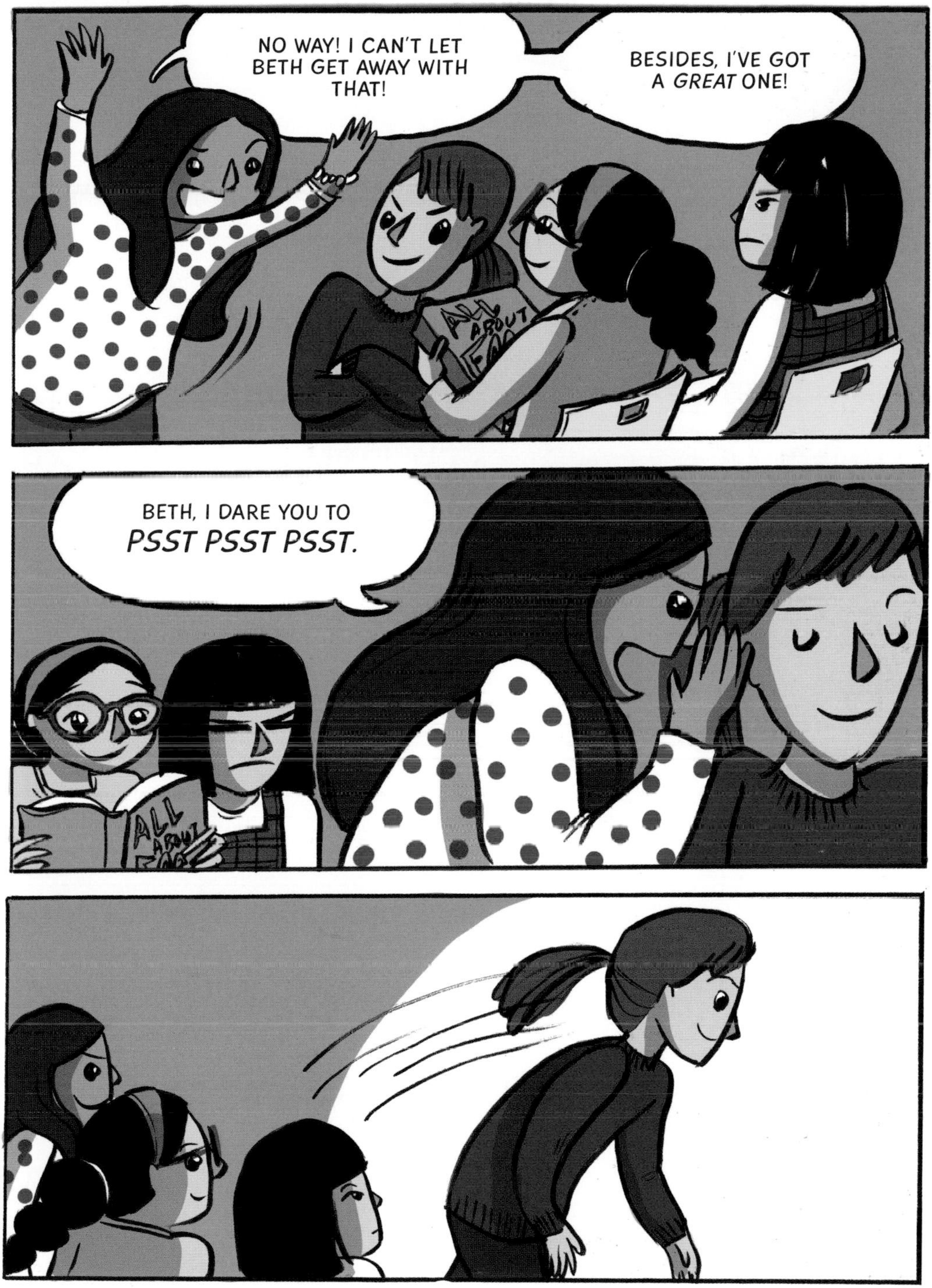
NO WAY! I CAN'T LET BETH GET AWAY WITH THAT!
BESIDES, I'VE GOT A *GREAT* ONE!
BETH, I DARE YOU TO *PSST PSST PSST.*

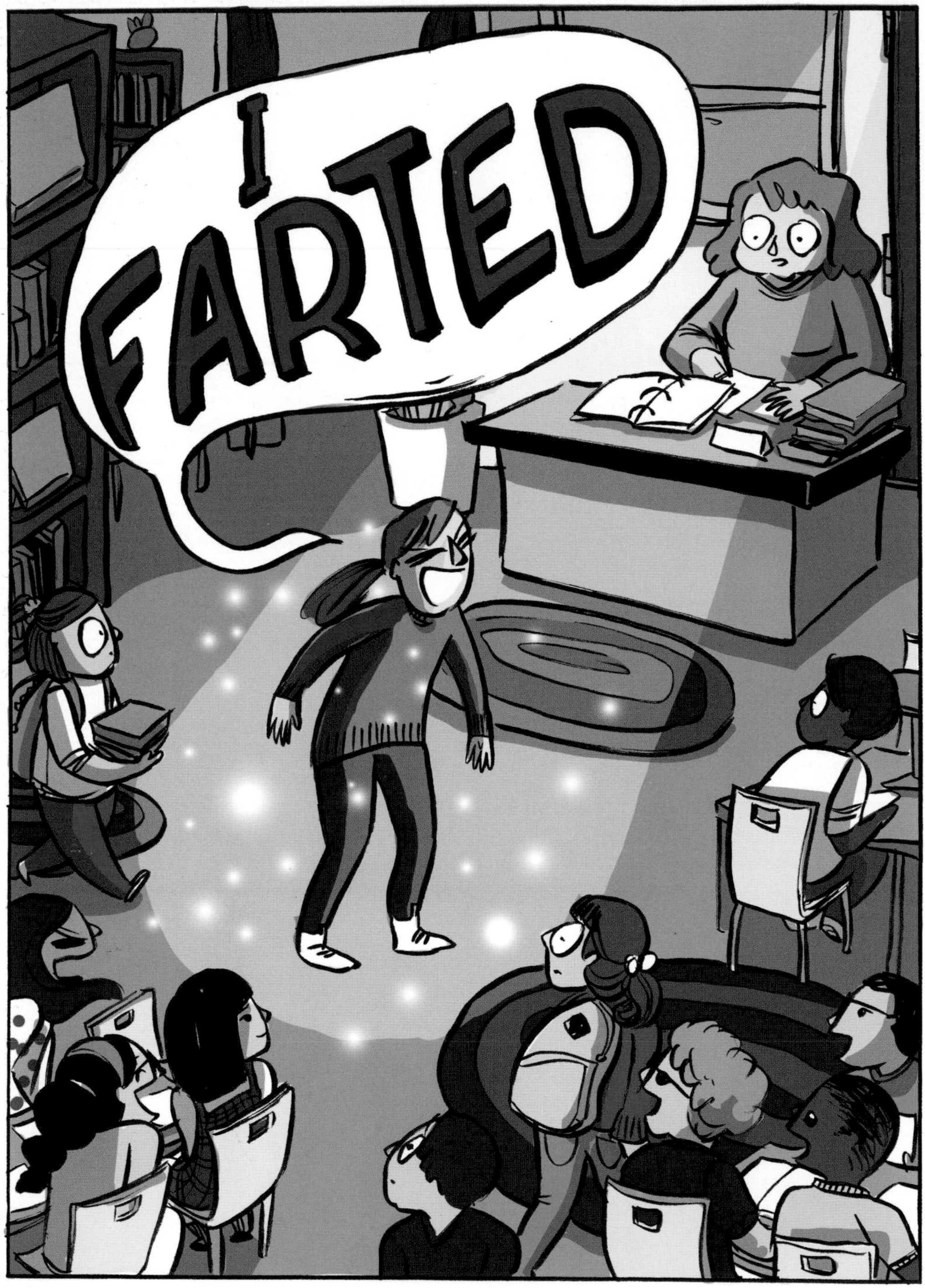
I FARTED

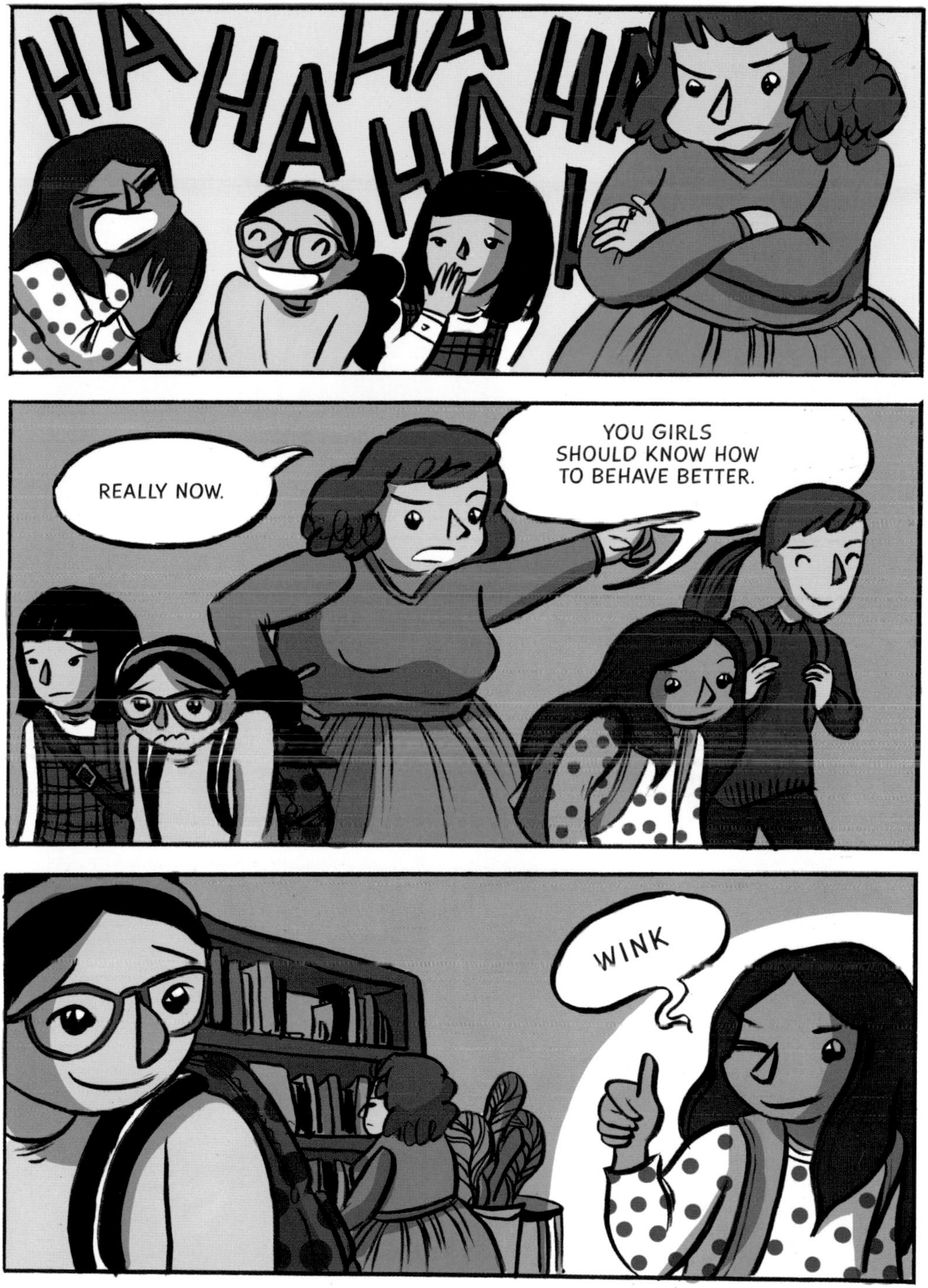
HA HA HA HA HA HA
REALLY NOW.
YOU GIRLS SHOULD KNOW HOW TO BEHAVE BETTER.
WINK

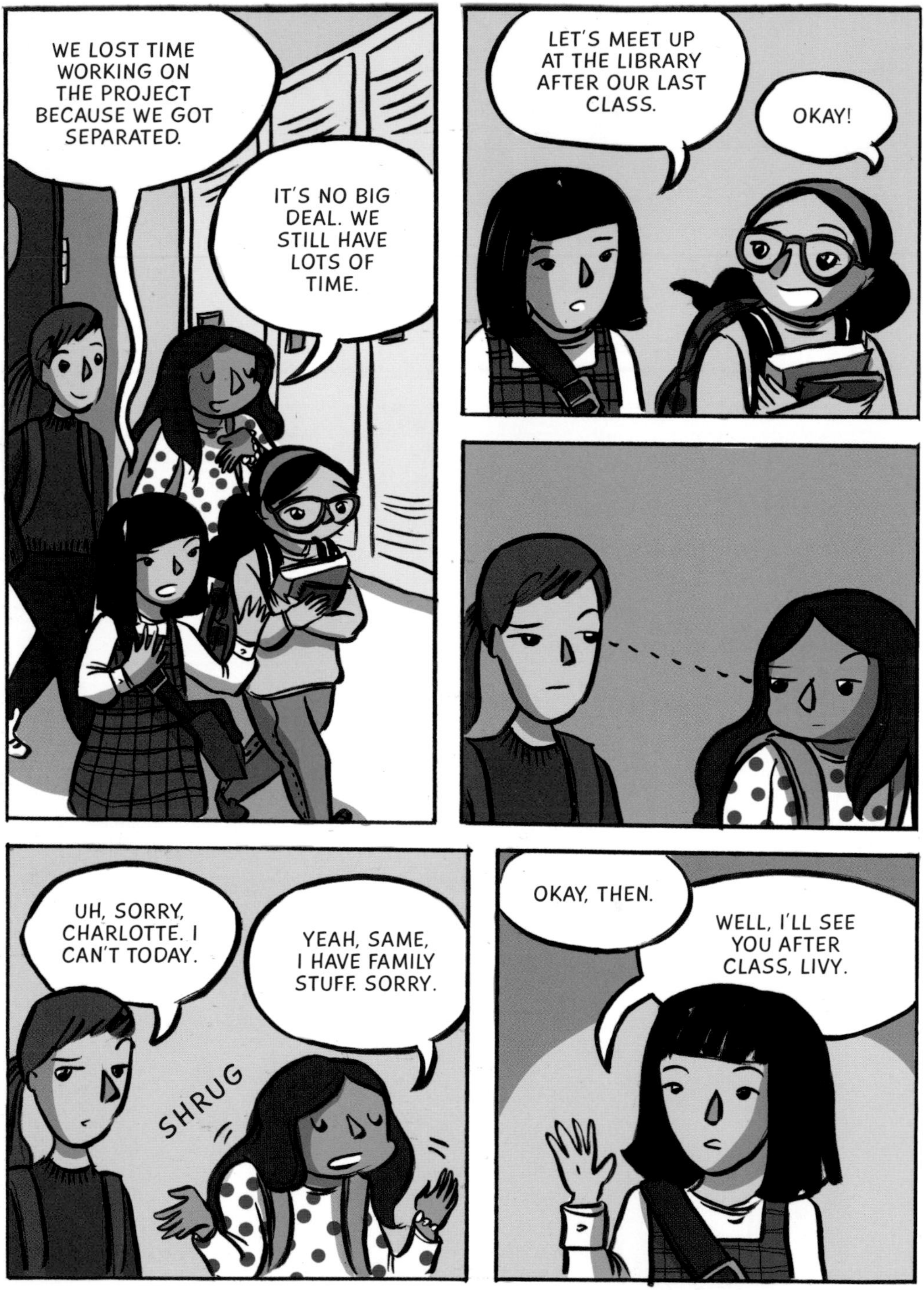
WE LOST TIME WORKING ON THE PROJECT BECAUSE WE GOT SEPARATED.
IT'S NO BIG DEAL. WE STILL HAVE LOTS OF TIME.
LET'S MEET UP AT THE LIBRARY AFTER OUR LAST CLASS.
OKAY!
UH, SORRY, CHARLOTTE. I CAN'T TODAY.
YEAH, SAME, I HAVE FAMILY STUFF. SORRY.
SHRUG
OKAY, THEN.
WELL, I'LL SEE YOU AFTER CLASS, LIVY.

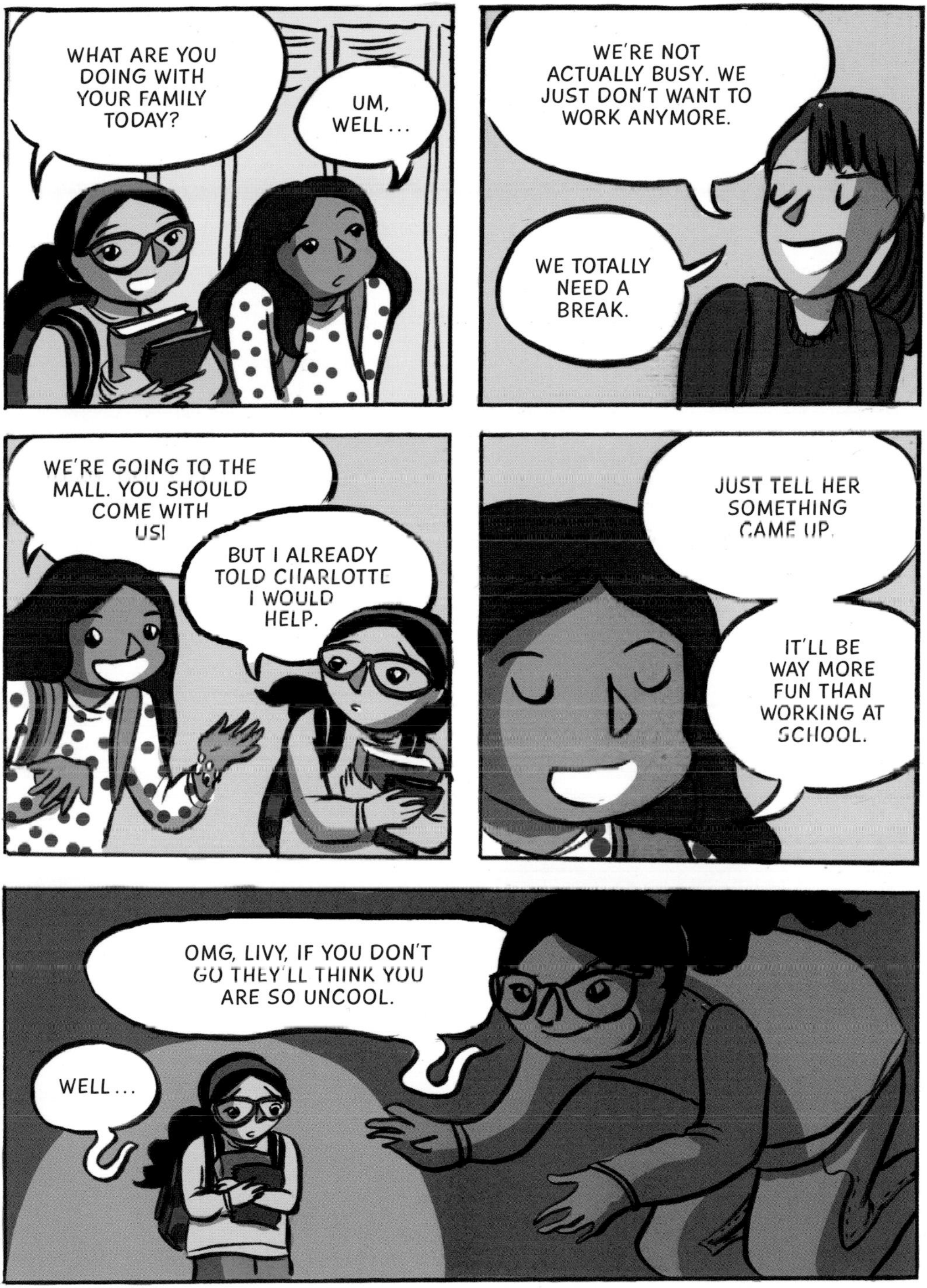
WHAT ARE YOU DOING WITH YOUR FAMILY TODAY?
UM, WELL...
WE'RE NOT ACTUALLY BUSY. WE JUST DON'T WANT TO WORK ANYMORE.
WE TOTALLY NEED A BREAK.
WE'RE GOING TO THE MALL. YOU SHOULD COME WITH US!
BUT I ALREADY TOLD CHARLOTTE I WOULD HELP.
JUST TELL HER SOMETHING CAME UP.
IT'LL BE WAY MORE FUN THAN WORKING AT SCHOOL.
OMG, LIVY, IF YOU DON'T GO THEY'LL THINK YOU ARE SO UNCOOL.
WELL...

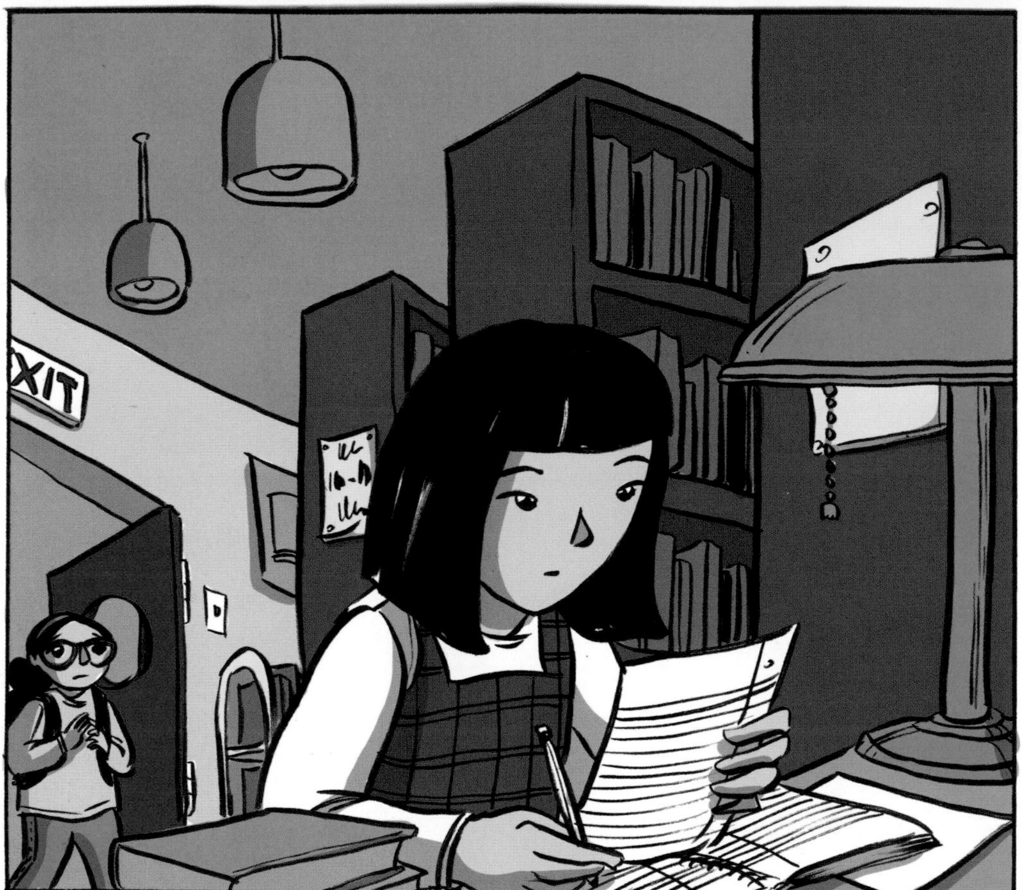
EXIT

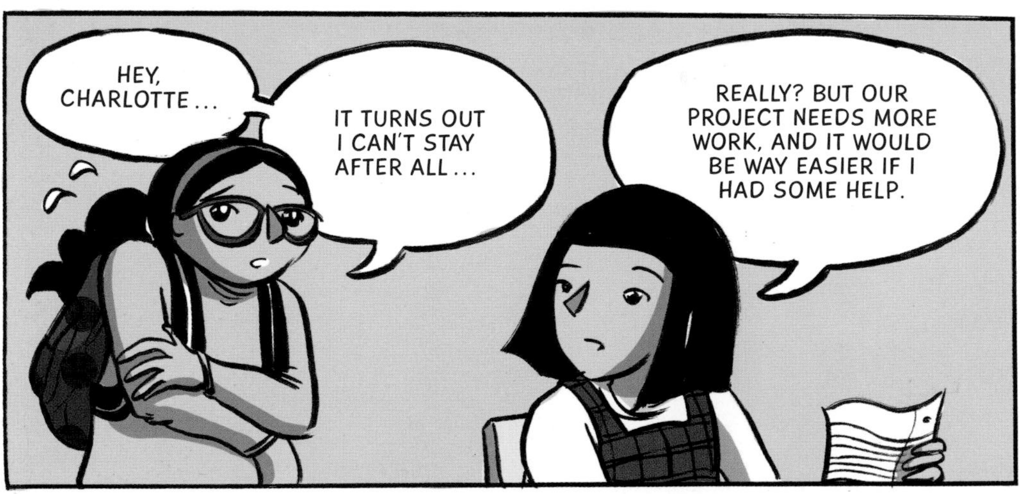
HEY, CHARLOTTE...
IT TURNS OUT I CAN'T STAY AFTER ALL...
REALLY? BUT OUR PROJECT NEEDS MORE WORK, AND IT WOULD BE WAY EASIER IF I HAD SOME HELP.

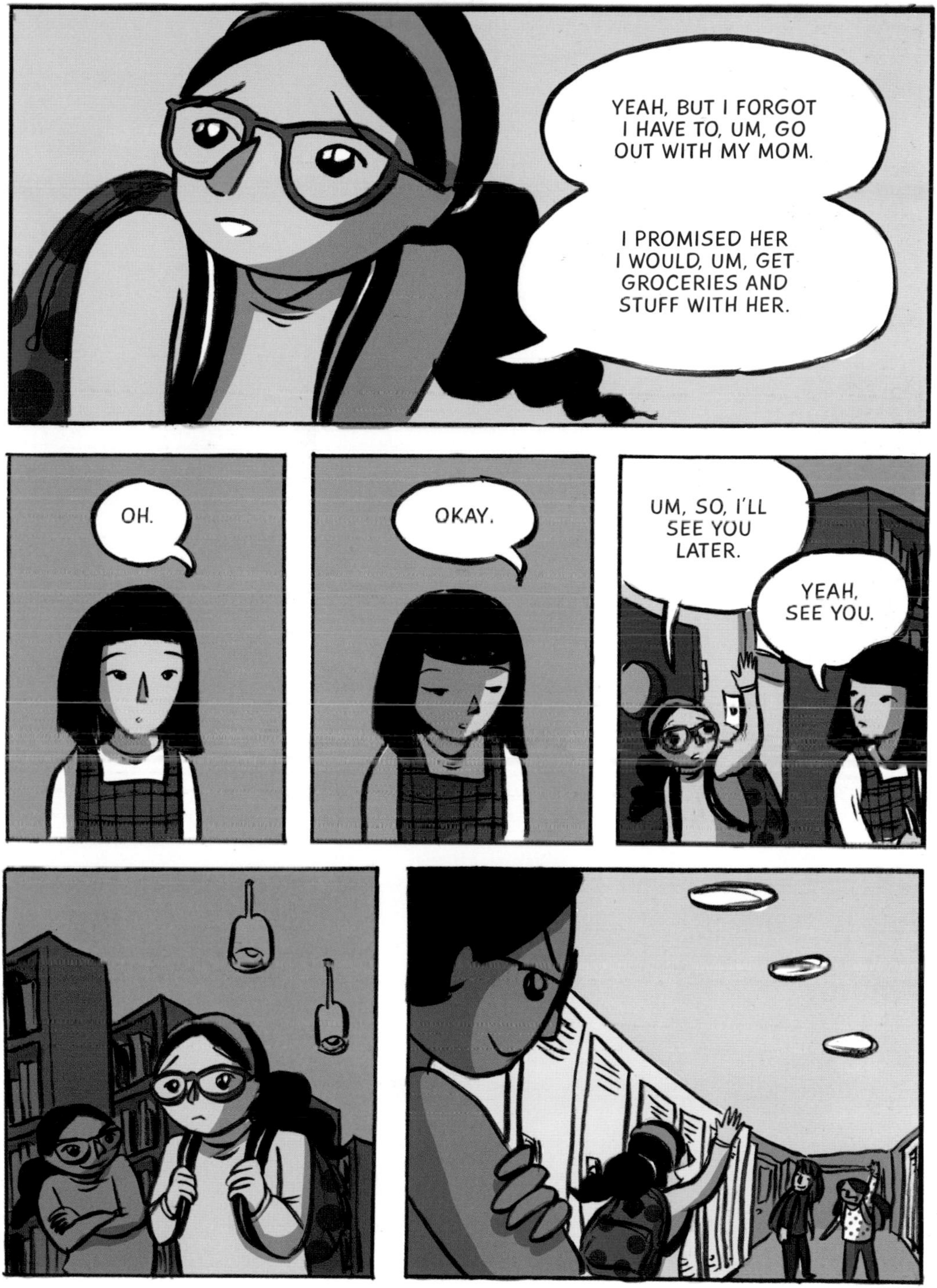
YEAH, BUT I FORGOT I HAVE TO, UM, GO OUT WITH MY MOM.
I PROMISED HER I WOULD, UM, GET GROCERIES AND STUFF WITH HER.
OH.
OKAY.
UM, SO, I'LL SEE YOU LATER.
YEAH, SEE YOU.

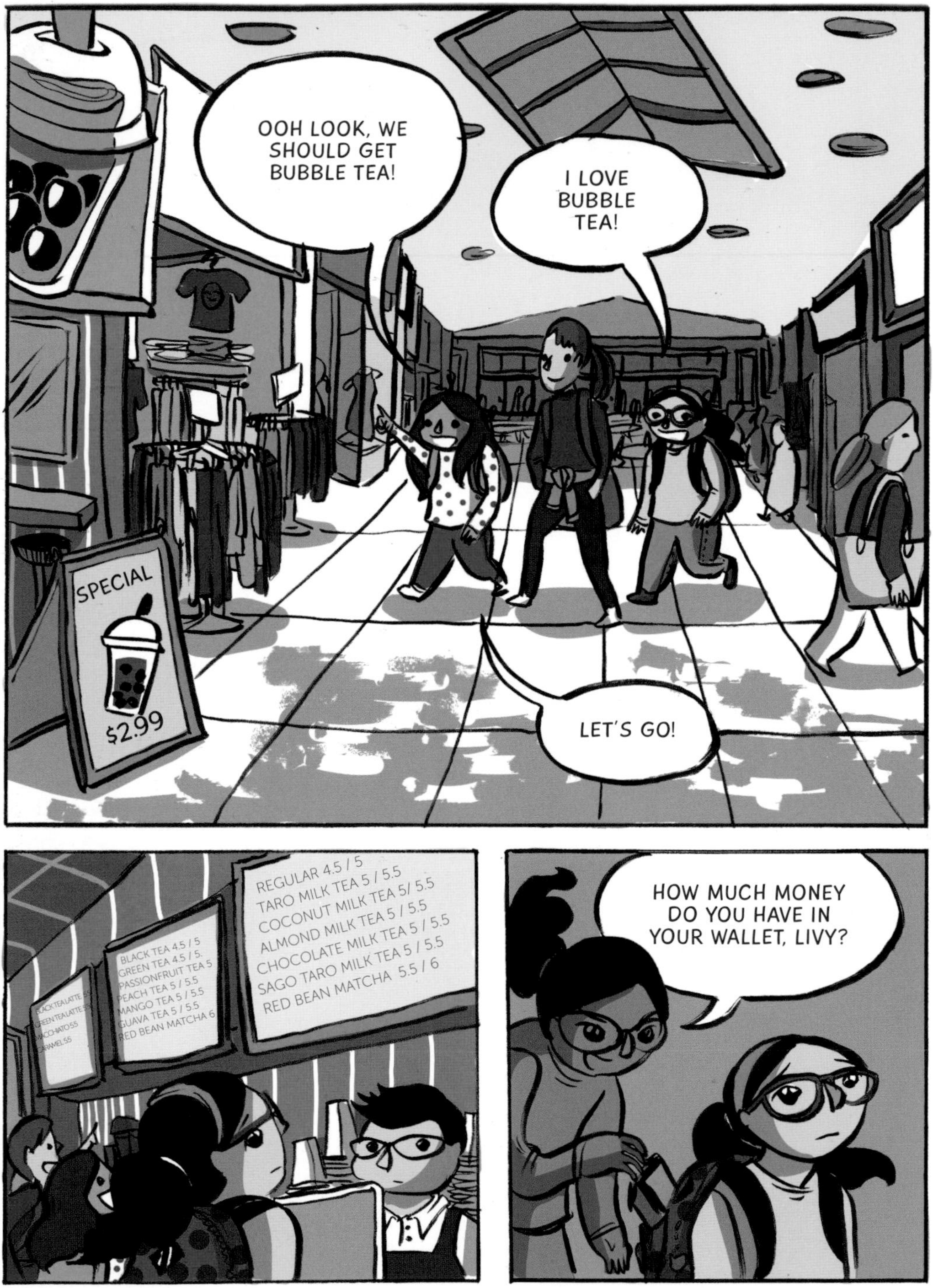
OOH LOOK, WE SHOULD GET BUBBLE TEA!
I LOVE BUBBLE TEA!
SPECIAL
$2.99
LET'S GO!
BLACK TEA 4.5 / 5
GREEN TEA 4.5 / 5.
PASSIONFRUIT TEA 5
PEACH TEA 5 / 5.5
MANGO TEA 5 / 5.5
GUAVA TEA 5 / 5.5
RED BEAN MATCHA 6
REGULAR 4.5 / 5
TARO MILK TEA 5 / 5.5
COCONUT MILK TEA 5/ 5.5
ALMOND MILK TEA 5 / 5.5
CHOCOLATE MILK TEA 5 / 5.5
SAGO TARO MILK TEA 5 / 5.5
RED BEAN MATCHA 5.5 / 6
HOW MUCH MONEY DO YOU HAVE IN YOUR WALLET, LIVY?

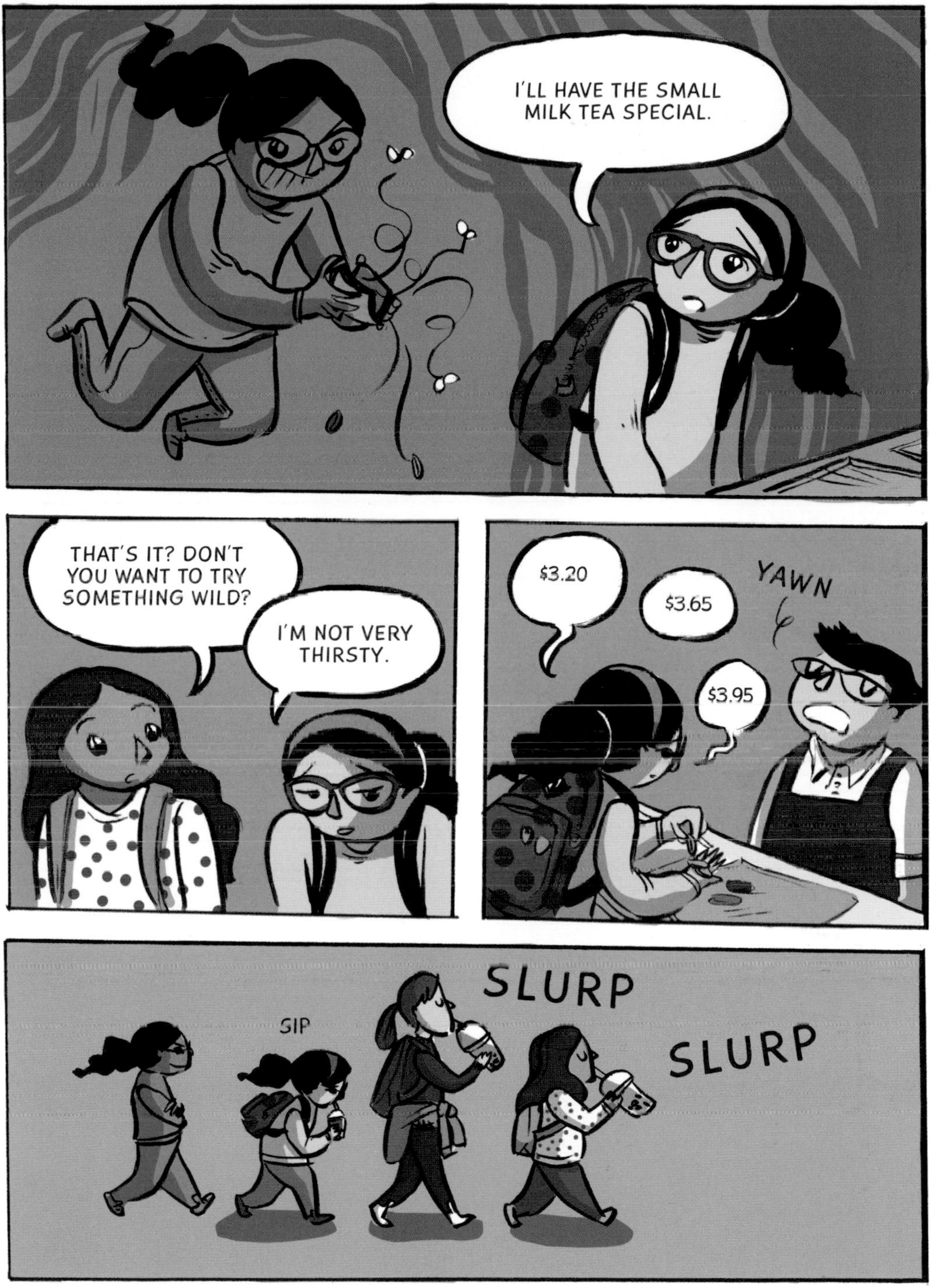
I'LL HAVE THE SMALL MILK TEA SPECIAL.
THAT'S IT? DON'T YOU WANT TO TRY SOMETHING WILD?
I'M NOT VERY THIRSTY.
$3.20
$3.65
YAWN
$3.95
SLURP
SIP
SLURP

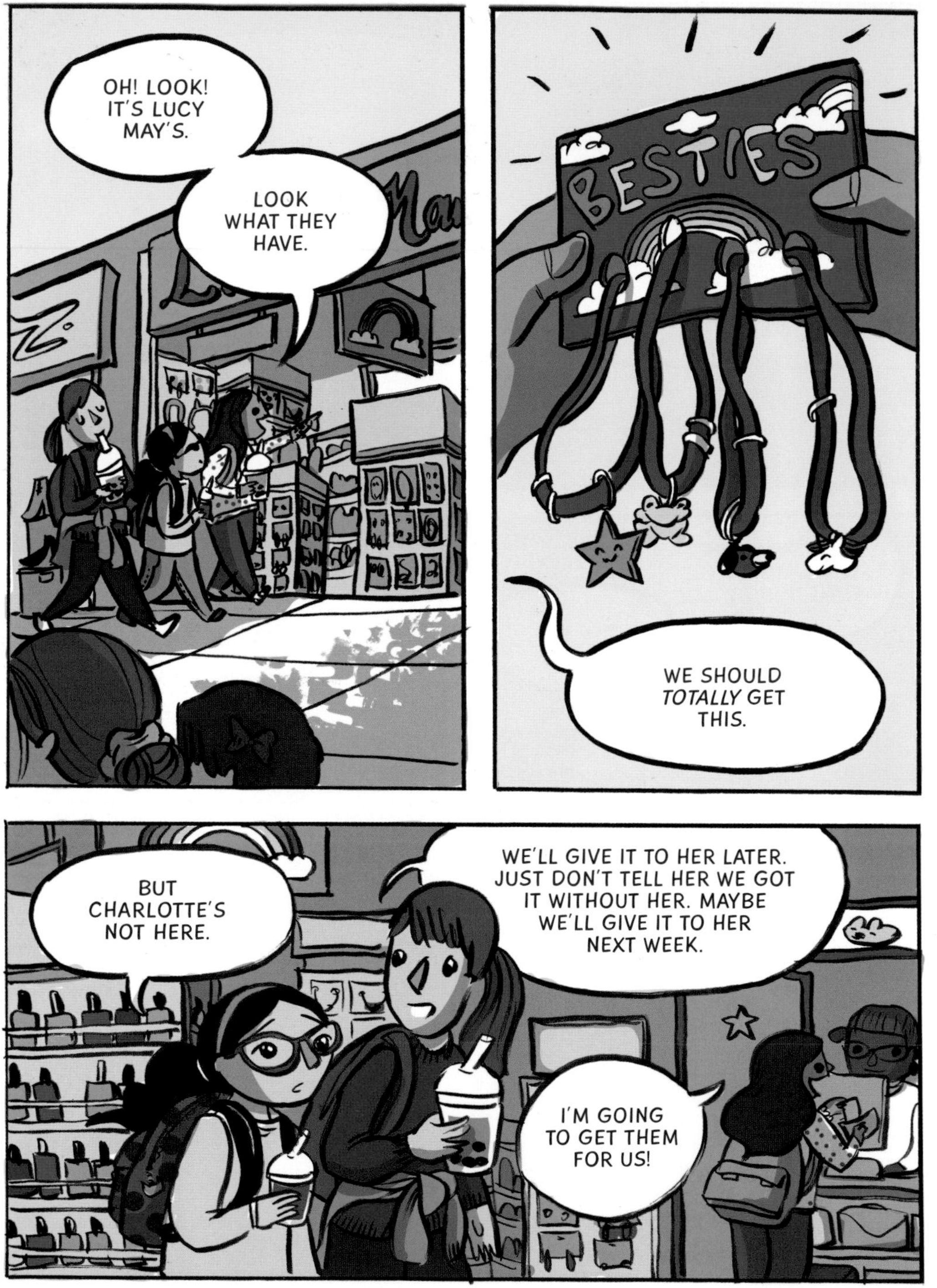
OH! LOOK! IT'S LUCY MAY'S.
LOOK WHAT THEY HAVE.
BESTIES
WE SHOULD *TOTALLY* GET THIS.
BUT CHARLOTTE'S NOT HERE.
WE'LL GIVE IT TO HER LATER. JUST DON'T TELL HER WE GOT IT WITHOUT HER. MAYBE WE'LL GIVE IT TO HER NEXT WEEK.
I'M GOING TO GET THEM FOR US!

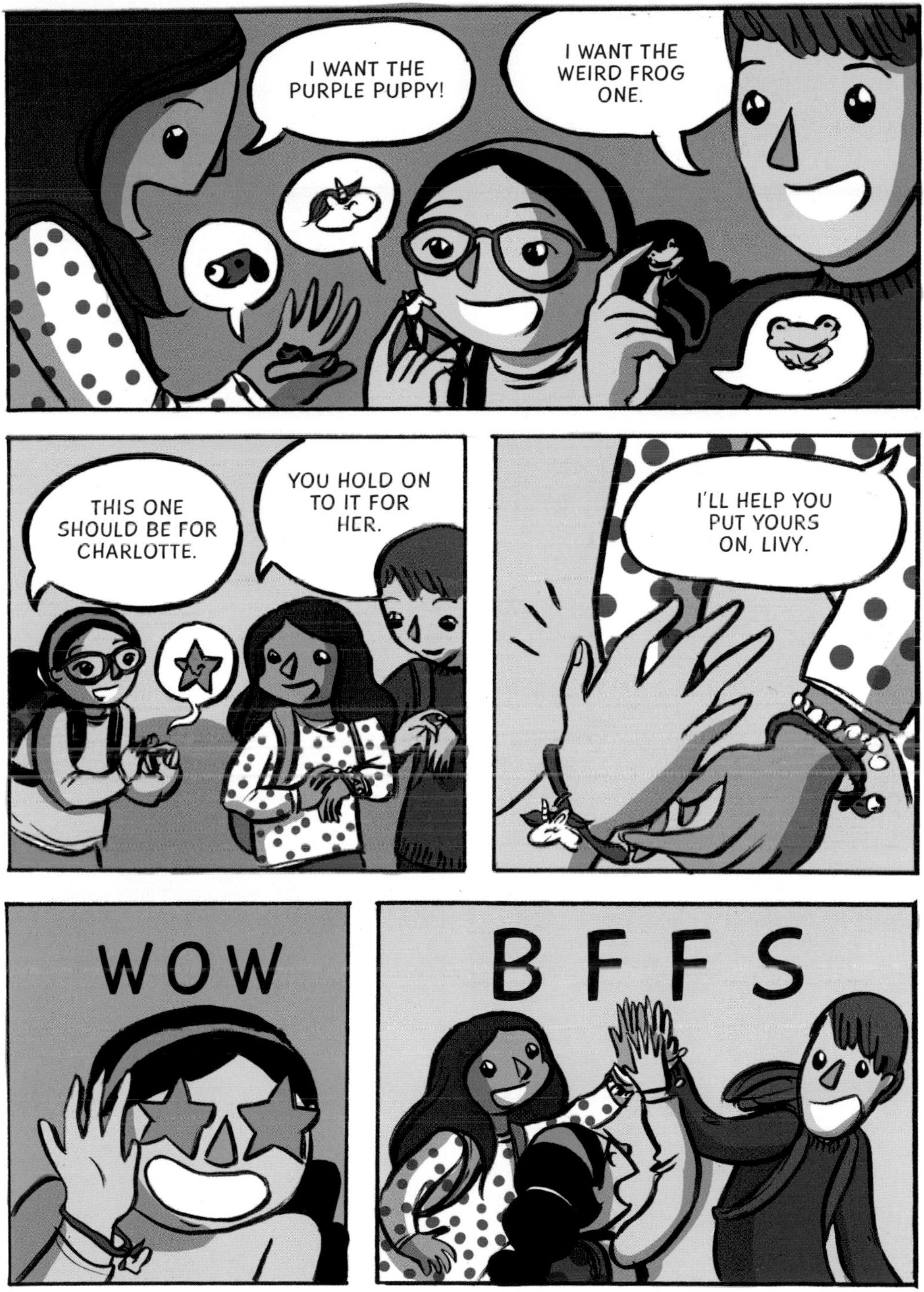
I WANT THE PURPLE PUPPY!
I WANT THE WEIRD FROG ONE.
THIS ONE SHOULD BE FOR CHARLOTTE.
YOU HOLD ON TO IT FOR HER.
I'LL HELP YOU PUT YOURS ON, LIVY.
WOW
BFFS

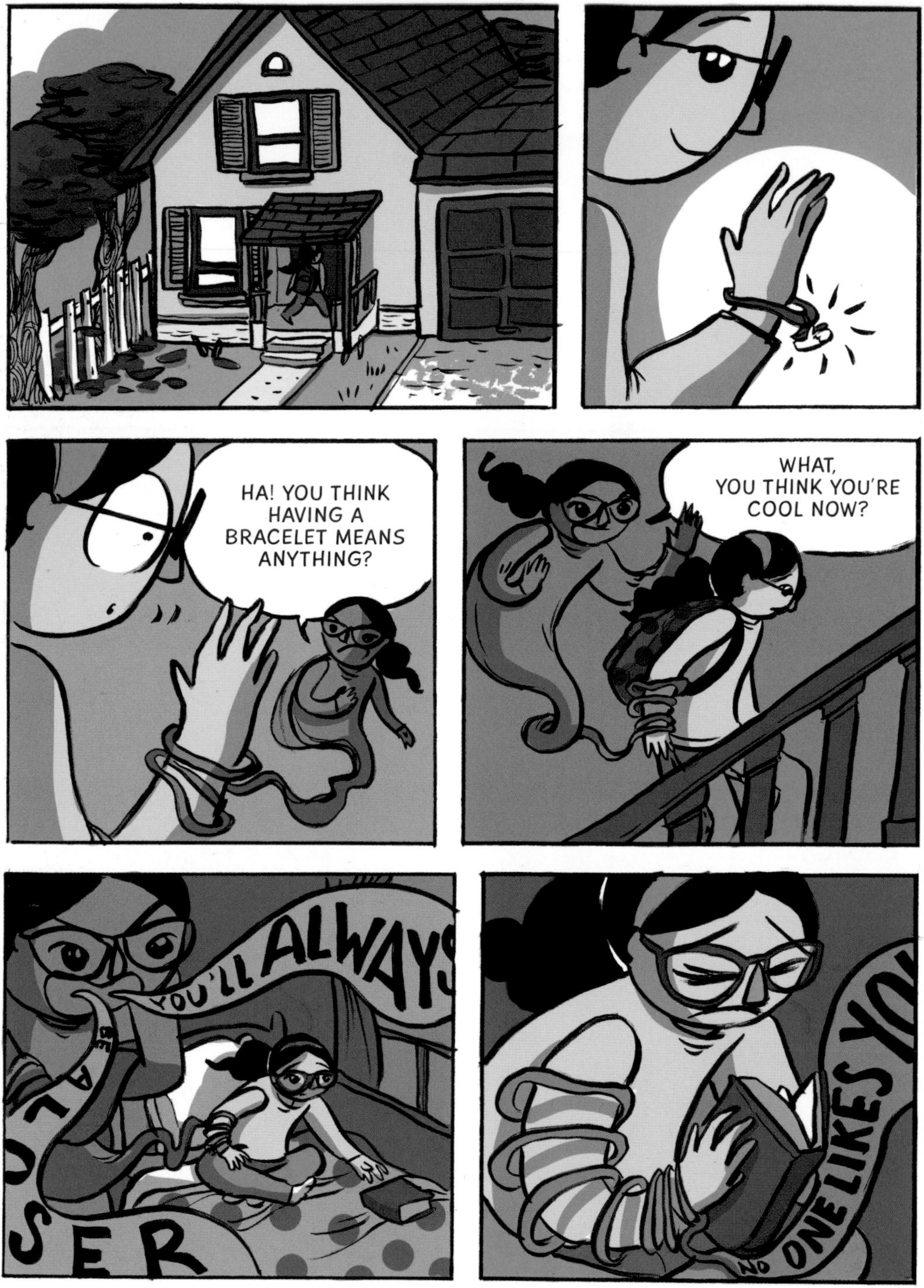

HA! YOU THINK HAVING A BRACELET MEANS ANYTHING?
WHAT, YOU THINK YOU'RE COOL NOW?
YOU'LL ALWAYS BE A LOSER
NO ONE LIKES YOU

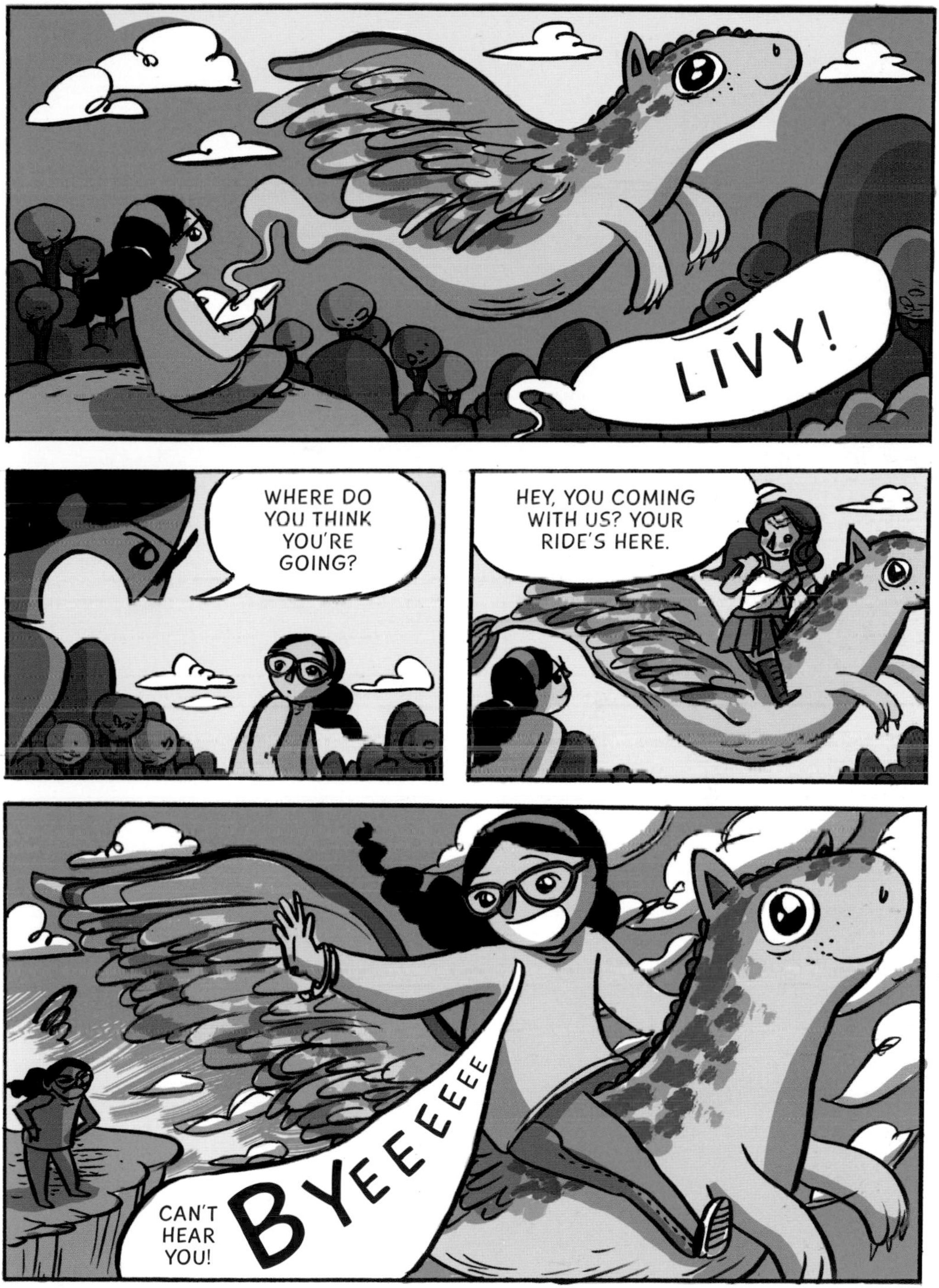
LIVY!
WHERE DO YOU THINK YOU'RE GOING?
HEY, YOU COMING WITH US? YOUR RIDE'S HERE.
CAN'T HEAR YOU!
BYEEEEEEE

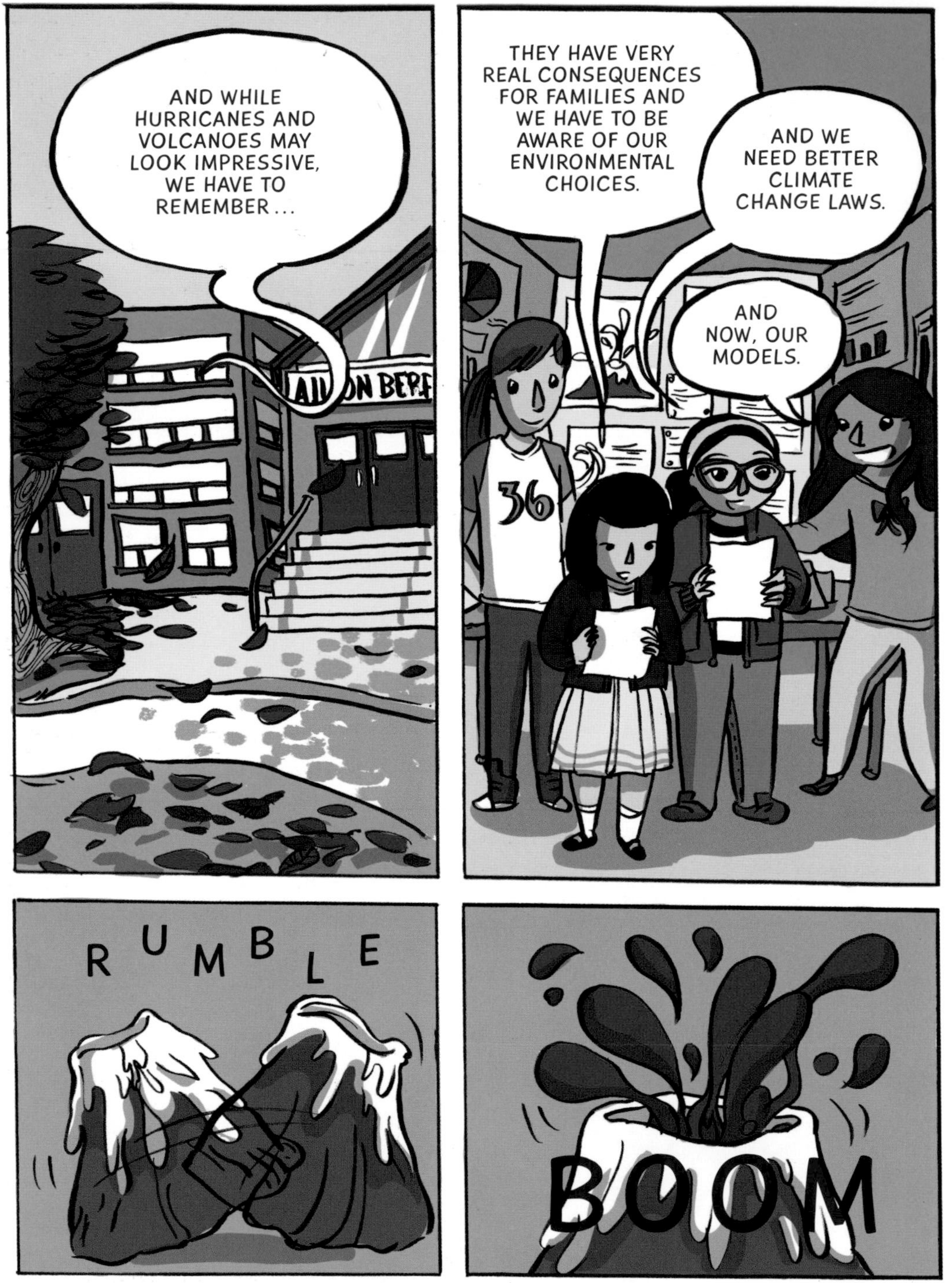
AND WHILE HURRICANES AND VOLCANOES MAY LOOK IMPRESSIVE, WE HAVE TO REMEMBER...
THEY HAVE VERY REAL CONSEQUENCES FOR FAMILIES AND WE HAVE TO BE AWARE OF OUR ENVIRONMENTAL CHOICES.
AND WE NEED BETTER CLIMATE CHANGE LAWS.
AND NOW, OUR MODELS.
RUMBLE
BOOM

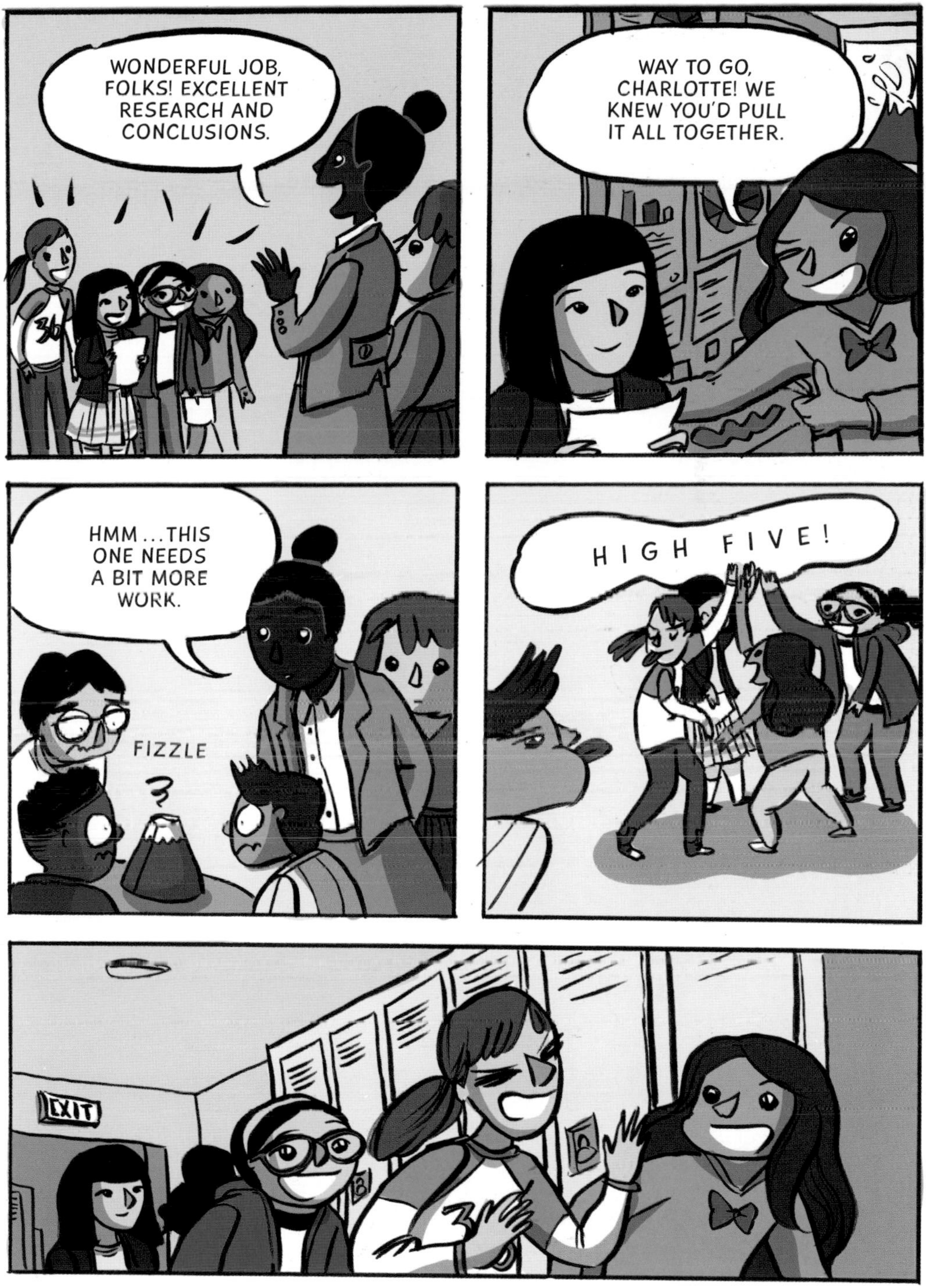
WONDERFUL JOB, FOLKS! EXCELLENT RESEARCH AND CONCLUSIONS.
WAY TO GO, CHARLOTTE! WE KNEW YOU'D PULL IT ALL TOGETHER.
HMM...THIS ONE NEEDS A BIT MORE WORK.
FIZZLE
HIGH FIVE!
EXIT

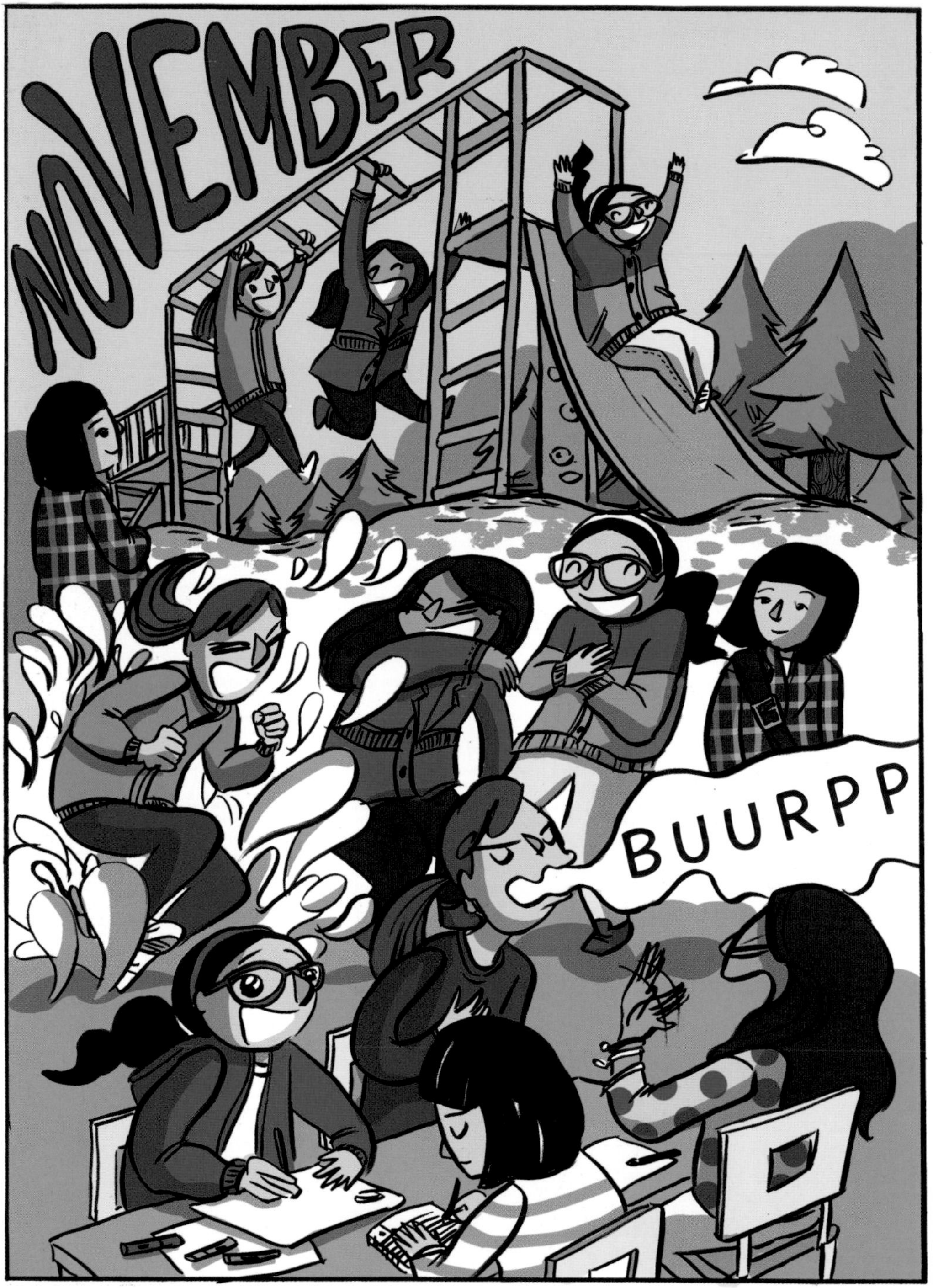
NOVEMBER
BUURPP

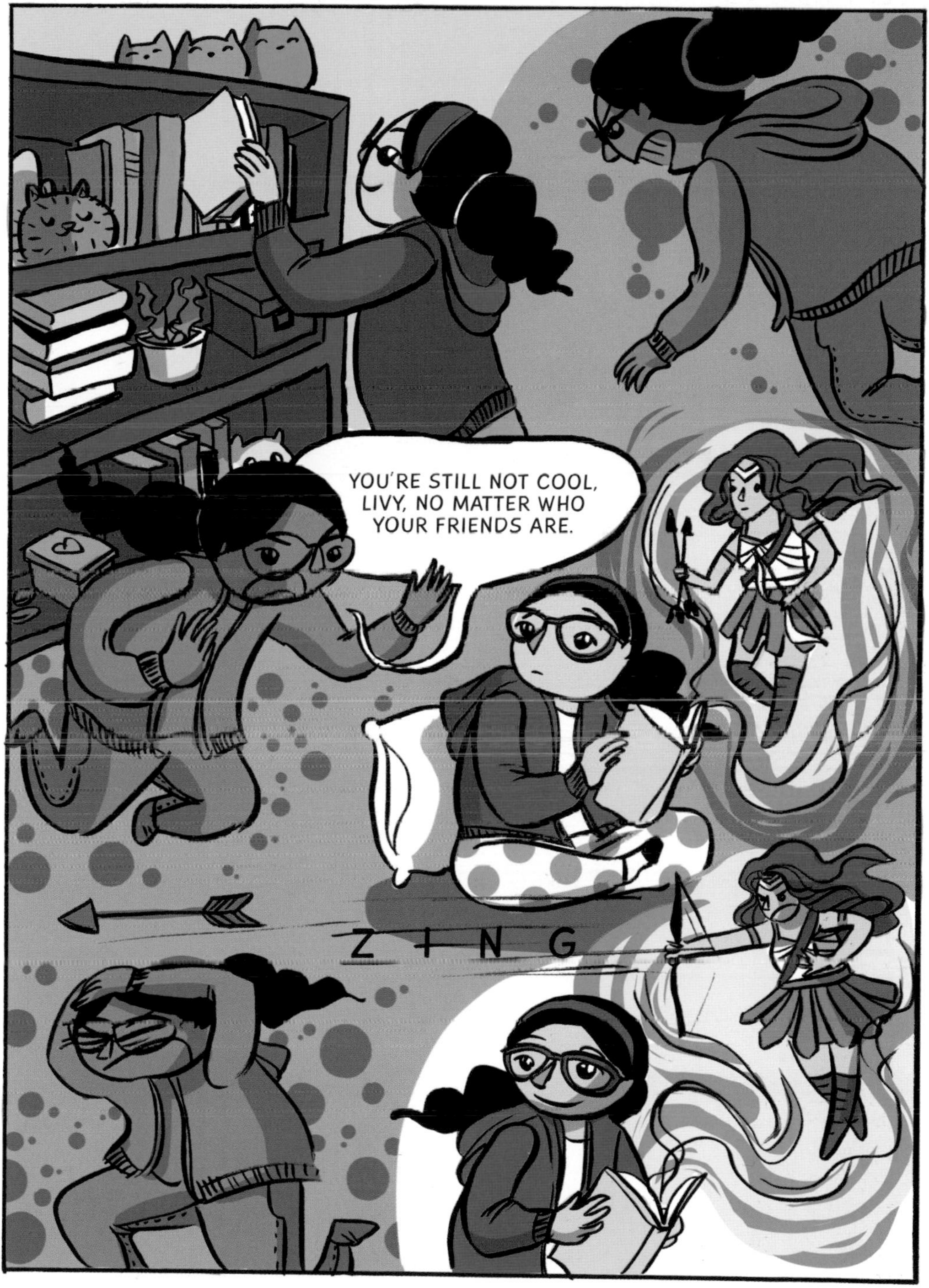
YOU'RE STILL NOT COOL, LIVY, NO MATTER WHO YOUR FRIENDS ARE.
ZING

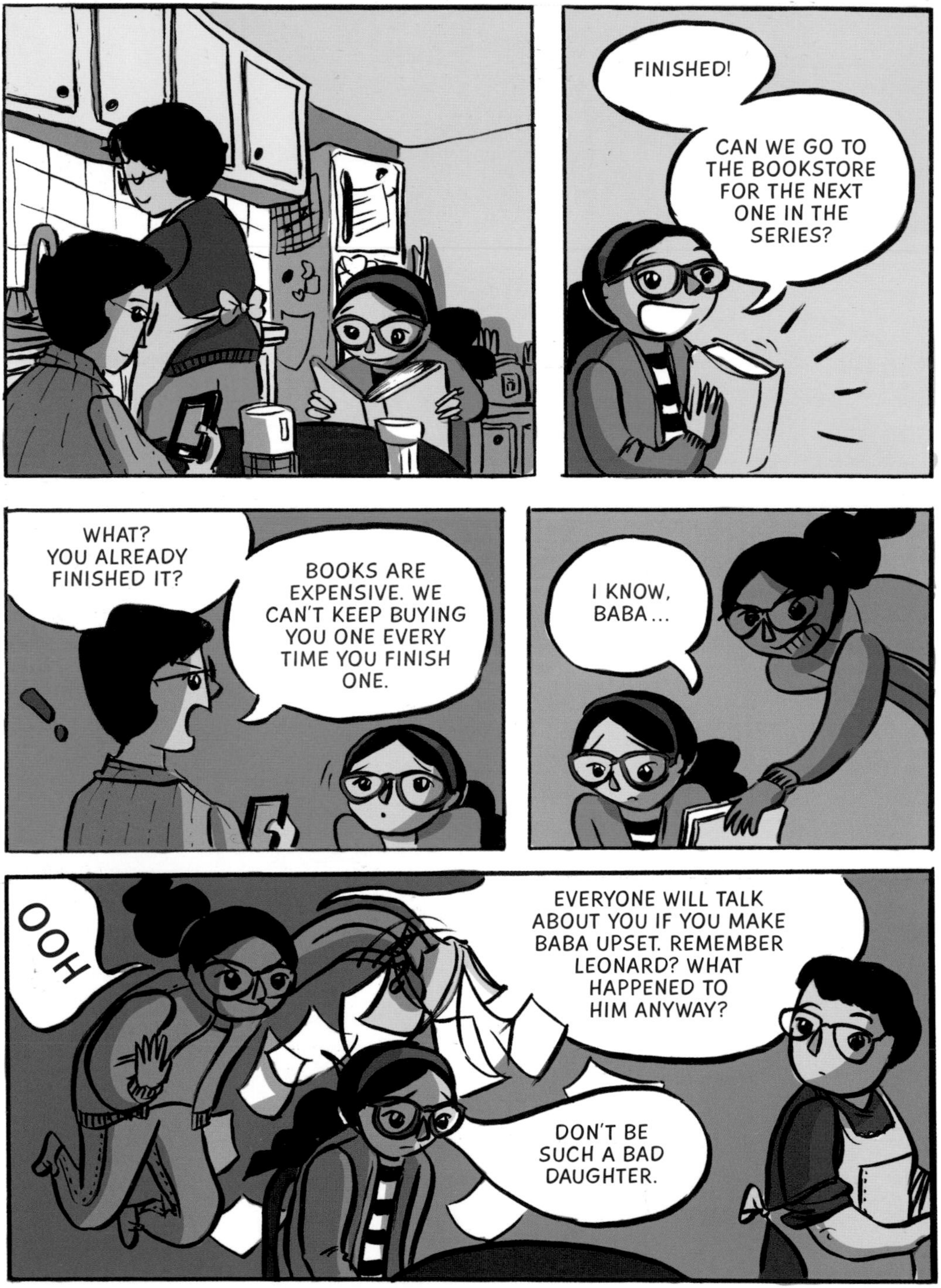
FINISHED!
CAN WE GO TO THE BOOKSTORE FOR THE NEXT ONE IN THE SERIES?
WHAT? YOU ALREADY FINISHED IT?
BOOKS ARE EXPENSIVE. WE CAN'T KEEP BUYING YOU ONE EVERY TIME YOU FINISH ONE.
I KNOW, BABA...
OOH
EVERYONE WILL TALK ABOUT YOU IF YOU MAKE BABA UPSET. REMEMBER LEONARD? WHAT HAPPENED TO HIM ANYWAY?
DON'T BE SUCH A BAD DAUGHTER.

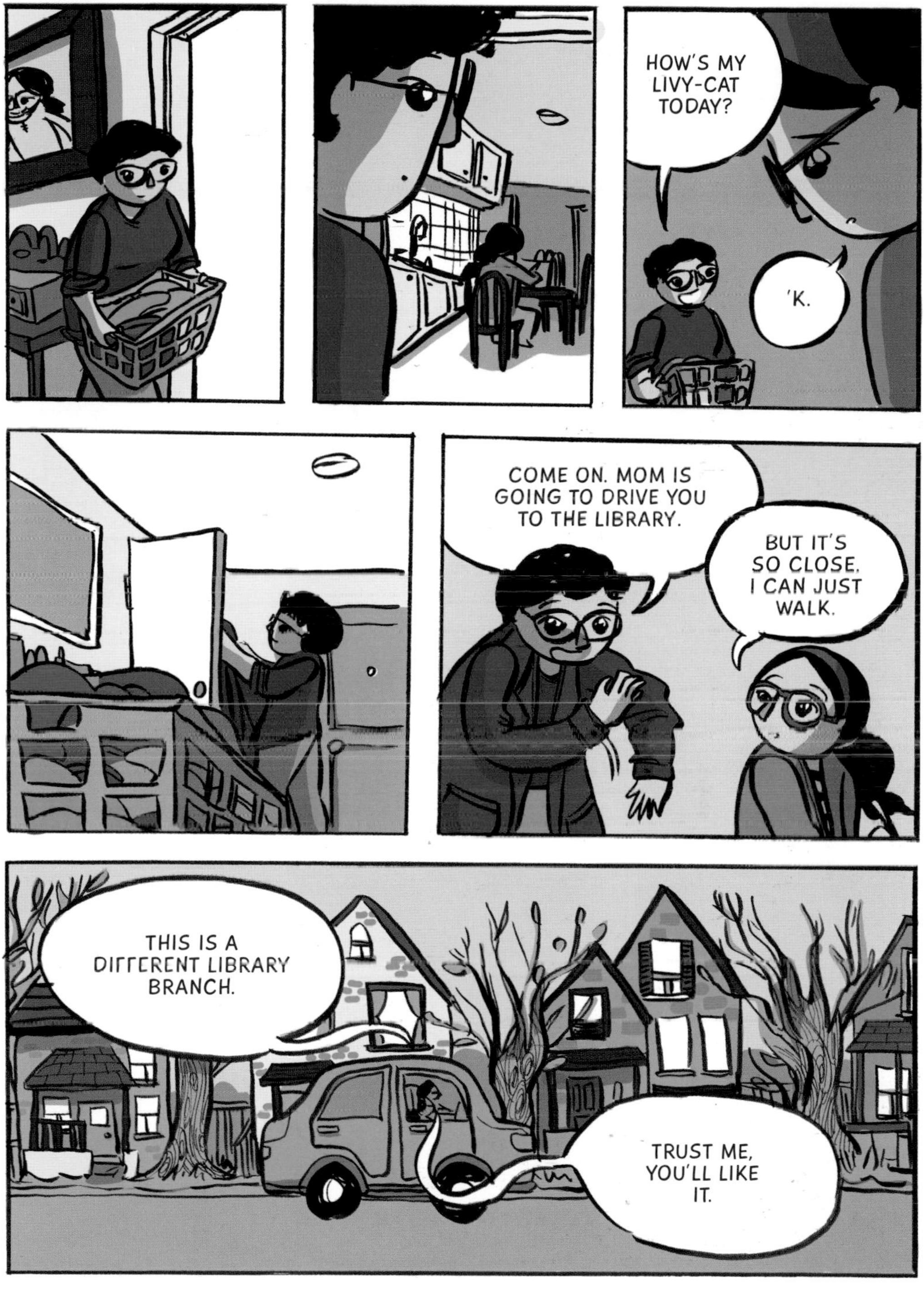
HOW'S MY LIVY-CAT TODAY?
'K.
COME ON. MOM IS GOING TO DRIVE YOU TO THE LIBRARY.
BUT IT'S SO CLOSE. I CAN JUST WALK.
THIS IS A DIFFERENT LIBRARY BRANCH.
TRUST ME, YOU'LL LIKE IT.

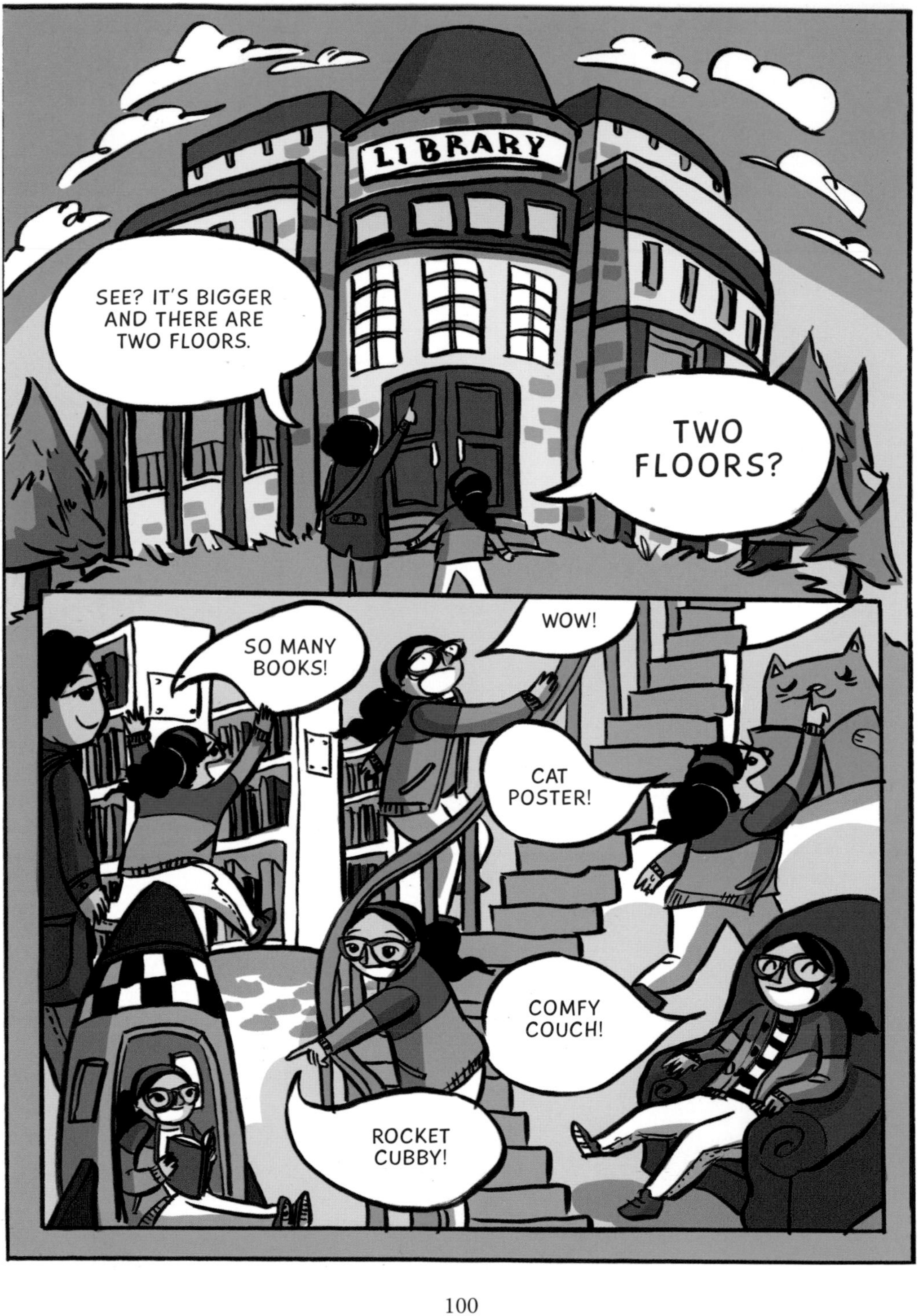
LIBRARY
SEE? IT'S BIGGER AND THERE ARE TWO FLOORS.
TWO FLOORS?
SO MANY BOOKS!
WOW!
CAT POSTER!
COMFY COUCH!
ROCKET CUBBY!

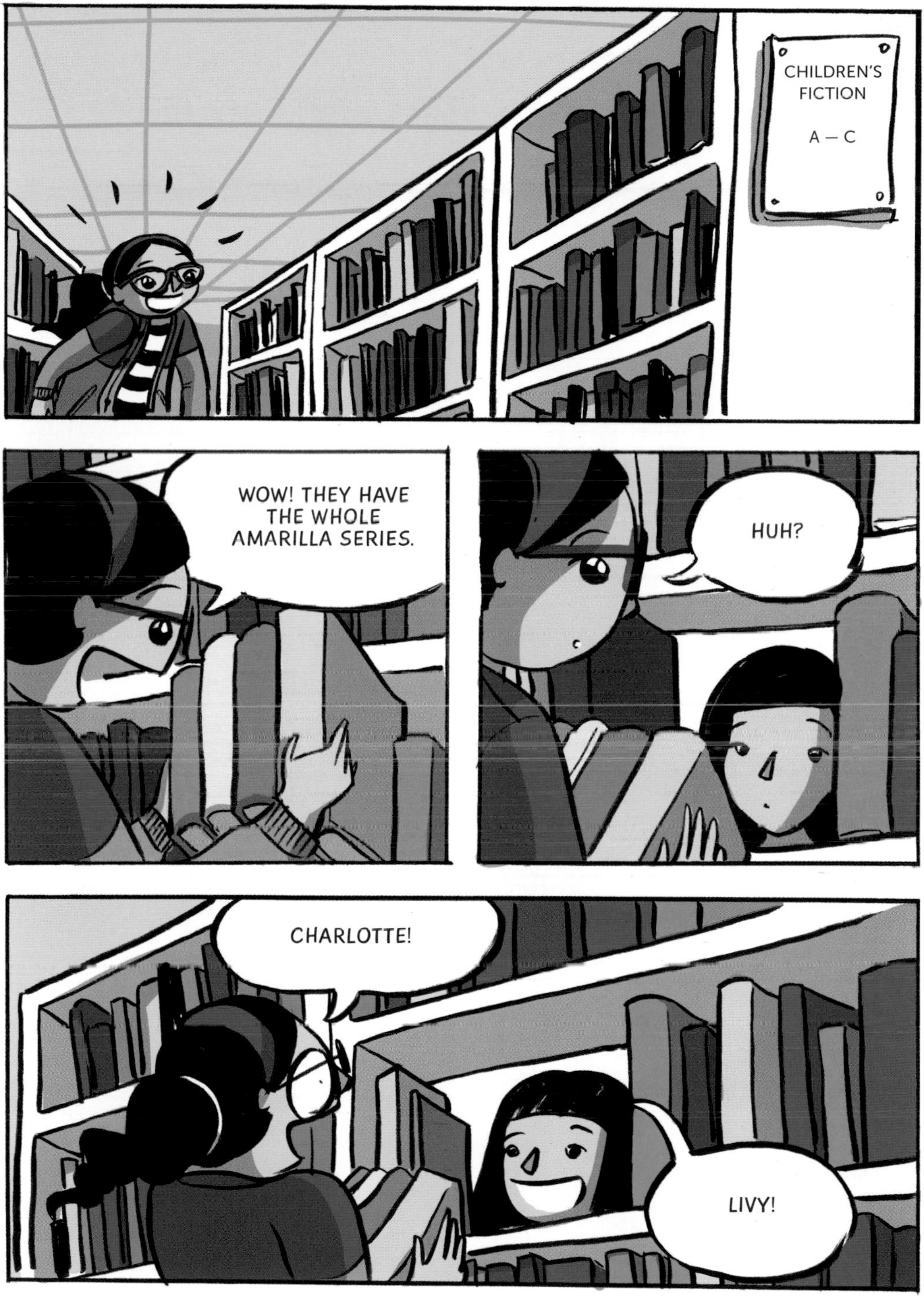
CHILDREN'S
FICTION
A — C
WOW! THEY HAVE THE WHOLE AMARILLA SERIES.
HUH?
CHARLOTTE!
LIVY!

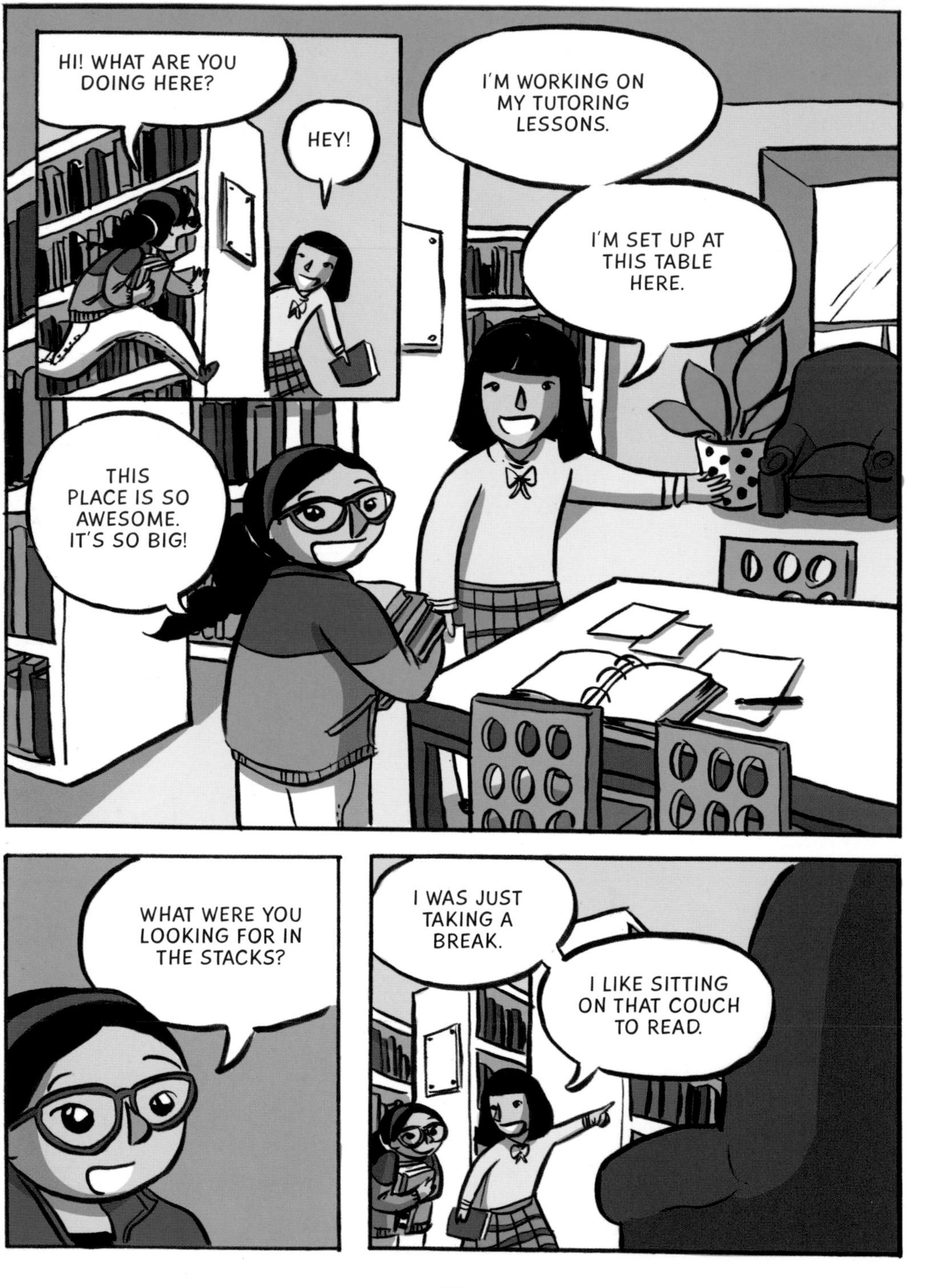
HI! WHAT ARE YOU DOING HERE?
HEY!
I'M WORKING ON MY TUTORING LESSONS.
I'M SET UP AT THIS TABLE HERE.
THIS PLACE IS SO AWESOME. IT'S SO BIG!
WHAT WERE YOU LOOKING FOR IN THE STACKS?
I WAS JUST TAKING A BREAK.
I LIKE SITTING ON THAT COUCH TO READ.

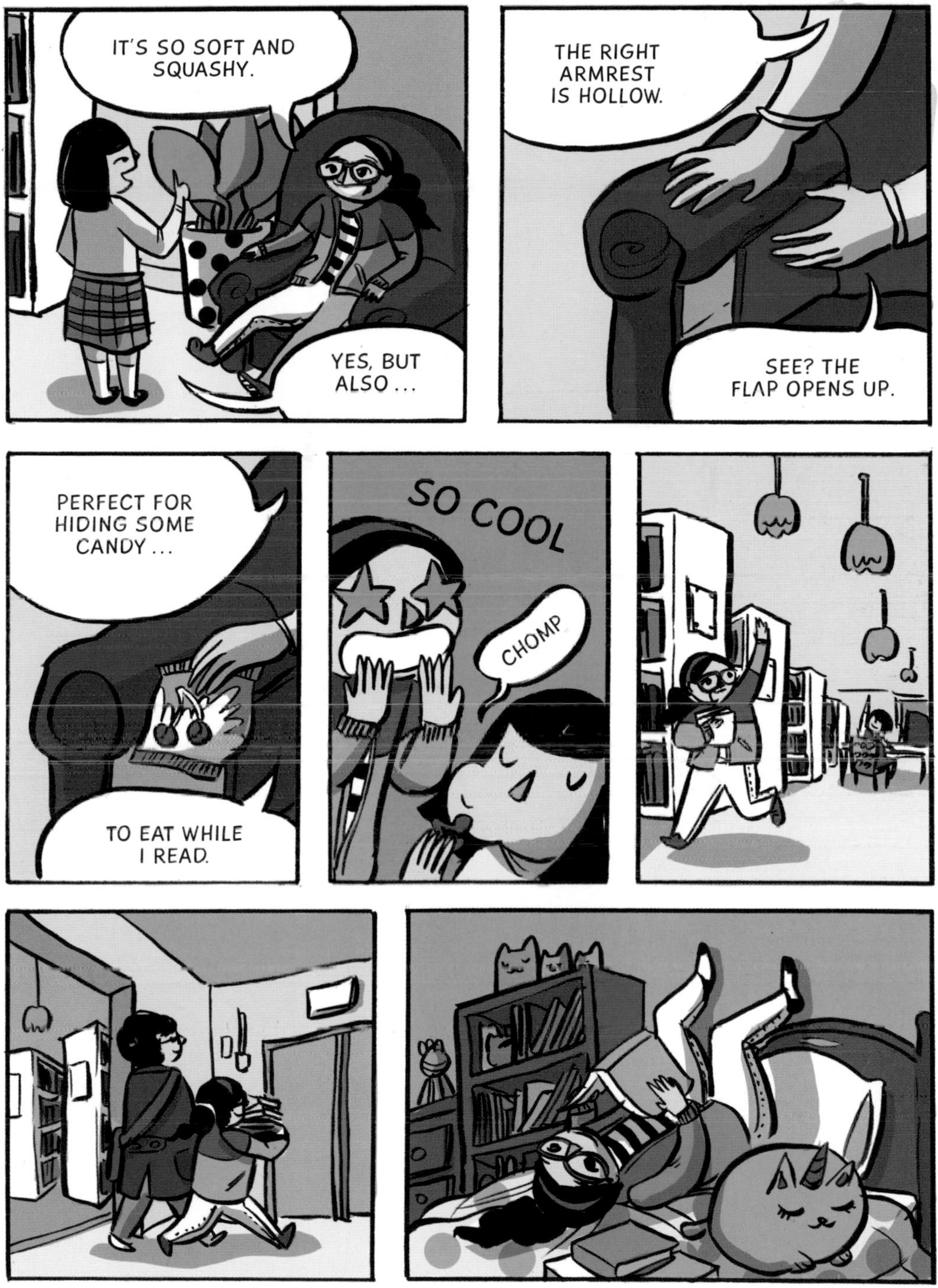
IT'S SO SOFT AND SQUASHY.
YES, BUT ALSO . . .
THE RIGHT ARMREST IS HOLLOW.
SEE? THE FLAP OPENS UP.
PERFECT FOR HIDING SOME CANDY . . .
TO EAT WHILE I READ.
SO COOL
CHOMP

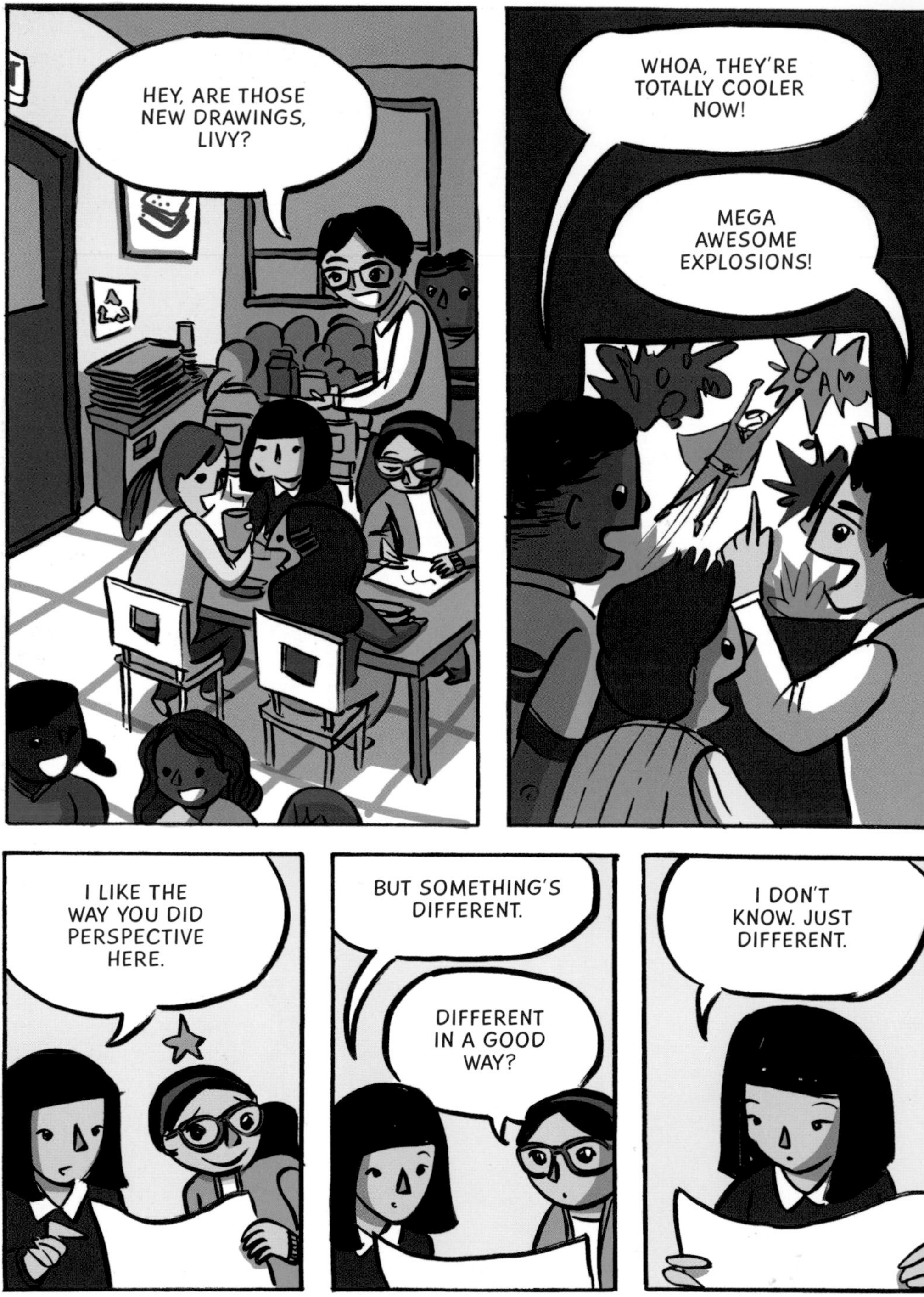
HEY, ARE THOSE NEW DRAWINGS, LIVY?
WHOA, THEY'RE TOTALLY COOLER NOW!
MEGA AWESOME EXPLOSIONS!
I LIKE THE WAY YOU DID PERSPECTIVE HERE.
BUT SOMETHING'S DIFFERENT.
DIFFERENT IN A GOOD WAY?
I DON'T KNOW. JUST DIFFERENT.

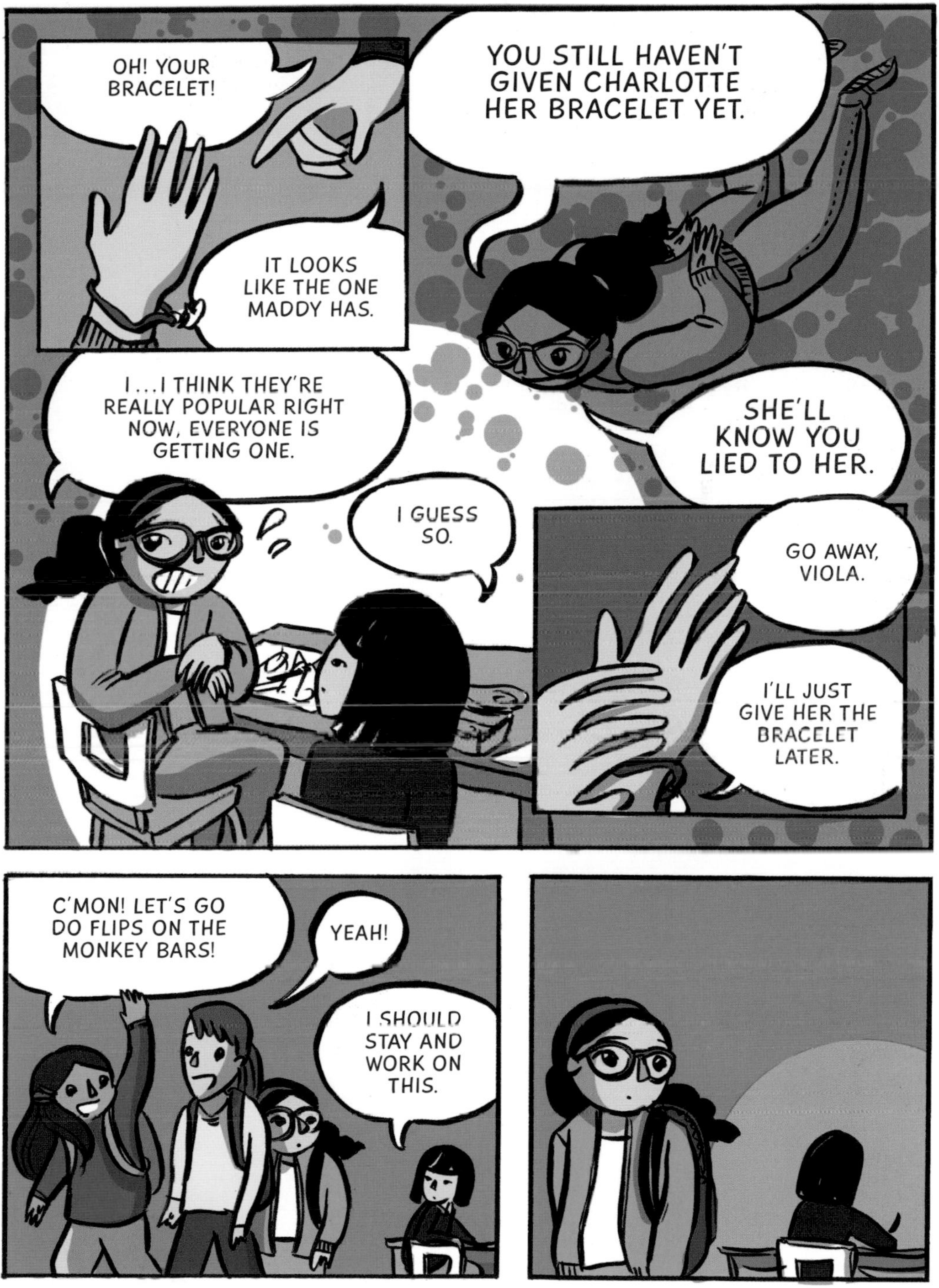
OH! YOUR BRACELET!
IT LOOKS LIKE THE ONE MADDY HAS.
YOU STILL HAVEN'T GIVEN CHARLOTTE HER BRACELET YET.
I...I THINK THEY'RE REALLY POPULAR RIGHT NOW, EVERYONE IS GETTING ONE.
I GUESS SO.
SHE'LL KNOW YOU LIED TO HER.
GO AWAY, VIOLA.
I'LL JUST GIVE HER THE BRACELET LATER.
C'MON! LET'S GO DO FLIPS ON THE MONKEY BARS!
YEAH!
I SHOULD STAY AND WORK ON THIS.

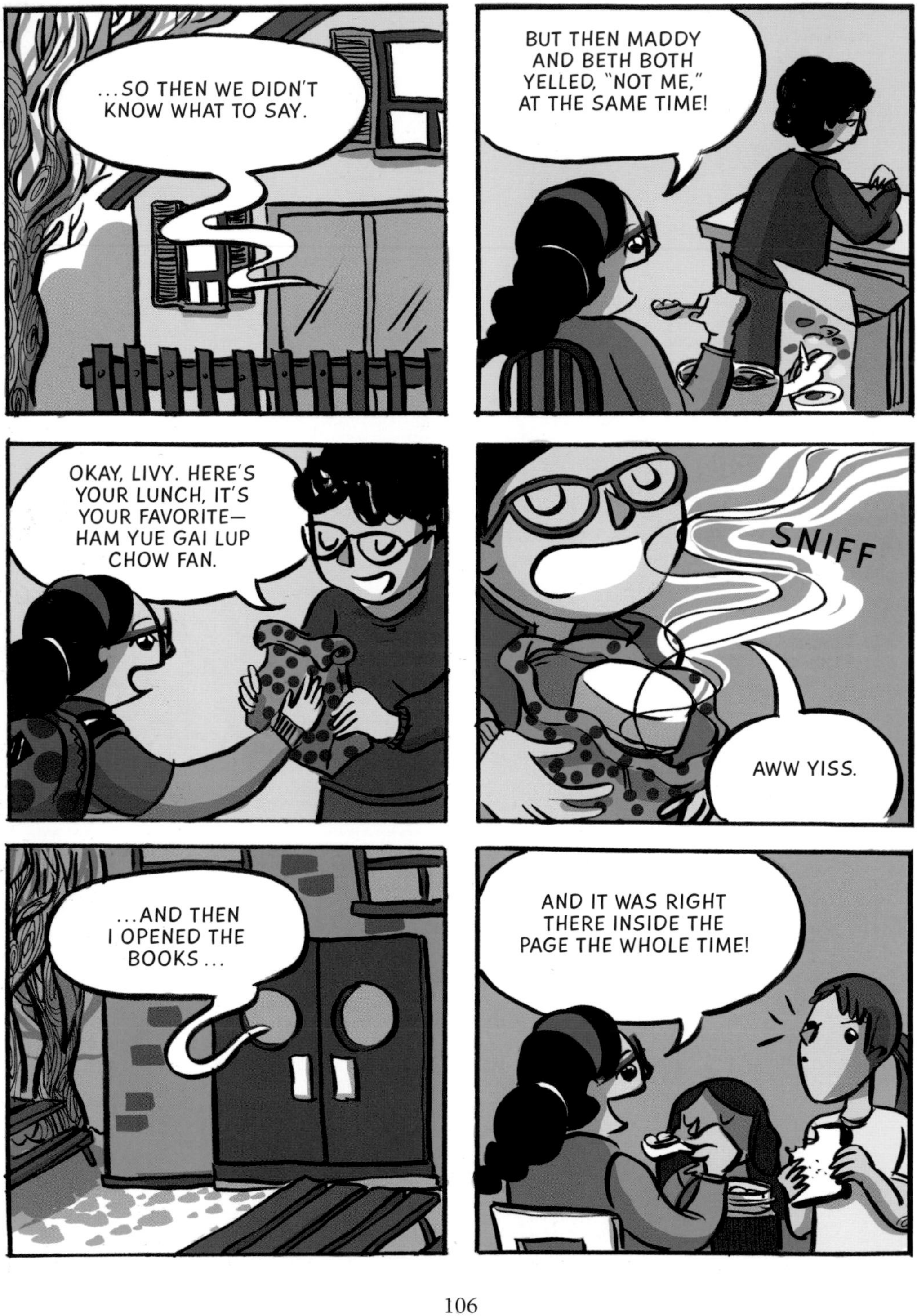
...SO THEN WE DIDN'T KNOW WHAT TO SAY.
BUT THEN MADDY AND BETH BOTH YELLED, "NOT ME," AT THE SAME TIME!
OKAY, LIVY. HERE'S YOUR LUNCH, IT'S YOUR FAVORITE— HAM YUE GAI LUP CHOW FAN.
SNIFF
AWW YISS.
...AND THEN I OPENED THE BOOKS...
AND IT WAS RIGHT THERE INSIDE THE PAGE THE WHOLE TIME!

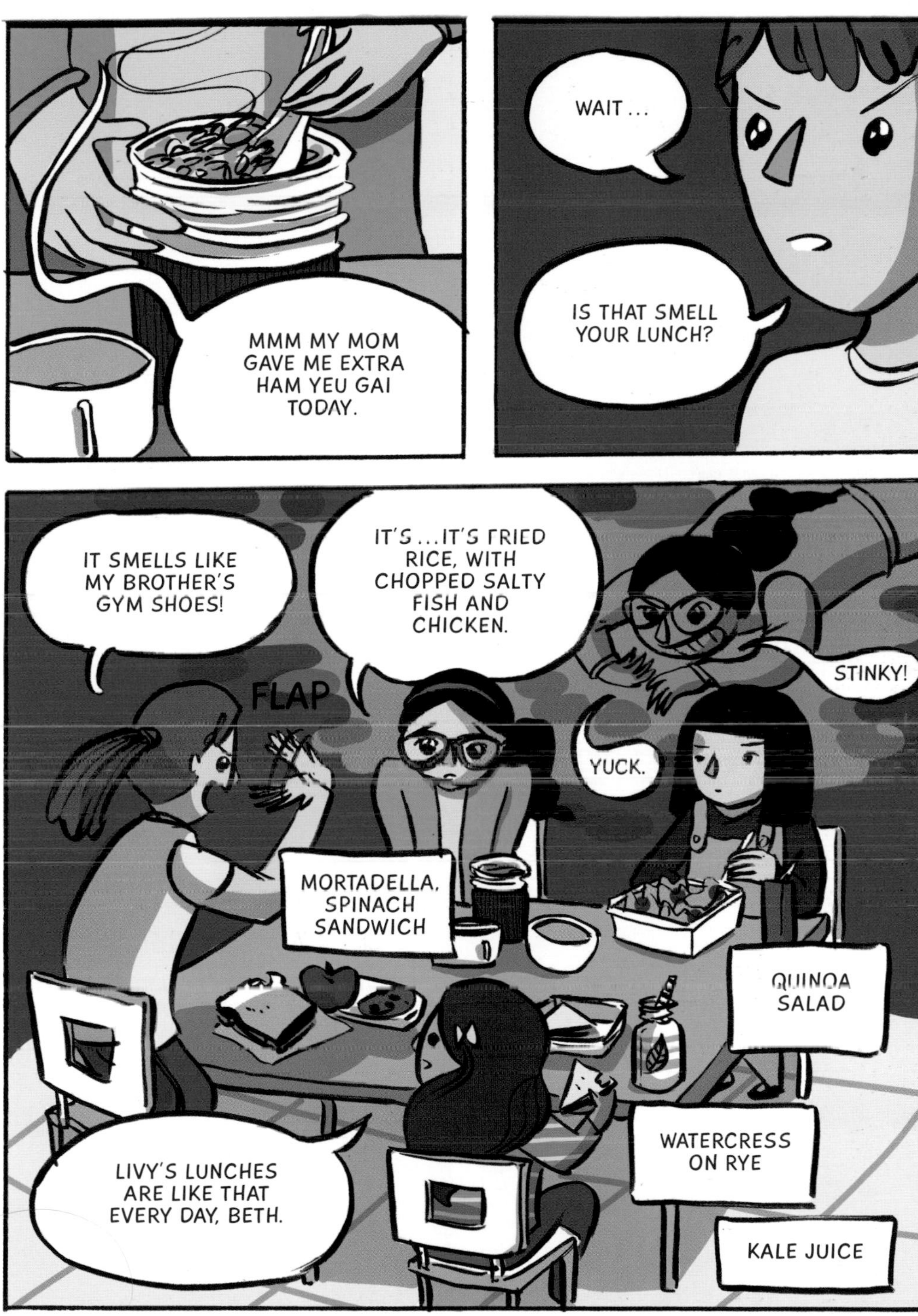
MMM MY MOM GAVE ME EXTRA HAM YEU GAI TODAY.
WAIT...
IS THAT SMELL YOUR LUNCH?
IT SMELLS LIKE MY BROTHER'S GYM SHOES!
IT'S...IT'S FRIED RICE, WITH CHOPPED SALTY FISH AND CHICKEN.
STINKY!
FLAP
YUCK.
MORTADELLA, SPINACH SANDWICH
QUINOA SALAD
WATERCRESS ON RYE
KALE JUICE
LIVY'S LUNCHES ARE LIKE THAT EVERY DAY, BETH.

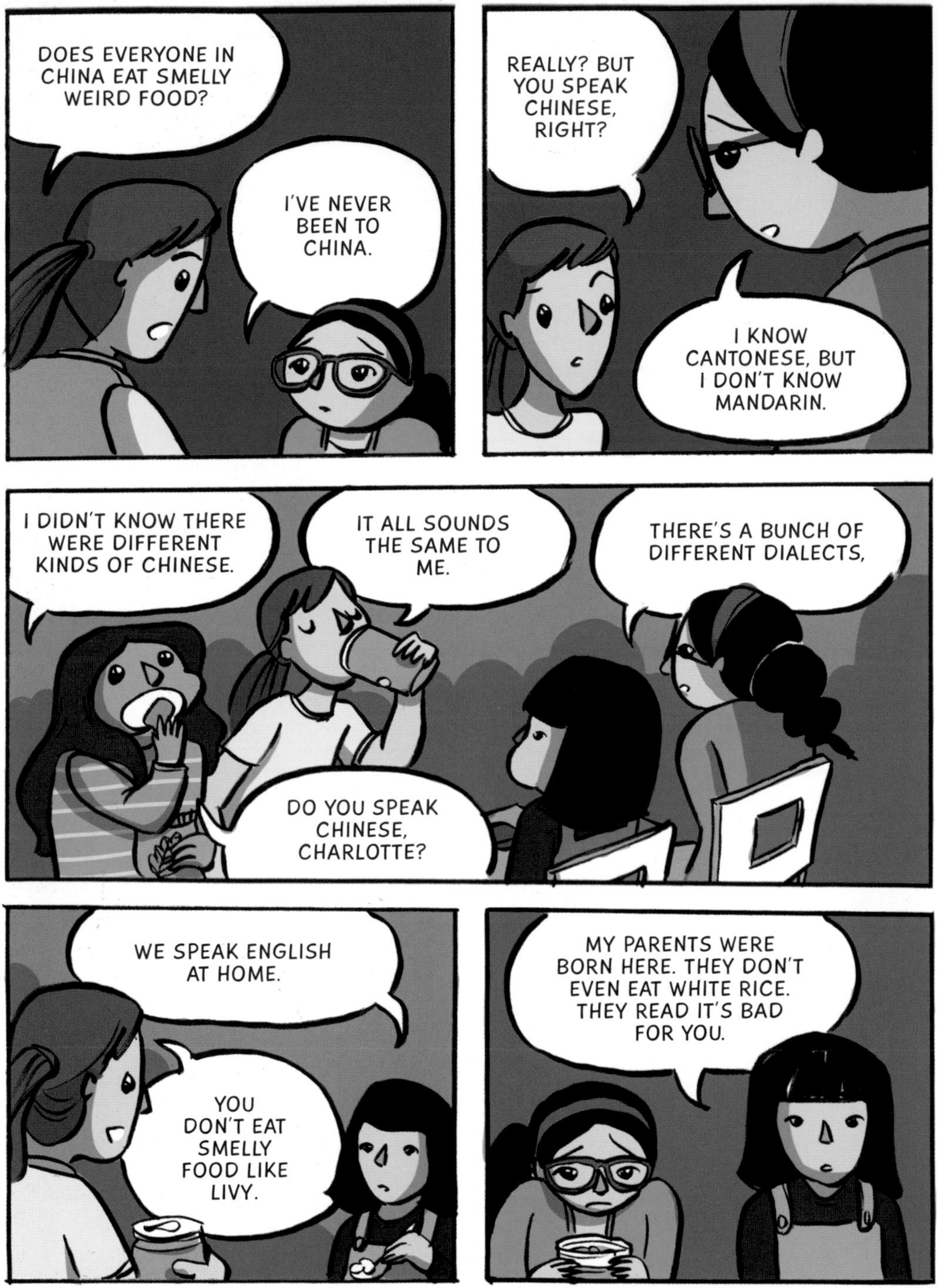

DOES EVERYONE IN CHINA EAT SMELLY WEIRD FOOD?
I'VE NEVER BEEN TO CHINA.
REALLY? BUT YOU SPEAK CHINESE, RIGHT?
I KNOW CANTONESE, BUT I DON'T KNOW MANDARIN.
I DIDN'T KNOW THERE WERE DIFFERENT KINDS OF CHINESE.
IT ALL SOUNDS THE SAME TO ME.
THERE'S A BUNCH OF DIFFERENT DIALECTS,
DO YOU SPEAK CHINESE, CHARLOTTE?
WE SPEAK ENGLISH AT HOME.
YOU DON'T EAT SMELLY FOOD LIKE LIVY.
MY PARENTS WERE BORN HERE. THEY DON'T EVEN EAT WHITE RICE. THEY READ IT'S BAD FOR YOU.

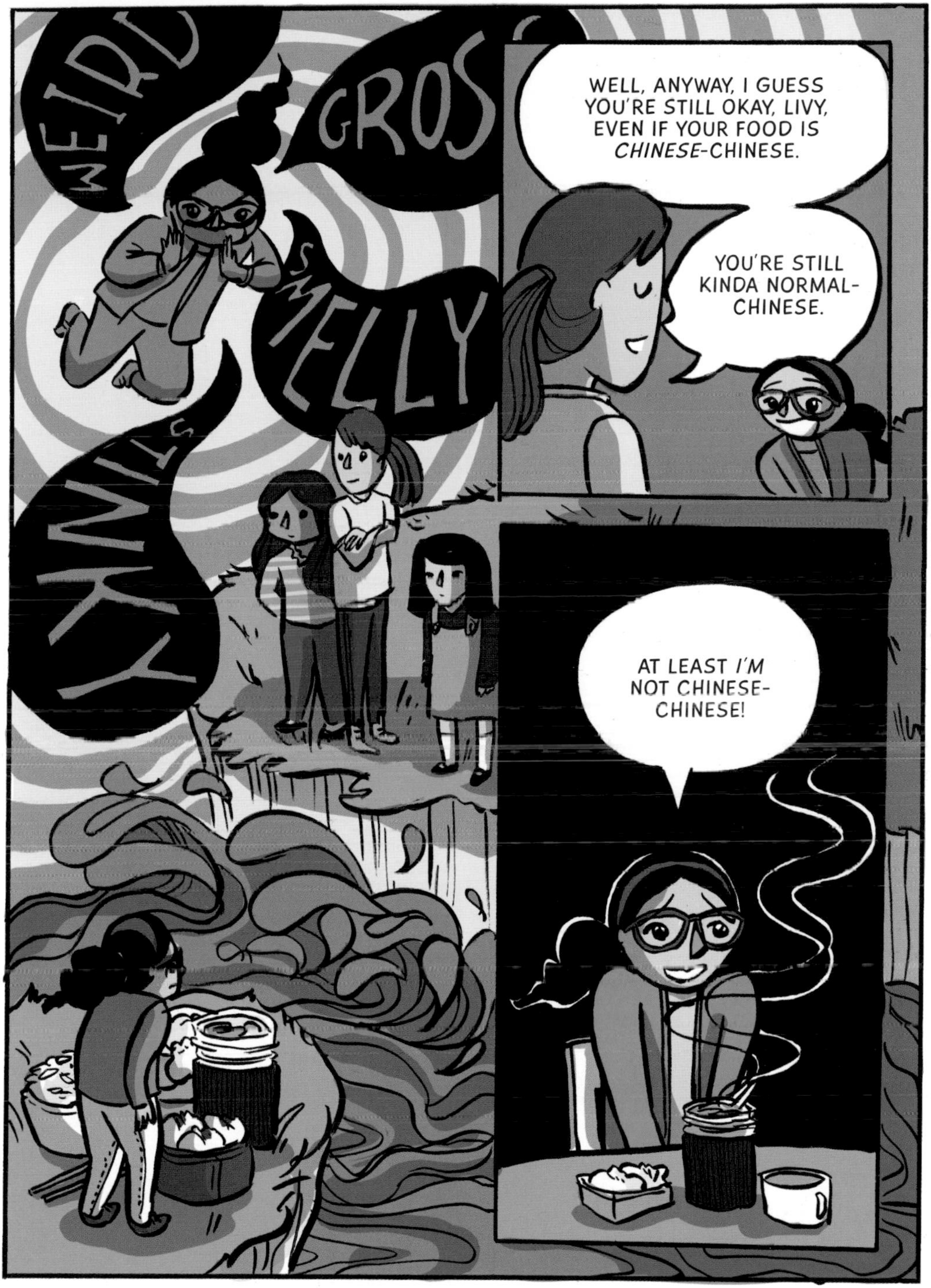
WEIRD
GROS
SMELLY
STINKY
WELL, ANYWAY, I GUESS YOU'RE STILL OKAY, LIVY, EVEN IF YOUR FOOD IS *CHINESE*-CHINESE.
YOU'RE STILL KINDA NORMAL-CHINESE.
AT LEAST *I'M* NOT CHINESE-CHINESE!

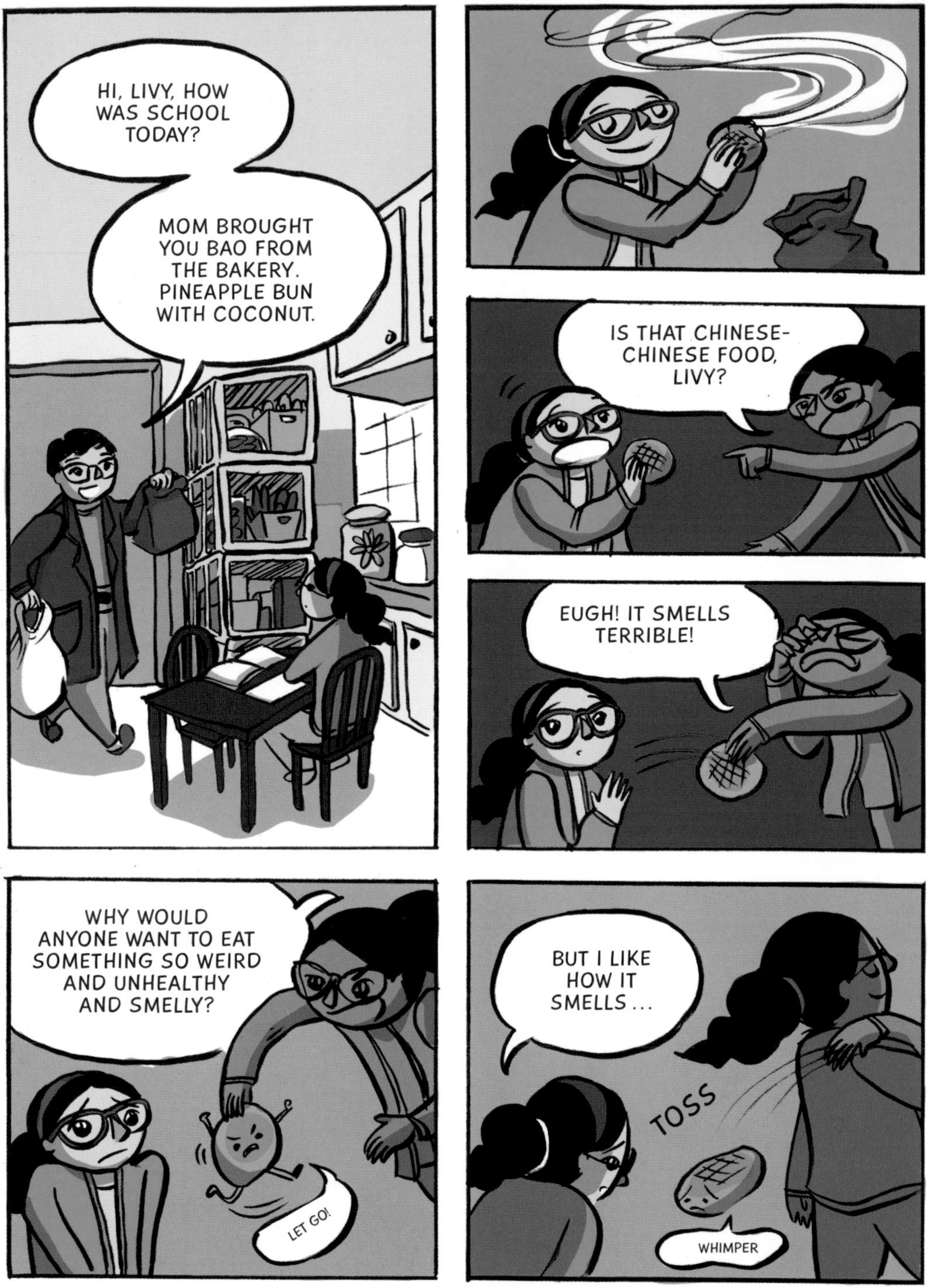
HI, LIVY, HOW WAS SCHOOL TODAY?
MOM BROUGHT YOU BAO FROM THE BAKERY. PINEAPPLE BUN WITH COCONUT.
IS THAT CHINESE-CHINESE FOOD, LIVY?
EUGH! IT SMELLS TERRIBLE!
WHY WOULD ANYONE WANT TO EAT SOMETHING SO WEIRD AND UNHEALTHY AND SMELLY?
LET GO!
BUT I LIKE HOW IT SMELLS . . .
TOSS
WHIMPER

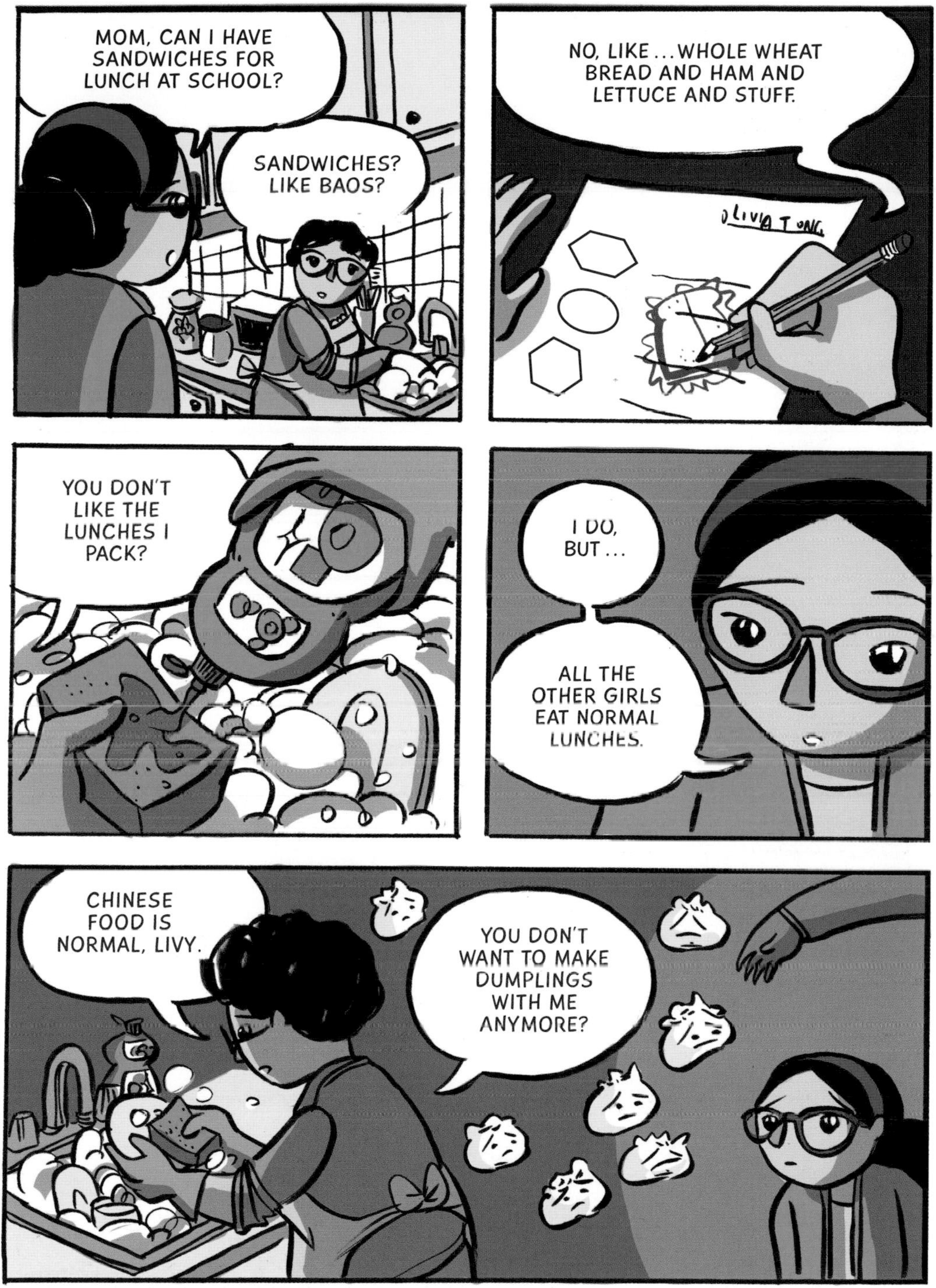
MOM, CAN I HAVE SANDWICHES FOR LUNCH AT SCHOOL?
SANDWICHES? LIKE BAOS?
NO, LIKE . . . WHOLE WHEAT BREAD AND HAM AND LETTUCE AND STUFF.
OLIVIA TONG
YOU DON'T LIKE THE LUNCHES I PACK?
I DO, BUT . . .
ALL THE OTHER GIRLS EAT NORMAL LUNCHES.
CHINESE FOOD IS NORMAL, LIVY.
YOU DON'T WANT TO MAKE DUMPLINGS WITH ME ANYMORE?

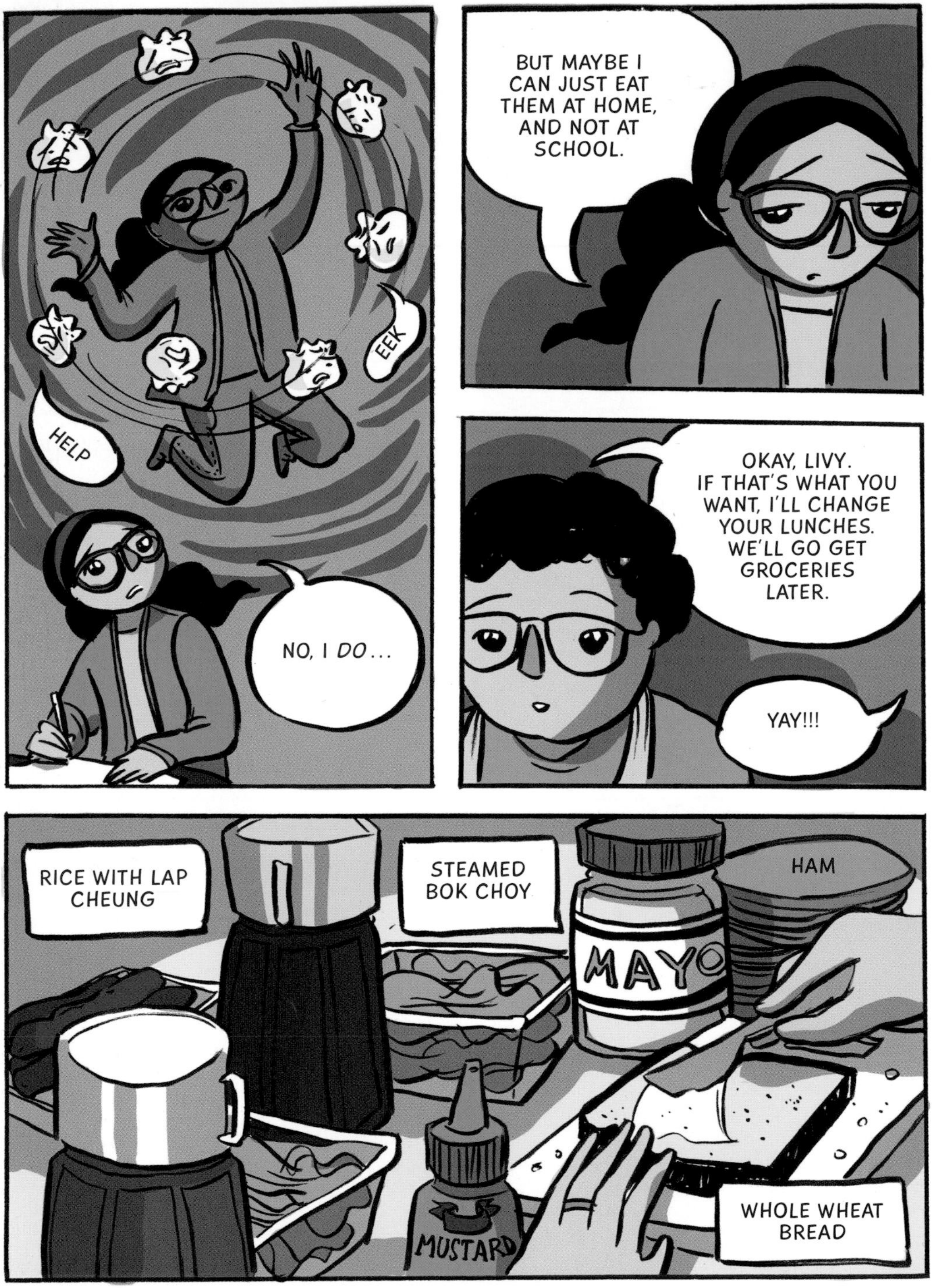
EEK
HELP
NO, I *DO*...
BUT MAYBE I CAN JUST EAT THEM AT HOME, AND NOT AT SCHOOL.
OKAY, LIVY. IF THAT'S WHAT YOU WANT, I'LL CHANGE YOUR LUNCHES. WE'LL GO GET GROCERIES LATER.
YAY!!!
RICE WITH LAP CHEUNG
STEAMED BOK CHOY
HAM
MAYO
MUSTARD
WHOLE WHEAT BREAD

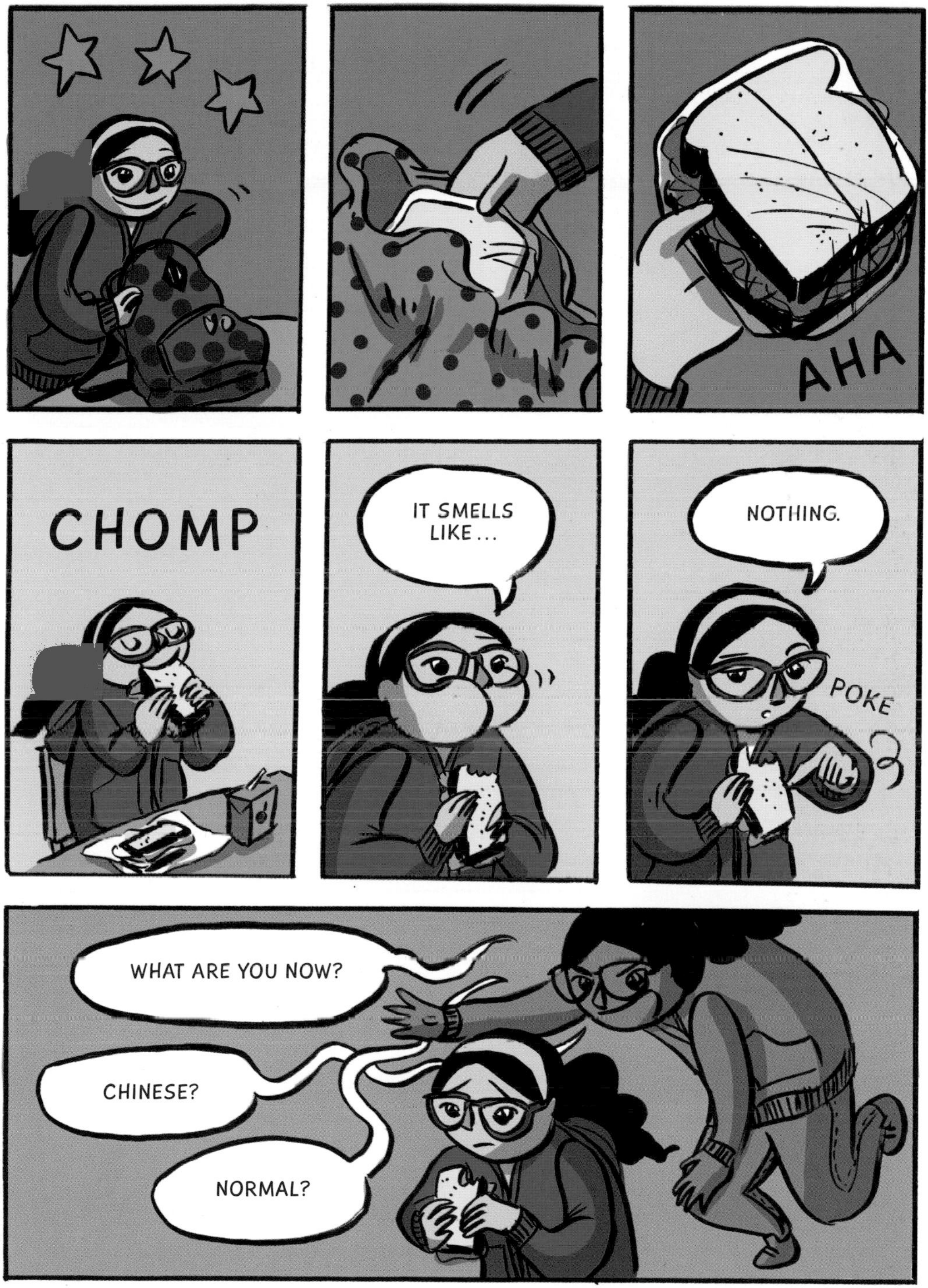
AHA
CHOMP
IT SMELLS LIKE...
NOTHING.
POKE
WHAT ARE YOU NOW?
CHINESE?
NORMAL?

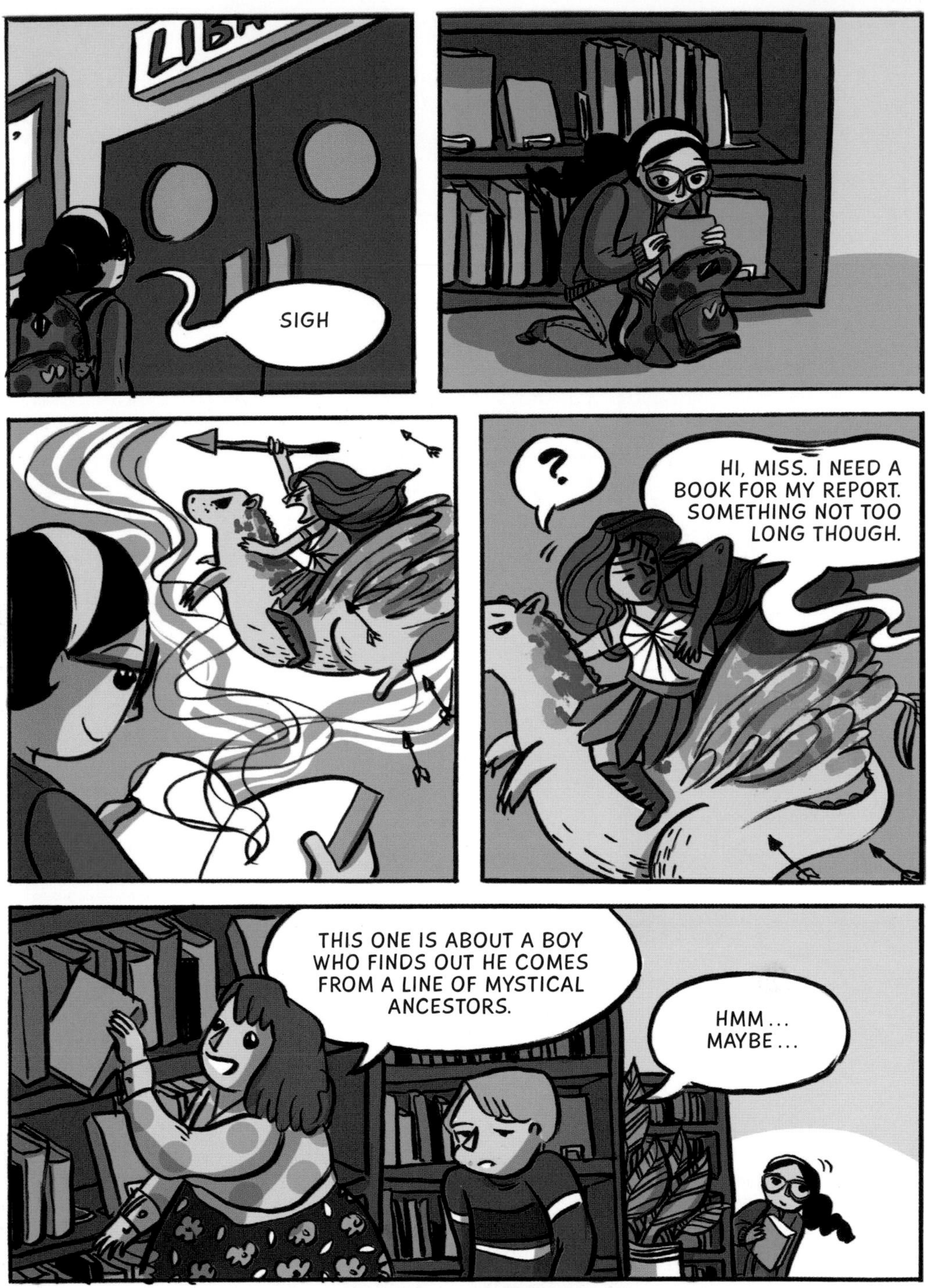
SIGH
?
HI, MISS. I NEED A BOOK FOR MY REPORT. SOMETHING NOT TOO LONG THOUGH.
THIS ONE IS ABOUT A BOY WHO FINDS OUT HE COMES FROM A LINE OF MYSTICAL ANCESTORS.
HMM… MAYBE…

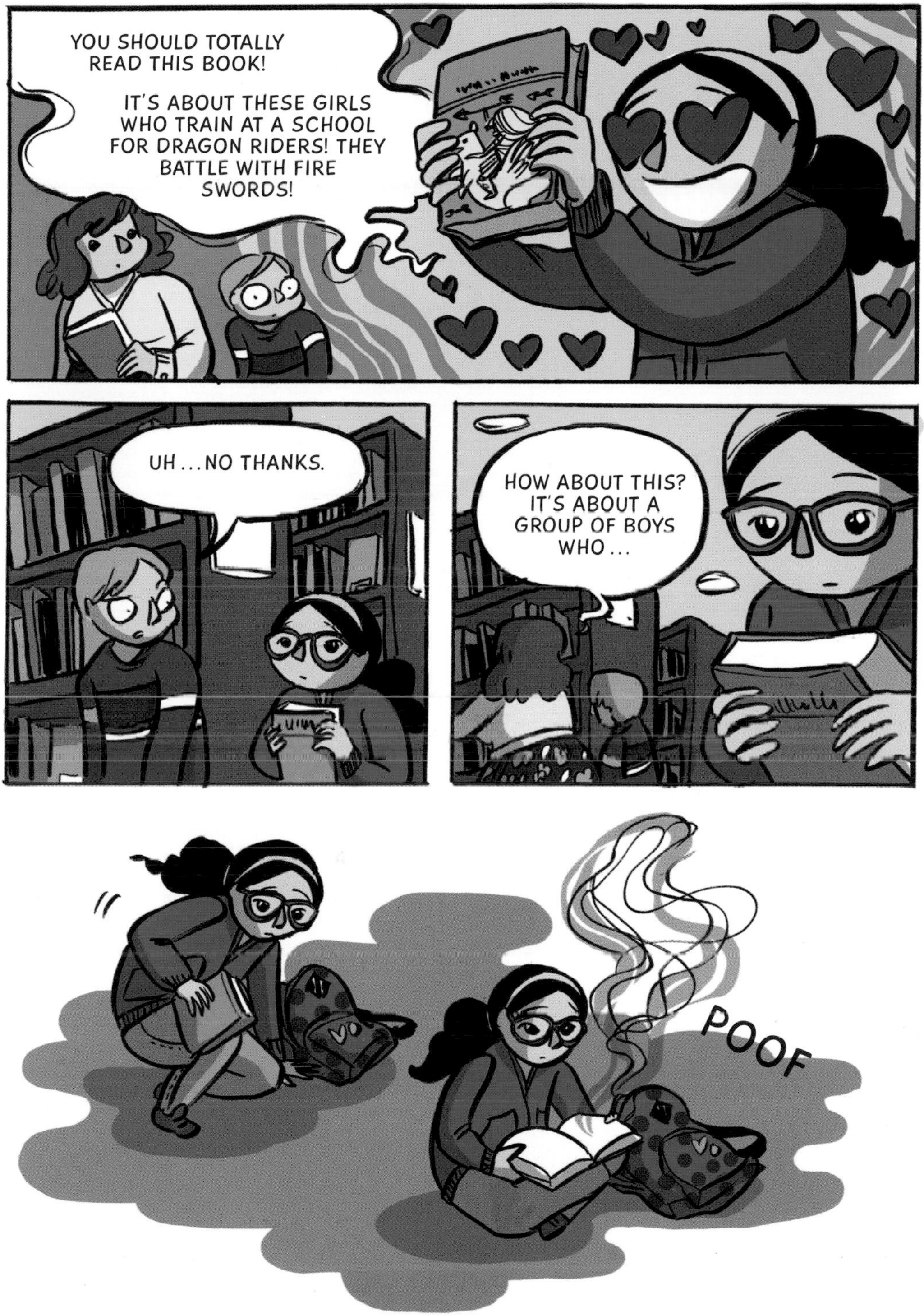
YOU SHOULD TOTALLY READ THIS BOOK!
IT'S ABOUT THESE GIRLS WHO TRAIN AT A SCHOOL FOR DRAGON RIDERS! THEY BATTLE WITH FIRE SWORDS!
UH . . . NO THANKS.
HOW ABOUT THIS? IT'S ABOUT A GROUP OF BOYS WHO . . .
POOF

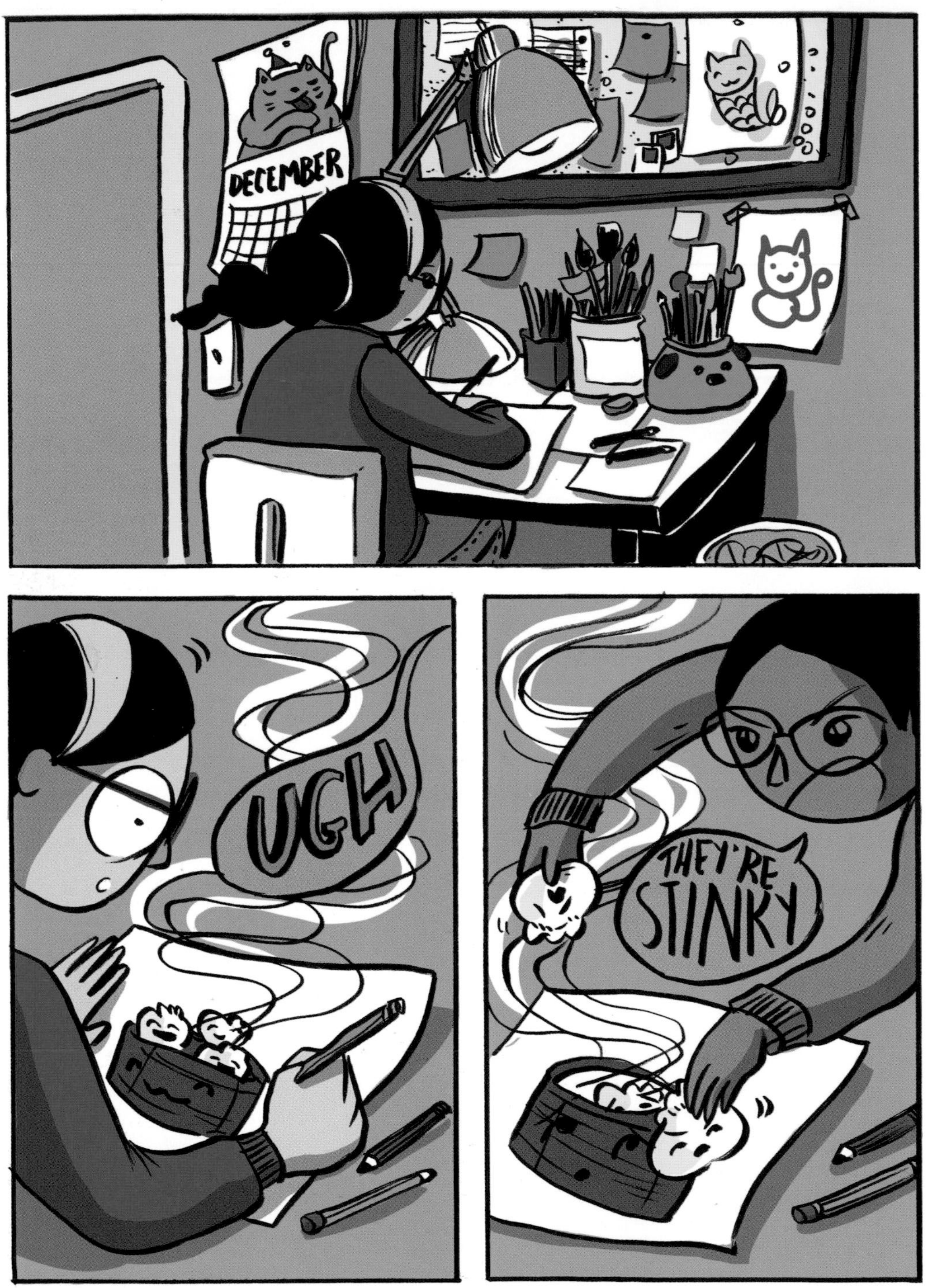
DECEMBER
UGH
THEY'RE STINKY

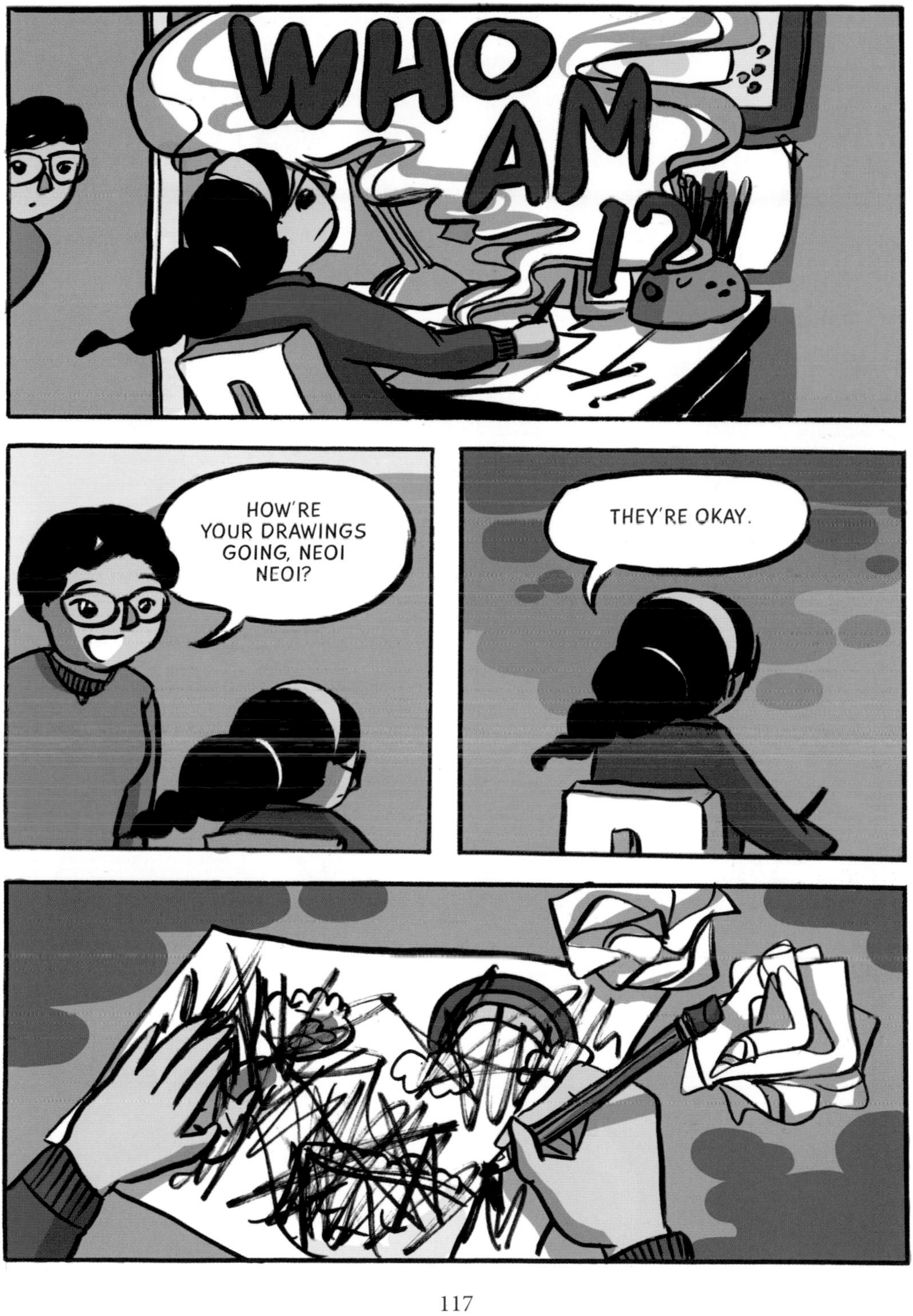
WHO AM I?
HOW'RE YOUR DRAWINGS GOING, NEOI NEOI?
THEY'RE OKAY.

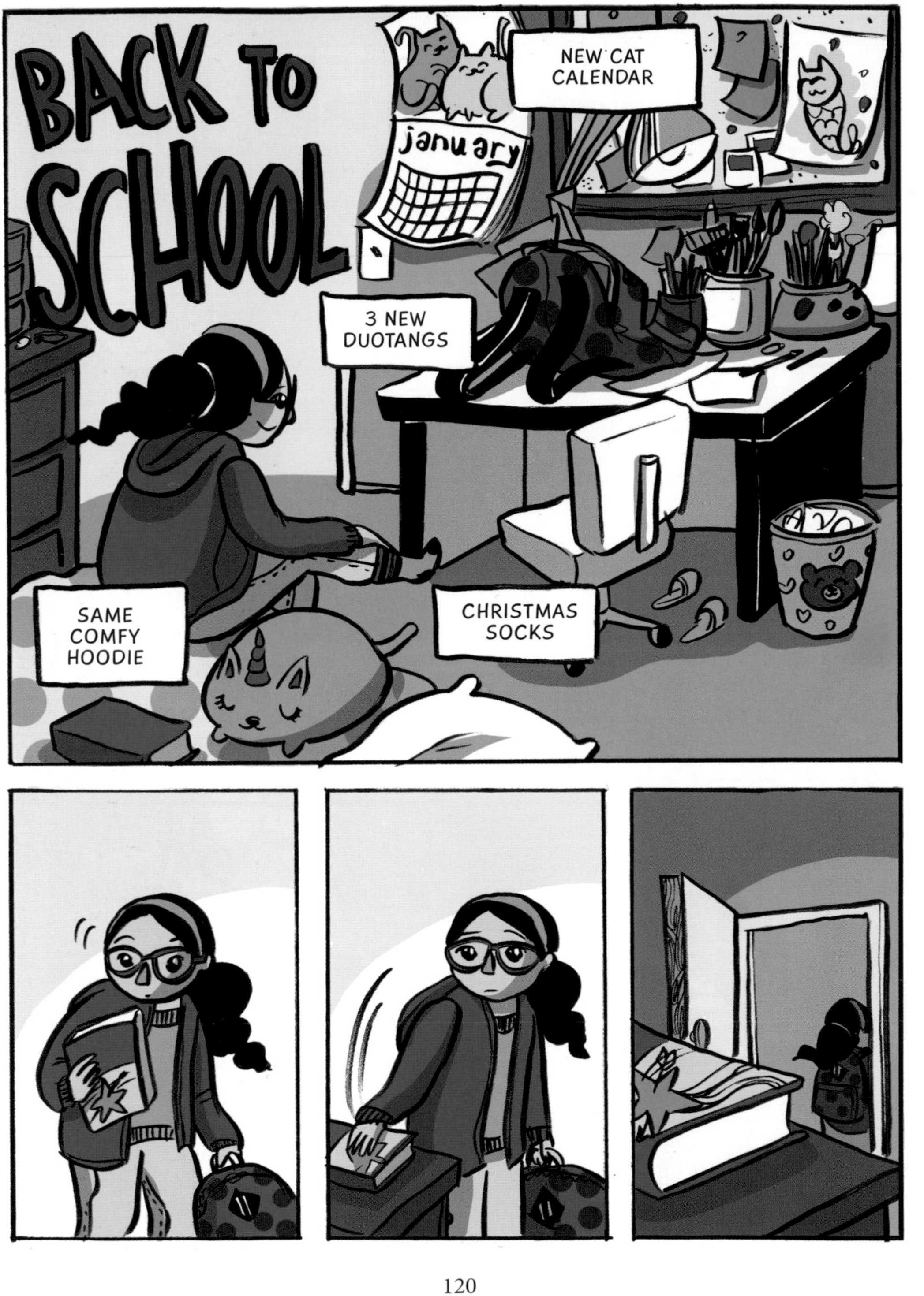
BACK TO SCHOOL
NEW CAT CALENDAR
january
3 NEW DUOTANGS
SAME COMFY HOODIE
CHRISTMAS SOCKS

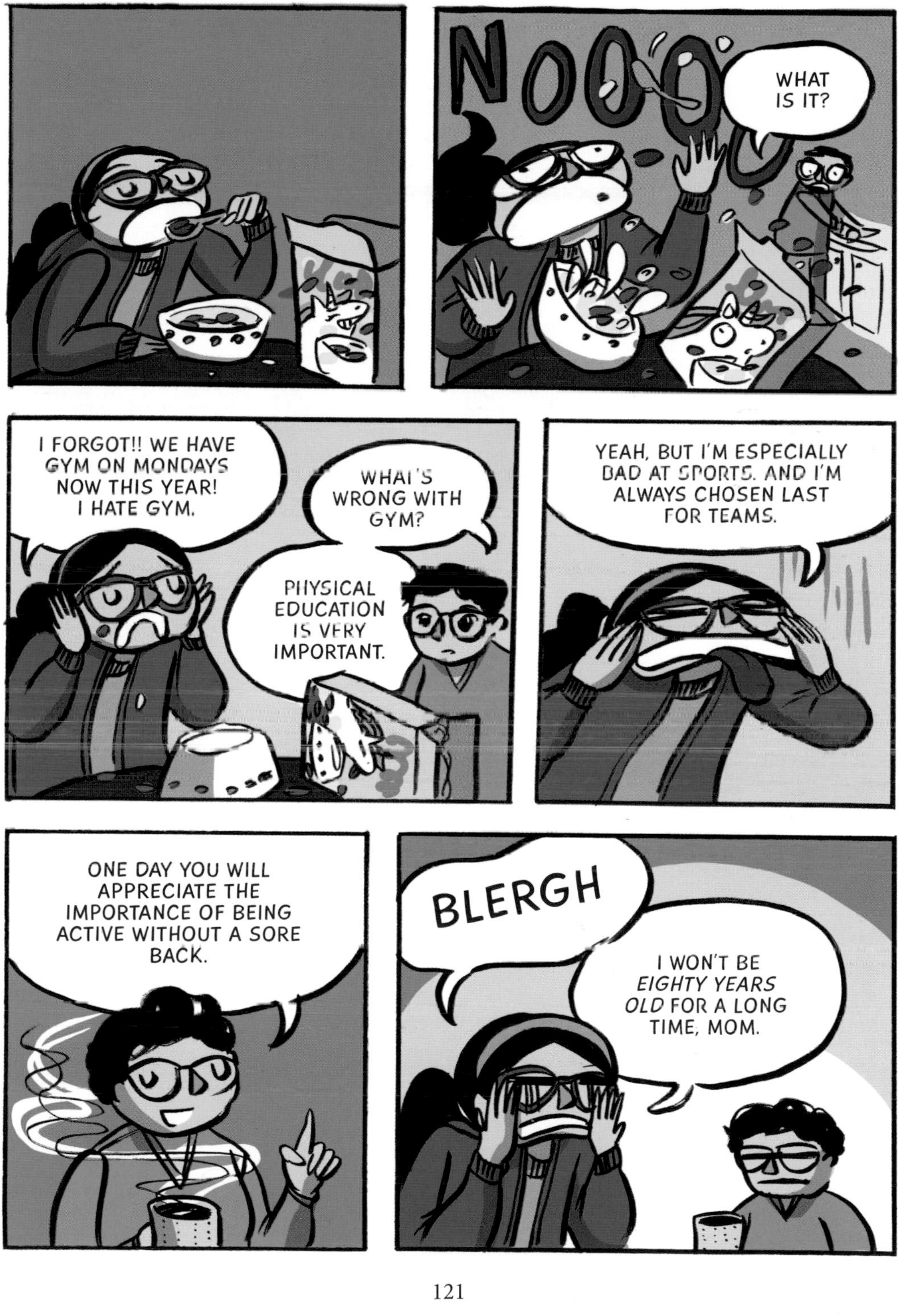
NOOOO
WHAT IS IT?
I FORGOT!! WE HAVE GYM ON MONDAYS NOW THIS YEAR! I HATE GYM.
WHAT'S WRONG WITH GYM?
PHYSICAL EDUCATION IS VERY IMPORTANT.
YEAH, BUT I'M ESPECIALLY BAD AT SPORTS. AND I'M ALWAYS CHOSEN LAST FOR TEAMS.
ONE DAY YOU WILL APPRECIATE THE IMPORTANCE OF BEING ACTIVE WITHOUT A SORE BACK.
BLERGH
I WON'T BE *EIGHTY YEARS OLD* FOR A LONG TIME, MOM.

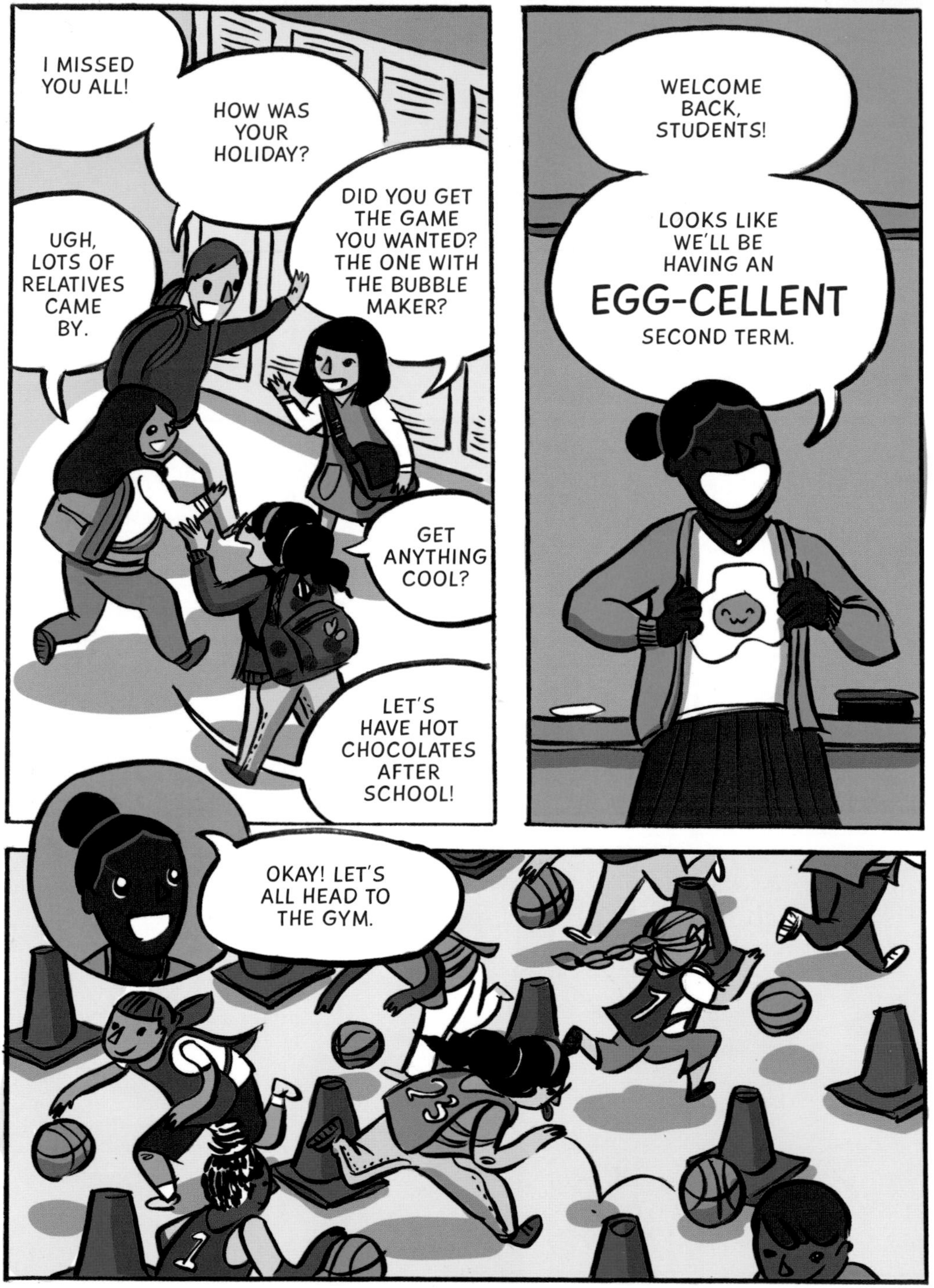

I MISSED YOU ALL!
HOW WAS YOUR HOLIDAY?
UGH, LOTS OF RELATIVES CAME BY.
DID YOU GET THE GAME YOU WANTED? THE ONE WITH THE BUBBLE MAKER?
GET ANYTHING COOL?
LET'S HAVE HOT CHOCOLATES AFTER SCHOOL!
WELCOME BACK, STUDENTS!
LOOKS LIKE WE'LL BE HAVING AN EGG-CELLENT SECOND TERM.
OKAY! LET'S ALL HEAD TO THE GYM.

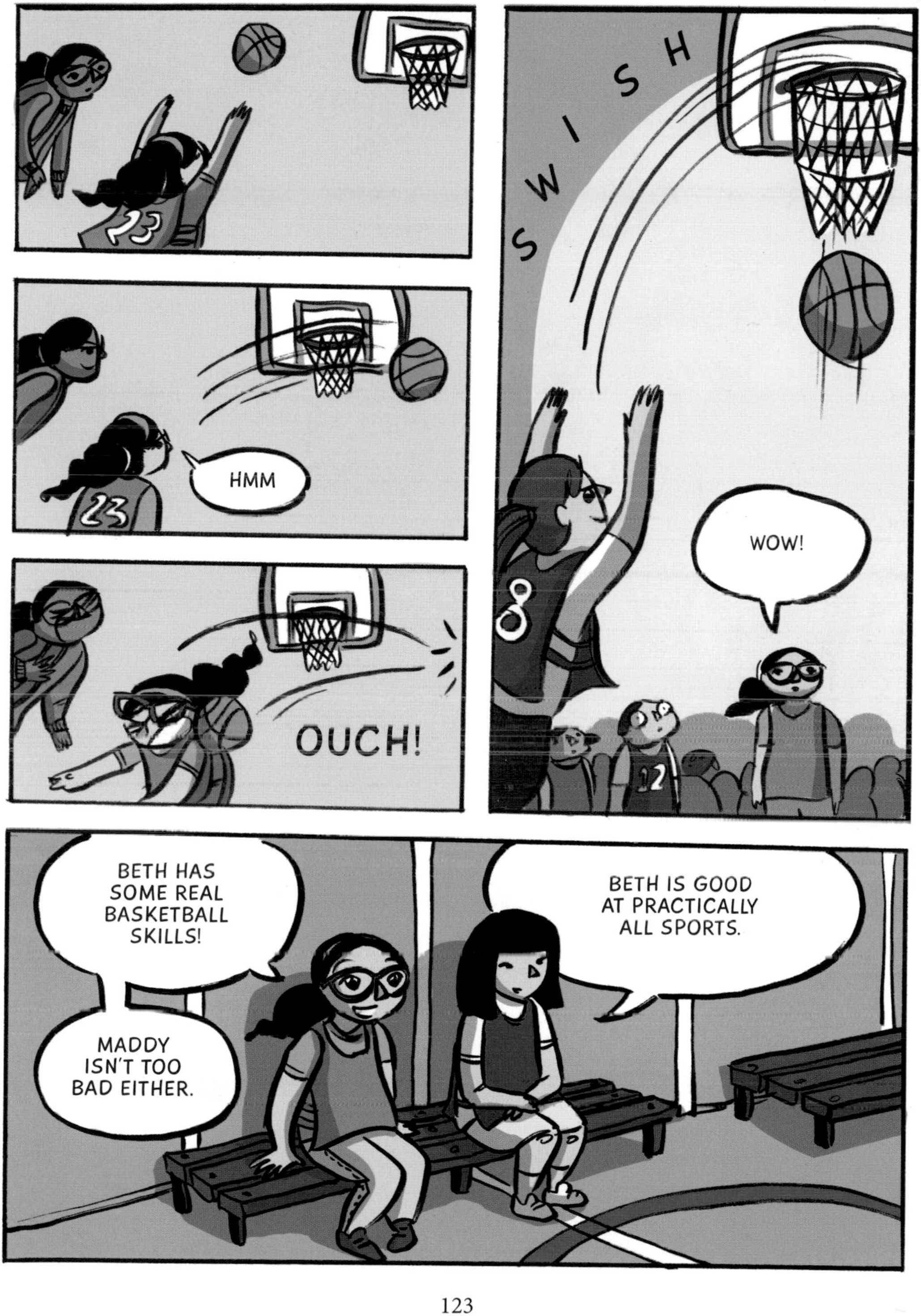
HMM
OUCH!
SWISH
WOW!
BETH HAS SOME REAL BASKETBALL SKILLS!
MADDY ISN'T TOO BAD EITHER.
BETH IS GOOD AT PRACTICALLY ALL SPORTS.

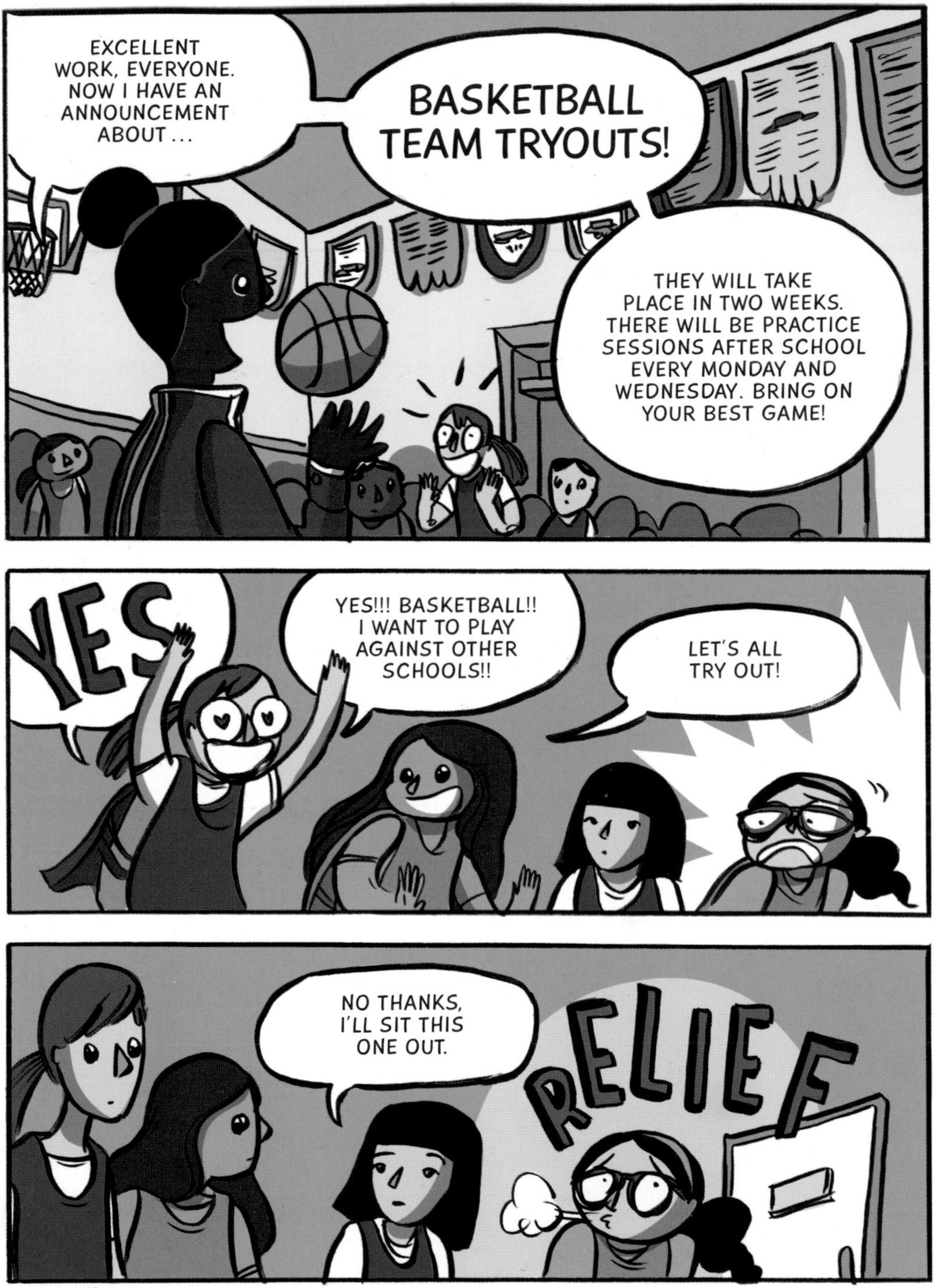
EXCELLENT WORK, EVERYONE. NOW I HAVE AN ANNOUNCEMENT ABOUT . . .
BASKETBALL TEAM TRYOUTS!
THEY WILL TAKE PLACE IN TWO WEEKS. THERE WILL BE PRACTICE SESSIONS AFTER SCHOOL EVERY MONDAY AND WEDNESDAY. BRING ON YOUR BEST GAME!
YES
YES!!! BASKETBALL!! I WANT TO PLAY AGAINST OTHER SCHOOLS!!
LET'S ALL TRY OUT!
NO THANKS, I'LL SIT THIS ONE OUT.
RELIEF

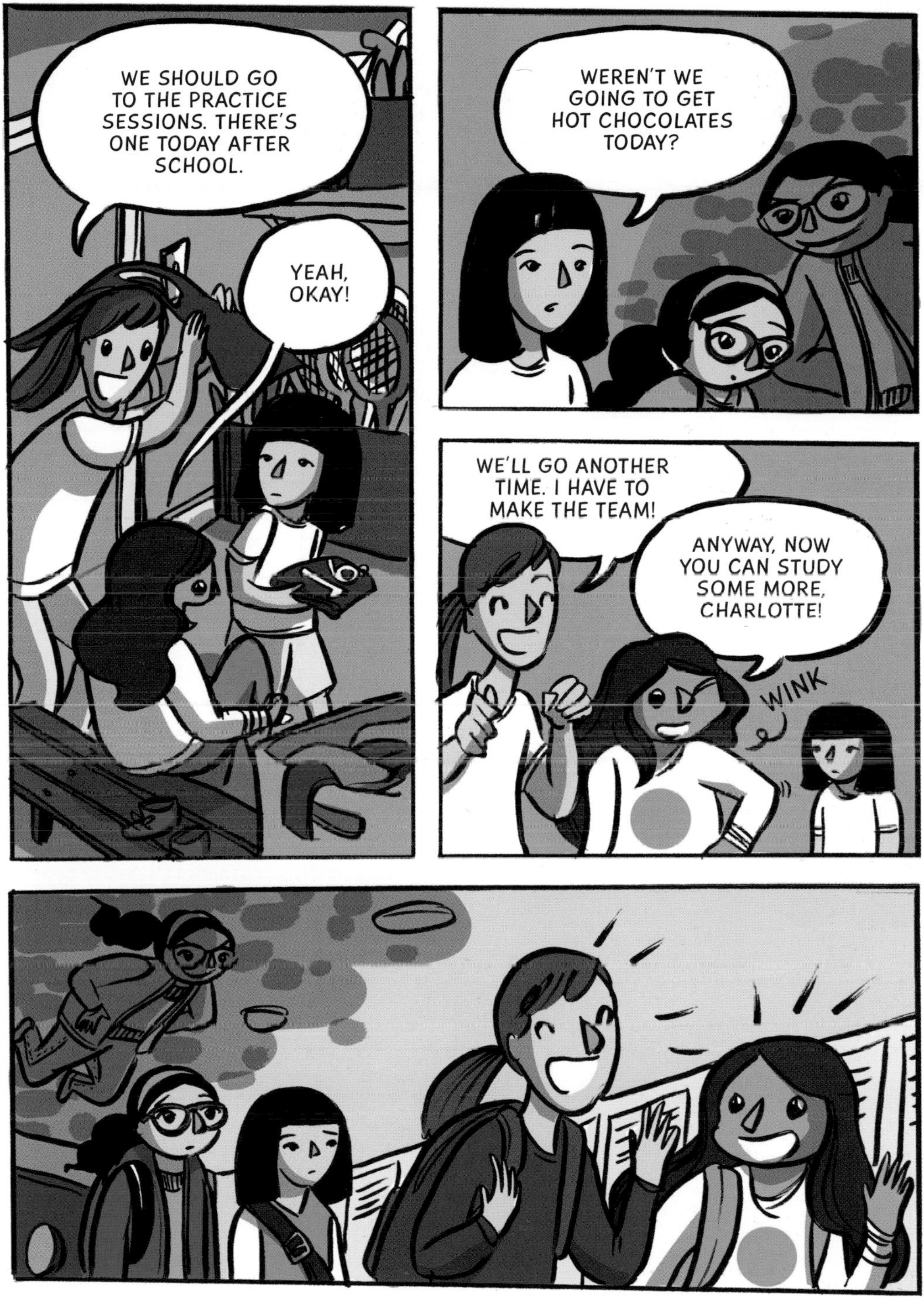
WE SHOULD GO TO THE PRACTICE SESSIONS. THERE'S ONE TODAY AFTER SCHOOL.
YEAH, OKAY!
WEREN'T WE GOING TO GET HOT CHOCOLATES TODAY?
WE'LL GO ANOTHER TIME. I HAVE TO MAKE THE TEAM!
ANYWAY, NOW YOU CAN STUDY SOME MORE, CHARLOTTE!
WINK

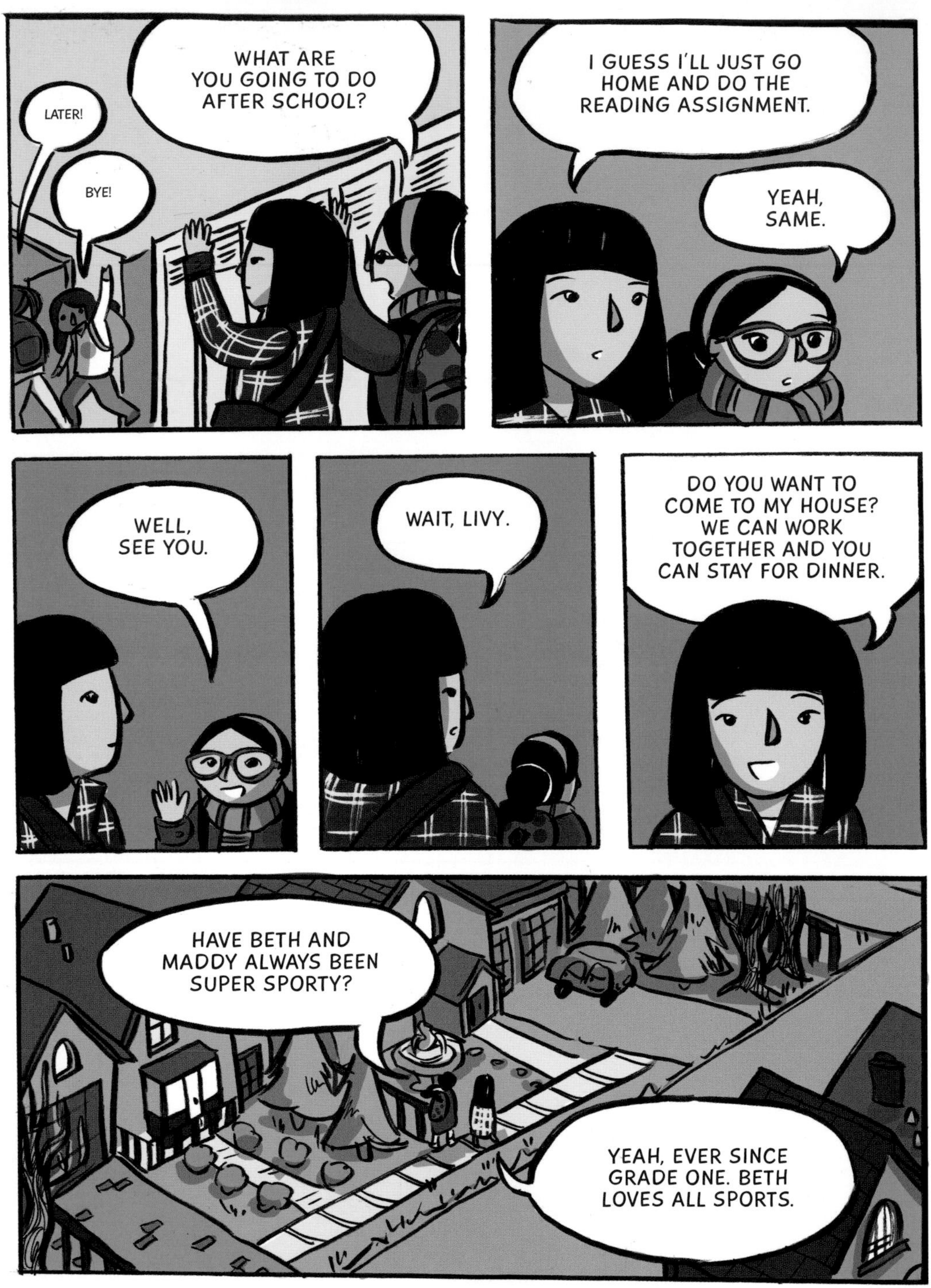
WHAT ARE YOU GOING TO DO AFTER SCHOOL?
LATER!
BYE!
I GUESS I'LL JUST GO HOME AND DO THE READING ASSIGNMENT.
YEAH, SAME.
WELL, SEE YOU.
WAIT, LIVY.
DO YOU WANT TO COME TO MY HOUSE? WE CAN WORK TOGETHER AND YOU CAN STAY FOR DINNER.
HAVE BETH AND MADDY ALWAYS BEEN SUPER SPORTY?
YEAH, EVER SINCE GRADE ONE. BETH LOVES ALL SPORTS.

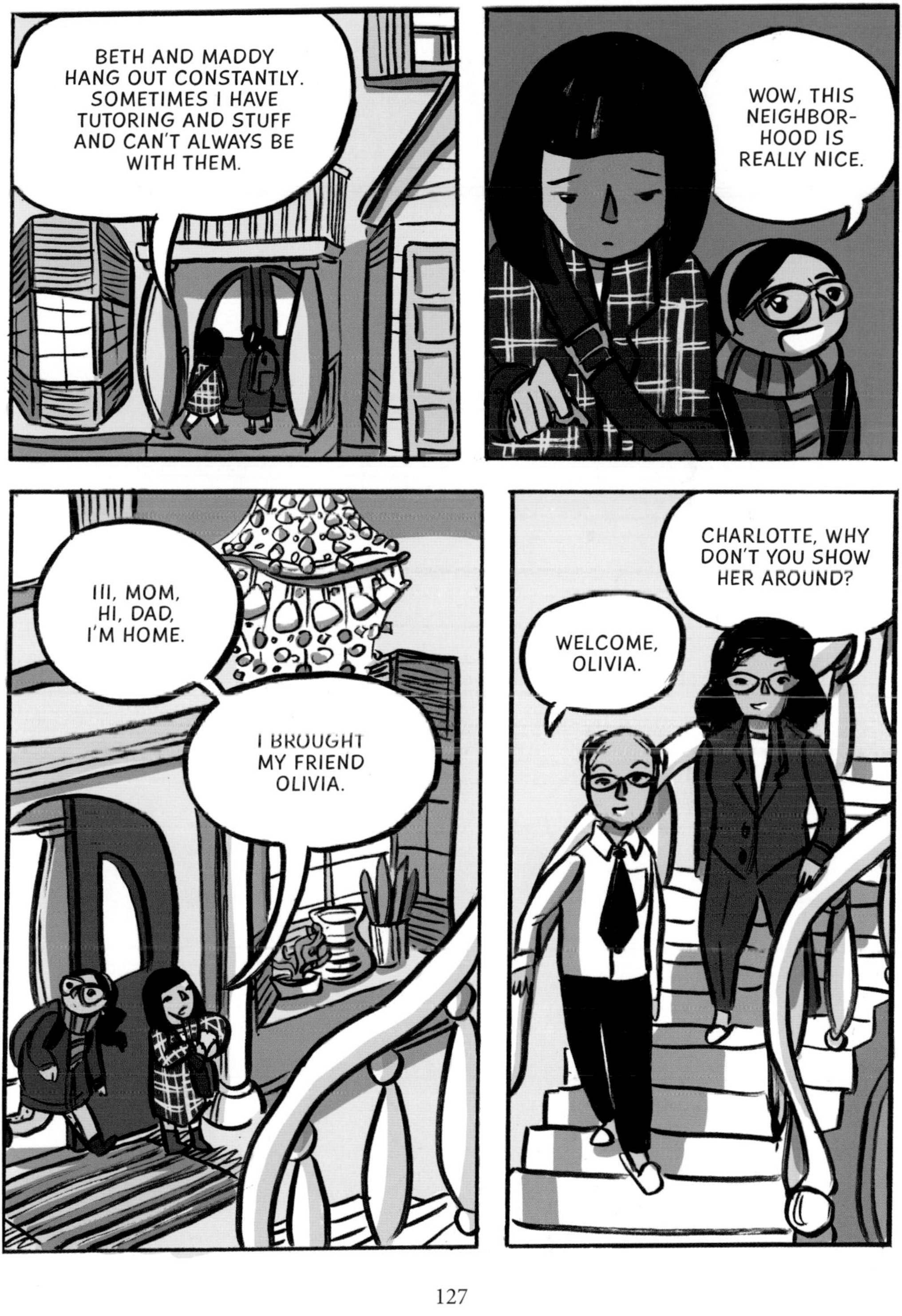
BETH AND MADDY HANG OUT CONSTANTLY. SOMETIMES I HAVE TUTORING AND STUFF AND CAN'T ALWAYS BE WITH THEM.
WOW, THIS NEIGHBOR-HOOD IS REALLY NICE.
HI, MOM, HI, DAD, I'M HOME.
I BROUGHT MY FRIEND OLIVIA.
CHARLOTTE, WHY DON'T YOU SHOW HER AROUND?
WELCOME, OLIVIA.

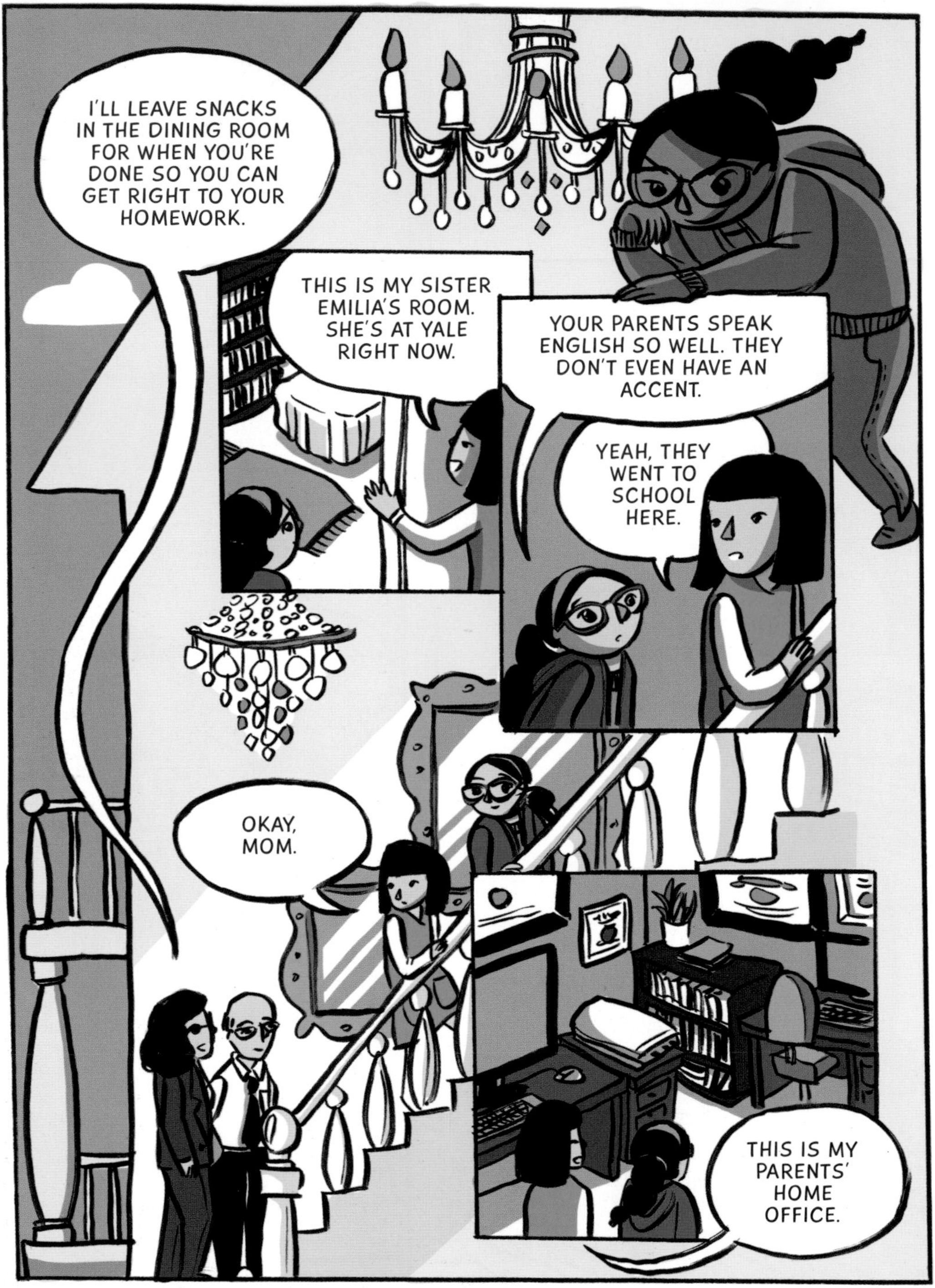
I'LL LEAVE SNACKS IN THE DINING ROOM FOR WHEN YOU'RE DONE SO YOU CAN GET RIGHT TO YOUR HOMEWORK.
THIS IS MY SISTER EMILIA'S ROOM. SHE'S AT YALE RIGHT NOW.
YOUR PARENTS SPEAK ENGLISH SO WELL. THEY DON'T EVEN HAVE AN ACCENT.
YEAH, THEY WENT TO SCHOOL HERE.
OKAY, MOM.
THIS IS MY PARENTS' HOME OFFICE.

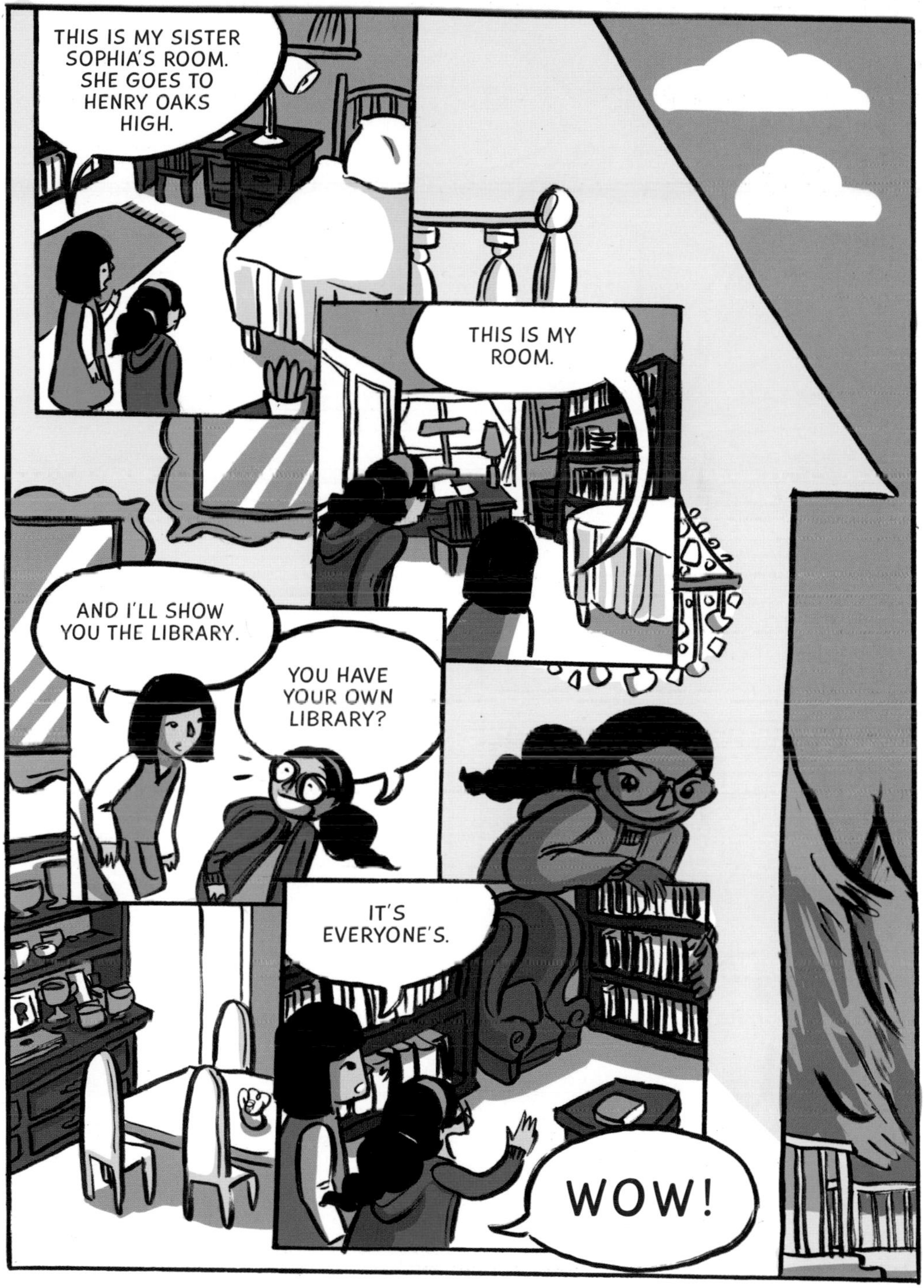
THIS IS MY SISTER SOPHIA'S ROOM. SHE GOES TO HENRY OAKS HIGH.
THIS IS MY ROOM.
AND I'LL SHOW YOU THE LIBRARY.
YOU HAVE YOUR OWN LIBRARY?
IT'S EVERYONE'S.
WOW!

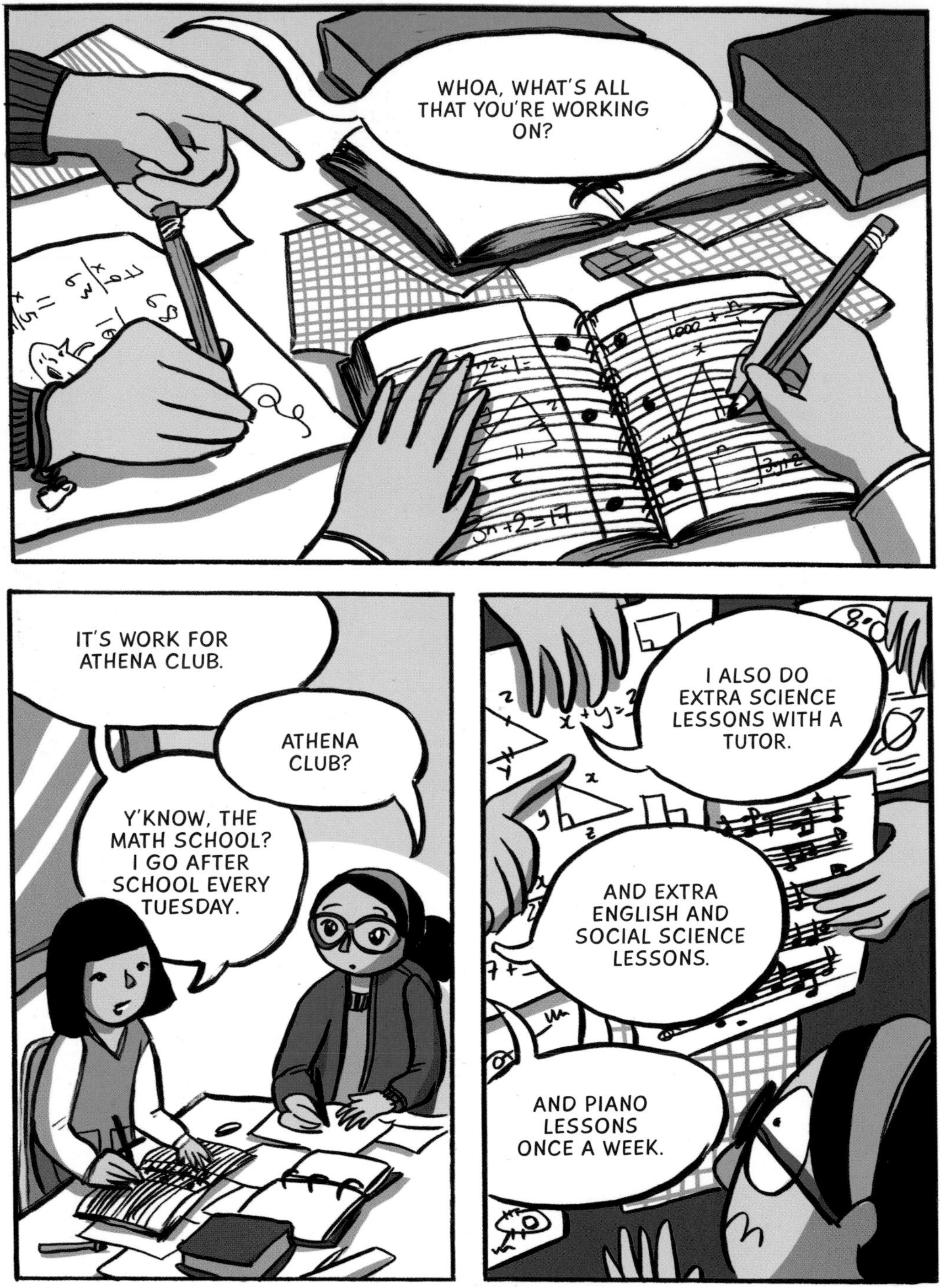
WHOA, WHAT'S ALL THAT YOU'RE WORKING ON?
IT'S WORK FOR ATHENA CLUB.
ATHENA CLUB?
Y'KNOW, THE MATH SCHOOL? I GO AFTER SCHOOL EVERY TUESDAY.
I ALSO DO EXTRA SCIENCE LESSONS WITH A TUTOR.
AND EXTRA ENGLISH AND SOCIAL SCIENCE LESSONS.
AND PIANO LESSONS ONCE A WEEK.

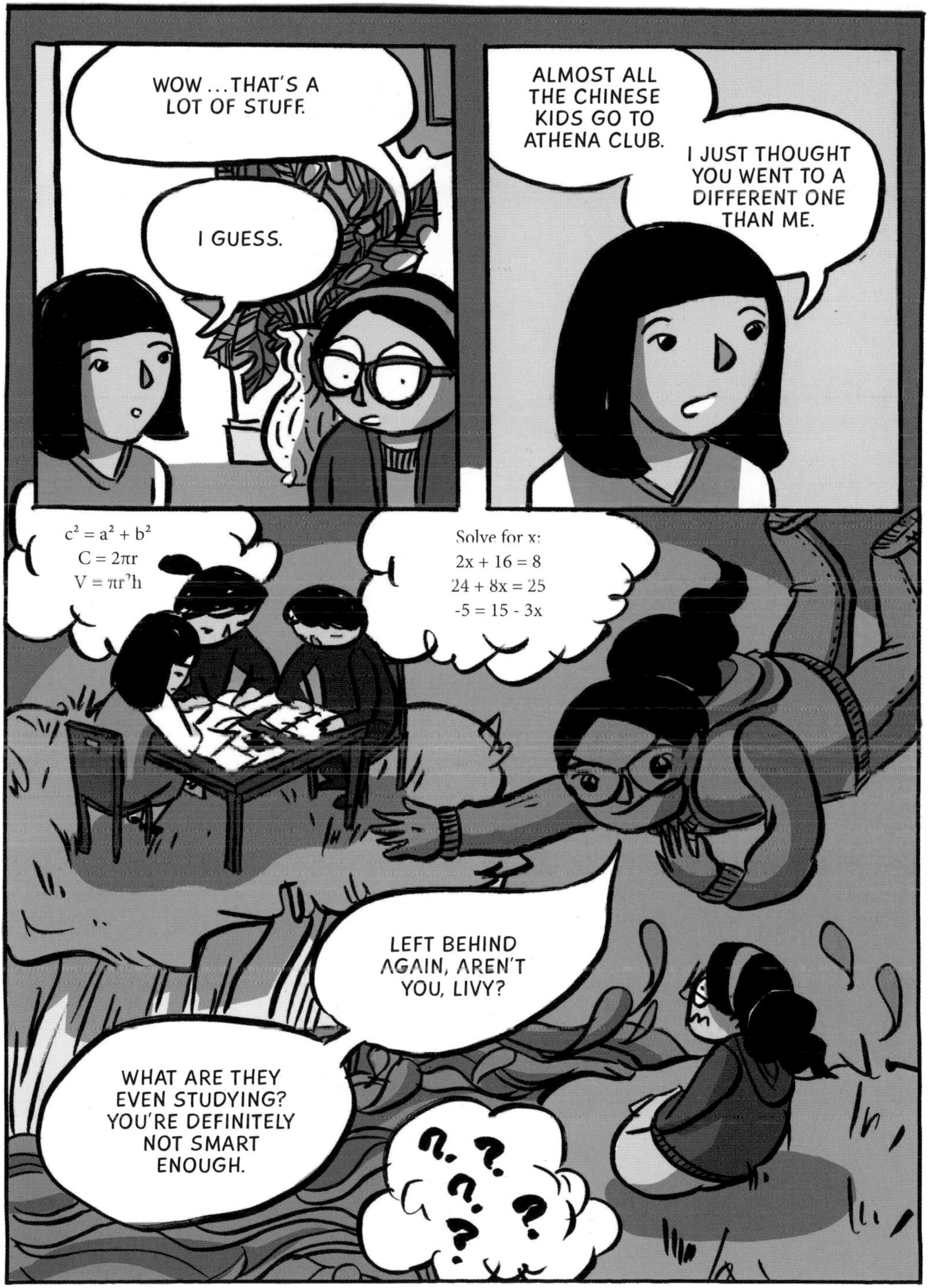
WOW ...THAT'S A LOT OF STUFF.
I GUESS.
ALMOST ALL THE CHINESE KIDS GO TO ATHENA CLUB.
I JUST THOUGHT YOU WENT TO A DIFFERENT ONE THAN ME.
$c^2 = a^2 + b^2$
$C = 2\pi r$
$V = \pi r^2 h$
Solve for x:
$2x + 16 = 8$
$24 + 8x = 25$
$-5 = 15 - 3x$
LEFT BEHIND AGAIN, AREN'T YOU, LIVY?
WHAT ARE THEY EVEN STUDYING? YOU'RE DEFINITELY NOT SMART ENOUGH.
? ? ? ? ? ?

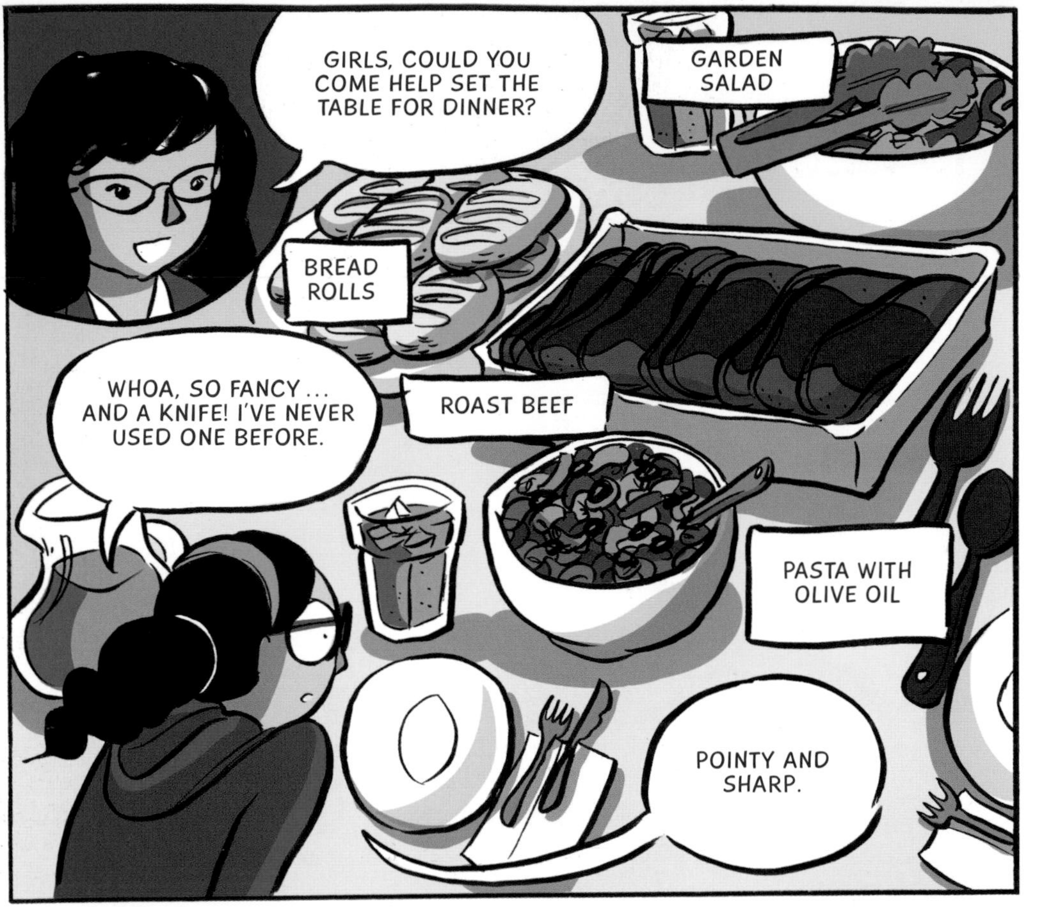
GIRLS, COULD YOU COME HELP SET THE TABLE FOR DINNER?
GARDEN SALAD
BREAD ROLLS
ROAST BEEF
WHOA, SO FANCY . . . AND A KNIFE! I'VE NEVER USED ONE BEFORE.
PASTA WITH OLIVE OIL
POINTY AND SHARP.

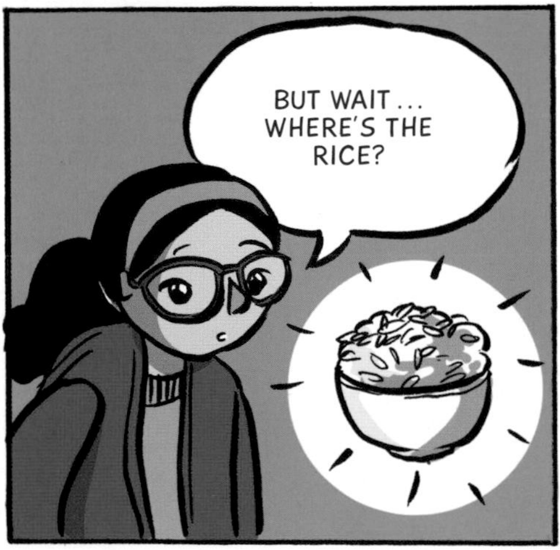
BUT WAIT . . . WHERE'S THE RICE?

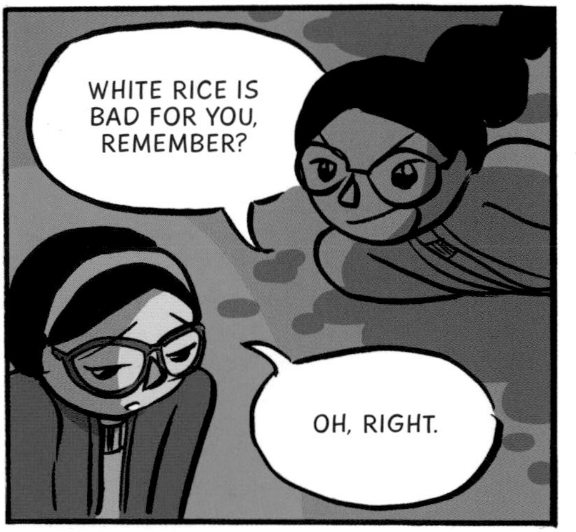
WHITE RICE IS BAD FOR YOU, REMEMBER?
OH, RIGHT.

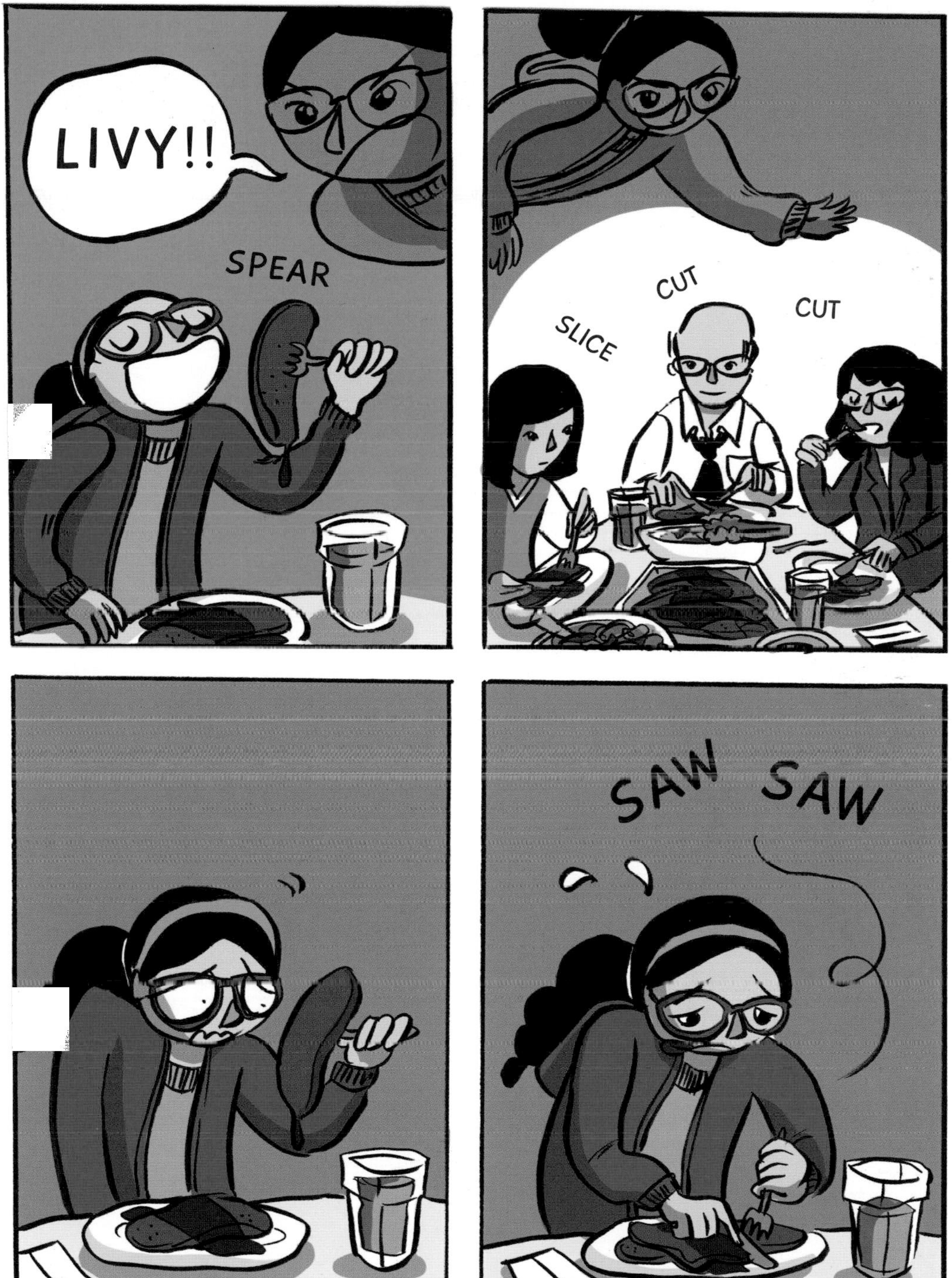
LIVY!!
SPEAR
SLICE
CUT
CUT
SAW
SAW

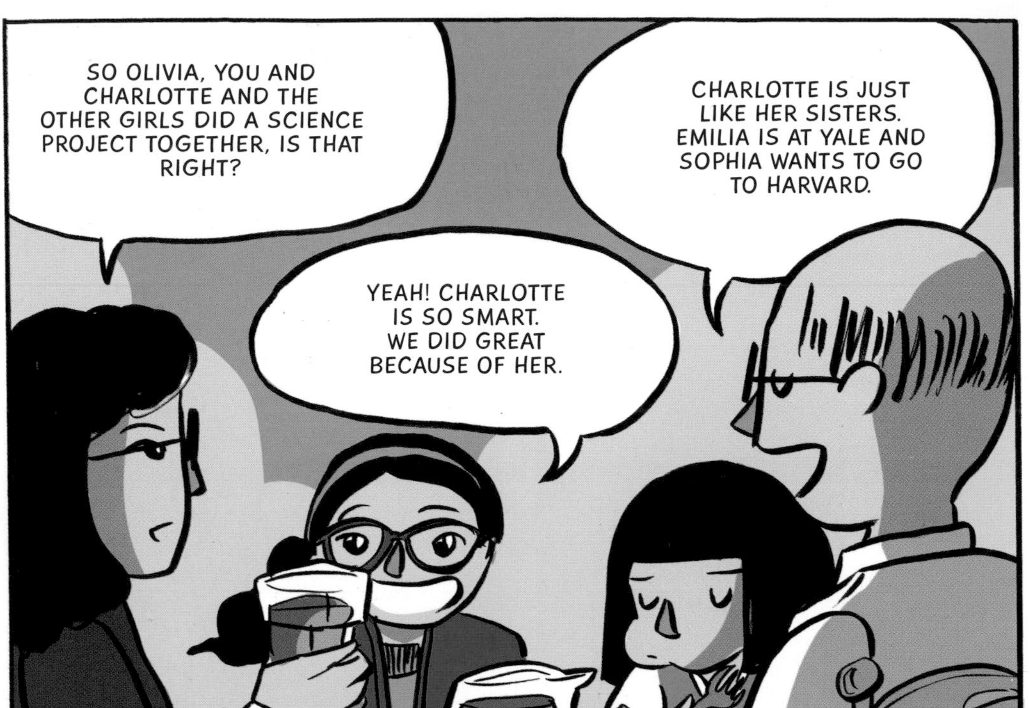
SO OLIVIA, YOU AND CHARLOTTE AND THE OTHER GIRLS DID A SCIENCE PROJECT TOGETHER, IS THAT RIGHT?
CHARLOTTE IS JUST LIKE HER SISTERS. EMILIA IS AT YALE AND SOPHIA WANTS TO GO TO HARVARD.
YEAH! CHARLOTTE IS SO SMART. WE DID GREAT BECAUSE OF HER.

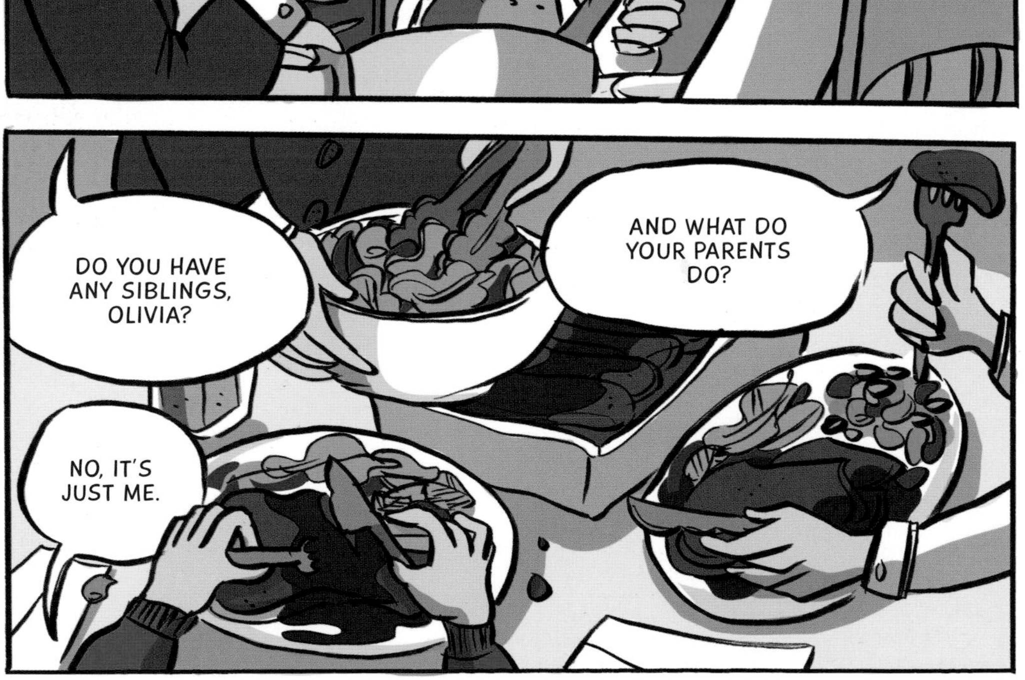
DO YOU HAVE ANY SIBLINGS, OLIVIA?
AND WHAT DO YOUR PARENTS DO?
NO, IT'S JUST ME.

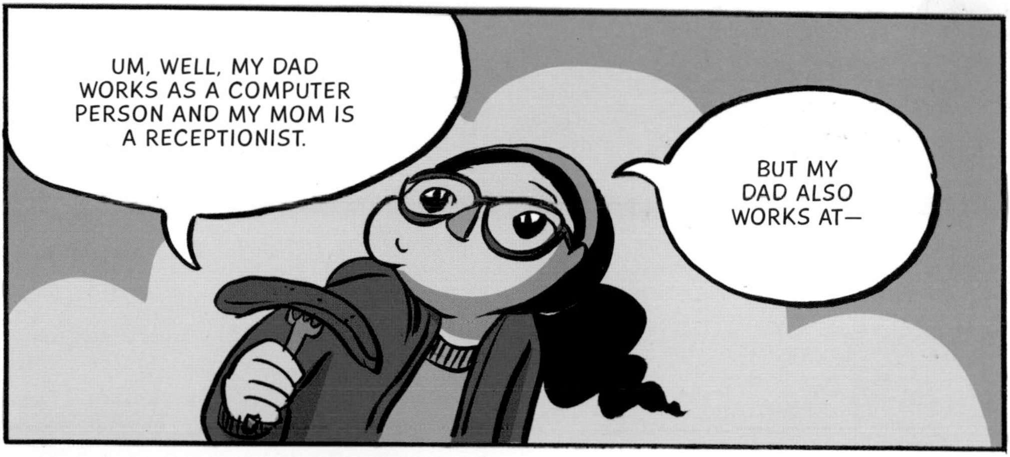
UM, WELL, MY DAD WORKS AS A COMPUTER PERSON AND MY MOM IS A RECEPTIONIST.
BUT MY DAD ALSO WORKS AT—

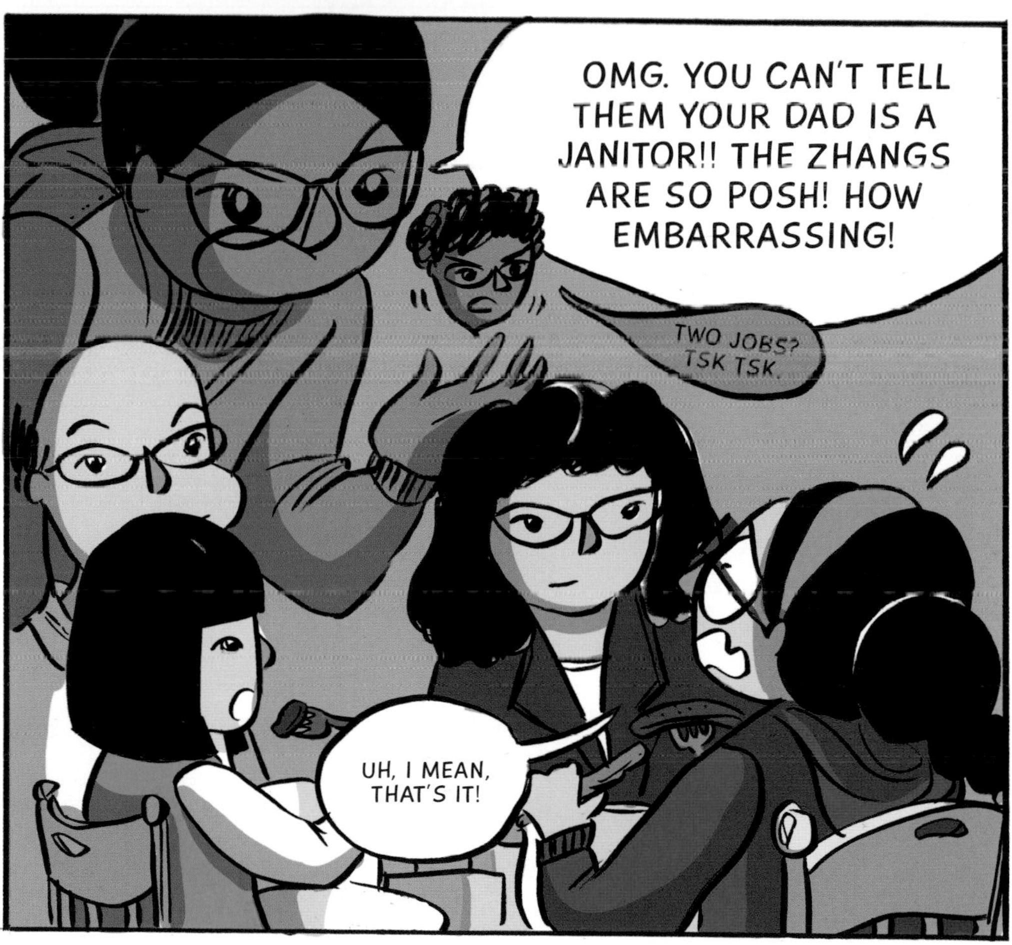
OMG. YOU CAN'T TELL THEM YOUR DAD IS A JANITOR!! THE ZHANGS ARE SO POSH! HOW EMBARRASSING!
TWO JOBS? TSK TSK.
UH, I MEAN, THAT'S IT!

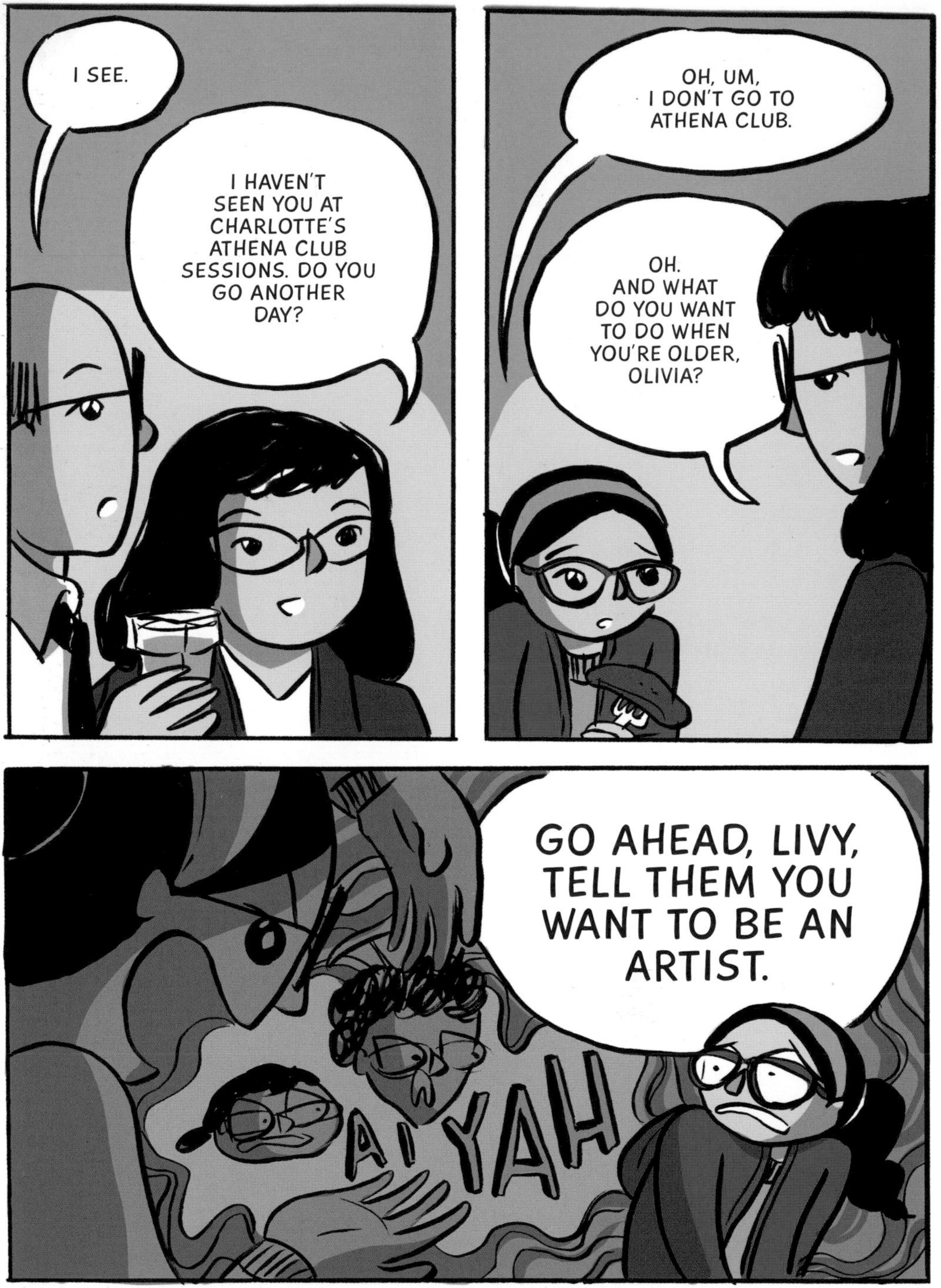

I SEE.
I HAVEN'T SEEN YOU AT CHARLOTTE'S ATHENA CLUB SESSIONS. DO YOU GO ANOTHER DAY?
OH, UM, I DON'T GO TO ATHENA CLUB.
OH. AND WHAT DO YOU WANT TO DO WHEN YOU'RE OLDER, OLIVIA?
GO AHEAD, LIVY, TELL THEM YOU WANT TO BE AN ARTIST.
AIYAH

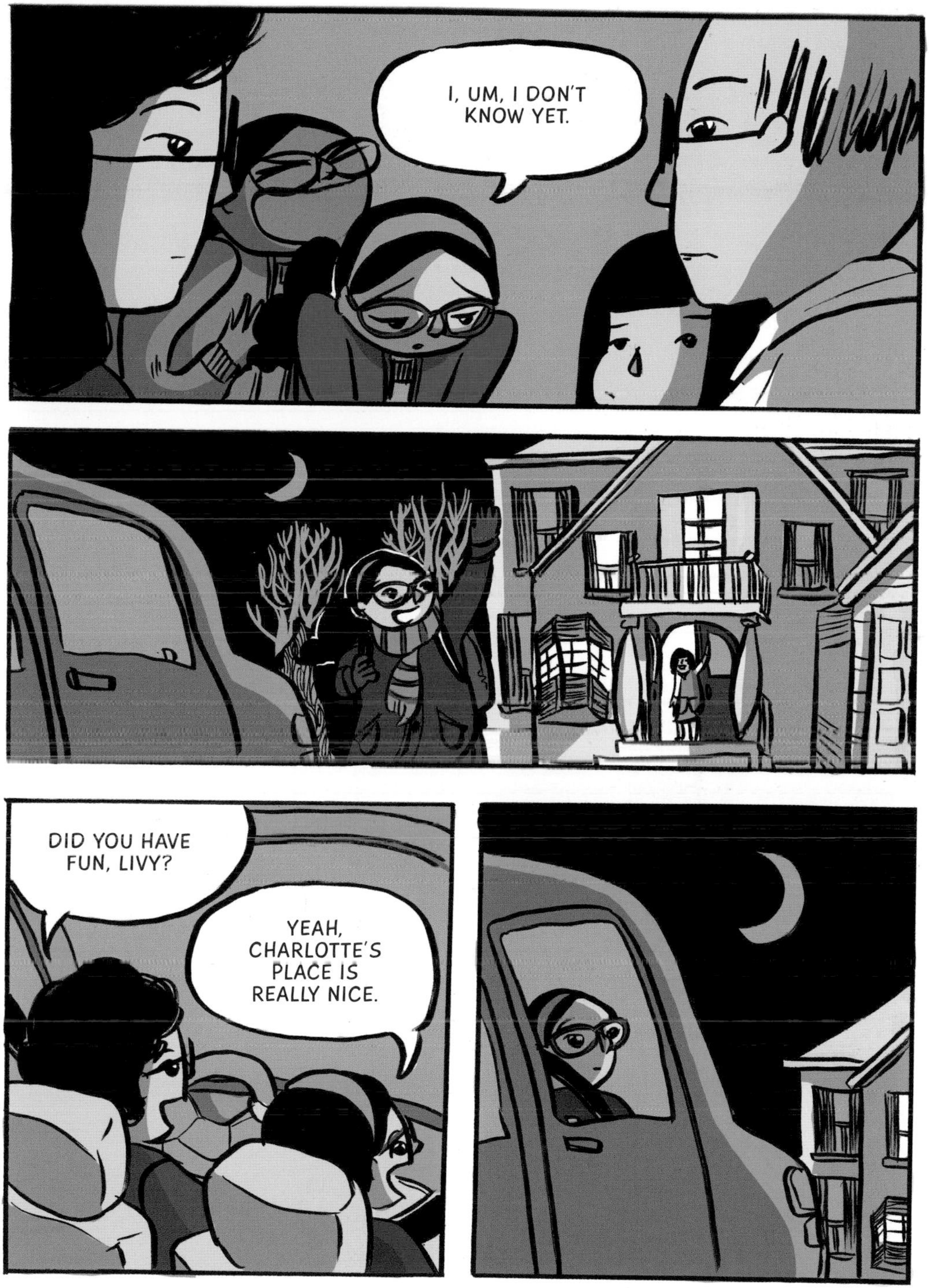
I, UM, I DON'T KNOW YET.
DID YOU HAVE FUN, LIVY?
YEAH, CHARLOTTE'S PLACE IS REALLY NICE.

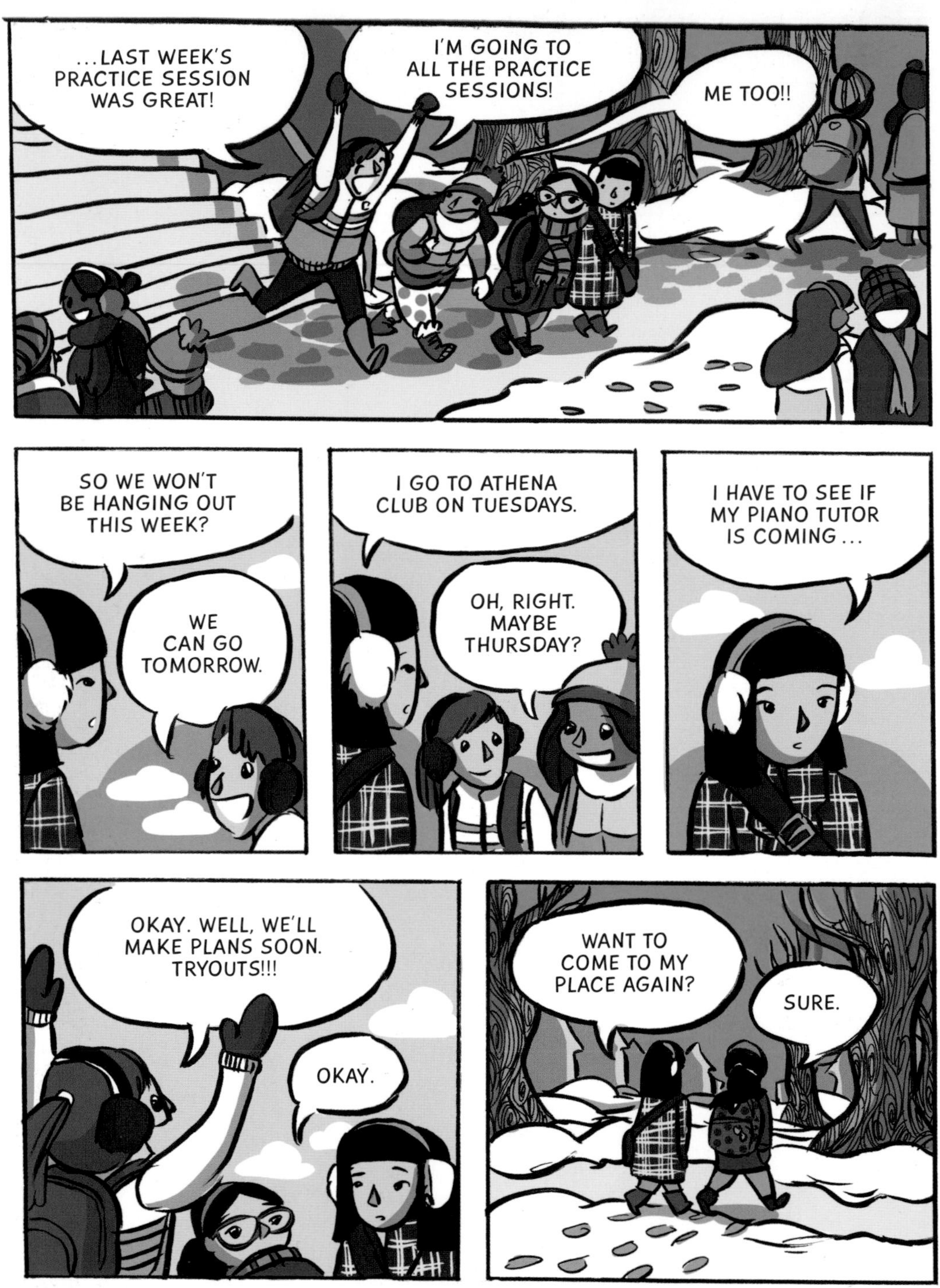
...LAST WEEK'S PRACTICE SESSION WAS GREAT!
I'M GOING TO ALL THE PRACTICE SESSIONS!
ME TOO!!
SO WE WON'T BE HANGING OUT THIS WEEK?
WE CAN GO TOMORROW.
I GO TO ATHENA CLUB ON TUESDAYS.
OH, RIGHT. MAYBE THURSDAY?
I HAVE TO SEE IF MY PIANO TUTOR IS COMING...
OKAY. WELL, WE'LL MAKE PLANS SOON. TRYOUTS!!!
OKAY.
WANT TO COME TO MY PLACE AGAIN?
SURE.

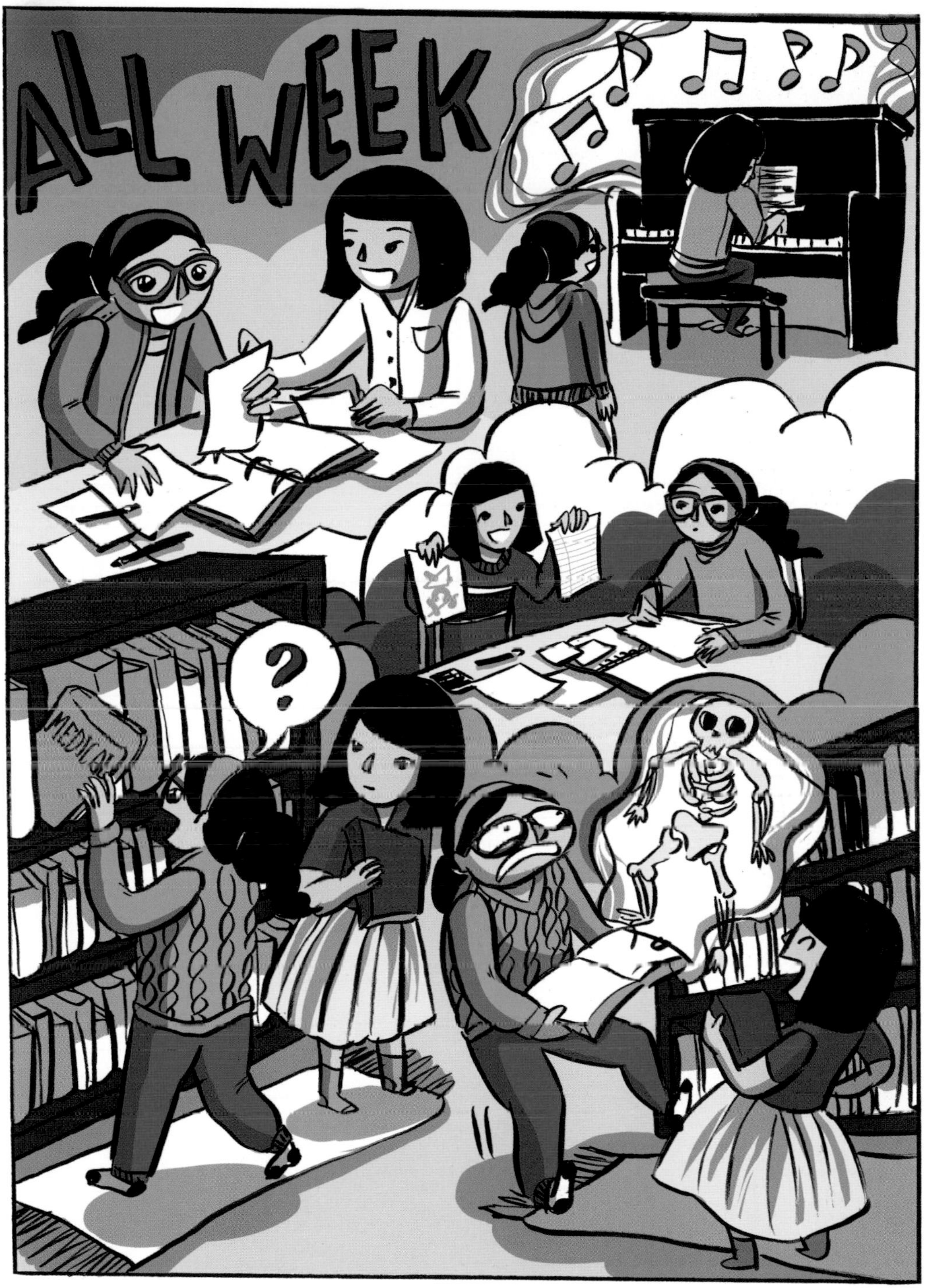
ALL WEEK
?
MEDICAL

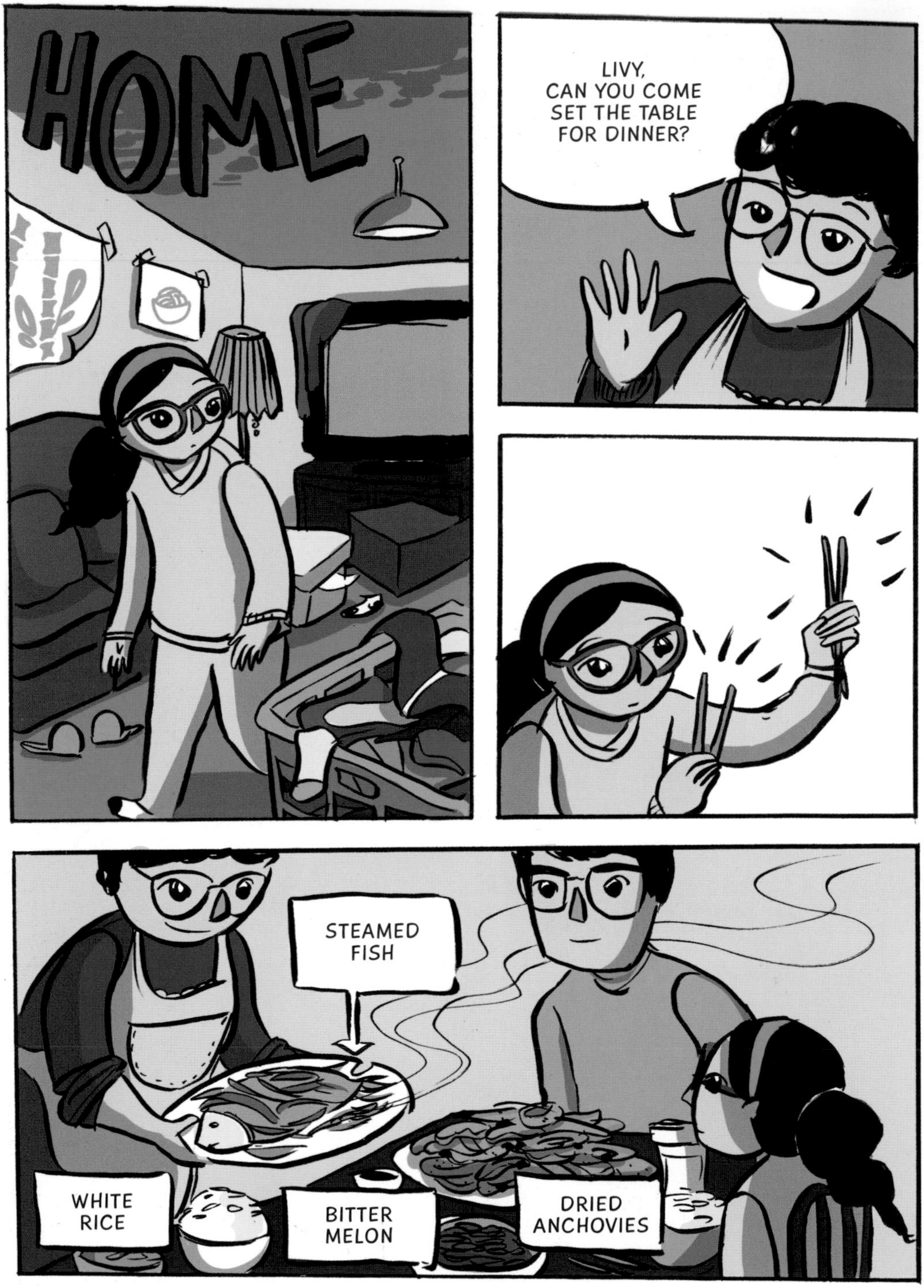
HOME
LIVY, CAN YOU COME SET THE TABLE FOR DINNER?
STEAMED FISH
WHITE RICE
BITTER MELON
DRIED ANCHOVIES

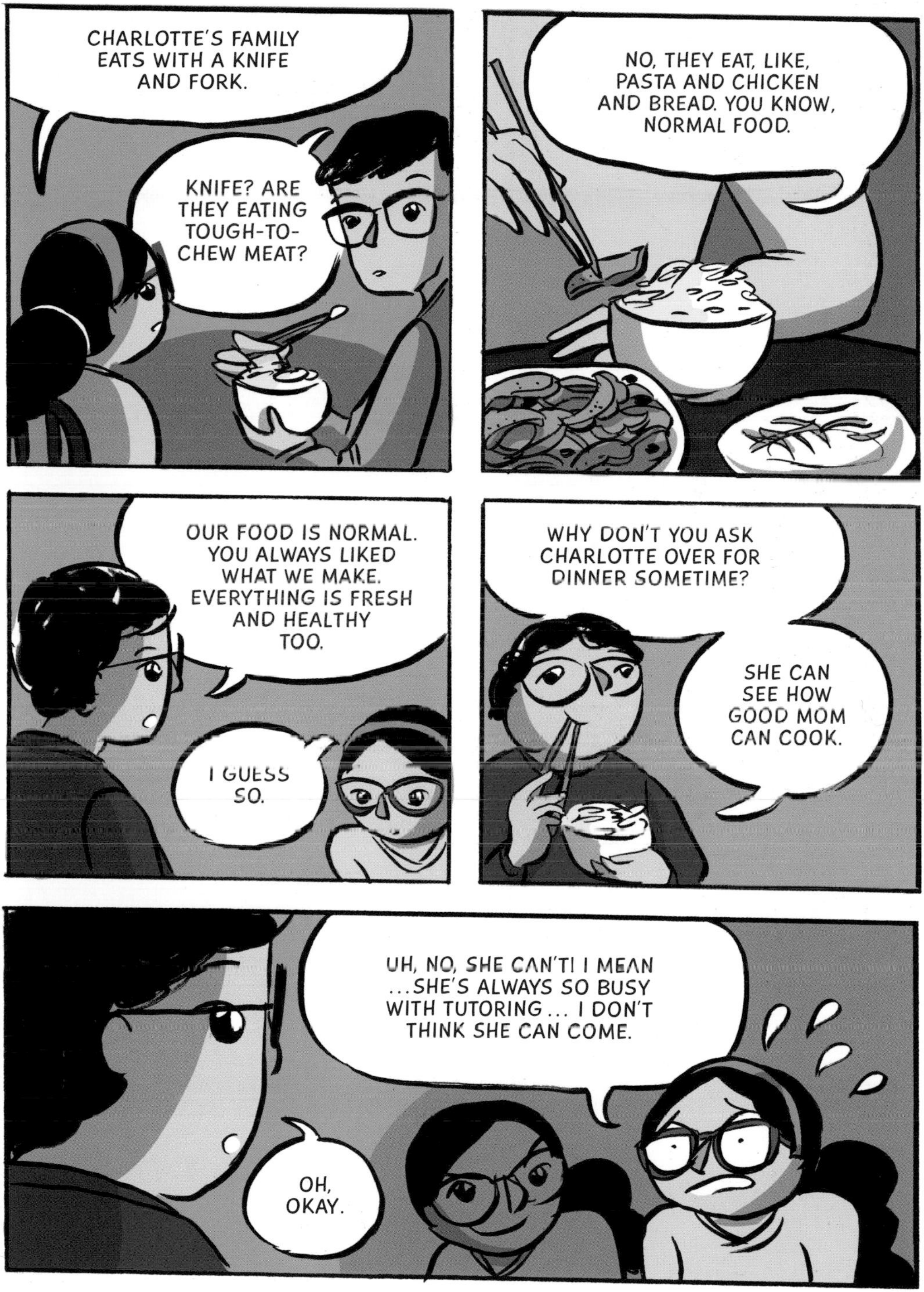
CHARLOTTE'S FAMILY EATS WITH A KNIFE AND FORK.
KNIFE? ARE THEY EATING TOUGH-TO-CHEW MEAT?
NO, THEY EAT, LIKE, PASTA AND CHICKEN AND BREAD. YOU KNOW, NORMAL FOOD.
OUR FOOD IS NORMAL. YOU ALWAYS LIKED WHAT WE MAKE. EVERYTHING IS FRESH AND HEALTHY TOO.
I GUESS SO.
WHY DON'T YOU ASK CHARLOTTE OVER FOR DINNER SOMETIME?
SHE CAN SEE HOW GOOD MOM CAN COOK.
UH, NO, SHE CAN'T! I MEAN ...SHE'S ALWAYS SO BUSY WITH TUTORING... I DON'T THINK SHE CAN COME.
OH, OKAY.

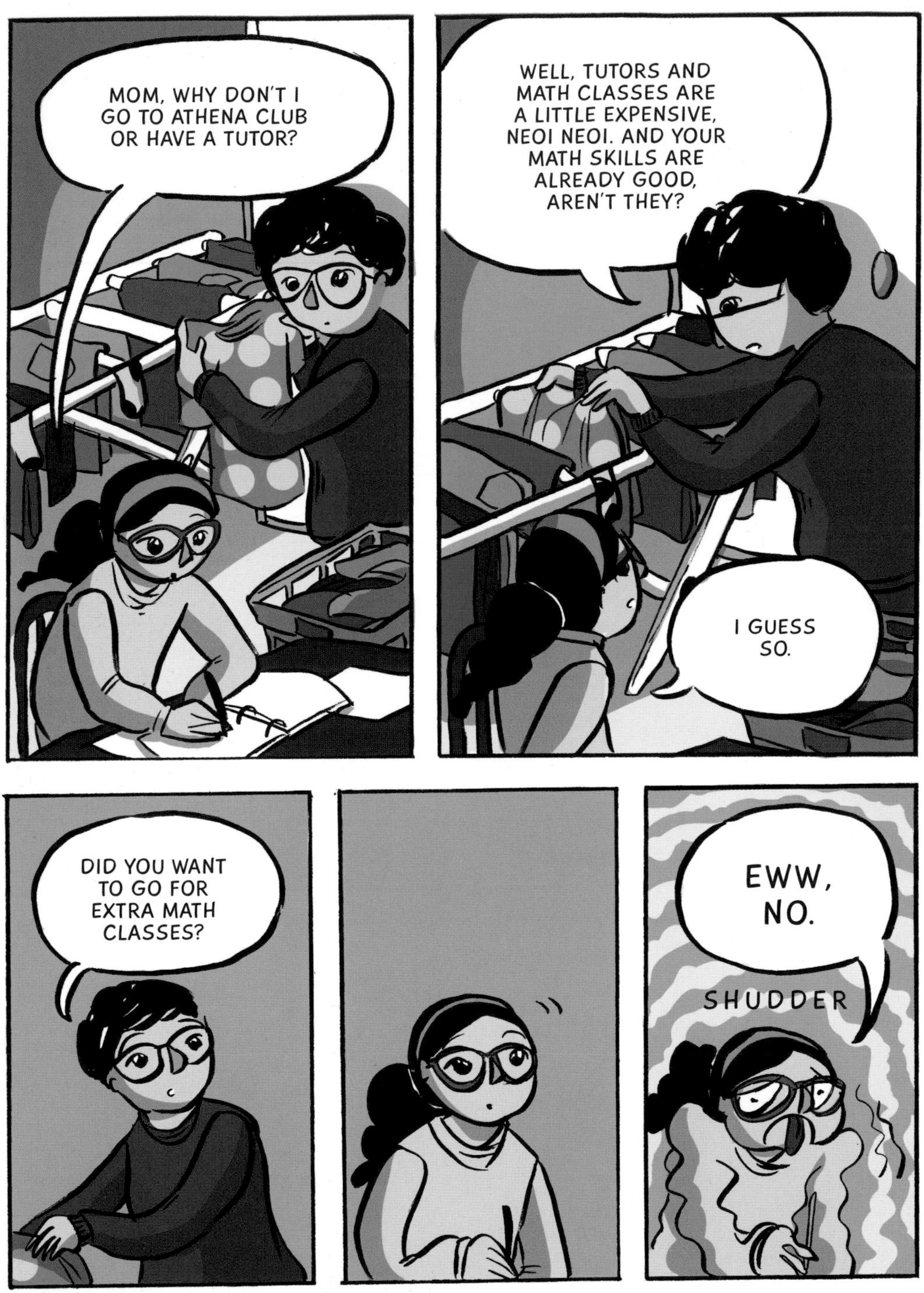
MOM, WHY DON'T I GO TO ATHENA CLUB OR HAVE A TUTOR?
WELL, TUTORS AND MATH CLASSES ARE A LITTLE EXPENSIVE, NEOI NEOI. AND YOUR MATH SKILLS ARE ALREADY GOOD, AREN'T THEY?
I GUESS SO.
DID YOU WANT TO GO FOR EXTRA MATH CLASSES?
EWW, NO.
SHUDDER

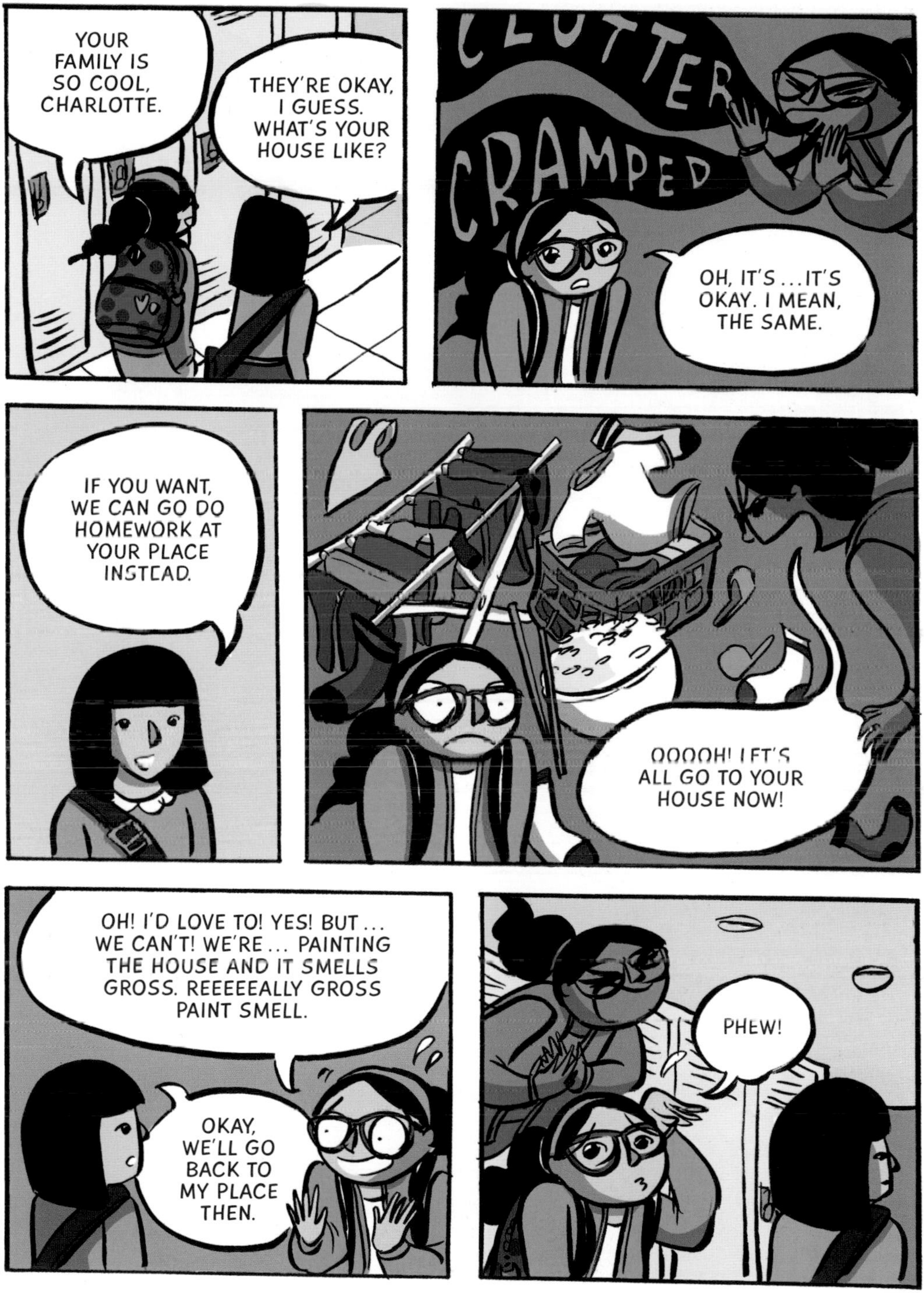
YOUR FAMILY IS SO COOL, CHARLOTTE.
THEY'RE OKAY, I GUESS. WHAT'S YOUR HOUSE LIKE?
CLUTTER
CRAMPED
OH, IT'S ... IT'S OKAY. I MEAN, THE SAME.
IF YOU WANT, WE CAN GO DO HOMEWORK AT YOUR PLACE INSTEAD.
OOOOH! LET'S ALL GO TO YOUR HOUSE NOW!
OH! I'D LOVE TO! YES! BUT ... WE CAN'T! WE'RE ... PAINTING THE HOUSE AND IT SMELLS GROSS. REEEEEALLY GROSS PAINT SMELL.
OKAY, WE'LL GO BACK TO MY PLACE THEN.
PHEW!

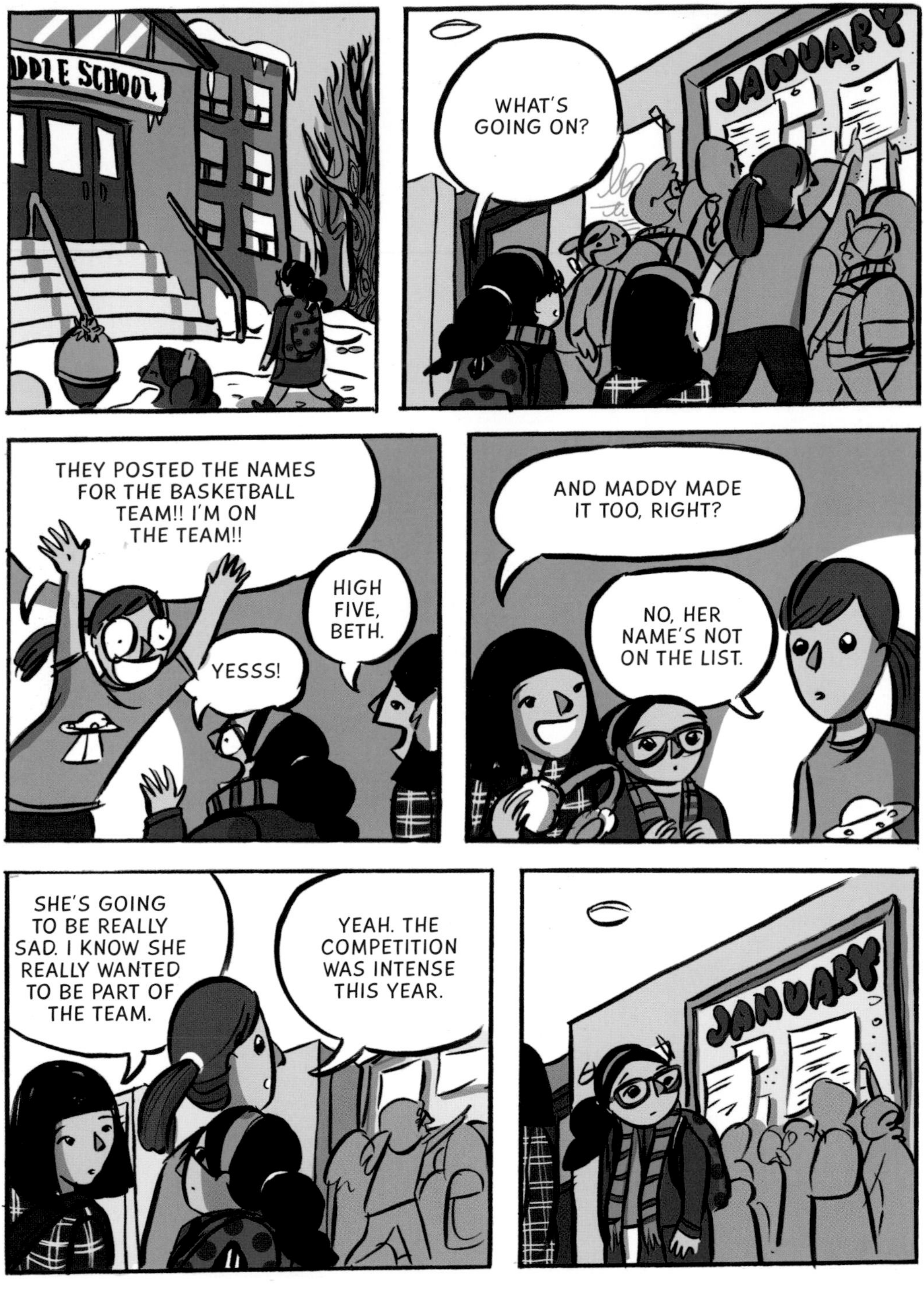
DDLE SCHOOL
WHAT'S GOING ON?
JANUARY
THEY POSTED THE NAMES FOR THE BASKETBALL TEAM!! I'M ON THE TEAM!!
YESSS!
HIGH FIVE, BETH.
AND MADDY MADE IT TOO, RIGHT?
NO, HER NAME'S NOT ON THE LIST.
SHE'S GOING TO BE REALLY SAD. I KNOW SHE REALLY WANTED TO BE PART OF THE TEAM.
YEAH. THE COMPETITION WAS INTENSE THIS YEAR.
JANUARY

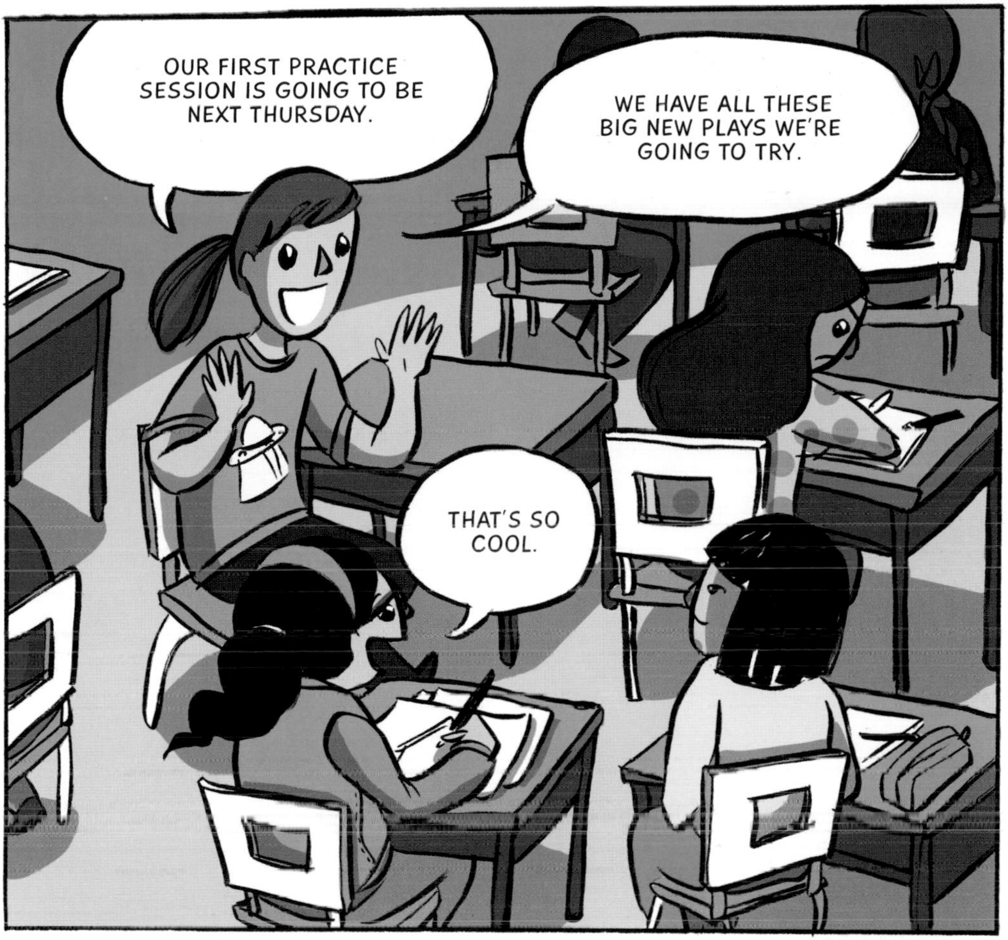
OUR FIRST PRACTICE SESSION IS GOING TO BE NEXT THURSDAY.
WE HAVE ALL THESE BIG NEW PLAYS WE'RE GOING TO TRY.
THAT'S SO COOL.

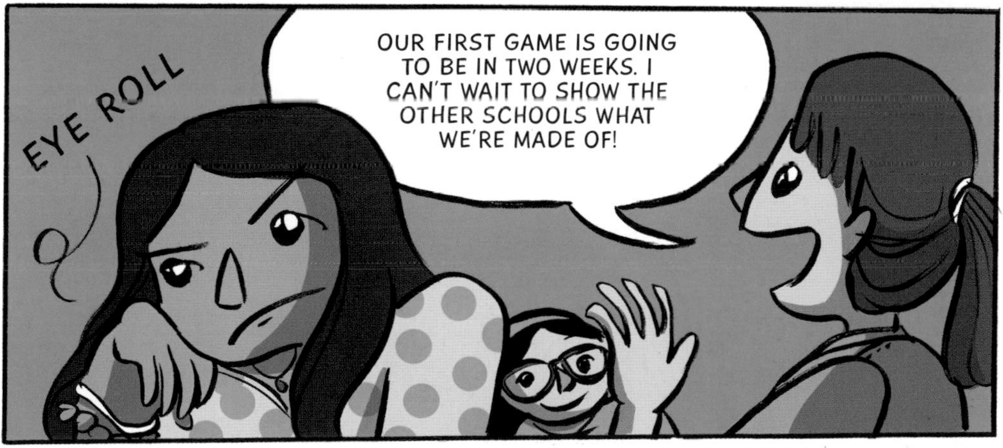
OUR FIRST GAME IS GOING TO BE IN TWO WEEKS. I CAN'T WAIT TO SHOW THE OTHER SCHOOLS WHAT WE'RE MADE OF!
EYE ROLL

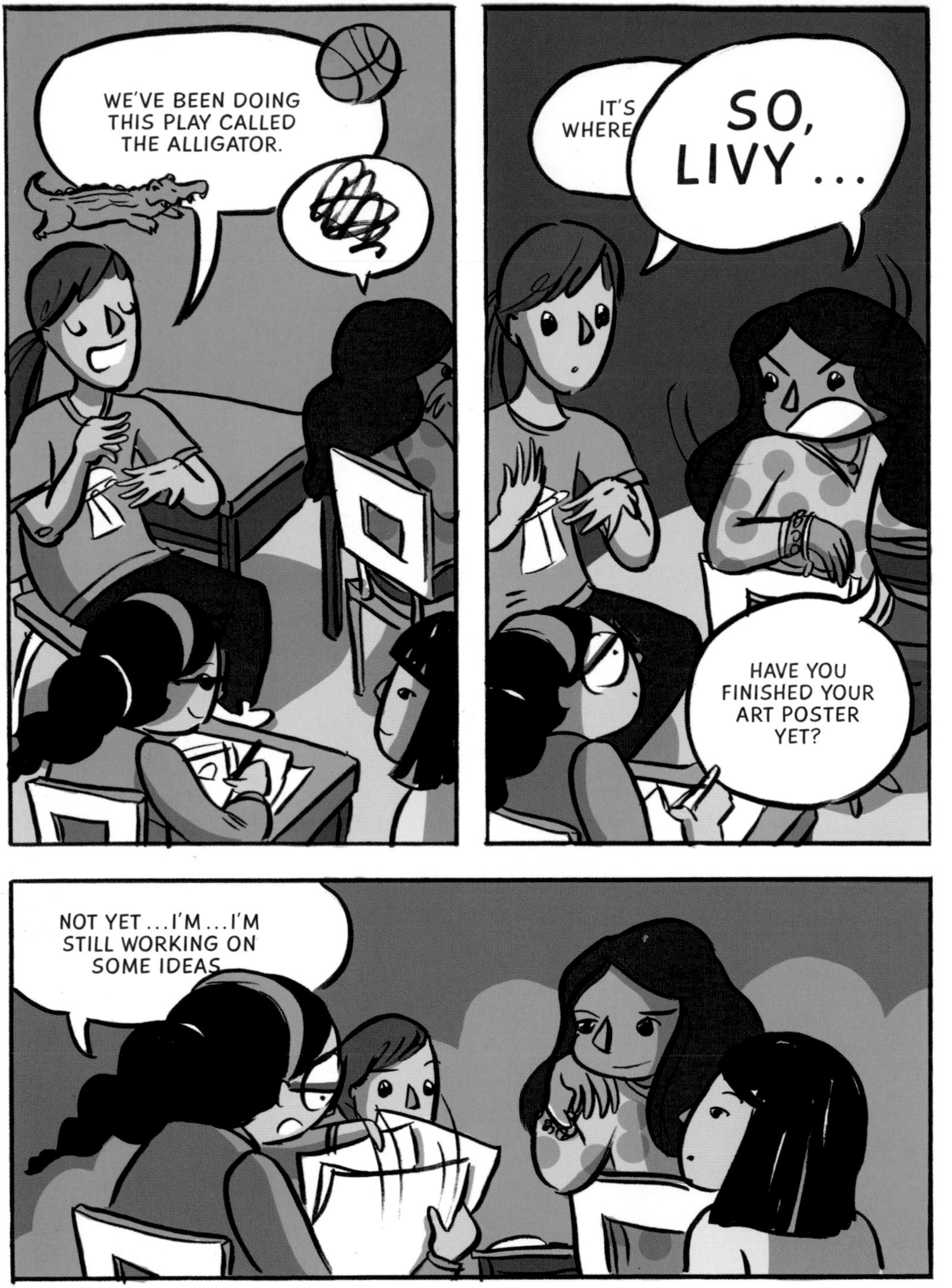
WE'VE BEEN DOING THIS PLAY CALLED THE ALLIGATOR.
IT'S WHERE
SO, LIVY ...
HAVE YOU FINISHED YOUR ART POSTER YET?
NOT YET ... I'M ... I'M STILL WORKING ON SOME IDEAS

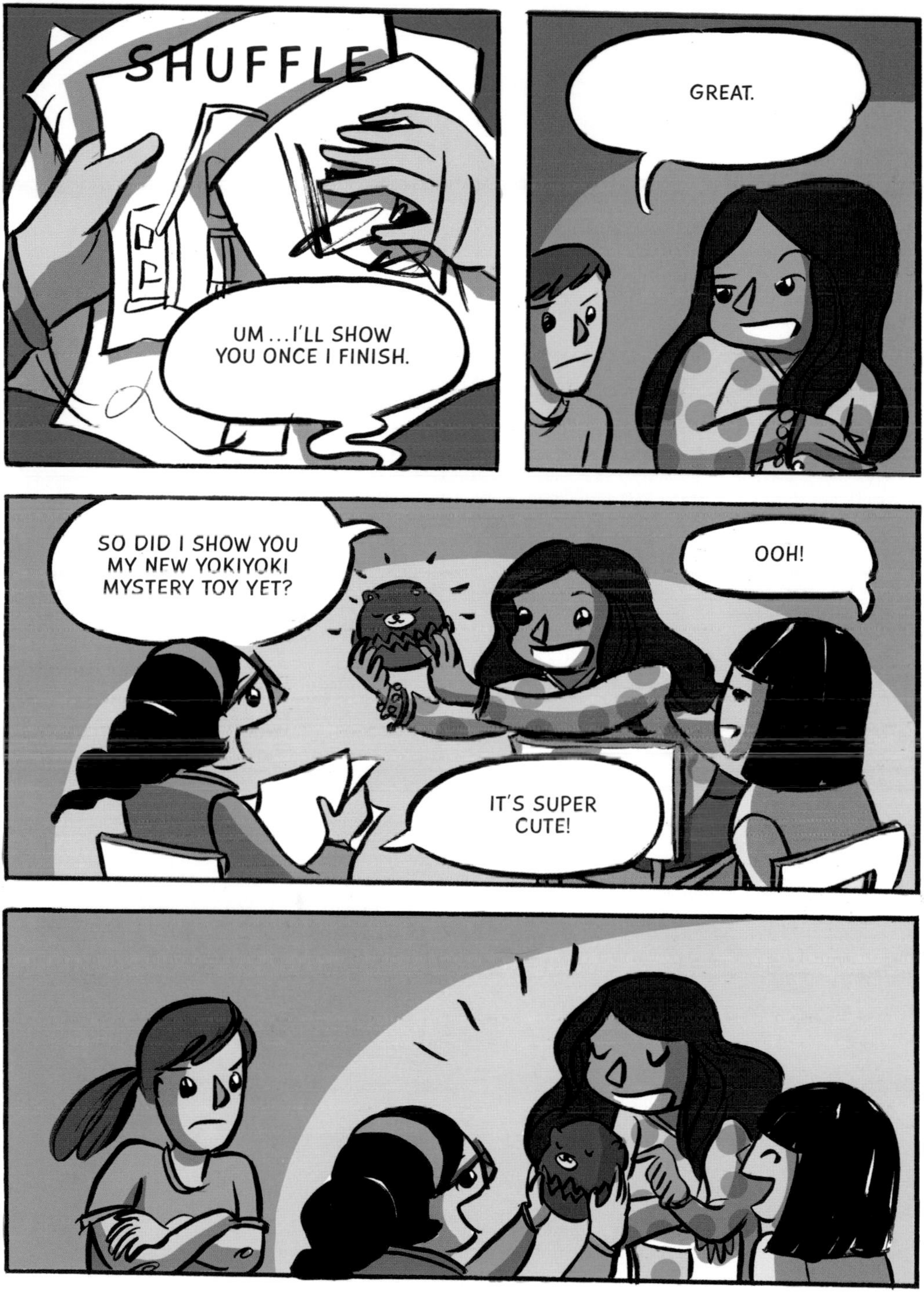
SHUFFLE
UM . . . I'LL SHOW YOU ONCE I FINISH.
GREAT.
SO DID I SHOW YOU MY NEW YOKIYOKI MYSTERY TOY YET?
OOH!
IT'S SUPER CUTE!

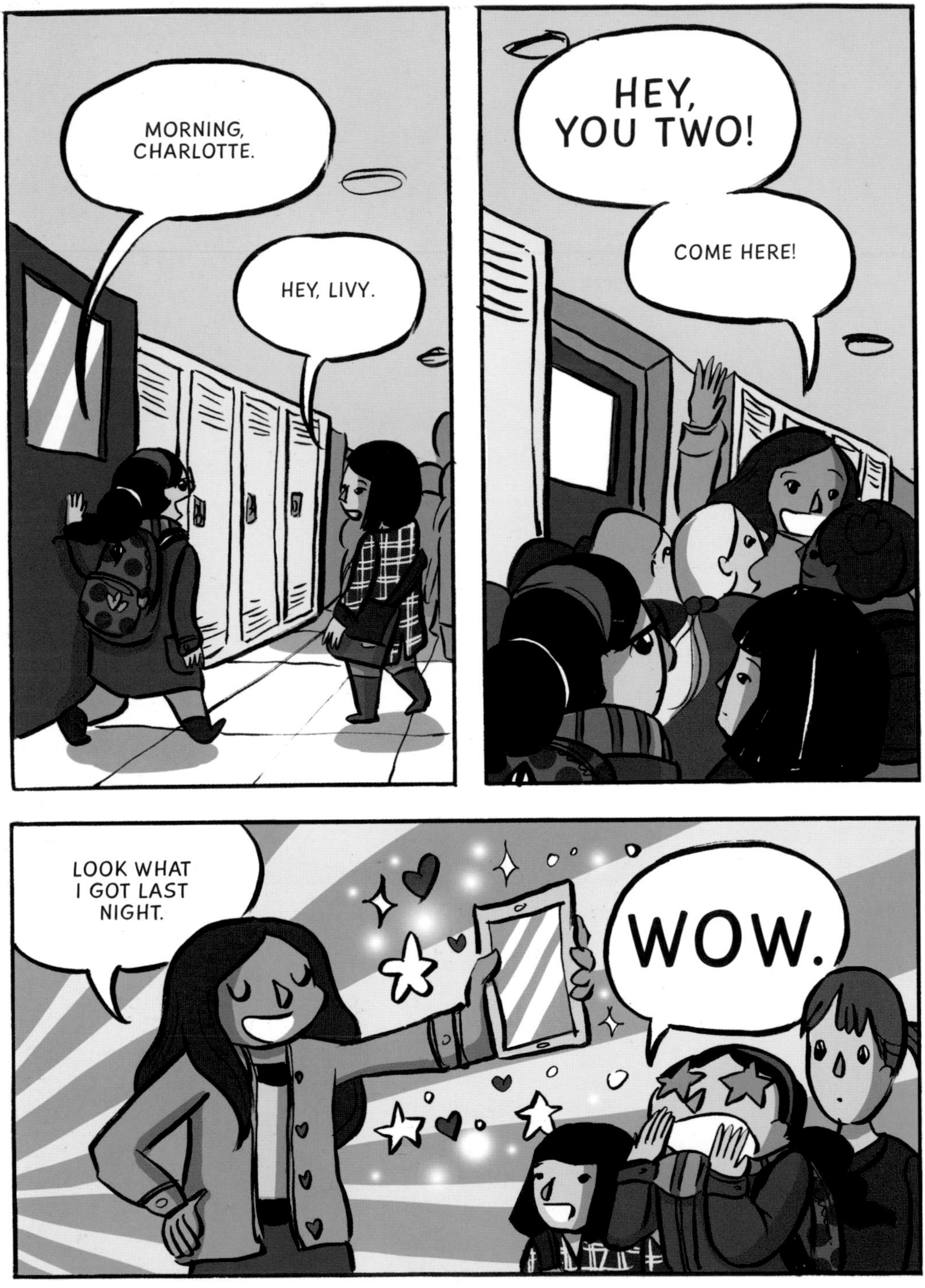
MORNING, CHARLOTTE.
HEY, LIVY.
HEY, YOU TWO!
COME HERE!
LOOK WHAT I GOT LAST NIGHT.
WOW.

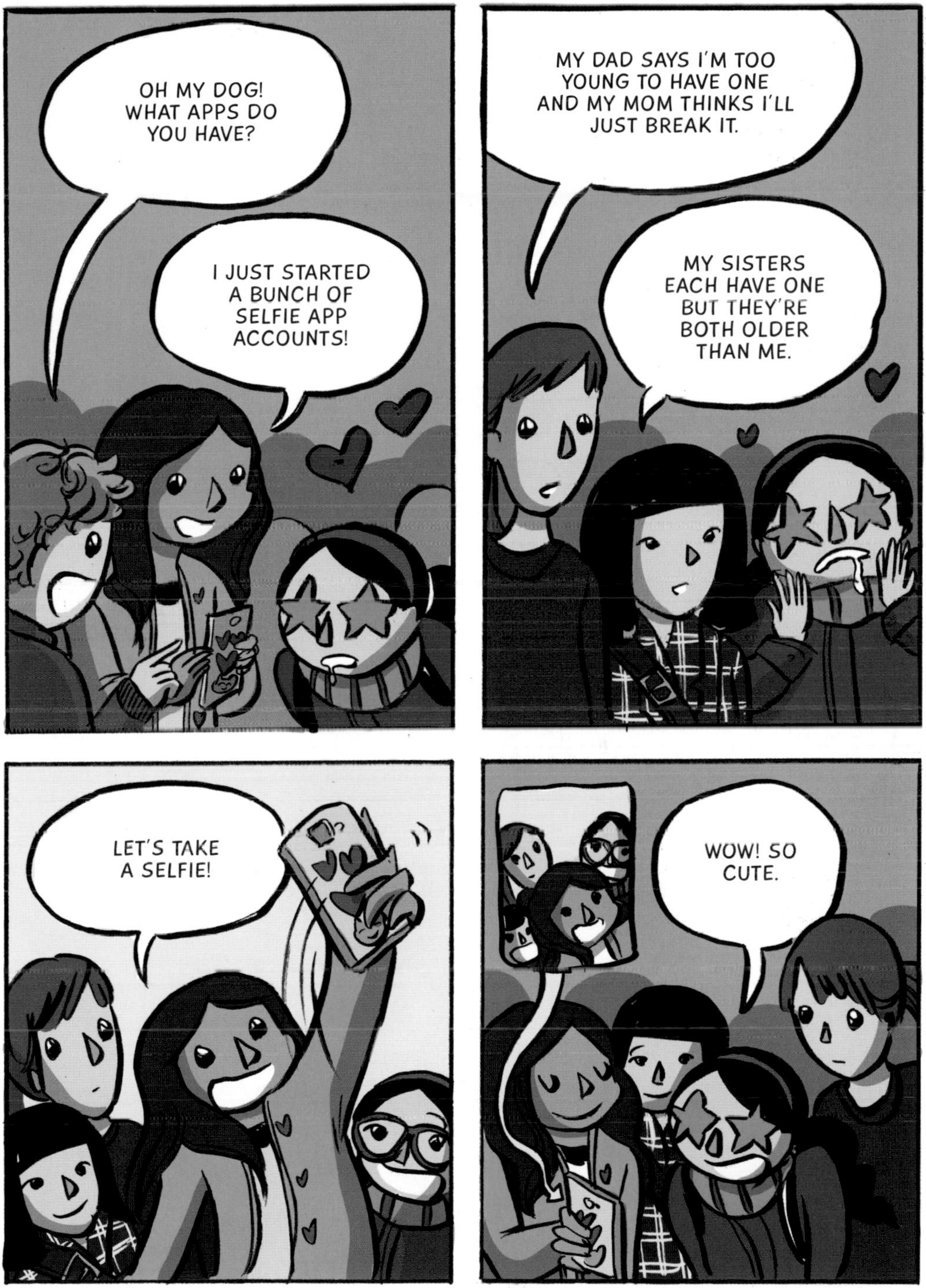
OH MY DOG! WHAT APPS DO YOU HAVE?
I JUST STARTED A BUNCH OF SELFIE APP ACCOUNTS!
MY DAD SAYS I'M TOO YOUNG TO HAVE ONE AND MY MOM THINKS I'LL JUST BREAK IT.
MY SISTERS EACH HAVE ONE BUT THEY'RE BOTH OLDER THAN ME.
LET'S TAKE A SELFIE!
WOW! SO CUTE.

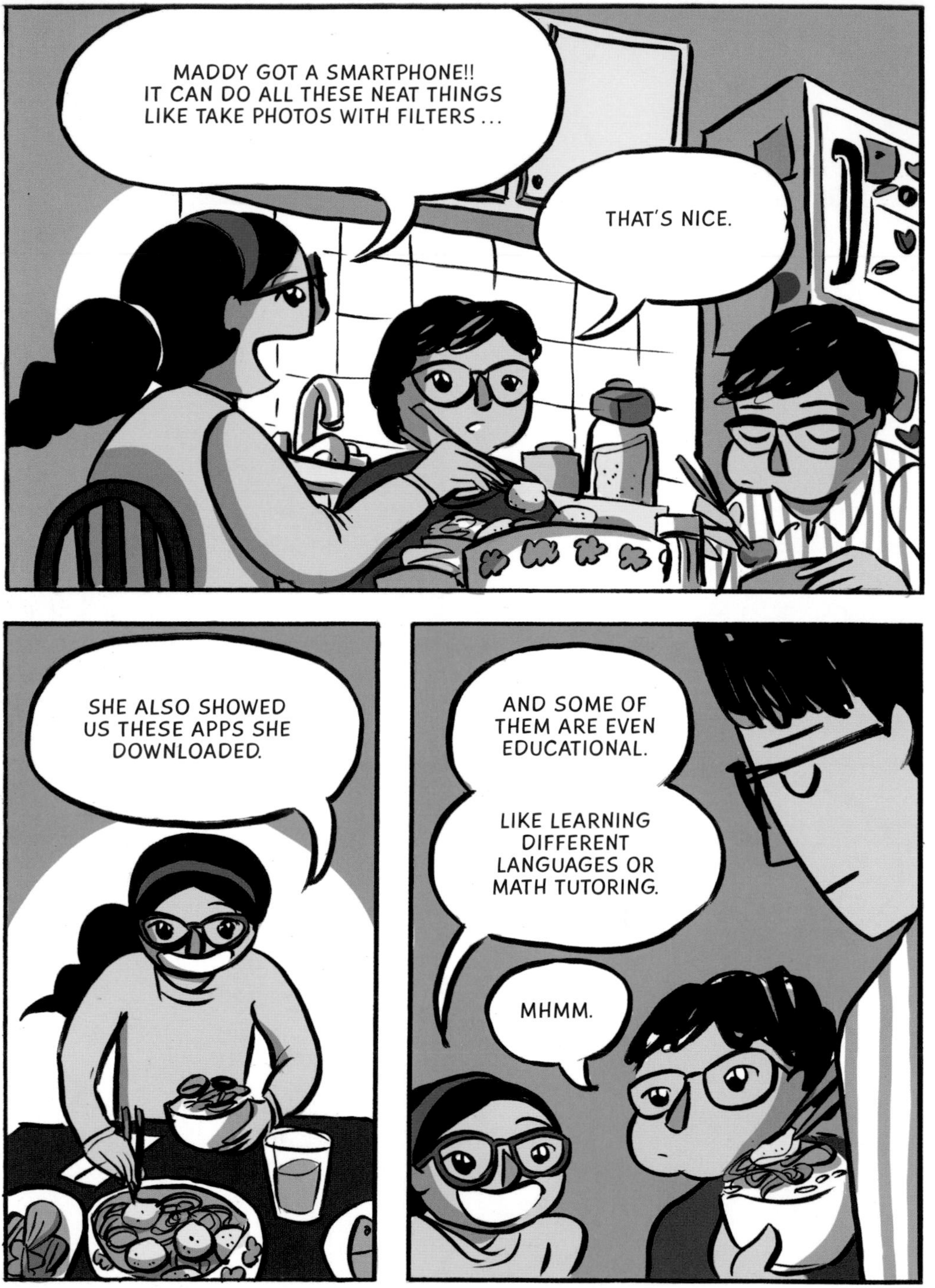
MADDY GOT A SMARTPHONE!! IT CAN DO ALL THESE NEAT THINGS LIKE TAKE PHOTOS WITH FILTERS . . .
THAT'S NICE.
SHE ALSO SHOWED US THESE APPS SHE DOWNLOADED.
AND SOME OF THEM ARE EVEN EDUCATIONAL.
LIKE LEARNING DIFFERENT LANGUAGES OR MATH TUTORING.
MHMM.

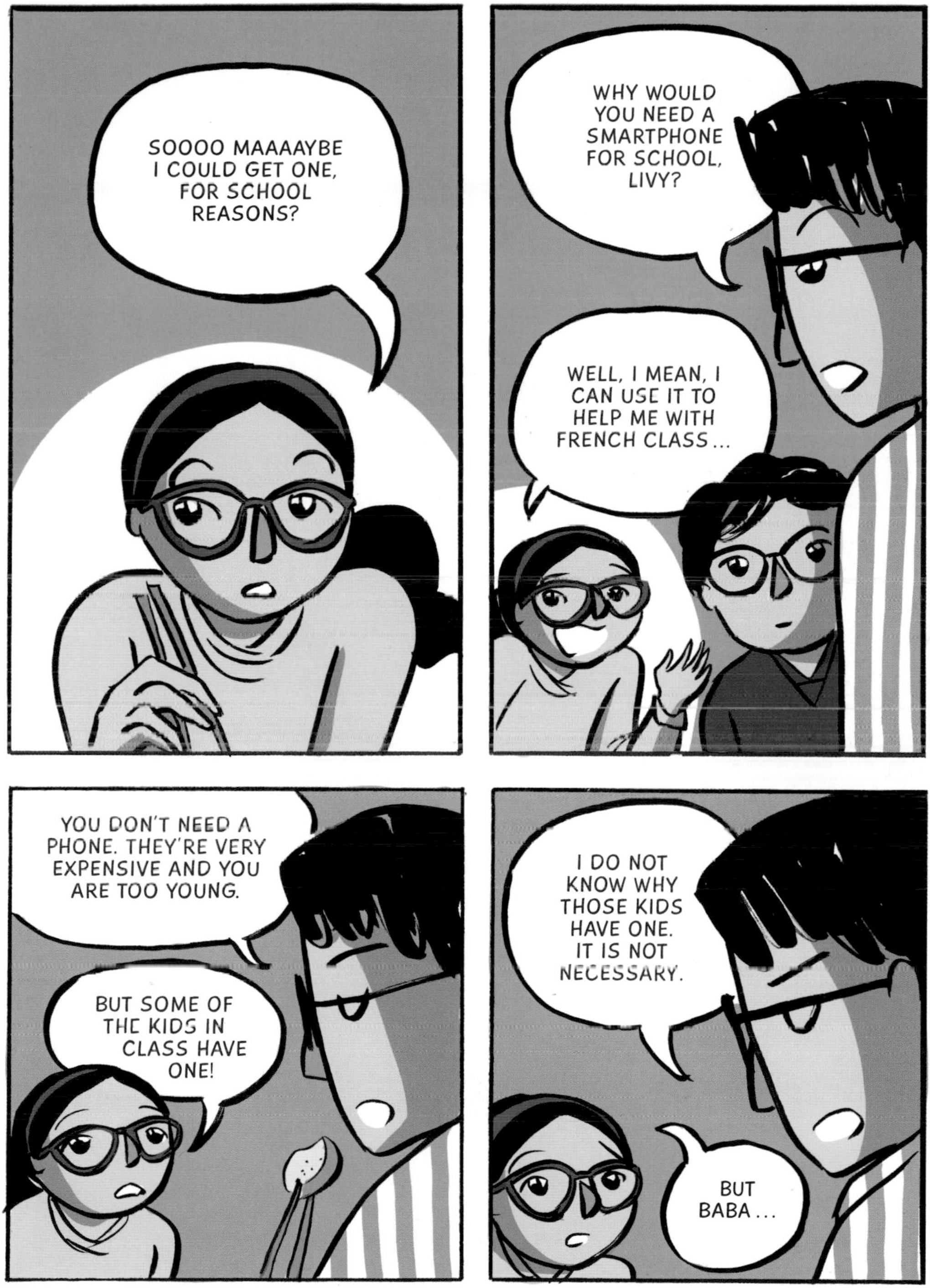
SOOOO MAAAAYBE I COULD GET ONE, FOR SCHOOL REASONS?
WHY WOULD YOU NEED A SMARTPHONE FOR SCHOOL, LIVY?
WELL, I MEAN, I CAN USE IT TO HELP ME WITH FRENCH CLASS...
YOU DON'T NEED A PHONE. THEY'RE VERY EXPENSIVE AND YOU ARE TOO YOUNG.
BUT SOME OF THE KIDS IN CLASS HAVE ONE!
I DO NOT KNOW WHY THOSE KIDS HAVE ONE. IT IS NOT NECESSARY.
BUT BABA...

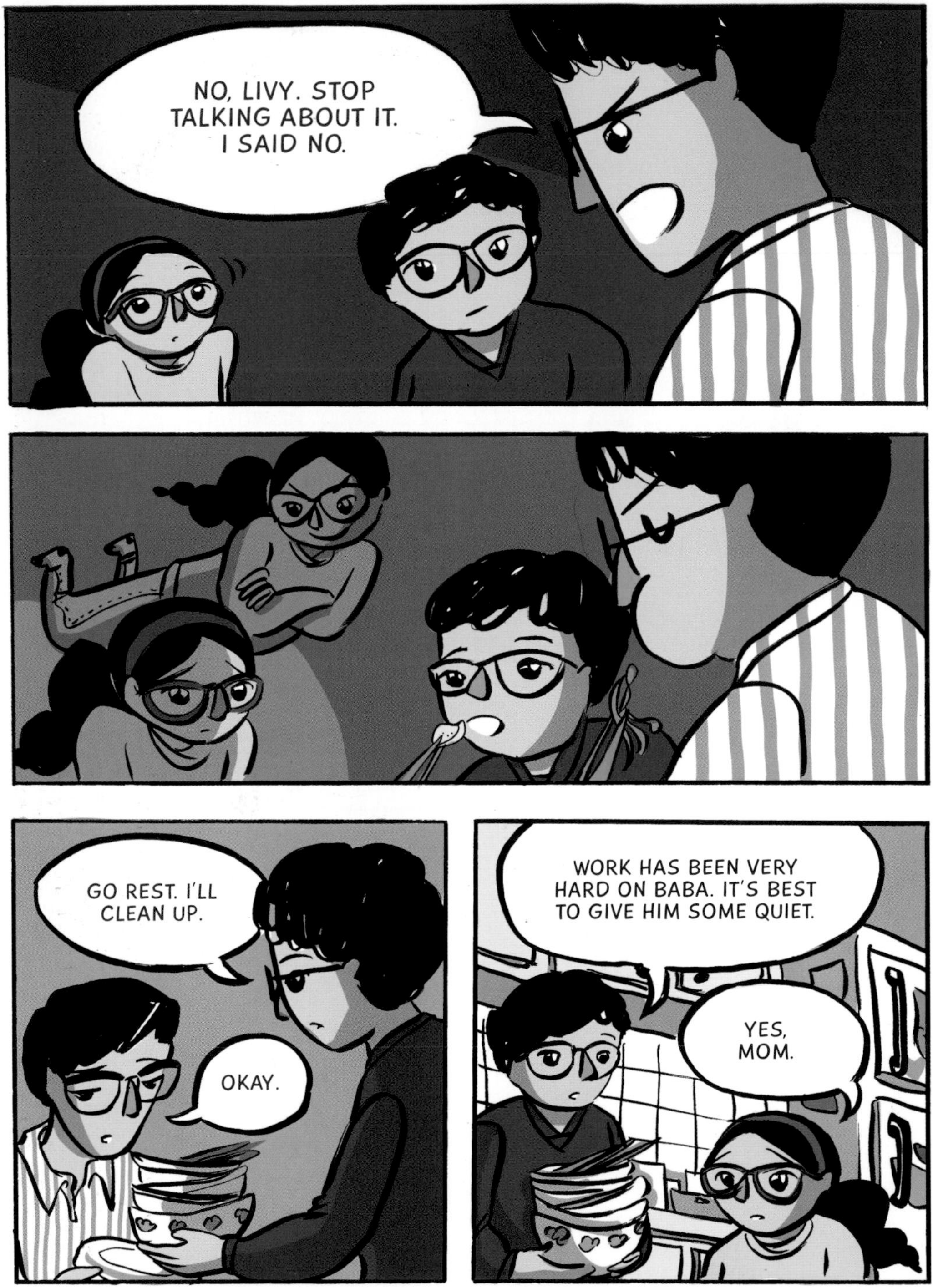
NO, LIVY. STOP TALKING ABOUT IT. I SAID NO.
GO REST. I'LL CLEAN UP.
OKAY.
WORK HAS BEEN VERY HARD ON BABA. IT'S BEST TO GIVE HIM SOME QUIET.
YES, MOM.

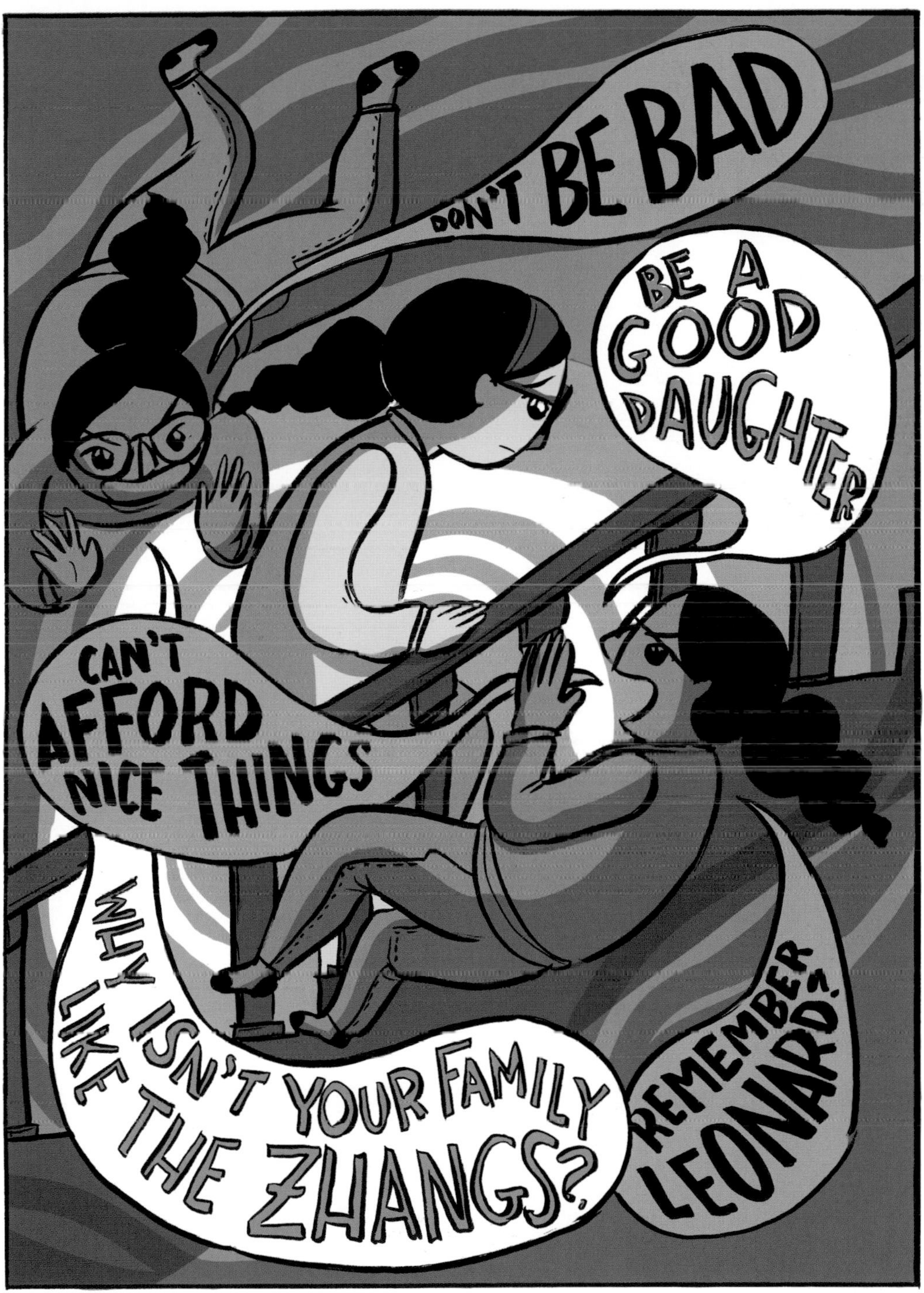
DON'T BE BAD
BE A GOOD DAUGHTER
CAN'T AFFORD NICE THINGS
WHY ISN'T YOUR FAMILY LIKE THE ZHANGS?
REMEMBER LEONARD?

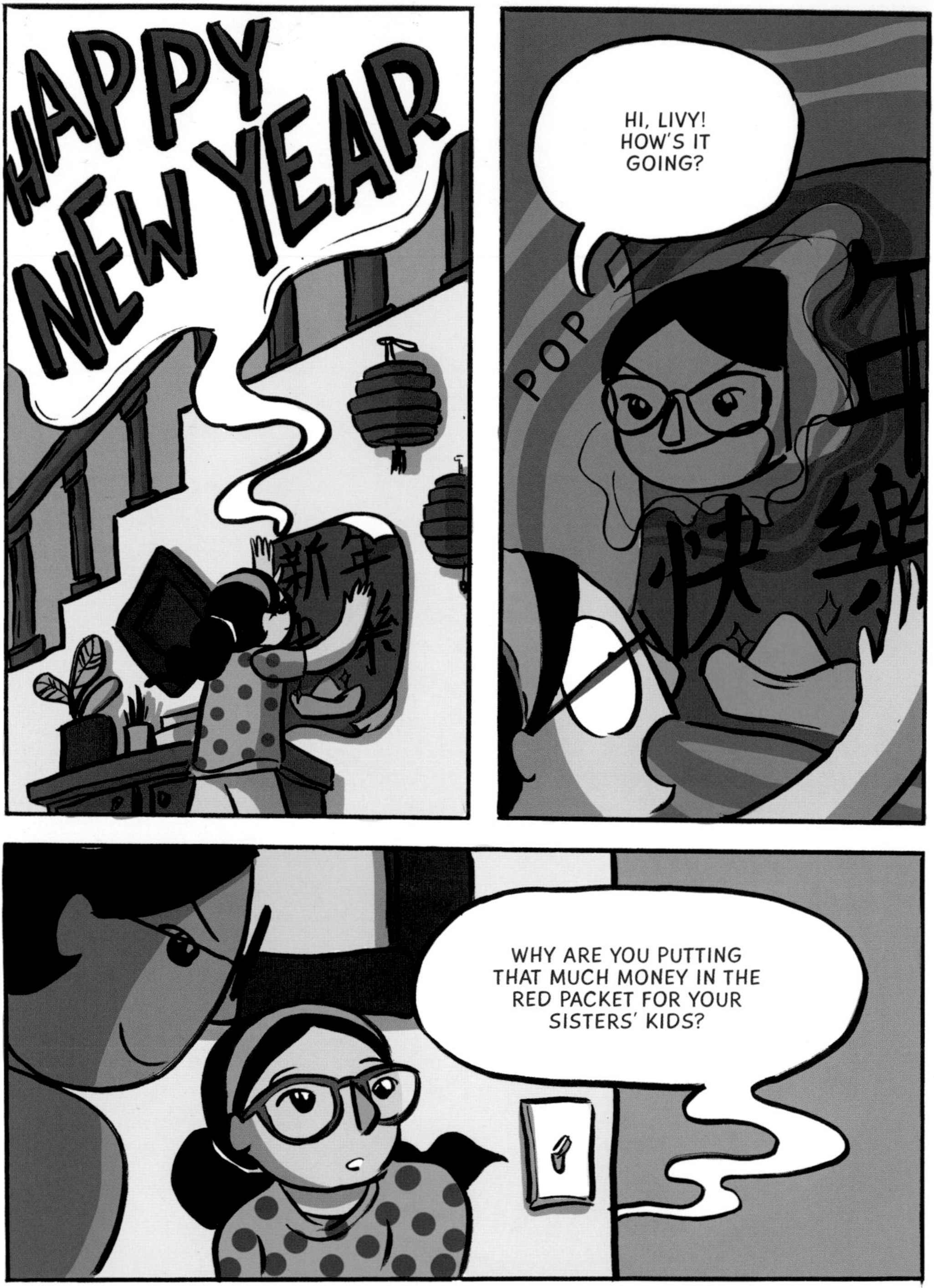
HAPPY NEW YEAR
HI, LIVY! HOW'S IT GOING?
POP
WHY ARE YOU PUTTING THAT MUCH MONEY IN THE RED PACKET FOR YOUR SISTERS' KIDS?

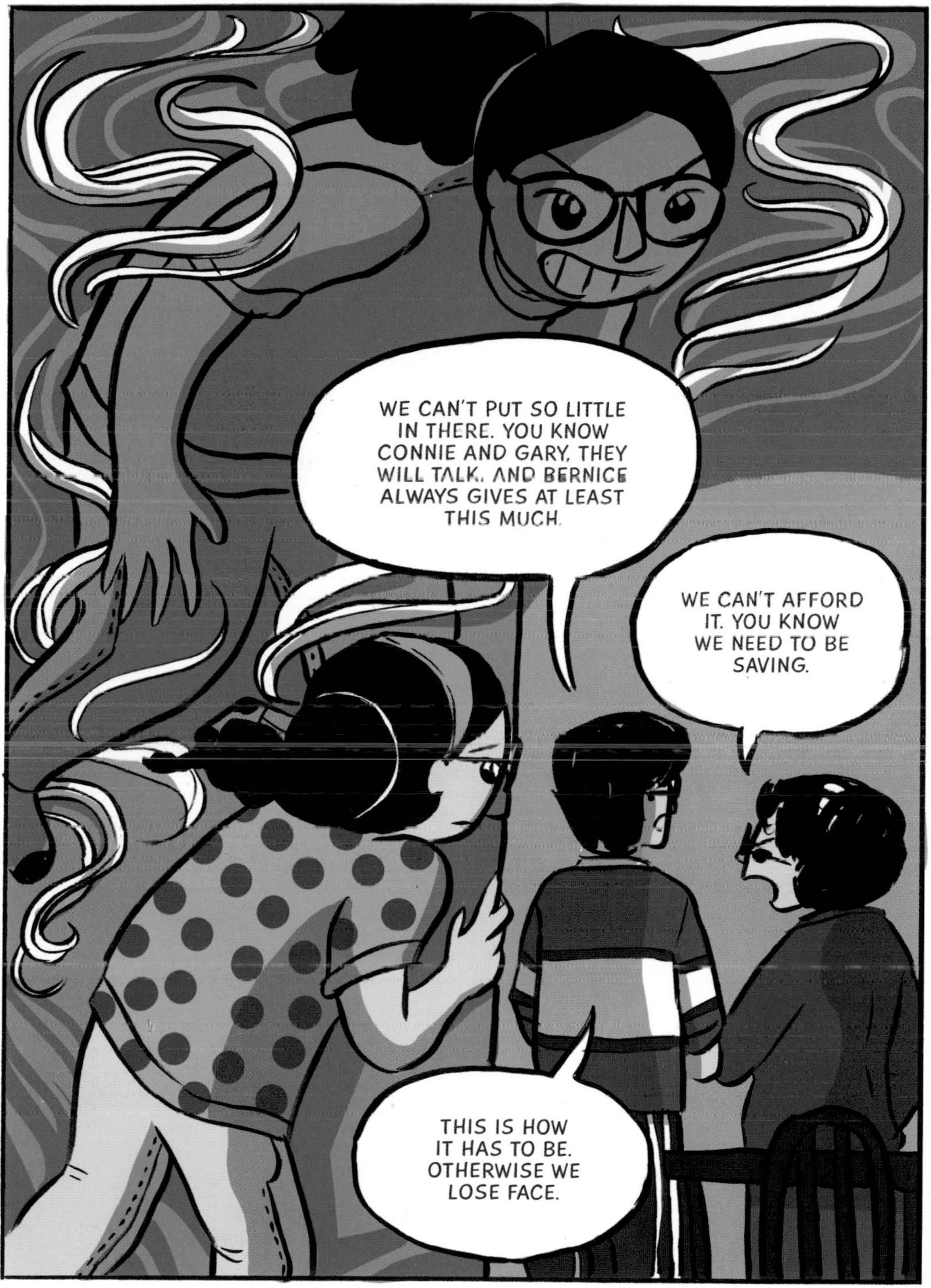
WE CAN'T PUT SO LITTLE IN THERE. YOU KNOW CONNIE AND GARY, THEY WILL TALK. AND BERNICE ALWAYS GIVES AT LEAST THIS MUCH.
WE CAN'T AFFORD IT. YOU KNOW WE NEED TO BE SAVING.
THIS IS HOW IT HAS TO BE. OTHERWISE WE LOSE FACE.

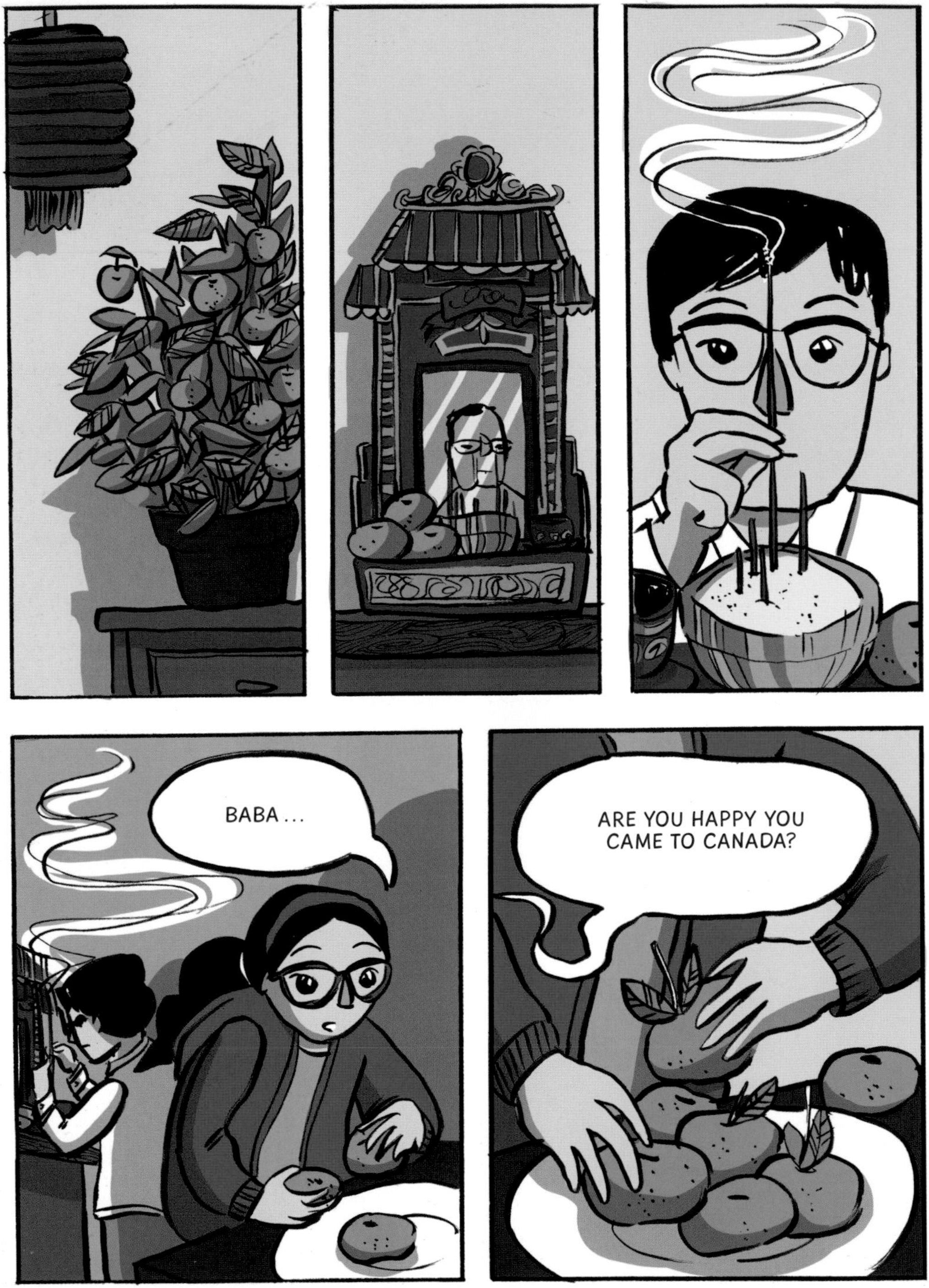
BABA . . .
ARE YOU HAPPY YOU CAME TO CANADA?

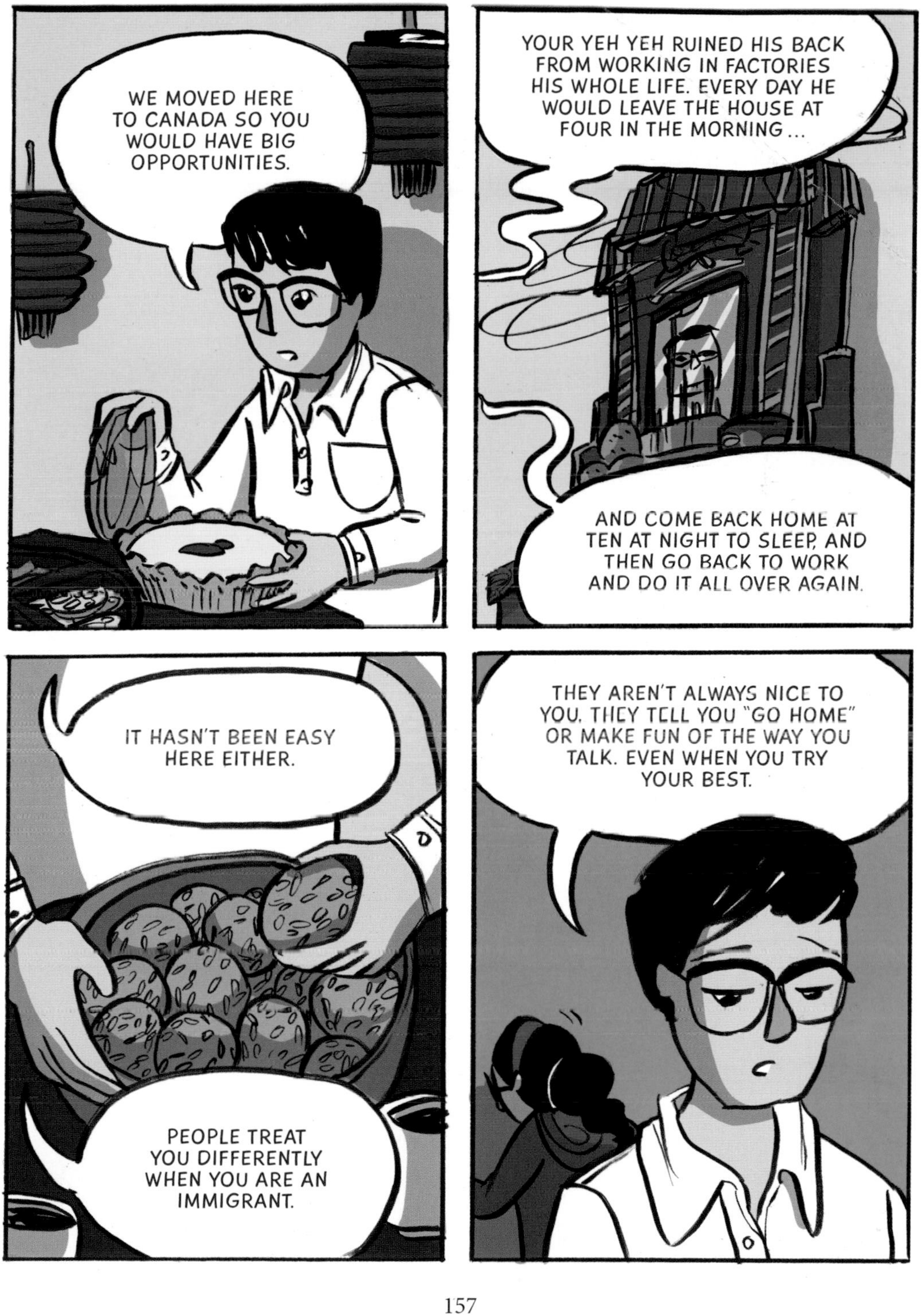
WE MOVED HERE TO CANADA SO YOU WOULD HAVE BIG OPPORTUNITIES.
YOUR YEH YEH RUINED HIS BACK FROM WORKING IN FACTORIES HIS WHOLE LIFE. EVERY DAY HE WOULD LEAVE THE HOUSE AT FOUR IN THE MORNING...
AND COME BACK HOME AT TEN AT NIGHT TO SLEEP, AND THEN GO BACK TO WORK AND DO IT ALL OVER AGAIN.
IT HASN'T BEEN EASY HERE EITHER.
PEOPLE TREAT YOU DIFFERENTLY WHEN YOU ARE AN IMMIGRANT.
THEY AREN'T ALWAYS NICE TO YOU. THEY TELL YOU "GO HOME" OR MAKE FUN OF THE WAY YOU TALK. EVEN WHEN YOU TRY YOUR BEST.

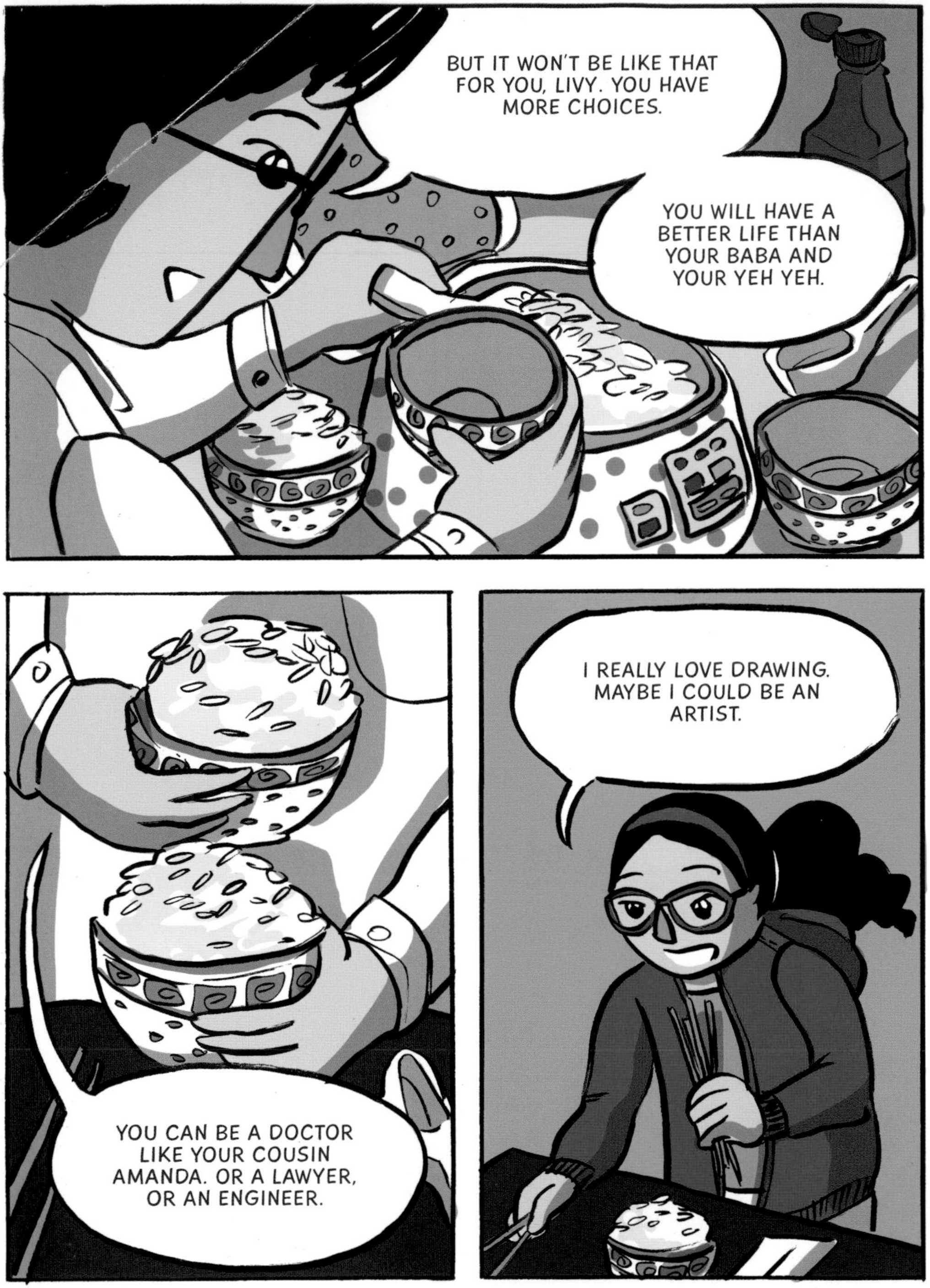
BUT IT WON'T BE LIKE THAT FOR YOU, LIVY. YOU HAVE MORE CHOICES.
YOU WILL HAVE A BETTER LIFE THAN YOUR BABA AND YOUR YEH YEH.
YOU CAN BE A DOCTOR LIKE YOUR COUSIN AMANDA. OR A LAWYER, OR AN ENGINEER.
I REALLY LOVE DRAWING. MAYBE I COULD BE AN ARTIST.

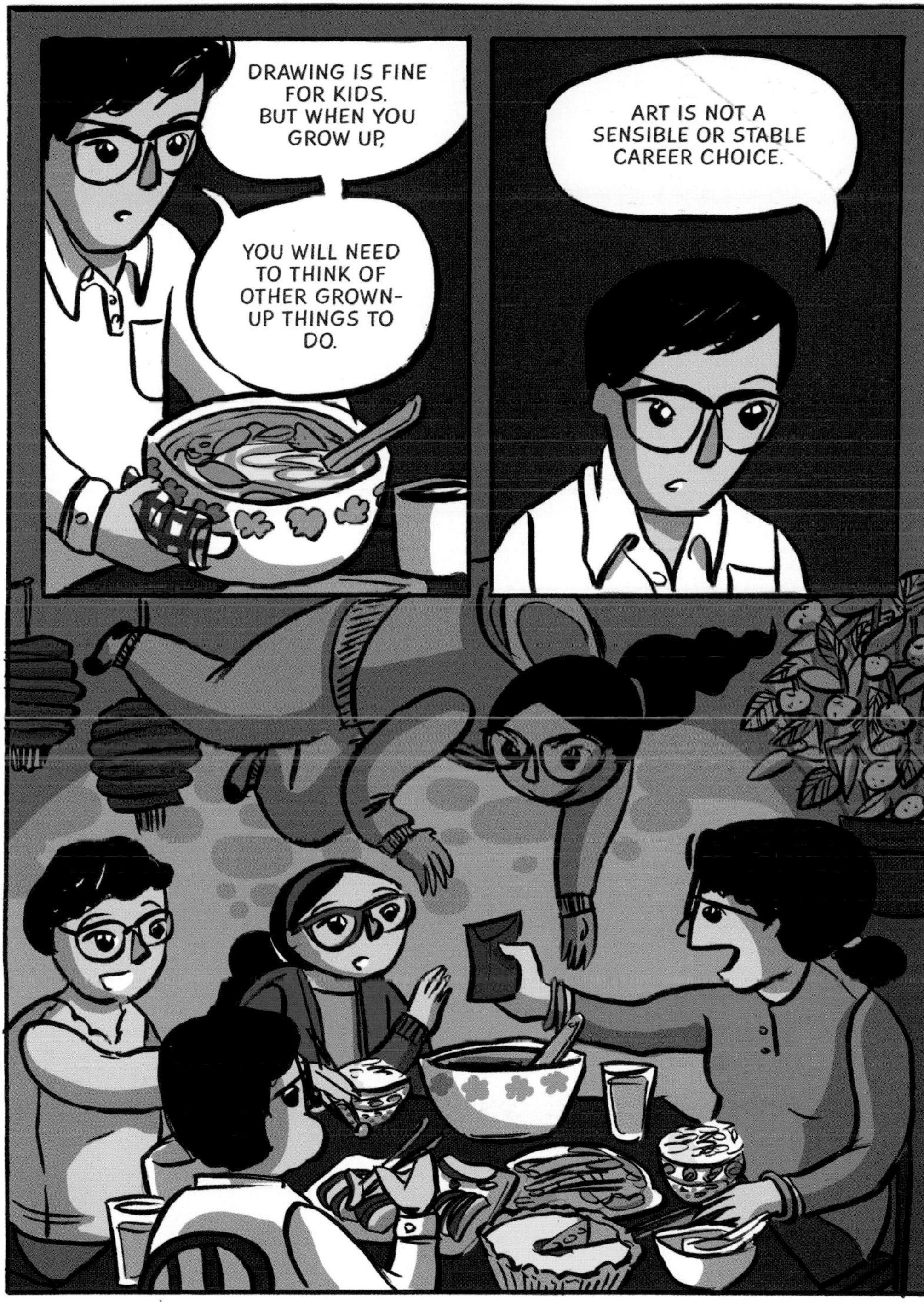
DRAWING IS FINE FOR KIDS. BUT WHEN YOU GROW UP,
YOU WILL NEED TO THINK OF OTHER GROWN-UP THINGS TO DO.
ART IS NOT A SENSIBLE OR STABLE CAREER CHOICE.

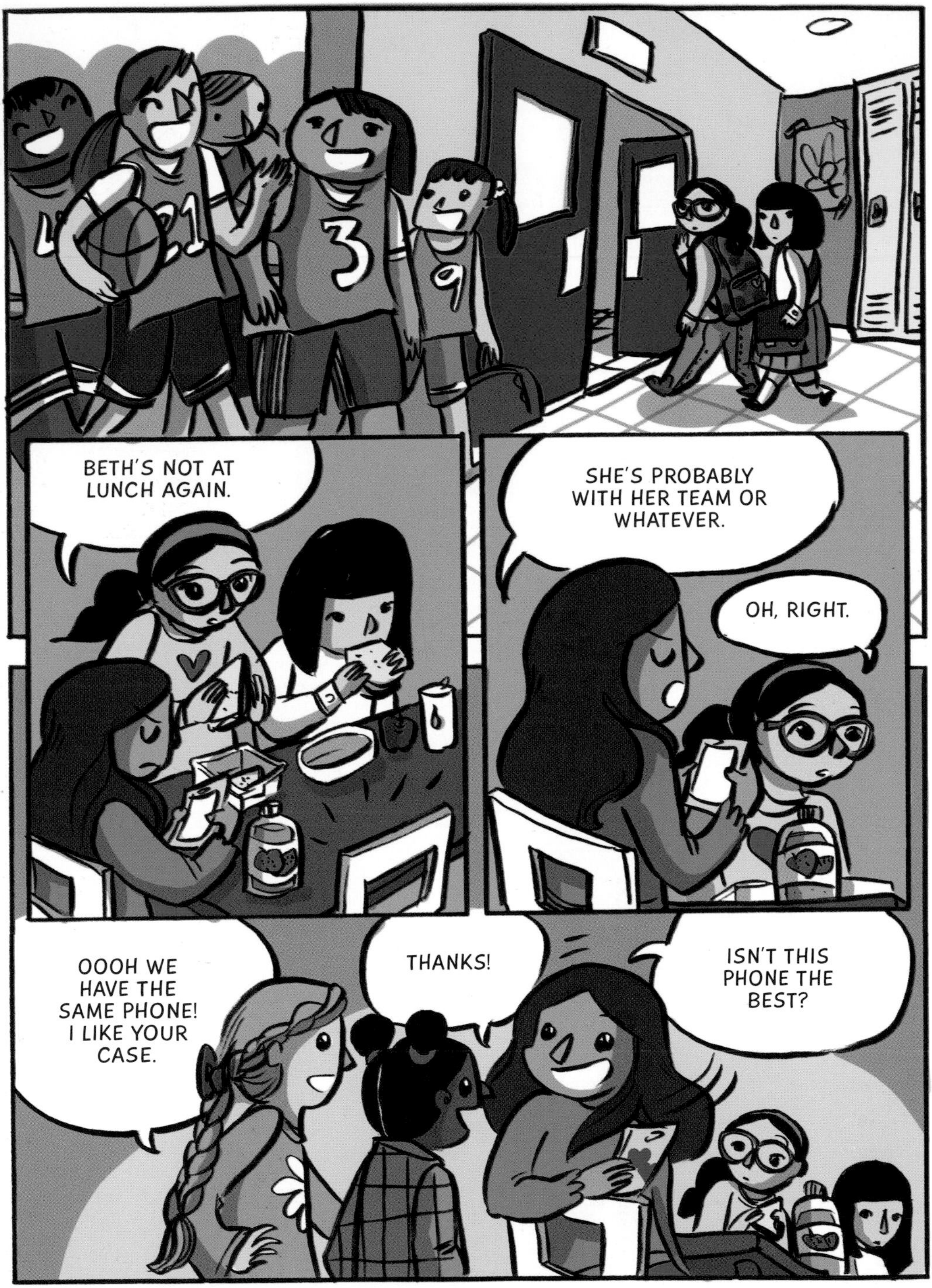
BETH'S NOT AT LUNCH AGAIN.
SHE'S PROBABLY WITH HER TEAM OR WHATEVER.
OH, RIGHT.
OOOH WE HAVE THE SAME PHONE! I LIKE YOUR CASE.
THANKS!
ISN'T THIS PHONE THE BEST?

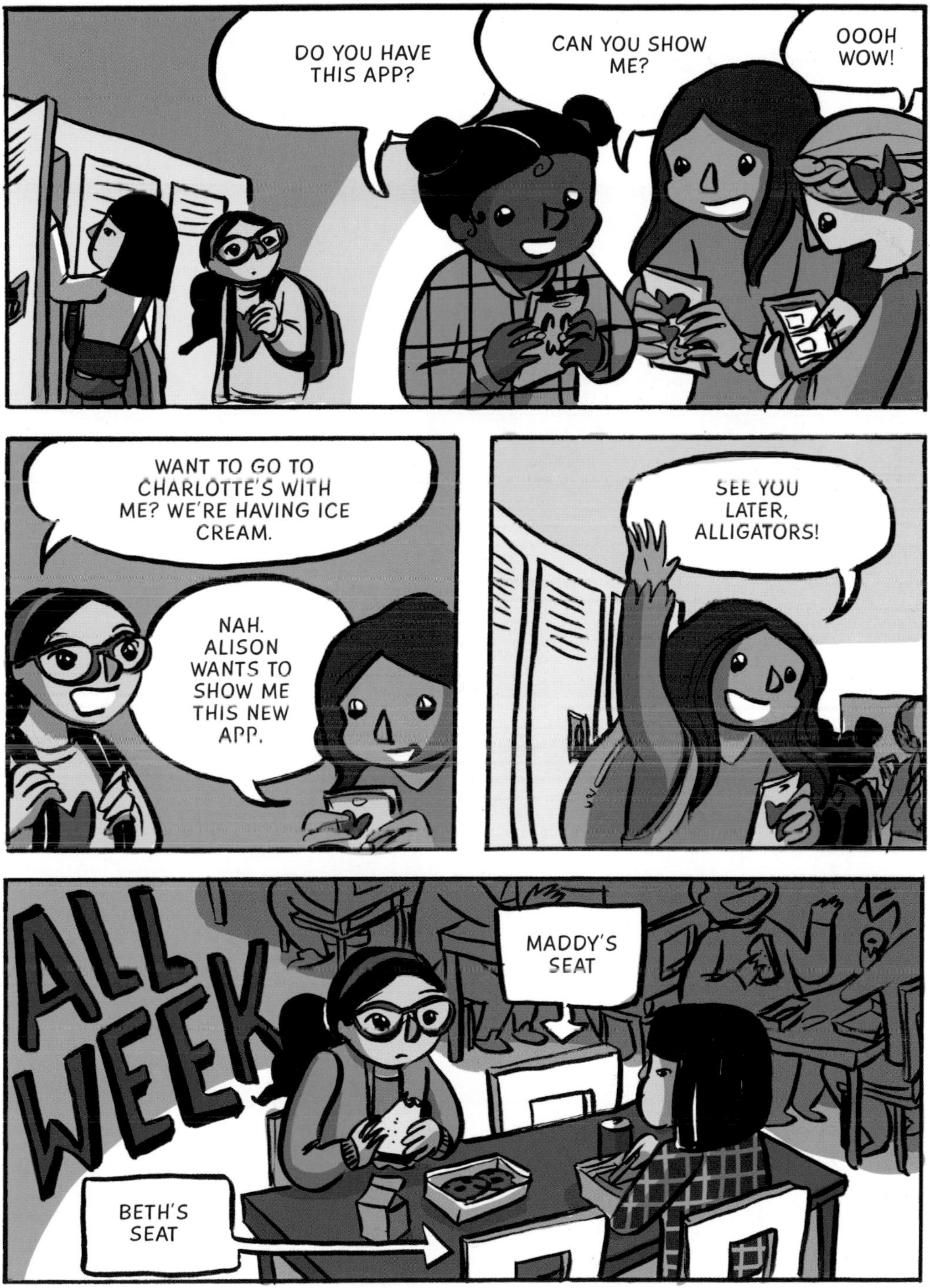
DO YOU HAVE THIS APP?
CAN YOU SHOW ME?
OOOH WOW!
WANT TO GO TO CHARLOTTE'S WITH ME? WE'RE HAVING ICE CREAM.
NAH. ALISON WANTS TO SHOW ME THIS NEW APP.
SEE YOU LATER, ALLIGATORS!
ALL WEEK
MADDY'S SEAT
BETH'S SEAT

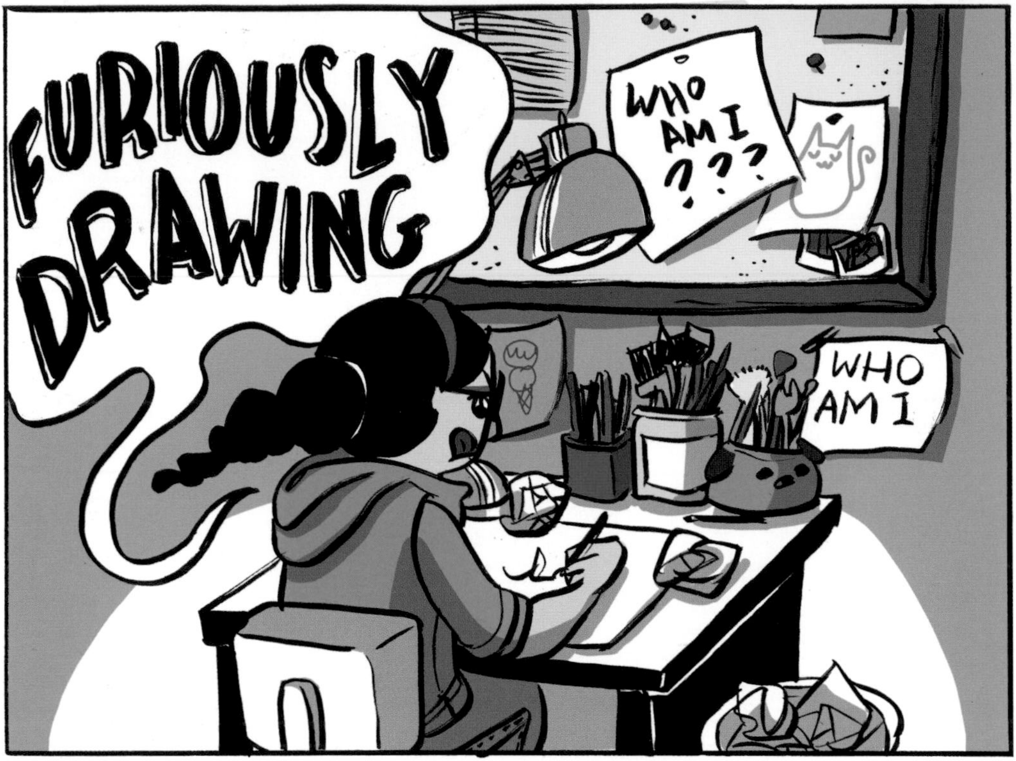
FURIOUSLY DRAWING
WHO AM I ???
WHO AM I

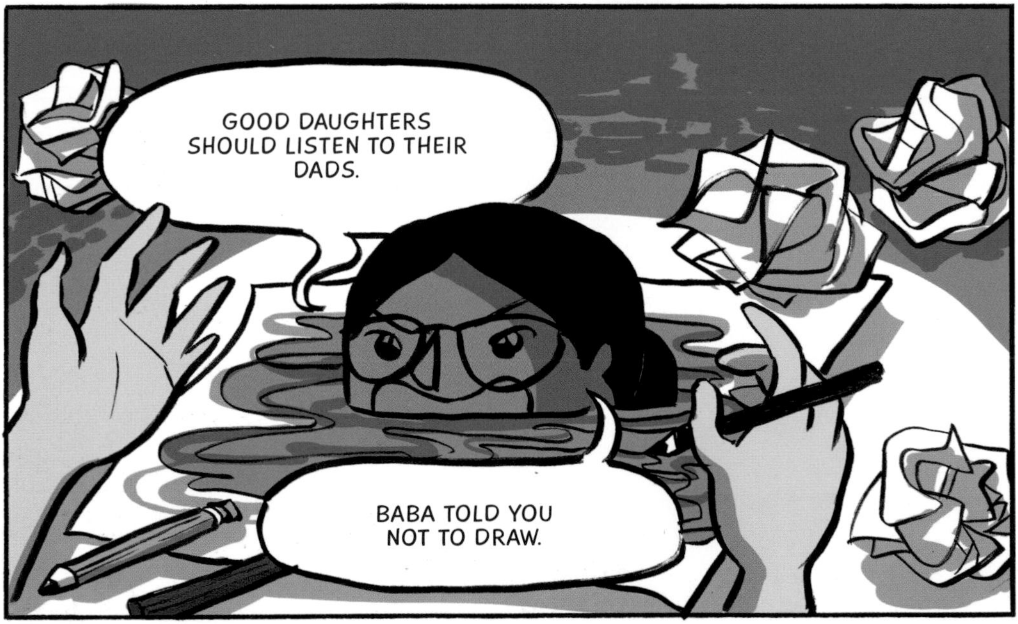
GOOD DAUGHTERS SHOULD LISTEN TO THEIR DADS.
BABA TOLD YOU NOT TO DRAW.

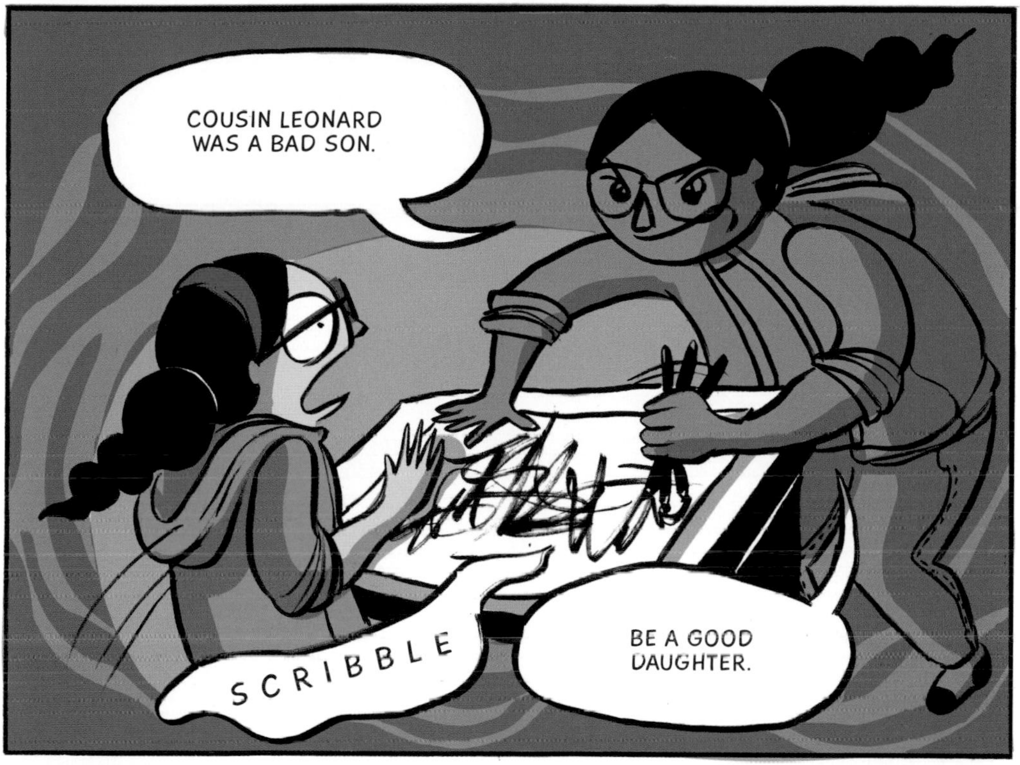
COUSIN LEONARD WAS A BAD SON.
SCRIBBLE
BE A GOOD DAUGHTER.

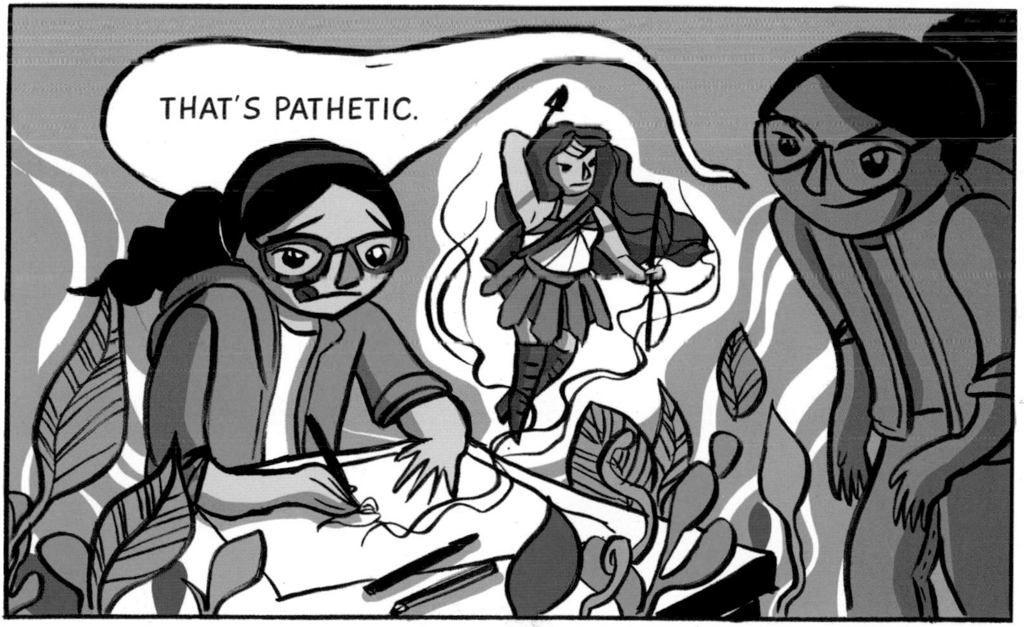
THAT'S PATHETIC.

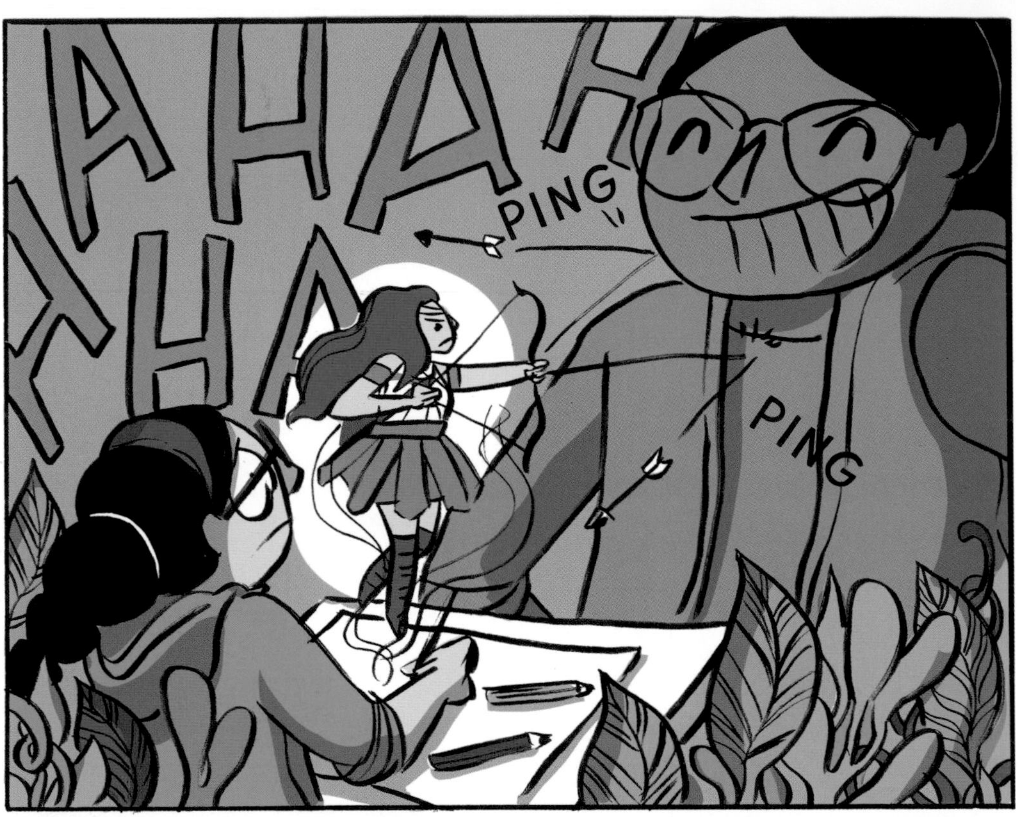
HAHAHA
HA
PING
PING

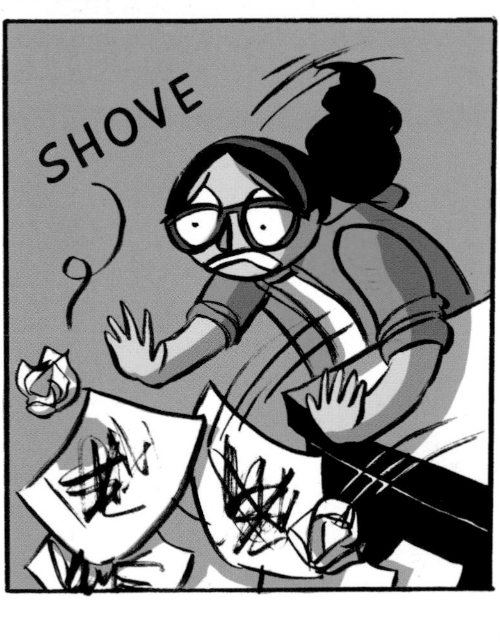
SHOVE

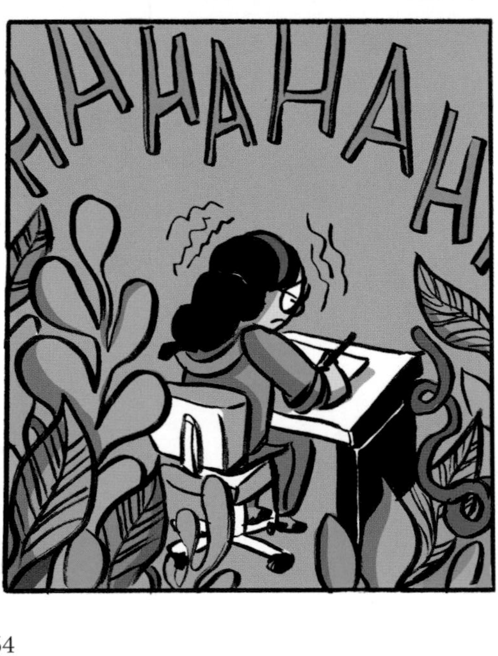
HAHAHAHA

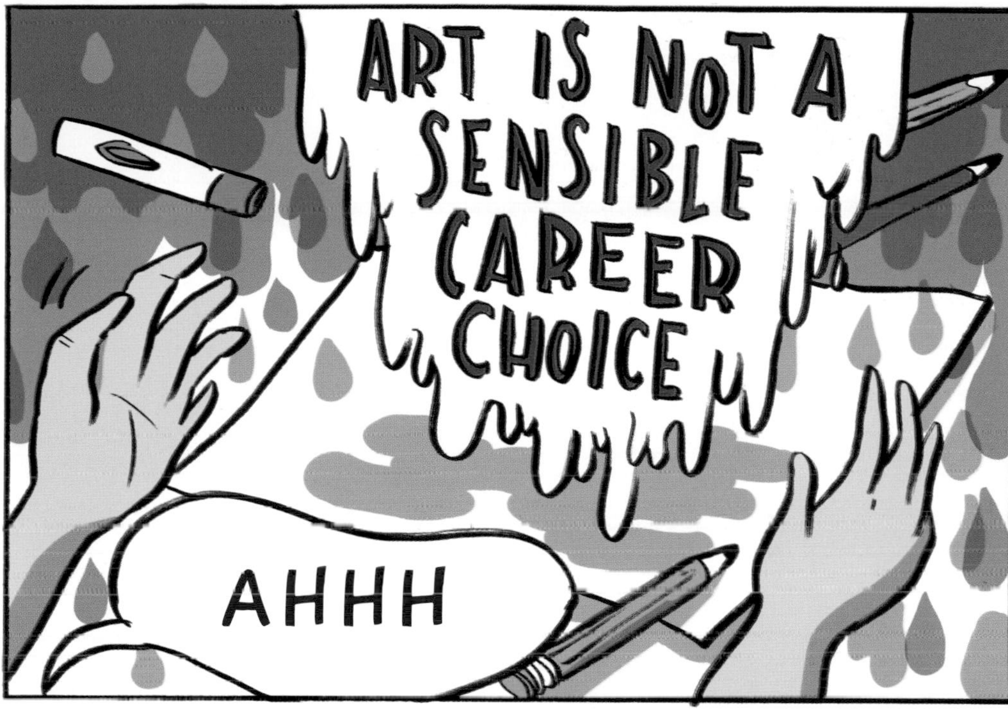
ART IS NOT A SENSIBLE CAREER CHOICE
AHHH

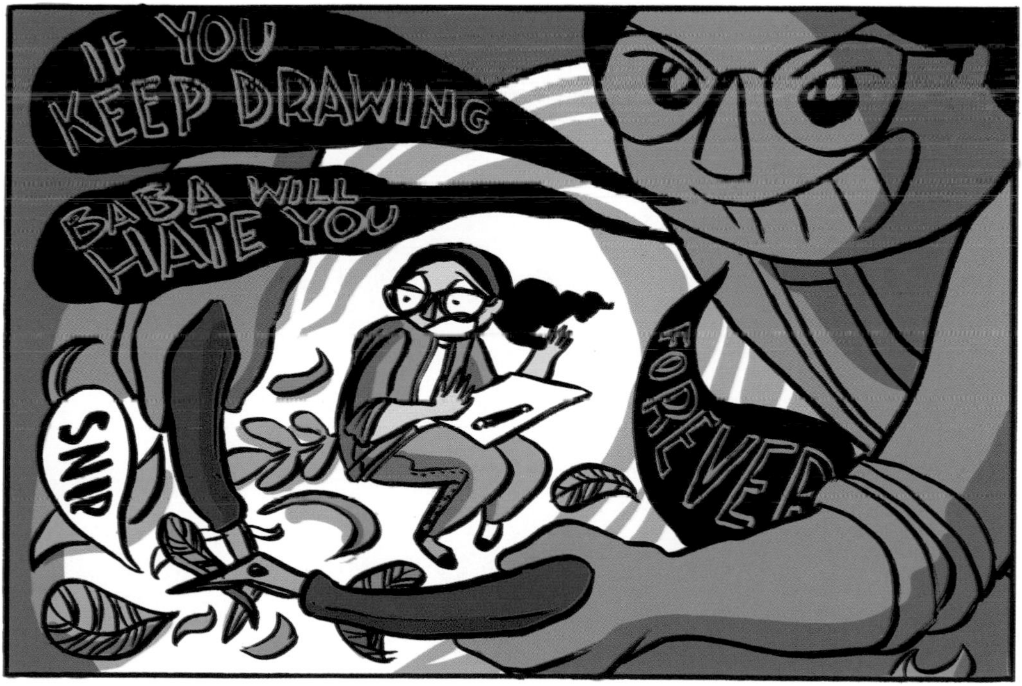
IF YOU KEEP DRAWING
BABA WILL HATE YOU
FOREVER
SNIP

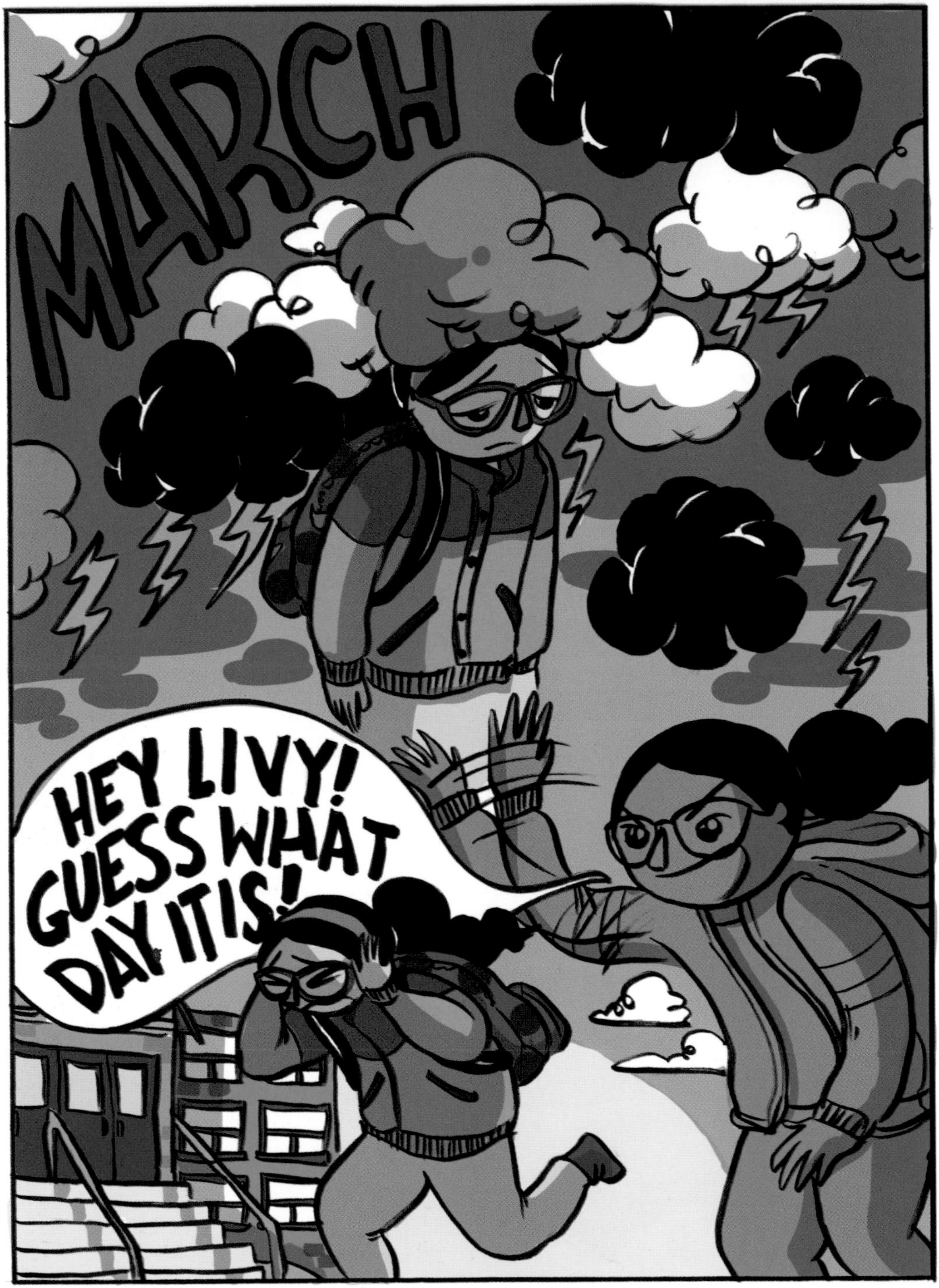
MARCH
HEY LIVY! GUESS WHAT DAY IT IS!

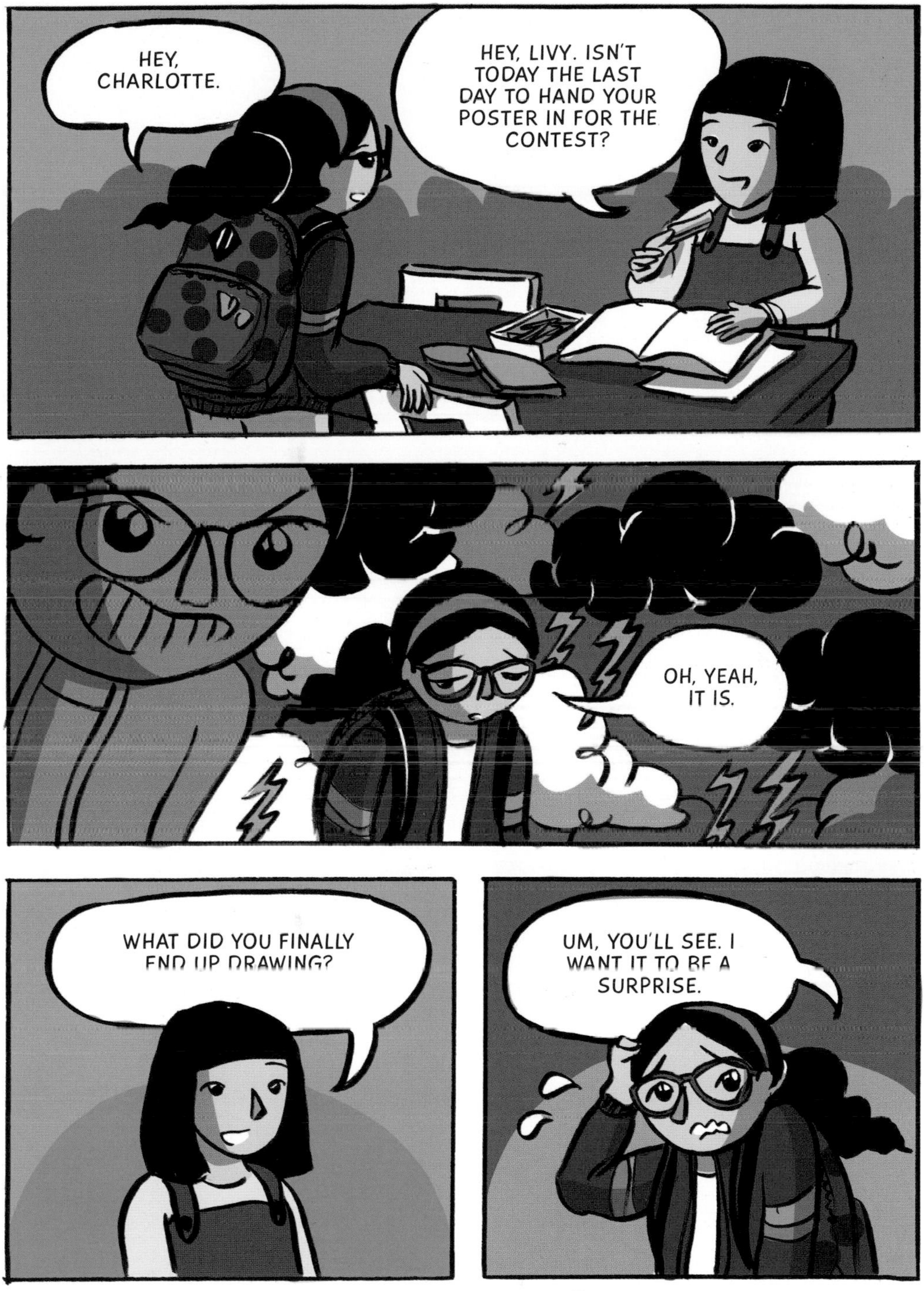
HEY, CHARLOTTE.
HEY, LIVY. ISN'T TODAY THE LAST DAY TO HAND YOUR POSTER IN FOR THE CONTEST?
OH, YEAH, IT IS.
WHAT DID YOU FINALLY END UP DRAWING?
UM, YOU'LL SEE. I WANT IT TO BE A SURPRISE.

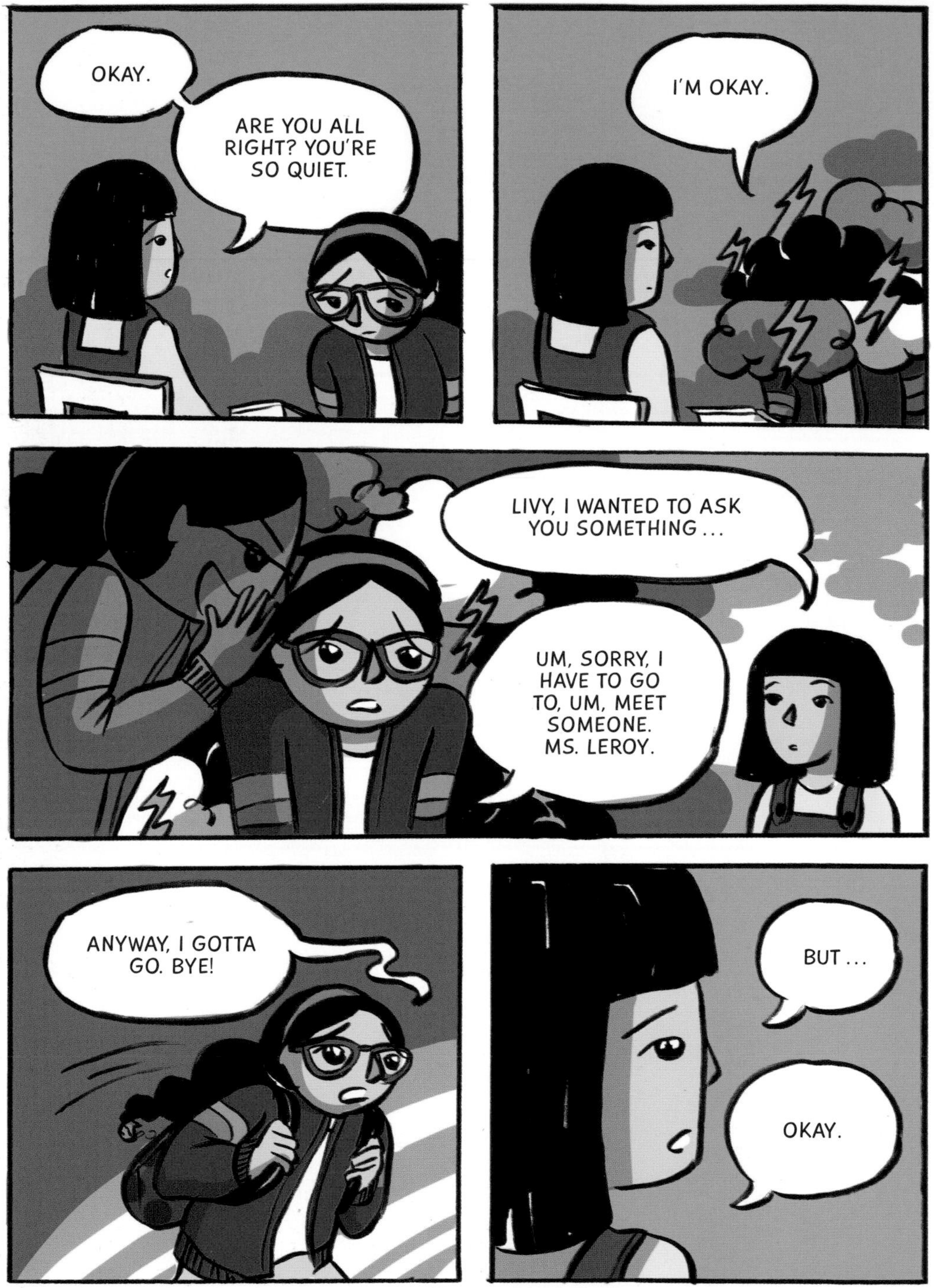
OKAY.
ARE YOU ALL RIGHT? YOU'RE SO QUIET.
I'M OKAY.
LIVY, I WANTED TO ASK YOU SOMETHING ...
UM, SORRY, I HAVE TO GO TO, UM, MEET SOMEONE. MS. LEROY.
ANYWAY, I GOTTA GO. BYE!
BUT ...
OKAY.

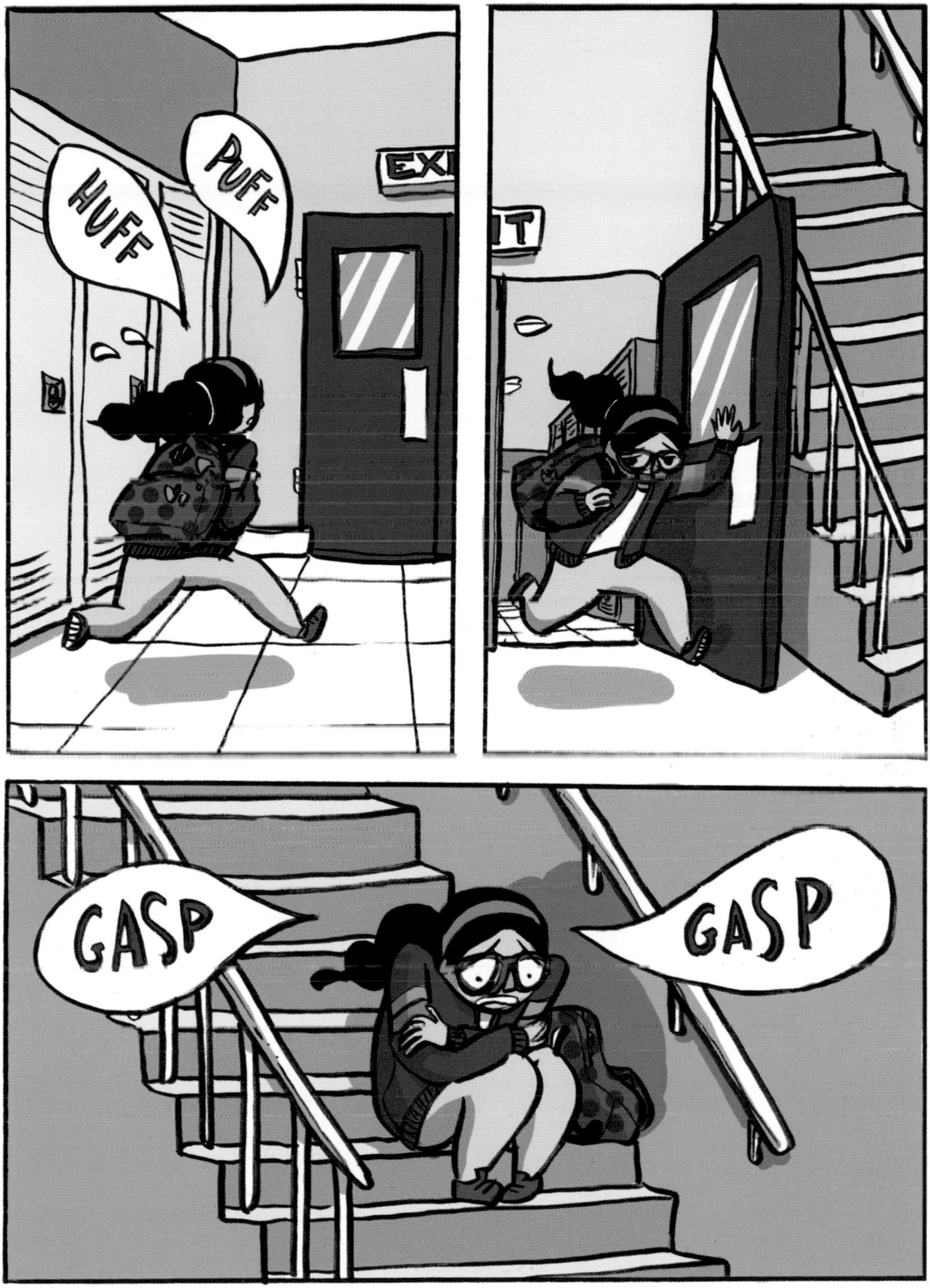
HUFF
PUFF
EXIT
GASP
GASP

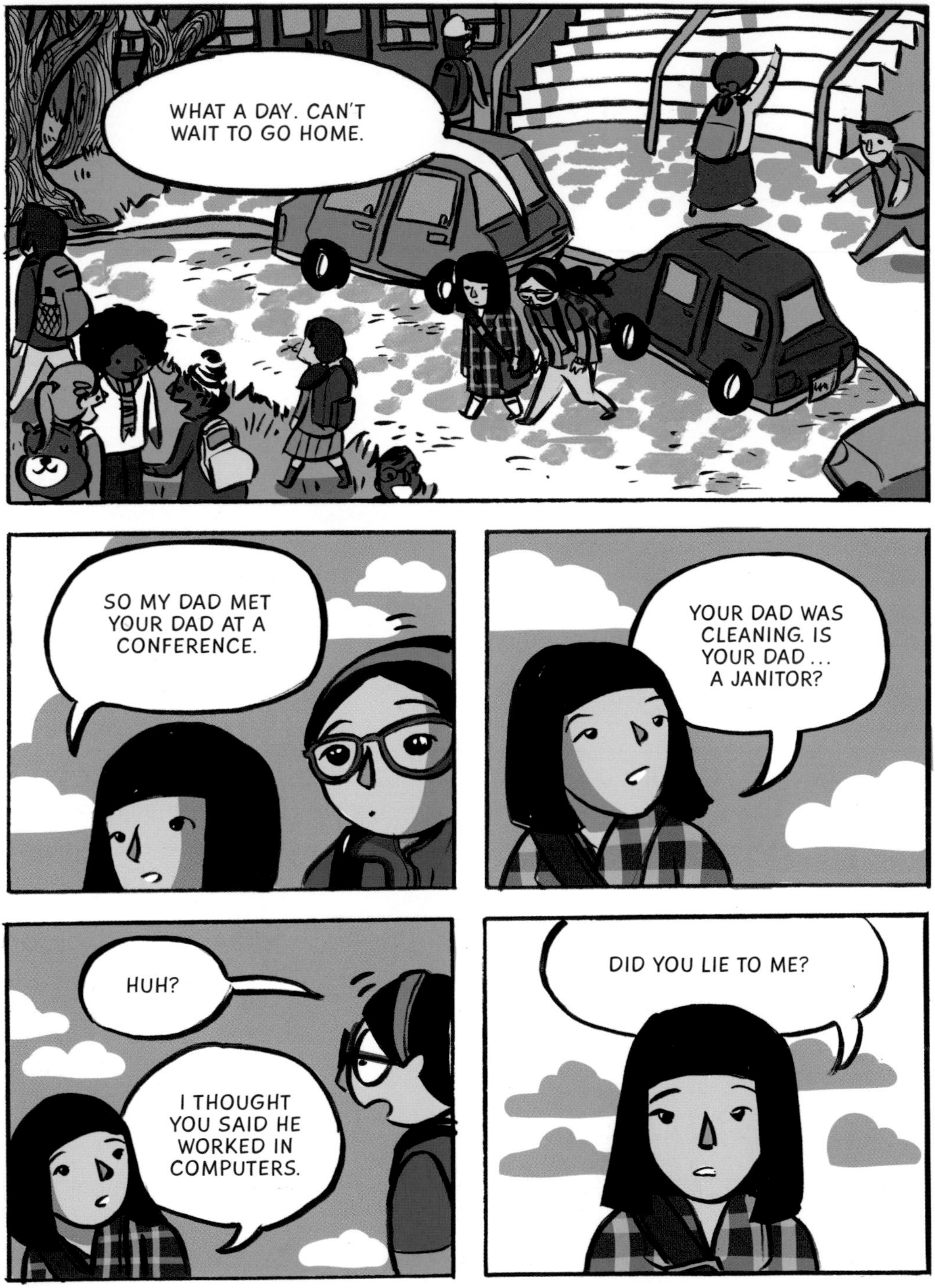
WHAT A DAY. CAN'T WAIT TO GO HOME.
SO MY DAD MET YOUR DAD AT A CONFERENCE.
YOUR DAD WAS CLEANING. IS YOUR DAD . . . A JANITOR?
HUH?
I THOUGHT YOU SAID HE WORKED IN COMPUTERS.
DID YOU LIE TO ME?

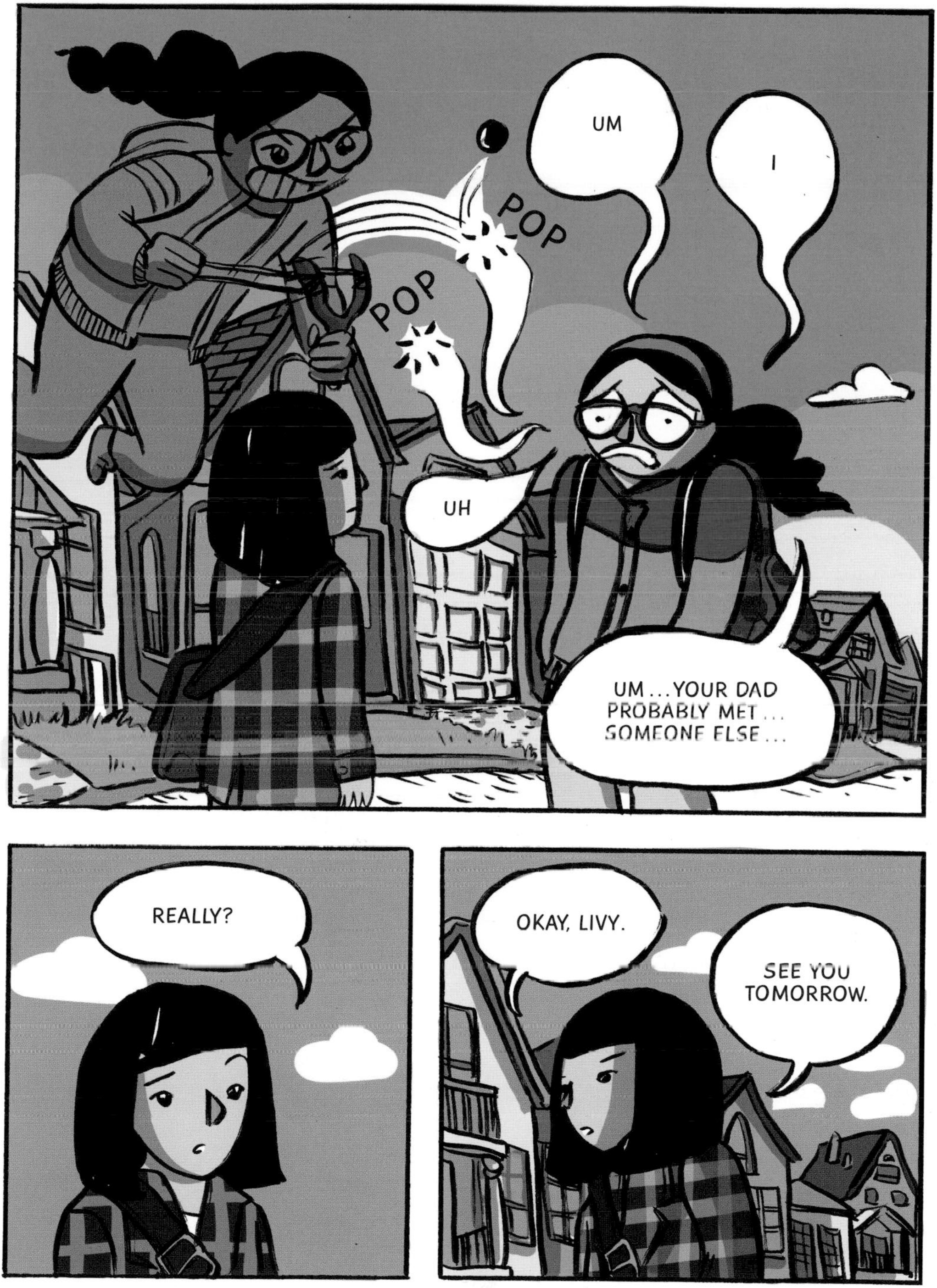
UM
I
POP
POP
UH
UM ... YOUR DAD PROBABLY MET ... SOMEONE ELSE ...
REALLY?
OKAY, LIVY.
SEE YOU TOMORROW.

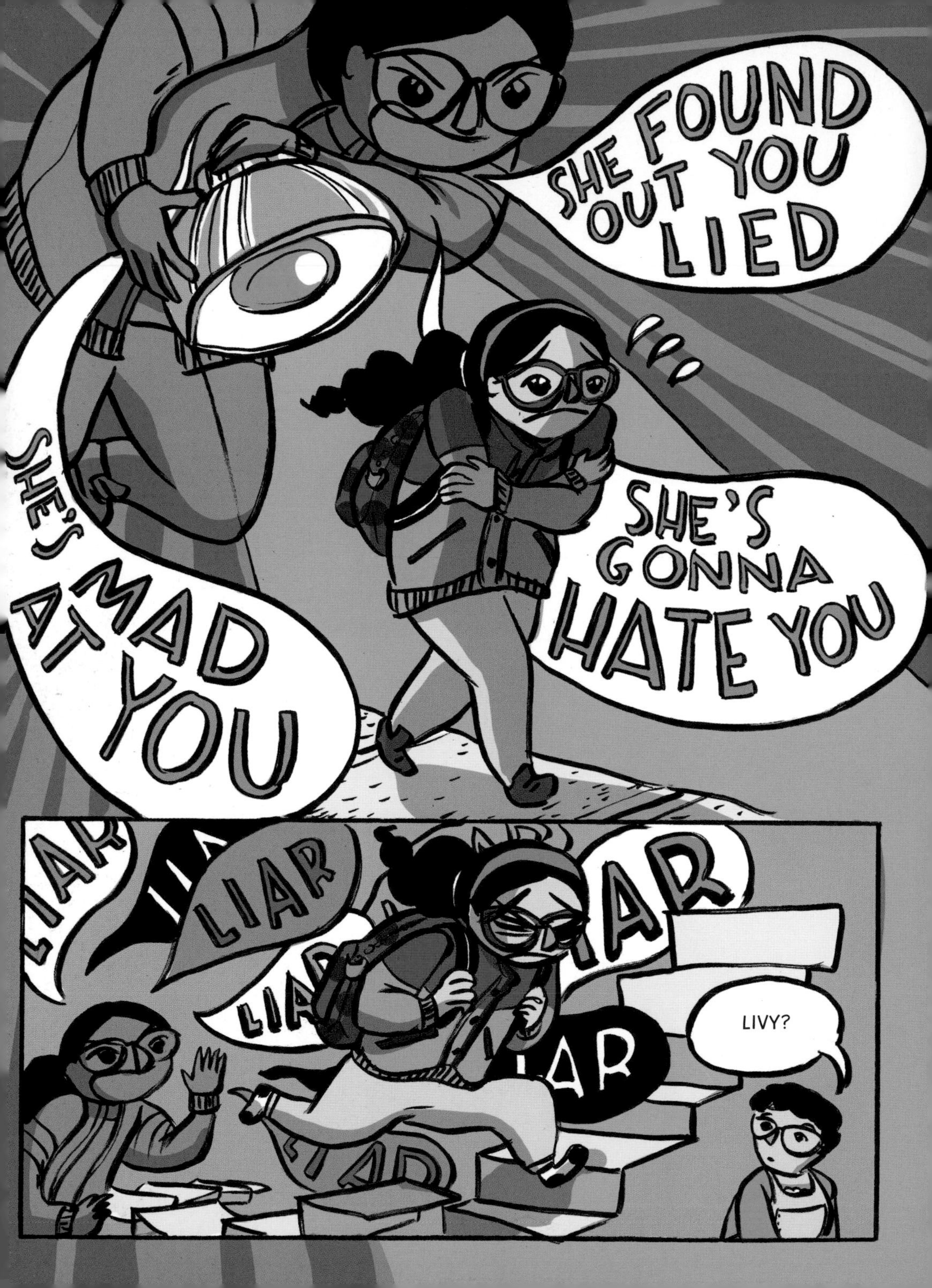
SHE FOUND OUT YOU LIED
SHE'S MAD AT YOU
SHE'S GONNA HATE YOU
LIAR
LIAR
LIAR
LIAR
LIVY?

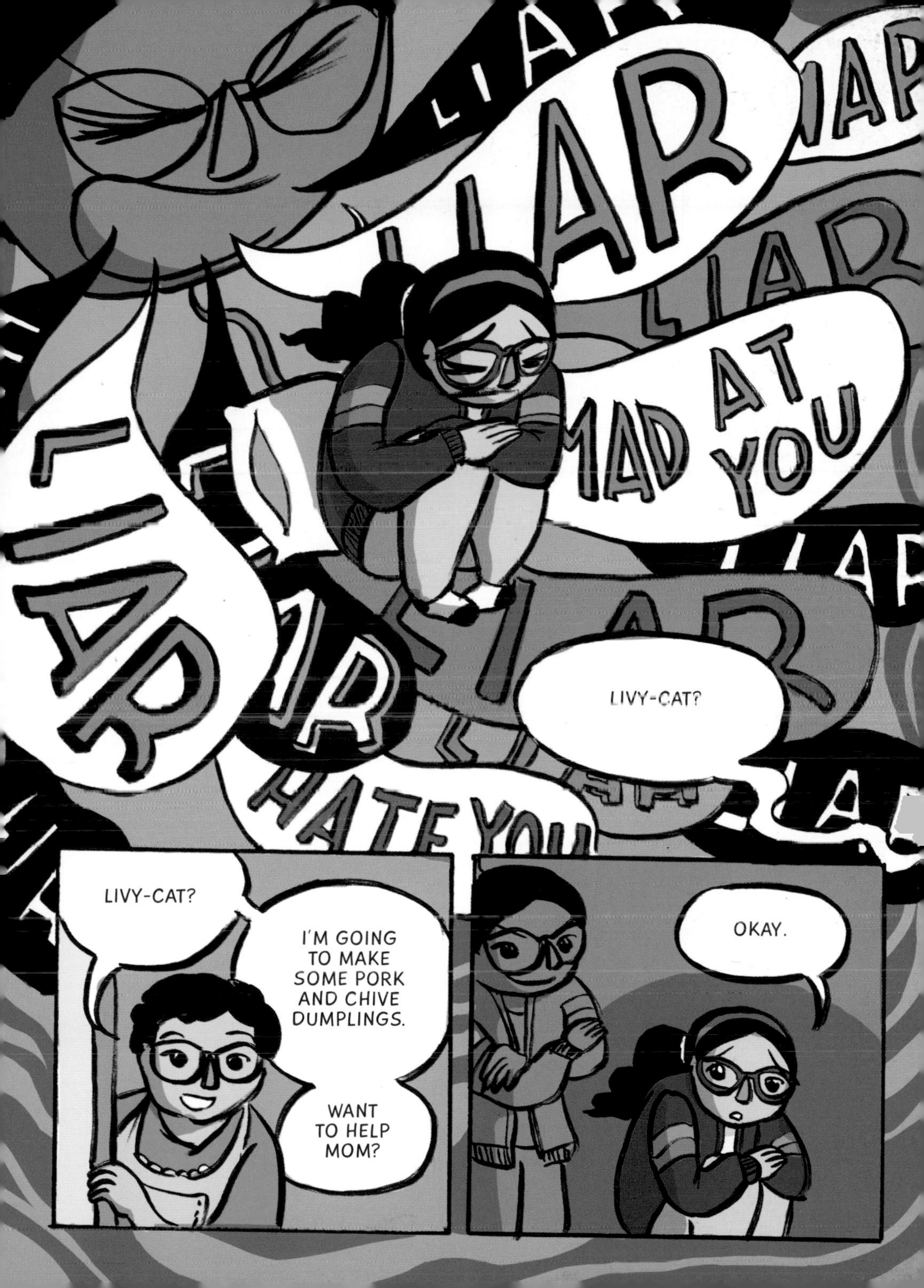
LIAR
LIAR
LIAR
MAD AT YOU
LIAR
LIAR
HATE YOU
LIVY-CAT?
LIVY-CAT?
I'M GOING TO MAKE SOME PORK AND CHIVE DUMPLINGS.
WANT TO HELP MOM?
OKAY.

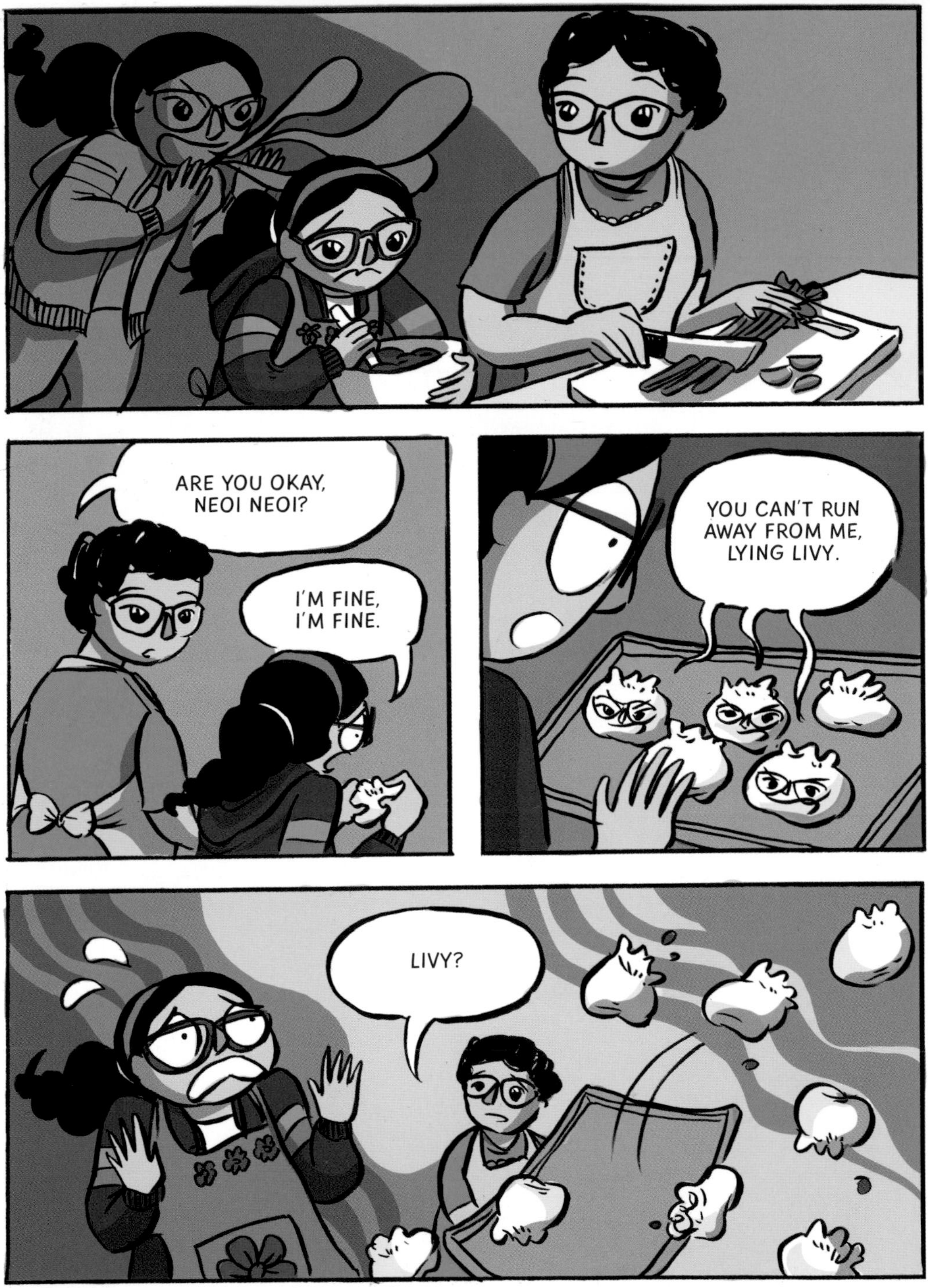
ARE YOU OKAY, NEOI NEOI?
I'M FINE, I'M FINE.
YOU CAN'T RUN AWAY FROM ME, LYING LIVY.
LIVY?

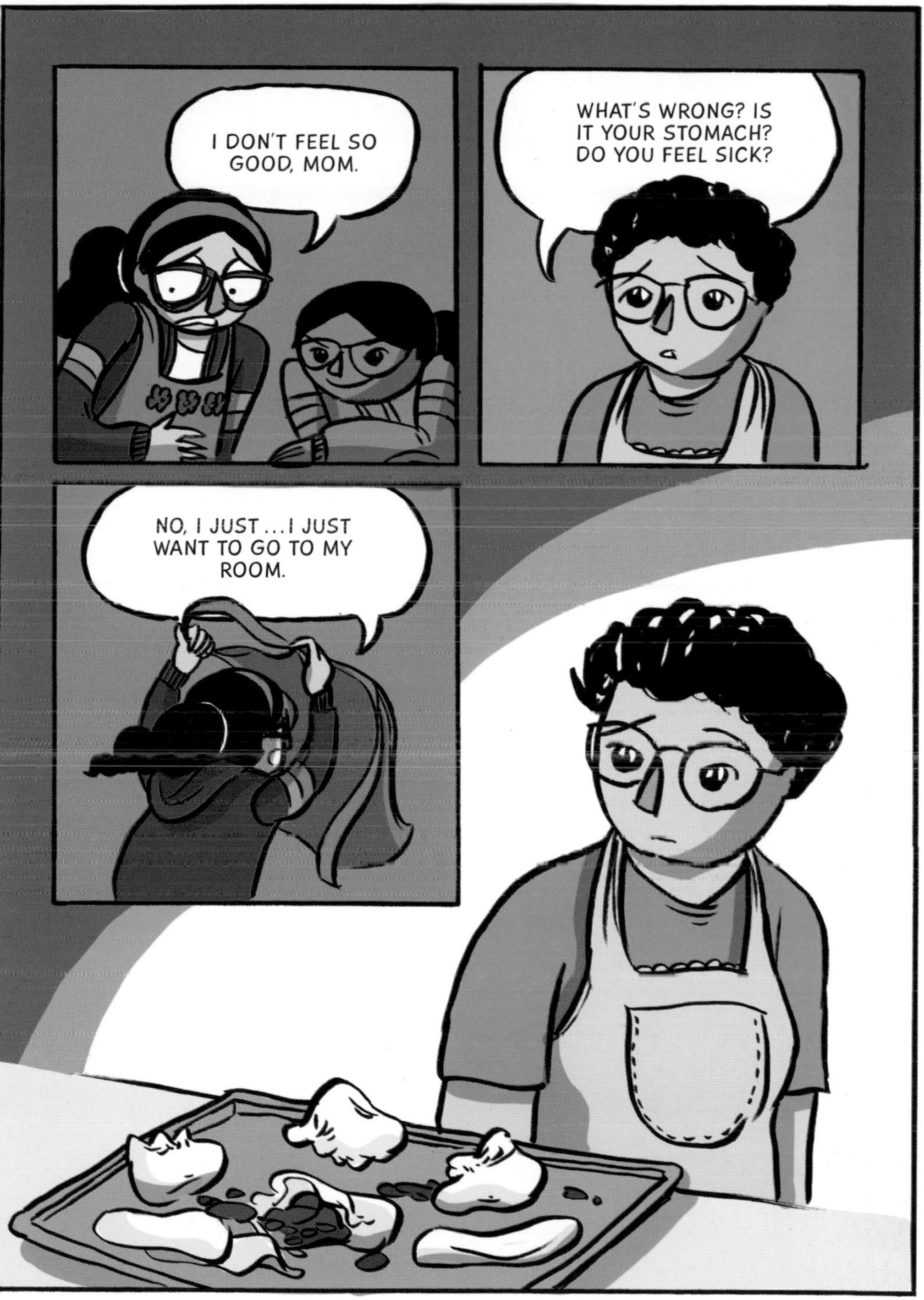
I DON'T FEEL SO GOOD, MOM.
WHAT'S WRONG? IS IT YOUR STOMACH? DO YOU FEEL SICK?
NO, I JUST . . . I JUST WANT TO GO TO MY ROOM.

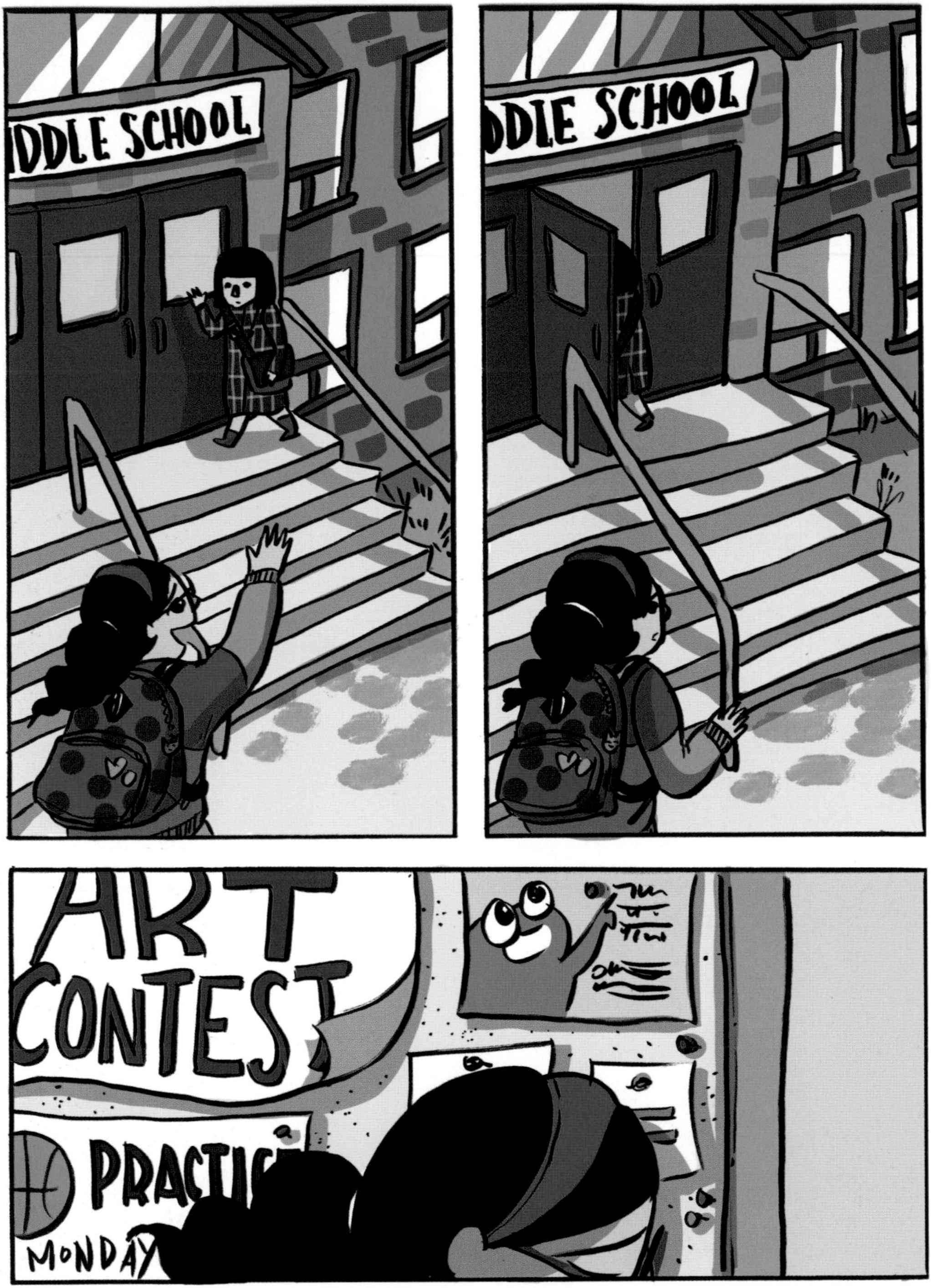
DDLE SCHOOL
DDLE SCHOOL
ART
CONTEST
PRACTIC
MONDAY

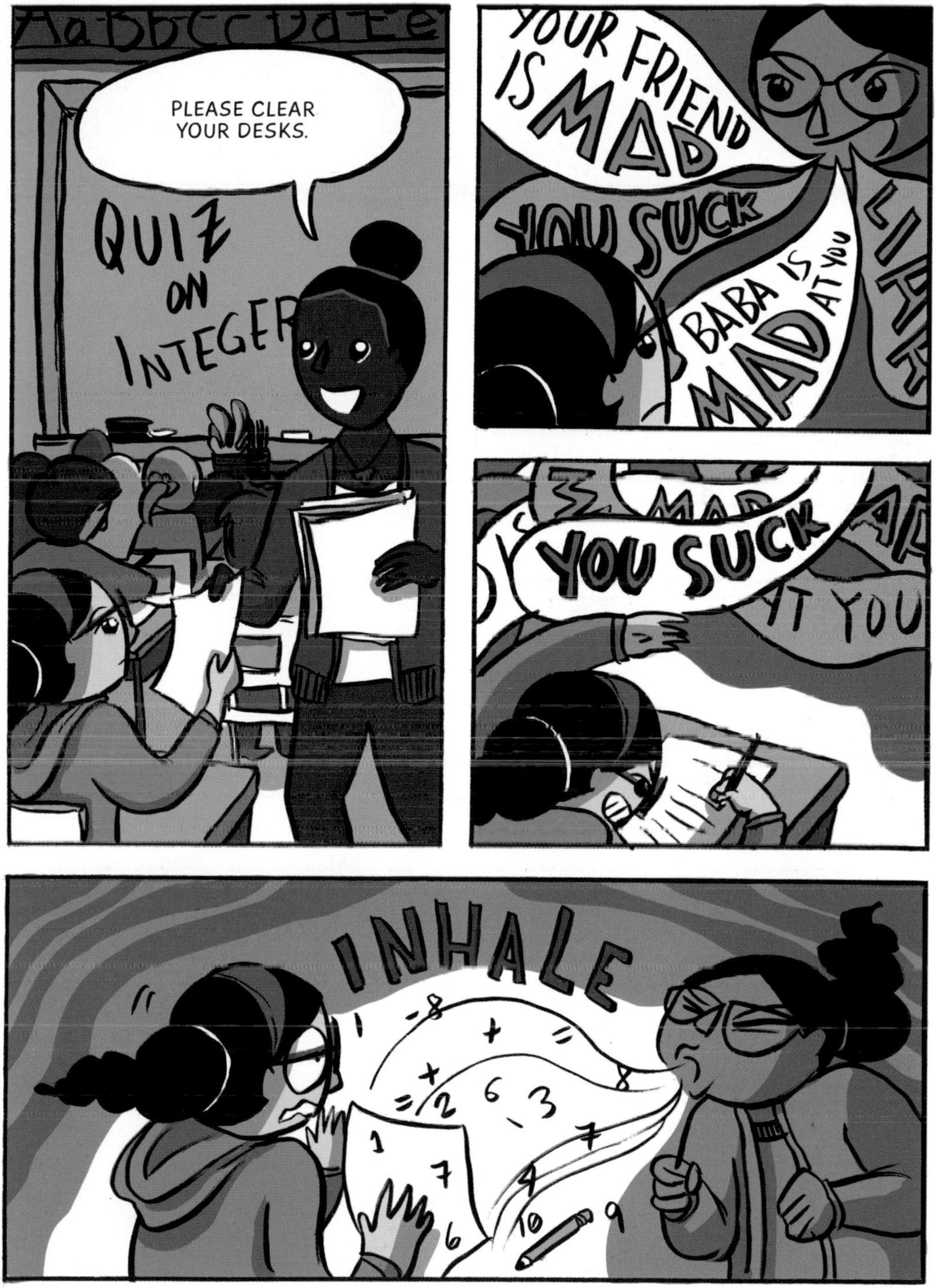

PLEASE CLEAR YOUR DESKS.
QUIZ ON INTEGER
YOUR FRIEND IS MAD
YOU SUCK
BABA IS MAD AT YOU
LIAR
YOU SUCK
AT YOU
INHALE

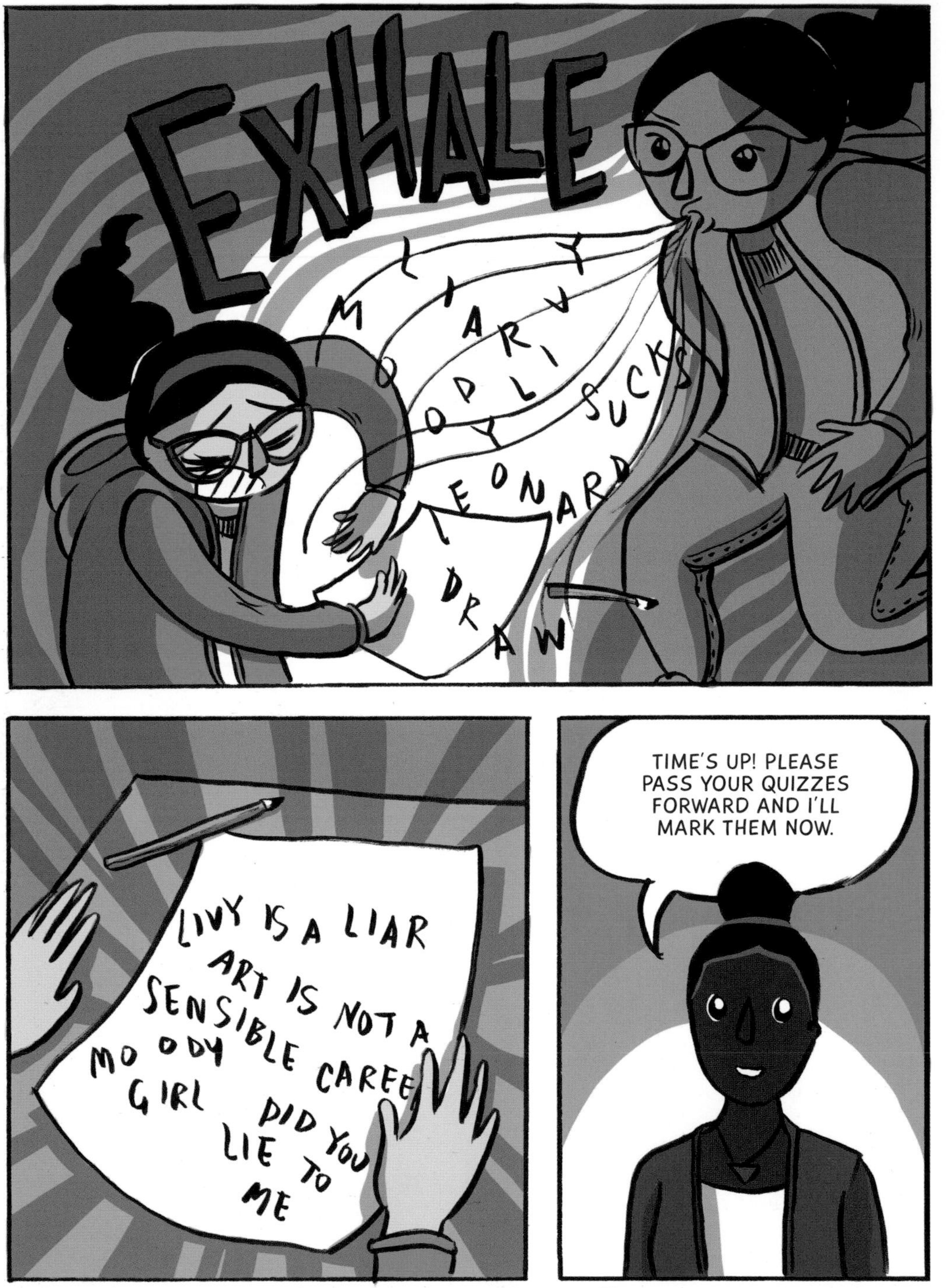

EXHALE
SUCKS
LEONARD
DRAW
LIVY IS A LIAR
ART IS NOT A SENSIBLE CAREE
MOODY GIRL
DID YOU LIE TO ME
TIME'S UP! PLEASE PASS YOUR QUIZZES FORWARD AND I'LL MARK THEM NOW.

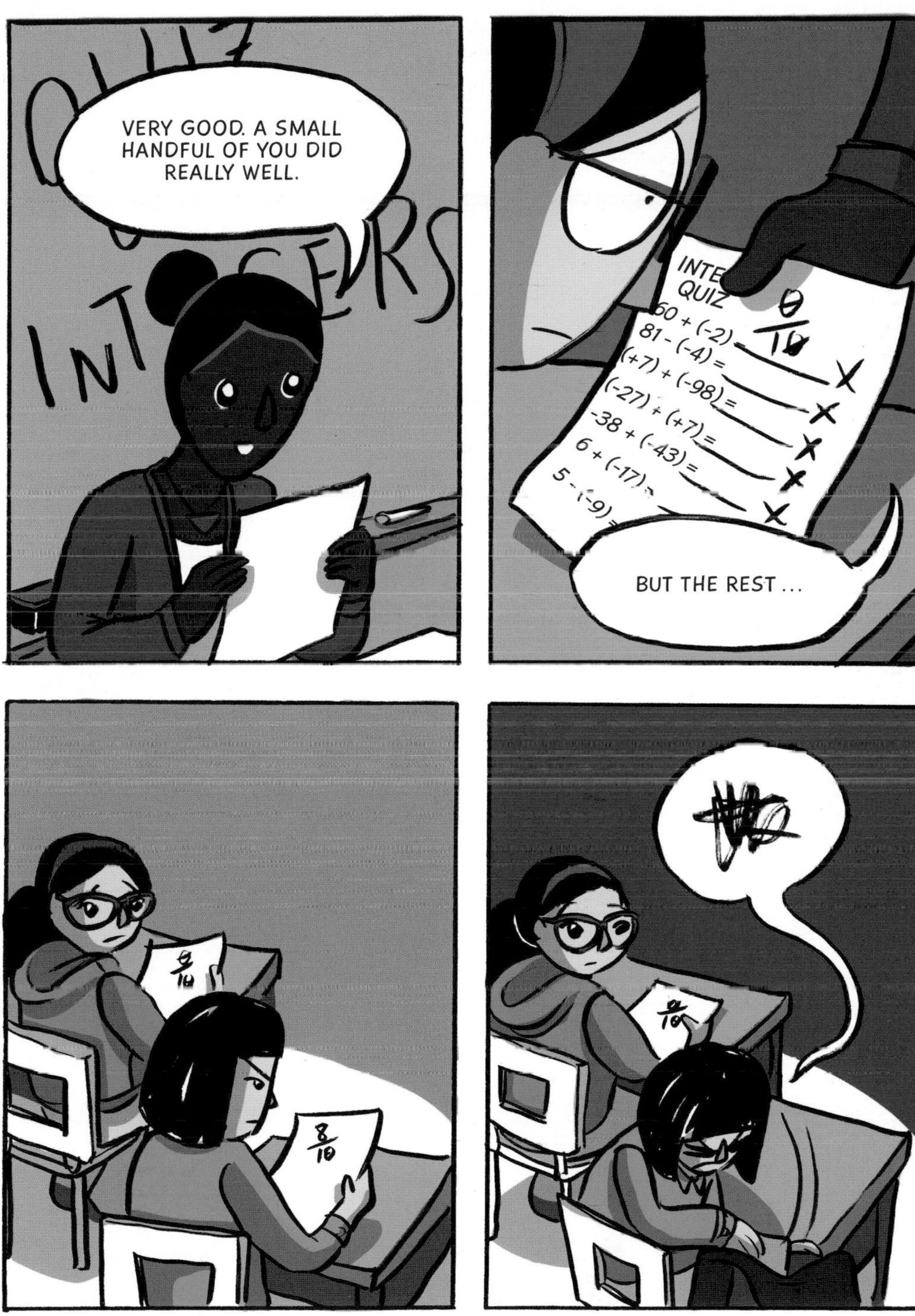
VERY GOOD. A SMALL HANDFUL OF YOU DID REALLY WELL.
INTE
QUIZ
60 + (-2) =
81 - (-4) =
(+7) + (-98) =
(-27) + (+7) =
-38 + (-43) =
6 + (-17) =
BUT THE REST . . .

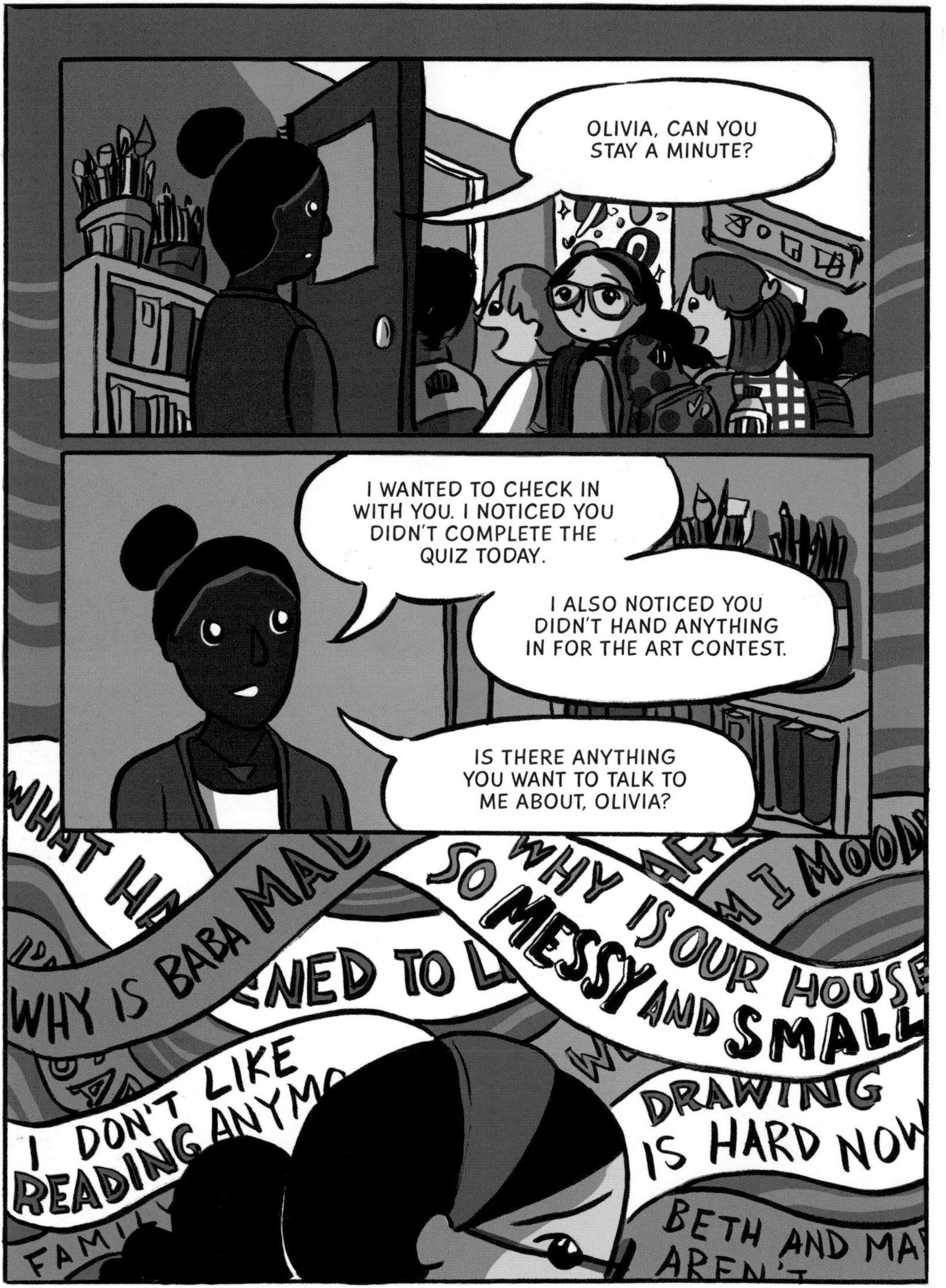
OLIVIA, CAN YOU STAY A MINUTE?
I WANTED TO CHECK IN WITH YOU. I NOTICED YOU DIDN'T COMPLETE THE QUIZ TODAY.
I ALSO NOTICED YOU DIDN'T HAND ANYTHING IN FOR THE ART CONTEST.
IS THERE ANYTHING YOU WANT TO TALK TO ME ABOUT, OLIVIA?
WHY IS BABA
SO MESSY AND SMALL
WHY IS OUR
I DON'T LIKE READING
DRAWING IS HARD NOW
BETH AND

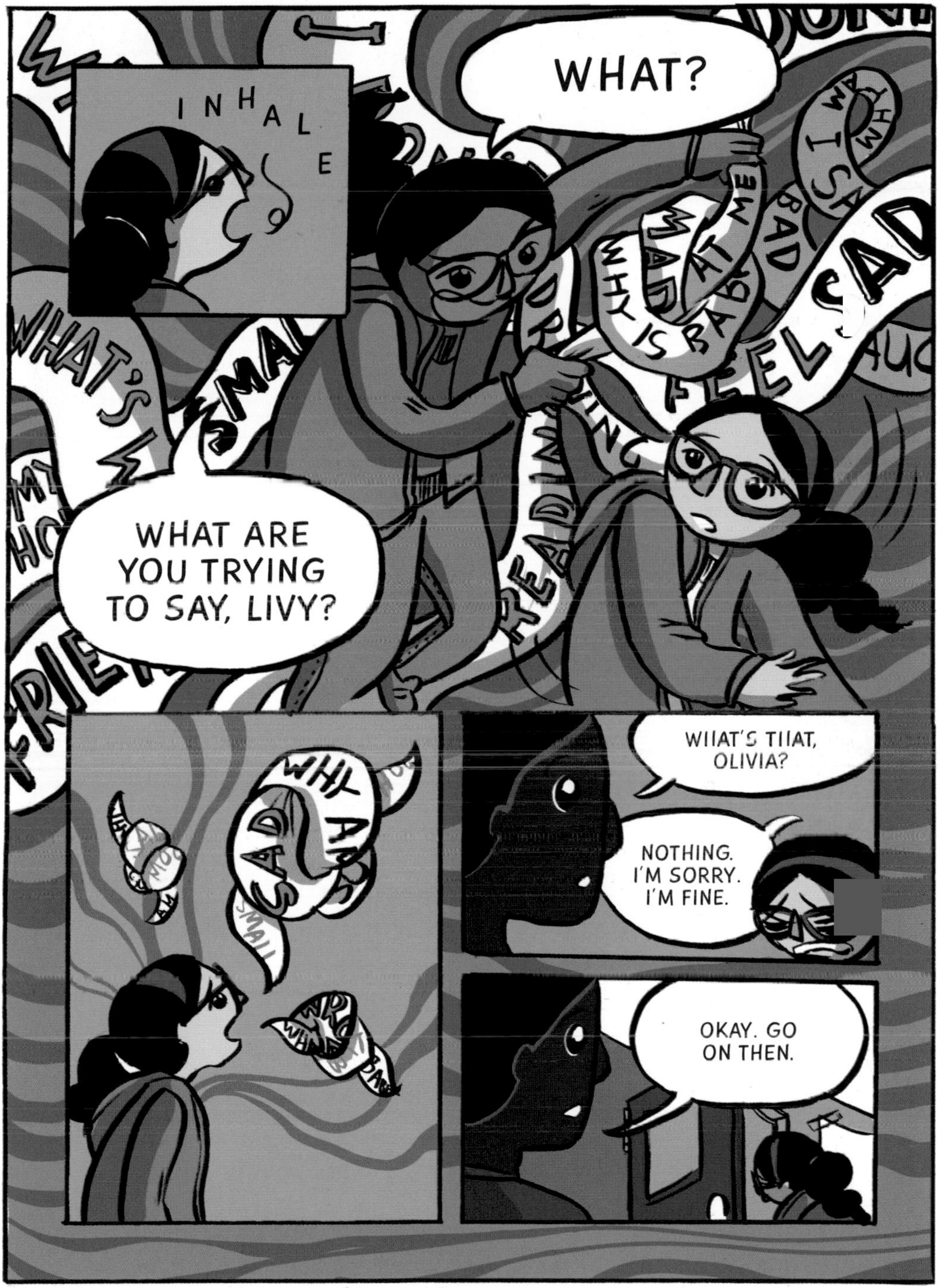
INHALE
WHAT?
WHAT ARE YOU TRYING TO SAY, LIVY?
WHAT'S THAT, OLIVIA?
NOTHING. I'M SORRY. I'M FINE.
OKAY. GO ON THEN.

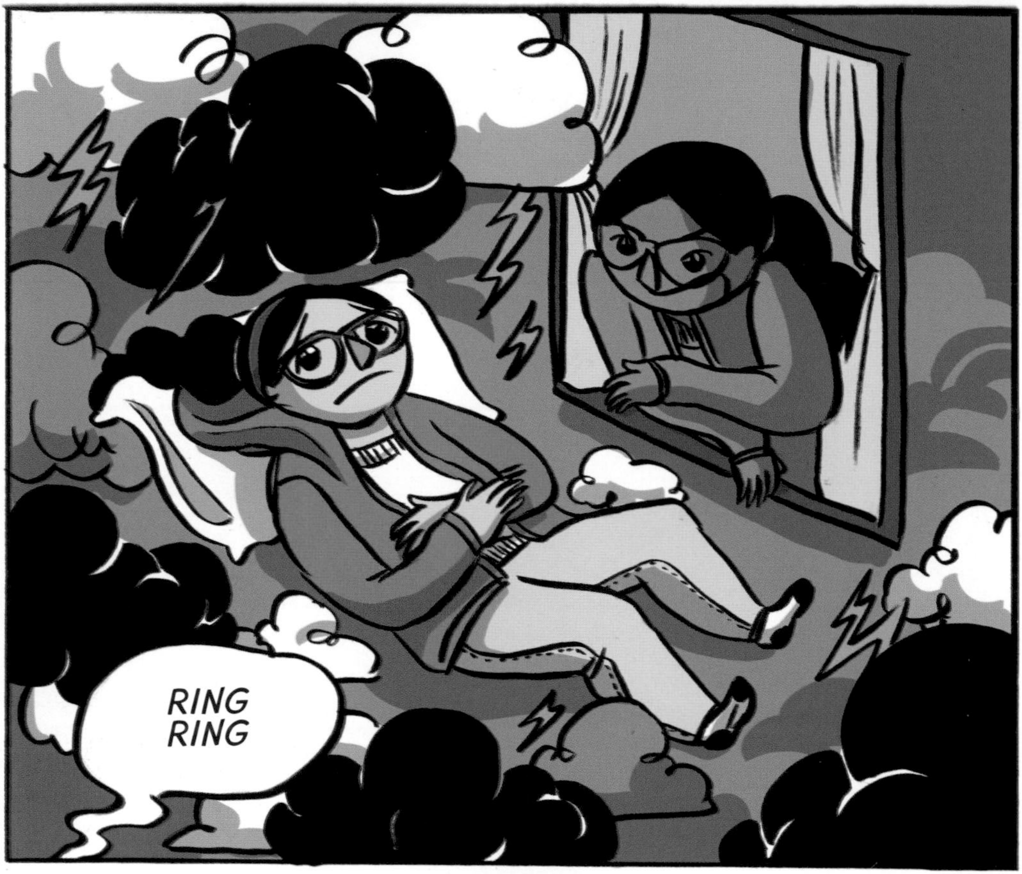
RING
RING

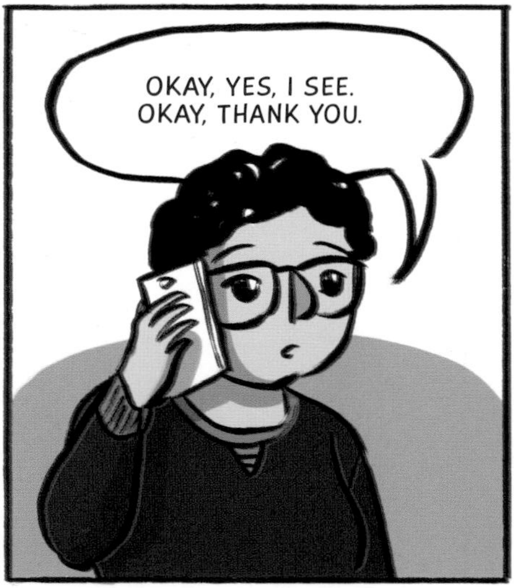
OKAY, YES, I SEE. OKAY, THANK YOU.

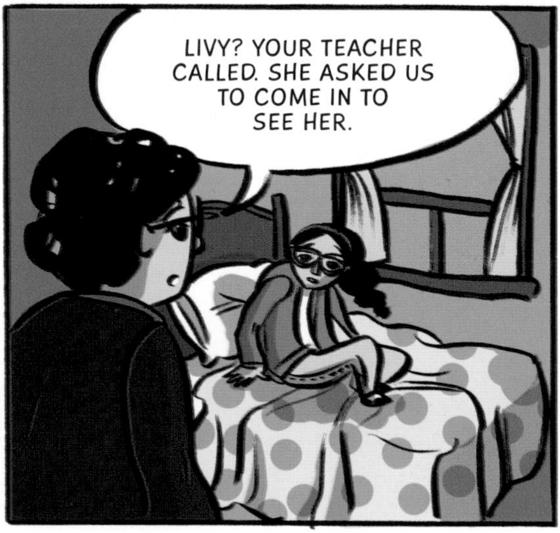
LIVY? YOUR TEACHER CALLED. SHE ASKED US TO COME IN TO SEE HER.

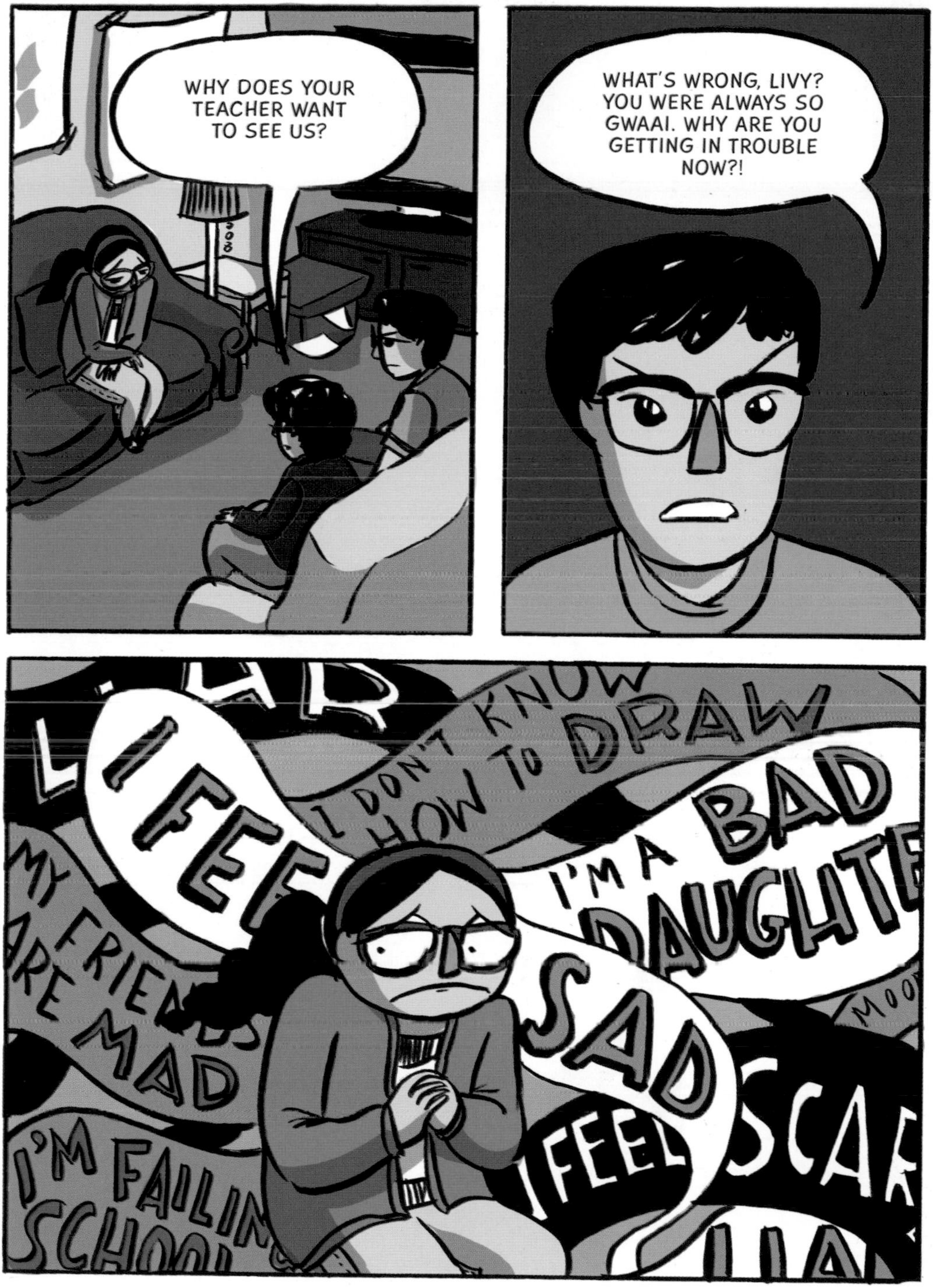
WHY DOES YOUR TEACHER WANT TO SEE US?
WHAT'S WRONG, LIVY? YOU WERE ALWAYS SO GWAAI. WHY ARE YOU GETTING IN TROUBLE NOW?!
I FEE
I DON'T KNOW HOW TO DRAW
I'M A BAD DAUGHTE
MY FRIEN ARE MAD
SAD
I FEEL SCAR
I'M FAILIN SCHOO

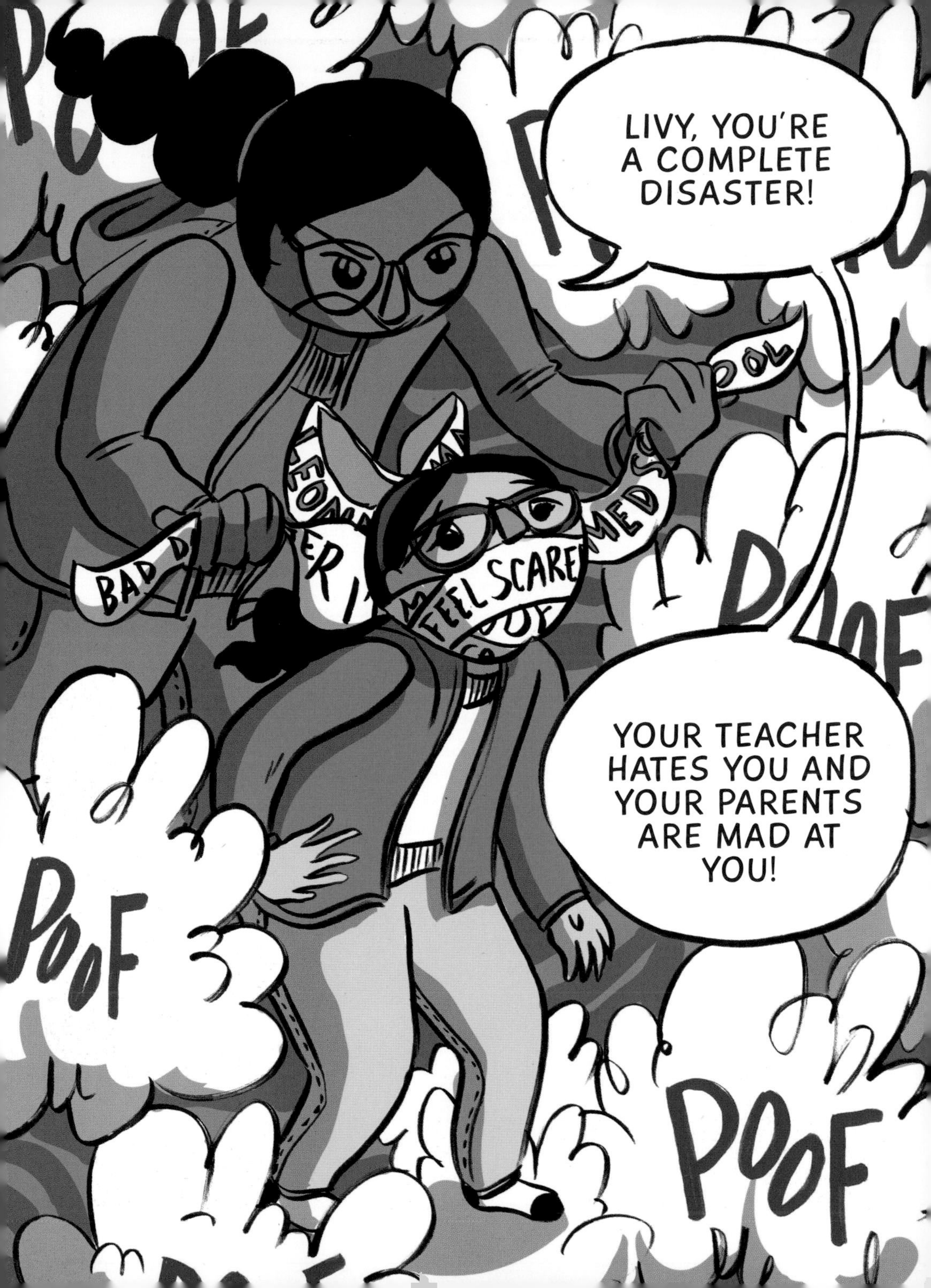
LIVY, YOU'RE A COMPLETE DISASTER!
YOUR TEACHER HATES YOU AND YOUR PARENTS ARE MAD AT YOU!
FEEL SCARED
POOF
POOF
POOF

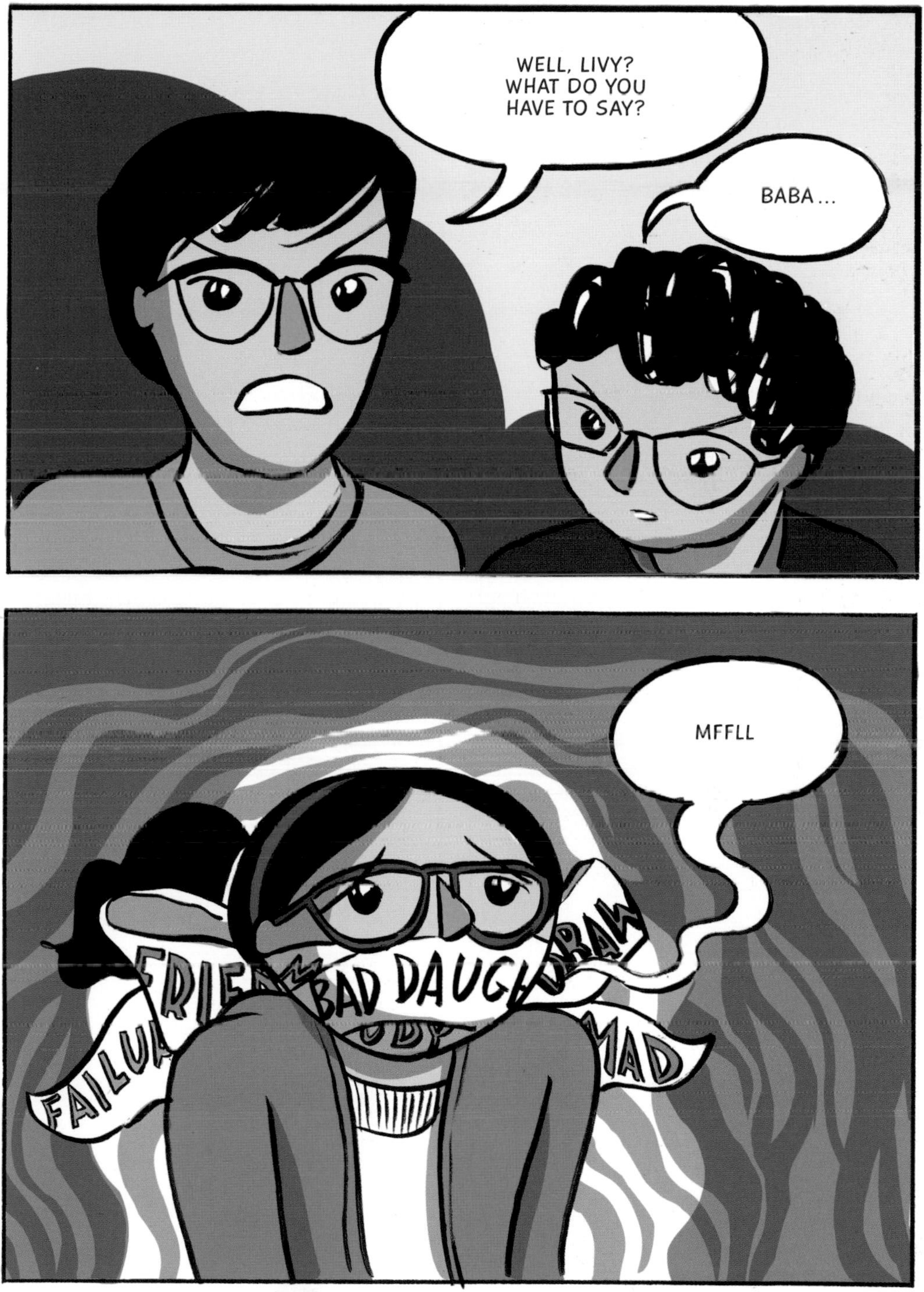
WELL, LIVY? WHAT DO YOU HAVE TO SAY?
BABA...
MFFLL
BAD
DRAW
MAD

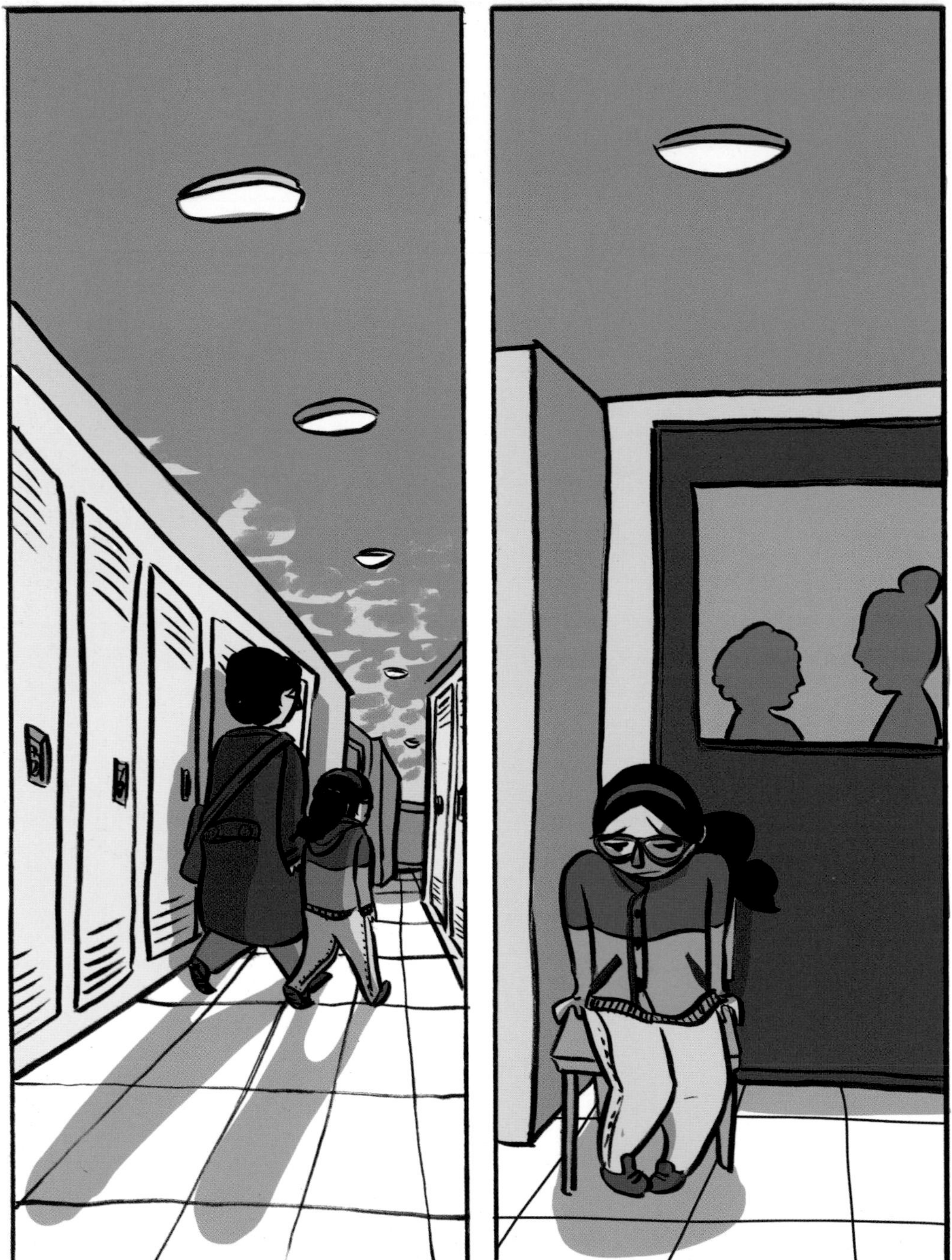

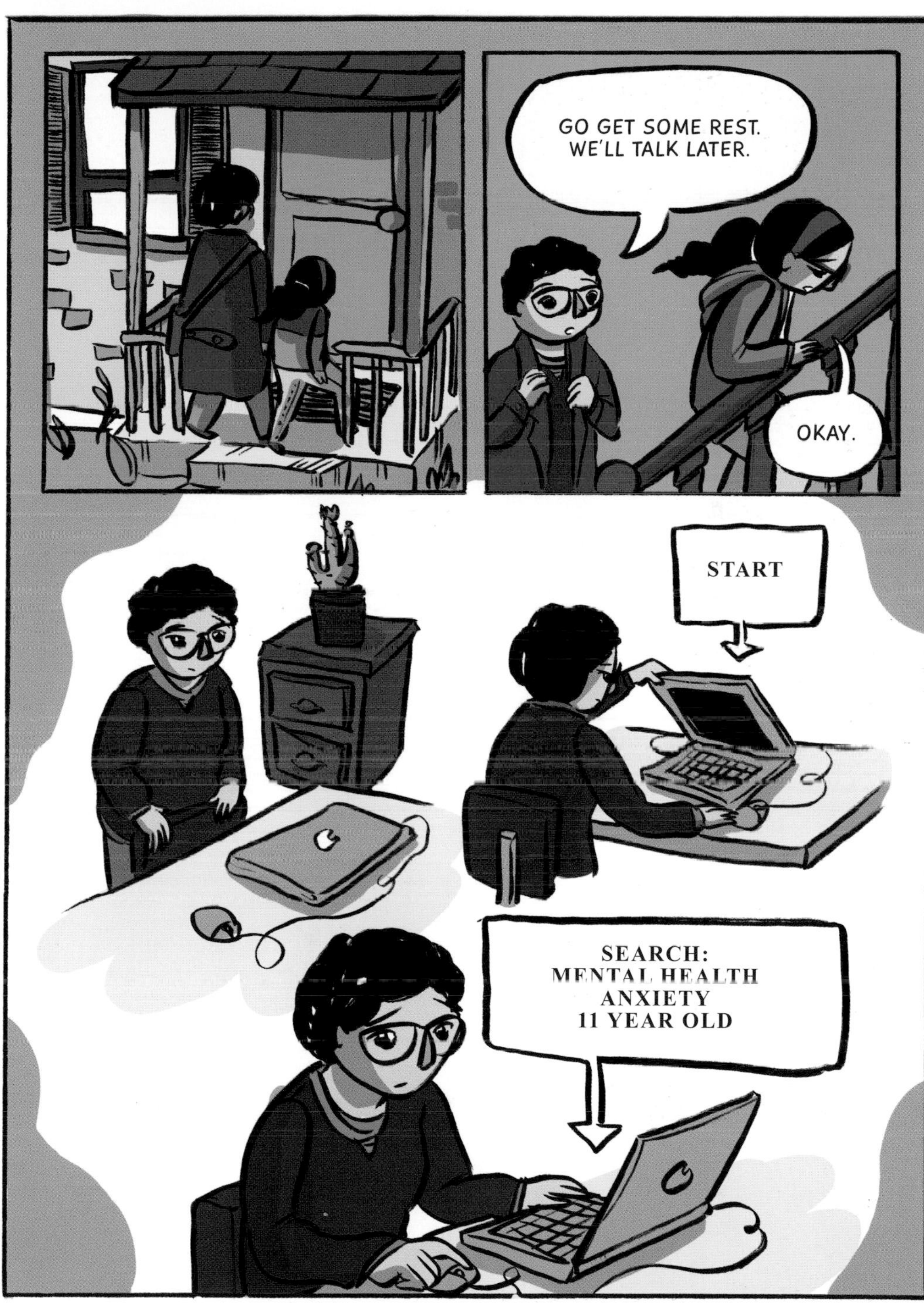
GO GET SOME REST. WE'LL TALK LATER.
OKAY.
START
SEARCH: MENTAL HEALTH ANXIETY 11 YEAR OLD

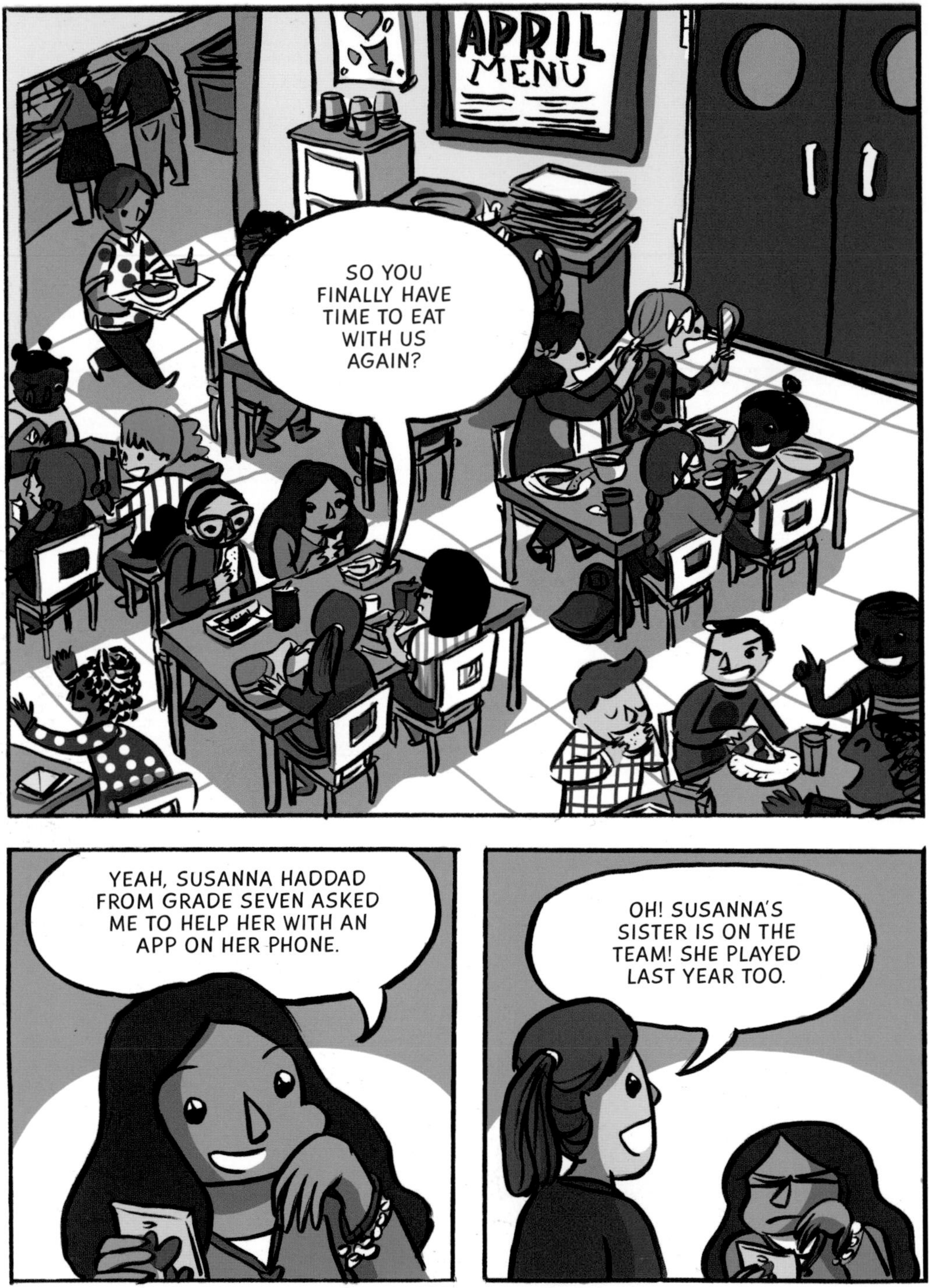
APRIL MENU
SO YOU FINALLY HAVE TIME TO EAT WITH US AGAIN?
YEAH, SUSANNA HADDAD FROM GRADE SEVEN ASKED ME TO HELP HER WITH AN APP ON HER PHONE.
OH! SUSANNA'S SISTER IS ON THE TEAM! SHE PLAYED LAST YEAR TOO.

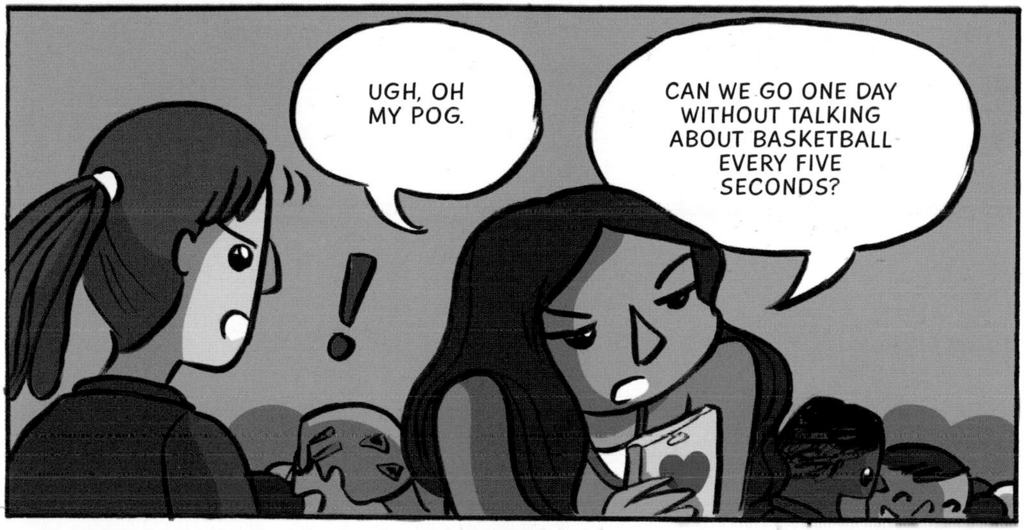
UGH, OH MY POG.
CAN WE GO ONE DAY WITHOUT TALKING ABOUT BASKETBALL EVERY FIVE SECONDS?

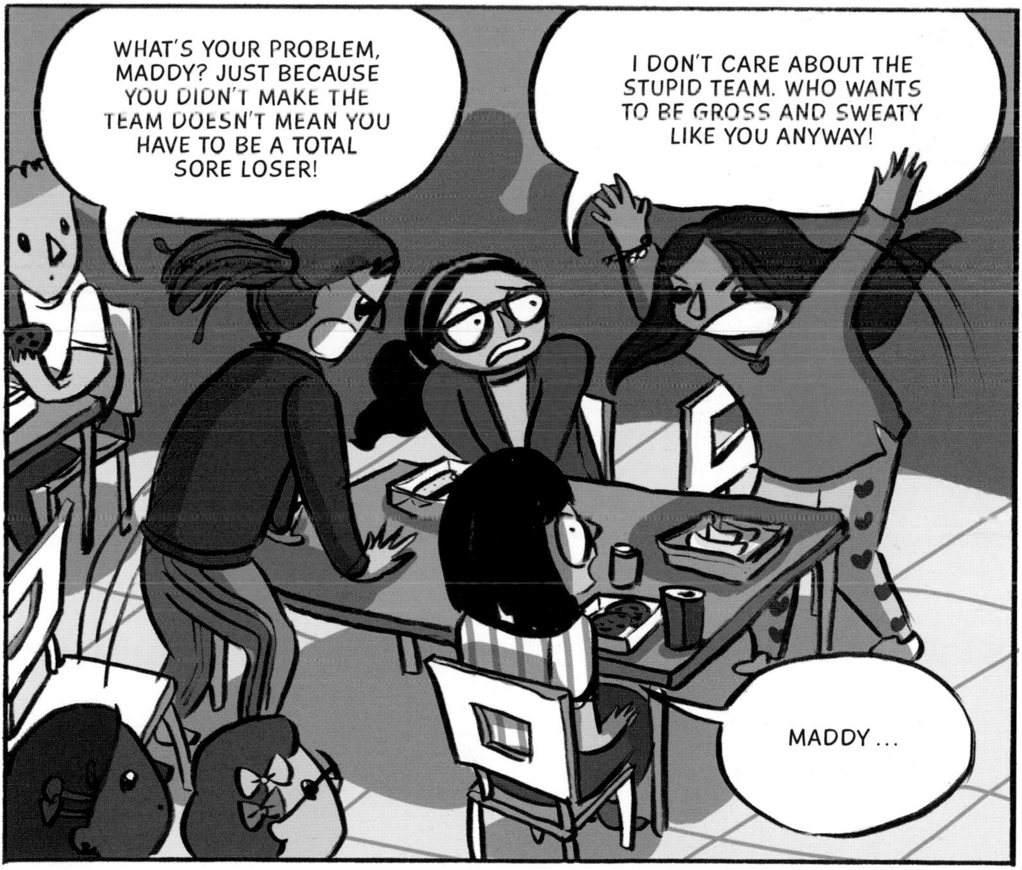
WHAT'S YOUR PROBLEM, MADDY? JUST BECAUSE YOU DIDN'T MAKE THE TEAM DOESN'T MEAN YOU HAVE TO BE A TOTAL SORE LOSER!
I DON'T CARE ABOUT THE STUPID TEAM. WHO WANTS TO BE GROSS AND SWEATY LIKE YOU ANYWAY!
MADDY . . .

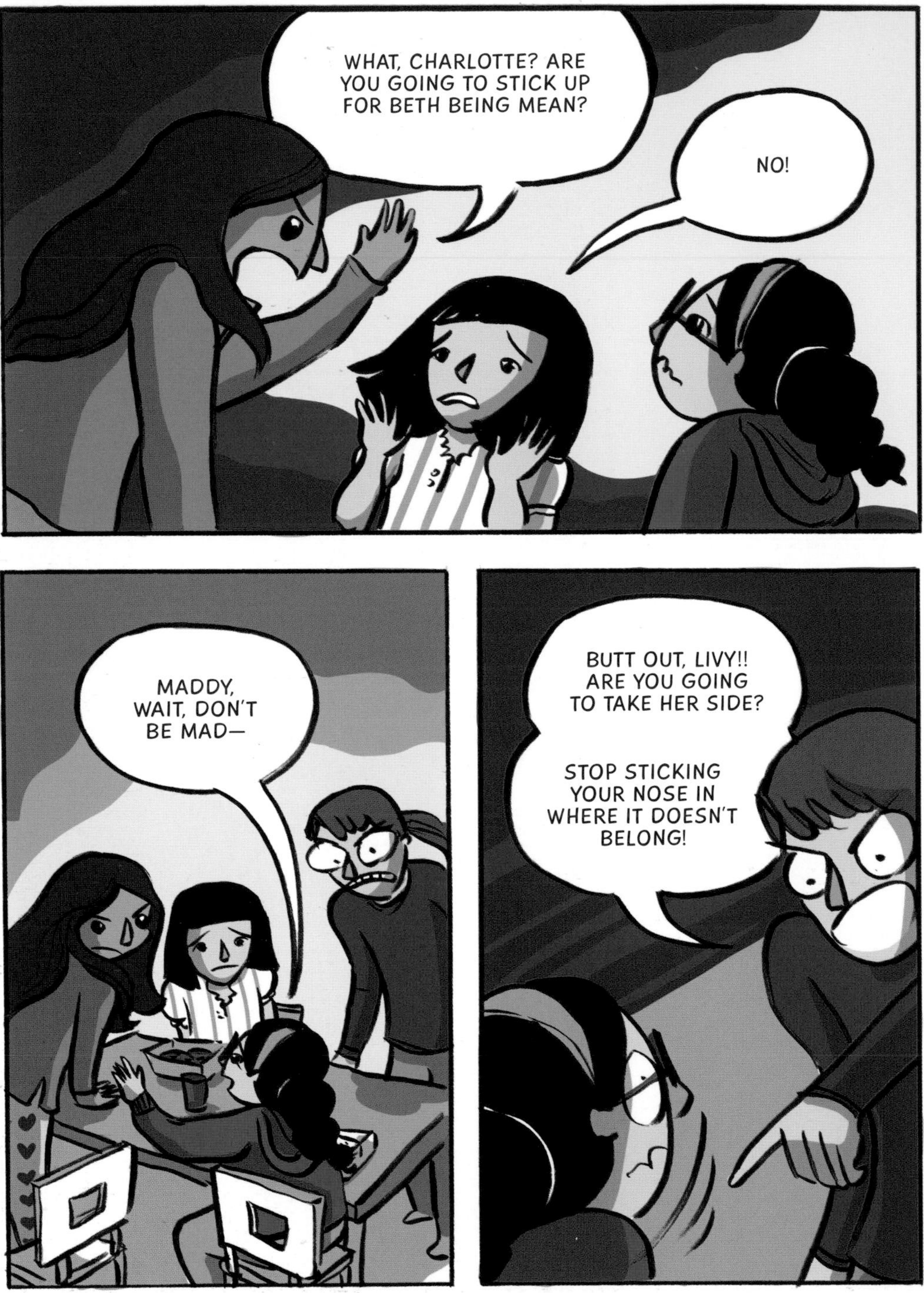
WHAT, CHARLOTTE? ARE YOU GOING TO STICK UP FOR BETH BEING MEAN?
NO!
MADDY, WAIT, DON'T BE MAD—
BUTT OUT, LIVY!! ARE YOU GOING TO TAKE HER SIDE?
STOP STICKING YOUR NOSE IN WHERE IT DOESN'T BELONG!

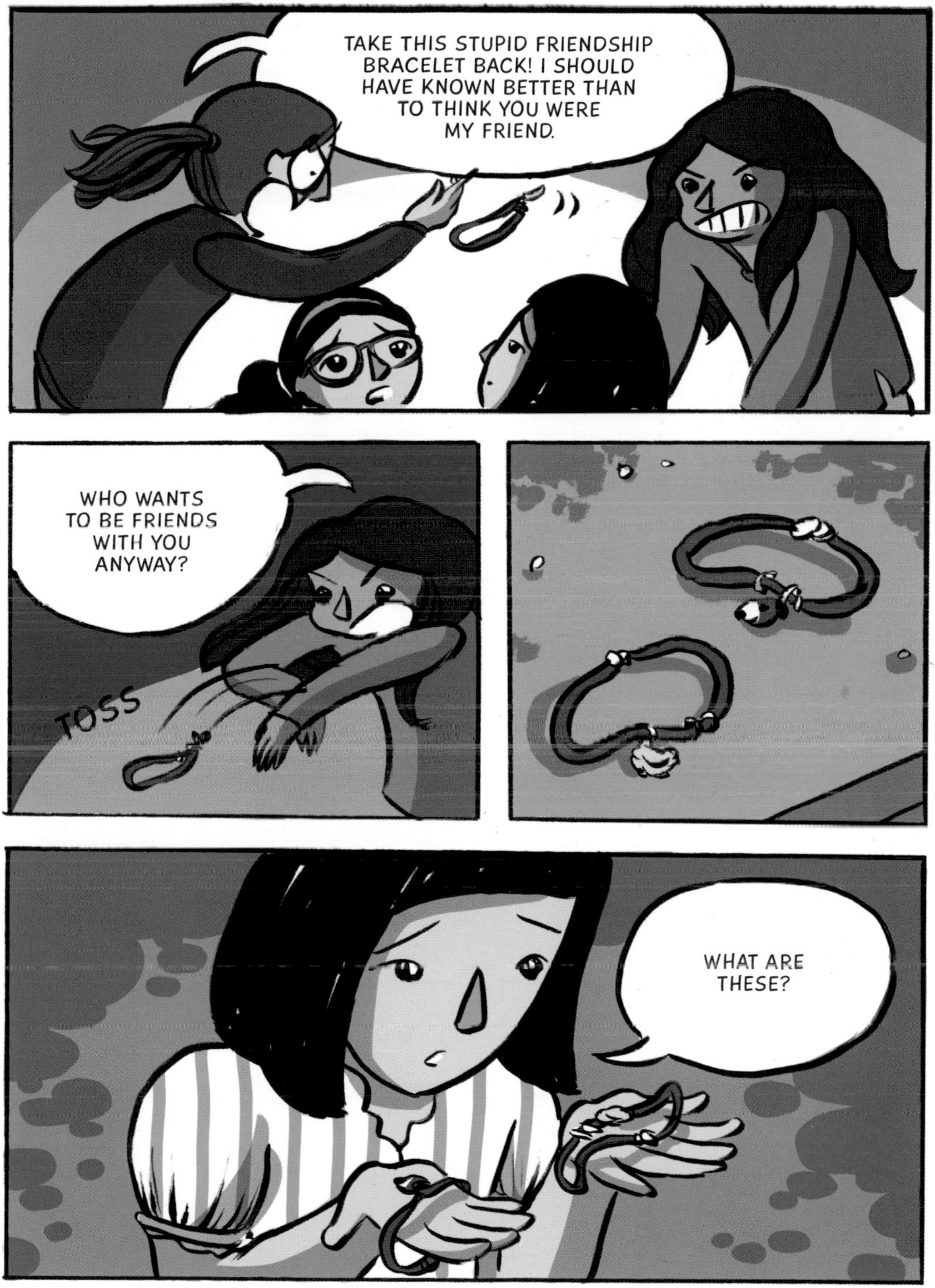
TAKE THIS STUPID FRIENDSHIP BRACELET BACK! I SHOULD HAVE KNOWN BETTER THAN TO THINK YOU WERE MY FRIEND.
WHO WANTS TO BE FRIENDS WITH YOU ANYWAY?
TOSS
WHAT ARE THESE?

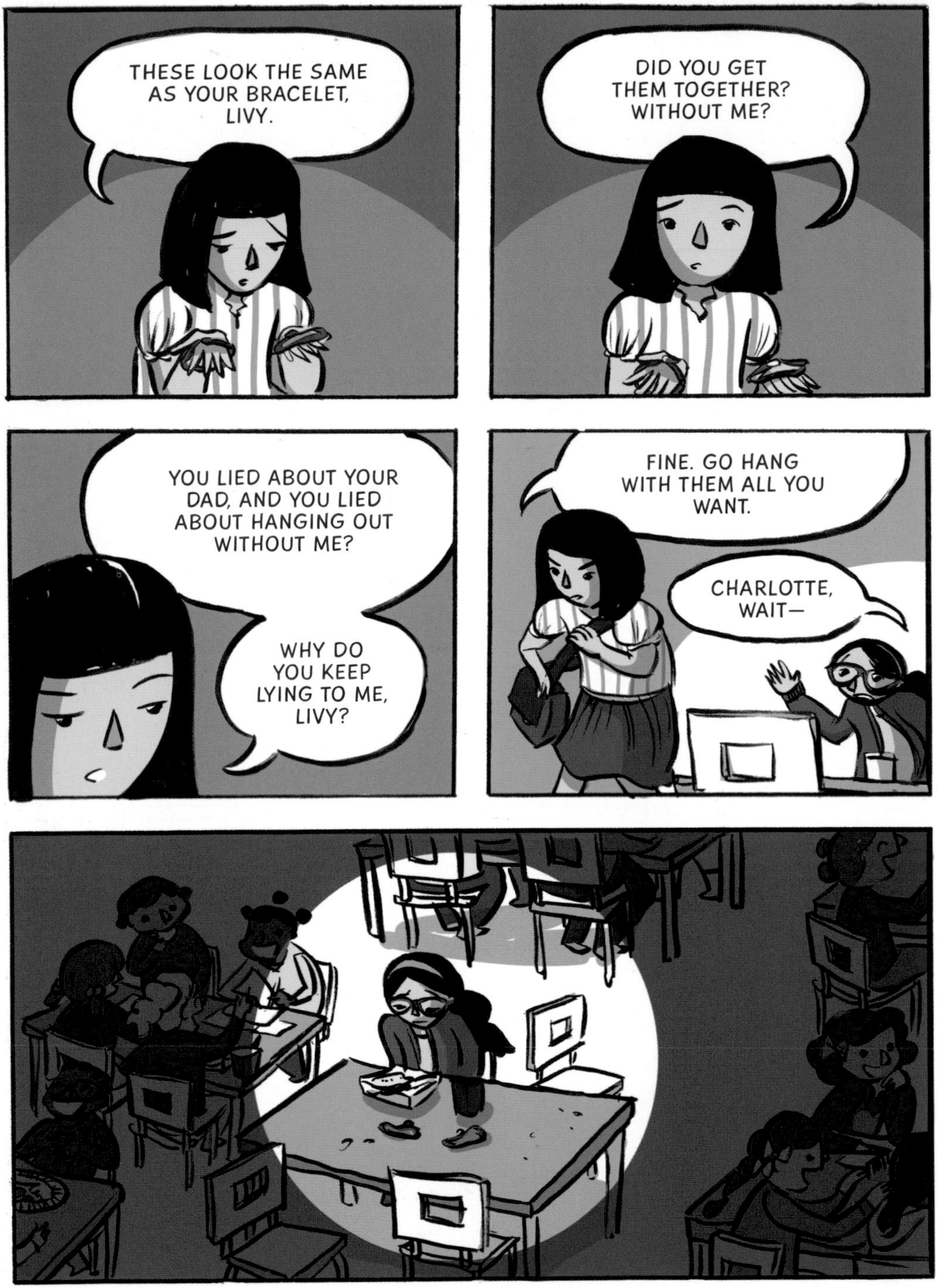
THESE LOOK THE SAME AS YOUR BRACELET, LIVY.
DID YOU GET THEM TOGETHER? WITHOUT ME?
YOU LIED ABOUT YOUR DAD, AND YOU LIED ABOUT HANGING OUT WITHOUT ME?
WHY DO YOU KEEP LYING TO ME, LIVY?
FINE. GO HANG WITH THEM ALL YOU WANT.
CHARLOTTE, WAIT—

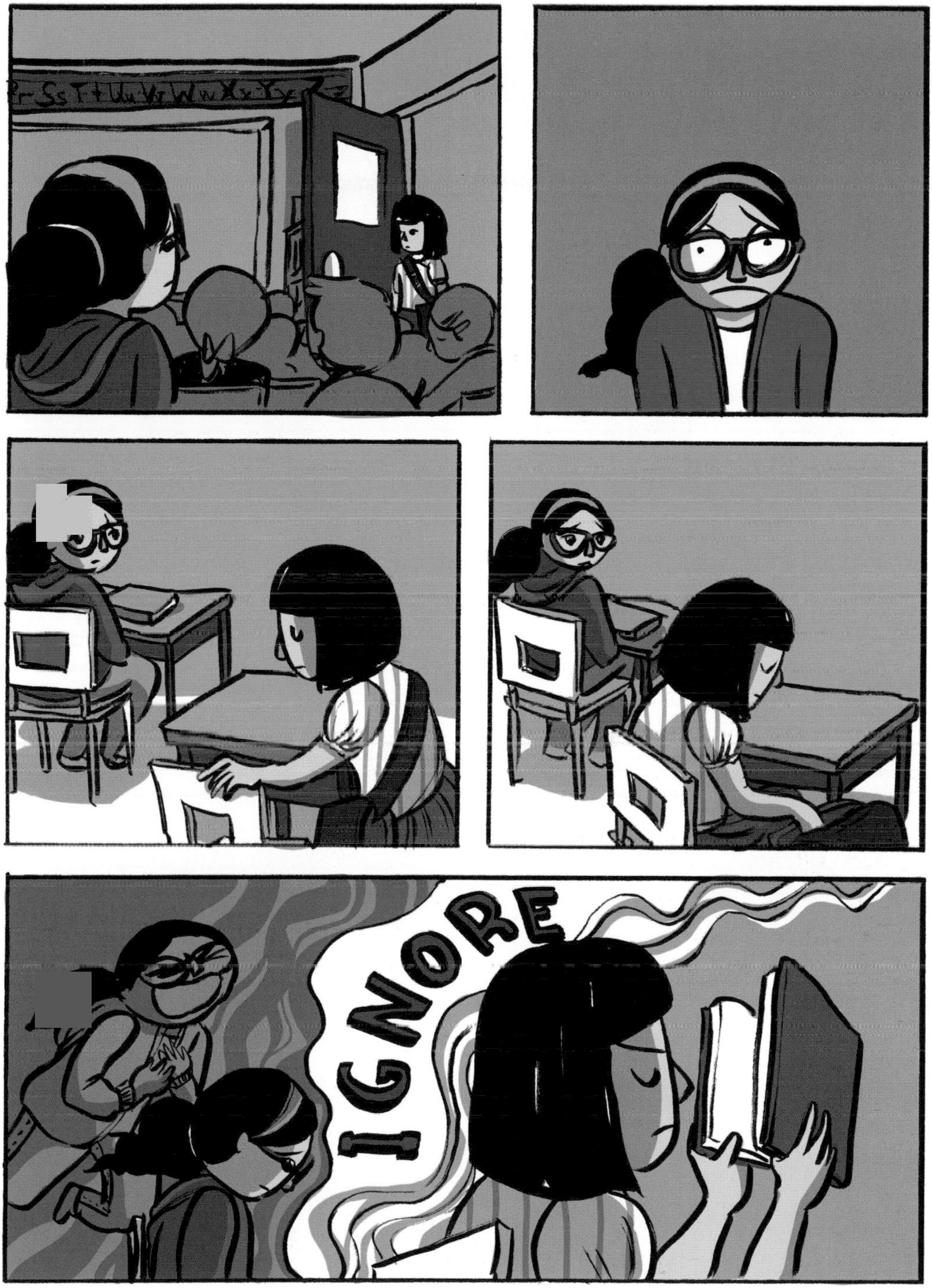
IGNORE

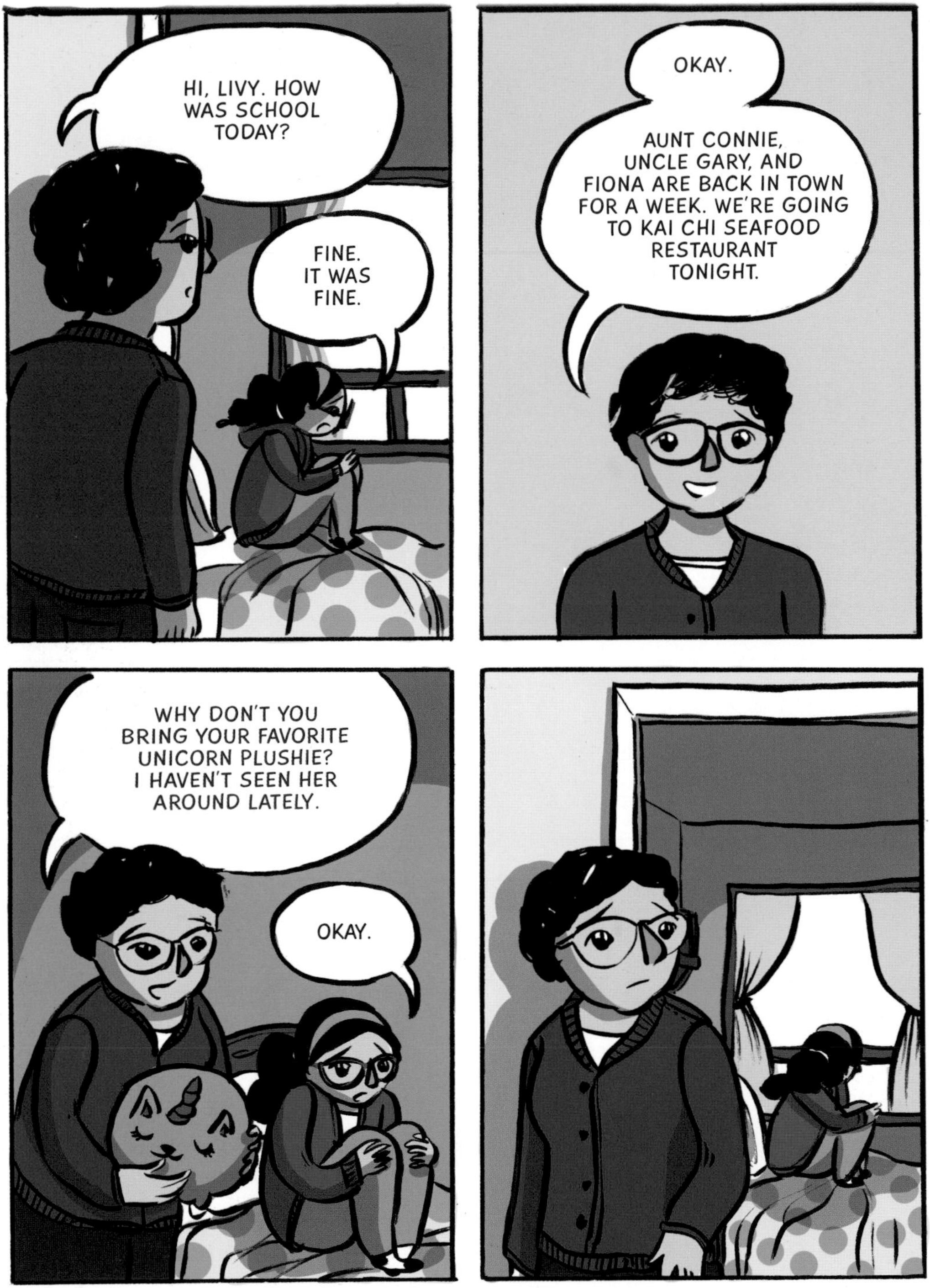
HI, LIVY. HOW WAS SCHOOL TODAY?
FINE. IT WAS FINE.
OKAY.
AUNT CONNIE, UNCLE GARY, AND FIONA ARE BACK IN TOWN FOR A WEEK. WE'RE GOING TO KAI CHI SEAFOOD RESTAURANT TONIGHT.
WHY DON'T YOU BRING YOUR FAVORITE UNICORN PLUSHIE? I HAVEN'T SEEN HER AROUND LATELY.
OKAY.

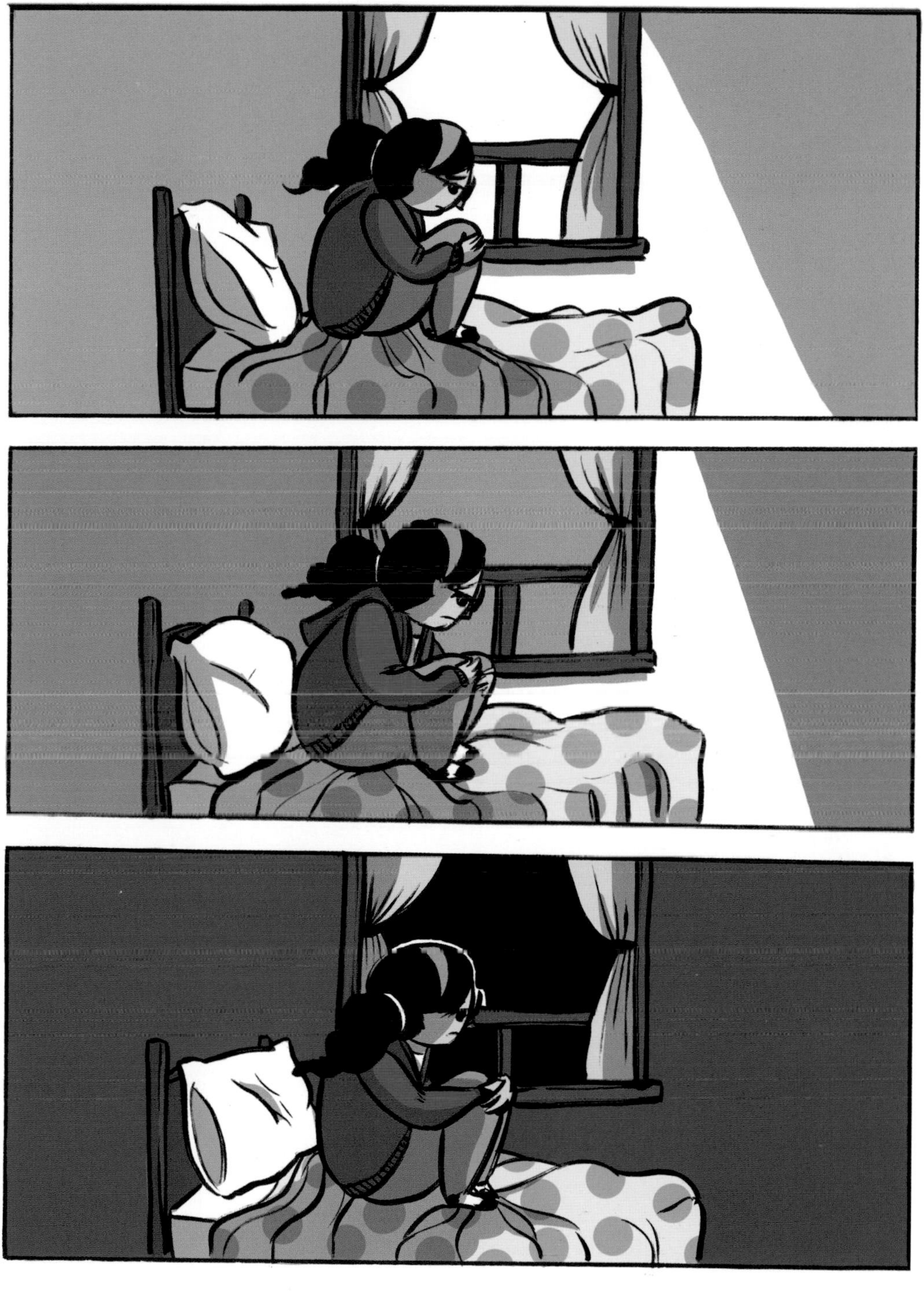

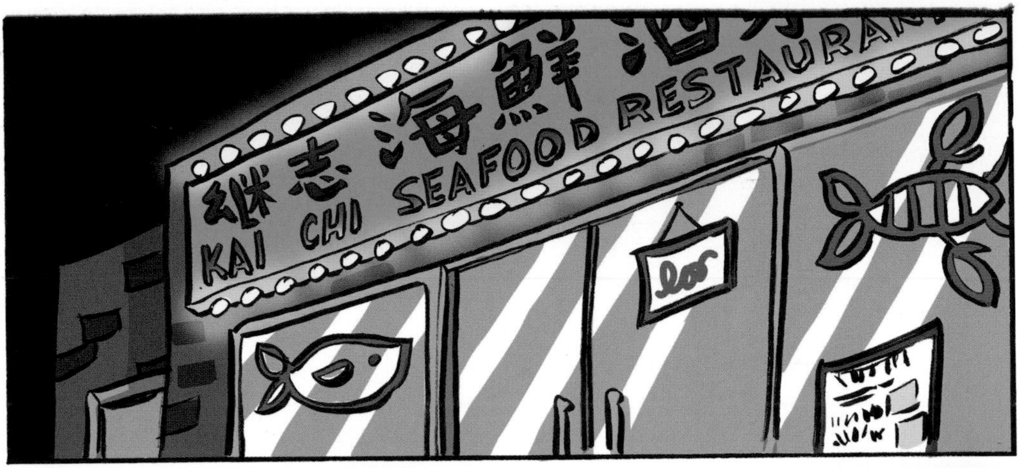

KAI CHI SEAFOOD RESTAURANT

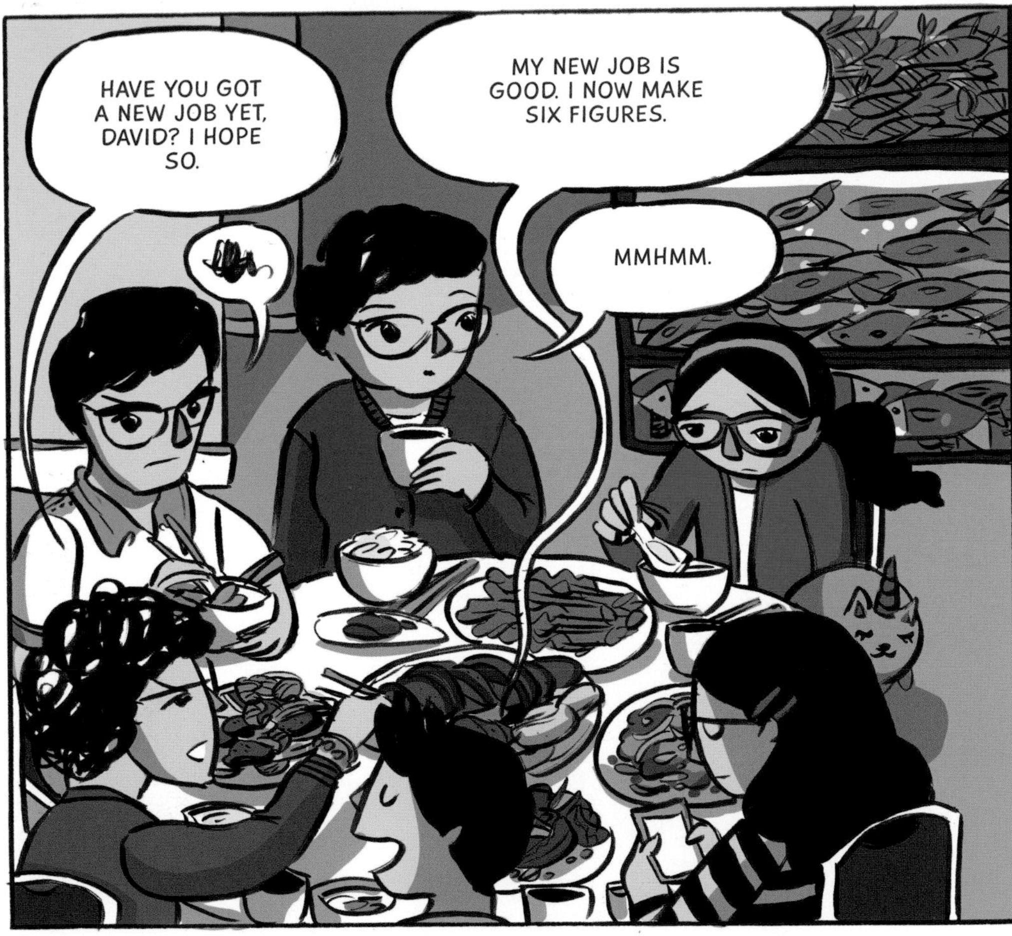

HAVE YOU GOT A NEW JOB YET, DAVID? I HOPE SO.
MY NEW JOB IS GOOD. I NOW MAKE SIX FIGURES.
MMHMM.

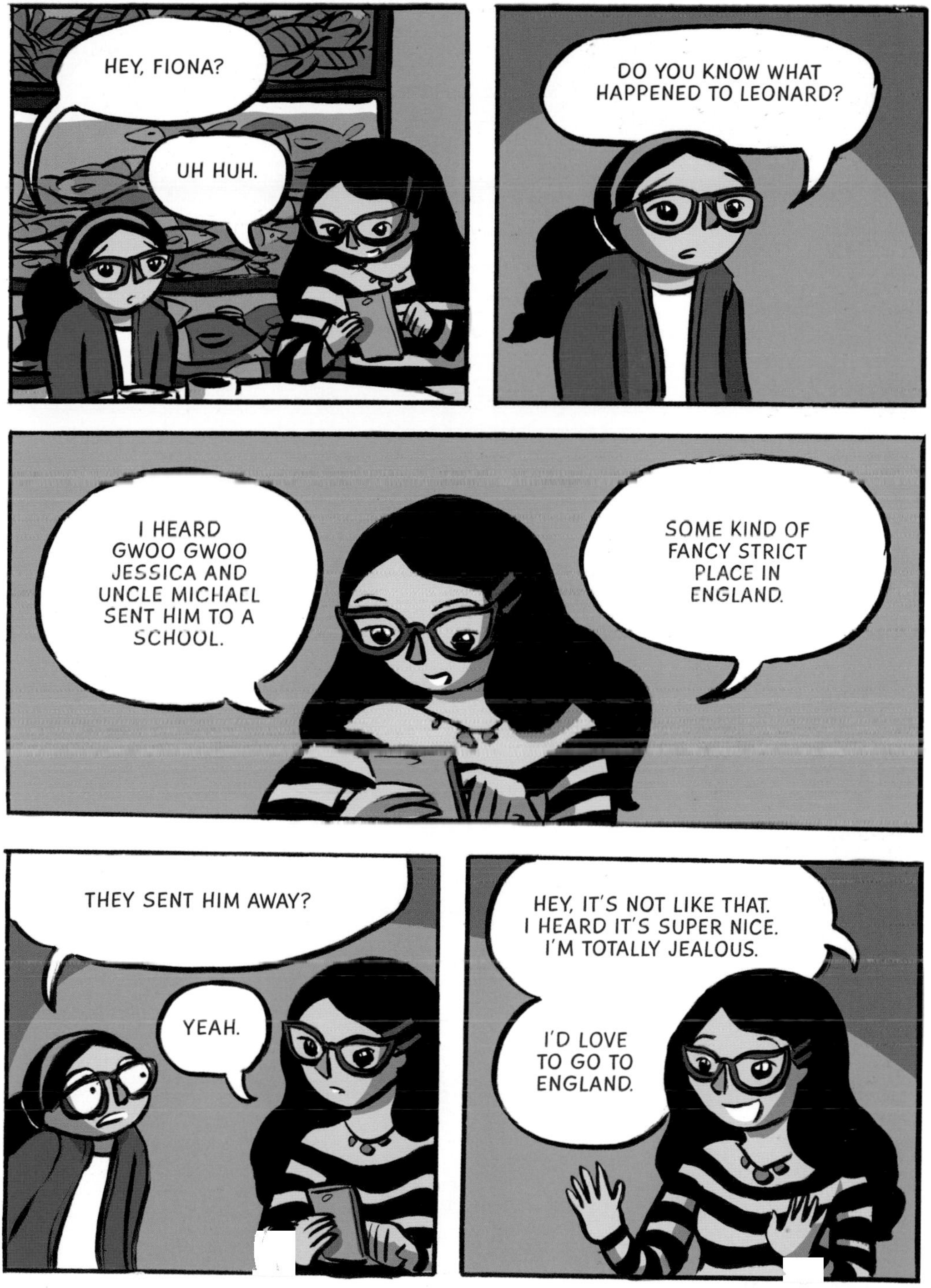
HEY, FIONA?
UH HUH.
DO YOU KNOW WHAT HAPPENED TO LEONARD?
I HEARD GWOO GWOO JESSICA AND UNCLE MICHAEL SENT HIM TO A SCHOOL.
SOME KIND OF FANCY STRICT PLACE IN ENGLAND.
THEY SENT HIM AWAY?
YEAH.
HEY, IT'S NOT LIKE THAT. I HEARD IT'S SUPER NICE. I'M TOTALLY JEALOUS.
I'D LOVE TO GO TO ENGLAND.

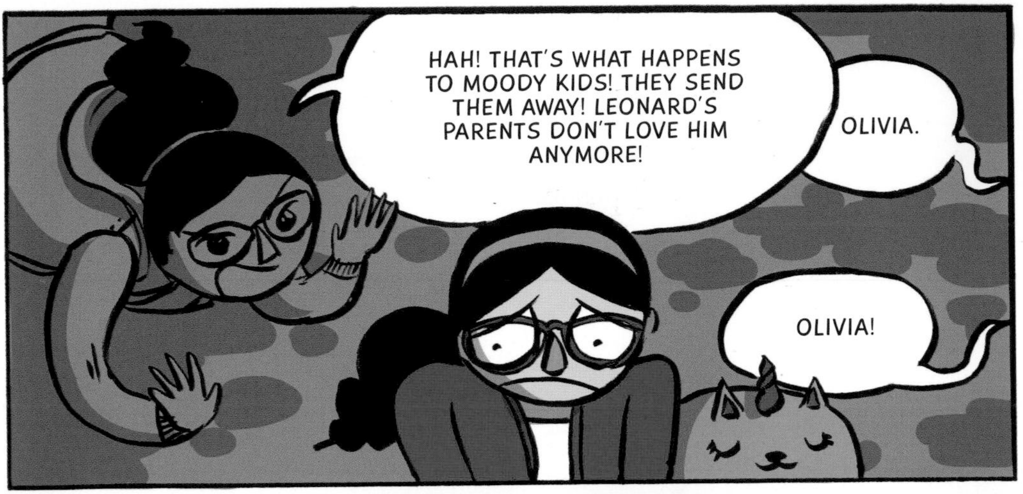
HAH! THAT'S WHAT HAPPENS TO MOODY KIDS! THEY SEND THEM AWAY! LEONARD'S PARENTS DON'T LOVE HIM ANYMORE!
OLIVIA.
OLIVIA!

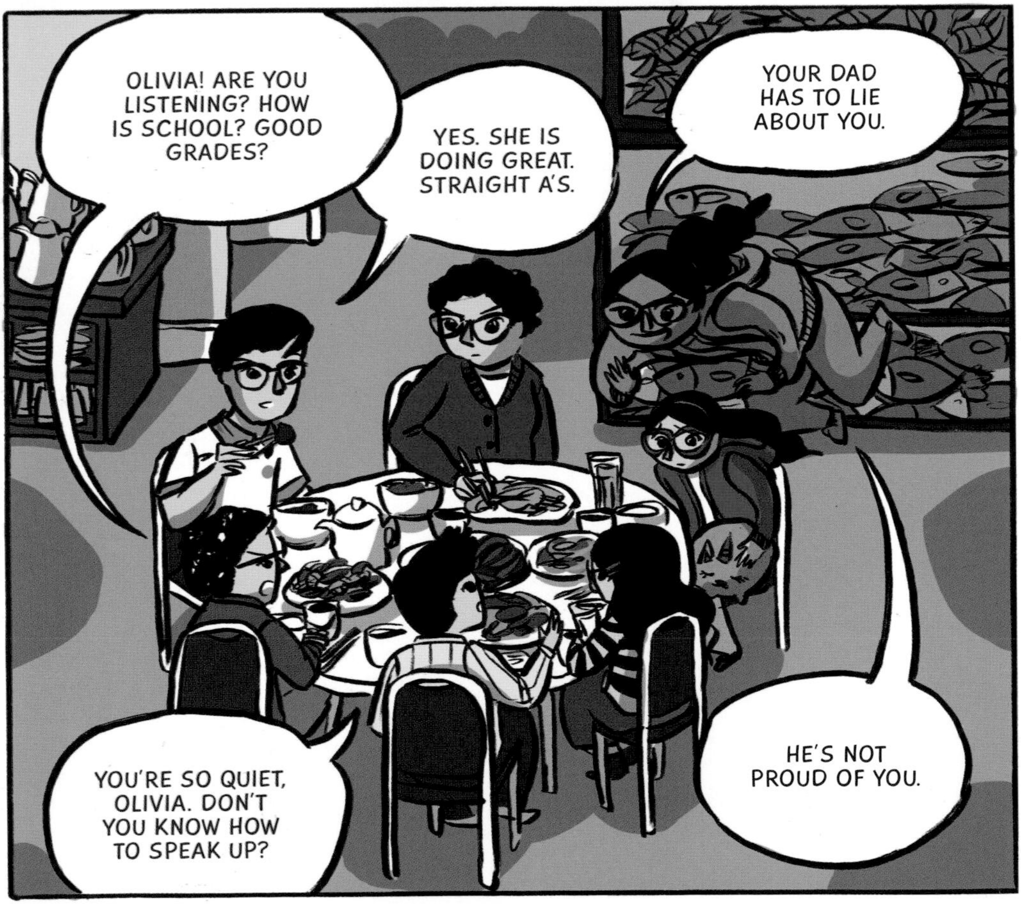
OLIVIA! ARE YOU LISTENING? HOW IS SCHOOL? GOOD GRADES?
YES. SHE IS DOING GREAT. STRAIGHT A'S.
YOUR DAD HAS TO LIE ABOUT YOU.
YOU'RE SO QUIET, OLIVIA. DON'T YOU KNOW HOW TO SPEAK UP?
HE'S NOT PROUD OF YOU.

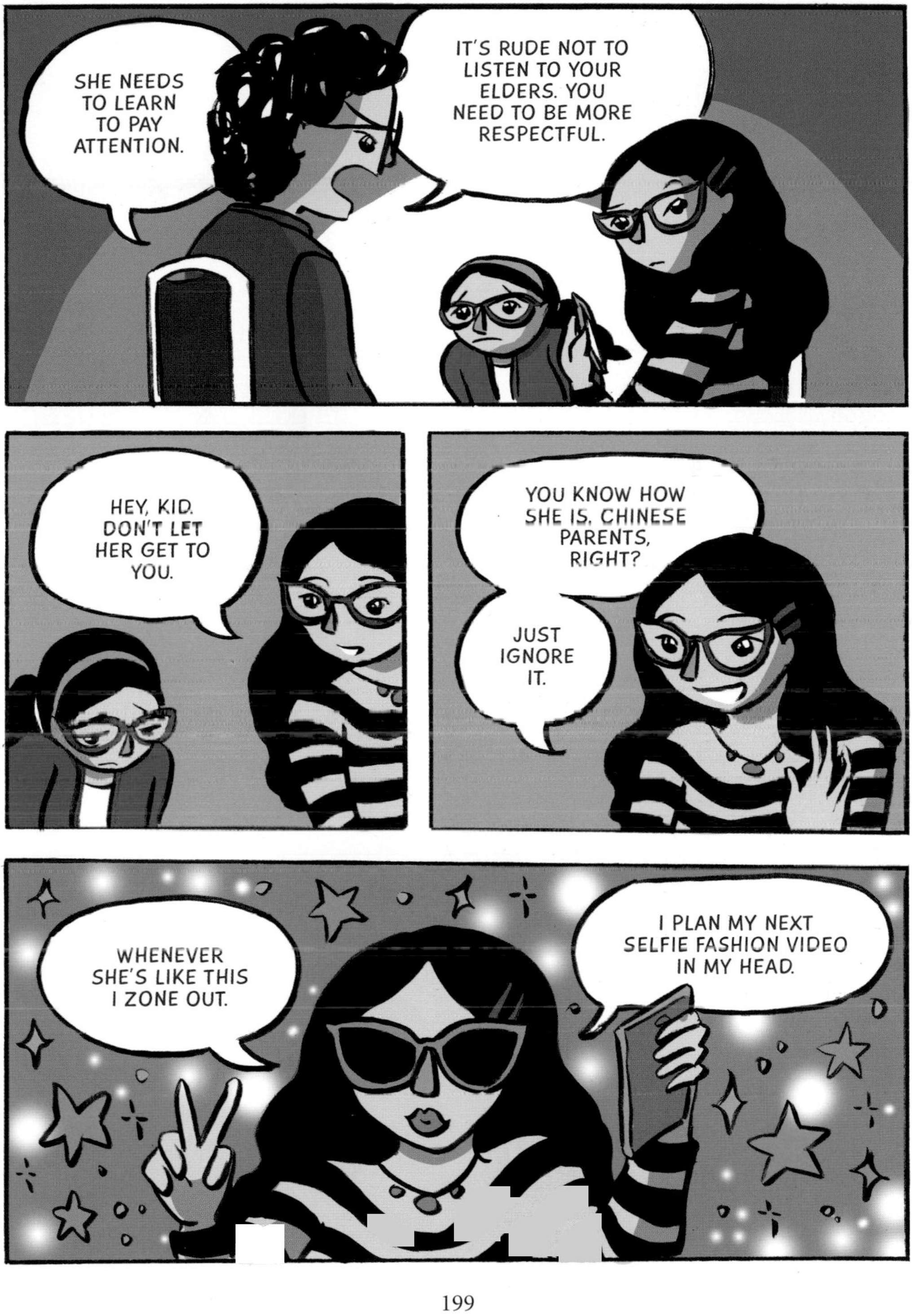
SHE NEEDS TO LEARN TO PAY ATTENTION.
IT'S RUDE NOT TO LISTEN TO YOUR ELDERS. YOU NEED TO BE MORE RESPECTFUL.
HEY, KID. DON'T LET HER GET TO YOU.
YOU KNOW HOW SHE IS. CHINESE PARENTS, RIGHT?
JUST IGNORE IT.
WHENEVER SHE'S LIKE THIS I ZONE OUT.
I PLAN MY NEXT SELFIE FASHION VIDEO IN MY HEAD.

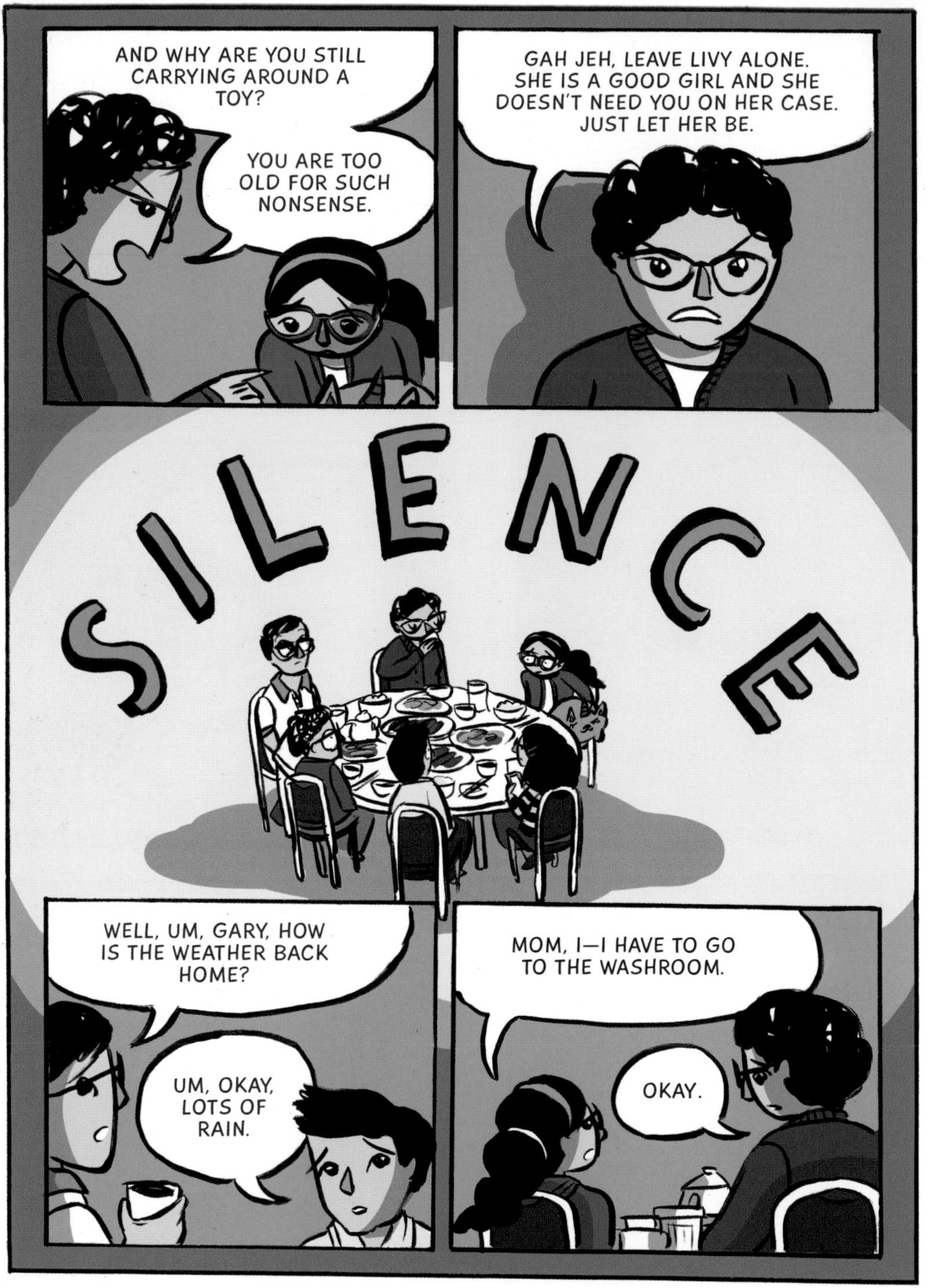
AND WHY ARE YOU STILL CARRYING AROUND A TOY?
YOU ARE TOO OLD FOR SUCH NONSENSE.
GAH JEH, LEAVE LIVY ALONE. SHE IS A GOOD GIRL AND SHE DOESN'T NEED YOU ON HER CASE. JUST LET HER BE.
SILENCE
WELL, UM, GARY, HOW IS THE WEATHER BACK HOME?
UM, OKAY, LOTS OF RAIN.
MOM, I—I HAVE TO GO TO THE WASHROOM.
OKAY.

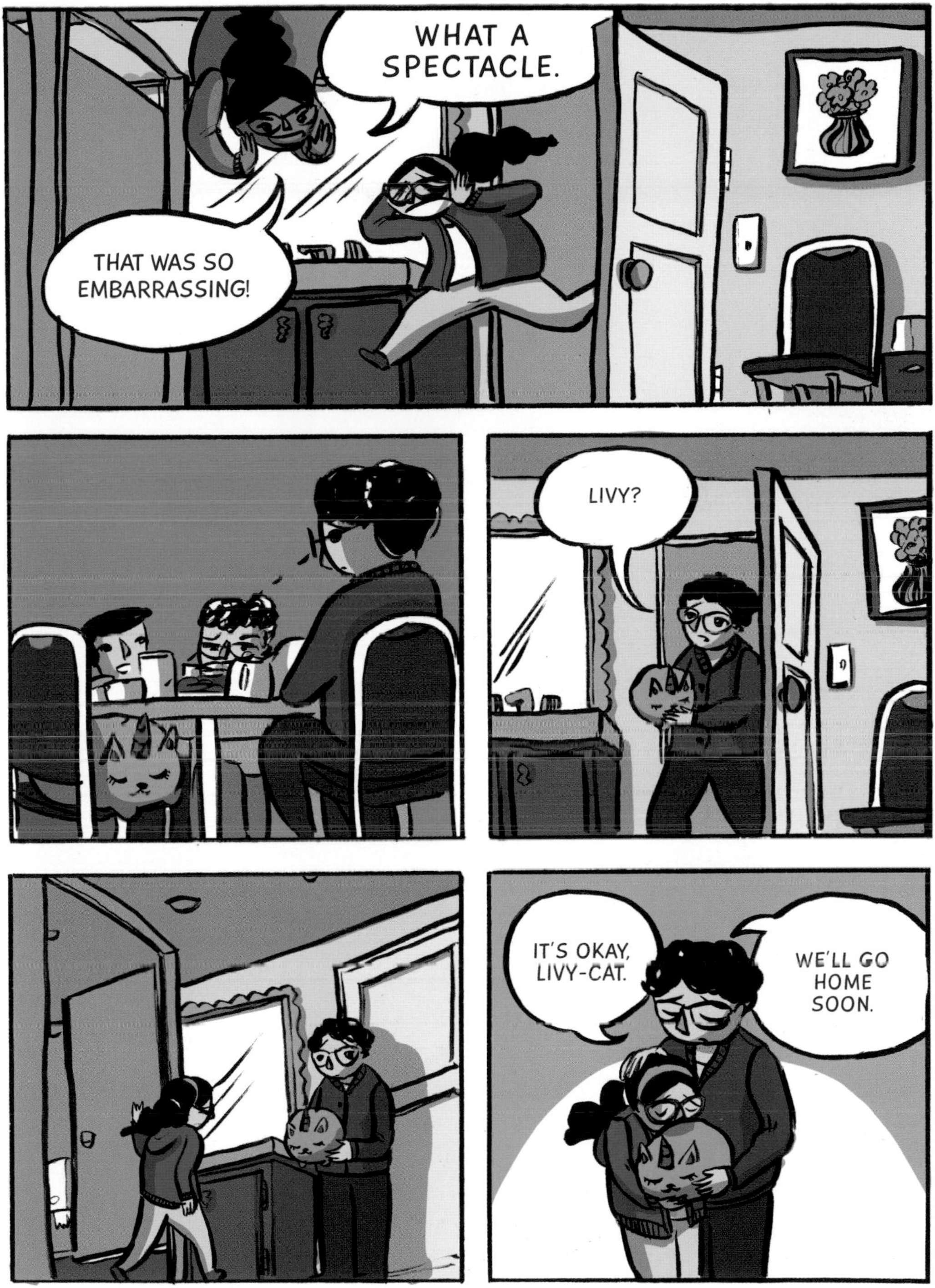
WHAT A SPECTACLE.
THAT WAS SO EMBARRASSING!
LIVY?
IT'S OKAY, LIVY-CAT.
WE'LL GO HOME SOON.

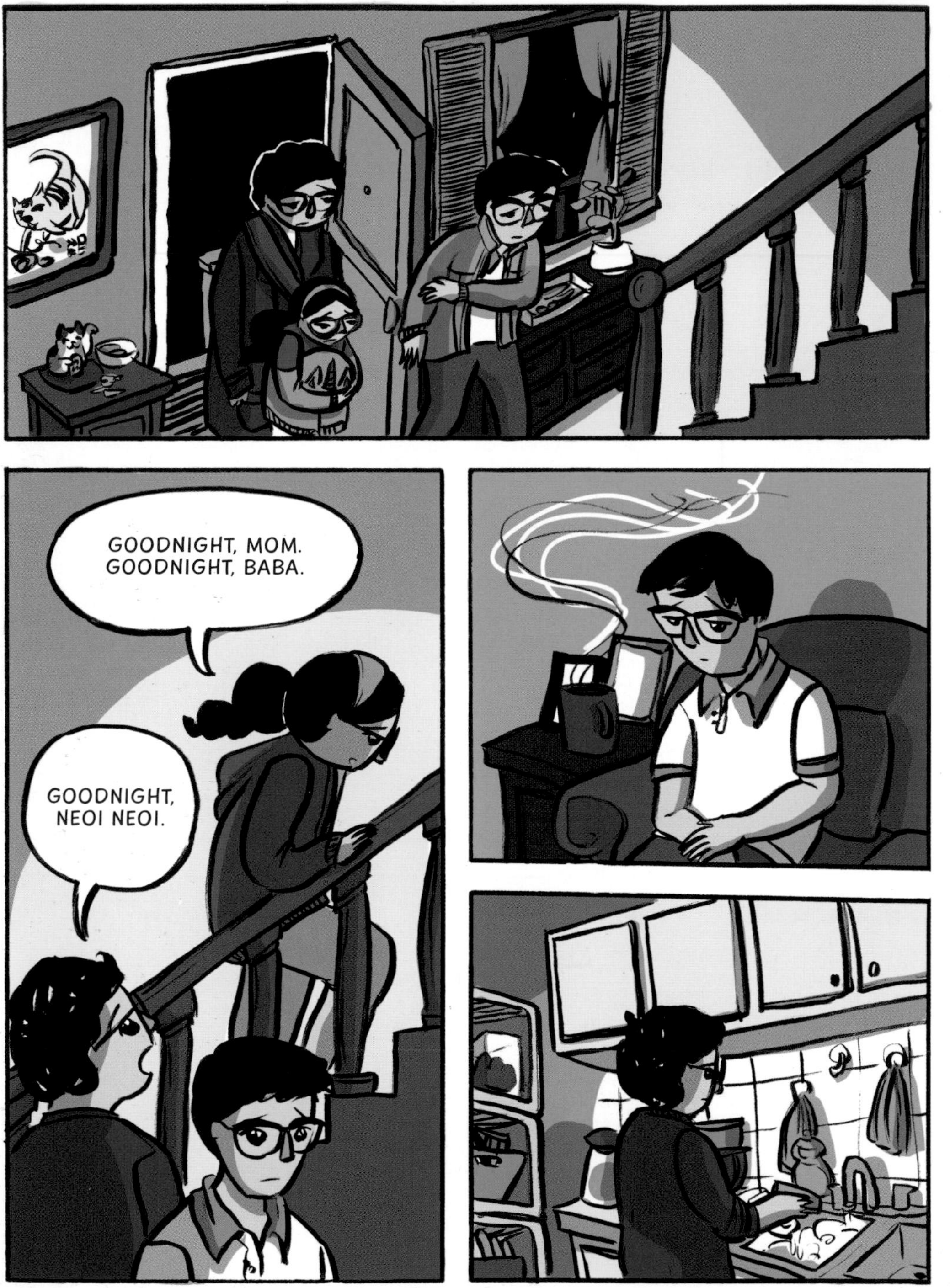
GOODNIGHT, MOM. GOODNIGHT, BABA.
GOODNIGHT, NEOI NEOI.

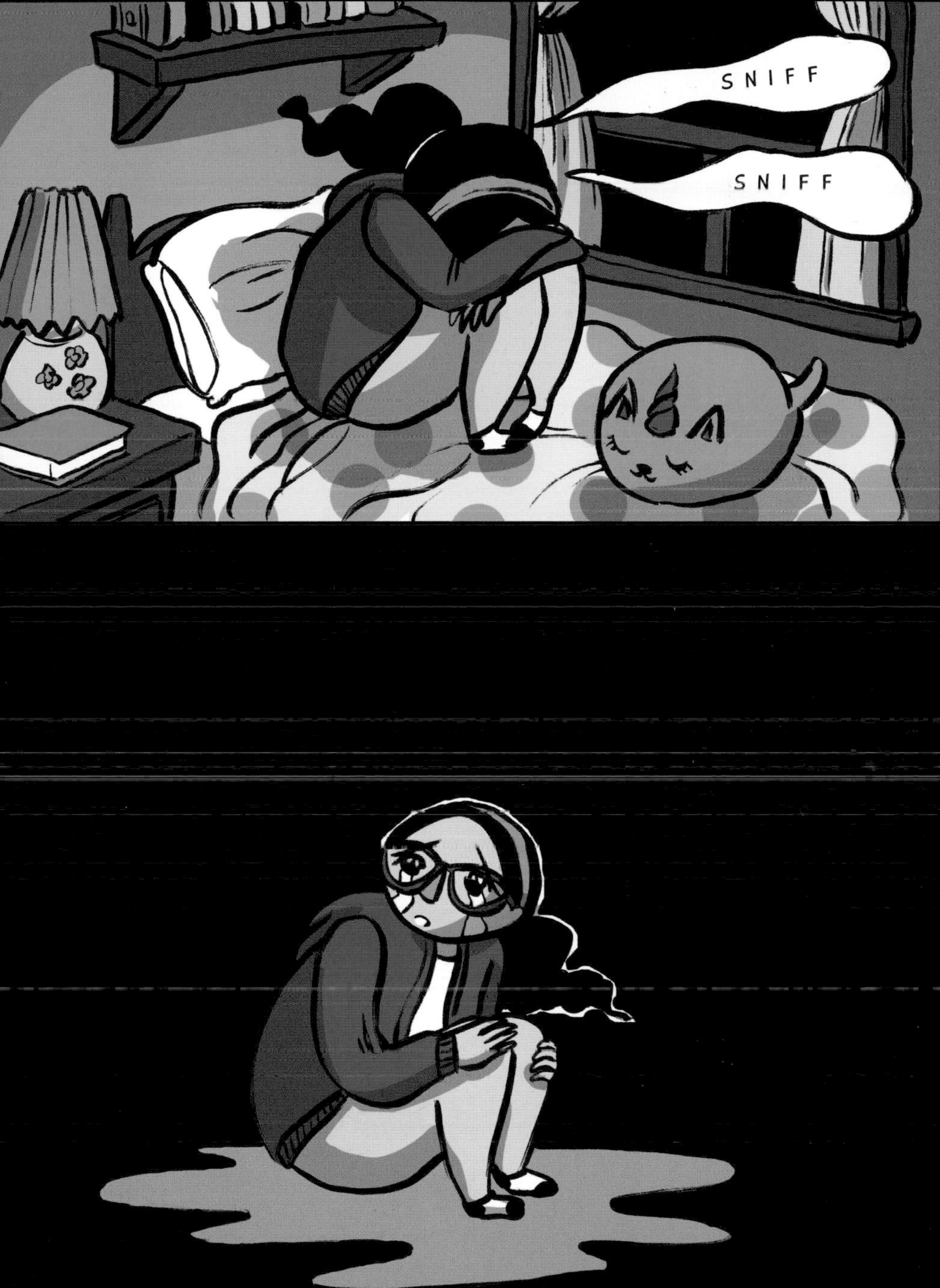
SNIFF
SNIFF

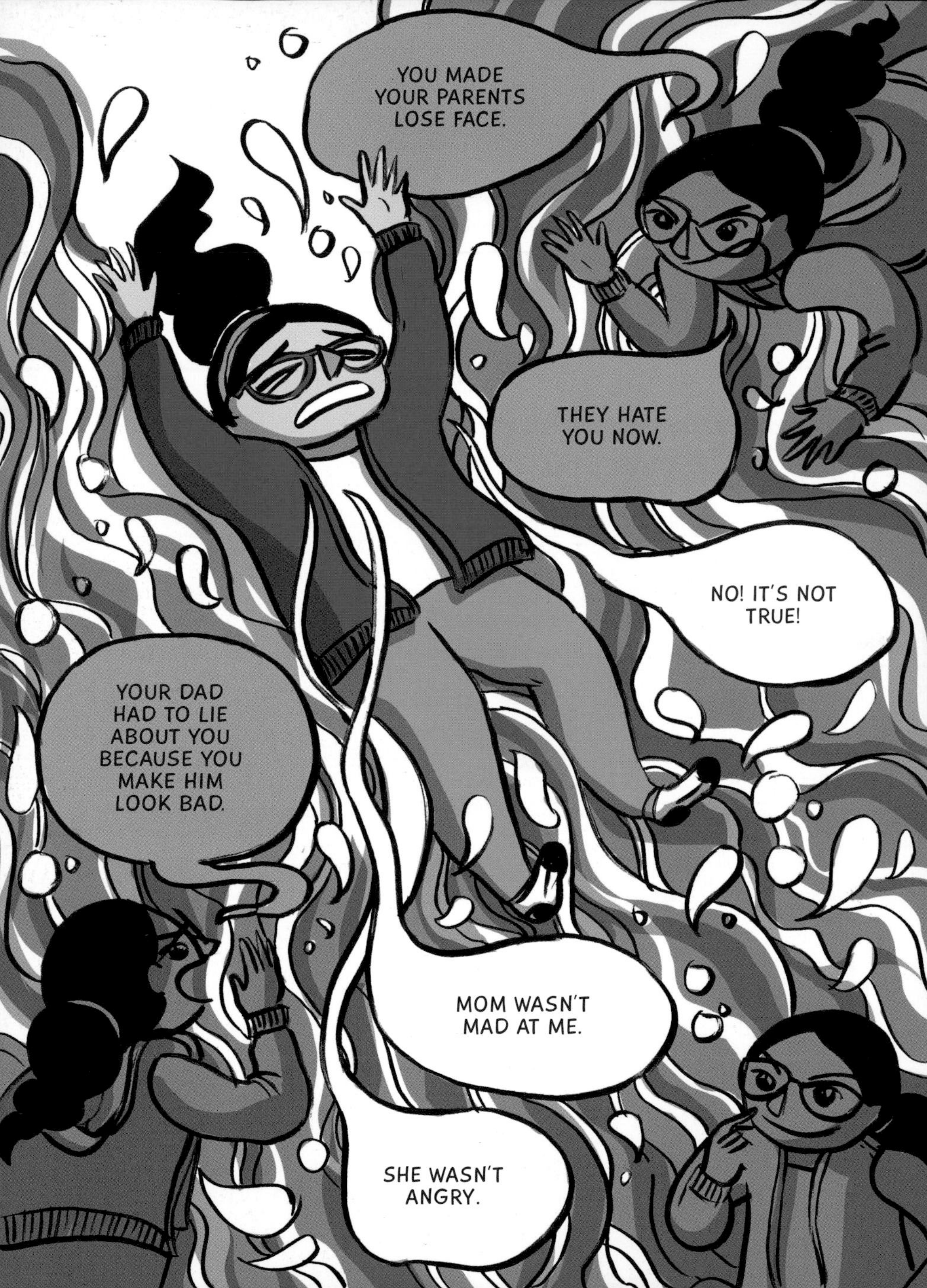
YOU MADE YOUR PARENTS LOSE FACE.
THEY HATE YOU NOW.
NO! IT'S NOT TRUE!
YOUR DAD HAD TO LIE ABOUT YOU BECAUSE YOU MAKE HIM LOOK BAD.
MOM WASN'T MAD AT ME.
SHE WASN'T ANGRY.

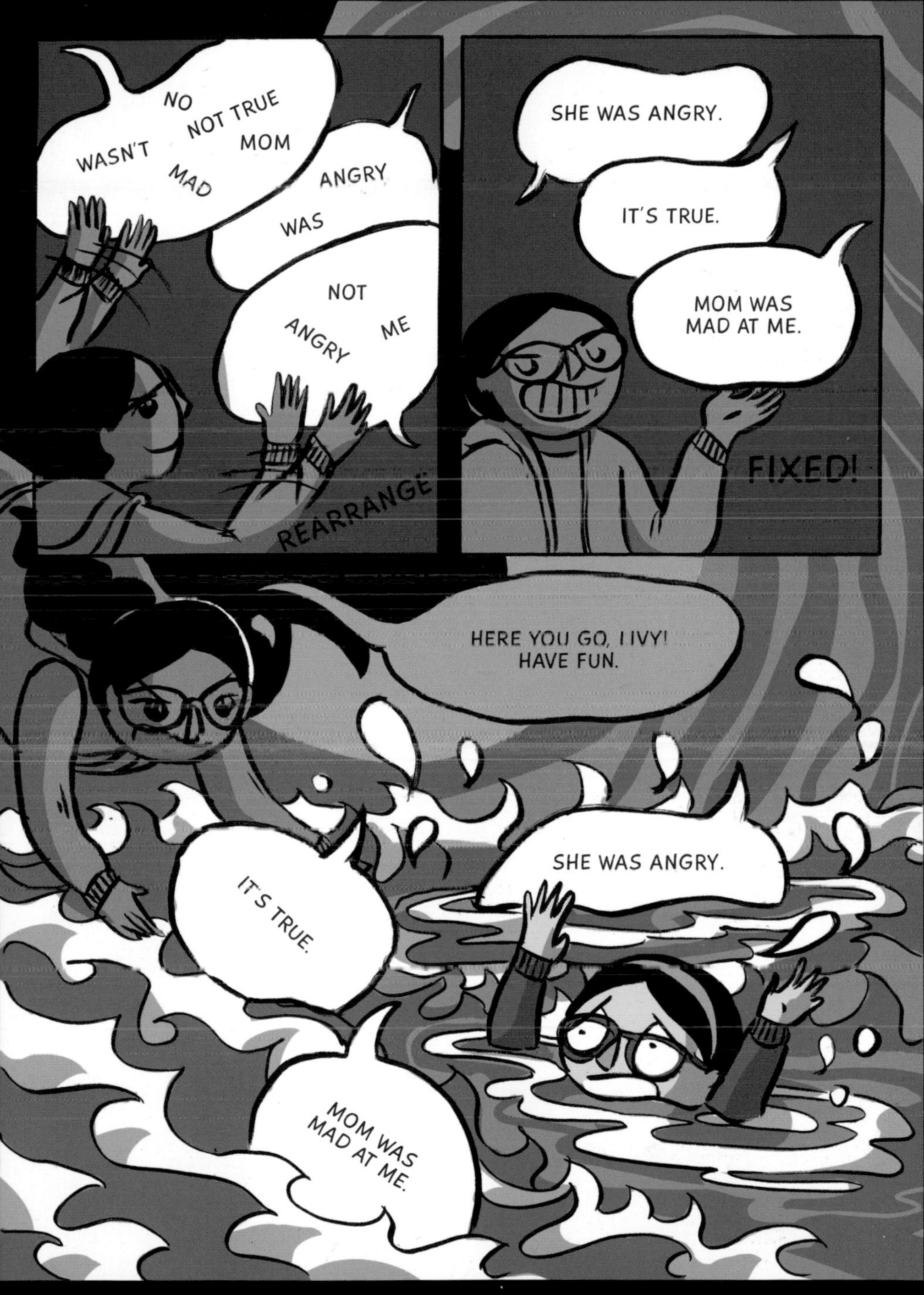
NO
NOT TRUE
WASN'T
MOM
MAD
ANGRY
WAS
NOT
ANGRY
ME
REARRANGE
SHE WAS ANGRY.
IT'S TRUE.
MOM WAS MAD AT ME.
FIXED!
HERE YOU GO, LIVY! HAVE FUN.
IT'S TRUE.
SHE WAS ANGRY.
MOM WAS MAD AT ME.

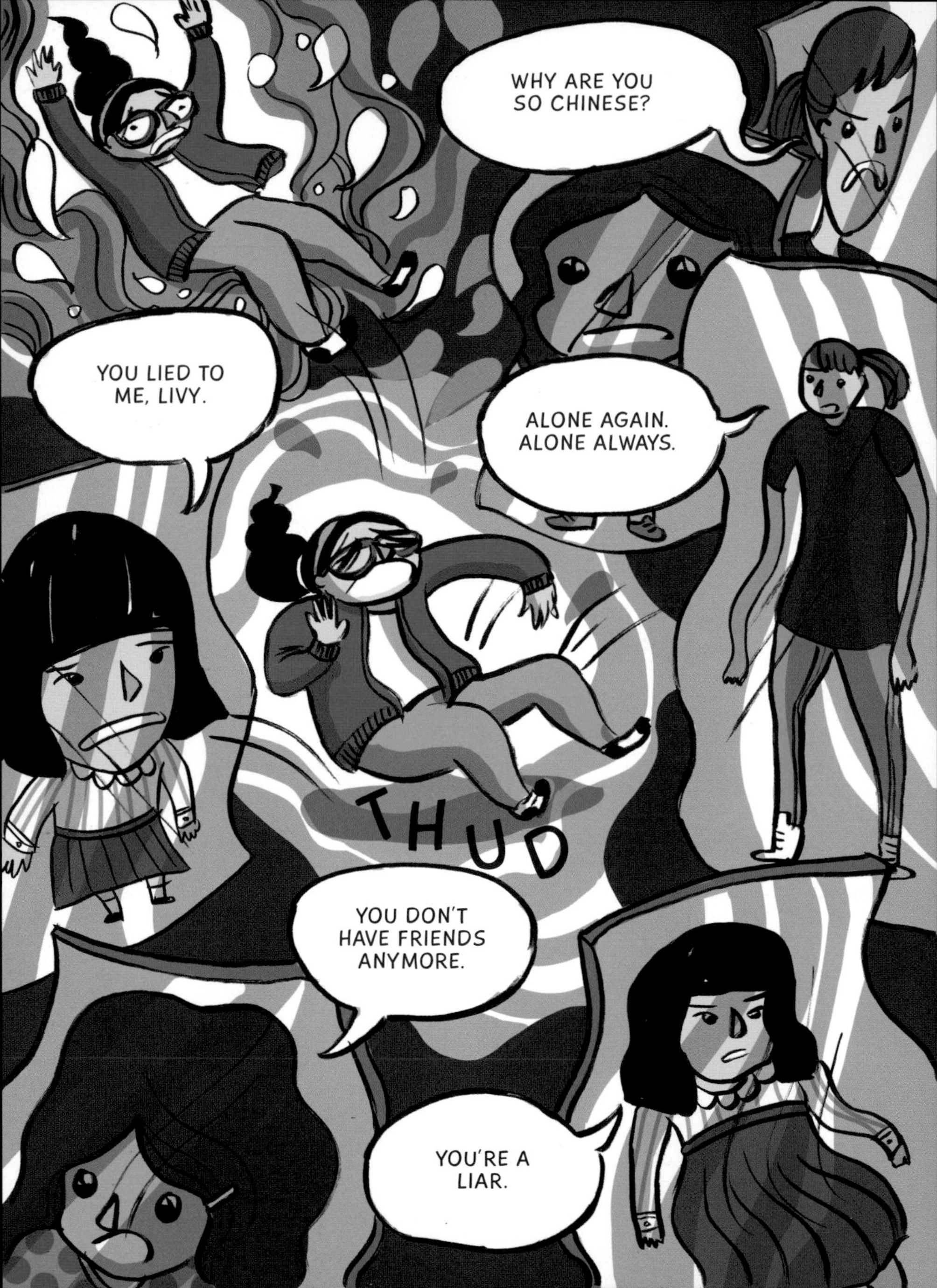
WHY ARE YOU SO CHINESE?
YOU LIED TO ME, LIVY.
ALONE AGAIN. ALONE ALWAYS.
THUD
YOU DON'T HAVE FRIENDS ANYMORE.
YOU'RE A LIAR.

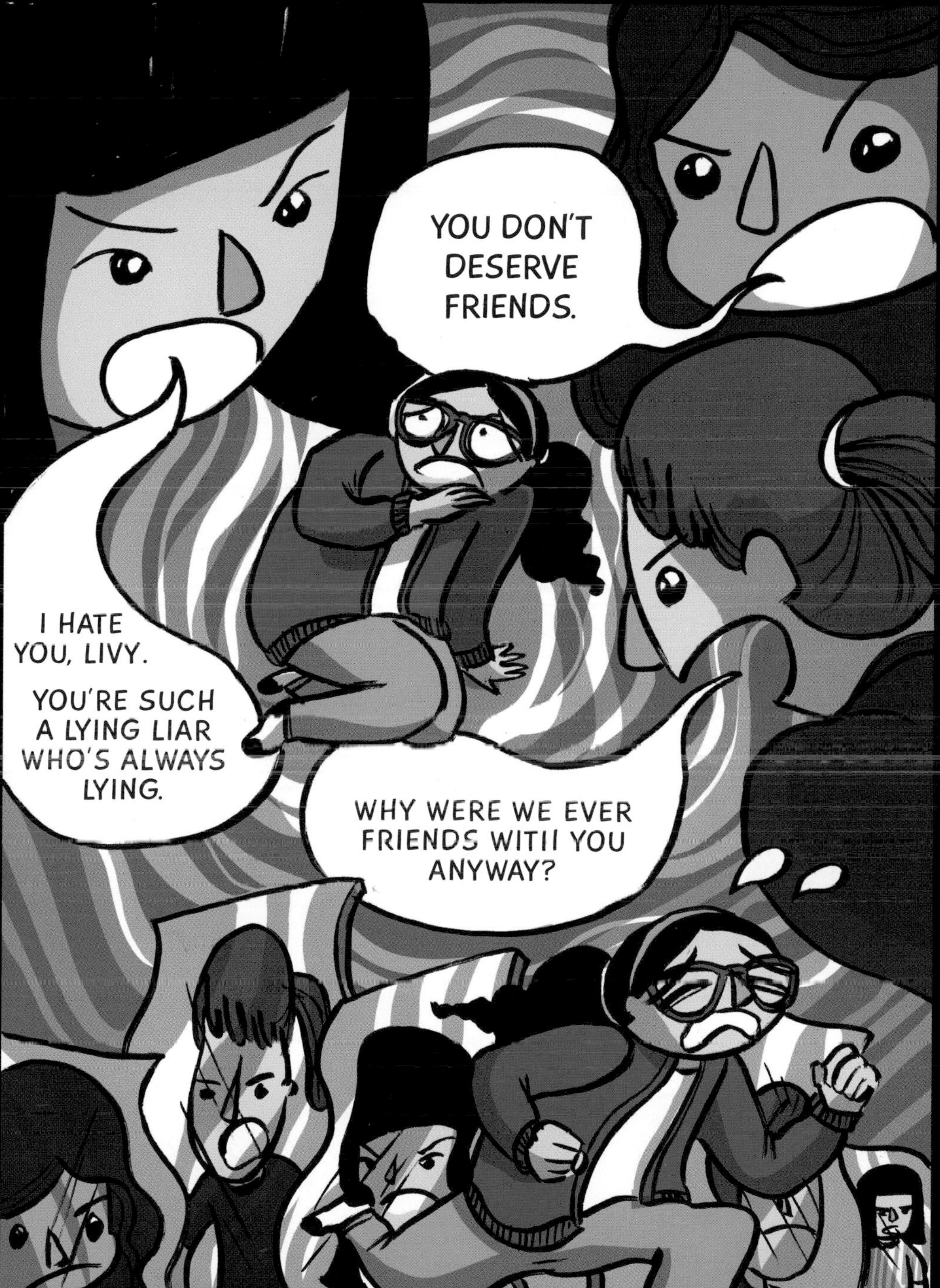

YOU DON'T DESERVE FRIENDS.
I HATE YOU, LIVY.
YOU'RE SUCH A LYING LIAR WHO'S ALWAYS LYING.
WHY WERE WE EVER FRIENDS WITH YOU ANYWAY?

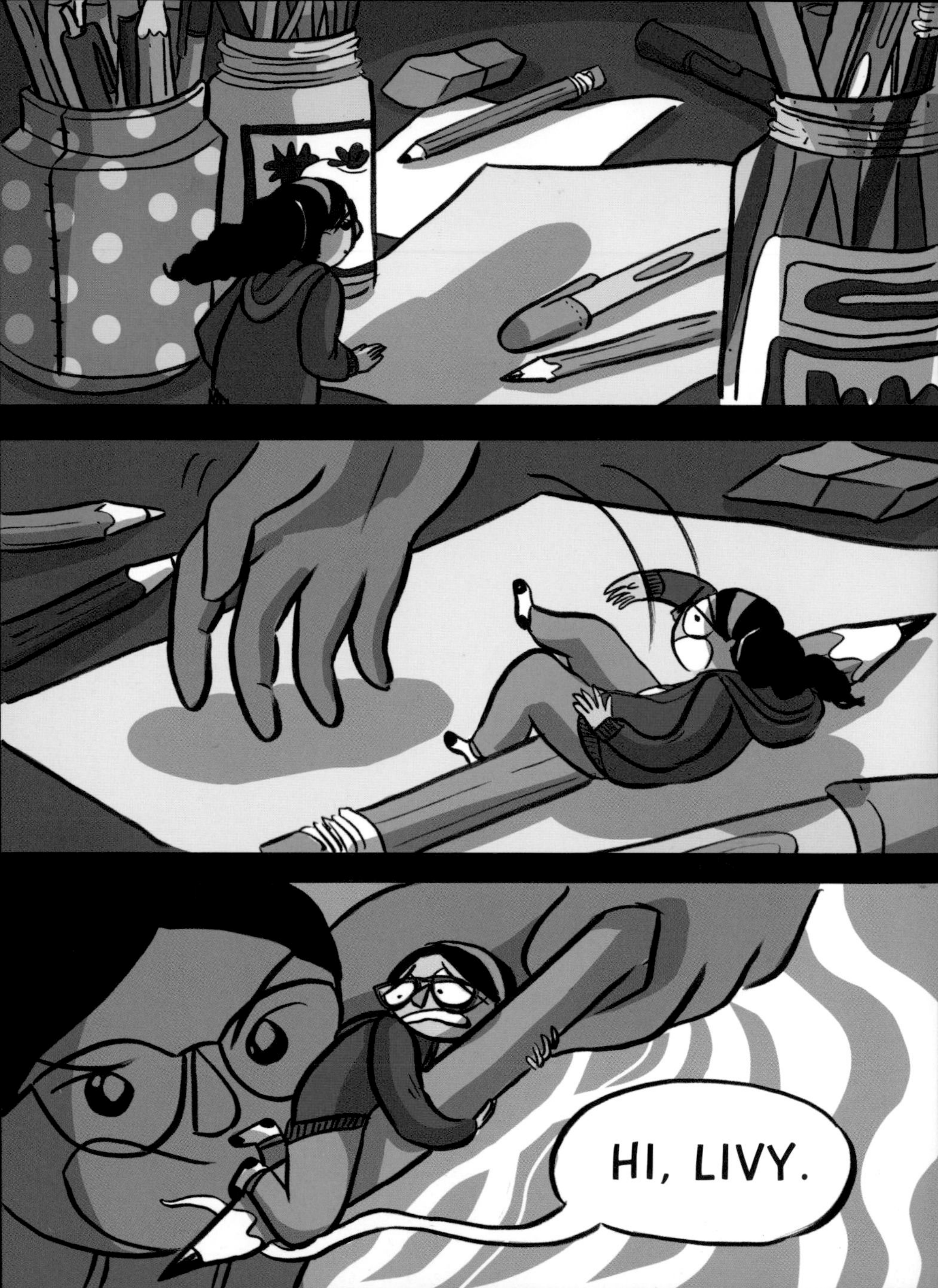
HI, LIVY.

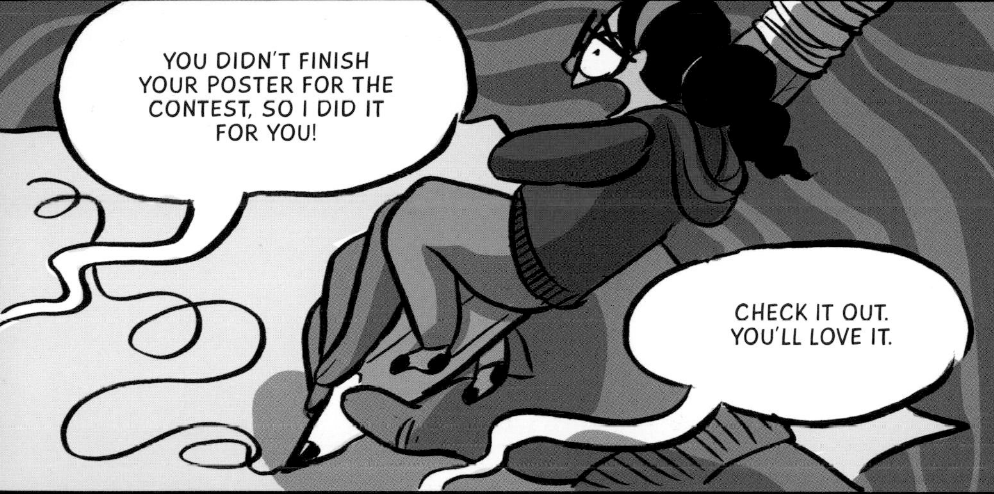
YOU DIDN'T FINISH YOUR POSTER FOR THE CONTEST, SO I DID IT FOR YOU!
CHECK IT OUT. YOU'LL LOVE IT.

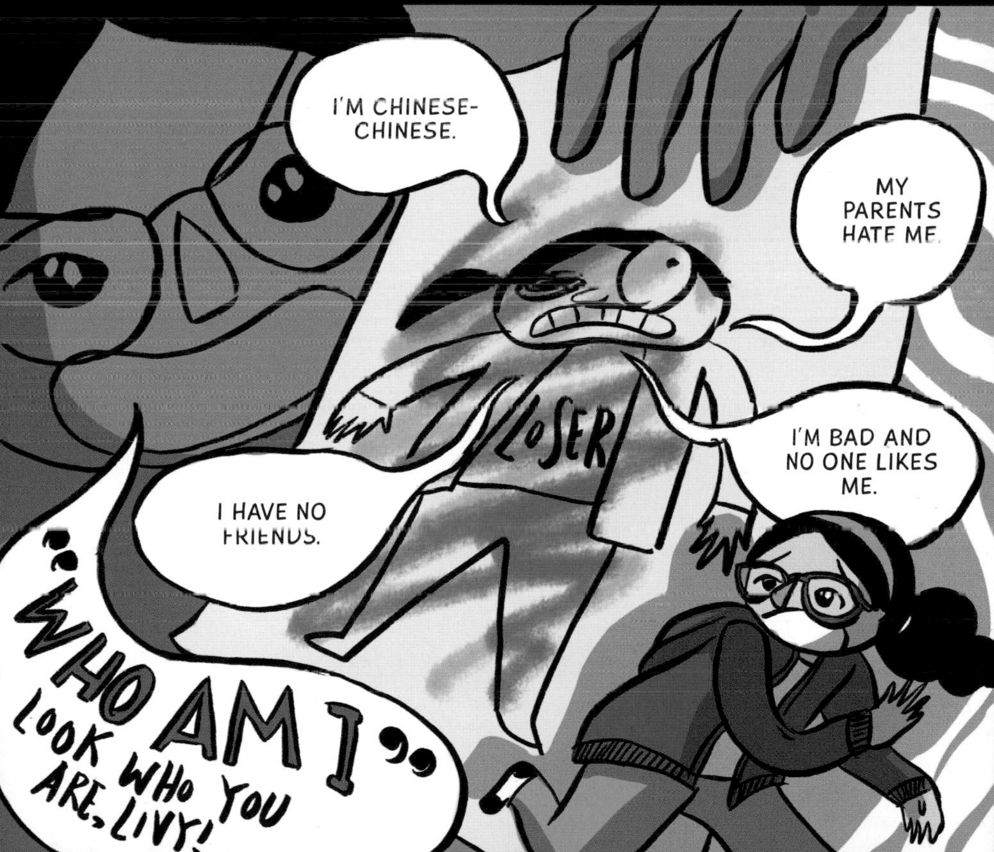
I'M CHINESE-CHINESE.
MY PARENTS HATE ME.
LOSER
I'M BAD AND NO ONE LIKES ME.
I HAVE NO FRIENDS.
"WHO AM I"
LOOK WHO YOU ARE, LIVY!

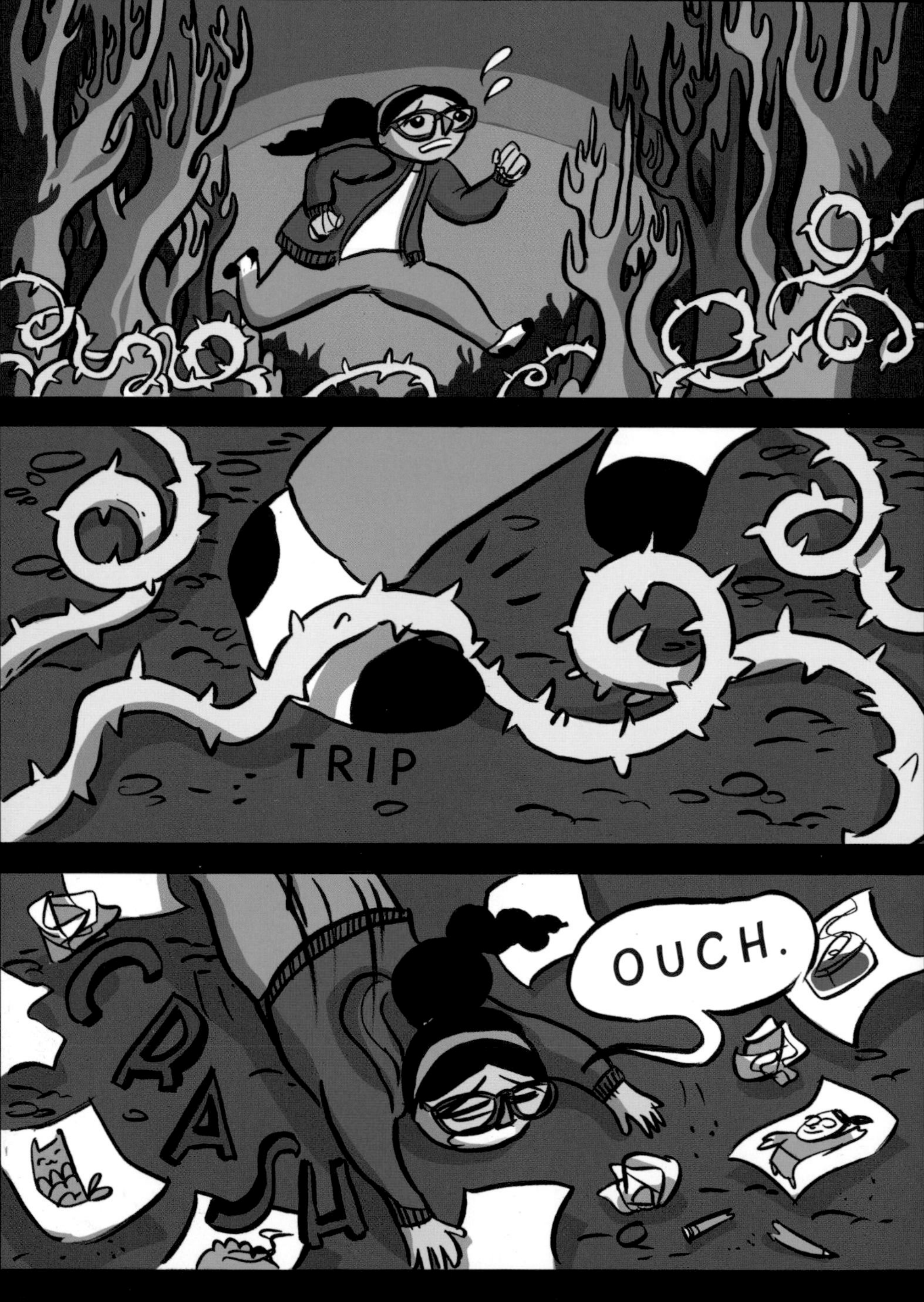
TRIP
CRASH
OUCH.

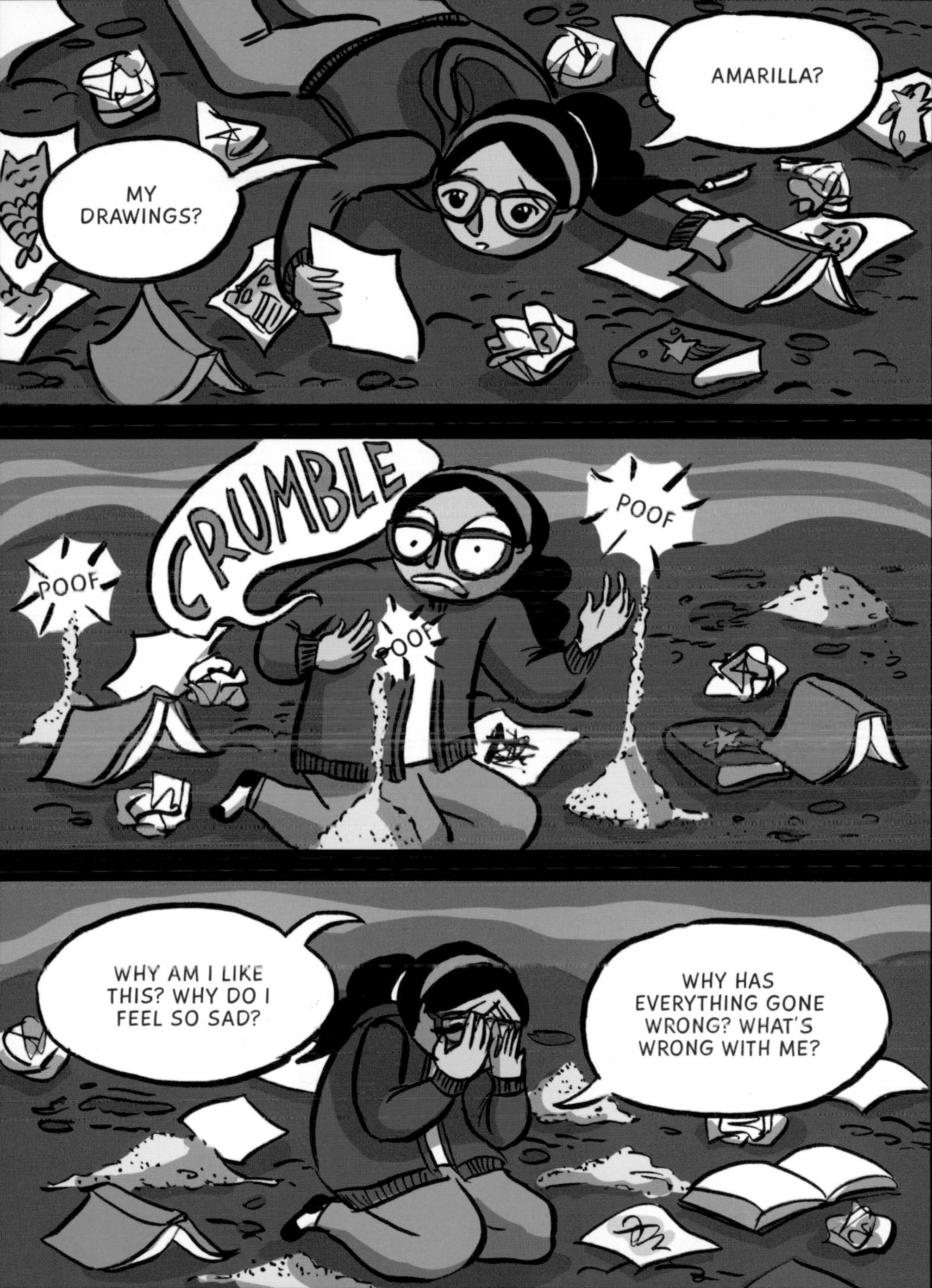
AMARILLA?
MY DRAWINGS?
CRUMBLE
POOF
POOF
POOF
WHY AM I LIKE THIS? WHY DO I FEEL SO SAD?
WHY HAS EVERYTHING GONE WRONG? WHAT'S WRONG WITH ME?

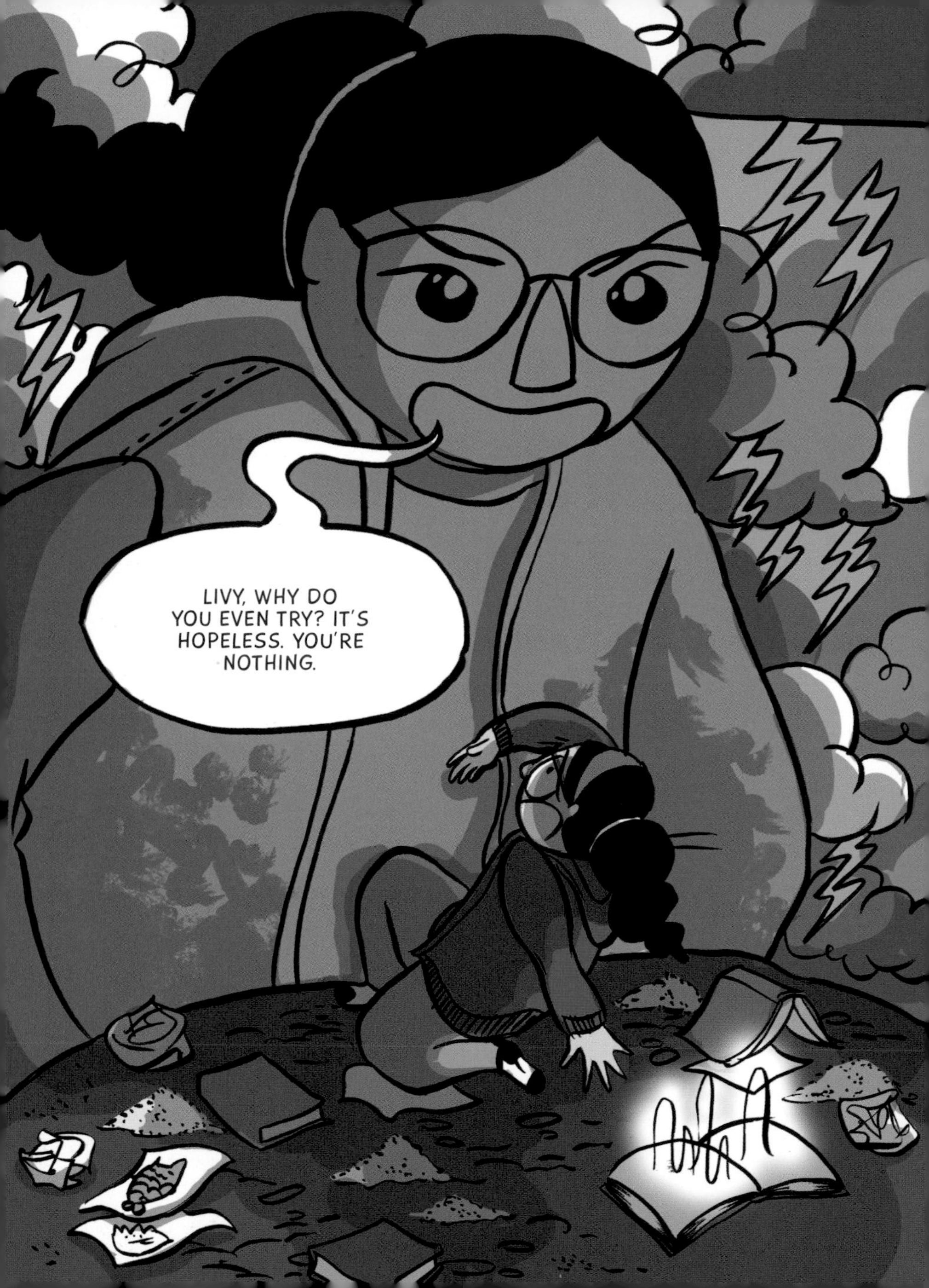
LIVY, WHY DO YOU EVEN TRY? IT'S HOPELESS. YOU'RE NOTHING.

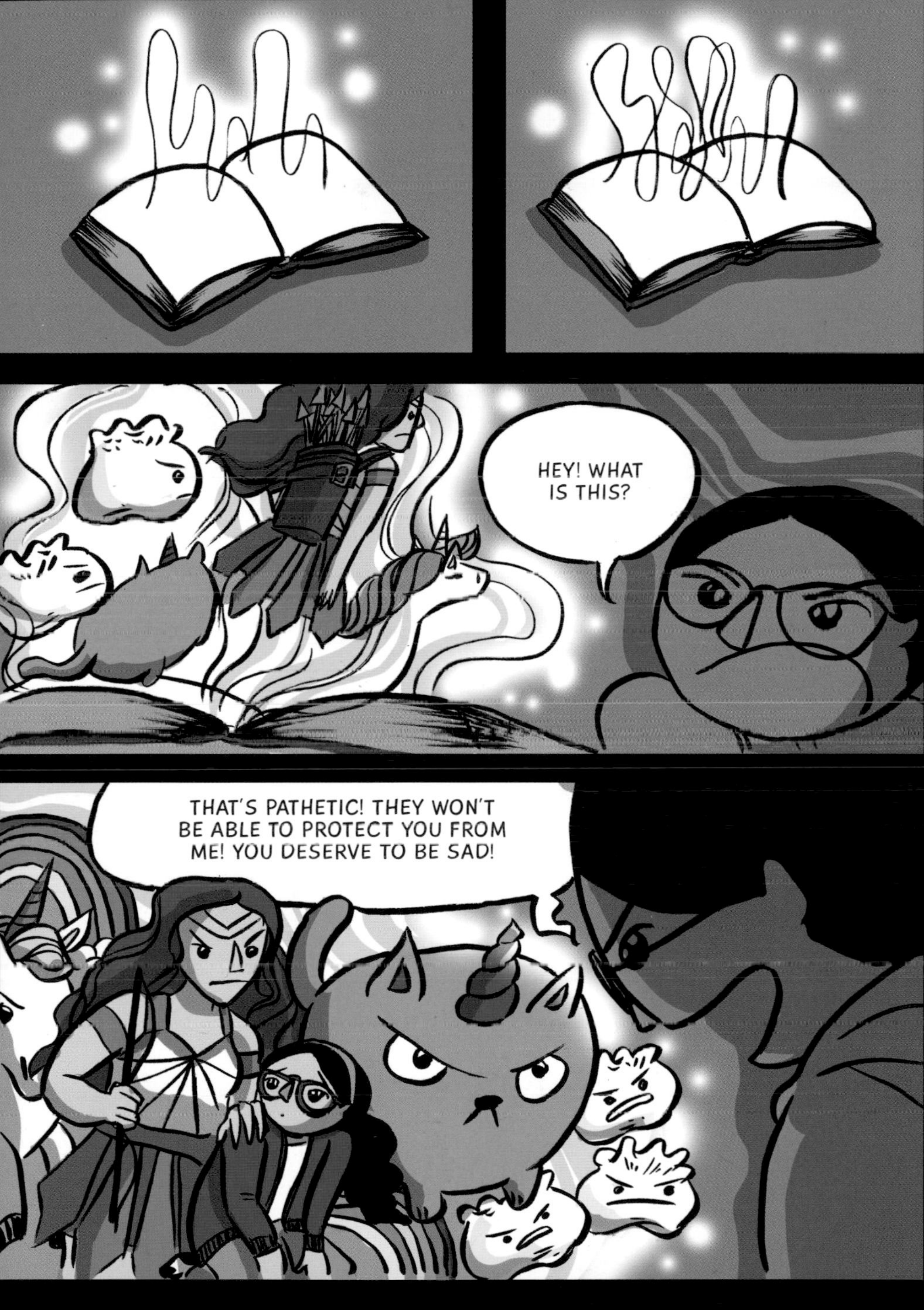
HEY! WHAT IS THIS?
THAT'S PATHETIC! THEY WON'T BE ABLE TO PROTECT YOU FROM ME! YOU DESERVE TO BE SAD!

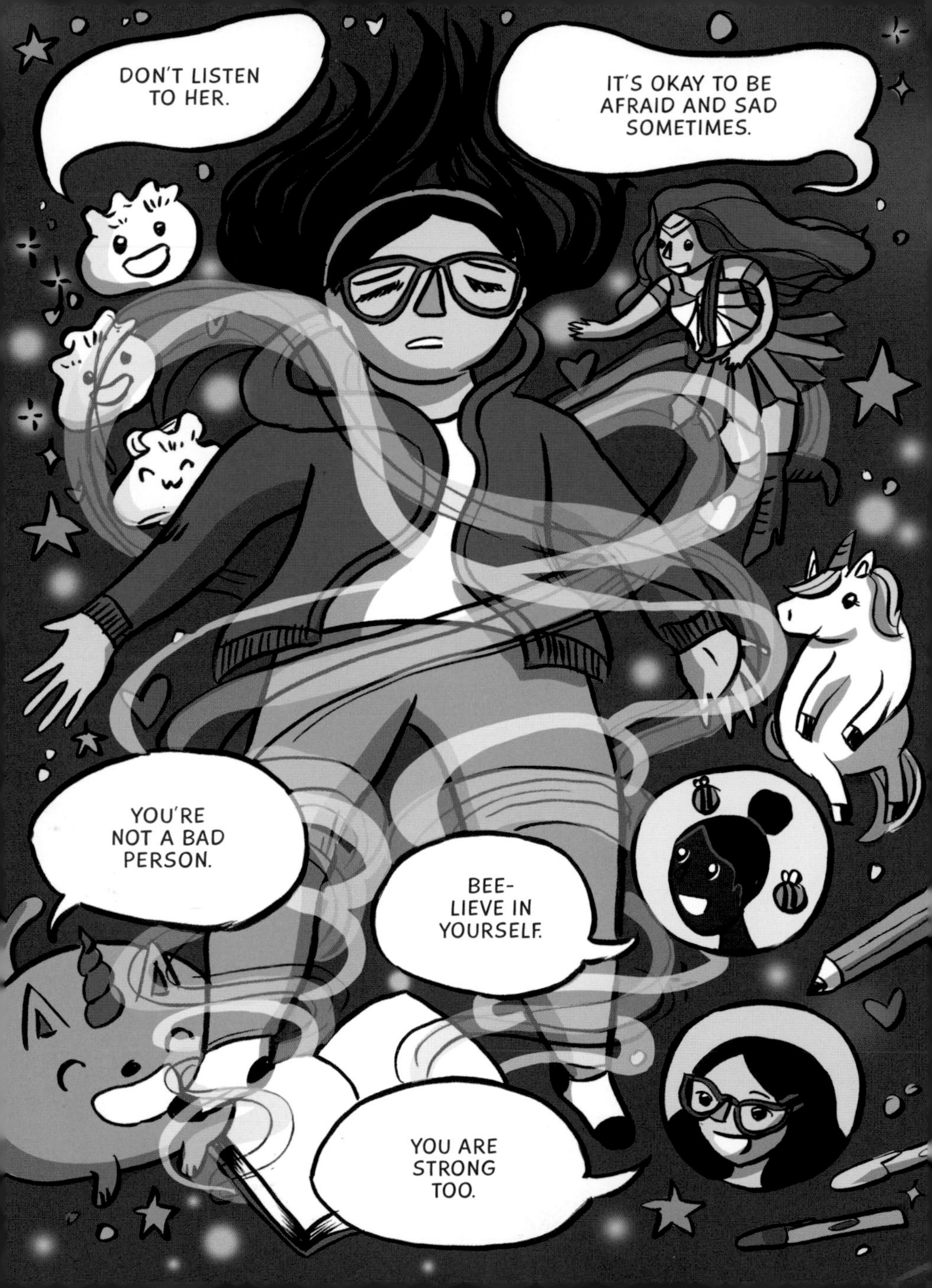
DON'T LISTEN TO HER.
IT'S OKAY TO BE AFRAID AND SAD SOMETIMES.
YOU'RE NOT A BAD PERSON.
BEE-LIEVE IN YOURSELF.
YOU ARE STRONG TOO.

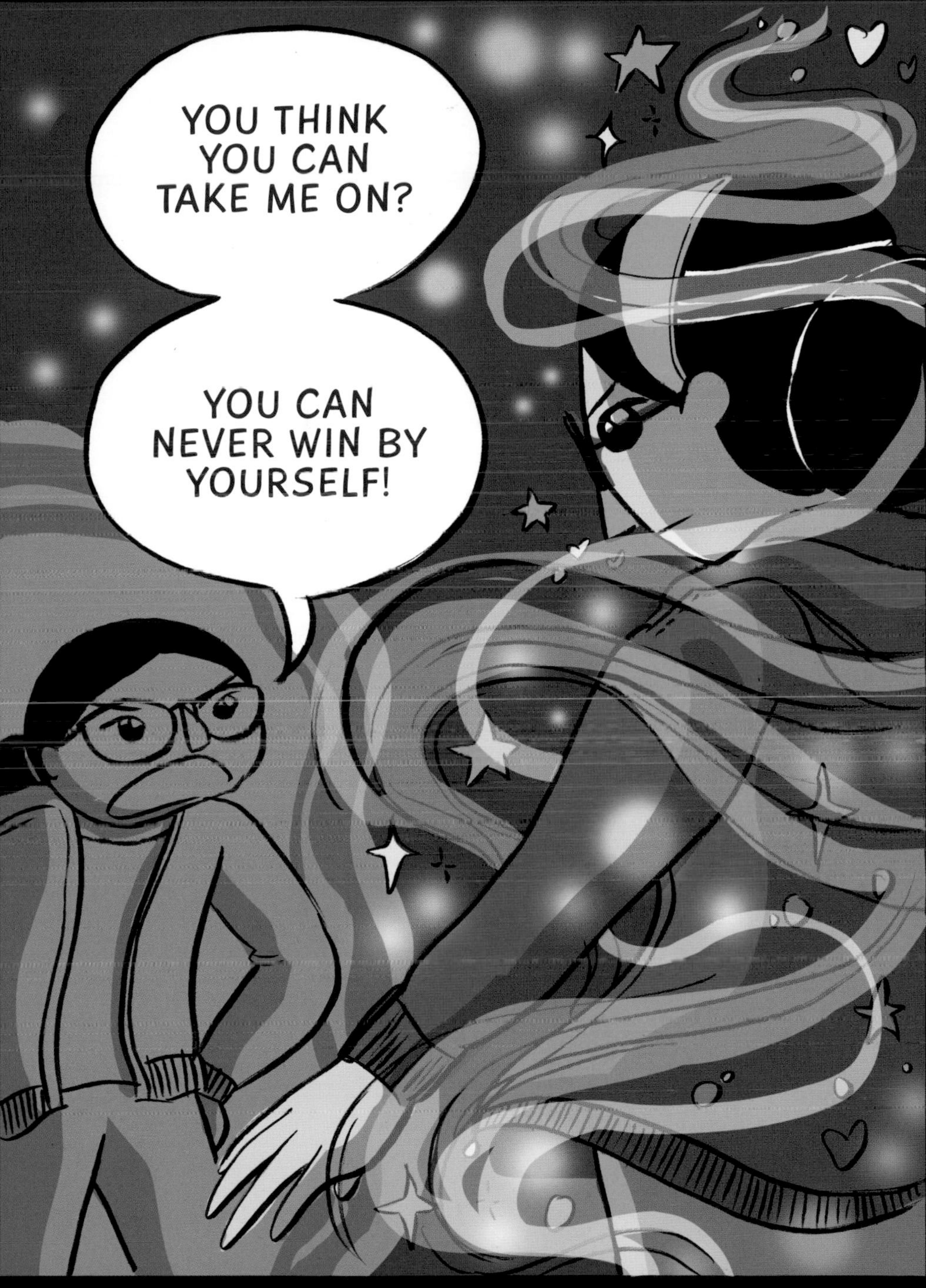
YOU THINK YOU CAN TAKE ME ON?
YOU CAN NEVER WIN BY YOURSELF!

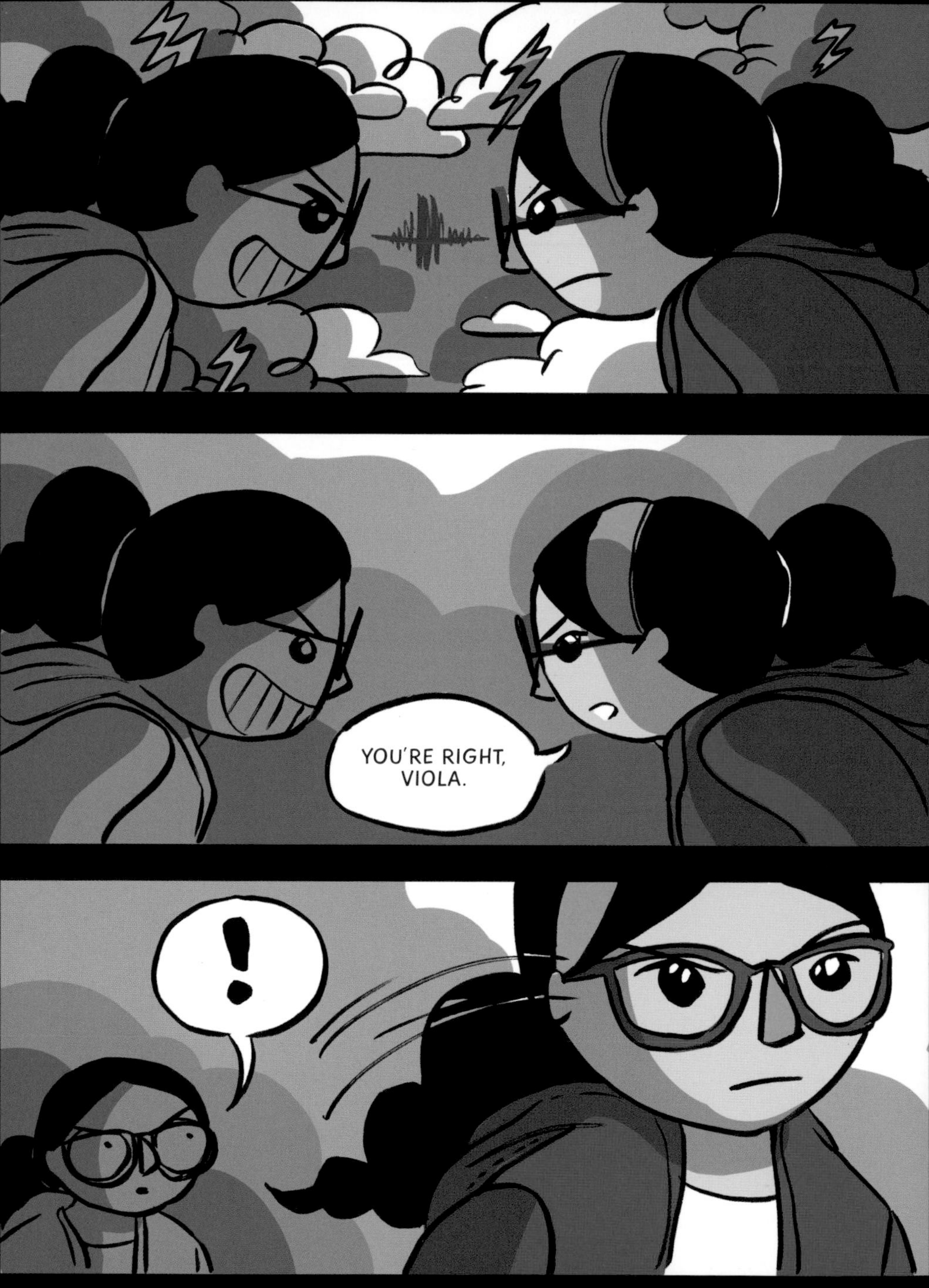
YOU'RE RIGHT, VIOLA.
!

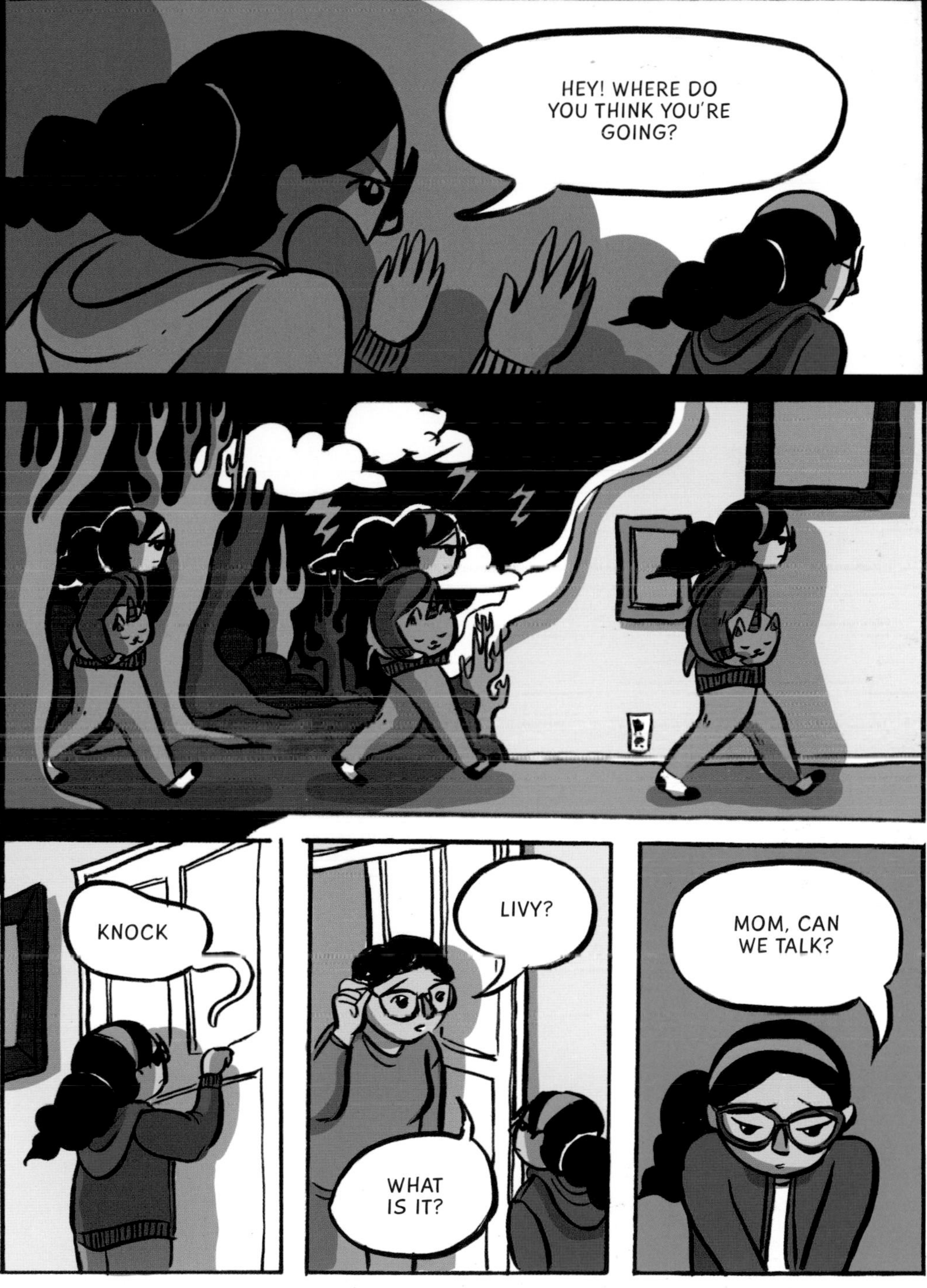
HEY! WHERE DO YOU THINK YOU'RE GOING?
KNOCK
LIVY?
WHAT IS IT?
MOM, CAN WE TALK?

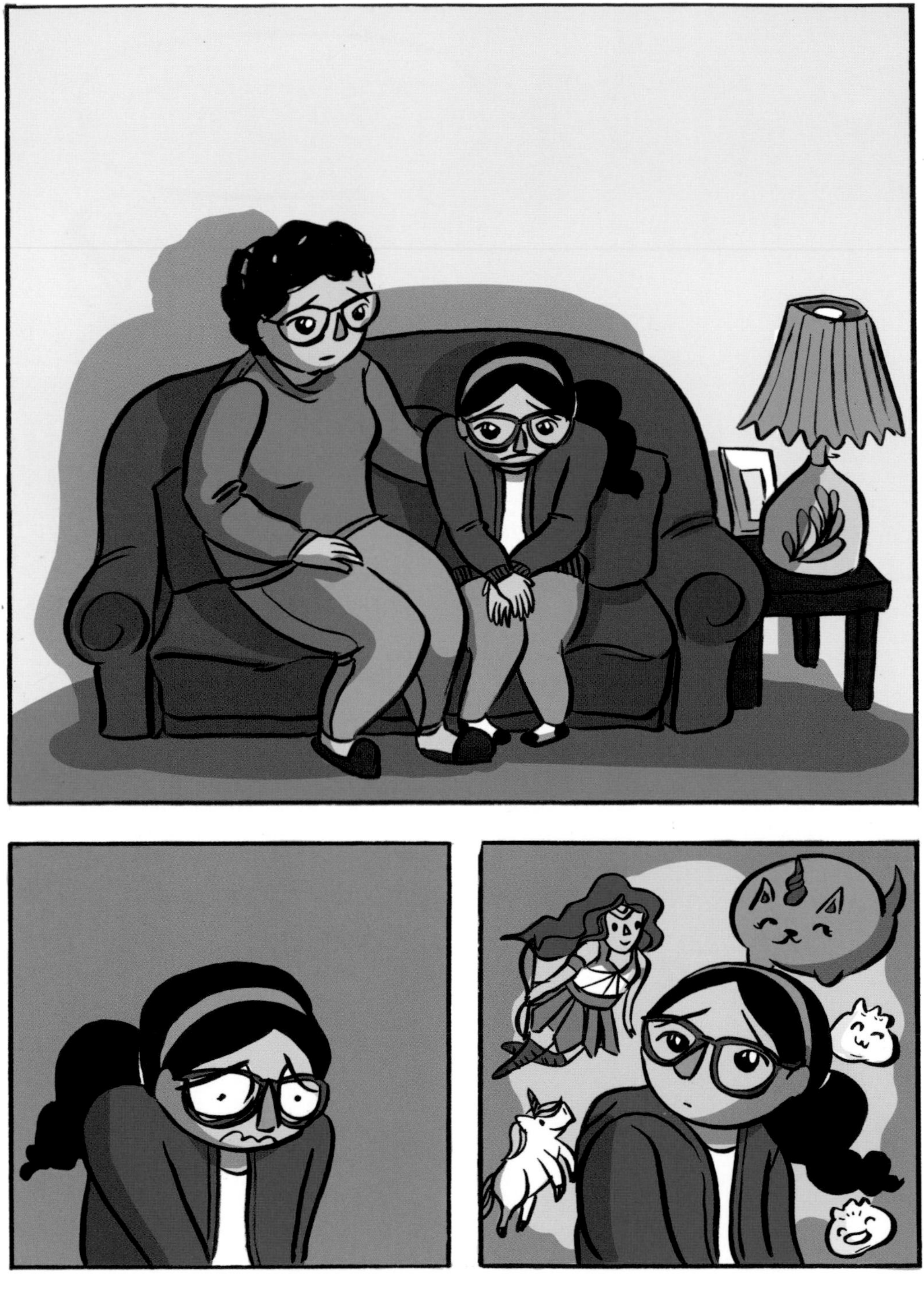

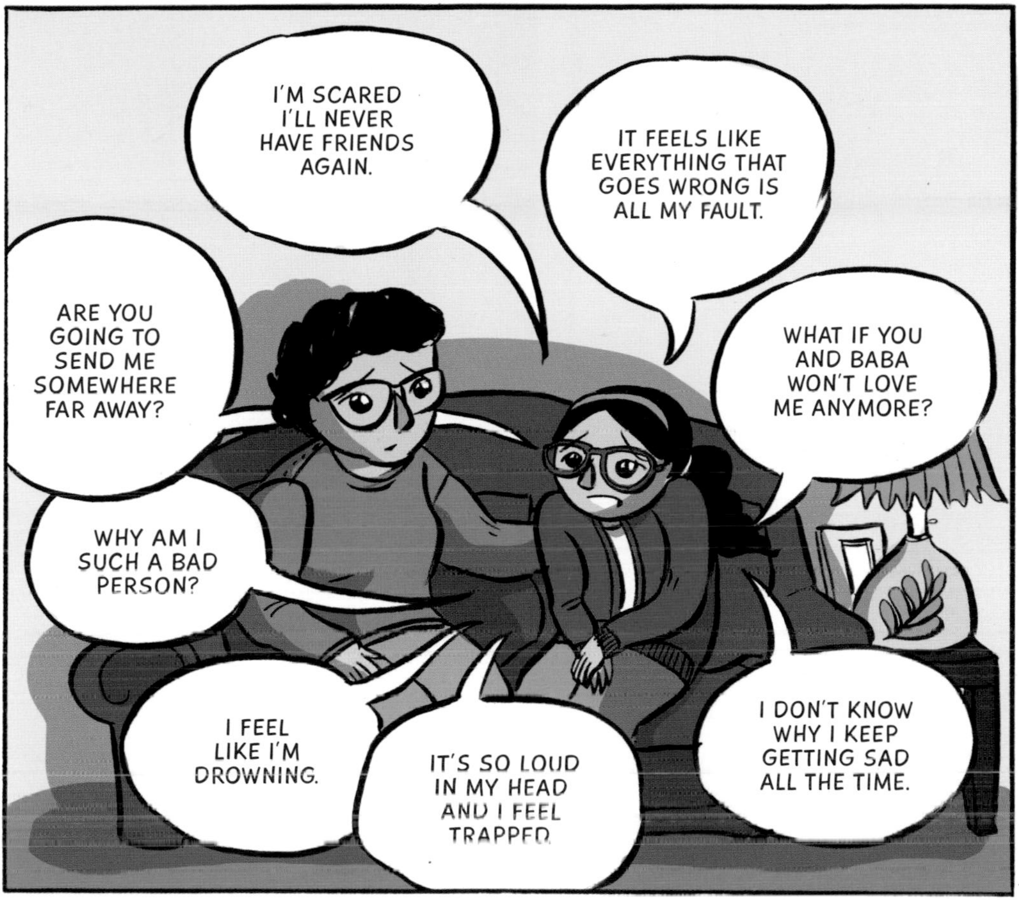
I'M SCARED I'LL NEVER HAVE FRIENDS AGAIN.
IT FEELS LIKE EVERYTHING THAT GOES WRONG IS ALL MY FAULT.
ARE YOU GOING TO SEND ME SOMEWHERE FAR AWAY?
WHAT IF YOU AND BABA WON'T LOVE ME ANYMORE?
WHY AM I SUCH A BAD PERSON?
I FEEL LIKE I'M DROWNING.
IT'S SO LOUD IN MY HEAD AND I FEEL TRAPPED.
I DON'T KNOW WHY I KEEP GETTING SAD ALL THE TIME.

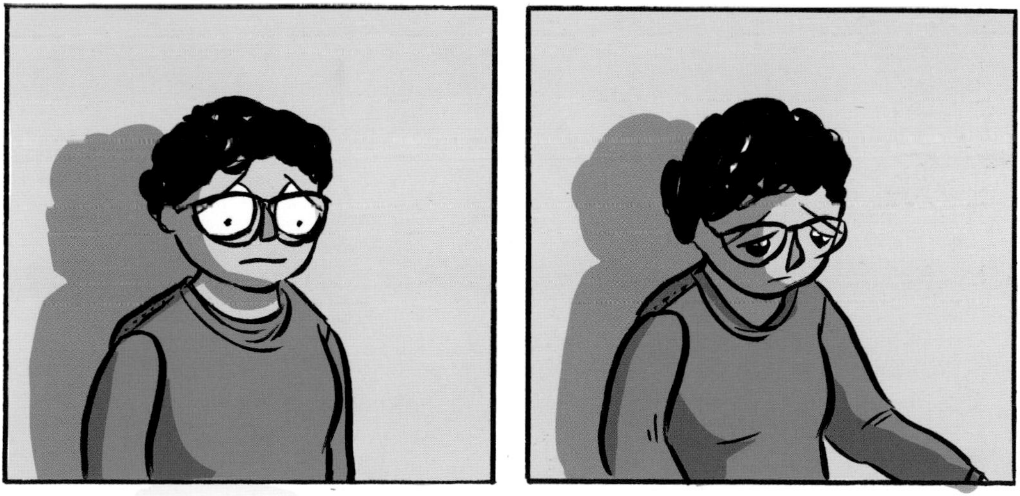

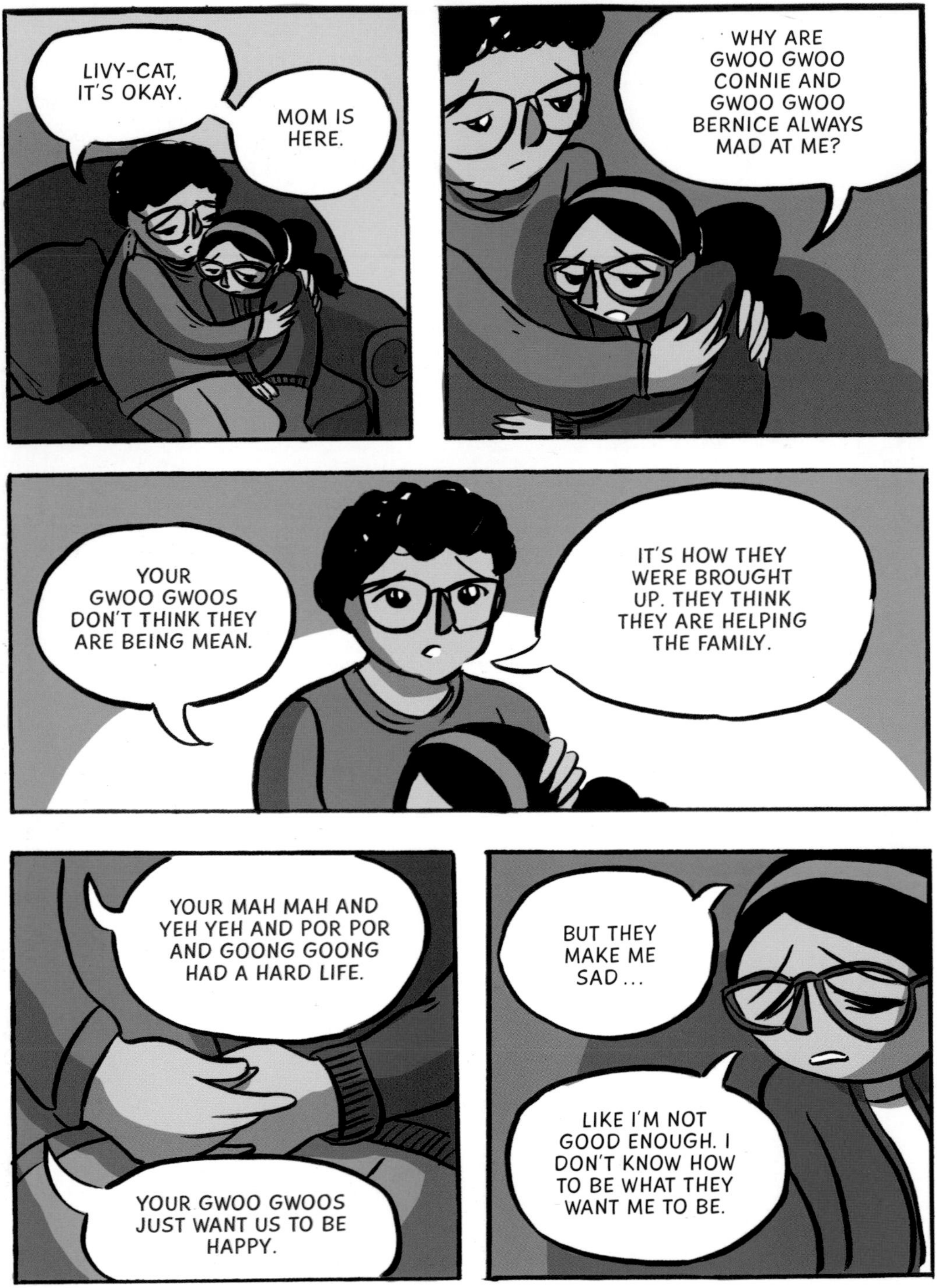
LIVY-CAT, IT'S OKAY.
MOM IS HERE.
WHY ARE GWOO GWOO CONNIE AND GWOO GWOO BERNICE ALWAYS MAD AT ME?
YOUR GWOO GWOOS DON'T THINK THEY ARE BEING MEAN.
IT'S HOW THEY WERE BROUGHT UP. THEY THINK THEY ARE HELPING THE FAMILY.
YOUR MAH MAH AND YEH YEH AND POR POR AND GOONG GOONG HAD A HARD LIFE.
YOUR GWOO GWOOS JUST WANT US TO BE HAPPY.
BUT THEY MAKE ME SAD...
LIKE I'M NOT GOOD ENOUGH. I DON'T KNOW HOW TO BE WHAT THEY WANT ME TO BE.

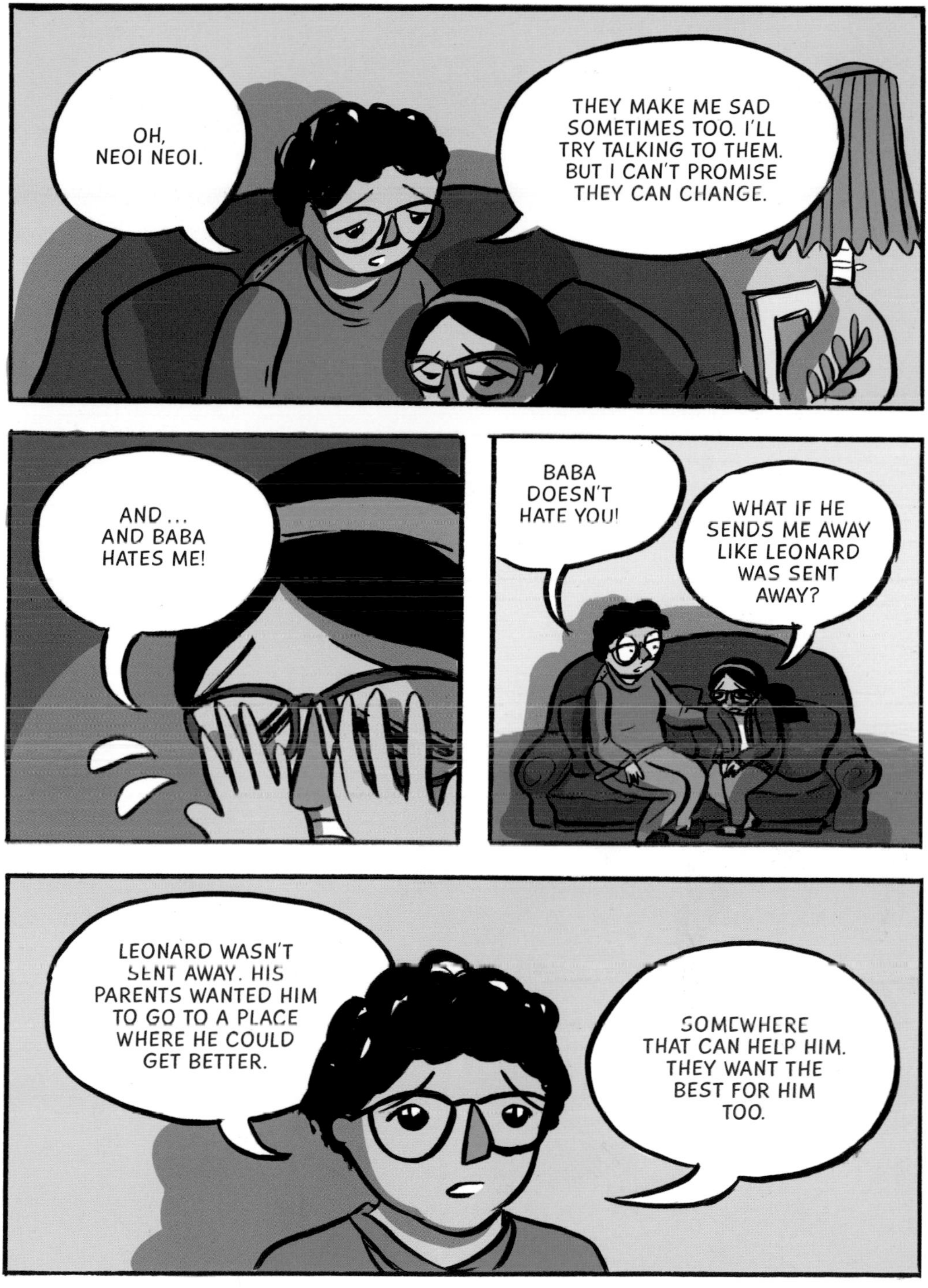
OH, NEOI NEOI.
THEY MAKE ME SAD SOMETIMES TOO. I'LL TRY TALKING TO THEM. BUT I CAN'T PROMISE THEY CAN CHANGE.
AND... AND BABA HATES ME!
BABA DOESN'T HATE YOU!
WHAT IF HE SENDS ME AWAY LIKE LEONARD WAS SENT AWAY?
LEONARD WASN'T SENT AWAY. HIS PARENTS WANTED HIM TO GO TO A PLACE WHERE HE COULD GET BETTER.
SOMEWHERE THAT CAN HELP HIM. THEY WANT THE BEST FOR HIM TOO.

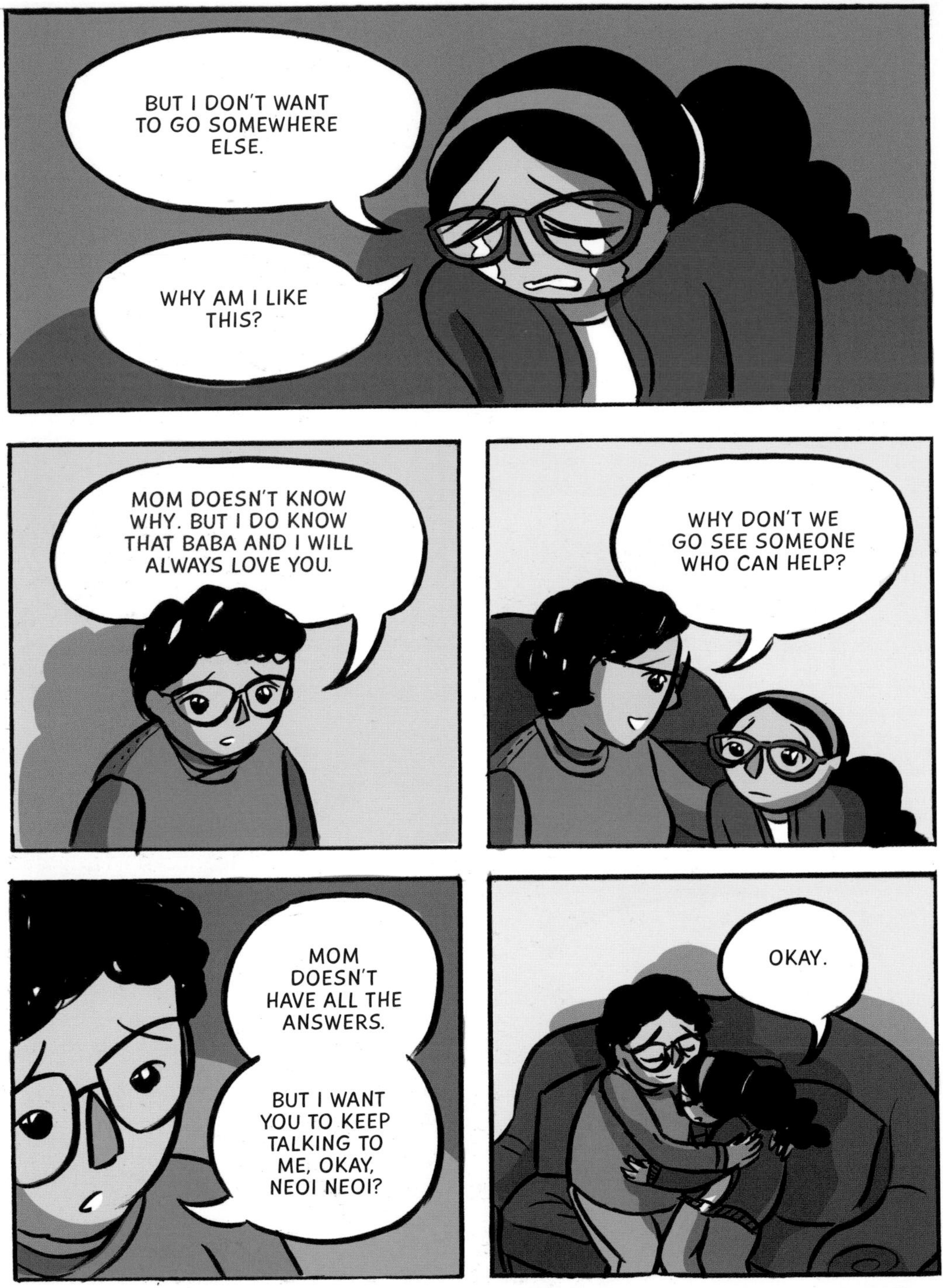
BUT I DON'T WANT TO GO SOMEWHERE ELSE.
WHY AM I LIKE THIS?
MOM DOESN'T KNOW WHY. BUT I DO KNOW THAT BABA AND I WILL ALWAYS LOVE YOU.
WHY DON'T WE GO SEE SOMEONE WHO CAN HELP?
MOM DOESN'T HAVE ALL THE ANSWERS.
BUT I WANT YOU TO KEEP TALKING TO ME, OKAY, NEOI NEOI?
OKAY.

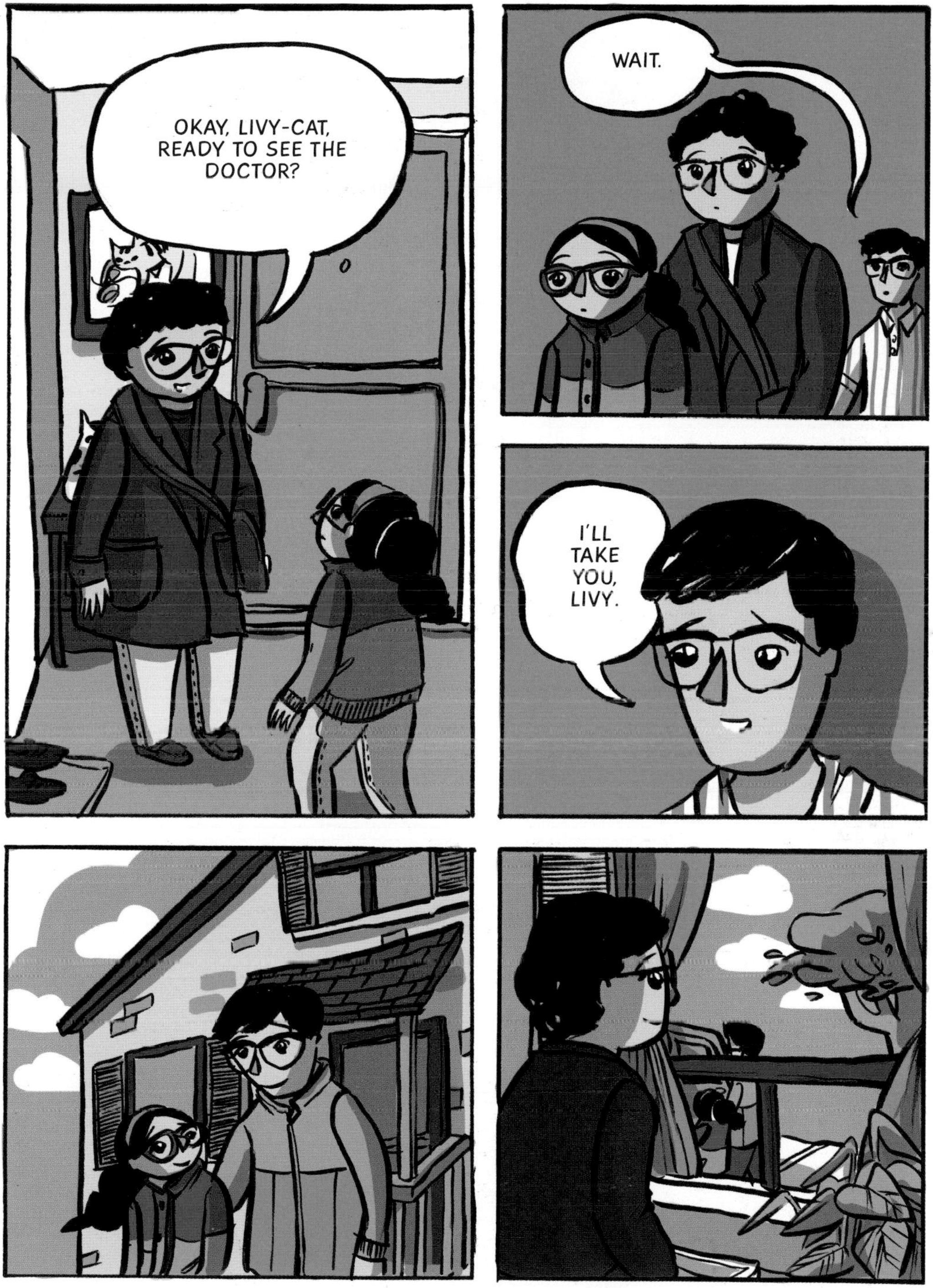
OKAY, LIVY-CAT, READY TO SEE THE DOCTOR?
WAIT.
I'LL TAKE YOU, LIVY.

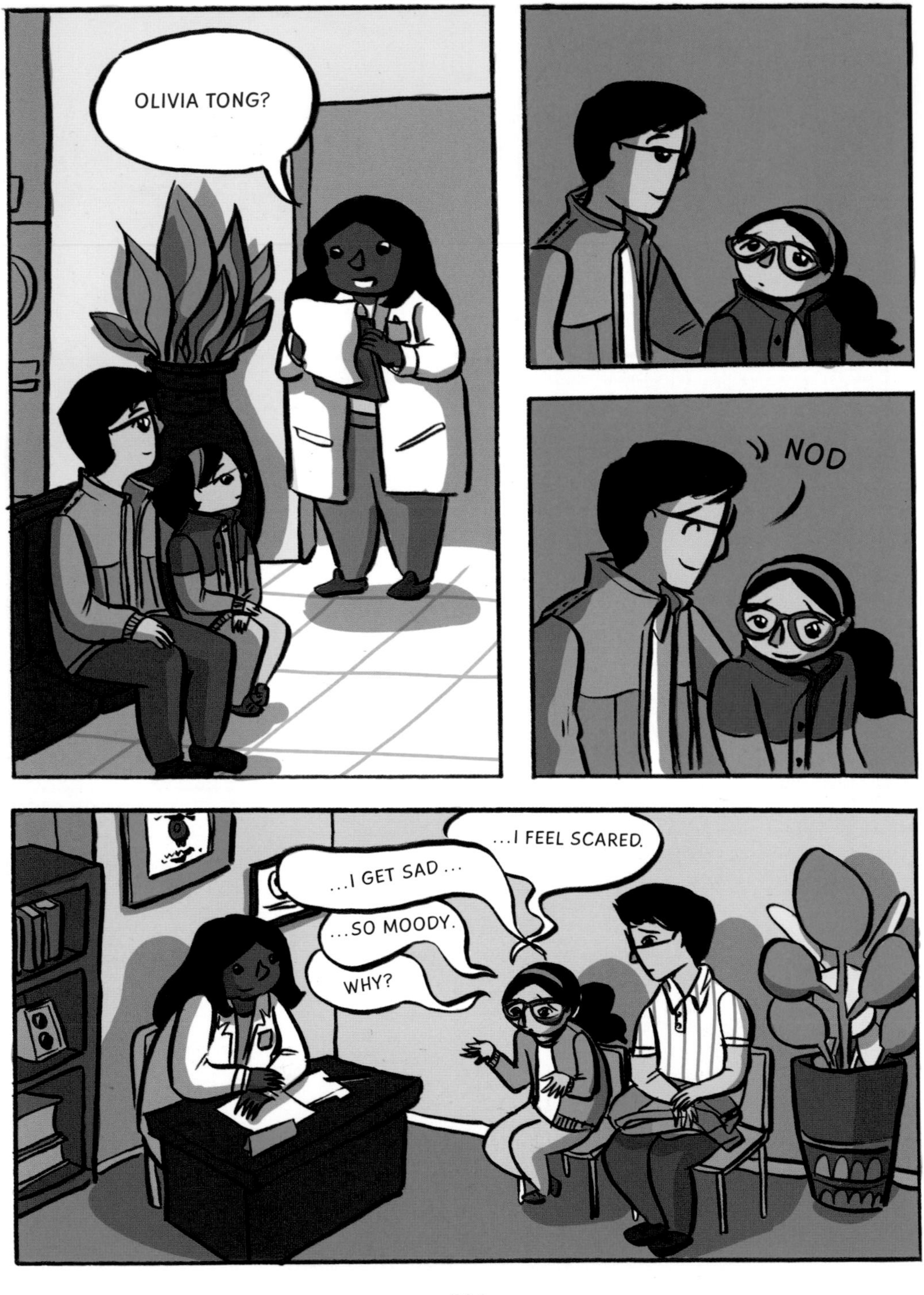
OLIVIA TONG?
NOD
...I FEEL SCARED.
...I GET SAD...
...SO MOODY.
WHY?

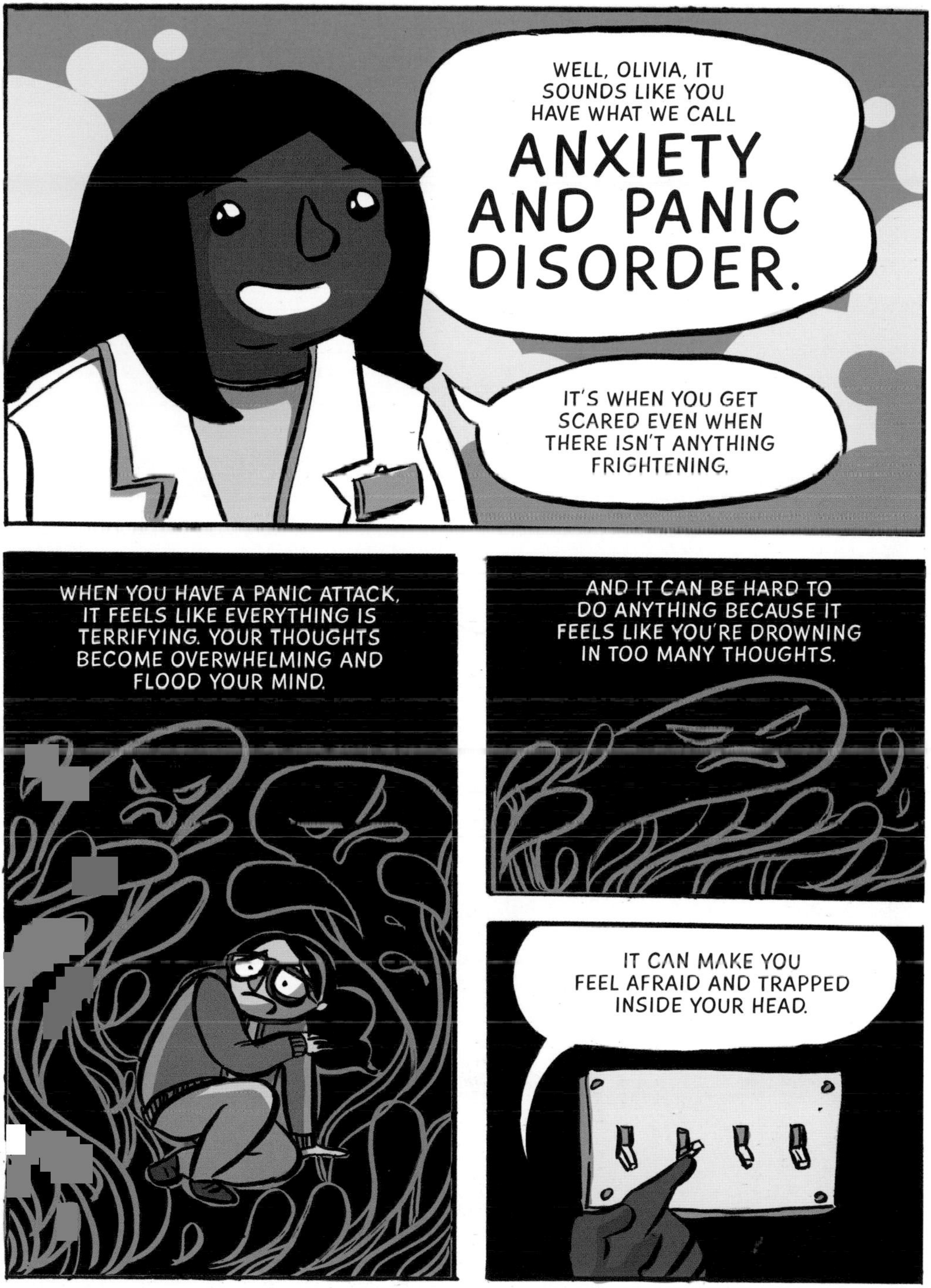
WELL, OLIVIA, IT SOUNDS LIKE YOU HAVE WHAT WE CALL ANXIETY AND PANIC DISORDER.
IT'S WHEN YOU GET SCARED EVEN WHEN THERE ISN'T ANYTHING FRIGHTENING.
WHEN YOU HAVE A PANIC ATTACK, IT FEELS LIKE EVERYTHING IS TERRIFYING. YOUR THOUGHTS BECOME OVERWHELMING AND FLOOD YOUR MIND.
AND IT CAN BE HARD TO DO ANYTHING BECAUSE IT FEELS LIKE YOU'RE DROWNING IN TOO MANY THOUGHTS.
IT CAN MAKE YOU FEEL AFRAID AND TRAPPED INSIDE YOUR HEAD.

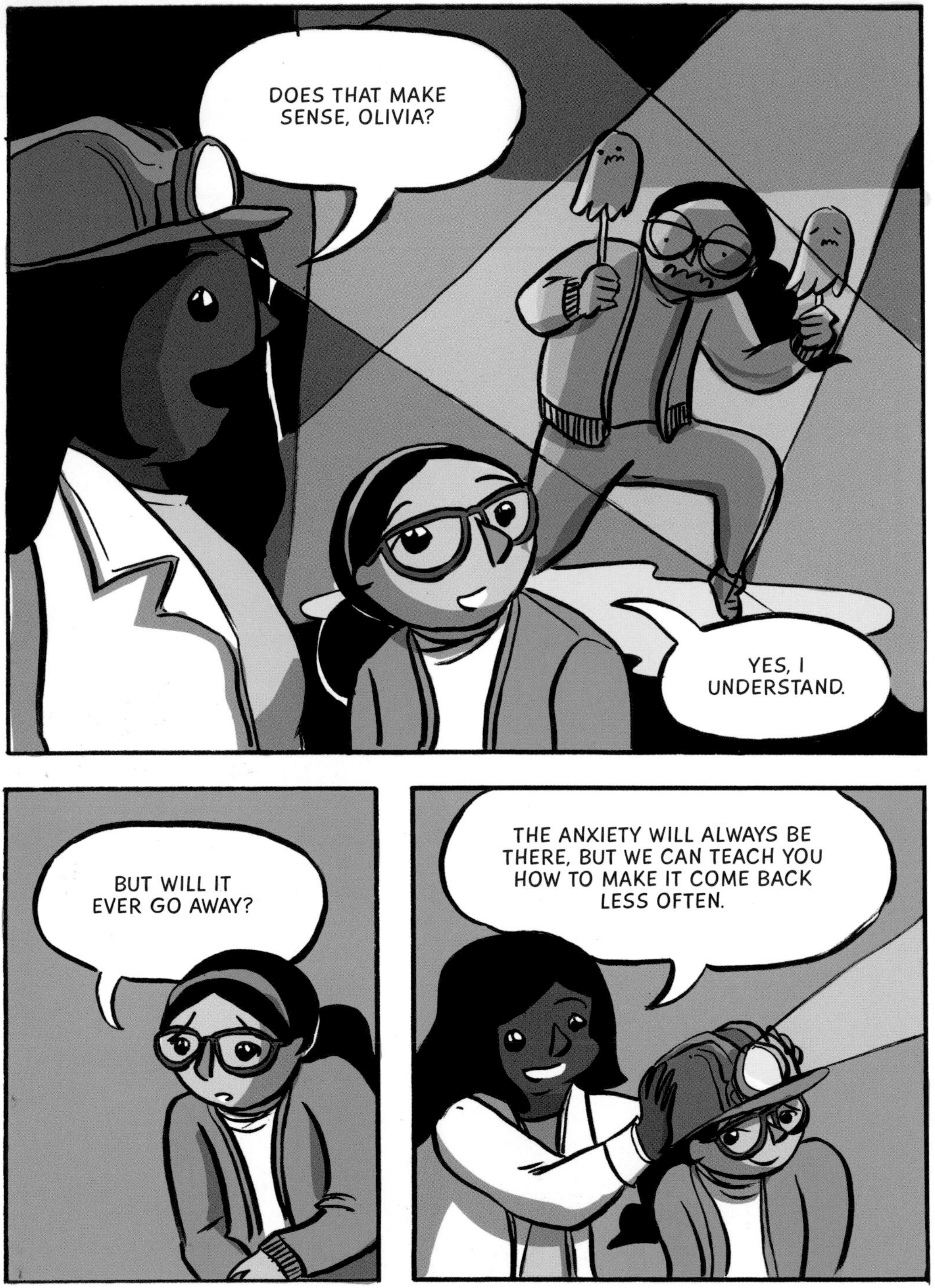
DOES THAT MAKE SENSE, OLIVIA?
YES, I UNDERSTAND.
BUT WILL IT EVER GO AWAY?
THE ANXIETY WILL ALWAYS BE THERE, BUT WE CAN TEACH YOU HOW TO MAKE IT COME BACK LESS OFTEN.

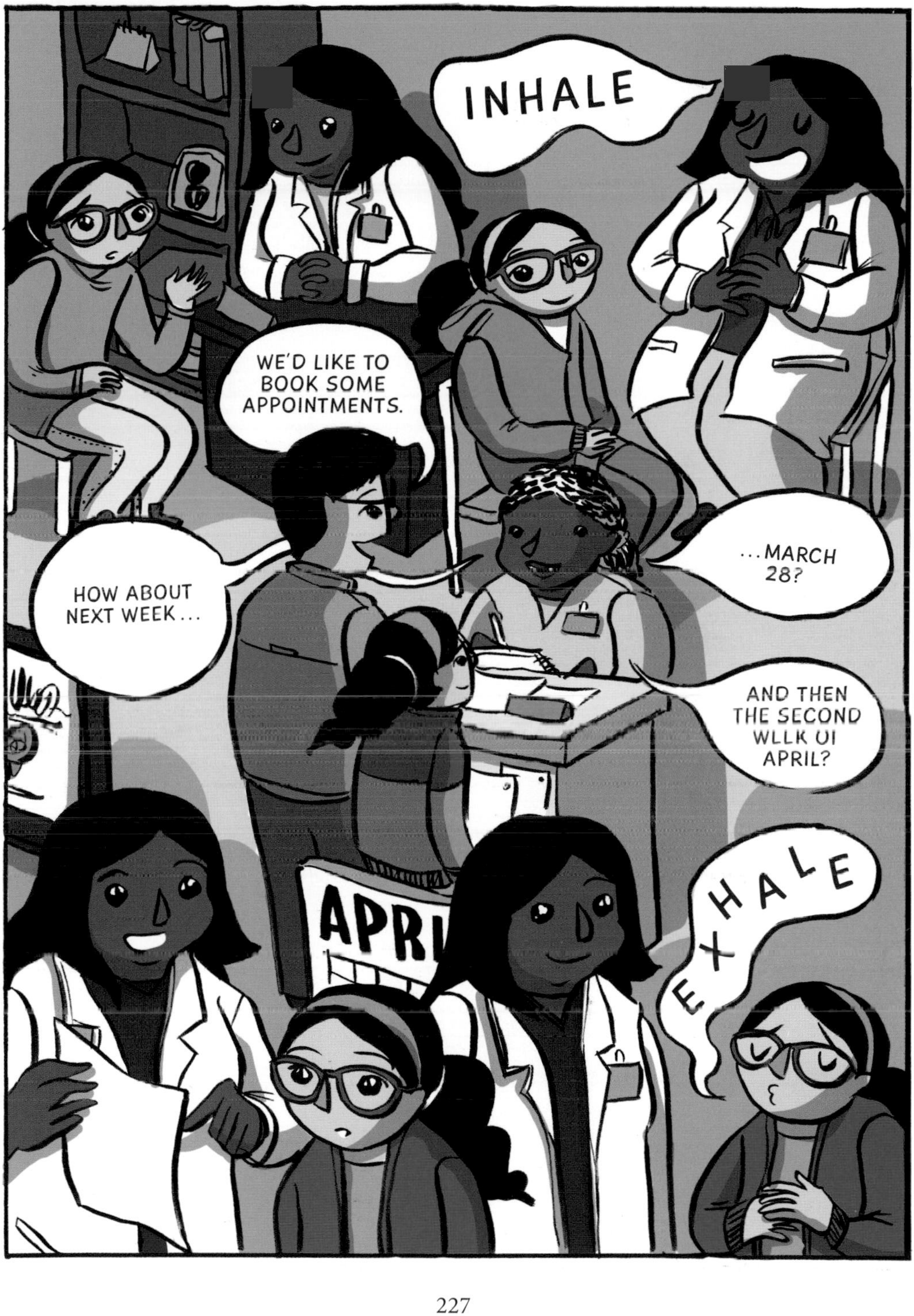
INHALE
WE'D LIKE TO BOOK SOME APPOINTMENTS.
HOW ABOUT NEXT WEEK...
...MARCH 28?
AND THEN THE SECOND WEEK OF APRIL?
APRI
EXHALE

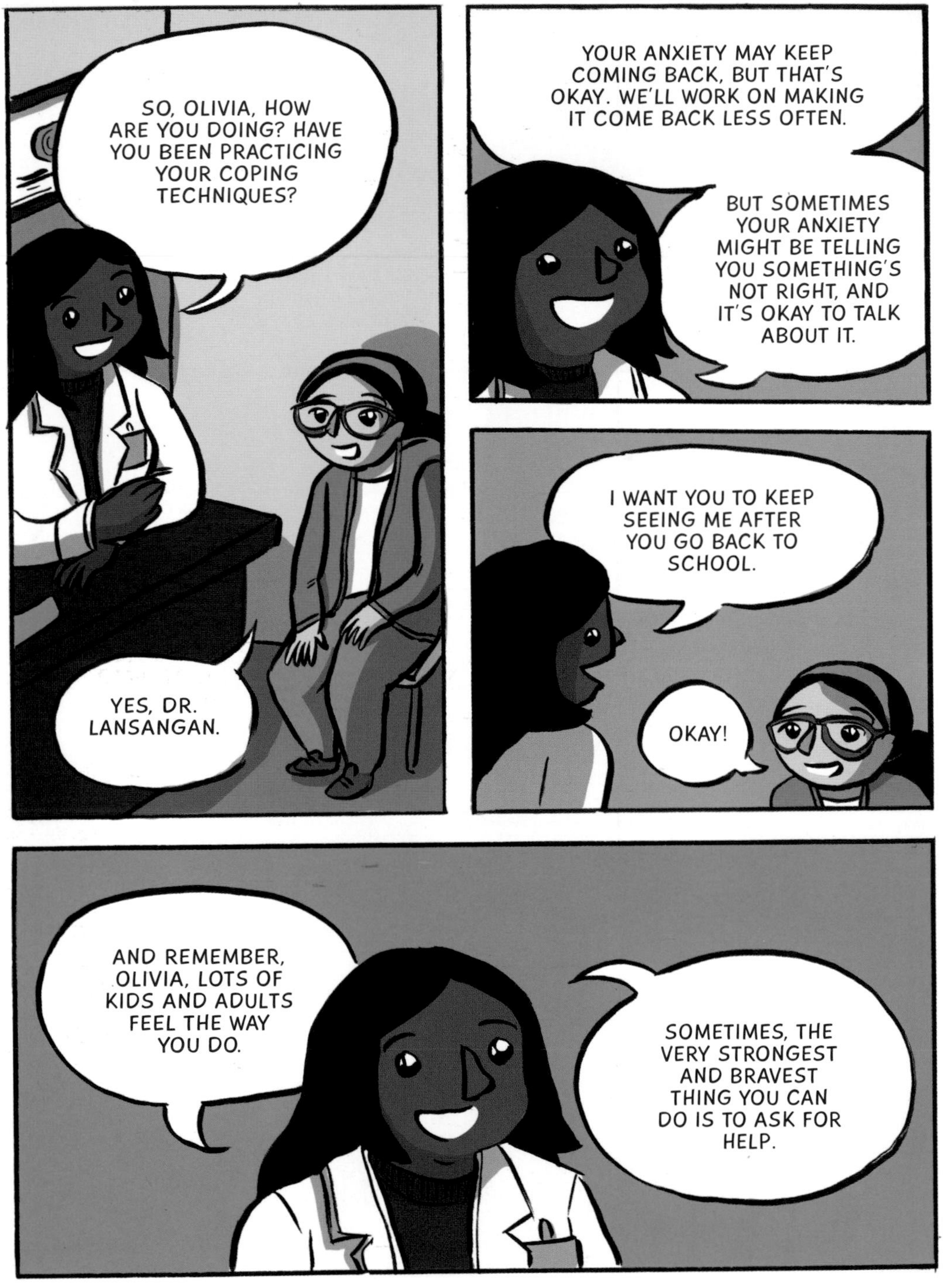
SO, OLIVIA, HOW ARE YOU DOING? HAVE YOU BEEN PRACTICING YOUR COPING TECHNIQUES?
YES, DR. LANSANGAN.
YOUR ANXIETY MAY KEEP COMING BACK, BUT THAT'S OKAY. WE'LL WORK ON MAKING IT COME BACK LESS OFTEN.
BUT SOMETIMES YOUR ANXIETY MIGHT BE TELLING YOU SOMETHING'S NOT RIGHT, AND IT'S OKAY TO TALK ABOUT IT.
I WANT YOU TO KEEP SEEING ME AFTER YOU GO BACK TO SCHOOL.
OKAY!
AND REMEMBER, OLIVIA, LOTS OF KIDS AND ADULTS FEEL THE WAY YOU DO.
SOMETIMES, THE VERY STRONGEST AND BRAVEST THING YOU CAN DO IS TO ASK FOR HELP.

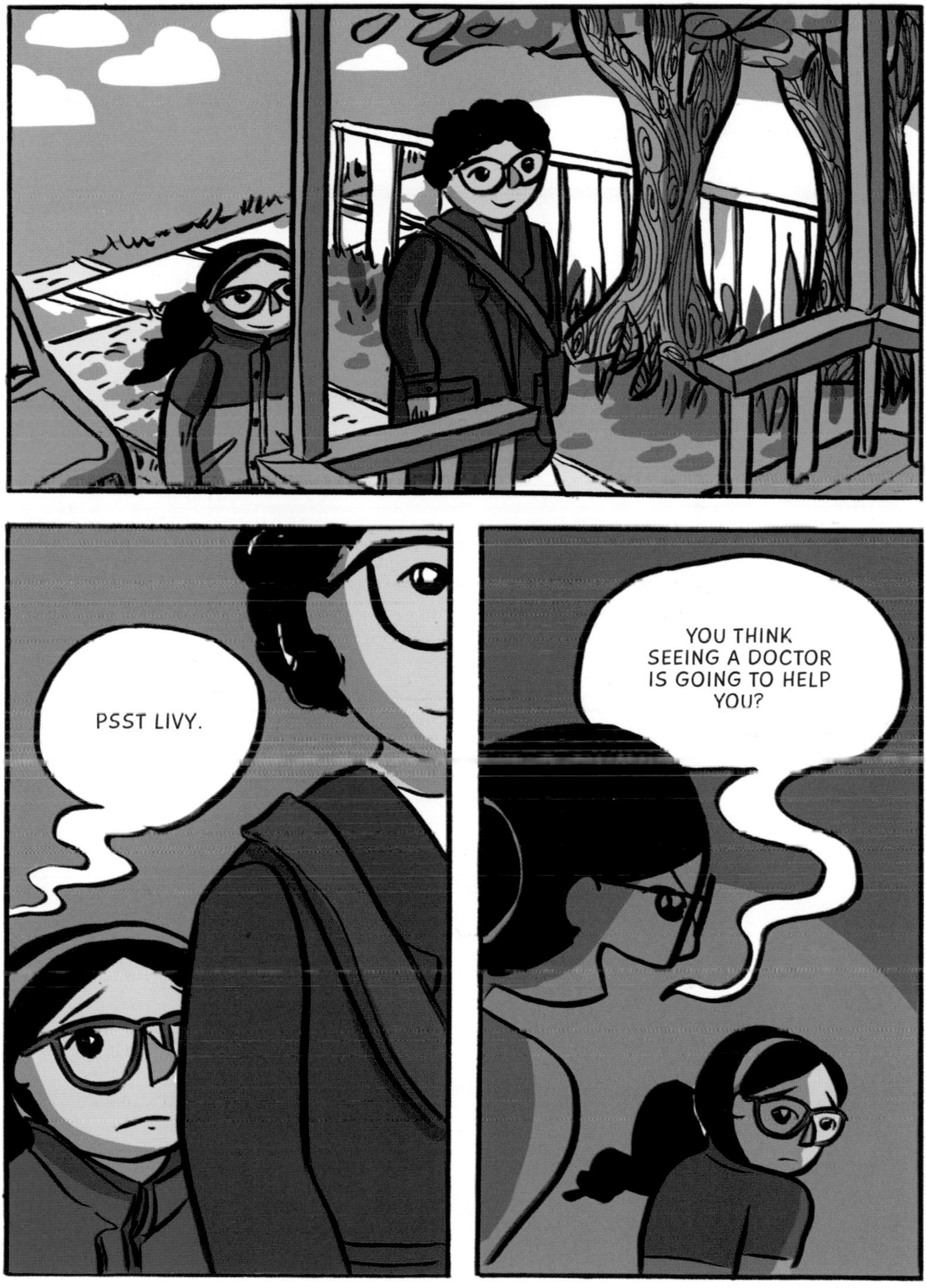
PSST LIVY.
YOU THINK SEEING A DOCTOR IS GOING TO HELP YOU?

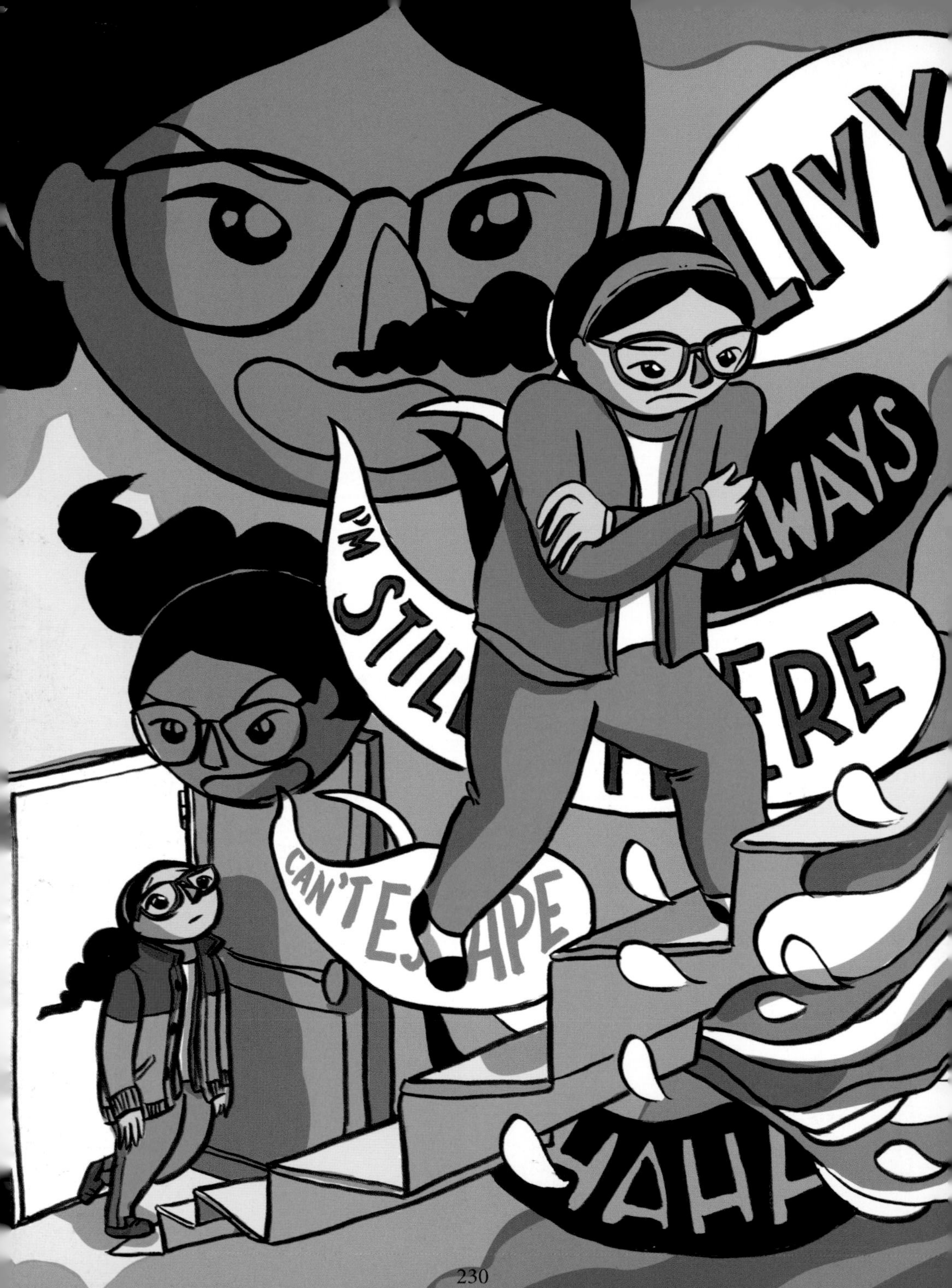
LIVY
I'M STIL
LWAYS
ERE
CAN'T ES APE
AHA

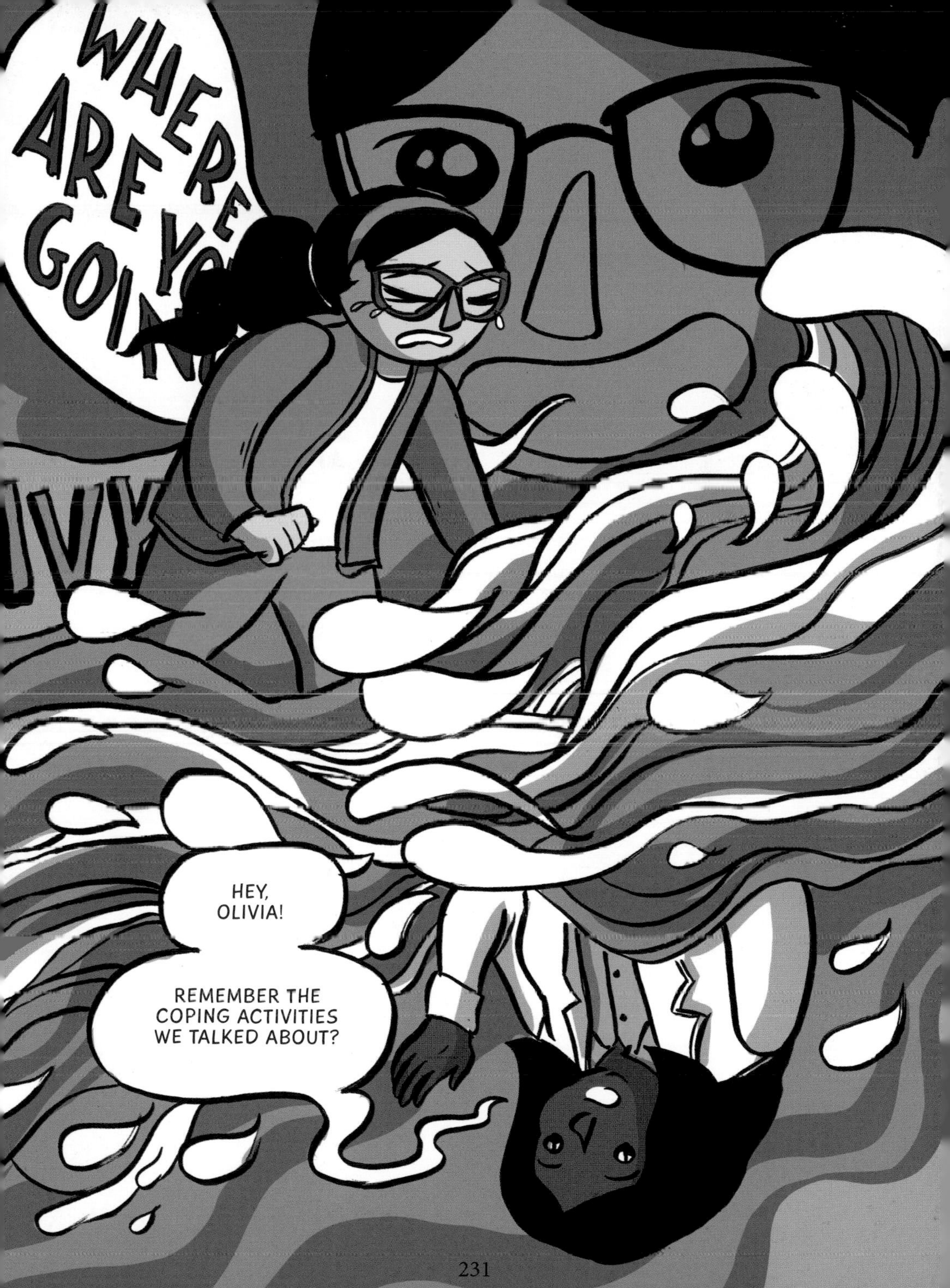
WHERE ARE YO GOIN
IVY
HEY, OLIVIA!
REMEMBER THE COPING ACTIVITIES WE TALKED ABOUT?

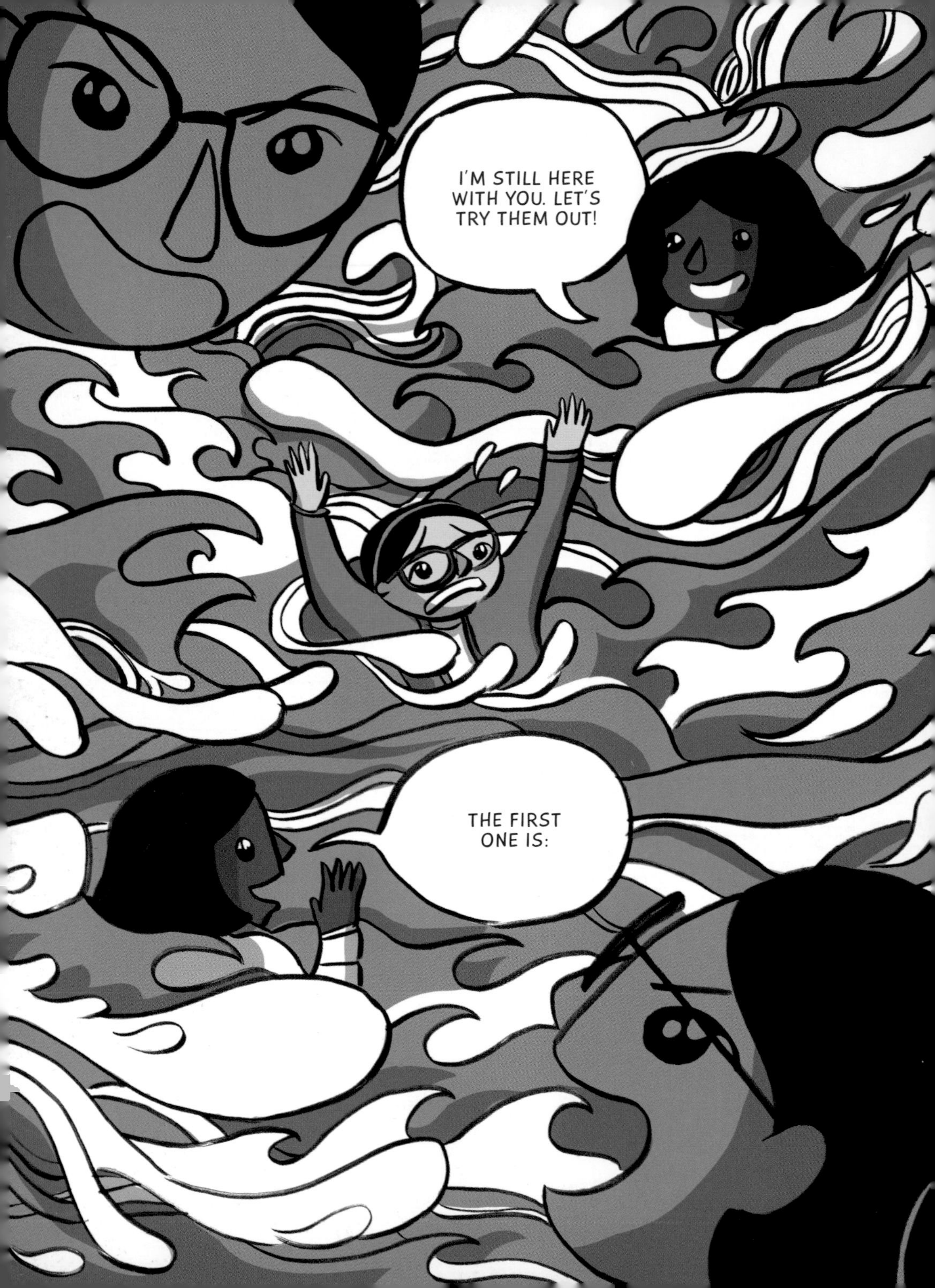
I'M STILL HERE WITH YOU. LET'S TRY THEM OUT!
THE FIRST ONE IS:

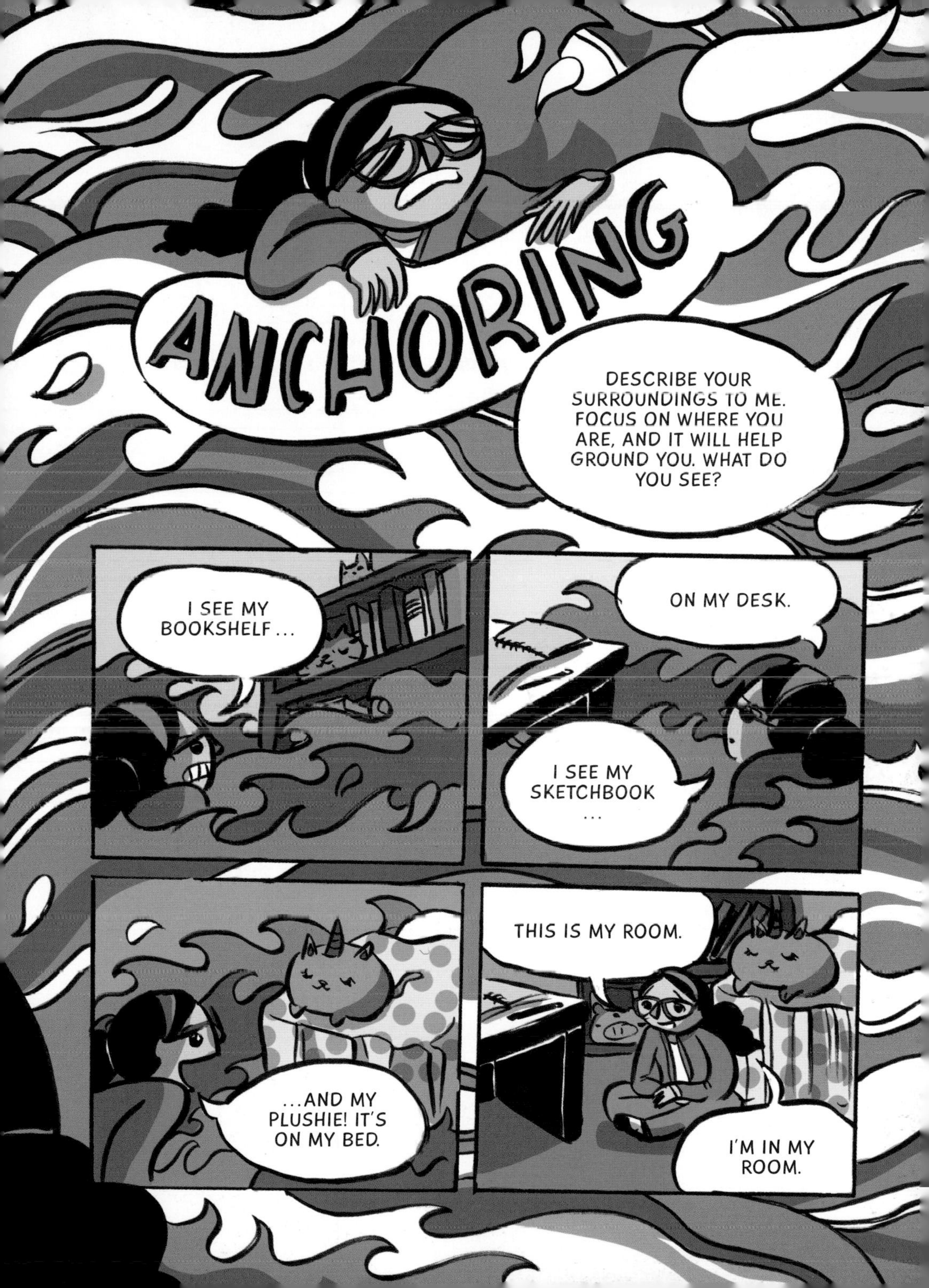
ANCHORING
DESCRIBE YOUR SURROUNDINGS TO ME. FOCUS ON WHERE YOU ARE, AND IT WILL HELP GROUND YOU. WHAT DO YOU SEE?
I SEE MY BOOKSHELF ...
I SEE MY SKETCHBOOK ...
ON MY DESK.
...AND MY PLUSHIE! IT'S ON MY BED.
THIS IS MY ROOM.
I'M IN MY ROOM.

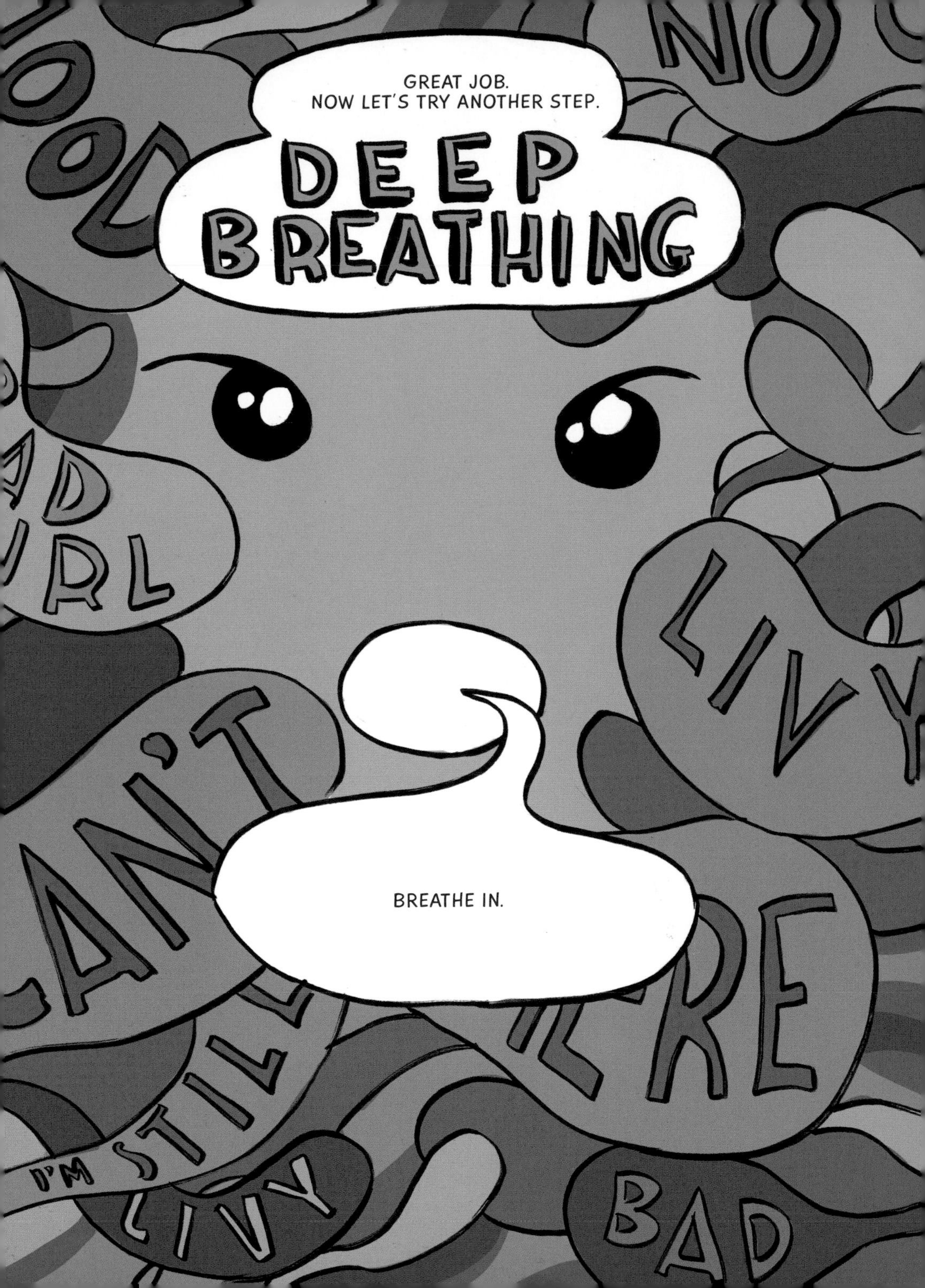
GREAT JOB.
NOW LET'S TRY ANOTHER STEP.
DEEP BREATHING
BREATHE IN.
LIVY
CAN'T
I'M STILL
LIVY
BAD

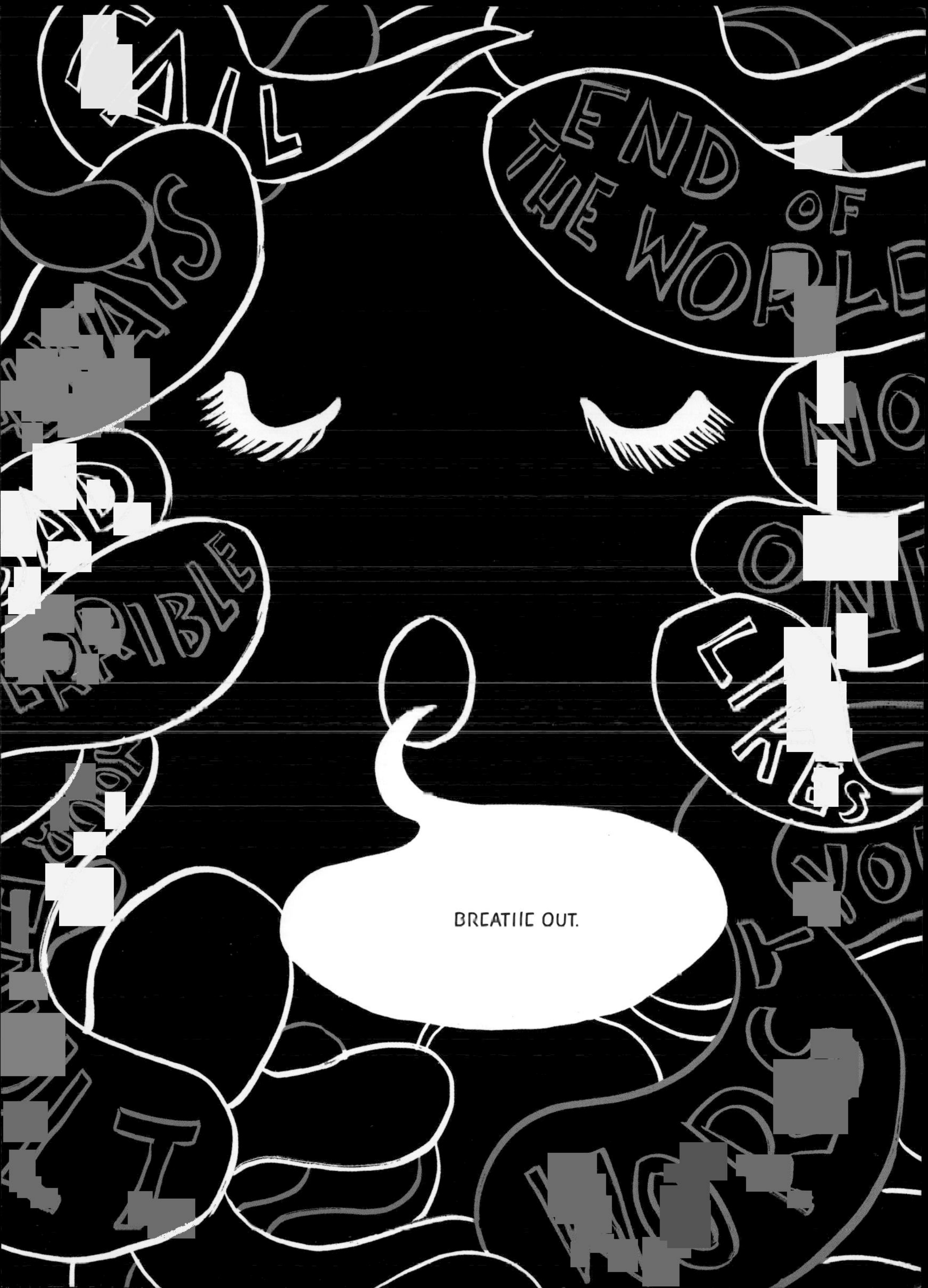
END OF THE WORLD
BREATHE OUT.

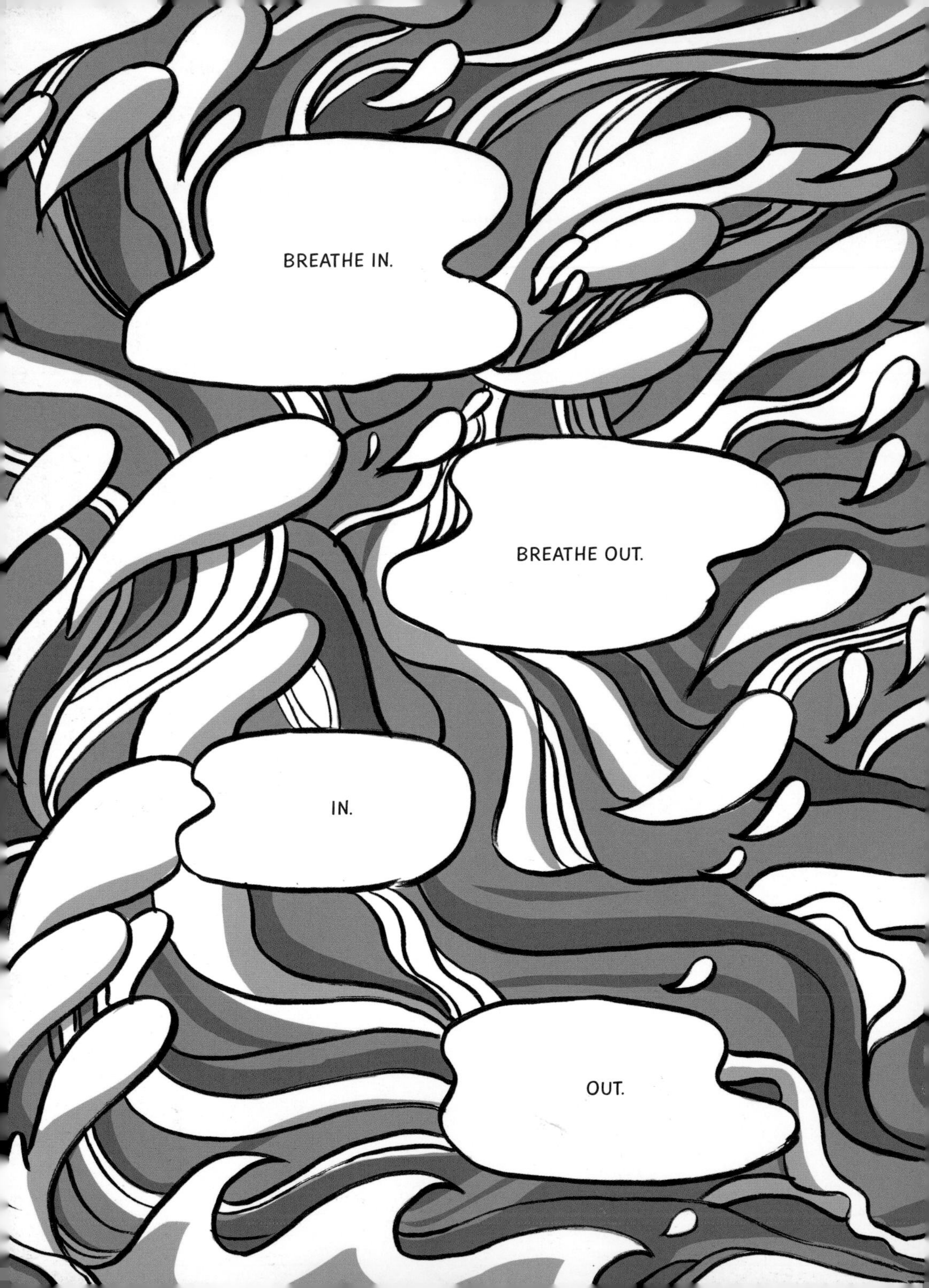
BREATHE IN.
BREATHE OUT.
IN.
OUT.

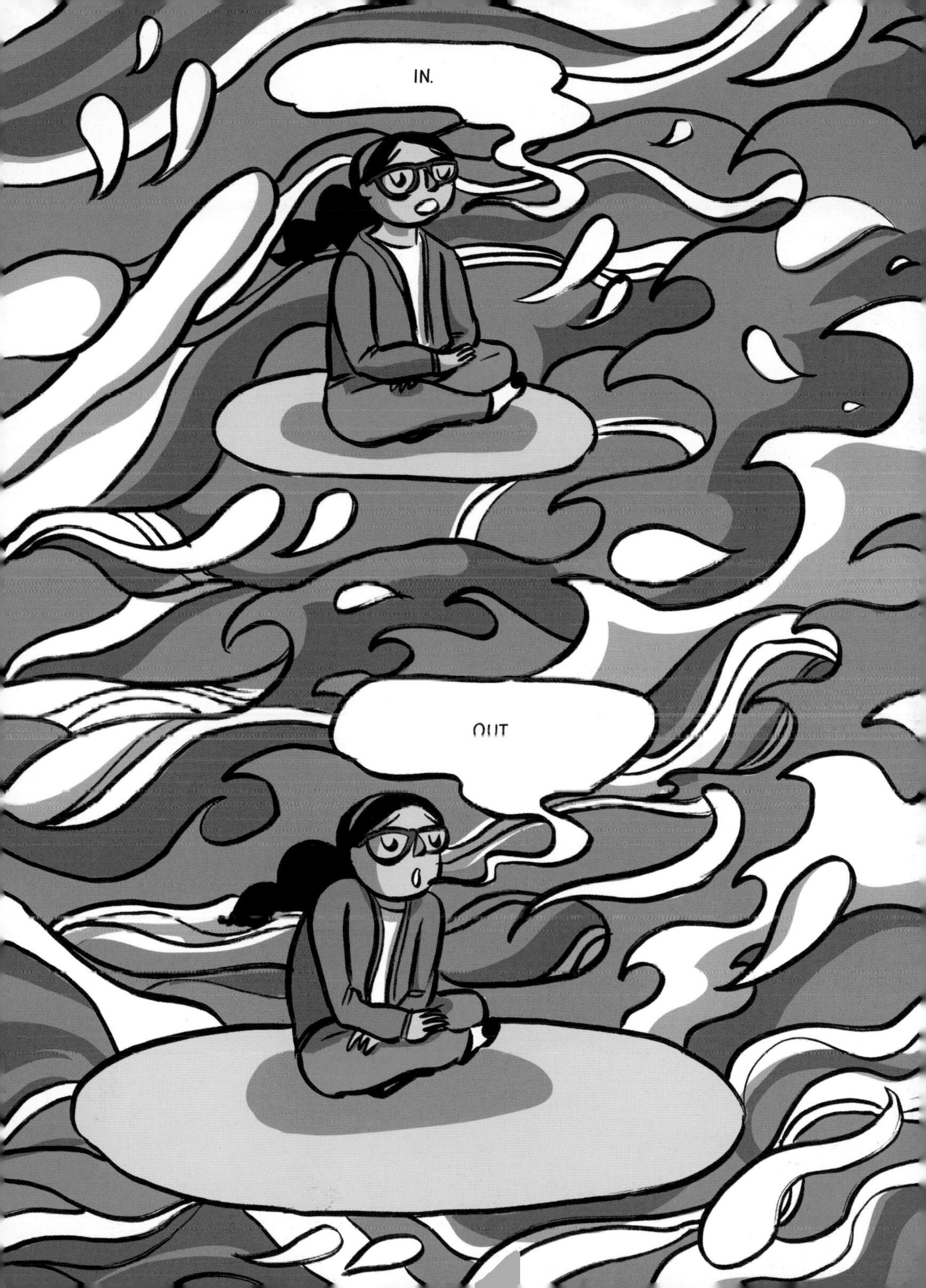
IN.
OUT

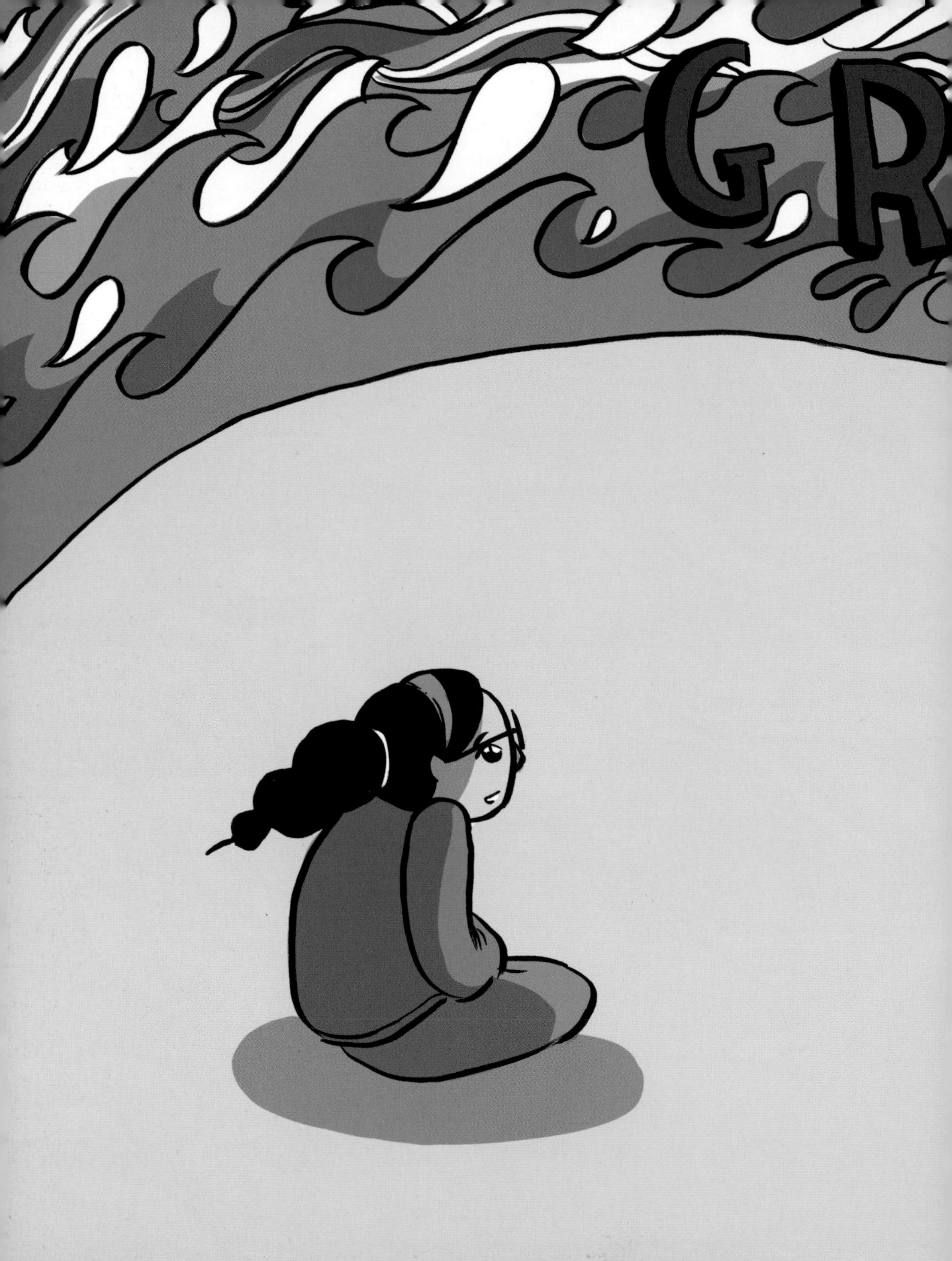
GR

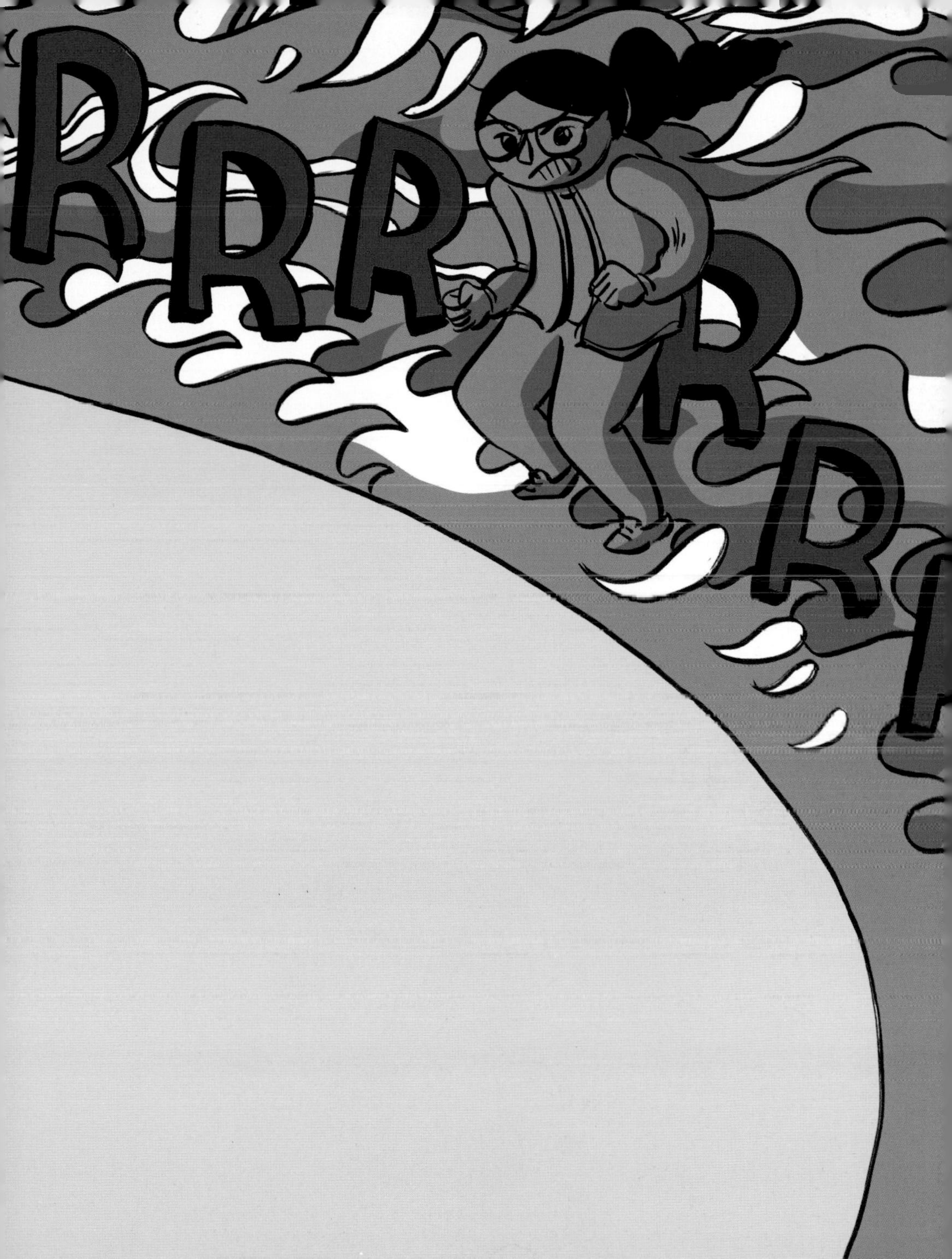
RRRRRR

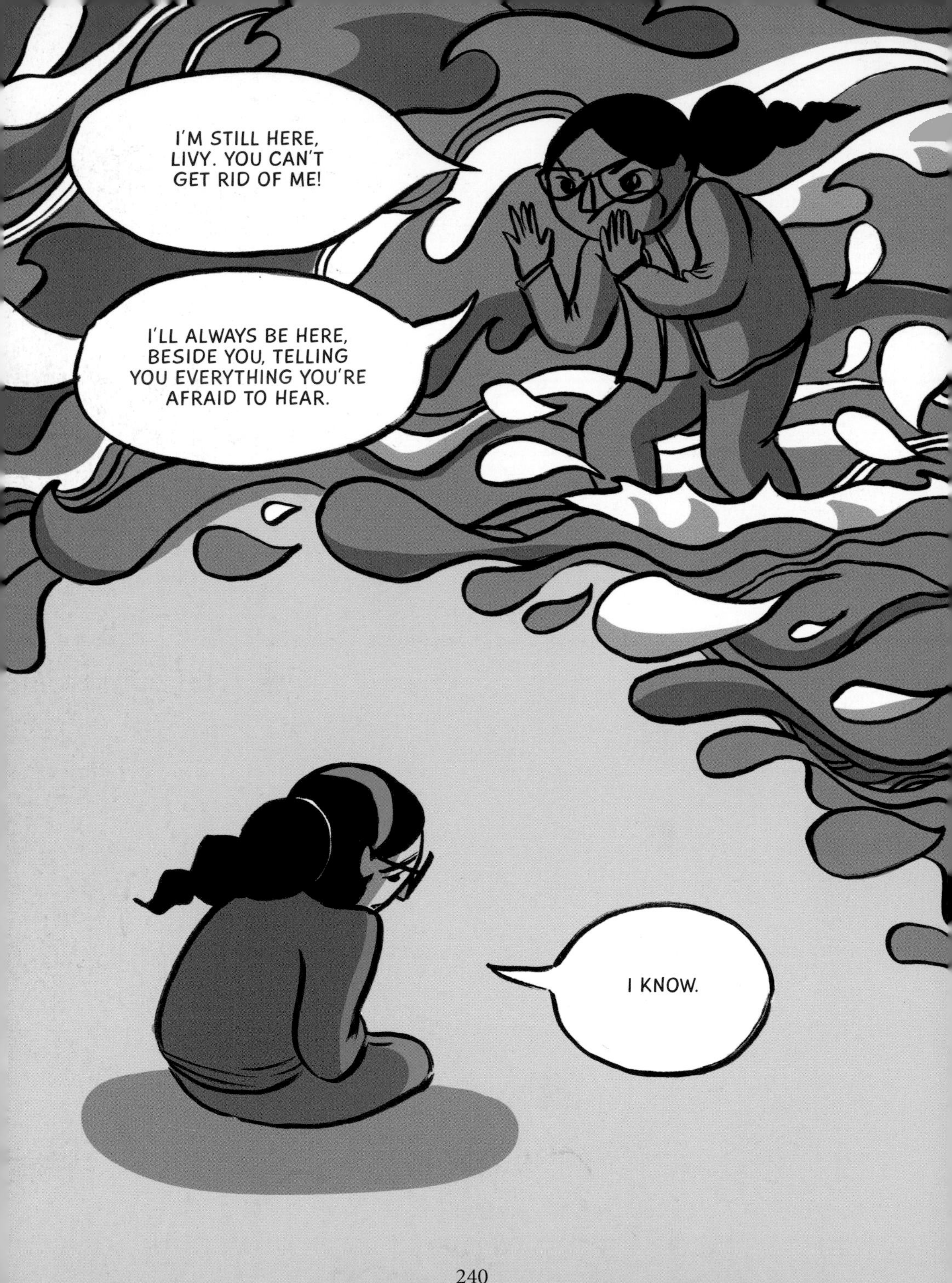
I'M STILL HERE, LIVY. YOU CAN'T GET RID OF ME!
I'LL ALWAYS BE HERE, BESIDE YOU, TELLING YOU EVERYTHING YOU'RE AFRAID TO HEAR.
I KNOW.

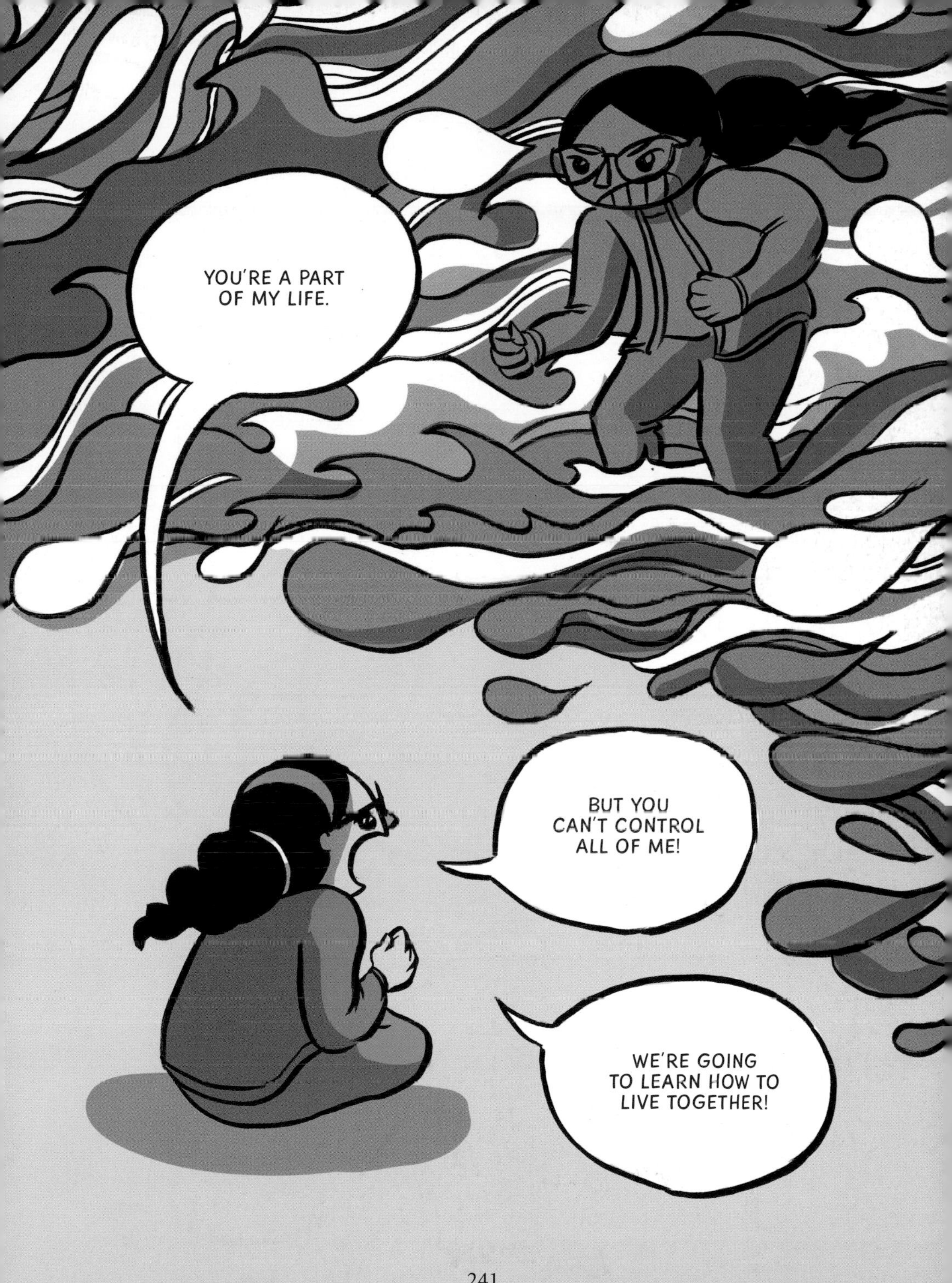
YOU'RE A PART OF MY LIFE.
BUT YOU CAN'T CONTROL ALL OF ME!
WE'RE GOING TO LEARN HOW TO LIVE TOGETHER!

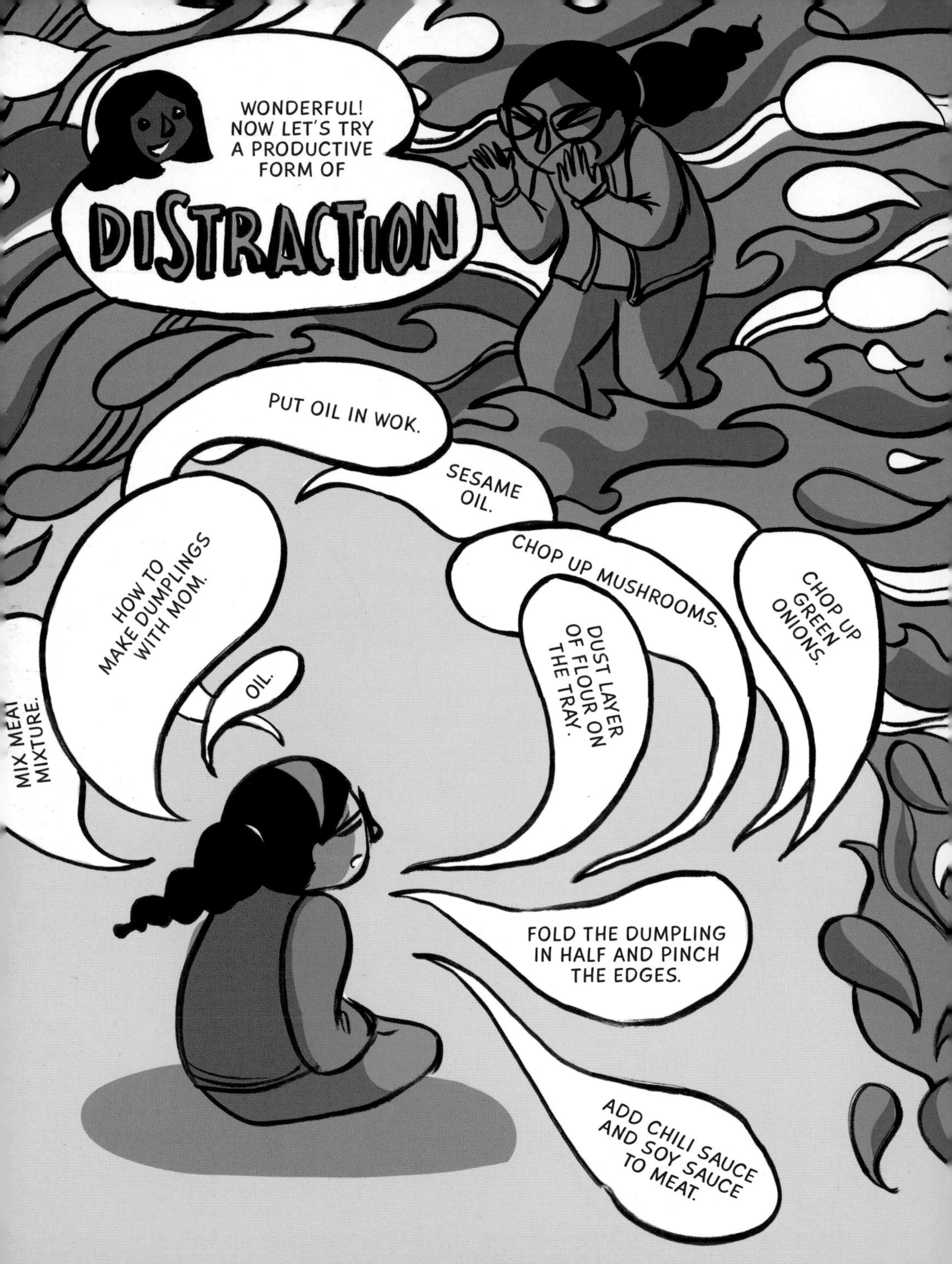
WONDERFUL! NOW LET'S TRY A PRODUCTIVE FORM OF
DISTRACTION
PUT OIL IN WOK.
SESAME OIL.
HOW TO MAKE DUMPLINGS WITH MOM.
MIX MEAT MIXTURE.
OIL.
CHOP UP MUSHROOMS.
DUST LAYER OF FLOUR ON THE TRAY.
CHOP UP GREEN ONIONS.
FOLD THE DUMPLING IN HALF AND PINCH THE EDGES.
ADD CHILI SAUCE AND SOY SAUCE TO MEAT.

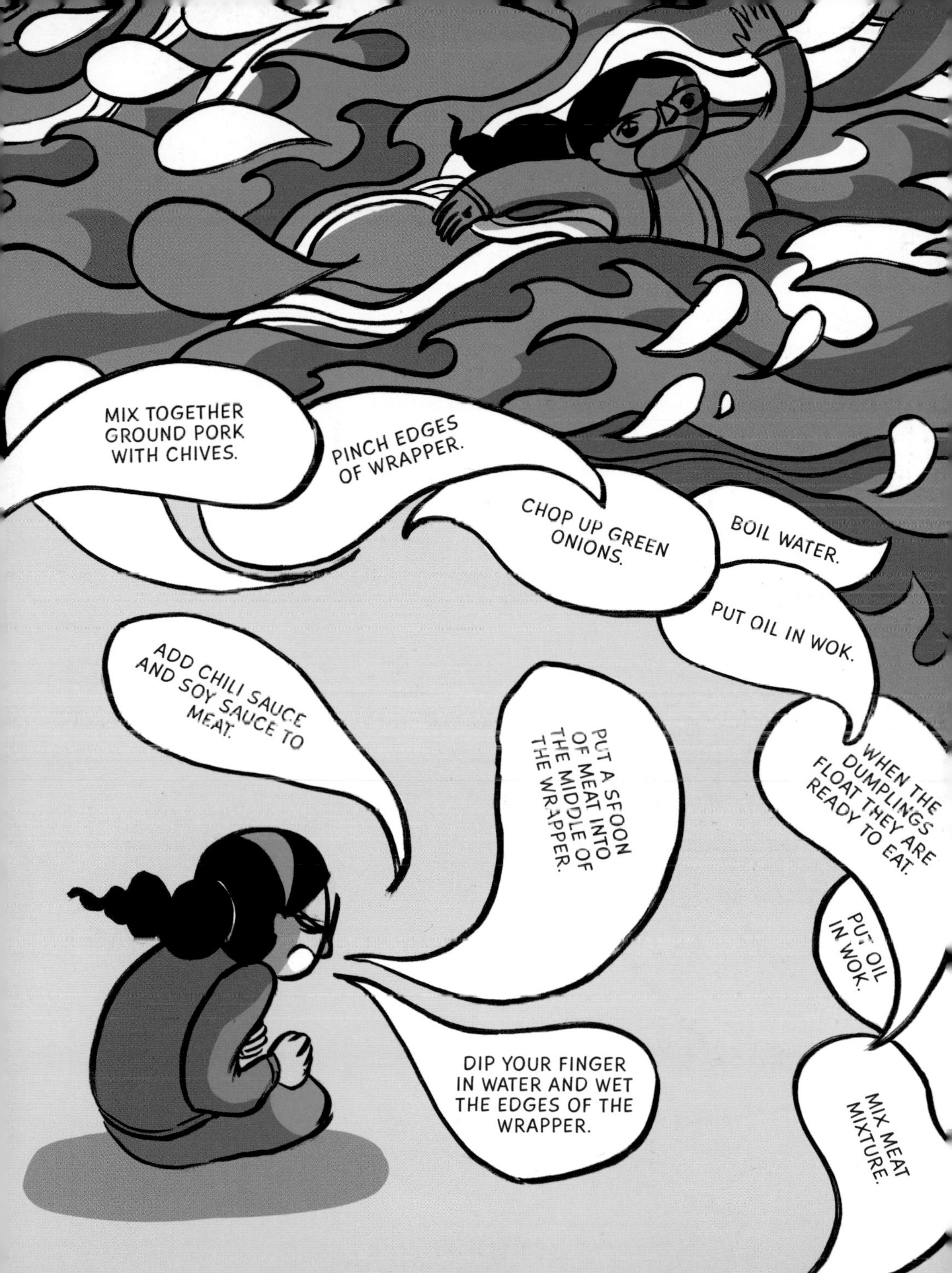
MIX TOGETHER GROUND PORK WITH CHIVES.
PINCH EDGES OF WRAPPER.
CHOP UP GREEN ONIONS.
BOIL WATER.
PUT OIL IN WOK.
WHEN THE DUMPLINGS FLOAT THEY ARE READY TO EAT.
PUT OIL IN WOK.
MIX MEAT MIXTURE.
DIP YOUR FINGER IN WATER AND WET THE EDGES OF THE WRAPPER.
PUT A SFOON OF MEAT INTO THE MIDDLE OF THE WRAPPER.
ADD CHILI SAUCE AND SOY SAUCE TO MEAT.

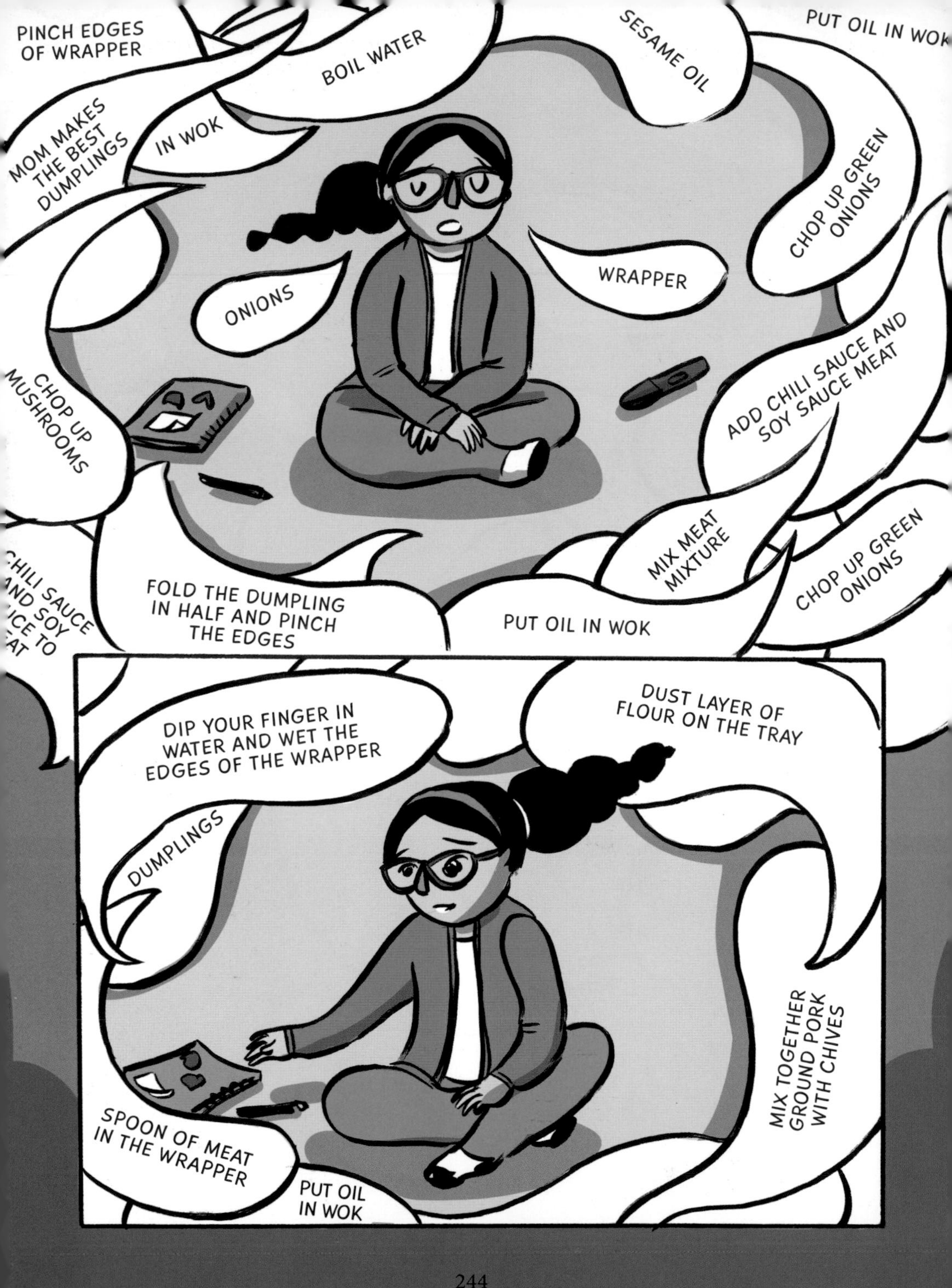
PINCH EDGES OF WRAPPER
BOIL WATER
SESAME OIL
PUT OIL IN WOK
MOM MAKES THE BEST DUMPLINGS
IN WOK
CHOP UP GREEN ONIONS
WRAPPER
ONIONS
CHOP UP MUSHROOMS
ADD CHILI SAUCE AND SOY SAUCE MEAT
MIX MEAT MIXTURE
CHOP UP GREEN ONIONS
FOLD THE DUMPLING IN HALF AND PINCH THE EDGES
PUT OIL IN WOK
DIP YOUR FINGER IN WATER AND WET THE EDGES OF THE WRAPPER
DUST LAYER OF FLOUR ON THE TRAY
DUMPLINGS
MIX TOGETHER GROUND PORK WITH CHIVES
SPOON OF MEAT IN THE WRAPPER
PUT OIL IN WOK

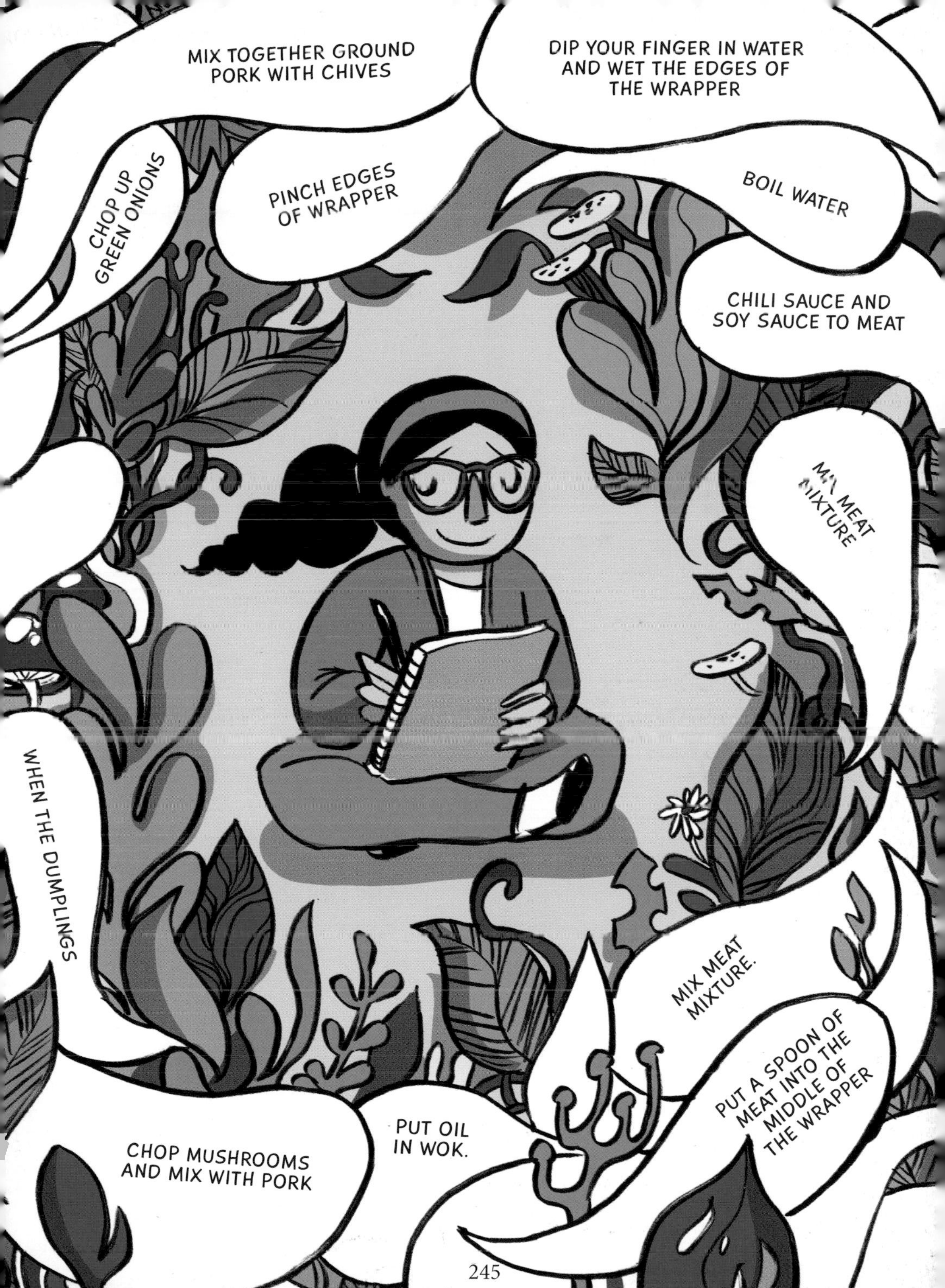
MIX TOGETHER GROUND PORK WITH CHIVES
DIP YOUR FINGER IN WATER AND WET THE EDGES OF THE WRAPPER
CHOP UP GREEN ONIONS
PINCH EDGES OF WRAPPER
BOIL WATER
CHILI SAUCE AND SOY SAUCE TO MEAT
MEAT MIXTURE
WHEN THE DUMPLINGS
MIX MEAT MIXTURE.
PUT A SPOON OF MEAT INTO THE MIDDLE OF THE WRAPPER
CHOP MUSHROOMS AND MIX WITH PORK
PUT OIL IN WOK.

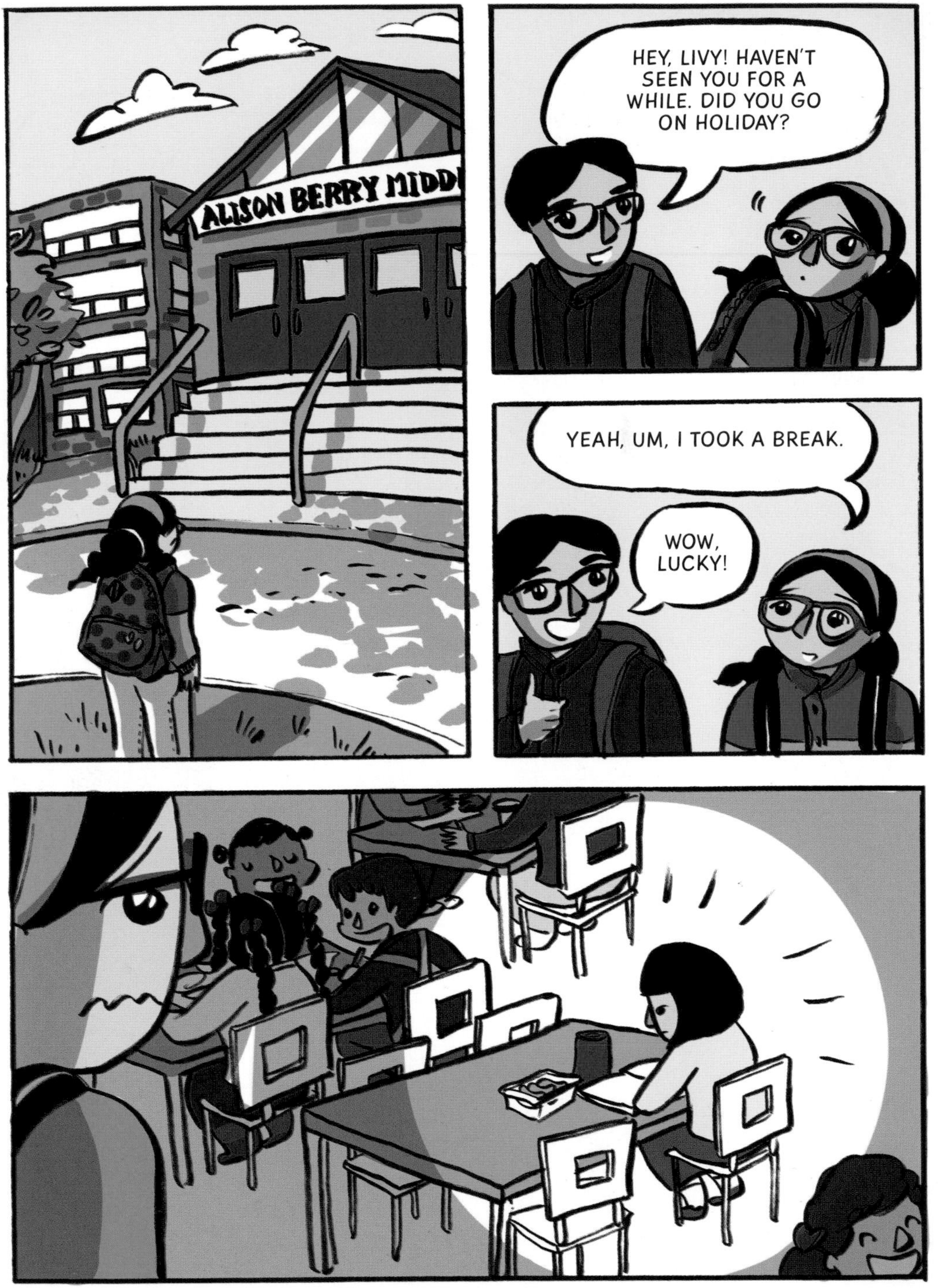
ALISON BERRY MIDD
HEY, LIVY! HAVEN'T SEEN YOU FOR A WHILE. DID YOU GO ON HOLIDAY?
YEAH, UM, I TOOK A BREAK.
WOW, LUCKY!

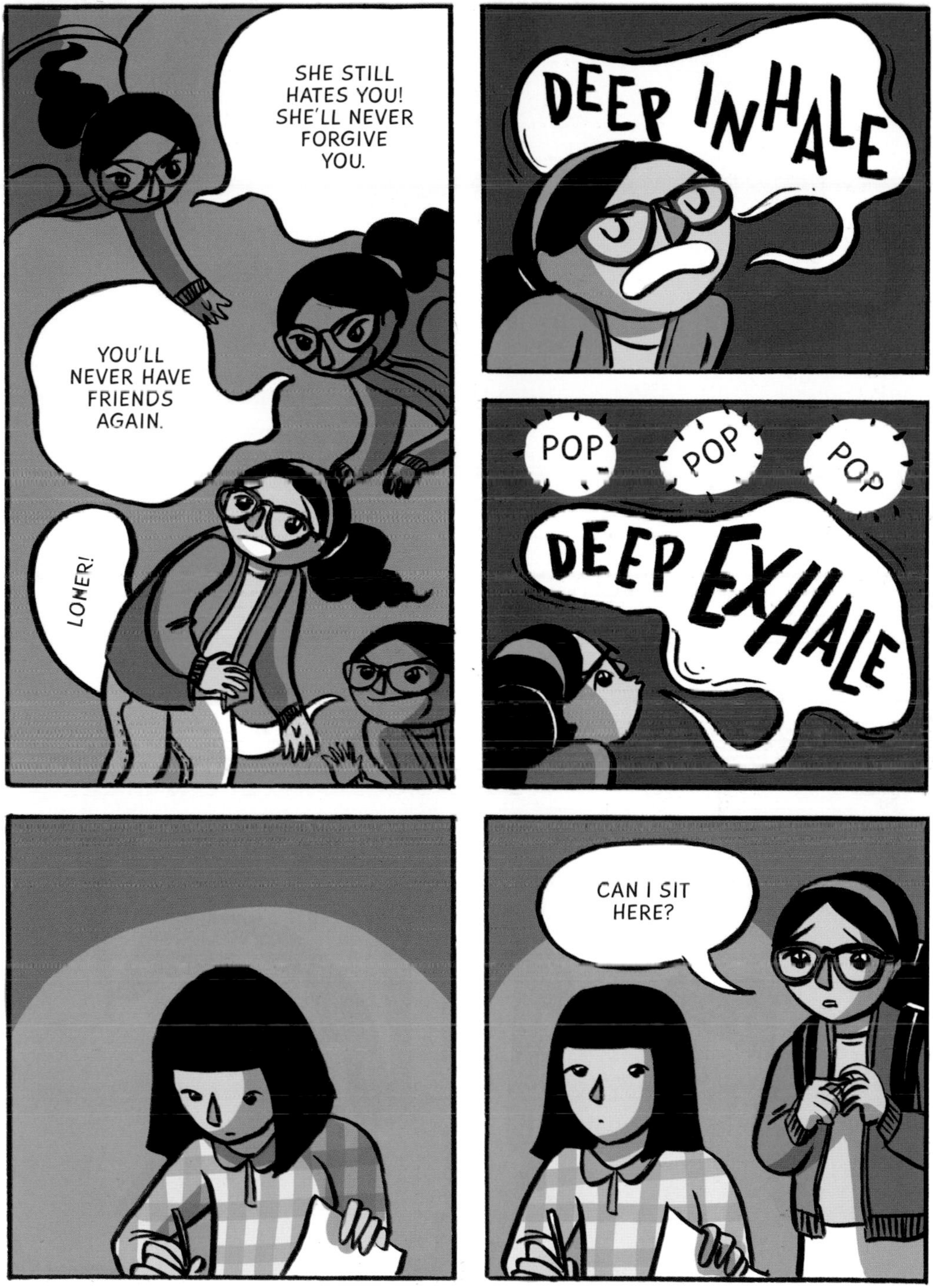
SHE STILL HATES YOU! SHE'LL NEVER FORGIVE YOU.
YOU'LL NEVER HAVE FRIENDS AGAIN.
LONER!
DEEP INHALE
POP
POP
POP
DEEP EXHALE
CAN I SIT HERE?

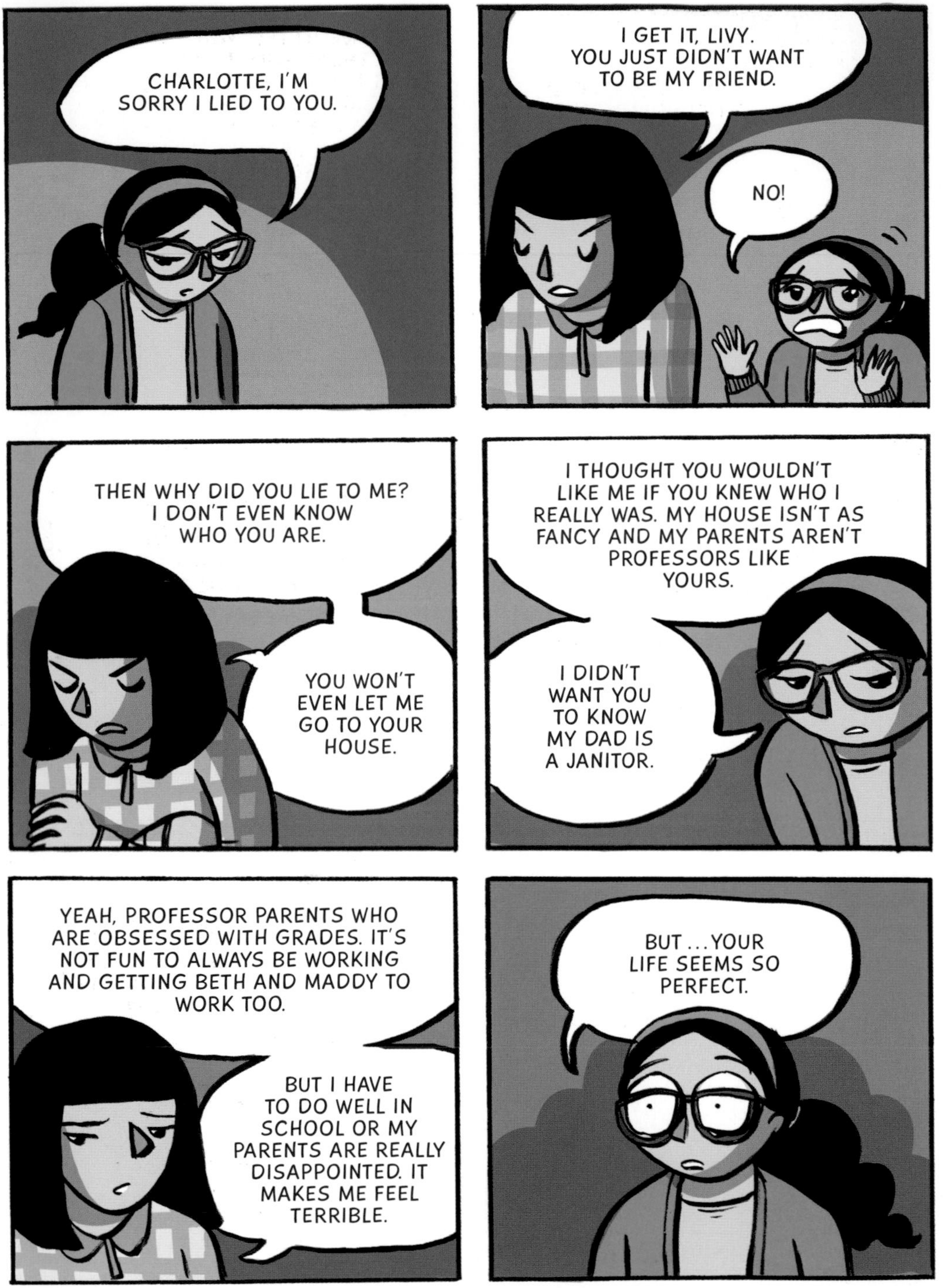
CHARLOTTE, I'M SORRY I LIED TO YOU.
I GET IT, LIVY. YOU JUST DIDN'T WANT TO BE MY FRIEND.
NO!
THEN WHY DID YOU LIE TO ME? I DON'T EVEN KNOW WHO YOU ARE.
YOU WON'T EVEN LET ME GO TO YOUR HOUSE.
I THOUGHT YOU WOULDN'T LIKE ME IF YOU KNEW WHO I REALLY WAS. MY HOUSE ISN'T AS FANCY AND MY PARENTS AREN'T PROFESSORS LIKE YOURS.
I DIDN'T WANT YOU TO KNOW MY DAD IS A JANITOR.
YEAH, PROFESSOR PARENTS WHO ARE OBSESSED WITH GRADES. IT'S NOT FUN TO ALWAYS BE WORKING AND GETTING BETH AND MADDY TO WORK TOO.
BUT I HAVE TO DO WELL IN SCHOOL OR MY PARENTS ARE REALLY DISAPPOINTED. IT MAKES ME FEEL TERRIBLE.
BUT . . . YOUR LIFE SEEMS SO PERFECT.

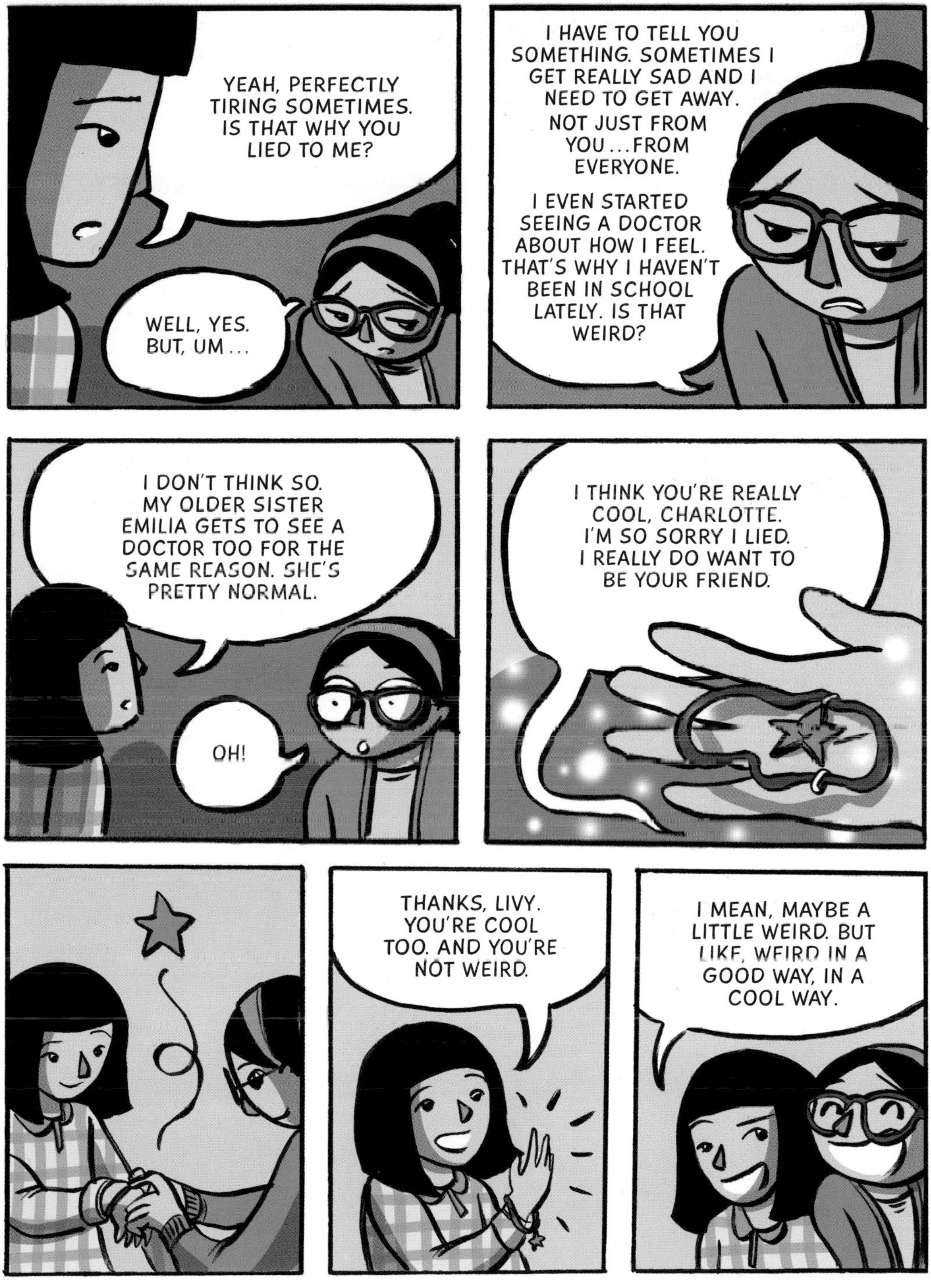
YEAH, PERFECTLY TIRING SOMETIMES. IS THAT WHY YOU LIED TO ME?
WELL, YES. BUT, UM ...
I HAVE TO TELL YOU SOMETHING. SOMETIMES I GET REALLY SAD AND I NEED TO GET AWAY.
NOT JUST FROM YOU ... FROM EVERYONE.
I EVEN STARTED SEEING A DOCTOR ABOUT HOW I FEEL. THAT'S WHY I HAVEN'T BEEN IN SCHOOL LATELY. IS THAT WEIRD?
I DON'T THINK SO. MY OLDER SISTER EMILIA GETS TO SEE A DOCTOR TOO FOR THE SAME REASON. SHE'S PRETTY NORMAL.
OH!
I THINK YOU'RE REALLY COOL, CHARLOTTE. I'M SO SORRY I LIED. I REALLY DO WANT TO BE YOUR FRIEND.
THANKS, LIVY. YOU'RE COOL TOO. AND YOU'RE NOT WEIRD.
I MEAN, MAYBE A LITTLE WEIRD. BUT LIKE, WEIRD IN A GOOD WAY, IN A COOL WAY.

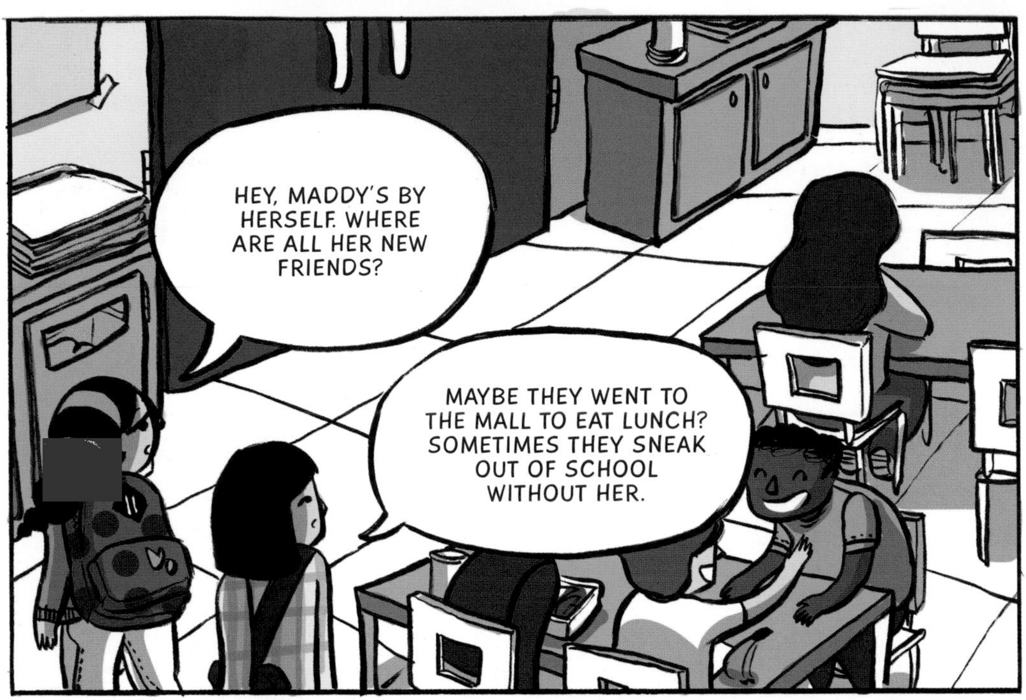
HEY, MADDY'S BY HERSELF. WHERE ARE ALL HER NEW FRIENDS?
MAYBE THEY WENT TO THE MALL TO EAT LUNCH? SOMETIMES THEY SNEAK OUT OF SCHOOL WITHOUT HER.

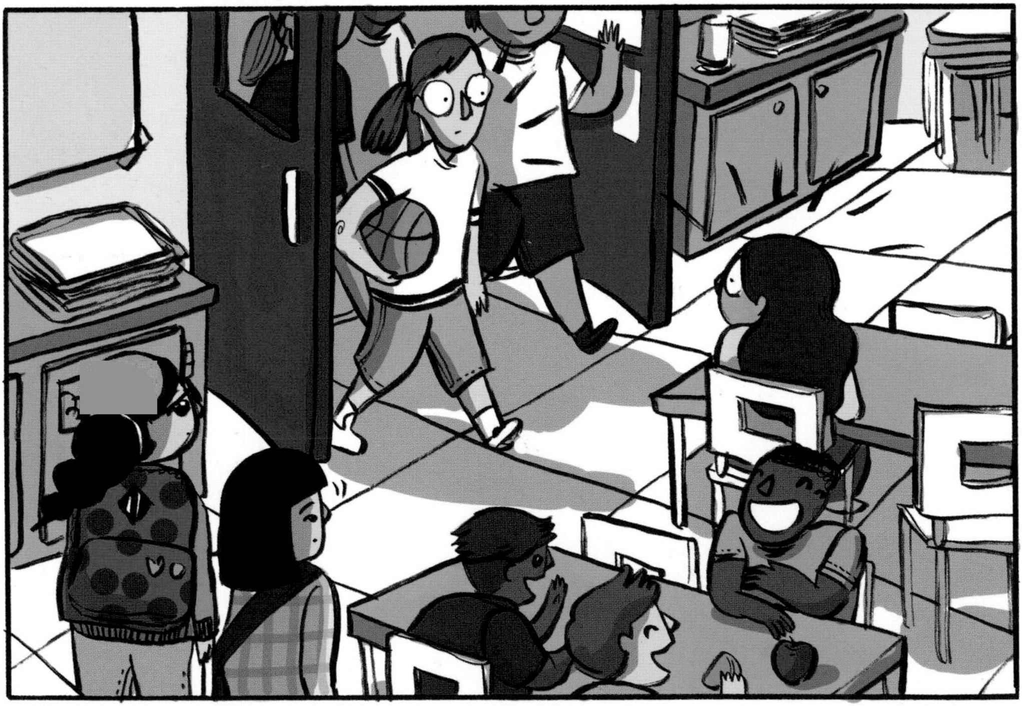

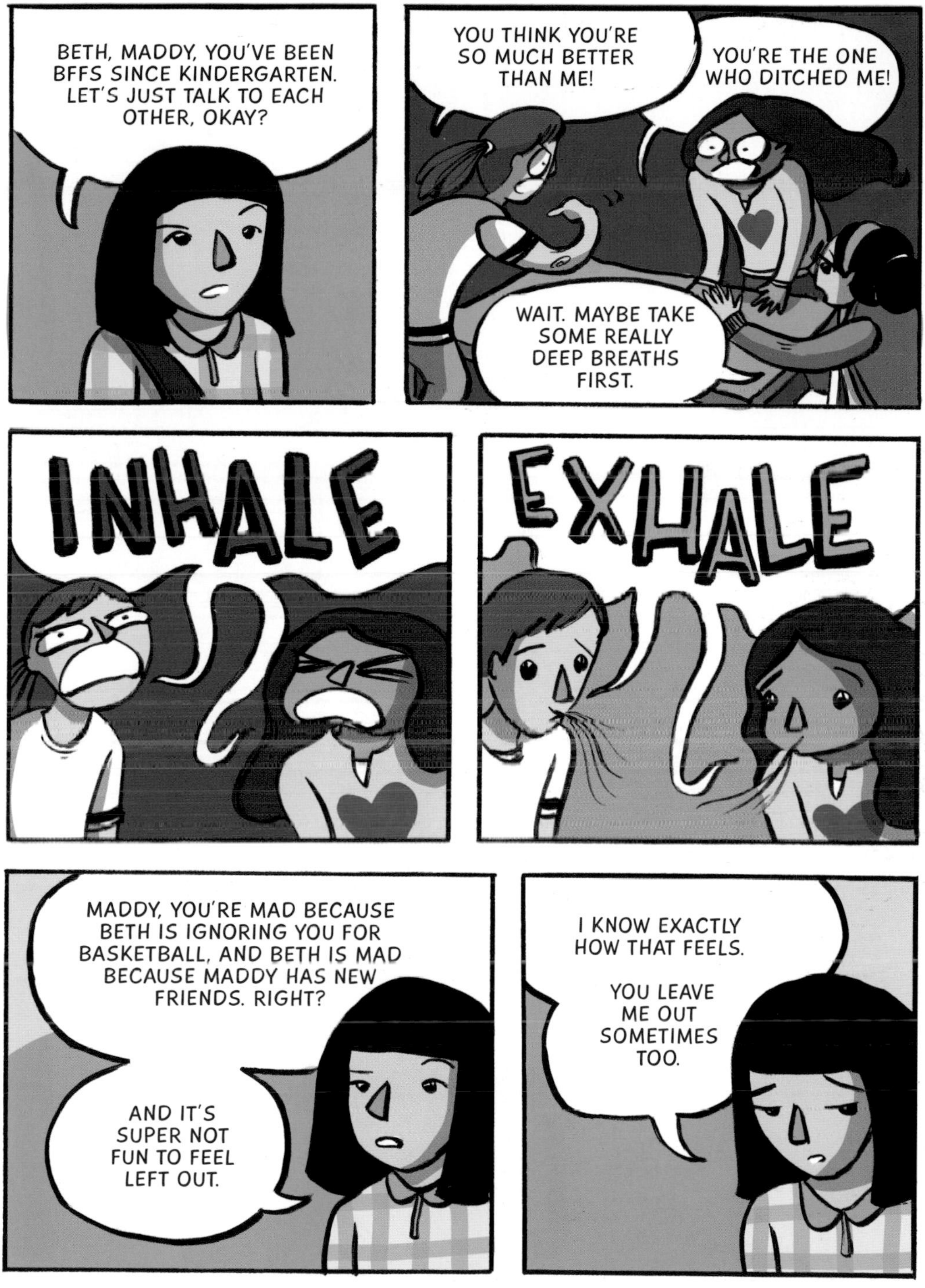
BETH, MADDY, YOU'VE BEEN BFFS SINCE KINDERGARTEN. LET'S JUST TALK TO EACH OTHER, OKAY?
YOU THINK YOU'RE SO MUCH BETTER THAN ME!
YOU'RE THE ONE WHO DITCHED ME!
WAIT. MAYBE TAKE SOME REALLY DEEP BREATHS FIRST.
INHALE
EXHALE
MADDY, YOU'RE MAD BECAUSE BETH IS IGNORING YOU FOR BASKETBALL, AND BETH IS MAD BECAUSE MADDY HAS NEW FRIENDS. RIGHT?
AND IT'S SUPER NOT FUN TO FEEL LEFT OUT.
I KNOW EXACTLY HOW THAT FEELS.
YOU LEAVE ME OUT SOMETIMES TOO.

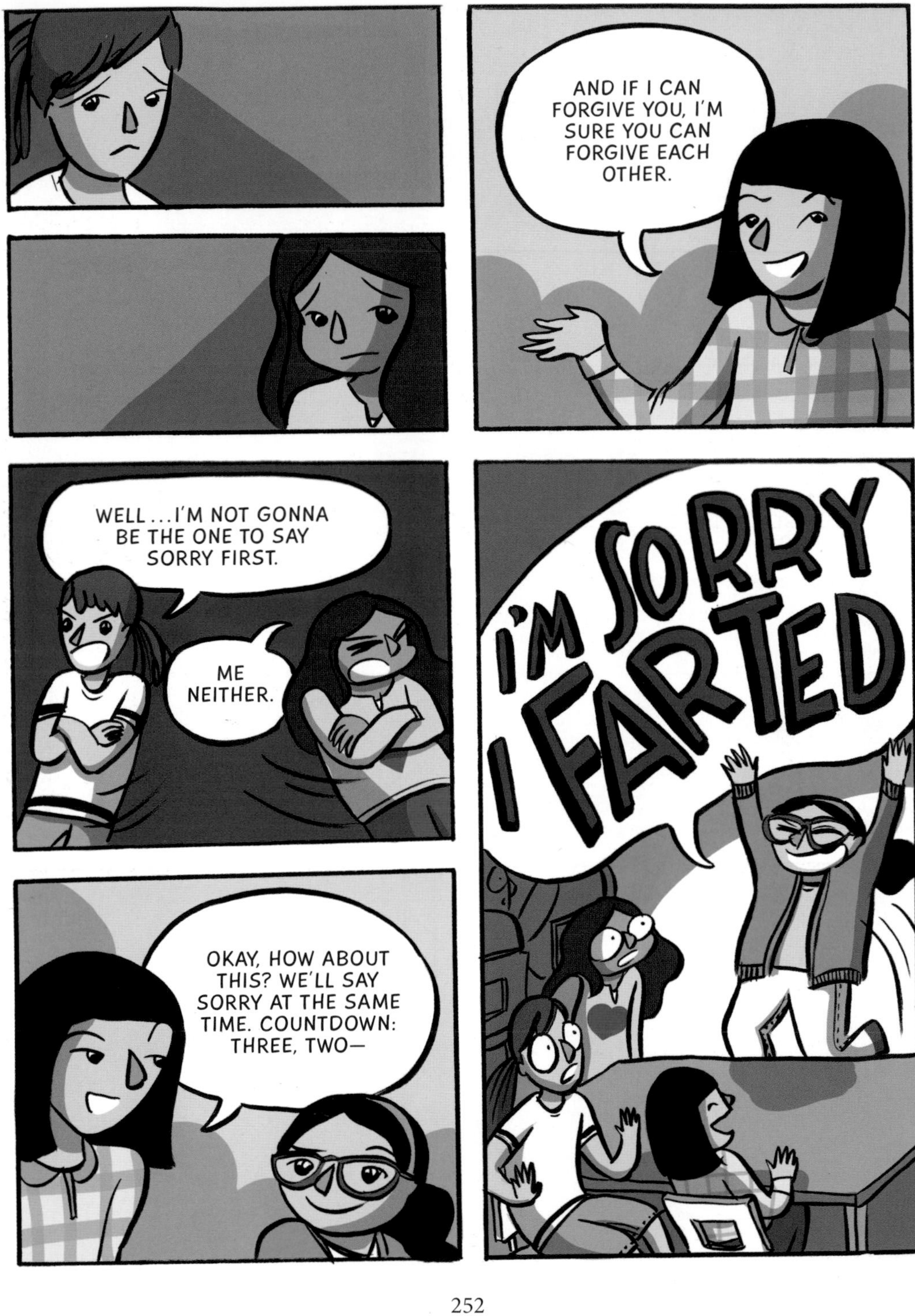
AND IF I CAN FORGIVE YOU, I'M SURE YOU CAN FORGIVE EACH OTHER.
WELL...I'M NOT GONNA BE THE ONE TO SAY SORRY FIRST.
ME NEITHER.
OKAY, HOW ABOUT THIS? WE'LL SAY SORRY AT THE SAME TIME. COUNTDOWN: THREE, TWO—
I'M SORRY I FARTED

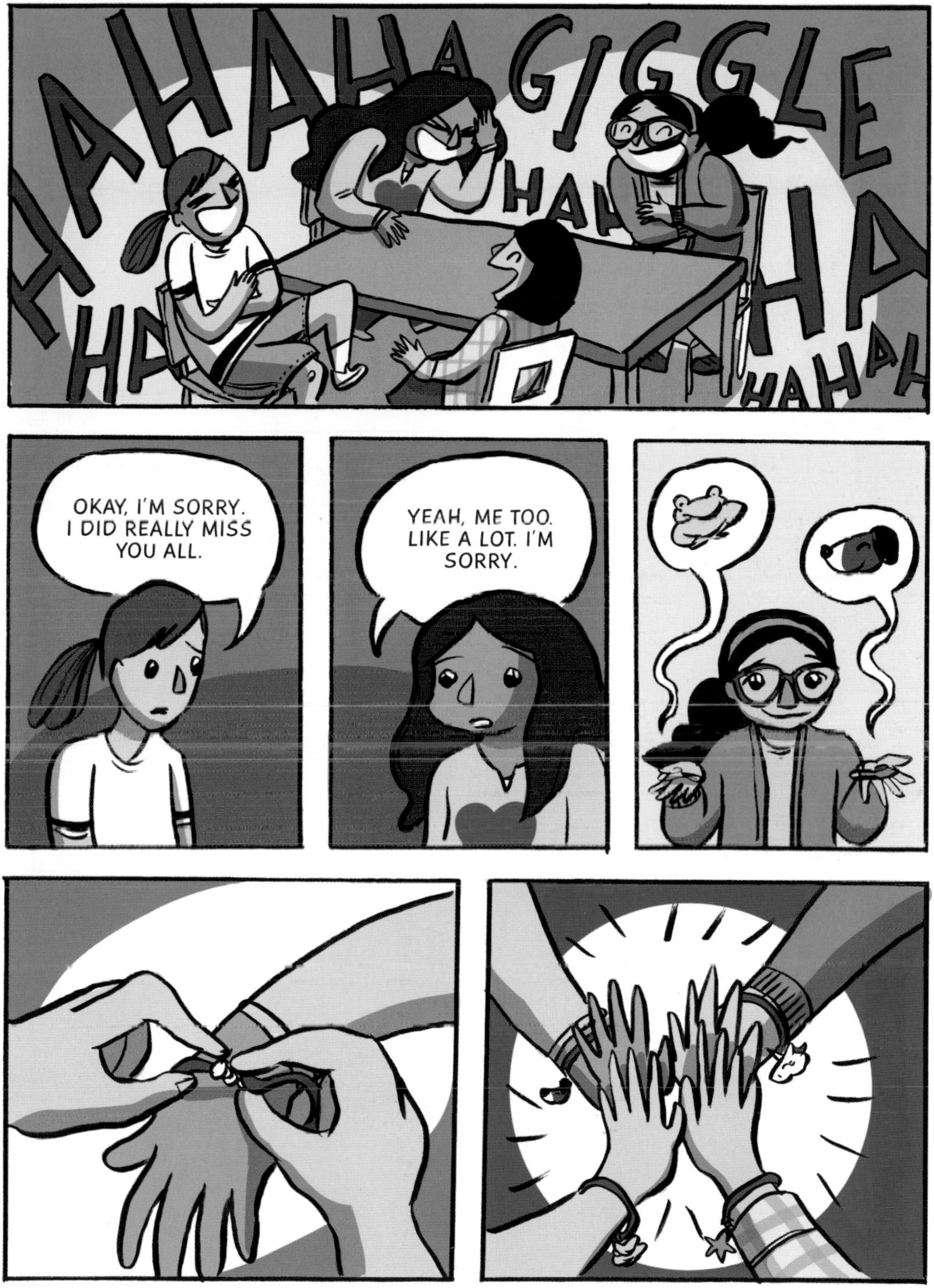
HAHAHA
GIGGLE
HAHA
HA
HAHAHA
HAHAH
OKAY, I'M SORRY. I DID REALLY MISS YOU ALL.
YEAH, ME TOO. LIKE A LOT. I'M SORRY.

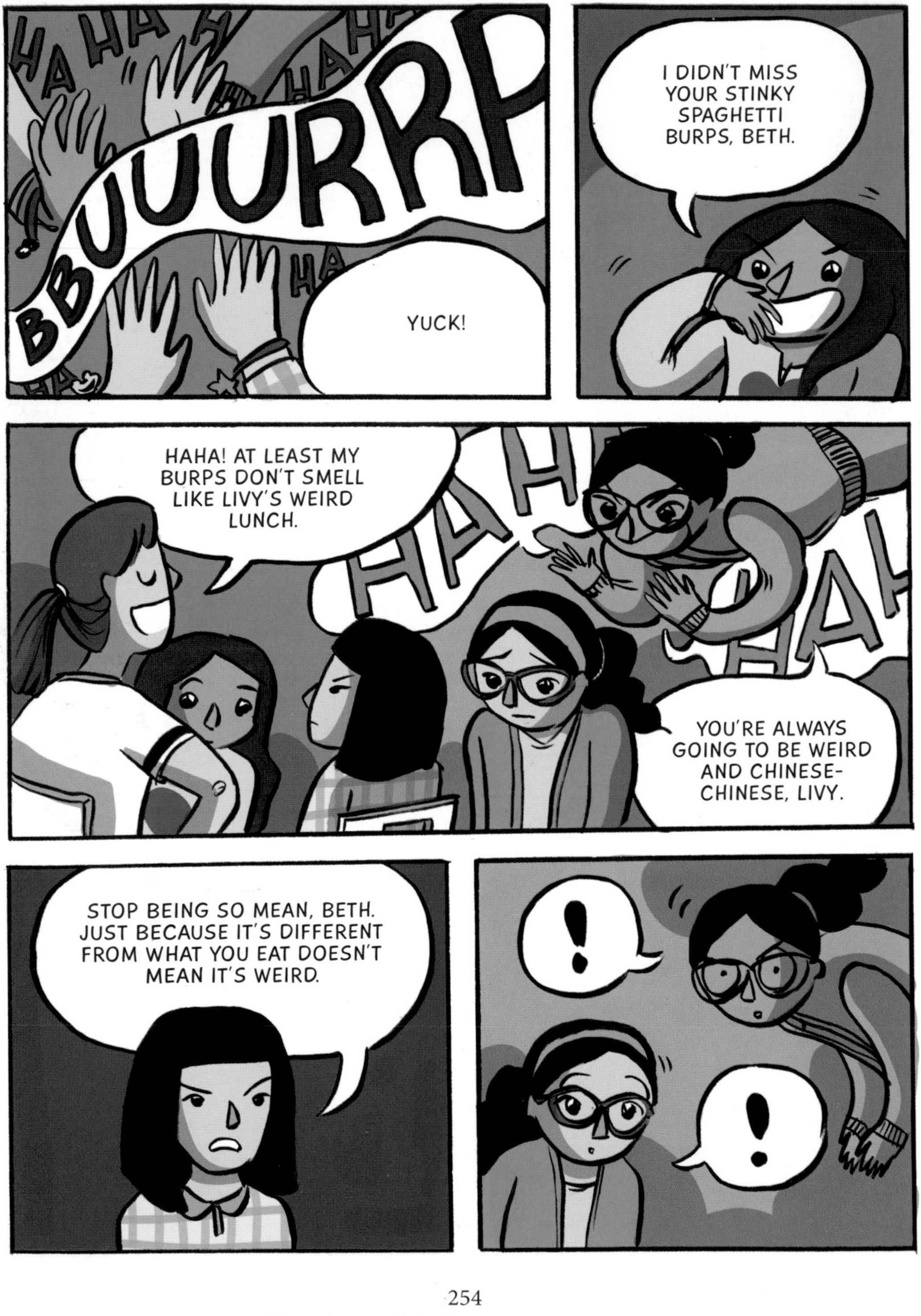
HA HA HA HA HA HA
BBUUURRRP
HA
YUCK!
I DIDN'T MISS YOUR STINKY SPAGHETTI BURPS, BETH.
HAHA! AT LEAST MY BURPS DON'T SMELL LIKE LIVY'S WEIRD LUNCH.
HA HA HA HA HA
YOU'RE ALWAYS GOING TO BE WEIRD AND CHINESE-CHINESE, LIVY.
STOP BEING SO MEAN, BETH. JUST BECAUSE IT'S DIFFERENT FROM WHAT YOU EAT DOESN'T MEAN IT'S WEIRD.
!
!

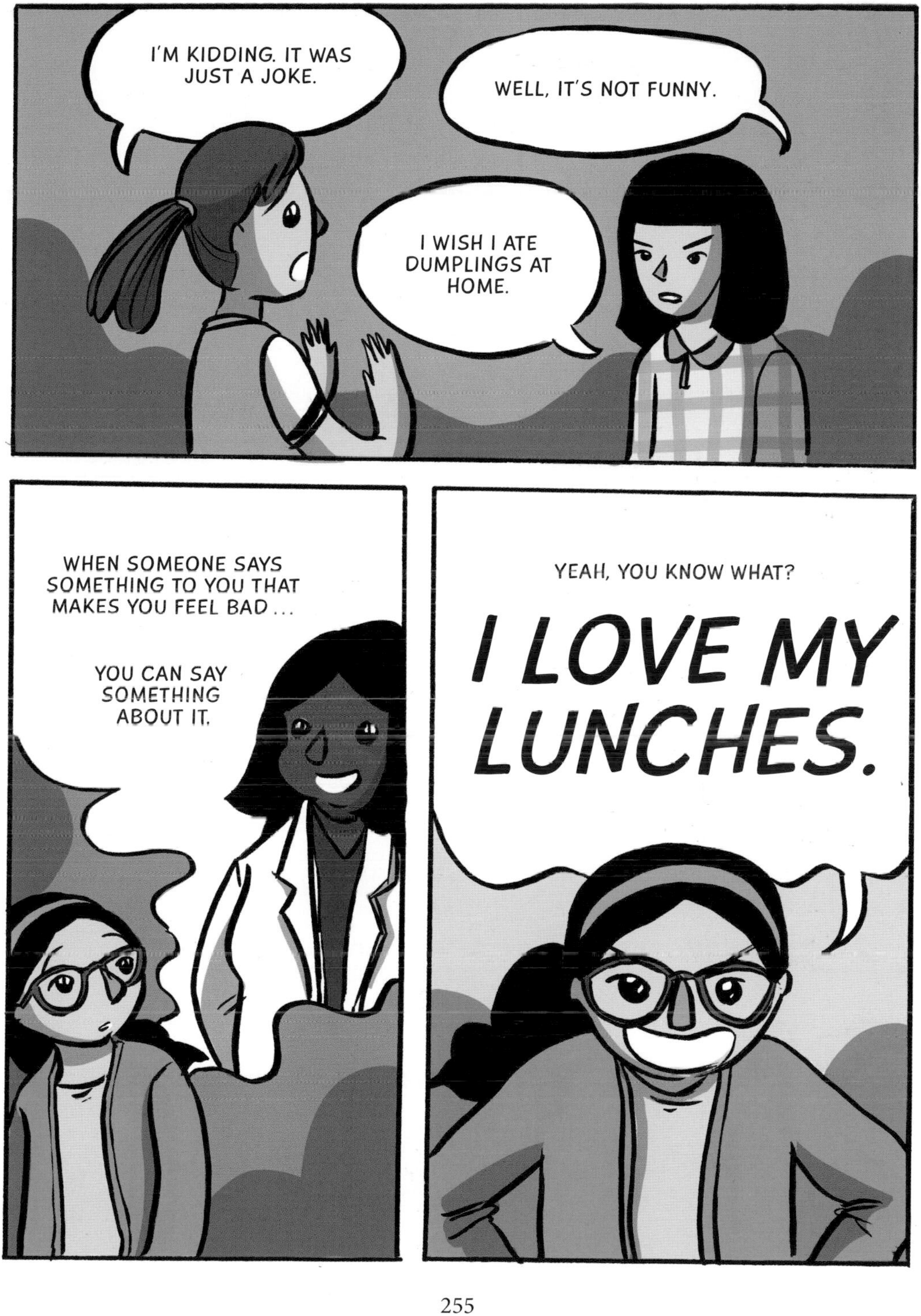
I'M KIDDING. IT WAS JUST A JOKE.
WELL, IT'S NOT FUNNY.
I WISH I ATE DUMPLINGS AT HOME.
WHEN SOMEONE SAYS SOMETHING TO YOU THAT MAKES YOU FEEL BAD . . .
YOU CAN SAY SOMETHING ABOUT IT.
YEAH, YOU KNOW WHAT?
I LOVE MY LUNCHES.

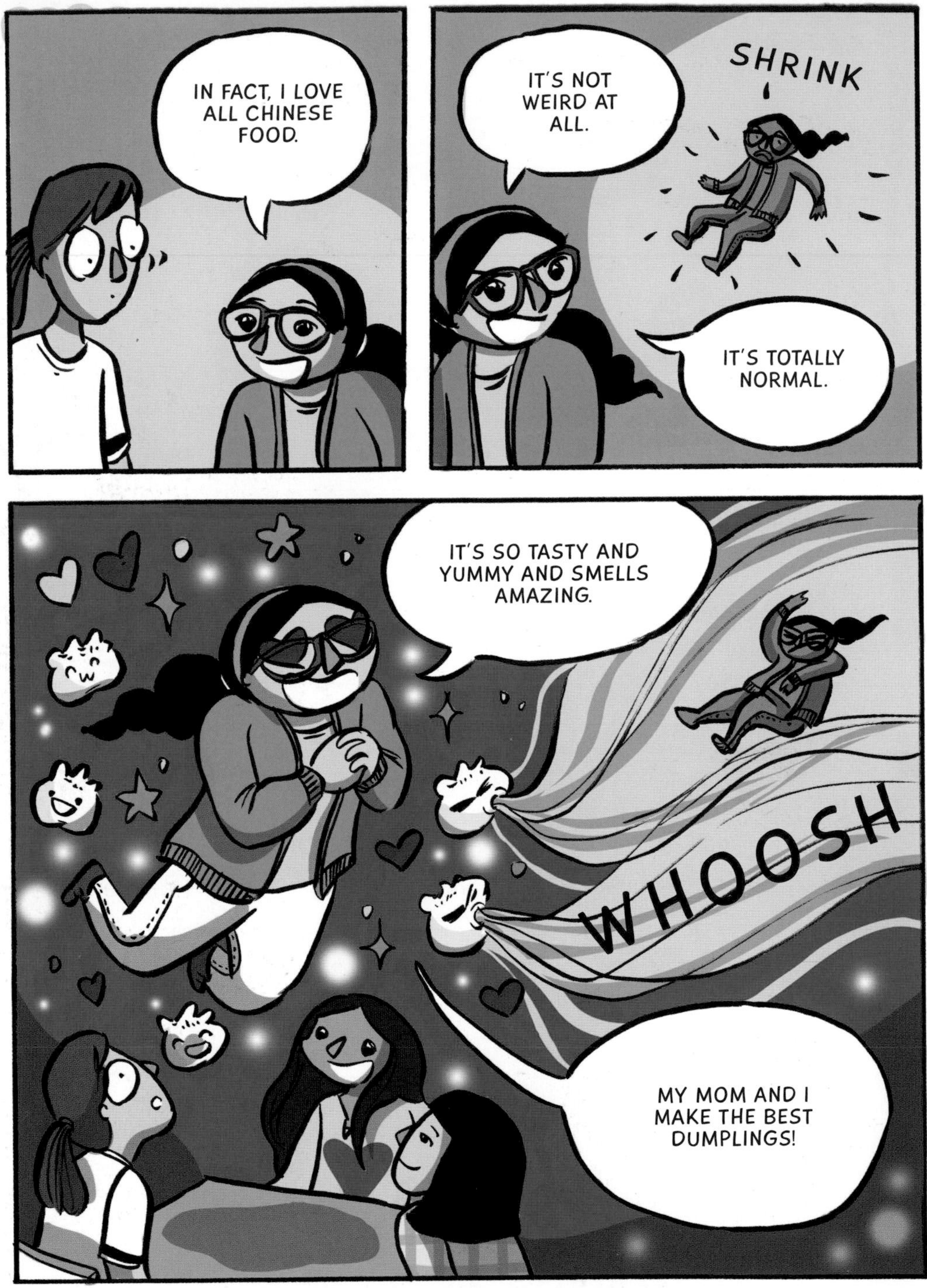
IN FACT, I LOVE ALL CHINESE FOOD.
IT'S NOT WEIRD AT ALL.
SHRINK
IT'S TOTALLY NORMAL.
IT'S SO TASTY AND YUMMY AND SMELLS AMAZING.
WHOOSH
MY MOM AND I MAKE THE BEST DUMPLINGS!

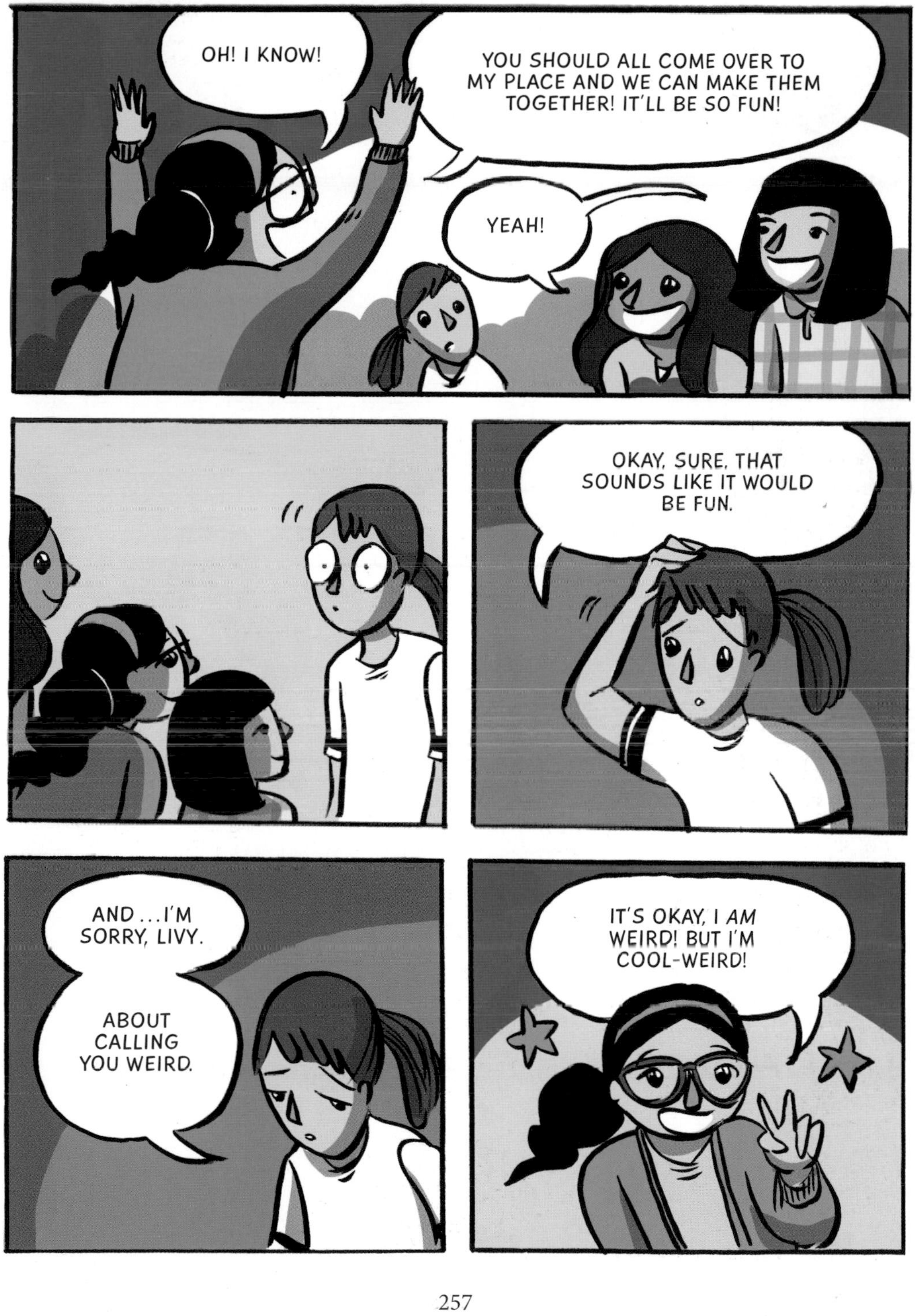
OH! I KNOW!
YOU SHOULD ALL COME OVER TO MY PLACE AND WE CAN MAKE THEM TOGETHER! IT'LL BE SO FUN!
YEAH!
OKAY, SURE, THAT SOUNDS LIKE IT WOULD BE FUN.
AND . . . I'M SORRY, LIVY.
ABOUT CALLING YOU WEIRD.
IT'S OKAY, I *AM* WEIRD! BUT I'M COOL-WEIRD!

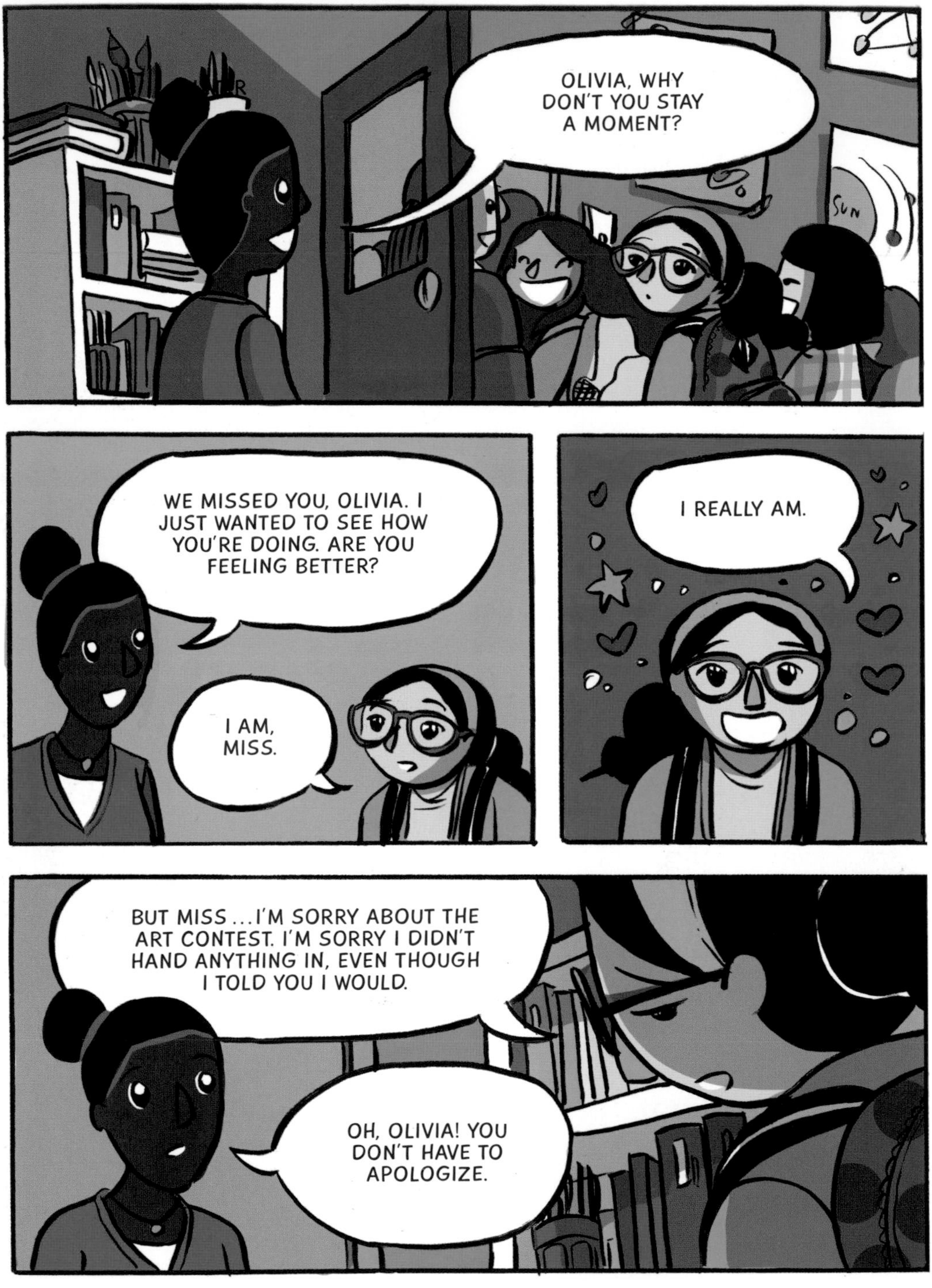
OLIVIA, WHY DON'T YOU STAY A MOMENT?
WE MISSED YOU, OLIVIA. I JUST WANTED TO SEE HOW YOU'RE DOING. ARE YOU FEELING BETTER?
I AM, MISS.
I REALLY AM.
BUT MISS ... I'M SORRY ABOUT THE ART CONTEST. I'M SORRY I DIDN'T HAND ANYTHING IN, EVEN THOUGH I TOLD YOU I WOULD.
OH, OLIVIA! YOU DON'T HAVE TO APOLOGIZE.

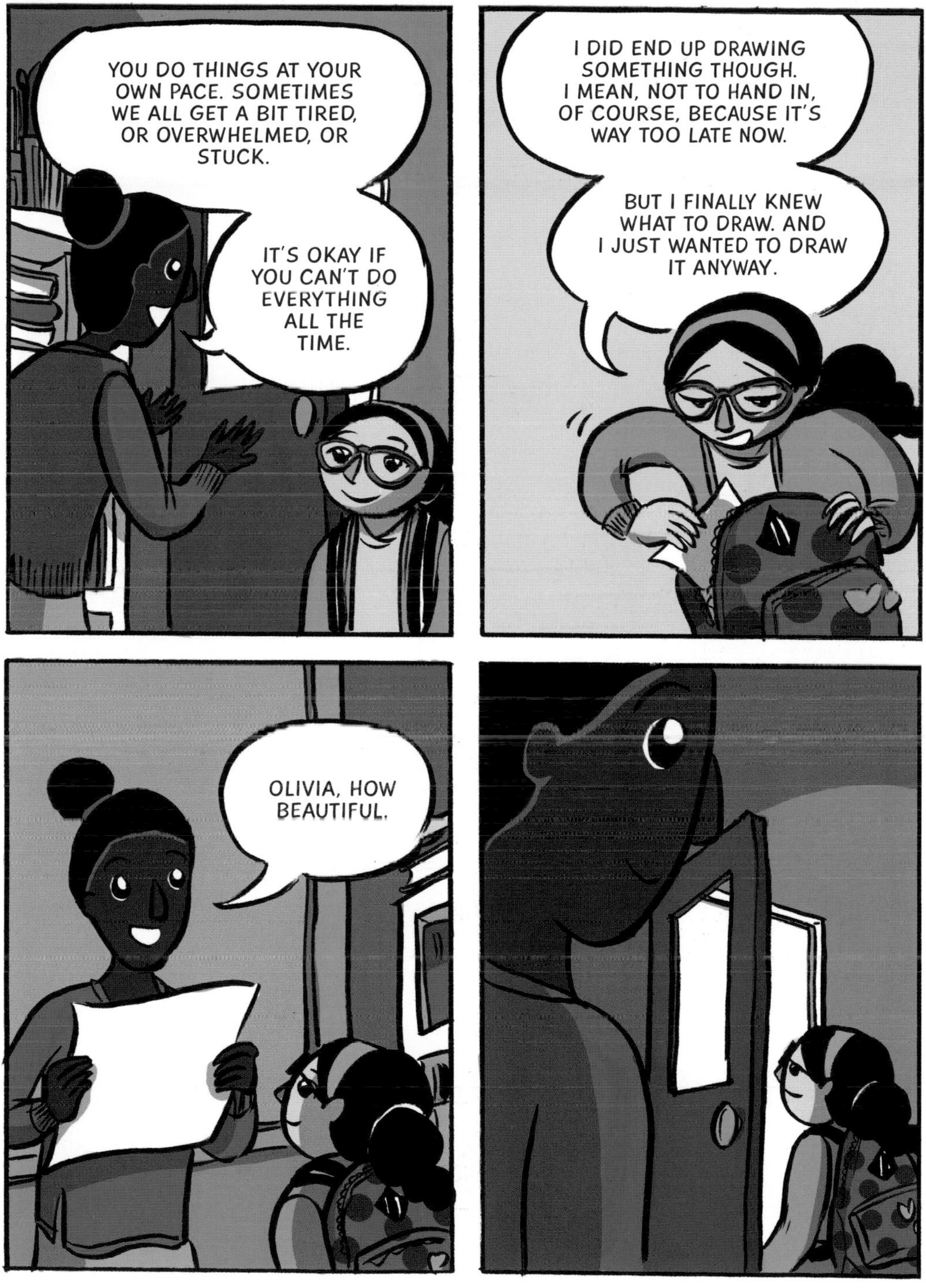

YOU DO THINGS AT YOUR OWN PACE. SOMETIMES WE ALL GET A BIT TIRED, OR OVERWHELMED, OR STUCK.
IT'S OKAY IF YOU CAN'T DO EVERYTHING ALL THE TIME.
I DID END UP DRAWING SOMETHING THOUGH. I MEAN, NOT TO HAND IN, OF COURSE, BECAUSE IT'S WAY TOO LATE NOW.
BUT I FINALLY KNEW WHAT TO DRAW. AND I JUST WANTED TO DRAW IT ANYWAY.
OLIVIA, HOW BEAUTIFUL.

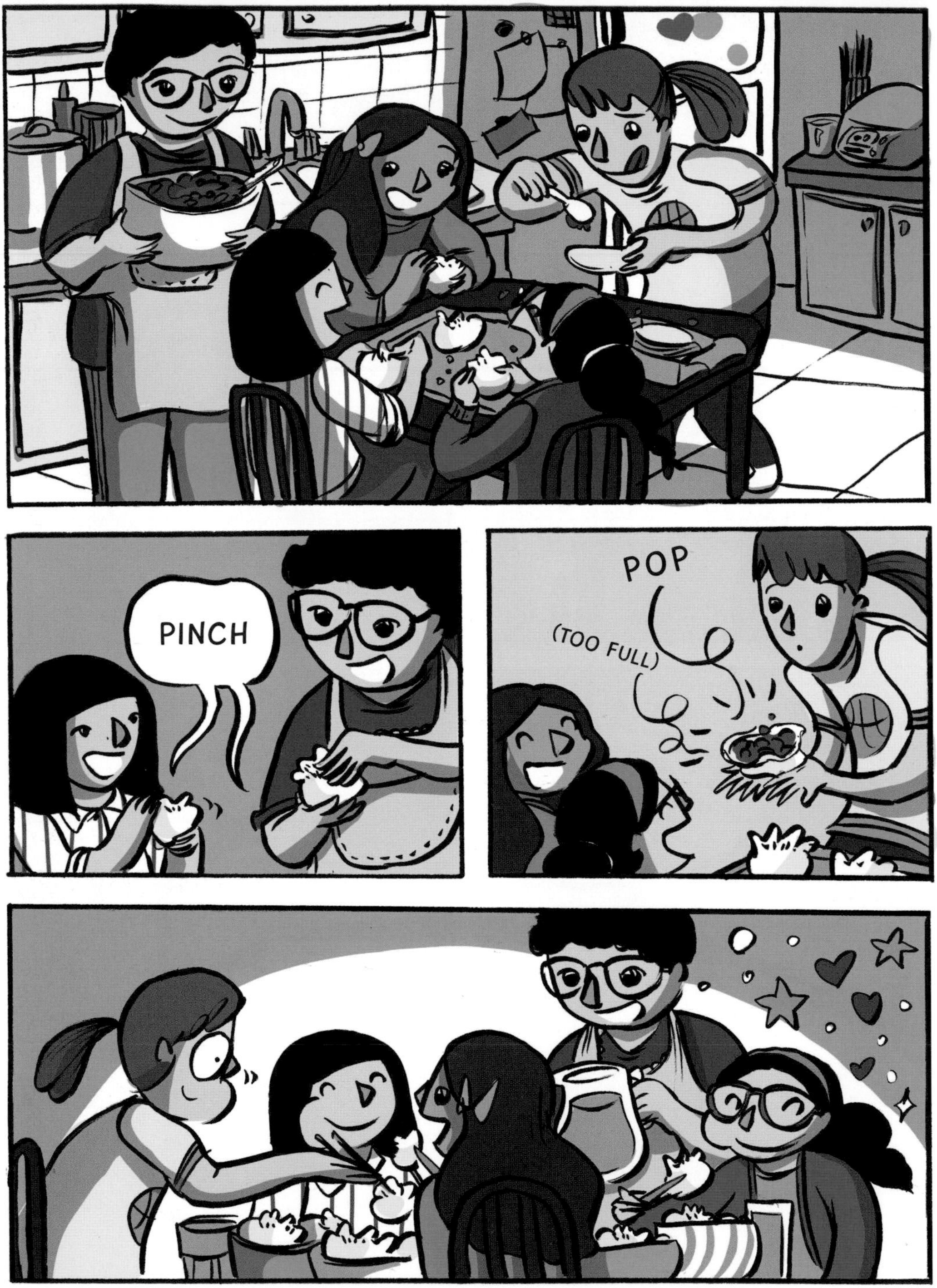
PINCH
POP
(TOO FULL)

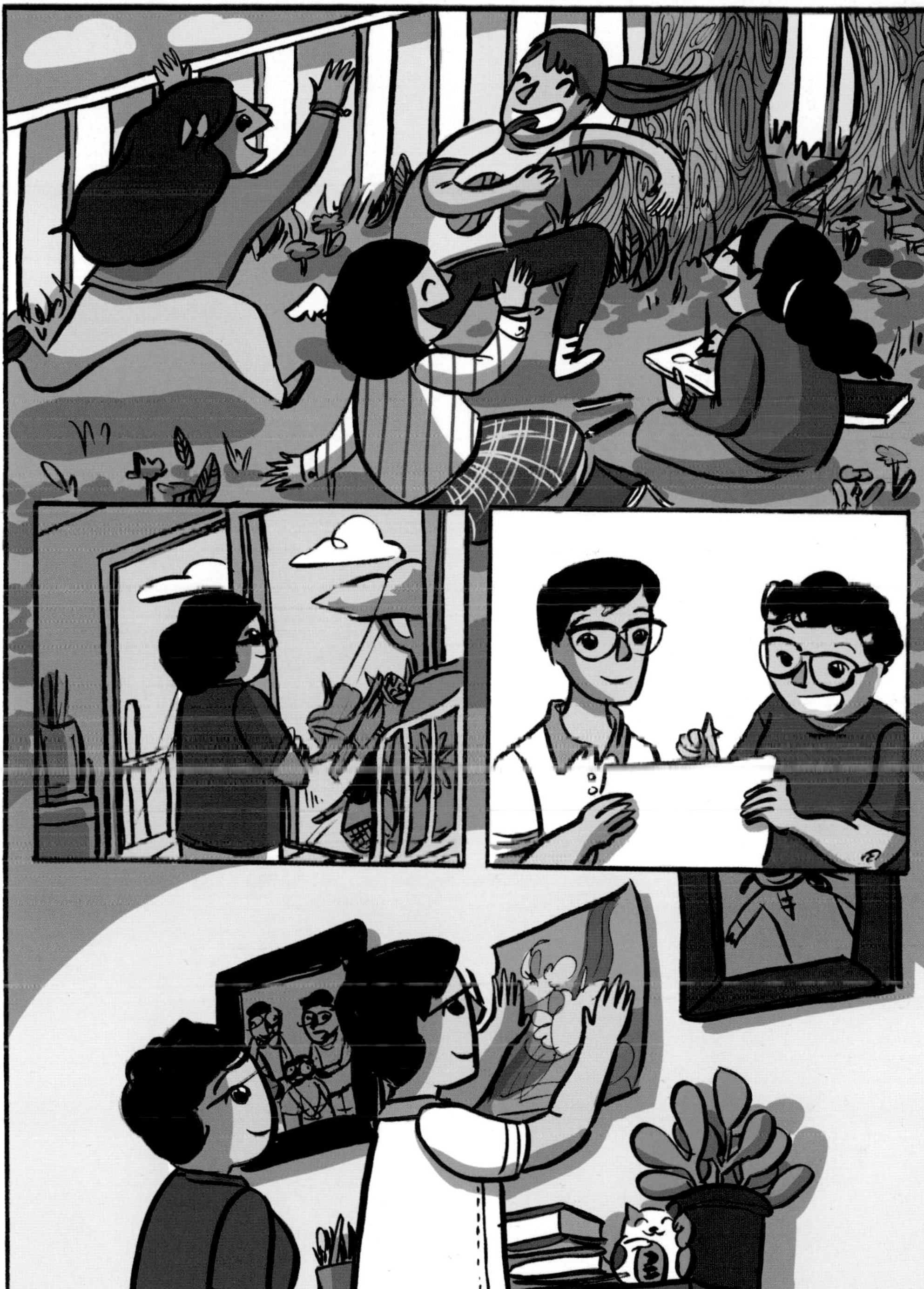

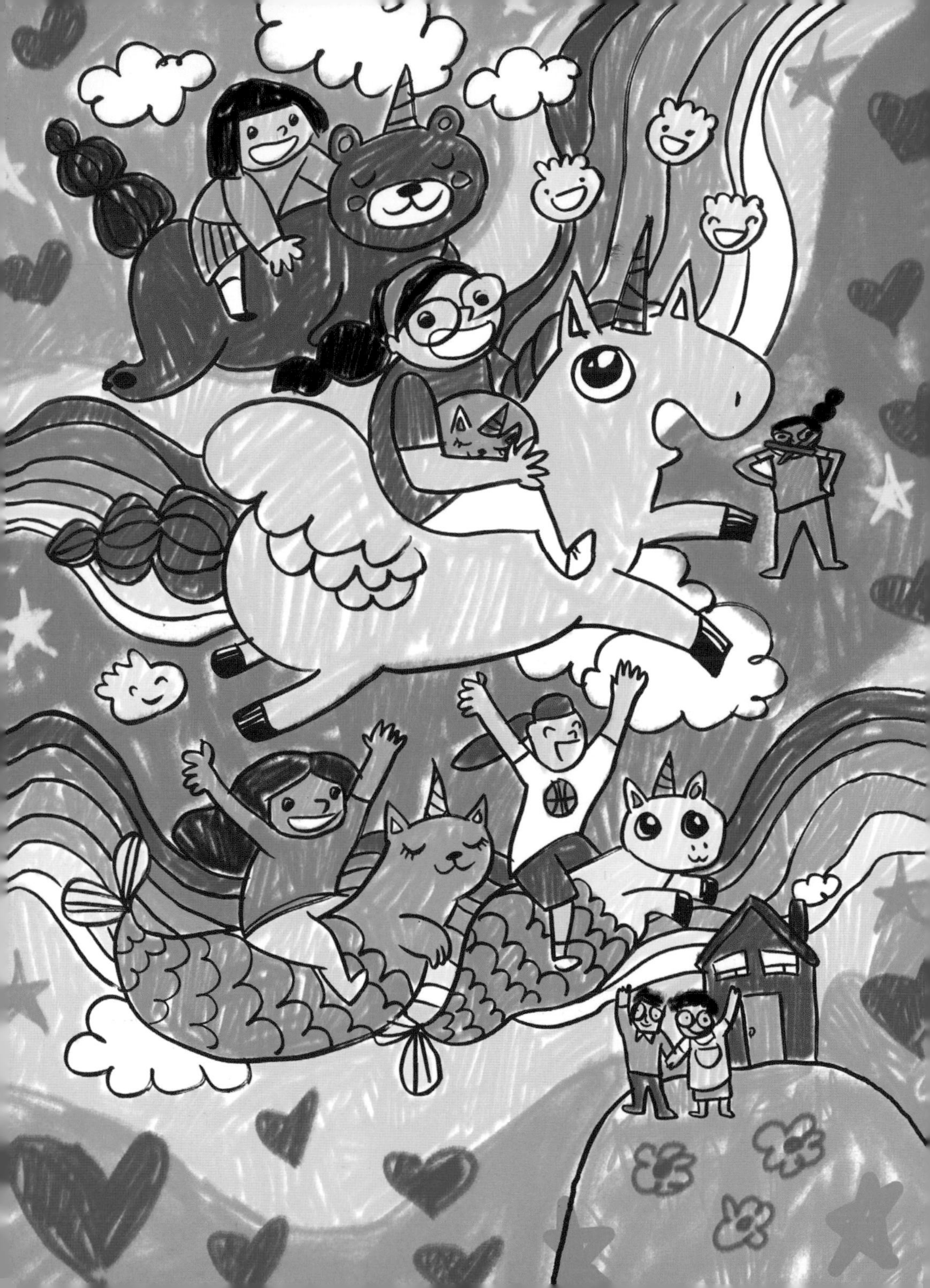

Author's Note

Living With Viola is fiction, but this isn't the kind of story you make up out of nowhere. A lot of it is inspired by things that actually happened to me.

My parents were both immigrants to Canada from Hong Kong. As I got older, I saw that immigrants were treated differently, and not always nicely. Other people would make fun of the way they spoke, or think that because they did some things differently it meant they were weird.

But just because something is unfamiliar doesn't mean it's bad or scary. It's important to be open and kind to everyone.

When I was in sixth grade (the same as Livy) I started having panic attacks and feeling nervous and sad all the time. I was sure bad things were going to happen because I was a bad person. I got really good at pretending I was okay on the outside, even while I was terrified on the inside. I didn't understand why I was always so scared.

My parents didn't know what was happening, either. They were very worried for me. They took me to see some doctors, and by the time I was about 16 I was diagnosed with anxiety disorder and panic disorder, with a bit of obsessive-compulsive disorder. Wow! When I finally knew what it was, it felt like the biggest relief. I wasn't alone, and there were things I could do to help me feel better, like cognitive behavioral therapy, medication, group sessions, and talking to people I could trust.

My anxiety didn't exactly exist outside of me the way Viola is with Livy. Often when I was scared, it was like hearing my own voice tell me I was horrible. After getting help, I realized you can't always believe everything you think about yourself. We're not always nice to ourselves, whether or not we have anxiety. But would you say the same things to people you love that you sometimes say to yourself? Thinking about my critical voice as an actual person helped me to say, "Hey, that's pretty mean. Why are you saying these things? They're not true."

When I was a kid, my favorite things to do were to draw and to read. I'm older now but those are STILL my favorite things. I also love pink sparkles and cat unicorn plushies, but I used to worry that liking things that are too "girly" or too "childish" were not cool. I even tried to change, but I didn't find much happiness trying to pretend to like things other people liked. And I realized that there are no girly things, or boyish things, or childish things. There are just things that make you happy.

If you ever feel scared or sad, or don't understand why you feel a certain way, talk to someone about it, like an adult you can trust. There are lots of people like you who understand how you feel and have gone through the same thing. You're not alone!

—Rosena Fung

Cantonese Glossary

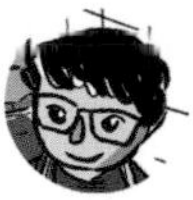

ah ma (a mā): a less formal way of saying mother

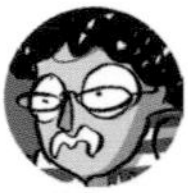

ai yah (ai ya): an exclamation expressing fear, shock, surprise, or dismay

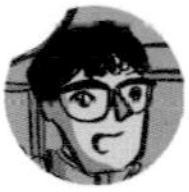

baba (bā bā): daddy

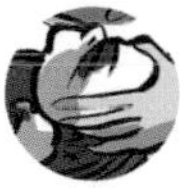

bao (bāau): A delicious bun stuffed with meat or sweet fillings like red bean, coconut, or custard. When steamed they are soft and white, when baked they are brown and glazed.

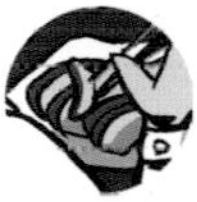

char siu (chā sīu): sweet red barbecue pork

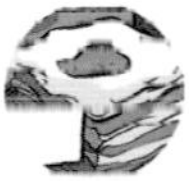

cheen chung goh (chīn chàhng gōu): A steamed dessert cake made of egg and custard in alternating layers. Literally translates to "thousand layer cake."

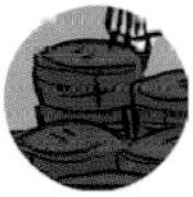

dim sum (dím sām): Usually eaten during yum cha, dim sum are small shared dishes like dumplings, buns, and other things that don't need to be cut with a knife to be shared by lots of people. They can be sweet or savory, and can be fried, baked, or steamed, often in stackable baskets brought to the table.

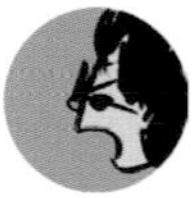

face (mín): Not literally a face! It means how you are perceived by others, having to do with respect or honor in social interactions. Face depends on prestige, roles, reputation, actions, and behaviors. You can "gain face" or "lose face" as a person and it affects how you are seen by others. You can also "give face" to someone with actions that demonstrate respect.

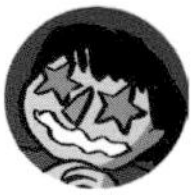

gah jeh (gā jē): older sister

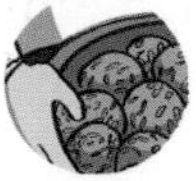

goong goong (gūng gūng): grandfather, specifically mother's father

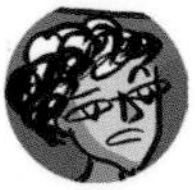

gwoo gwoo (gū gū): aunt, specifically father's sister

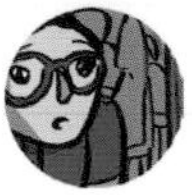

gwaai (gwāai): When pronounced with an upper high intonation, "gwaai" means good or obedient.

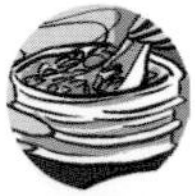

ham yue gai (hàahm ỳuh gāi): salted fish and chicken

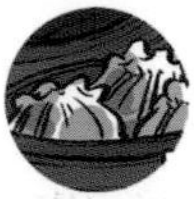

ham yue gai lup chow fan (hàahm ỳuh gāi lāp cháau faahn): salted fish and diced chicken fried rice

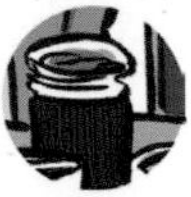

har gow (hā gáau): steamed shrimp dumpling made with a translucent wrapper. Often served together with siu mai.

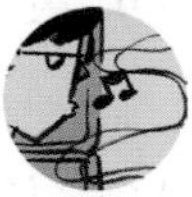

joh sun (jóu sàhn): good morning

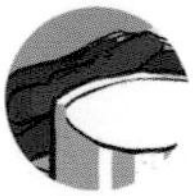

lap cheung (laahp chéung): dried red Chinese sausage

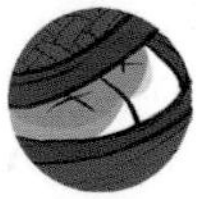

lau sah bao (làuh sā bāau): A dessert made of a steamed white bun full of hot and melting custard, and sometimes a salted egg. Literally translates to "leaking sand bun."

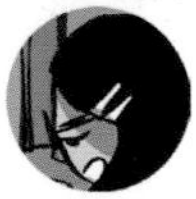

lei lah (lèih la): A response to being called, like "I'm coming!"

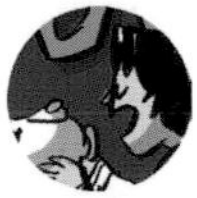

leng jai (leng jái): a handsome guy, often used to get someone's attention

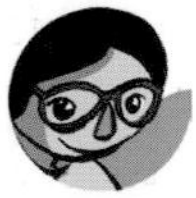

leoi (léui): a casual way to say neoi

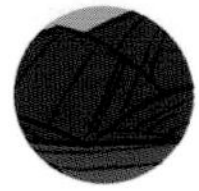

lo mai gai (noh máih gāi): sticky rice stuffed with fillings like diced chicken, lap cheung, Chinese black mushroom, salted egg, or shrimp, then steamed in a wrapped in lotus leaf

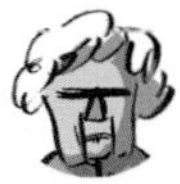

mah mah (màh màh): When said with a lower intonation, means grandmother, specifically father's mother. (With either an upward or upper high intonation, means mom.)

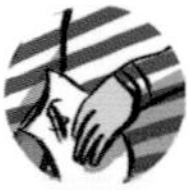

maai daan (màaih dāan): a way of asking for the check at the end of a meal

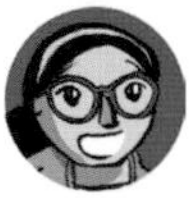

neoi (néui): Daughter. Neoi neoi (nèuih néui) is also daughter, but more endearing.

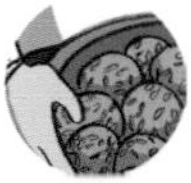

por por (pòh pòh): grandmother, specifically mother's mother

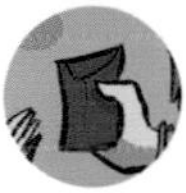

red packet: Also known as lai see (laih sih), it's a red envelope filled with money given by married couples to younger family members during special occasions like New Year's Day, weddings, graduations, and birthdays.

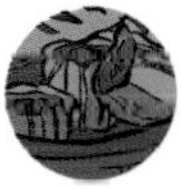

siu mai (sīu máai): A dumpling made of steamed pork in an open yellow wrapper. Sometimes includes mushrooms and diced shrimp, and often topped with orange fish eggs.

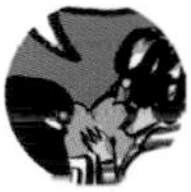

sot jor (sōt jó): an unkind and insulting way to talk about someone in reference to their mental health, kind of like saying "crazy"

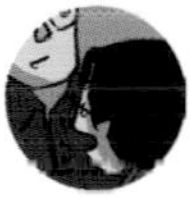

yeet hay (yiht hei): In some cultures, certain foods have "cold" energy, and some have "hot" energy (but not necessarily cold or hot in temperature!). If you have too much of one or the other, it will make you feel unwell, and you should eat the other kind of food to get a good balance back. Yeet hay literally translates to "hot air," and can describe "hot" foods (like fries, peanuts, or lychee) or how you feel after eating too much of it.

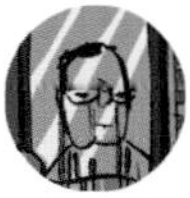

yeh yeh: grandfather, specifically father's father

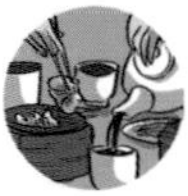

yum cha (yám chàh): Literally translating to drink tea, yum cha is a tradition of eating out between breakfast and lunchtime where large groups share dim sum and hot tea. Sometimes food is ordered off a list you fill out at the table, while other restaurants have servers push steam-heated carts full of fresh dim sum dishes to choose from.

Character Sketches

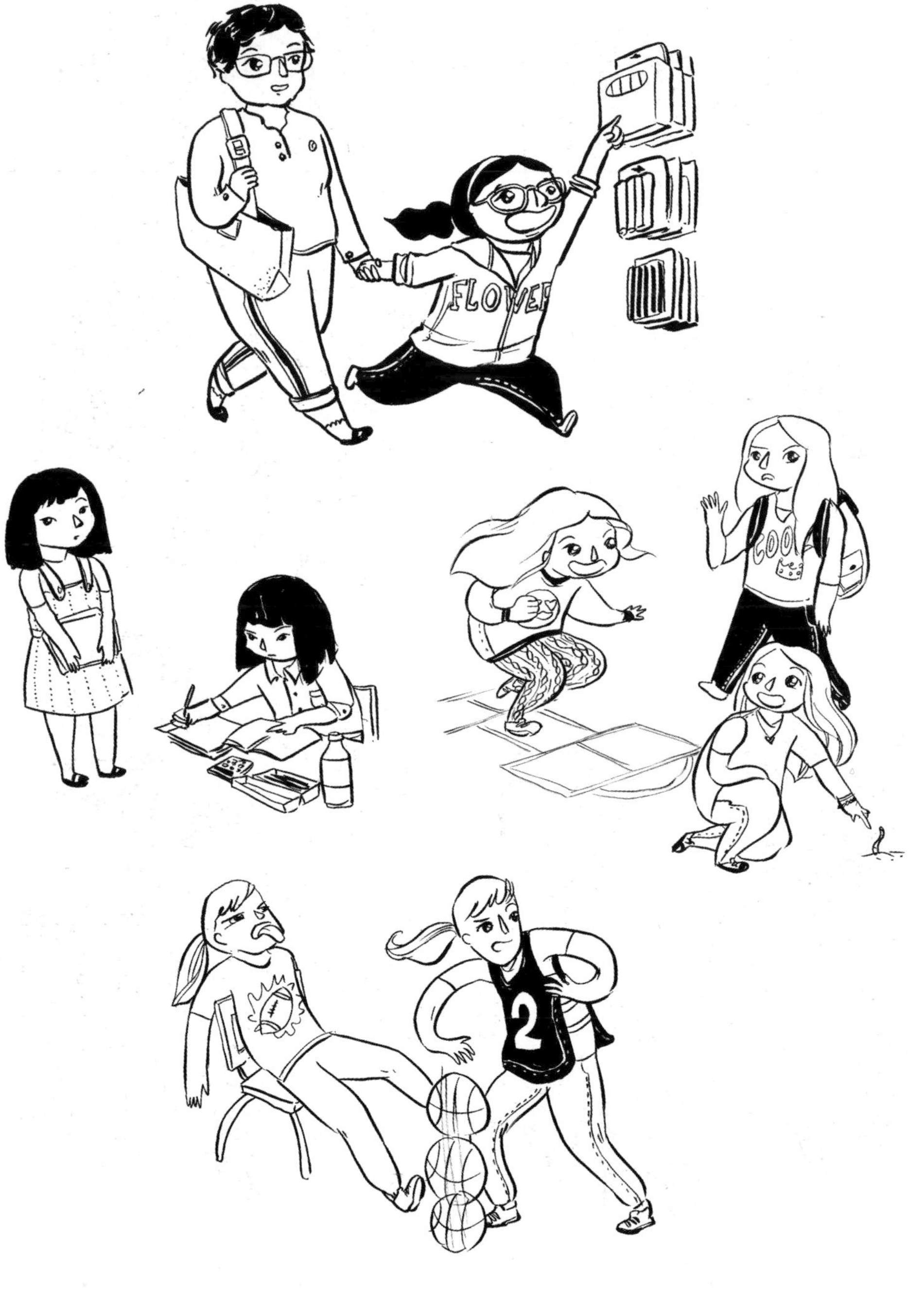
FLOWER
COOL
2

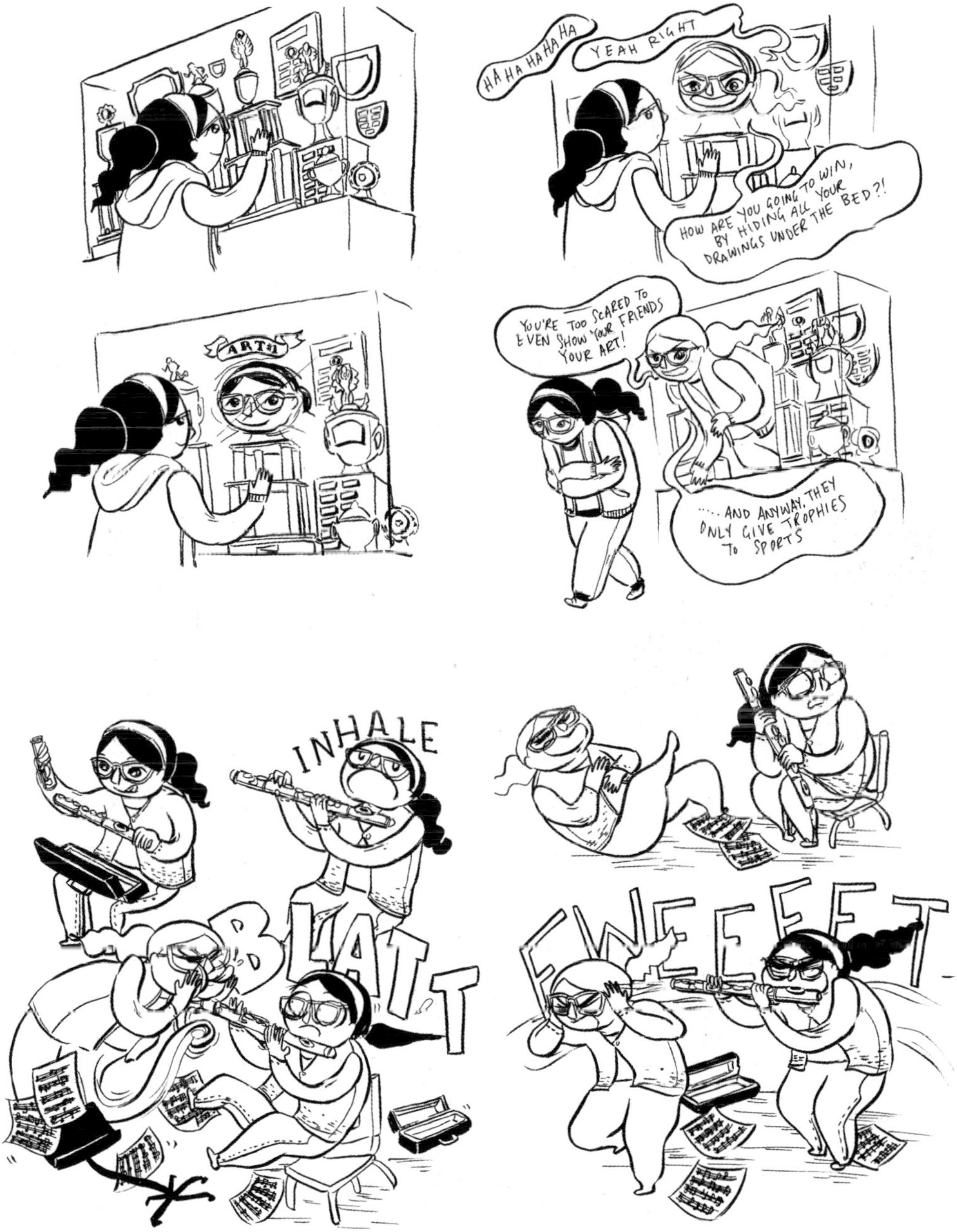
HA HA HA HA HA
YEAH RIGHT
HOW ARE YOU GOING TO WIN, BY HIDING ALL YOUR DRAWINGS UNDER THE BED?!
ART#1
YOU'RE TOO SCARED TO EVEN SHOW YOUR FRIENDS YOUR ART!
.... AND ANYWAY, THEY ONLY GIVE TROPHIES TO SPORTS
INHALE
BLATT
FWEEET

Acknowledgments

Living With Viola was created in Toronto/Tkaronto, the traditional territory of the Mississaugas of the Credit, the Anishinaabe, the Chippewa, the Haudenosaunee, and the Wendat peoples. The story of my family's immigration is inextricable from the history of First Nations peoples. I will never forget whose land I'm on, and the histories that are suffused in this ground.

This book could not exist without my extraordinary and sublime editor, Serah-Marie McMahon. Thank you for this journey together and for being my guiding star. Thank you to Annick Press: Katie Hearn, Rick Wilks, Paul Covello, Kaela Cadieux, Heather Davies, Brendan Ouellette, Gayna Theophilus, Asiya Awale, Amanda Olson, and the entire team.

So much love to Mike Rennick and my Deserres fam for being so supportive and for all the laughs. Thank you to the OCADU Illustration faculty team and to my amazing students. To my bff crew Suharu Ogawa, Derrick Chow, Orlando Grünewald, and Hannah Lee—your love and belief in me mean the world. Thank you, Annie Koyama and all my incredible friends, for your endless support.

This book is about family, and this story is the story of my family. Mom, Daddy, Jason Fung and Wendy Wang, and to the future generation of readers—Spencer, Kayleigh, and Luke. I love you all so much. Thank you to Julia and Octavio Medeiros and the entire family. Above all, thank you to my husband, Mark Medeiros, who never stopped believing in this and in me.